# On the Chin of a GIANT

I0590385

## Carmela Orsini Harmon

**On the Chin of a Giant**
Copyright © 2025 by Carmela Orsini Harmon

ISBN: 979-8993283302 (hc)
ISBN: 979-8993283319 (sc)
ISBN: 979-8993283326 (e)

All rights reserved. No part of this publication may be reproduced, distributed, or transmitted in any form or by any means, including photocopying, recording, or other electronic or mechanical methods, without the prior written permission of the author, except in the case of brief quotations embodied in critical reviews and other noncommercial uses permitted by copyright law.

The views expressed in this book are solely those of the author and reflect the author's own perspectives and experiences.

CARMELA ORSINI HARMON

Carmela Orsini Harmon
(912) 433-8125
burleyjaws@yahoo.com

To Jim, my first and greatest inspiration: Go with God, my love…

To our three sons, Ginger, eleven grandchildren and the most wonderful American/Italian parents and family on earth, all of whom taught me that sticking together, no matter what, we are the winners.

To Sister de Neri, may she rest in peace, who stirred my imagination like none other when she'd enter the class with directives such as "Give me 200 words on…nothing;" or "300 words on…a shoestring;" or "Write your own eulogy—and make it rhyme!"

To Candace Fralix and Brenda Clamp, who many years later, believed enough to invest in a first reading of this novel. And remained true friends after the rejection slip.

To my sister, Margie O. Kelly and niece, Carmela E. Orsini (Also; Too; Two; the Younger; the Lesser; the Littler—and admittedly, the Wiser,) for insisting this was a "good story" and encouraging me to work on the manuscript again. "What's not to like?" became my mantra.

To Mike Kelly and Peter Chiofalo, for keeping my Italian acceptable.

To my cousin, Ernestine R. Moody, and our flawlessly "principled" Maggie H. Mangan—talented ladies both—for helping to work out the plot-kinks and infusing my daily computer life with much laughter. Then tears of loss. A sad, "stupid" thing that…

To Dustin Ashcraft, an extraordinary photographer and his wife/ model, Amanda—who happens to be my eldest granddaughter. Thanks again, dear things. The costumed retakes of your wedding photos made perfect book covers.

My love and devotion to one and all…

# Contents

# PROLOGUE

Greeneville, Tennessee
1811

Bob Trott considered himself a sterling tribute to virility. Ink black hair, fashionably cropped to brush the collar, framed his square and symmetrically featured face. He had always been more heft than muscle, but well tailored clothing remedied his slight imperfections. Bob was plenty mean when he didn't get what he wanted, yet could also use charm to his best advantage. Charm won him a rich wife, albeit she'd just been jilted and was vulnerable. So what? With the birth of their daughter, he was, more or less, assured a place at the golden feed-trough. It was also his plan to impregnate the woman with as many children as it took to keep her out of his way, but the delivery had been difficult and his wife told she'd never conceive again. Had she died it would have served him better, for as the surviving parent, he could have manipulated untold sums before his daughter reached her majority. Not that he'd done badly for himself with the funds and businesses his wife's lawyers allowed him to handle. In fact, with some clever auditing, he was slowly accumulating a plump little nest-egg from places they'd never guess. It was becoming a damned bother though, keeping his wife and her law-buzzards ignorant of his more profound obsession.

No, Bob Trott was not a happy man. He had this one legitimate daughter, a string of bastards spread over several states, but not one male among them—and damn it, he wanted a son! He married money, by God, and husbandly rights should have given him freer rein in the dispersal and disposal of such. It would not do putting that wealth into the hands of yet another woman the lawyers could fawn over—even if it was his daughter. He needed to be heard. He needed to know the power of passing wealth to a boy who would always carry his name, and in turn, to know future generations would eventually refer to that fortune as his. It had reached the point where he was dipping into anything female and of child-baring age, determined his seed would catch, and that one of these times, a male heir would result. For years, his plan had been ready for this to occur. He'd simply steal the babe and take it back to his wife, claiming him to be an orphaned nephew, son of a tragically deceased brother. There'd be no way of checking the story either, as he'd made it clear to his worthless family never to intrude on the good thing he had going. And because his soft-hearted wife still lamented her lack of more children, she'd soon be clucking over his bastard just as he planned. Then, his life would be complete. Then, he could end his many "business" forays, which usually allowed a month or more for rutting, periodic checks during the requisite nine months, and as compensation for failure, an immediate new round of rutting elsewhere.

Three years past, and illegally so, he had even married a proper widow up in Tennessee, who already had a boy, so he wasn't asking anything of her she hadn't already done, now was he? At the time, he believed he'd chosen wisely too, as Margaret was well-bred and well-educated—an English-born schoolmarm, for God's sake—and with her intelligence and his cunning, their son would do him proud. His hopes ran so high, in fact, that he returned more frequently to her bed than all the rest combined. But she hadn't produced and Tom, her idiot nine year old, was a constant reminder that Margaret just wasn't doing right by him. It was a festering kind of resentment Bob had for Tom and it worsened with each failed attempt to impregnate his schoolmarm mother.

The caning he gave the boy for losing a footrace to a slave four years his senior was so richly deserved. Tom was white, after all, and honor should have demanded he rise to the occasion.

But mores the pity, Bob did teach him to swim. Tossing the boy into the river, his instructions were brief: "Swim or drown, damn you!" And when Tom would reach for the dock, looking wholly terrified, he took great pleasure in striking his fingers with a stick. "You aren't worth saving! Swim, little bastard—or die!" So the boy swam and though Bob knew it was done on the strength of icy fear and deep resentment, this was fine with him too.

Only once did Tom try to enlist help from his mother and Bob put an immediate stop to that! Yet again, catching the boy away from the house—and out of Margaret's hearing—Bob twisted Tom's thin little arm in a brutal hold, while simply explaining facts. "If you ever—*ever*—speak against me again, I will slit your damn throat! I'll bleed you dry in the hog pen and chop your body into fucking, little chunks! I'll feed what's left to the bitching dogs, and your poor-dear-mother will never know what became of her precious piss-ant son!"

Then, the bane of Bob's existence—his cursed, uncontrolled rages— brought it all to an end. He had come in near dawn, from a night of drink and carousing. He and Margaret had escalating words about it, and he was just drunk enough to use her lack of conception—and a son of his own—as ample justification for his behavior. Retaliating, Margaret blamed his lack of ability and demanded he leave her house for good. Infuriated, he attacked and her strength, being no match for his fury, she was for all intents, raped. But it wasn't done quietly and because she continued to scream at him, he set about whipping her with his belt. This brought Tom into the fray and while attempting to stop Bob, found himself flung onto the bed for a share of his mother's punishment. As best she could, Margaret curled herself over her son's smaller body, taking the worst of the blows, but had Bob not passed out he may well have killed them then and there. As it was, he lay like a slab of stone across her thighs, penning her down, and fearful of trying to move, she told Tom in urgent whispers to go for help.

"But what if he wakes up, Mama?" the boy's voice quaked. She was covered in bleeding welts—as was he—but it hurt more to see her that way. "He might get meaner if he finds me gone!"

"If you stay, we'll both be dead by morning. Now go, Tom—and be quick coming back!" she urged.

So Tom ran as fast as his young legs would move; he ran until he could not breathe; he ran until his heart wanted to explode. But it wasn't fast enough. In the company of the nearest neighbors, he returned to find Bob had departed, but not before beating his mother senseless with closed fists...

During Margaret's slow and agonizing weeks of recovery, Tom lived in dread of Bob Trott's return. Daily he prayed they could go somewhere his stepfather would never find. Then a few months later, Margaret told him—along with interested neighbors, who still stopped in regularly—that she had sold their farm and was taking her son back to her birthplace in England. Tom was a happy little boy as they boarded the east bound stage, while beside him Margaret now prayed her lies were enough to cover their trail. She would not be spending Tom's inheritance from the farm buying passage to England. But they did have to leave the area where Bob might come looking for her. And come he would, if ever he learned his savagery had left her pregnant.

In Ashville, North Carolina, Margaret switched their tickets for a coach heading south toward a destination she'd chosen with great care and purpose: Athens, Georgia. On arrival, she rented a small furnished house near the school Tom was to attend, and presenting herself there as newly widowed, inquired about a teaching position. She was hired, and they settled into their new home and community, hopefully, to stay.

Margaret wondered if she could love the child she carried—who by her calculation was due in mid September—but explaining to Tom what was to happen, left her a bit hopeful and much amused. As excited as she'd ever seen him, he said brightly, "I like babies, Mama!

And if it's alright with you, it's sure alright with me! —Hey, can I pick out the names?"

The months passed, and by May, Tom had chosen his favorites: Rebecca Claire, for two classmates he was sweet on; and Ethan Allen, a hero from his history book. So it was that on September. 10th, a fine and healthy Ethan Allen Joseph Scott was born—Margaret adding her first husband's given name as her gift; her way of binding the child to a better father than he had. And over the next few years, Allen became a great source of joy to them both. As a toddler, he lived at "Big Brer's" heels, imitating gestures and hanging on his every word as gospel. In turn, Tom's love for his younger brother grew fiercely protective, because like his mother, he always feared Bob Trott might still come looking for them…

In the winter of Tom's sixteenth year, a flu epidemic took Margaret. For days, she fought to recover but knowing fate was upon her, she used her fleeting moments of strength to compose a letter. That and a few precious documents she gave to her eldest from her deathbed.

"Son," she struggled in faltering breaths, "…not getting better. … Dying."

"No, —don't say that!" Tom fell to his knees beside her. "Mama, please don't say that!"

"Must finish…," she ran fevered fingers over his thick, dark hair. "So worried…; failed you."

"No you didn't—no!" his voice broke. "You're the best mother in the world!"

"Love you…," she handed him an envelope. "All I leave…; your legacy…; all in my heart." Then, closing her eyes, she peacefully surrendered her life.

Tom stared at his mother, unable to breathe himself. Surely, if he just waited, she would come to his bed and wake him from this terrible nightmare. But after what seemed an eternity, his mind began to accept what his heart could not. Obedient fingers were opening the envelope, drawing his eyes to the task. Inside, he found two marriage certificates, naming his father as groom on the first, and Trott on the second. There was also a small green account book, a legal looking page on which he saw his name amid therefore and wherefores he didn't understand. But all were dropped to the floor on finding her last missive. Now, fighting mightily against the tears threatening to cloud his vision, he read; and as he did, each word became indelibly imprinted, not only in his memory, but on his very soul.

*My Dearest Son,*

*Tonight, I feel so close to your father. That his early death denied you the chance to know him remains a deep regret for me. He was so happy to learn you were coming and proved his love in the wording of his will, before you were even born. I shall now attempt to do the same. You know why I could not hold on to the land he meant for you to have, but the money it brought is in a trust and over the years, I have managed to pay back the cost of moving us here, plus some extra as I was able to afford it. So, on your 18th birthday, you will receive your rightful inheritance—your manhood money.*

*Please, use it wisely. My best advice is this: let your first investment be in yourself, by getting a good education. That was my reason for bringing you to Athens; —my fondest wish being to see you graduate Franklin University here. Knowledge lasts, Tom. Knowledge guides. Knowledge minimizes failure and escalates success.*

*Then, as you have had so little, find true happiness. Make a good marriage, be faithful to it, and always—always—let there be love in your manner during good times and bad. Let there be love, and the children born of it will be more precious than gold. Such was the life I shared with your father. You are our love personified; our grandest gift to the world.*

*And you are my only hope for poor, little Allen. I have nothing to leave him but my love and your father's honorable name, borrowed though it be. In good conscience, I could not give him a share of your inheritance. You, of course, may do as you see fit on the matter. Just see that he is kept on the right path—and remember: whatever you do, he copies; wherever you go, he is likely to follow.*

*It troubles me greatly to lay such burdens on your young shoulders, but when you most need me, I will be with you in spirit. I know this, because of your dear father's presence beside me now, lending words to write and strength to face the inevitable.*

*In closing, I can but repeat: invest in yourself first; care for your brother; and always*

*Let There Be Love,*
*Mother*

Tom lowered the page and looked at Margaret once more. How could she place such trust in him? Without her, he felt no older or wiser than Allen. Didn't she know she was his bedrock; —his only claim to love in the world? Then, he wept: deeply; inconsolably; tears he had stored in his often bruised body and soul, through all the unhappy years. But when the tears dried, Tom found, that even in death, his mother had given him a new strength: the strength of manhood, and it proved itself durable in the years to come...

The brothers became board-around hirelings, moving from farm to local farm as work was needed. That they came as a pair was Tom's only request of each employer. Allen was of little help at the age of seven, but Tom made certain that both their shares of the work were done—and then some—so the request was never refused. The result of his extra effort was a steady growth in physical power. Also, from one farmer or another, he learned to hunt, to track and to shoot with admirable accuracy. Putting as much into his studies, he finished his secondary schooling with honors. But diligence was not his true motivation. As Tom saw it, caring for Allen meant more than a warm bed and food.

It meant having the conditioned body and supple mind it would take for a damn good fight, should Bob Trott even attempt a claim on his brother. There would be no more whipping, twisting or tossing Tom around. He owed himself and his mother no less…

At eighteen, Tom grew restless. He was now in charge of his inheritance, but what did he really want from or know about life? He could have started college—probably should have—but was loathe to spend money he wasn't yet used to having. So for over a year, he clerked the General Store, but found cow-towing to the whims of every customer went against his grain. He also considered buying his own farm, as by then he certainly knew how to run one, but this too, he found unappealing. His next endeavor was a job in the looming mills, where the sameness of the work drove him nearly insane. As he approached twenty, he came to believe his destiny must lie beyond his immediate horizons, so arranging for Allen's stay with one of his mother's friends and fellow teachers—who promised to keep the eleven year old current on his school work—Tom signed on with a railroad crew leaving for South Carolina. The first year, he spent laying track between Augusta and Charleston. The second, he was promoted to Crew Boss, then time-keeper, but as his mother predicted, Allen begged constantly to join him. It was then he decided to return to Athens and enter the University. If his brother was determined to follow his lead, the options had to be better than boredom, lint in his lungs, or living on the road without roots of any kind.

Tom did discover two interesting things about himself from his sojourn, though: women seemed drawn to him—which proved a fascinating distraction; and, surprisingly, he'd learned to manage money quite well. Without touching his inheritance, he'd saved enough to pay for his courses, and thereafter, only had to work the farms with Allen during the harvest and planting seasons.

So it was that in a little more than fours years, he graduated. And as he walked away, diploma in hand, he knew his mother was smiling for the warmth of it seeped right into his heart. "Well, Mama," he murmured, smiling too, "where do we go from here?"

# CHAPTER 1

Augusta, Georgia
July, 1829

M adam Maggie's Tavern, located between the main business thoroughfare and the Savannah River, was a profitable venture. This was due to the careful eye Maggie kept on the till and the hired muscle that stood ready to rid her establishment of disruptive patrons at the first sign of trouble.

She looked up from the column of figures she'd tried—twice now—to tally and wondered at her lack of concentration. It was early afternoon on a blistering hot day and already the tavern was half-full of paying customers, which usually foretold a busy night ahead. ... But something was amiss; something wanted to happen; and it had been this way since the man by the window arrived an hour before.

Maggie remembered that he'd paused in the doorway, suit coat slung over a shoulder, allowing his vision to adjust to the inside dimness. Then, as a smile crawled slowly over his mouth, he'd taken ale, the chosen table and sat watching the street traffic. He still was, and minding his own business as well, so why was she certain he held a vital piece of her puzzle?

She admitted finding him handsome, in a dark, rugged way, and that being so, the heat could do nothing to lessen his appeal. The thick broad shoulders and well muscled arms were only enhanced by his wilting, rolled sleeved, dress shirt. And rumpled as they were, his trousers fit extremely well over long strong thighs. The rich deep brown of his hair and the healthy tan of his skin were perfect foils for those Sapphire blue eyes too. In fact, everything about the man, to his smallest gesture, was confident, casual and easy to appreciate, even for a woman of her advanced years.

As curiosity sharpened, so did Maggie's senses. Glancing over the room again, she realized that but for a quaffing woman intent on a rye-tongued assault of her mate, there was now a definite lack of female participation being voiced in the crowd. The hired girl, who never shut her vulgar mouth, had done so; the whore in the corner, paid well for the fondling she received beneath the table, had grown impatient with the hand between her thighs; and the rest—young and old alike—now flushed and fanned and fumbled with anything their fingers touched.

Maggie nodded in awe. Such might be expected of the inexperienced, but those here were either bored wives out for a night of forbidden fun, or well-ridden prostitutes practiced in the art of procurement. And yet, some force held all in their places. Oh, they studied the stranger readily enough with guarded expressions and a multitude of expectant glances, but not one found the courage to approach him.

"...All this, set into motion by a smile?" Maggie uttered. But she could not doubt her conclusion. That smile had acknowledged the admiration shown him—and perhaps encouraged more private hopes, if his eyes happened to linger anywhere at all. Then without a single spoken word, somehow his will was asserted, making it clear he would set the terms. And in so doing, he'd left those hopes dangling about the room like so many newspaper drawings. ...*Not yet,* he may well have said. *The day is too hot and it's never good to rush these things. But evening isn't far away now. Then my dears; then we'll see...*

Thoroughly amused by the jealous eyes that followed, Maggie went to the stranger's table and refilled his glass. He thanked her politely... smiled again...and she nearly forgot to collect her tab. Seeking the safe-side of her bar, she was nonetheless forced to admit two additional things: when this man wanted more than ogling, it wouldn't go unrewarded; and that even-a-woman-of-her-advanced-age, was not immune to temptations of the flesh—one-sided though it would certainly and sadly this time have to be...

It was a tad cooler now. The sun had set and Maggie's tavern had quickly filled with a dense parade of the thirsty. For a growing while, the man by the window had wanted to order something stronger than ale, but service was not keeping pace with demand. He could have fetched it from the bar himself, but that would be at a certain cost of the table, so propping his boots on the opposing chair, he pondered how this dilemma might be solved. He then became aware of a presence before him and glancing up, saw a man of about his own years, with a lean athletic build, a slight auburn tinge to his unruly hair, and pure mischief dancing in ice-blue eyes—which were fastened, at the moment, on the boots in that empty chair.

"Sir?" the man spoke suddenly, "How thirsty are you?"

"...Very," a shrug accompanied response.

"Good! Just don't shuffle your feet." And melting into the crowd, he left the seated one to wonder at the brief exchange. But soon he returned, a bottle and two glasses in hand, to continue as if he'd never departed. "Thirsty enough to drink with an Irishman?"

"With the devil—if that's decent whiskey," the reply corresponded with the thud of boots hitting the floor.

"Then shake with Satan!" a hand was extended and the coveted chair claimed. "Michael Herb, sir, Captain of the Irish Mist, running between Savannah and Augusta. Docked earlier this afternoon and now thirstier than hell."

"Thomas Scott," reciprocated the other, "From Athens and here to find employment. ...So, do you live in Augusta?"

"Oh-hell-no!" Mike uncorked the bottle and poured two drinks. "Savannah is my lady-city. Augusta is just where I unload cargo and passengers before I get to reload, turn her around and head home. And what is it you do?"

3

"Well, I'm hoping to secure a teaching position—"

"A what?" The Captain's surprise was evidenced by an abrupt halt between glass and mouth. "I mean…I could have made several guesses, but that would not have been among them."

Tom's nod was one of perplexity. "I should be used to this by now—but just what is it people expect to see in a teacher?"

Mike made a show of thinking that over while merriment played at the corners of his mouth. "Hmm, I'd say, someone more on the meek side—which you don't seem in the least. And not one who looks as if he might rip a man in half—which you do!" Yes, the Captain was beginning to enjoy himself and that, of course, called for another round of drink.

"Those years at the University didn't come free," Tom countered. "I had to work my way through."

"Doing what? Hurling anvils over a Blacksmith Shop?" Mike laughed.

"Never tried that," Tom fought to contain a smile. "But there were farmers who would board my brother and me—and pay some for a good, hard worker."

"Worker—in the singular? What's wrong with your brother?"

"Not a damn thing," Tom surrendered a chuckle. "Allen was only a lad when we started our board-around—too young for anything more useful than getting in the way. But he's older now and pulls his fair share of the load."

"How old?"

"…Seventeen, if makes a difference. —Captain, have you ever considered Police work? You'd do one hell of an interrogation."

"Sorry," Mike had the grace to flush. "Learned at the knee of an expert. But I am curious: if you're moving here, what happens to Allen?"

"The plan is I get the job, a place to live and send for him. He completed his secondary schooling this spring and is finishing up some farm work now. But I want him back in Athens for the start of the fall college term. Or the spring term, at the very latest."

There was something final and decided in the way the last was said, causing Mike to suspect the brothers may have had words on the subject. And, as any good Irishman knows, a drink in commiseration is every bit as important as one for merry-making, so the bottle was tipped anew. "No other family?" he asked then.

"Not a soul," Tom nodded.

"Me either—no parents, that is. I do have a saintly Aunt and two fine Uncles. Anyway, any luck yet finding the job you want?"

"Not yet. I promised myself a brief holiday first, so for the last few days, I've just been enjoying Augusta."

"And the ladies here?" a twinkle brightened in the Captain's eyes.

"Mostly that, I suppose," Tom admitted.

"Oh-hell-yes! Augusta does have her fair share of *that*. —Now, take the buxom redhead over there. Have you noticed she keeps looking this way?"

"I have. And I did. Night before last."

Mike barked out a hardy laugh. "Well, damn—and I thought she wanted *my* attention. Sir, you have sorely wounded my self-image!"

"You didn't miss much," Tom consoled. "There must be two pounds of wadding in her bodice."

"The hell you say," Mike looked the woman over again. "You know, that's down right dishonest. I'd be upset had I paid for stuffing."

"Had I, I might agree."

Another surprise for the Captain to digest. "…You didn't pay, because she deceived you?"

"No, I just don't enjoy playing the game for money. It's more sporting after a bit of a chase."

"What chase? Hell, pay their price and they're willing."

"But doesn't eager make it better than willing? A lady demands respect and many a-time, wont give up her virtue no matter how hard you work at it. But treat a whore as you would a lady and she just might give up her price."

"And how often does that work for you?" Mike asked skeptically.

"I don't claim to be infallible, so let's put it this way: you are the first male I've spent an evening with in Augusta; and I still have most of the money I brought with me."

"Yeah?" Mike filled their glasses to the brim. "So tell me more about yourself, Thomas Scott. I think we're going to be very good friends. But then—oh, and then, do I have a challenge for you!"

It only took Mike the rest of the evening to talk Tom into accepting an offer that would, if nothing else, save him lodging fees. The Irish Mist would be docked for the remainder of the week, so why shouldn't Tom avail himself of an empty cabin? Besides, as the evenings were to be spent presenting themselves to the ladies at Delilah Delightful's Infamous Brothel, having Tom close enough for an accurate *on-the-house-tally* made perfect sense to the Captain. And the aforementioned challenge came on the third night, with an invitation to Tom from the illusive Delilah herself.

In the wheelhouse the following morning, both suffered similar headaches over coffee strong enough to melt lead. "She didn't charge you a cent either?" crowed Mike, as if deserving a portion of credit. "Not a damn cent? —Well, here son, you've earned a cigar!"

Tom accepted it, but had to wait for a light, as a beam of sun had sneaked over the window ledge and poked him right in the eye. "Now, Captain," he said, still wincing, "afterwards, I didn't take it as a compliment when Delilah offered a job with her escort service. Hell, I didn't know what that was, until she explained it."

"Opened your eyes to life in the city, did she?" Mike lit them both up now. "Well, friend, let me enlighten you further. What brought you to Delilah's attention was female curiosity. She wanted to know what her girls were whispering about. You impressed her. But first and foremost Delilah is a business woman, providing for peons like me, and purely doting on the whims of the rich—male and female alike. So, she must have seen a chance to fatten her purse by adding you to her stable of Gent-rentals," he smirked, and it seemed to ignite that teasing eye twinkle. "Hell, Tom, just think about that! How many men can brag that a whorehouse Madam offered a job with pay? Push for it, and she'd likely throw in a supply of preventative sheaths—rich lady's choice: the popular salt-cured linen or silk; the costly oiled goat-gut; or the uncomfortable, but reusable leathers. Now that, old son, could be a big fucking deal!"

"Wouldn't leave home without one," Tom laughed. But gearing-up—and on demand, no less—held some really bad connotations and sure as hell wasn't anywhere close to his reason for coming to Augusta. He'd buy his own damned sheaths too—as dictated by need and resulting from a session of good, old fashioned, male to female body-rubbing lust.

Yet somewhere between the nocturnal activities, they also found time for some rousing debates, traded life stories and learned respect for the best in their opposite personalities. Tom tended to be a loner, a worrier, to look for underlying motives and then to analyze the things people said and did. Above all, he tried to avoid trouble whenever possible. In Mike's world, worry was an alien notion and often, he'd create situations solely to provide the amusements or results he craved. He wasn't reckless about it…exactly…but neither was patience among his virtues. He simply and truly believed in the luck of the Irish and expected the world to grant full enjoyment of his privileged status.

Already, and at full steam ahead, the Captain had launched his next scheme. A word here, a promise of prominent endorsement there, and he was close to convincing Tom to settle in Savannah instead. Then after reading in the Herald that the Augusta school, where Tom was to present a letter of introduction, had burned to the ground further convincing wasn't needed. Mike appreciated this twist of fate—he really did—though to his way of thinking, the favor granted was only his due, sterling fellow that he was.

"You'll love Savannah," he assured Tom, caressing the word as if speaking of a woman. "She's a queen and a vixen, my man, and there's not another like her. Soon enough, you'll see…"

The morning of departure was a busy one for Captain Michael Leonard Herb. After seeing that the loading and storage of his cargo was started, he would have to return to the wheelhouse for final checks and rechecks of his charts, cargo, luggage and passenger lists.

Standing along the railing of a bow-end deck on the main level, Tom amused himself with watching the passengers board. As it was too warm to remain in their cabins, they were nesting in groups beneath a string of awning squares, thoughtfully provided by the boat Captain. One lady, in particular, held his interest because from the moment of arrival, she set out to make herself the center of attention, first by refusing to share her spot of shade with anyone but Jenny, her servant/ chaperone; and then because everyone in hearing distance had learned Jenny's name from the number of times she'd been called on to see to the girl's comfort; and lastly, because she preened and posed, adjusted and readjusted, until satisfied all males present had eyes glued longingly on her. She was a beauty—Tom freely admitted that—but the proud erectness of her posture, the very tilt of her chin, said she too was aware of her breeding; her pale skinned, white-blonde softness; and most of all, her effect on the masculine gender. Indeed, she was reveling in the awe-struck expressions about her, while smiling benevolently at the less beautiful and more disapproving ladies there. All of which said to Tom that manor-born she might be, but she was also a spoiled pampered wench, and with every inch of her delicate frame, adored both roles entirely.

It was after the normally cocky and confident Captain had presented himself, only to retreat from her flirtatiousness nearly speechless, that Tom added to his evaluation. ...*Satin and sandpaper*, he catalogued the look in her searching, black-brown eyes. ...*Very expensive satin, and perhaps, the coarsest of sandpaper.* The notion grew when a still-flustered Mike asked his company in the wheelhouse, for while turning to follow, he felt...or sensed...her eyes upon him now. He stood for it only as long as it took to reach the stairs. Pausing there, he returned her blatantly assessing stare and kept staring, matching her gaze spark for spark, until her lashes lowered on reddened cheeks.

The Captain was lighting a cigar when Tom entered the door. "Pretty little colleen, huh?" he asked, offering Tom one too.

"Very," he answered, accepting it. There was no doubting who Mike meant or that he had more to say, but was searching for a place to begin. "So tell me about Ransom O'Rourke's daughter," Tom lit his smoke while making a helpful suggestion. "He's a banker in Savannah, isn't he?"

"You've already asked questions?" Mike tried for surprise, but defensiveness crept in too.

"No, but she did cause a stir out there and wives tend to gossip when their husbands ogle another woman. I just listened, Captain."

"Damned old biddies," Mike muttered. "Well, if you haven't guessed, I want Nicole O'Rourke—and I mean to have her. The problem is…I need her father's approval on the whole damn thing."

"That would be obliging of him," Tom laughed, not knowing what else to say.

Mike laughed too. "It sure as hell would be," he nudged his friend toward a compact dining unit. "Sit down and hear me out, will you? We have a little time before they're finished loading the cargo. …I want your opinion, because I truly do love Nicole—and because if there is one thing I'm deadly serious about, it's wedding her."

"…All right," Tom nodded, tucking away reservations as he tucked himself into a chair.

"Let me tell you about Ransom first, then," began the Captain. "He is a banker and one hell of a fine man. —You'll like him, Tom. And lest you think I'm aiming a rung too high up the social ladder, Ransom and I are practically partners."

"*Practically* how?" Tom wondered aloud.

"The Irish Mist and most of the profits thereof. You see, last year I won this boat in a poker game—luckiest damn night of *my* life, for sure. Then, I heard O'Rourke had booked passage and when I learned why, I rehired the crew and kept the appointment. …It was quite a journey, my man," he paused for a puff and a chuckle. "I threw around every nautical term I knew, kept Ransom's glass full of good Irish whiskey, and thanked God for the able men running the damn boat! Anyway, he was going to set up an export deal with some mills near Augusta and naturally, I talked myself in. I told him I'd bring the stuff down-river for him; that if business was good enough, I'd pull my other boat out of dry-dock and organize a round-robin of exclusive Herb-O'Rourke traffic."

"Your other boat?" Tom injected, letting Mike's billing order slide. "—You have two of these paddle-wheelers?"

"I only said *boat*," Mike grinned. "The point is, O'Rourke liked my proposal and I saw no reason to tell him the Shamrock was just a sailing sloop. But friend, if he wants another wheeler, I'll buy one; or steal it; —or wish one down from heaven."

"Or up from hell," Tom uttered in appropriate awe.

"Oh-hell-yes!" the Captain agreed. "But I've made us a nice profit so far and convinced Ransom I am reliable; —this time, enough to be trusted with his daughter's safe return from her visit. Little by little then, I hope to win complete approval—and where Nicole is concerned, especially."

"But if she was staying in Augusta…," Tom puzzled. "I mean, if you love the girl, why didn't you call on her there?"

"I thought about it; —damn, how I did," vowed the Captain. "I wanted to take her from her cousin's house and parade her all over town; to show her one hell of a good time; —one she'd never be able to forget. But you know what that would have to include. No, this time—with this girl—I have to play it straight. She means that much to me."

Tom had to ask. "And Nicole? Is she willing to wait until you win approval?"

"I've loved her for as long as I can remember," Mike took a turn with hesitation, "…but I was always just part of the crowd that surrounded her; …and you witnessed our first one-on-one meeting today."

"The first—damn, Captain! Then how can you be talking marriage?"

"Wait now!" the Irishman rushed on. "Listen to the rest before doubting my sanity. I've spent a lot of time finding out about her. She has a wild streak and is a God-awful flirt—which worries Ransom to no end—but that's as far as it's gone."

Again, Tom had to ask. "As far as *what* has gone?"

"Hell, you know what I mean! But I've questioned every one of her beaus—cleverly, through the bottom of a bottle, where tongues are apt to loosen—and the closest she came was a half-ass cousin who swore she pretended sleep when he sneaked in for a few late nights of fondling. He won't be coming back, though. I've taken care of that already."

"Still, Mike," Tom proceeded carefully. "Your efforts say that you don't trust her; that you do have doubts."

"What is there to doubt? I am going to be the only man in her life," the Captain insisted, yet paused anew. "...I know she is overdue for the big fall, but not to some horny boy. Tom, that I couldn't stand; —not when I know I can wed her and keep her. What's more, Ransom knows it will take a firm hand to guide Nico and that I have one." Mike had finished and looking at Tom, who looked at the toes of his boots, waited for him to speak. "Well?" he urged when it didn't happen. "...What do you think?"

Tom sent him a level gaze. "Honestly?"

"Straight as the road to hell. You'd get the same from me."

"Well...I think your intentions are good; —damn near noble considering the week we just spent in Augusta." Then, snuffing out the cigar, he nodded. "But this whole thing sounds like a novel: dashing young Captain woos and weds beautiful lady to the everlasting delight of her rich—and worried—father. ...So where is your margin for error, Mike? You admitted that Nicole is spirited—with a wild streak, you said. You also admitted to wanting her badly, but not without benefit of marriage. Just how do you plan to keep her interested, but at arm's length—and away from the beaus and cousins—until Ransom approves you? It's not going to happen overnight and if you'll forgive my saying so, she is not going to make it easy for you."

"Oh-hell-no, it won't be easy!" the Captain turned to humor. "I will probably be forced to lay a parcel of wenches getting through it. But hell, for Nicole—anything!"

"That's mighty thin ice for a hot blooded Irishman," Tom cautioned.

But there the conversation ended, for Nicole O'Rourke appeared at the wheelhouse door to accept Mike's earlier issued, but badly bungled, dinner invitation for the evening. She also insisted on an introduction to Tom. And once more, he felt the singe of her eyes as he spoke his greetings; saw that she hoped to rekindle an answering spark in his. When he kept it neutral, she wasn't deterred. Rather, as he formally raised her hand to his lips, she stepped closer, causing her full skirts to rustle against his trouser leg. But Tom would have sworn it was the rasping of sandpaper…

Many miles down river, when the Irish Mist moored for the night and most of the passengers had retired to their beds, Tom took a stroll along a shore road where the air was cool and scented with honeysuckle. By accident, he topped a levy which put him on eye-level with the wheelhouse windows. Not at all by accident—and mostly because Jenny dozed peacefully outside the closed door—he stopped for a moment to watch. He couldn't hear the dialogue between the pair inside, but it wasn't hard to guess.

Dressed in a skin pink gown, dipping dangerously into her bust, Nicole flitted from the wheel to the dials asking insipid questions. Mike still sat at the supper table, arms folded across his chest. …*To keep his hands out of trouble*, Tom mused. Then she moved from view, but returned holding a whiskey decanter. *Oh no*, the Captain nodded. *Please?* she cooed, coming closer. *No, I think not*, he straightened in the chair. *Just a little?* she measured. *Absolutely not!* he shifted again. *But Captain*, she pled and dropped to the floor at his knees, her cleavage displayed precisely for his admiration.

"Oh hell," Tom groaned, heading back to the boat. If Mike loved the girl as deeply as he professed, he wouldn't be able to resist… Well, the problem was, even had Nicole's behavior been totally innocent—which it wasn't—her body certainly was not either. "Hell," he repeated, trying to remember that the Irishman did seem to lead a charmed life. He just wouldn't worry about it more. But he did…

Still later, Mike knocked at Tom's door, bringing the same decanter and elation enough to make a Tent Preacher anxious to pass the collection plate. Between liberally poured toasts, he deemed the evening a *great success*. He and Nicole were now on a first name basis; she had accepted several invitations to accompany him about Savannah… though she did call the plan their *exciting, wicked secret*—wasn't that the oddest thing? And, best of all, entirely on her own, she kissed him goodnight—not once, but three times!

When the Irishman finally took leave, Tom lay on his bunk, staring at the ceiling. He had wanted to share his friend's enthusiasm, but there was no mistaking the invitation he'd seen in Nicole's eyes. It ran deeper than flirtation, or spirit, or whatever the Captain chose to call it. There was hunger there too; raw and unleashed…

But determents from him would prove useless because fervor, such as Mike's, was blind to all but it's own bright flame and could only be extinguished from within. And, not that it mattered one damn way or the other, but he wondered who had won the tussle between Mike, Nicole and that decanter. If she did, then Captain Herb had just failed his first test in guidance with a firm hand…

# CHAPTER 2

The Irish Mist arrived in Savannah at four in the afternoon, but dusk loomed before Mike had finished his business and joined Tom in a tavern just up the narrow river-front street. Over a thirst-quenching ale, he said when Ransom arrived to collect his daughter, she had asked permission to invite the *so-charming* Captain to dinner one night soon. "So-charming—that's what she called me!" he said in high spirits. "But damn it, good news makes me hungry—always has—and I'm ready to go find some supper."

As they made the steep cobblestoned climb from the river, Mike was extolling the merit of something with the dubious name of *hushpuppy*, but on entering a narrow park running the length of a bluff he called Yamacraw, Tom had to stop for his first look at the city.

Maybe he imagined the pleasant sensation in the fading light of day…maybe…but he did see Savannah as a woman. And tonight, she was playing the vixen. Her perfume oozed heavy and sweet from a multitude of flowers; her eyes sparkled in glowing street lamps; and swishing her skirts in the rustle of palmetto fronds, she breathed suggestive night winds in his ear. Yes, the city was very much alive. And impatient. For while he continued to observe, she drummed her fingers through the clopping of hoof beats along the street. She had offered her warmth and wanted response. Tom laughed—he couldn't help it—but then had to assure the curious Captain, as well as his lady-city, that he'd likely enjoy Savannah very much indeed.

14

Crossing Bay Street, they turned east and it wasn't long before Mike pointed out their destination: The Pirate's House. As they approached, a lively concertina bid them welcome though Tom found the tune at odds with the ghostly grey clapboard exterior, for the place stood nestled in a grove of towering moss-draped oaks and seemed caught in the long gauzy swatches of a web. Shadows swam past grimy window panes, lending the look of badly strained eyes—eyes that had, perhaps, seen too much and would gladly have closed their pale blue shutters forever, had they not hung awry on the hinges. The place fairly reeked of aged mustiness and history pleading to speak…

On entering, they ordered a drink and Mike revealed the purpose of the visit while they enjoyed it. He'd come to collect the concertinist, one Miss Candace de Shoka, a local with three passions in life: the concertina, which earned a few extra coins; her work, which brought in a great many more; and both of which, allowed her employer to indulge her personal weakness for the Captain of the Irish Mist. It was also known by most, she would have considered it an insult should Mike offer her coins. They had, after all, been first time lovers and from the age of 15, had been at it, pretty much, ever since.

"So who is for a good supper?" Mike asked as the trio rode south in a rental buggy. After a time, they stopped before a place that had once been a private home. Now, torches and black pots of blooming petunias graced the sides of the doorway. Above it, hung a simple sign reading Seafest. Tantalizing aromas drifted to greet them from a back yard kitchen, convincing Tom he was ready to try any fare they offered—including the dreaded hushpuppy.

It was during his attack on a second seafood platter, that the obvious coolness of the small, pretty, auburn-haired serving woman piqued his curiosity. "…A jealous lady friend, Captain?" Tom asked quietly. For having finished eating, Mike was busy making dessert of Candace's ear.

"No, that's Kathleen Morgan; —or Kathy to most," he answered in like tone. "She's a widow—been widowed for two years now. Her husband left her with five small sons and a lot of debts. Anyway, there are stories about her. You see, a real bastard—name of Sam Lucas—owns

15

this place and a lot more in Savannah. Some say Kathy's husband owed him a large sum of money and he's making her work it off here. Others say she's Sam's mistress. All I know for certain is that every man on the prowl in this city has tried lifting her skirts—myself, included—and there's been no bragging done yet. Maybe, she's scared of crossing Lucas; maybe, she's happy being his bitch; or maybe, she just doesn't give a damn about men anymore," Mike shrugged. "Who knows?"

Candace shot a look of disbelief in Kathy's direction. And fondling the concertina, as she had been during the ride over and throughout the meal, she snuggled all the closer to her Captain. "Why fool with her?" she asked huskily. "I care for you, Mike—always have. Take me for a walk and I'll show you how much."

"Oh-hell-yes!" he grinned, drawing the girl to her feet. "If you'll excuse us, Mr. Scott, I've just found a place to drain some of that damn river. Finish your supper now—and don't be in a rush. We'll be close by." So saying, he led Candace away, the concertina dangling from her hand like a snake.

…*Five children*, Tom thought as he peeled a boiled shrimp. "And so small," he uttered aloud.

"You've surely heard about things in small packages," said Kathy, placing a tray on the table. "The smaller ones are always tastiest."

"I…are," Tom stammered, "—Were you speaking to me?"

Kathy glanced over the now vacant room as if that truly should be obvious and then began to stack dishes. "Yes," she decided to answer anyway, "I said the smaller sized shrimp taste better."

"Well, thank you, Miss," he chuckled, "but I was talking about a lady. —Not these shrimp."

"Oh!" she said and blushed. "I'm sorry, sir—very sorry," she laughed a bit too, but in a strained way, as if she didn't do it often.

"Please, sit down here and help me finish this meal," Tom pulled back a chair. "—Please?" he repeated. "My friend has deserted me and I've never enjoyed eating alone."

"Well…I don't expect more customers tonight," she hesitated nervously. "…Let me dismiss the cooks and lock up out there. Then, maybe I—I'll stay until your friends come for you."

16

"Good," he nodded. "And bring fresh ale for us both, will you?"

Kathy returned and while they sat eating shrimp and making light conversation, Tom studied her. Her hands were never at rest, but the ruse was not enough to hide their nervous tremble. When their eyes chanced to meet, she would blush looking quickly aside, proving Mike wrong on at least one point: she did give-a-damn about men. Time now to learn more.

So holding a freshly shelled morsel before him, he addressed it. "Shrimp, my name is Tom Scott. And since you brought this lady and me together, would you kindly introduce her?" Then reaching forward, he fed it to Kathy.

Cheeks scarlet with color, she lowered her eyes yet again. "I'm Kathleen Morgan," she said, just above a murmur.

"Well, Kathleen Morgan," he smiled, "Mike told me you have five children—which, for your slender size, I find hard to believe."

She busied herself brushing imaginary crumbs from the table. "I see. ...And what else did Mike say?"

"A lot. And nothing," he shrugged. "Only what he's heard."

"But you believed him, I'm sure," she said defensively.

"I believe you've had a rough time. ...No, you don't seem very happy to me."

"Rough?" she managed, her eyes remaining downcast. "Yes, I've had a very rough time."

"I'd like to hear your side of it," he urged.

"Why?" she glanced at him sharply. "Do you expect me to bare my soul—and then everything else? After two years of hell, am I supposed to be that grateful someone finally considered I might have a side to tell?"

So, there was a spark of life beneath those pent emotions. "Whoa, now," Tom countered. "I've suggested no more than conversation and you are half way up the wall."

She paused, reining hard on that spurt of defiance. "I'm sorry. I just get so...tired of the men that gossip brings in here. Why should you be any different?"

17

"I'm not. And I am," he met and held her gaze for the first time. "You are a beautiful woman, and like any other man, I'm attracted by that. But I'm not here because of gossip and I don't want anything you're not willing to give—be it your story, your friendship, or your-everything-else. You have a problem you're unhappy about. I am willing to listen, if it helps. Beyond that, the decision is yours and I don't intend to pressure you. …Fair enough?"

"Maybe," she said slowly. "…Yes, maybe it would help to talk. I haven't with anyone but Sam in so long—and he has no patience with the things that bother me." Then, inhaling raggedly, she made a brief start. "To put it bluntly, Mr. Scott, I am being used by a married man and there's nothing I can do about it—or would do now, if I'm being honest. It's too late for me, but not for those I love." She didn't trust that she wasn't about to see or hear the usual condemnations and lewdness she'd heard before.

But all he said was, "Tom—Kathy, please call me Tom." And because he'd chosen that as most important in all she'd admitted, she felt free to pour out the rest of the story.

Kathy's husband had owned a riverboat and for many good years, provided his family with a growing income. That profit was coveted by Sam Lucas, who made several friendly offers to buy Jamie Morgan out. The offers were refused, but the cordial tactics continued until Lucas learned his prey had a fondness for betting. He then invited Jamie for an evening of gambling at his club and before morning, Lucas owned the boat lock, stock and barrel staves.

Next Lucas suggested that Jamie captain the boat for him, but at a salary far below what was fair and needed—and knowing Jamie would have to accept, as the river was the only work he knew. When debts begin to mount, Lucas stepped in again, with loans at high rates of interest, driving the unfortunate man even deeper into his hands. Then Lucas also insisted on employing Kathy, claiming her salary as a bar maid his due. It mattered not that Jamie became despondent and started to drink heavily, or that his free time was spent watching in helpless frustration, as his wife warded off drunken advances in the low-life tavern where Lucas had placed her.

"And, when Jamie was on the river," Kathy added, "Sam was there propositioning me more persistently than all the rest. I turned him down, but lived in fear that Jamie would suspect Sam's motive—or what may have been his motive from the start."

"It does sound that way," Tom agreed, "As if Lucas ruined your husband to get to you. ...Damn. What happened then?"

"I've come to doubt even that," Kathy remarked. "Anyway, two years ago, the fever hit Savannah and in Jamie's weakened condition," she sought control. "...Well, he died almost overnight, leaving me at Sam's mercy."

Tom knew, up-close, some of the misery she felt and reaching, he gave a rub and comforting pats to her shoulder.

"Jamie had been gone less than a month, when Sam appeared on my doorstep," she continued. "He brought gifts for my sons; plied them with fatherly words and promises; and all the while, I prayed he felt some guilt for our dire situation. But in that same soothing voice, he demanded my submission. He threatened to put my home on the auction block unless he got it. He could have, too—still could—because Jamie was forced to turn over the deed to satisfy one of Sam's loans. So with my children playing at his feet, he told me I'd lose them too; that he'd use his influence as a trustee at Bethesda Boy's Home and see them taken because I wouldn't be able to provide shelter or support. ...And, through it all, that smile was still on his lips, but his eyes were cold as death," she shuddered, covering her face briefly with her hands. "Tom, I wanted to scream; to beat him with my fists! But... there sat the boys, laughing and enjoying themselves for the first time in a long while. I just couldn't cause them more strife—or risk losing them altogether—so I agreed," she lowered her head. "I could not fight it any more."

Tom lifted her chin on his fingers, urging her to straighten. "And this has been going on for two years?"

"Yes!" tears spilled over her lashes. "He made of me the married man's whore society ladies snub and to whom men feel free to show their baser sides."

19

"You're his victim and nothing more," Tom corrected. "…So, what about Sam's wife? Does she snub you too—or doesn't she know?"

"Neither his wife or daughter knows. They still believe what they were told: that Sam is allowing a poor widow to work off her debts at a charitable pace. Those two kind ladies bring food and clothing to my home all the time—and it breaks my heart to deceive them so! To make it worse, Sam is enrolling my oldest two in a fine school this year—and guess who insisted he do it? His wife! It's such a tangle and I'm stuck with it," she made brief swipes at wet cheeks. "But some good has come from their visits. It has stopped Sam from invading my home—and thankfully, while the boys are still too young to be swayed by his influence; …or to ask what Mama and Uncle Sam are doing together at night."

"If not in your home, then what arrangement did he make; — an Inn?"

Kathy's laugh was brittle. "The honorable Samuel T. Lucas would not be seen in public with me! No, he bought this place and had it done-over. Down here, I run his business. Upstairs…he ruins my life."

"I'm surprised you haven't tried to kill the bastard," Tom watched her dab at tears with a table napkin.

"If I were alone in the world, he would already be dead. But there is more to tell: In talking with his wife, I believe I learned the true reason Sam came after Jamie, then me—and it wasn't just about taking over our business or the boat. When Mrs. Lucas met my children, she said Sam had mentioned how cute they were, and how they both regretted not having a son of their own to love. And there I sat with five! Remember, I said he came bearing gifts and making them promises? It's possible he expected to step in and play father to my boys while bedding their mother—and still go home to his wealth and fine possessions."

"That's a lot to take in, Kathy," Tom leaned to the back of the chair.

"Maybe, but it's not important. As long as I can keep Sam coming here—to the Seafest—and away from the house, he can use my body as he wants. Mrs. Lucas has already said she'd see to it he paid to school *all* my sons—which is the only hope I have of giving them a better life than this. …So, the tangle tightens."

"Damn, that is complicated," Tom came forward again. "But is it enough for you; —as a woman, I mean?"

"It has become an alliance for my children's security."

For a second time, Tom held her gaze. "You didn't answer my question."

"Well, other than the ugly talk and the ugly men who come with it, it has been enough," she managed. "…Until you walked in here tonight," she added, embarrassed by this admission.

Tom raised both her hands to his lips and smiled. "That was an invitation, I hope."

"Yes," her voice softened to match the soft pink of her blush, "I think it was."

"I don't want to cause you more problems. …What would happen if Lucas finds out about this?"

"I don't know," she traced a finger down his cheek. "But he will be out of town for another week."

Catching that finger, he drew it across his mouth. "And do you have a key to that upstairs room?"

"I do—yes!" she whispered, moving around the table to kiss him briefly. "Give a few minutes before you come?" Then, locking the front door too, she went toward another door, pausing there to point the way.

Tom rose to look from a window. No sign of the Irishman or Candace and her dangling squeezebox. But should they return to find the door locked, Mike would know what it meant. Then, heading up the stairway, he came to a surprised halt on finding himself in an office. A large desk sat in the center of the room, with a chair behind and another before it. The windows were heavily draped in purple velvet, as was a windowed door to an outside stairway, on which he rechecked the thrown bolt. On the far wall, stood a whiskey cabinet framed with paintings signed by an M. Lucas, and Tom thought them quite good. The opposite wall was a solid unit of book lined shelves. It all seemed very business like, and he wondered if Lucas enjoyed taking Kathy on the carpet. He also wondered where she was and called her name.

21

At the same moment, a section of the bookcase swung open and she stepped from a concealed room. She wore only a filmy white gown, as evidenced by three feminine and alluring shaded areas showing through it. She had also loosened her hair and its auburn color caught the radiance of the lamplight. "Come in," she made a soft plea. "Please, please come in."

Tom went to her, watching for acceptance as he gathered her hair in his hands. A gentle downward tug tilted her face to his, and he kissed her warm cheeks; the tip of her nose; her closed eyelids. Lifting Kathy, he entered the secret room, then paused at what lay before him. For there sat the most enormous bed he'd yet to see, its size twice glorified in mirrored side walls, which then reflected the shimmer of sconce lights across a yellow satin spread. ...A most inviting playground. Looking upward, he saw that the ceiling above the bed had been windowed-in and moon glow spilled in with passionate suggestions as well. Heeding all, he nudged the door shut and holding Kathy close against his chest, allowed her feet a sliding seek for the floor. With a smile, which she returned, and slow, deliberate moves, he untied the ribbon at the top of her gown, peeled it from her shoulders, and ran curious palms over the tops of the rounded breasts still pressed firmly against his shirt. Taking a backward step, encouraging the gown to whisper its way downward from her body, he stood gazing upon her naked form and nodded approval as he reached to play with a small, tightened nipple.

Kathy's cheeks were deeply flushed, and her eyes bright with tears. "Tom, I have not wanted this for two years. Now, I can't wait—not a moment longer!" And closing her arms about him, she sought his mouth with an urgency he'd seldom felt in a woman.

She wanted him on the bed, and so they went. She wanted to undress him, and did in the midst of their many and varied embraces. She wanted his hands to roam her, and he gladly obliged. Then, drawing herself over him, guiding him to her pleasure, it wasn't long before she collapsed on his chest, allowing him to take the lead and his fill of her. For a time, they lay in silence, released from the realities of life, each unwilling to return from that place.

22

"Thank you," Kathy murmured at last.

Turning her onto the bed, they lay nose to nose. "You do deserve more than we've done here," he injected the words between small kisses he was placing on her face.

"Please…not tonight," she held a finger to his lips. "This has been a big step for me, Tom. …I hope you can understand that."

"I said no pressure and I meant it," he assured her. "But send word when you feel so inclined. I'm staying with Mike for the present."

"Aboard the Irish Mist?" she asked. And with his nod, a strange smile touched her mouth. "How very ironic," she said sitting up. "Anyway, you'd best leave now. I have much to do before going home."

"It's late to be on the streets," Tom said, reaching for his shirt.

"I won't be," she leaned on an elbow to watch him dress. "When Sam took me out of his tavern, he set up this business on the street directly behind my house. He paid a hefty price to do it, too, and even gave me a maid for the children—which, of course, freed me to do the bastard's bidding." Then, she laughed, and it sounded less strained. "Oh, Tom, you must be good for me. Did you hear what I called him? I've never dared to before—not aloud!"

Once on the street again, Tom followed the sound of the concertina toward a shrub laden square on the corner and called out to the Captain.

"Here, Tom!" came an answer. "Come see something you won't believe."

Wading through a head-high bank of Azaleas, he found Mike sprawled on a patch of grass, while Candace stood before him, nude from the waist down.

"Sit," invited the grinning Irishman. "You've got to see this—and here; have a cigar."

Tom went to his knees, unsure of what to expect, as Candace began to play her concertina and move in a kind of dance. He lit the cigar just as she gave a violent jerk of her lower body and a small object hit him in the chest. Holding the match to see what it was, he was

23

rapidly pelted twice more, and now three, bantam egg-size, shriveled green orbs lay nesting in the grass. ...So, she'd packed herself..., and with each jerk of up-tilted hips..., "spit" them out again? "Damn!" he muttered, singeing his fingers on the forgotten match flame. "—What the hell are those things?" he asked with all the astonishment Mike could have hoped for.

"Seed pods," answered the Captain jovially. "Come off the Angel's Trumpet bush in her Granny's yard. Candace, being the industrious lass that she is, collects the pods, planes the husks smooth and preserves them in her own secret formula. I was there once, when Granny asked if she'd made a lot of money from harvesting seed, and Candace said—all innocent and sweet, *Not yet, Granny. I'm still figuring out how deep to plant them.*"

"Mike, no...," Tom chuckled, sensing the onset of blarney.

"So, Granny asked how deep she'd tried it already and Candace says, *Oh, maybe six or seven inches.* Then Granny told her, *It's better when you can take it bit deeper, but do keep them in their own furrow and away from other things planted in your bed.*"

"Captain, would you stop?" Tom pled through eye-watering mirth.

"And Candace says, *Well that's odd, Granny, because I do put them in my furrow—in a nice, neat little row; one behind the other. But I've had* just as much luck with the ones I stuff right-up-under-my-bush."

By then, on the flat of his back, Tom had yielded to laughter; and Mike, wearing his Irish pride of story telling in the broadest of smiles, watched as Candace finished the exercise he'd just decided to call The Dance of the Horticulture Fairy...

Later, on the forward deck of the Irish Mist, Tom related Kathy's story as he and the Captain nursed a drink before retiring.

"I told you Sam Lucas was a damn bastard," swore the Captain. "I won the Irish Mist from him in a poker game, you know—luckiest damn night I'll ever hope to have—and ever since, he's had it in for me too. He wanted that deal I made with Ransom for himself."

Remembering Kathy's words, Tom asked, "Mike, was this boat once owned by Jamie Morgan?"

"Yes, and now that I know the truth of how he lost it, my feud with Lucas seems all the sweeter. He should be denied the fortune I'm making, because he ruined a good man for a chance at it."

"Things do have a way of coming full circle," Tom searched the heavens for the North Star "And, he deserves to lose Kathy too. That would make for a perfect ending."

"Don't count on it," Mike nodded. "In spite of everything, Sam is still a skirt chaser. —But that was the damnedest thing, Tom. See, a few years back, he had a real bad case of the Mumps. Overnight, his hair turned that silvery gray; —caused from high fever, or something. Then, by the time he could leave the sick-bed, he'd lost close to forty pounds too and didn't even look like the same man—doesn't to this day. Wears that bush of hair to his damned shoulders and hasn't gained back an ounce of weight either; —looks like a piece of dried fruit with a clump of Spanish moss lobbed on top, if you ask me. People joked, saying he was his wife's 2nd husband, but that she should have chosen better, because this one was as rotten inside as the first. Anyway, it's also said the disease left him sterile. No proving that, I guess, but before he was sick, he had more bastards than you can imagine. Then afterwards, nary a one according to those who keep track of such things," he paused for a needed sip. "Know what else? I heard he was terrified the next thing to go would be getting his pecker to stay up, so he became a damn humping machine, taking on more women than before. Hell, he still does —and he must be nearing fifty. So, no, don't look for Sam Lucas to give up his play-pretties—and especially Kathy, I'm afraid."

"Which begs a question, my informative friend," said Tom. "If Lucas is so powerful and corrupt, why would he stay away from Kathy's home because the wife might find out? ...Or, maybe she already knew and went there herself trying to catch him. But that doesn't make sense either. If she knew about Kathy's home, it stands to reason she'd know about the room above the Seafest. ...So, what would make it all right for her husband to see Kathy in one place but not the other?"

"Hell, Tom, you think too much," Mike grumbled. "But all else aside, are you going to see Kathy again?"

"If she wants," he replied. "I told her to send word here." And a note arrived from Kathy the next day—the first of many to follow...

# CHAPTER 3

---

Mike was damned proud of his success on the river. And the best part was the money. He purely loved making a whole lot of money! Yet, during this particular week, he wasn't too upset that the Irish Mist would have to remain dockside for needed repairs. Ever the optimist, he just deemed it the perfect time for showing Tom all there was to love about Savannah.

They began with a visit to his motherly Aunt Mary Ernestine and very Irish Uncle Pat—a Captain, himself, with the City Police. The pair had raised their nephew from the age of three and over a delicious Sunday afternoon dinner, regaled Tom with stories of that harrowing experience.

The next stop of the day was preceded by a perilous climb up the crumbling walls of Fort Wayne. From the top, Tom had a slightly elevated view of the city to the west and south. To the north, at the base of the bluff, ran the river. To the east, over the marsh and just at a bend in the Savannah, Mike pointed out the ramparts of Fort Jackson.

"The one there was the second fortification built to protect the city. Fort Wayne was first." And with pride burning bright in his eyes, he added, "It's why the settlement around us—including the home we just left—is called the Old Fort Irish Section."

Then as it was nearby, they finished off the evening at The Pirate's House. Over drinks at the bar, Tom asked about the history there and with one arm draped about Candace, Mike began an abbreviated sketch that was soon taken over by the bartender and several patrons.

Enlivened with much drama and gusto, they spun tales of marauding pirates who'd once walked the same plank floors; lifted glasses at the same bar; of women captured off the city streets and shamefully used above-stairs; of unwary men, fed drug-laced rum and their unconscious bodies carried through a basement tunnel to the river; of pirate boats there, lying in wait of a full crew before taking to the seas again; of those who dared protest captivity and how they were tossed overboard many miles out in the ocean; of one man who was unable to return to Savannah for 30 years; of the many who never did come home; of residing, tormented ghosts, who never left. And, as one tale led to another, Tom decided it had been a most memorable day…

On Monday, the Captain rented another buggy and just after the repair crew arrived at the boat, they set out on a tour of the main thoroughfares, stopping for a walk through the ornate lobby and gardens of the new DeSoto Hotel. Then they drove to the South for a look at Oglethorpe Barracks and lunched with a gunnery sergeant who'd been a classmate of Mike's. It was nearing three o'clock when they started back, and the Captain chose a route that had them weaving around a series of squares, much like the one where Candace had performed.

"Other than slowing us down in this heat," Tom questioned, "what is the purpose of all these squares?"

"Savannah was the first planned city in the Union, my boy," Mike explained. "The streets, lots and squares were plotted before the first damn tree was cut. Within the original city walls, there were four squares, which served as practice fields for the militia and gathering places for the folks living around them. Fire was a real danger then too, so the squares had community ovens to reduce the risk of house fires and community wells for drinking water—and putting out those fires if they happened anyway. Today, there are a dozen or more squares, but they're being made into greens or parks and the wealthy are building their mansions around them as fast as they can lay hold of property rights." And now he was holding the horse to a snail's pace. "The one over there—that big one—belongs to Ransom O'Rourke. This one on the right, here, is home to Samuel T. Lucas, bastard at large."

Mike continued speaking, but Tom's attention had fastened on the Lucas place. It was stuccoed and Spanish in design, with high wrought-iron balconies, arched windows and recessed doors. The house reeked of wealth, down to its precisely manicured shrubs. And as he watched, a lovely middle aged woman in a lavender gown—a woman as perfectly groomed and polished as her surroundings—paused on the front steps to adjust the wide brim of her hat before joining a carriage of ladies at the curb. ... *The wife?* he wondered, and for no reason he could discern, a twinge of apprehension wiggled up his spine...

"Tom?" Mike was saying. "You weren't paying a damn bit of attention. I'm not talking for my health here, son."

"Sorry," Tom chuckled, for Mike's portrayal of a snit wasn't very good. "Would you care to begin anew?"

"Oh-hell-no!" he declined. "You've heard my plan already and as we both have invitations for the evening, we'd best move along."

"...So, you received the expected dinner invitation from Nicole?" Tom guessed. "Is that the reason for the drive-by—and what you were trying to tell me?"

"Not just yet," the Captain said testily—and this time it was real. "No, while you're with Kathy tonight, I'll be with Candace—and she damned-well better make a job of it!"

Tom let the matter drop, as he knew Mike took his frustration over Nicole to Candace, who likely believed he truly needed her. Sad situation, that...

Tuesday's treat was a late performance at the famed Savannah Theater, so dressed in their best, Tom and Mike sat in the hushed audience awaiting the start of the play. But Tom found the quiet akin to a drug after a full day of knocking, hammering and banging from the ardent repairmen aboard the Irish Mist. Yawning, far more than was socially acceptable, he scanned the richly attired gathering, hoping for a reviving point of interest. He soon discovered, all on his own, another of Savannah's attributes. He was surrounded, happily, by beautiful women of all ages and sizes—like the young woman in the balcony just above them. He'd been granted a fairly good look, when she leaned forward trying to gain someone's notice with a waved greeting. And even in the subdued theater lighting, her smile had been…well, enchanting. It made him want to smile too. Then, the Captain was introducing the Curry's, a pair of ravishing brunette sisters, who invited them to a cast party after the play. Oh yes, Tom was wide awake now, and more than glad he'd come…

Mike chose Wednesday to show Tom some of Savannah's industries. It began with an up-river drive along the Savannah, to Hermitage Plantation, for a look at the domed ovens that baked the Savannah gray bricks made from clay dredged from the river bottom. Next, they drove east of the city, to the docks at Thunderbolt and observed the shrimpers and fishing fleets come and go after haggling prices over their catch with vendors waiting to buy. Then, in town, they spent some time at a foundry, watching the wrenching procedure used to make the ornate wrought-iron pieces that adorned many of the city's homes and explored the river front warehouses so bulging full of cotton, cane sugar, turpentine and bourbon casks, ready for foreign export on ships standing ready to load. That evening, escorting Barbara and Brenda Curry again, they went to dinner, then rode out to Barbees where Savannah's summer society often slipped away for an evening of dancing.

Tom was instantly impressed, for after passing through an entry room, they stood on a huge, roofed pavilion that extended over the brackish waters of the Skidaway River. On the three open sides, there were long rows of bench-seating against the guard railings, but nothing more to impede the free-flowing breeze. Colored lanterns bobbled in the rafters overhead, bathing everything and everyone in a kaleidoscope of romantic hues. He was smiling in approval, but as the present musical-set wound to a halt, he felt his smile broaden on its own—and realized he'd just seen that young lady from the theater balcony among the large crowd of dispersing dancers. For several minutes, he tried to find the direction she'd taken, but a new dance-set was starting, and his attention was kidnapped by the lady he brought.

Later, while sharing a cup of cider with Barbara, he again spotted the girl on the far side of the floor—and this time, he did not relinquish his gaze. While his date chattered and he nodded at what he hoped were appropriate intervals, he watched the girl just over the top of Barbara's head. ...*Willowy, but full bosomed figure; hair color hard to discern in this dappled lighting—as it was in the theater too. But some shade of blonde,* he thought... Then Barbara's laughter brought his attention back to her—which, truth be told, was really beginning to grate on his nerves. He kept wondering who that young lady was. Mike would know, surely, but the chance to ask never arose, and when it did, she had already departed.

The question plagued Tom late into the night. Why did he feel a sense of loss on finding the girl had left the dance? How could a woman he'd only seen twice—and never met—have such a startling effect on his senses? But Lord, that smile...

He saw Kathy the next evening and felt certain here was the cure for his nonsensical preoccupation. Yet, at the height of their passion, *she* returned to his mind and it wasn't Kathy he made love to but *her!* Tom left the Seafest thoroughly upset with himself. Where women were concerned, obsession wasn't an allowed emotion. He gave pleasure; they gave him pleasure—a fair and equal exchange. But he had used Kathy wrongfully just now, and for some insane reason, he felt cheated...

"Captain!" he roared, taking the boat stairs two at a time. "Are you ready to leave?" Mike had promised a round of the River Street taverns for Thursday night, and Tom was in sore need of a drastic change of mental environment. It was in this mood, that he greeted their jaunt, game for any scheme the Irishman had in mind. Or so he thought…

They had just watched the performance of a Turkish dancer and been improperly-impressed by her rigorous gyrations and scantily clad brown body. But all plans were put on hold, the moment one Mr. Bernard Brown appeared on the scene.

"Hey, Bernie, join us for a drink!" called the Captain. And a rather pleasant looking lad, who'd clearly had enough to drink, staggered to their table. "Sit down here," Mike pulled back a chair. "And meet my friend Thomas."

"Pleasur'; real pleasur'," Bernie slurred, and at Tom's nodded response, the boy fell, more than sat, into the offered seat.

"Well, what dastardly thing have you been up to?' Mike smiled, filling Bernie's glass to the brim.

"Notta' thing. Notta' a God-damn-thing! That Turish' bishes' not selling! Or else she didn't like the siza' my tool—I showed-er', you know. She looked and said *Nope*! The God damn bish."

"Don't take it personally," Mike's eyes sparkled with inspiration. "That whore must be stretched as wide as a watermelon. Why, it would take a stud horse to fill her. —And hell, boy, you've still got some growing to do!" Then, leaning closer, he continued in a soft, sly voice. "You do know you can make your prick grow? —And I'm not talking about a God damn hard-on."

"How?" Bernie stared. "How you make it grow?"

And now, Tom was staring too.

"Well, it won't happen with an old well-hole like the Turk. You'll need a young woman, with strong, tight muscles, that will grab hold and make you work like hell to get it back."

"I—I bet-cha' right! —I bet-cha' are!" sputtered Bernie.

"Hell, I know I am," the Captain winked at Tom—who was searching really hard for Mike's purpose. "Why, I'm living proof! —Hey, son, can I offer you another drink?" And, as he poured them a new one, he started in again. "…So, speaking of pretty, young things, I hear you've been seeing a lot of Nicole O'Rourke lately."

"Well, I'll-be-damned," Tom uttered audibly and flopped against the chair back.

"Yesh', I have," Bernie nodded. "The O'Rourke's been out to Hollow Oak since Sunday—bowf' of um'. And tomorra' night, I'm to be Nico's dinner eshcort' for the welcome-back ole' Ransom's giving at home."

Mike scooted his chair in closer. "Listen," he was almost whispering, "Perhaps I shouldn't tell you this—I mean, Miss O'Rourke is the daughter of a prominent man. ...But then, so is your father and considering her yen for you, maybe I should say something."

"For me? —Nico has a yen for me?" the lad asked eagerly.

"Well, I did bring her home from Augusta, you know, and she mentioned your name several times—yes, *several*," Mike emphasized. "Then, just today, I heard she told her servant, Jenny, she could barely resist, if you wanted to touch her."

"But...but I tried—ever' day since Sunday!" vowed Bernie. "She jus' kept running and laffin'; or else she'd cry. Then I truly felt turrable'—I mean, jus' turrable'!"

"All the same, she must want you to or she wouldn't have said what she did," Mike encouraged. But Tom saw his knuckles whiten on the chair arm. "You should do something about it too. At that dinner tomorrow night, you should get her alone—maybe in some shady spot of her courtyard? Then you should pet her in just-the-right-places—and hold her there until she's begging for more!"

"Do-ya' think she would? I mean, if she can't resis' me, she would—wouldn't she?"

"You'll see," Mike prodded. "Start with that little blonde and soon you'll have a stump-thick dick; a hundred women after it; and just as many yard-children."

"Work like hell—jus' to get it back!" Bernie repeated his favorite part. "Well, I'm gonna' do it, by-God-damn—Nico will be mine for the taking!"

"Good lad!" Mike clapped his shoulder a might too generously. "Believe me, Bernie, you will *never* forget tomorrow evening."

And he spoke the truth, for early Friday morning, Mike paid a visit to Ransom O'Rourke's office. When he left, a most grateful father was planning to catch young Mr. Brown in an act that would forever ban him from the premises…

Friday evening. The Friday evening. The one on which Mike had hoped to be among the arriving dinner guests at Nicole's party. He would have greatly appreciated seeing Bernie tossed out on his ear too. He'd never expected to attend as her escort—it was too soon for that—but he was disappointed that she'd forgotten to include him so quickly. As a result, his mood was churly and when Tom left to see Kathy, he stayed aboard the Irish Mist to bathe his ego in a new bottle of Bourbon. Later, he heard Tom come in and having grown bored with his own company, walked over to offer him a drink too. Tom accepted, saying he'd join the Captain in the wheelhouse when he'd changed into more comfortable clothing.

It was a cloudy night, limiting the moon to a faint glow, but Mike thought little of it as he started back along the upper deck. Blindfolded, he could have navigated every inch of his boat. Then, from down on the narrow flat dock, he heard his name called. There were shadows aplenty covering the area and one street lamp that shown no more brightly than the hampered moon. But again, he thought little of it, as his senses had been marinated in Bourbon. At the bottom of the stairs, he heard his name a second time in what sounded like a heavy French accent. More curious than ever, he crossed the gangway, searching the deep pockets of darkness tucked around and between the cargo stacked off to the left. Just in front of that, veiled in paler shadow, he spotted a man now, bent double and moaning as if in great pain. Concerned, he hurried forward—and right into the most terror filled predicament of his life.

Out of those pit black shadow pools, four more men leapt upon him. In the next second, he was lifted and slammed hard to his back, knocking the air from his lungs in a whoosh! Gagged and pinned,

34

one man on each limb, he tried in vain, for breath enough to protest. Amid the dots dancing before his eyes, a face swam into focus close to his own and a wicked looking knife came sliding up between their noses. "Candace will want you no longer," hissed the accented voice. "We fix this now and forever!" With that sobering thought—and the feel of the knife sawing away at his belt—Mike began to struggle in frantic earnest...

Tom started from his cabin looking forward to the offered drink, but on hearing muffled cries for help, he quickly evaluated the scene on the dock below, even as he climbed the railing, chose his target and jumped, feet first, in that direction.

The knife wielding Frenchman hovering at Mike's midsection, was there one moment, then gone: knocked cold; sandwiched between the dock and the force of Tom's weight. Taking advantage of the chaos, Mike wrenched free a leg, only to plant an angry booted blow to the stomach of the man who'd held it. Tom wrestled the assailants from Mike's arms, flinging them far and wide, while the Captain threw an even more furious blow to the jaw of the man on his other leg. Scrambling upright, jerking the gag from his mouth, he gave Tom a hurried warning. "Watch their damned feet!"

Back to back now, they saw only two adversaries with will left for battle, but one had pried the knife from his fallen comrade's grip. Circling slowly, the French sailors muttered curses and launched an effective series of short, quick kicks and lunging, straight-armed jabs. It was an unfamiliar, almost teasing method of fight, meant to confuse and it did. Mike's shirt was soon a crisscross of blood stains, where the blade scored his chest with taunting deliberation. Tom took a painful kick to the ribs and a hard jab to his head that left both eyes watering. But seeing a second attempt on the way, he flung both arms up beneath an extended air borne leg, flipping the off-balanced man and hearing the snap of bones when he landed face-down, in an ungainly pile.

At this, the knifer let out a cry of rage, charging forward, the knife aimed directly at Mike's groin. Side stepping, the Captain still took a gash to the thigh, but the sailor never knew it, as Tom hammered a two-fisted chop to the back of his neck—to which Mike added a well earned knee to a French groin—and he folded in an unmoving heap.

Once the weapon was removed from the man's limp fist, Tom straightened to look around. All five sailors lay on the dock, unconscious and in various stages of injury. "An unusual evening, Captain," he wiped perspiration from his brow. "Or is this standard fare for a Friday night in Savannah?"

"Oh-hell-no!" Mike came back. "We Old Fort Irish see more action on a dull week night. …Just the same, thanks, Tom," he added seriously. "They were about to take my most prized possession."

"Can't help but wonder why?"

"Candace. They must have wanted her services. But the little twit refuses all offers when I'm in town—enjoys throwing it in their faces, too. I've told her to stop or she'd get us both killed," Mike took an irritated step forward, only to wince sharply at noting his injury for the first time. "Damn! Get me aboard before I bleed to death! Then, go for Uncle Pat and his boys before these bastards crawl away. Damn, my leg hurts! —Tell Uncle Pat to bring a Doctor too!"

It was dawn before Mike's wound was patched and the police had finished their investigation. In his cabin again, Tom was hoping to finally get some sleep, when Mike hobbled in wearing his plotting expression.

"What now?" Tom asked, unsure if he was annoyed or amused.

"I'm having company after while," the Captain's grin widened. "Miss Nicole O'Rourke and her father—and I want you to usher them to my sick-bed. Then, you can sleep or whatever, so get up, my man!"

"I can't say you won't get away with this, because you probably will," Tom nodded. "But how do you know they're coming?"

"Because I sent Uncle Pat to tell them how bravely I defended that cargo load on the dock—and Ransom just happens to own the stuff. He'll come, Tom. He's that kind of man. And I'm hoping Nicole will too—if only to see me in bed."

"Is that the story you gave Captain Pat? You're charging the Frenchmen with attempted robbery?"

"Well, had they succeeded with their plan, I daresay I would have been robbed of an irreplaceable treasure," the grin turned devilish. "But yes, attempted robbery, plus two counts of attempted murder—yours and mine—and whatever else it takes to have the bastards deported or hung—I really don't care which. Now come along, Thomas. We have a scene to create!"

When finished, the Captain wore a nightshirt and lay propped in his bed against three pillows. Protruding from beneath the sheet, his injured leg rested on a fourth. It had been over-dressed in a bandage running down past his knee—and with a talent to be envied by ancient mummy wrappers. He added drama to the show by undoing more shirt buttons to better display the blade scratches on his chest. On the nightstand was an artful arrangement of pill boxes and salve jars; and the window shutters were slanted so the cabin was just shafted in light. For Ransom's use, a table beside a large easy chair held glasses and a decanter of Irish whiskey. For Nicole though, a small straight chair was more strategically placed near the bed.

With a cigar in one hand and a drink in the other, the Captain nodded approval. "This should do it. What do you think?"

"Do what?" Tom shrugged.

"By damn, Tom—I thought you'd guess! I'm ready to start seeing Nicole on a regular basis now."

Tom looked over the room and back to the Captain with a chuckle. "Wouldn't it be simpler to knock on her door with candy and flowers?"

"No—oh-hell-no! She'll be coming to *my* door first and I hope to keep her coming—even if I have to fake a couple of relapses. Now, take this glass and cigar away—and the bank draft on my desk? The workmen swore to be finished by ten, so pay them and get that damn noisy bunch off this boat!" Then snuggling into his pillows, he mumbled as if Tom were no longer there. "An injured man shouldn't have to listen to such racket. An injured man should lay here and practice ill expressions. *Poor, Michael,* she'll say. *Poor, poor Michael.* —Damn leg! Damn, it hurts!"

As expected, the O'Rourke's pulled up to the landing just before noon. Nicole was dressed in white, her hat an angelic cloud of white netting. But the purity of the outfit sharply contrasted the hot, lusty look she gave Tom as he assisted her from the carriage.

"Miss O'Rourke, it's good to see you again," he kept his manner cordial. "I hope you've been well since last we met?"

"I have, thank you," she held to his hand with a cloying squeeze. "But quite busy. Yes, I truly meant to ask you—and Captain Herb, of course—for dinner long before now. We've time, yet to get better acquainted though…haven't we?" And this came with fluttering lashes meant to sway the heart.

"Dinner would be a treat," he ignored all else and turned to extend a hand to her father. "Mr. O'Rourke, I'm Thomas Scott. It's a pleasure to meet you, sir."

"How is Mike?" Ransom responded with a firm handshake and clear, intelligent eyes that matched the sincerity of his tone. And as Mike had already predicted, Tom liked the man right away.

"Well…it would cheer him considerably to know you are here," he avoided a lie while they boarded and moved toward the stairway. "The Captain did have a close call, sir, but I believe he'll survive the mending."

"Yes, he's too proud to be beaten—too Irish!" Ransom laughed, guiding his daughter before him as they followed Tom up.

"And too good a friend to lose," Tom added, glancing over his shoulder, just in time to catch Nicole openly admiring the fit of his trousers. On reaching the top then, he stepped aside ushering both the O'Rourke's before him.

"Exactly his feeling toward you," Ransom said. "Mike told me he persuaded you to come to Savannah, Mr. Scott—filled me in on your background too. In your field, University graduates are as rare as hen's teeth around here. Come see me when you're ready to find a position. I can promise some interesting interviews."

"Thank you, sir, I'll do that soon," Tom nodded. "I've a financial matter I want settled too and your advice would be greatly appreciated."

They now stood before Mike's cabin, and Tom could still feel Nicole's inspecting gaze. He met her eyes and watched as eagerness spread to the corners of her mouth. "Miss, O'Rourke," he made a purposeful pause, "…Perhaps you had rather wait out here while we go in."

That stopped whatever game she was playing. "…What on earth for?" she puzzled.

"Well, Captain Herb isn't dressed—not to receive a lady. He's flat on his back and his wounded limb is…well, exposed, you see."

"Oh, then I must see him!" she almost spoke too quickly, proving Mike correct that she'd come to see a man in bed. "—I mean, he treated me most kindly on the trip from Augusta," she issued a hurried explanation, "And I will not desert my new, dear friend in his time of need."

"That's truly admirable," Tom nodded, seeing that Ransom believed her, even if he didn't. But likely, the man seldom heard his daughter express concern for anything more serious than looking her best for the next social event. Nevertheless, he opened the door, led the O'Rourke's to the waiting Irishman's bedside and excused himself from their presence…

# CHAPTER 4

From the riverfront, Tom strolled about the city paying no particular attention to direction. Yet, on finding himself in the square facing the Lucas home, weariness seemed to overtake him. After such a night, with no sleep and an aching bruise the size of saucer on his ribcage, all he wanted was a moment of rest. So settling on a deeply shaded bench, he was content to gaze over the lush green park in quiet abandon. But the respite was short lived…

"I mean it, Lucy—I could just kill Sam Lucas!" vowed an angry female from behind a tall, dense clump of Azaleas. "With my bare hands, I could kill him!"

"Mandria! —He's your father!" scolded the younger Lucy voice. "Why would you say such a terrible thing?"

"Because—damn it—he's seeing another woman!" the reply came with effort. "And she is awful—a whore from the streets, with dyed black hair and cheap, heavy make-up!"

"Oh dear," squeaked the other, while Tom felt relief. That was by no means, a description of Kathy. "Maybe you shouldn't be telling me this?" Lucy added hopefully.

"Well, we've been friends almost from birth and I have to talk with someone, Lucy! Mother refuses to discuss it—though she saw them yesterday evening as plainly as I did!"

"No, your father is in Charleston—remember? You couldn't have seen him yesterday!"

"But we did—in his office and he was undressing that damn woman!" her anger built again. "Then he had the nerve to come home this morning claiming he'd just arrived on the night coach!"

"Oh dear me!" Lucy gasped. "And your mother saw… Oh, Mandy, what did she say?"

"Mother said not a word; —not the first word! Father never knew we were there. She just closed the door quietly, and led me away. I thought she must be in shock, but when I tried to bring it up later, she refused to say or hear a word against him. She just said she'd take care of *things* and not to worry about it!" There was a pause here, and a ragged intake of breath. "But when he came in this morning, she poured his coffee; asked about his trip—and even brought him the damn newspaper, as if nothing at all had happened. And I'm telling you, Lucy, the longer I sat there, the angrier I became with both of them!"

"Why? Your mother didn't do anything," Lucy defended.

"But that's exactly it! Don't you see? By remaining silent, she all but condoned his behavior—and made a damn mockery of everything she's ever taught me! Words—just words she refuses to live by!"

"Yes, but she is a real good person," Lucy spoke now in staccato. "There isn't a mean bone in her body, and you know it!"

"Not much backbone either," the reply was fraught with disappointment. "Well, I have no intention of being that weak. —I am going to make him pay for what he did!"

"H…how?" the squeak was back, along with a pinch of apprehen-sion.

"Maybe by taking up his ways. —Yes, maybe I'll give him something to think about; …like finding me half-naked in someone's arms; —and preferably, someone he detests!"

"That is crazy—just plain crazy!" Lucy sounded frightened here.

"I could do worse," insistence strengthened resolve. "I could have an affair. I could tout it all over town too—and really disgrace him!"

"Mandria Lucas!" It was strongly declared. "You would not do that! —You know good and well you wouldn't!"

"Why not?" She led the way through the bushes, slapping furiously at the branches. "He got away with it! No one reproached him! Who

41

will reproach me, then—my mother?" she laughed bitterly. "Not my mother!" And moving on, she was never aware of Tom's presence, though she passed within touching distance of where he sat.

But Lucy saw his shadow-wrapped form and her expression went quickly from a nervous smile to a curious frown while trying to determine what he might have heard. Tom looked away in apparent disinterest, which must have satisfied, for she hurried up the walk jabbering after Mandria again. "Wait! You wait—Mandy, wait right there!" And when Mandria stopped abruptly at the curb, she all but ran into her. "Listen, you've never talked this way before!" she hopped about, her voice rising, then falling to a near whisper. "You know you wouldn't...*lay down* with a strange man. You know good and well you wouldn't!"

Mandria looked at her flustered little friend and relented all that she could. "We'll talk more later—on the island, all right? Now, come along and I'll fix us a nice cup of tea."

Lucy glanced back at Tom, who seemed to be watching a pigeon, and running to catch up, tagged Mandria's heels all the way to the house. "You'll think of a better way," the jabber continued. "You really, really will. You'll think of something more—well, more sensible, because you are just a real sensible person!"

...Disinterest? Tom wondered how he'd pulled that off. He was nearly numb with surprise, but disinterested? Not a chance. Mandria Lucas—Sam Lucas' daughter—was the girl he had not been able to banish from his thoughts. He sat there a while longer digesting all he'd heard. "So, the saga of Sam Lucas continues," he uttered aloud. ...*Would the man grieve the loss of his daughter's respect; —of her virtue, if she chose to disgrace him?* he thought. Lucas had shown no qualms about destroying Jamie Morgan; Kathy was virtually his prisoner; and according to Mike, they were but two among many victims. ... *Yet, it isn't Sam's conscience the lady hopes to wound,* Tom concluded. *She's aiming for her father's pride—and damn, but that could prove dangerous...*

Nonetheless, he tried her name on his tongue. "Mandria," he said, remembering the smiles she had cost him with each one of hers. But in truth, he found her equally exciting in anger. Odd thing, that.

"...M. Lucas," he recalled the signature on the paintings in the Seafest office and wondered if she'd done them. "Mandy," a tan and green image swept passed, followed by the scent of honeysuckle. ...Yes, she'd smelled of honeysuckle when hurrying by; her dress had been green, matching the angry green shards in her eyes; ...and sun-kissed skin, nearly the same shade as her tan hair. Not a combination easily dismissed. That, however, was no longer an option...

When Tom returned to the Irish Mist, Mike lay in wait, eager to report the outcome of his sick-bed strategy. In elated terms he said it had been Nicole who convinced Ransom of his needed convalescent care; she who insisted the O'Rourke's owed him a debt for saving the cargo from those nasty old thieves; and she who said the least they could do, was have Jenny bring in healthy meals each day. When Ransom readily agreed, she pushed for paternal permission to accompany the maid—just occasionally—to make certain the Captain's recovery progressed well.

"It was a hell of a lot of fun," Mike chuckled. "—Though, I don't know when it was I lost control of my own damn scheme. Nico just took over and all I had to do was lay here looking pitiful! But you know me. I never receive a gift in one hand without extending the other one too. So my boy, when the leg heals a bit more, we are making that trip to the coast I promised you—but with an extra passenger. See, I told Ransom—and it's true—that you've never seen the ocean; and as repayment for Nicole's thoughtfulness about my welfare, asked if she might accompany us. He made stipulations, of course, but damn if he didn't give his consent! Now, all I have to do is survive those fine O'Rourke meals, the stews Aunt Mary Ernestine will be sending for sure, and come out of this without looking like a fattened Christmas goose!"

...*Oh well*, Tom nodded, putting aside the questions he had wanted to ask about Mandria. It was useless to vie for Mike's attention when it was so focused on Nicole O'Rourke. *Later, perhaps...*

Tom had not heard from Kathy since Lucas returned three days before. Worried about her, he went by the Seafest during business hours, ordered a drink he didn't want and sat waiting at the bar for her find a spare minute away from the chatty lunch crowd in the adjoining room. He wasn't leaving until she did either, because the first things he noted were the bruises on her wrists; that her hands trembled again; and how she kept a constant eye on both the front door and the one to the stairway…

"Mister, you want a shine?" asked a small voice at his elbow.

Tom turned to face two bright-eyed, red haired boys peeking over the large wooden box they carried, and knew at once, they were Kathy's children. Across their crate, block letters advertised their service.

SHOE BLACKS (2 ½ c. a shoe)

"So," he grinned, "what happens if you meet up with a carnival type—let's say, a man with shoes on three feet; or maybe a pirate, with a peg leg and only one foot in need of a shoe? At 2 ½ cents each, how would you collect for those shines?"

The youngsters looked at each other and laughed. "Either way, we'd do them for free—compliments of the Morgan brothers!" announced the eldest. "People would like that."

"Yeah, com-mer-ments of the Morgan brothers," agreed the other boy.

"That shows good business sense—and excellent logic," Tom nodded. "So I'll take your very best shine."

"Hey, thanks, Mister!" they chimed, producing a mountain of rags, cans and brushes from their box.

As they set to work, Tom saw that the youngest was getting more polish on himself than where it belonged. "Got yourself a new partner?" he asked the oldest.

"Yes sir, I do. See, me and Rob are going to school this year and Mama said they'll have a Candy Kitchen there. We want to buy some everyday too, so we figured with both us working, we could save up and do it."

"And Mama would be Kathy?" Tom sought confirmation.

"It's the hair again, Jamie," the words were squeezed from the corner of Rob's mouth.

"Yes, sir, she's our Mama—and Rob's right about the hair. People guess who we are every time."

"Well, are you earning a lot of candy money?" Tom quizzed.

"Enough, but we could use more," Jamie answered. "We got little brothers at home and they like candy too."

"Might keep them out of ours that way," added Rob. "If it don't, I'll have to eat mine up before I get home, I guess."

Tom was enjoying himself, though it was with a touch of nostalgia for childhood days spent with his own little brother. "How old are you business tycoons?" he asked then.

"I'm ten and Rob, here, is eight," Jamie replied.

"Eight-and-a-half!" Rob contended from behind an over-sized rag. "—Jamie, I'm eight and a half."

At this point, Kathy returned with a scolding. "Boys! You'll have to stay outside with that polish. The ladies in the dining room will complain about the smell—and I've told you this before!"

"Oh, Mom," Jamie countered. "People won't stop outside—and Uncle Sam said we could come in here. He said no lady would be in a bar anyway."

"Yeah, Mom," Rob joined in, neither aware of the slight given their mother. "People just don't think about dirty shoes when they're all stuffed with food."

"...Well, if Sam gave you permission," Kathy hedged, her eyes returning to watch the doors. "But do stay out of the dining room, all right?"

"We will," Jamie promised, as Kathy hurried out again. "Let's see how you're doing there, Rob. Yeah, just buff the toe a little bit more, but that's real good." Then he said to Tom, "Rob learns pretty quick don't he, Mister?"

"I'd say so," he answered, handing money to the boy and watching him count back the change. "Correct to the penny, so you get to keep that for a tip. You know what else? If you were in my school, I'd make you my assistant in math class."

"Are you a teacher?" Jamie asked. "'Cause I wouldn't mind none if you taught me."

"Finally:—someone who believes I could be!" Tom looked heavenward and laughed. "Boys, did you know most people think a good teacher has to have warts and gout?"

"Well I'm glad you don't, sir," Jamie laughed too.

"What's gout?" Rob asked, looking at a wart on his thumb.

But Kathy had returned. "Never mind, now," she steered the pair toward the door. "Run along—but be inside the house before dark." And giving both a quick kiss, she watched for a moment as they lugged their box down the steps. Then, looking to see that the diners were still occupied with their plates and their conversations, she went behind the bar and began drying and shelving a tray of glasses—but didn't relax her watch on the entryways and never once looked at Tom, lest it appear they were conversing.

"Kathy, you seem frightened," he began, accepting her rules for their talk. "Are you all right?"

"I'm so sorry about this, but if Sam comes back…," her voice broke and she darted another glance toward the doors.

"You want to end it between us." he said—and it wasn't a question.

"Tom, I must! On Friday, you hadn't been gone thirty minutes when he came. And he knows things aren't the same as they were. He said I was…too happy and he'd find out why and fix it. He will, too. If we're caught, I could lose everything that matters." She raised a quaking hand to swipe at a single tear.

"And the bruises? …Has he hurt you?"

"My whole life hurts!" she shrugged. "But I'll survive—and you just met two of my five reasons."

"…Why do you stay?" he asked pointedly. "Don't you have family somewhere—anywhere—who'd take you in?"

Kathy straightened, drawing a bit of courage about her that was even more tattered than the rag with which she continued to dry glasses. "There is no family and nowhere I can hide with five children that Sam wouldn't find. He promised me that," her mouth firmed. "So I choose to stay, Tom, and for both our sakes, we have to part ways."

Had Tom reached for her hand, he knew she would have pulled away. "Kathy, look at me—please?" he bid for her gaze instead. And didn't continue until he held it. "I am still your friend. If you ever need help—if it finally becomes more than you can handle—I want your promise to call on our friendship for any favor. ... Will you give that much to take with me?"

Tears welled again, but her posture remained rigid. "Thank you—for being my friend," she struggled.

"I want that promise," he insisted.

But an assenting nod was all she could manage before turning to hurry away...

The Captain's recovery was a thing to marvel. It had been a week since the injury occurred and pleasing him to no end, Nicole had come with each of Jenny's meal deliveries. Of course, this was unknown to her father; and of course, she took further advantage, sending Jenny on various errands, which allowed for the addition of bed snuggles and stolen kisses to the menu. Mike very carefully indulged what he believed natural curiosity. But that, according to his logic, also necessitated Candace's night time visits as reward for his saintly day-time behavior.

Tom had his own reason for wanting to see Nicole aboard and throughout that week, made it a point to stop by at some time during each of her stays. If he wanted to know more about Mandria Lucas, what better place to start than with her neighbor from across the square? So tucking his inquiries into guarded corners of conversation, he learned Mandria was in her twenties; had refused several marriage proposals—which greatly upset her father; that she enjoyed reading, painting, music, dancing and "browning her skin" as Nicole put it with great distaste.

"I love Mandy dearly," she'd added just today, "but she really doesn't care about important things. She came to my dinner last week, of course, and she does go to nearly all the dances, but she never attends our Ladies Club—not even the High Teas!" And because her opinion seemed of value, she offered more. "Do you know she won't even keep a personal servant? Why, I couldn't live a day without Jenny."

A chuckled nod of certainty was heard from that one as she unpacked the Captain's lunch.

"That does seem unusual," Tom commented, trying not to hang on every word. "—Would you look at that platter of fried chicken?" he steered attention away from his purpose. "Jenny, I'll hug your neck if there's an extra piece for me," he teased.

Jenny laughed aloud and rolled her eyes at him, while Nicole instantly presented a large crispy chicken breast—but didn't get the promised hug. Mike just lifted an eyebrow. It wasn't like him to remain silent through all this and Tom knew there would soon be a reckoning.

It didn't take long. Once Nicole had departed for the day, the Captain's hobbled search found Tom seated on the main deck, boots propped on the guardrail, enjoying a cigar.

"Want something to go with that?" Mike dropped onto another chair, as he presented the bottle and glasses he brought with him.

"Don't mind if I do," Tom agreed.

With drinks poured, Mike lit his own cigar and for about a minute and a half, they sat looking out at the river in companionable silence. "Mind if I ask you something?" he said suddenly.

"Ask away," Tom shrugged. To be fair, it may have taken the Captain a full two minutes to fire off his question. "Not that my lack of permission would stop you," he added with a chuckle.

"All right, then. Why all the questions about Mandy Lucas? You've been at it all week and I didn't know you'd met her."

"I haven't."

"No?"

"Yet."

"Oh?"

Tom looked at his too-wise friend and conceded. "Since trying to keep anything from you, is like trying to keep it from God, all right then, I'll tell you." And confessing all, he started with Kathy ending their affair; moved to his growing fascination with a girl he hadn't met; and concluded with the discoveries he'd made in the park square. "So, do you know Mandria, Captain? Is she seeing anyone special?"

"We've a nodding acquaintance—same as I had with Nicole. But as you can imagine, Sam didn't give her much leeway in choosing friends," he paused, allowing time for the horn of a passing tug to fade. "I grew up on the streets, while she spent summers at Marsh Haven—that's the Lucas plantation. Come the winters, she was sent to one finishing school or another. And those proposals Nico spoke of? It's said Sam arranged them and not a man in the lot was under sixty."

"But all wealthy, of course," Tom uttered. "…Well, at least she had the sense to refuse them."

"Yeah, for all the good it did her. No one bucks Sam Lucas and goes unscathed—not even his own daughter—which keeps me on my toes, I'll tell you. Anyway, since Mandy refused his choices, he has refused any of hers. It's also said he threatened a few with bodily harm or financial ruin when her interest grew stronger than he liked."

"So he still hopes to marry her to money," Tom handed over his glass for a refill.

"And isn't that ironic? Sam runs over-town with his pants open, but expects Mandy to make a *proper* marriage," he replenished his own drink too. "…Well, it seems Mr. Lucas is in for a huge surprise. —You making a bid if Mandy goes up for grabs?"

"I don't know, Mike," Tom answered. "She is incredible, but how much longer can I avoid locking horns with Sam Lucas? You are my best friend and he has it in for you; I slept with his prize mistress; and now his daughter catches my eye? …I've a feeling I wouldn't be on his list of favorite people."

"So? To hell with him! If you want the girl, go after her. It would serve Lucas right—and likely do her more good than not." Then he switched on that eye twinkle. "Son, there's an old Irish saying that goes: Now I lay me *not* to sleep; —and the more damn *lays,* the better!"

"Never mind that," Tom said with a chuckle. "Just get your Leprechauns to introduce us. I'll take it from there."

"Sure you will. I'd put wagers on you, my friend! ...But, if it's Leprechauns you want, I just might know the right one," he finished, leaning his head back on the chair.

"Nicole?" Tom ventured.

"Is mine," he smiled, closing his eyes. "Now, go somewhere so I can think."

"One thing more: I ate the last of your Aunt Mary Ernestine's stew. Will you tell her I really enjoyed your supper?" And, when Mike's only response was the wag of an index finger, Tom heaved a sigh and left, but knowing when this Captain was at the wheel, the boat always went to the port he chose, regardless of time, tide or Leprechauns...

# CHAPTER 5

Such a fine day it was for sailing, with the winds holding steady, the sun tap dancing on the flat, low surface of the eastern horizon, and Captain Herb at the wheel of the Shamrock. A blinding glare rose off the river, causing him to squint badly, but he wore the broadest of smiles. For beside him, sat Nicole O'Rourke, looking quite lovely and ready as a lady could be for a Saturday of adventure.

The bodice of her sky-blue gown was a crisscross of cummerbund laces, snipping her waist to nothing. Her hair, pinned away from her face, and adorned with matching blue ribbons, hung in white blonde waves down her back. Complete with blue floral appliqués, she carried a parasol, twirling it prettily. Jenny, the eternal chaperone, held a picnic basket, though it too was draped with cloth slightly darker in hue than Nicole's dress.

Tom was also smiling as he took in the openness of the landscape. Unlike the swampy savannas he'd noted on the way from Augusta, the salt marsh was a maze of untutored tidal streams, intermingled with islands that had magically rooted in the midst of the gold reed sea. Along the mud banks, tiny fiddler crabs crawled sideways on disjointed legs. Mackerel and trout leapt from the water, flipping their tails before landing again with loud whapping sounds. Cranes, herons and snow white egrets—some balanced on a single, spindly leg—fluffed their feathers in apparent boredom and ignored the passing of time as well as the billowing flap of the Shamrock's mainsail. Overhead, seagulls drifted the air currents, diving and gliding, climbing and gliding, etching patterns on the early morning sky with pointed, finger-tipped wings.

Jenny enjoyed none of this beauty. Knotting her skirts to the boat rail, she clutched the woven hamper to her mammoth bosom and mumbled in prayerful monotones. "Don't let no shocks eat me, Lord. Ah won't fool with that Benjamin no more. Please, sweet Jesus, just save me."

"For goodness sake, Jenny!" laughed Nicole. "Do be quiet now." But the Negress mumbled on while the boat sailed ever eastward through miles of waving, rustling marsh grass that carpeted both sides of the river.

After a time, Mike pointed off to the right. "See that construction project? It's to be a federal fort—Fort Pulaski, they say."

"For Count Casmir Pulaski of Poland," Tom looked back over his shoulder for a better view. "Killed here during the Revolution, wasn't he?"

"Why, yes he was!" Nicole sought attention. "Interested in history, Mr. Scott? —Or is the making of it more to your taste?" her tone became sly. "Yes, a man like you, would love cutting a wide path across those annuals, wouldn't he?"

"That's *annals* to you, Tom," Mike's amusement was evident. Yet, ever willing to vie for Nicole's notice, he pointed again. "Look forward, me-darlin'! There's the Tybee lighthouse. —And Jenny, there isn't a shark or a whale in sight!"

"*Whales!*" Jenny shrieked. "Ah forgot about whales! Oh, Lord—oh, my sweet God! 'Member how you save Jonah? Now, don't go forgetting old Jenny! Please, Lord, please don't—please!"

"What lighthouse did you say?" Tom asked over the growing litany.

"Tybee—it's an Indian word meaning salt."

"They used to duel down here too," Nicole said helpfully. "But Tybee has lost its romantic charm to all but fishermen now. And those who want to leave the city for a while," she added in a bored urban tone. "Personally, I've never understood such cravings."

"I do!" Mike injected. "I spent a lot of summers here with my Uncle Denny and loved every minute of it."

"Well, Daddy does too," she admitted. "We have a cabin on Back River, but its just so damp and sandy, I've never enjoyed going there."

"What a shame," Mike feigned disappointment. "That would have been the perfect place for an early breakfast."

"Do it!" the words erupted from Jenny. "Go at the cabin, sir! We going to get swept to sea and lost for God-sure! Please, Cappin' Mike—please, get Jenny to land!"

"We should, you know," the Captain pled his own case to Nicole. "She's not looking well and we're just coming into the mouth of the river."

"The mouth of hell!" Jenny screeched. "Oh, my good forgiving God! Lord, save me! God, save me! —Jesus, you get in there too! Save me, somebody! Save Jenny from the shocks' and whales!"

"Well, alright then. I suppose she could do with a rest," Nicole patted Jenny's arm.

But Tom saw no sympathy in the gesture. More likely, she was imagining the daring possibilities of a cozy repast, alone with two eligible males. *And Mike had called Candace a twit*, he thought...

The Captain took a firmer hold on the wheel as the boat suddenly lunged into the tide, and for an instant, Tom feared his hold on reality had slipped over-board. Clear to the horizon, melting into the sky, the sea engulfed his vision. Patches of cloud shadow skimmed the surface in one direction, while the water rose and fell in another. It was a dizzying, humbling sensation that left him feeling minutely insignificant—like a speck of flesh colored lint, clinging to an enormous azure spread. And the Atlantic was definitely a woman too; all women collectively; the ultimate Amazon. For where Savannah had enticed with sauciness and warmth, the sea commanded the senses, making it known she'd tolerate no challenges in her domain. And Tom, as centuries of men before him, bowed to her awesome power. In answer, Atlantic revealed her smile in the curls of myriad sun-sparkled whitecaps, bidding him a conqueror's welcome...

Jenny had been wailing again when Tom returned from his tryst with the sea.

"Be calm now," Mike was soothing her, as he eased into a southward swing that had them skirting the shore. "Jenny, if the Lord won't save you, I will. For the love of God, I will—if only for some peace and quiet!"

But Jenny had passed beyond comfort or prayer. As the miles swept by, her smooth, brown skin paled to the color of tarnished brass; and tears streamed from her tightly closed eyes. She didn't open them once until they were anchored in the calmer waters of Back River, and it wasn't until she was settled in the dinghy for the short row to shore that she began to revive in the much subdued tone of a converted sinner. "Lord, Ah' see the road you wants me on. Get me to it, God. Sit my feets on your good sweet earth and leave these demon waters behind."

Mike hopped ashore and pulled the bow after him, assisted by tiny waves that licked at the sand with a slurping sound. Once Jenny was off-loaded, Tom was instructed to lift Nicole out to the waiting Captain. He obliged, but even with Mike's arms securely about her, she continued to cling to Tom's neck—and smiling the entire time, nearly toppled him from the boat. The Captain was not pleased. Striding to where Jenny stood, he deposited Nicole—none too gently—before returning to Tom at the same agitated pace.

"Please, Miss Nico," Jenny caressed the ground with grateful, patting feet. "Can Ah just lay me down somewheres? My poor old body be weak with pen-a-tence' and pain."

"Yes…well," Nicole waited to watch the show of male muscle as the men beached the dinghy. "Yes, I know the very spot for you. But here—do carry this heavy basket." She then led the way up a dune path, making frequent stops to peevishly shake the sand from her shoes. From the top, she turned to call back. "Mike, do you know which cabin it is?"

"I know!" he yelled, and when she was beyond hearing, added under his breath, "I sure as hell do-know-which-cabin. I know about everything that belongs to Nicole O'Rourke—and in her. Especially that, damn her!"

"…Captain, you said it wouldn't be easy," Tom reminded him.

"No, you said that—and damn it, you were right! But it's myself I'm angry with, here. I know what a tease she is and still I let her make me behave like a school-boy!"

"She behaved no better," Tom countered. "But you do have the advantage of experience, so why not educate her. If nothing else, scare the hell out of her."

"How? I can't beat her; and I can't bed her—not yet, damn, it!"

"Does she have to be sure of that? When she starts in again—and she will—make it clear you can take her and might."

"But I don't want to offend Nicole. She is a lady," Mike said as they started the trek toward the cabin.

"And this lady thrives on titillation. She is a flirt, but likes being flirted with too. That is the Captain Herb she wants to see. Do you realize you never cuss around her, when *damn* and *hell* come as natural to you as your own name? Mike, just be yourself; cocky and damn proud of the man you know you are. Then…if things don't work out, it won't be because you weren't true to yourself."

Stopping at the crest of the dune, the Captain stuffed his hands in his pockets and took a deep breath. "Damn," he grinned. "Damn," he munched on the word. "Hell, that tastes pretty good!" he concluded, laughing his way down the other side.

They came upon a row of houses, some two-storied and rambling; some small—as was the white block one they were approaching. While passing through the yard, a familiar groan rose from a gazebo. "…Please, Lord, don't let go," Jenny muttered even in slumber. "Old Jed, Lord? It be just one man at the time now…"

From the front doorway, Nicole led them to a table where a breakfast of buns, butter, jam and tea awaited. And as they began to eat, Tom wondered at her notion of a damp-and-sandy-cabin. One large room served as kitchen, dining and living areas. On the South corner was a private bedroom; and next to that, a curtained wall partitioned off a second chamber. The floors and walls were whitewashed and over a rock faced fire place on the North wall, hung a detailed map of Savannah, the surrounding rivers, marsh creeks and islands. In all, it was a clean airy place with large windows to let in the breeze and sunlight. By comparison, the cabins he had known as a boy were hewn from logs, mortared with mud, the floors being hard packed dirt and the windows small to keep out the bitter winds of long and often, snowy winters. Reaching for a third bun, he also realized how hungry he'd been and wondered aloud, at the size of his appetite.

"It's the salt air," Mike explained, ready now, to test Tom's advice. "You'll stay hungry the whole *damn* time you're here—hungry, and romantic as *hell*!"

Nicole blinked, looking to Mike for an apology. It didn't come. She looked next at Tom, expecting him to issue a reprimand. When that didn't happen either, she burst into delighted laughter.

"Food's gone," Mike patted his stomach like a friar. "Now, let's go for a walk on the front."

"Oh Mike, no," she pled. "My shoes are full of sand already, and I'm quite sure they're ruined. Why couldn't we…just-stay-here?" she delivered this last in sultry tones.

"So take your shoes off," he returned an unaffected shrug. "We're going to."

That sat her up straight in the chair. "Go barefoot?" she gasped. "Like a—a common gypsy?"

"Oh-hell-yes!" he tilted her chin on his fingers. "If you still expect to see my side of Savannah—and me-darlin,' it's a damn-site wilder than yours—you'll do as I tell you, or our deal is off."

Fascinated with such boldness, Nicole left her chin where it was. "…All right, Captain—sir," she cooed. "Barefoot it will be."

"Then hop to it, gypsy woman! Times a wasting!" he clapped. And giggling, Nicole skipped off to the bedroom in a hurry. "—Take off half those damn petticoats too," he called, sending Tom a wink. Yes, the Captain was definitely back!

Returning to Back River, they moved toward the sea at the water's edge. Nicole remained in high spirits, reciting every tale she knew about gypsies—until noticing the sand caked on the dampened hem of her gown. Then vigorously batting and shaking the offensive stuff from the dress, she uttered a string of complaints.

"Come here!" Mike took her arm firmly. "So what if your dress is muddy? Who the hell is watching? And who the hell cares?"

"Well," she hesitated, "...I guess no one in—in *hell* cares a bit!" And elated by her own daring, she splashed Mike with water, and finding that fun, splashed Tom too.

"All right, Miss O'Rourke!" the Captain scooped her from her feet. "You are about to be baptized!"

"No, Michael!" she screamed as he waded into the river. "Please, Michael, no!" she kicked and squirmed and laughed all the more.

"Yes, Michael, yes!" he knelt, pulling her under to the waist.

Clinging with both arms about his neck, Nicole ceased her protests, for the moving water was bringing them together in places she hadn't considered. "Captain," she said warmly, as her hold on him tightened, "if we were gypsies, and you, my wild young lover, would you kiss me now, with great passion?"

"Yes, I suppose I would," he nodded.

"Well?" she closed her eyes and offered her mouth.

Mike looked at her, wanting to capture those lips, but knew her game had become too serious, too quickly. "Sea witch," he gently pecked a kiss on the tip of her nose and followed it with a dribble of water. "You know this isn't the place," he motioned his head toward Tom—who was trying not to watch their exchange.

But he could not help hearing every word and when Mike steered Nicole back to shore, Tom couldn't tell if she was pleased or not with what had transpired. There were no certainties with this girl, which bothered him more than anything else about her. So far...

A cooling breeze arose as they continued their walk. It grew steadily stronger, and once they had rounded a point, all were pinned to the spot by a howling wind that plastered their clothing against them. And Tom was again caught in the lure of Atlantic. Nothing he'd read or imagined prepared him; no painting, no poetry or studied narration pictured it justly. He was looking at the crest of a high tide and it was easily one of the most awesome sights he could remember. Defying sense or description, words tumbled through his mind, as numerous as the waves, which threatened to swallow the earth in a mouth spewing great, hissing showers of foam. The thunderous crash and deafening roar; the intensity of the currents and strength of cross-currents; the varied, staggered patterns of constant, explosive movement—all combined to form a sea gone totally mad!

"Come on, you two!" Mike called over the wind-roar. "There's a tavern up the beach. We'll have ale and wait for the tide to ebb."

"A tavern!" exclaimed Nicole. "But what will I do? I can't go into a tavern—now can I?"

"As long as I'm with you—yes!" Mike answered, leading her by the hand.

"Looking like this?" she tried showing her wet, clinging skirt—which he had already appreciated.

"You look beautiful," he laughed, devilment dancing in his eyes. "Now, come along—damn it!" And come she did, with excitement shining in hers.

On entering, Tom stopped to place their order at the bar, while Mike seated Nicole next to a window. Opening wide a pair of shudders, he nodded approval, as his purpose was two-fold: the strong breeze would freshen the stale inside-air—which Nicole might find offensive; and as importantly, they would be afforded a perfect view of the beach—which very soon now, could prove most entertaining.

As Tom joined them, bringing full glasses of ale, he noticed Nicole's interest in the activity at another table. There, a group of men pitched coins down the front of woman's low-cut blouse and loudly applauded when each took a turn fishing them out—and that part, the woman was enjoying most of all.

Hugging Mike's arm against her, Nicole whispered, "Captain, … do they know we can see what they're doing?"

"They know," he answered, handing her a glass, in hopes it would prove a distraction.

"Well, I never," she uttered, looking again. Then she leaned in close with another question. "Have you ever played that game in a tavern, Mike?"

"I'm not so generous, Nico," he nodded. "I don't share my special ladies with anyone. —Now, drink your ale, gypsy."

Flattered, she wanted to hear more. "Do I sip it—the way you taught me with the whiskey that night on your boat?"

...*Well, that answers a question I've long wondered about, doesn't it?* Tom thought, stretching his legs out before him.

"Your first ale too?" grinned the Captain. "Damn, how many firsts are we to share? But, yes, sip until you grow accustomed to the flavor and strength."

"That can be said about many, many things," her eyes came to rest on Tom. "Sir, have you some spare change?" she asked sweetly.

"Yes," he answered cautiously. "...Why?"

Nicole strove for a wicked smile while raising the glass to her lips. "You just seem the type. I thought *you* might want to join our friends over there."

"And deny you the pleasure of my company?" he honestly attempted muzzling sarcasm, but wasn't certain he had. "Surely, you jest."

Undeterred, still smiling and still gazing at Tom, she slowly licked the foam from her lips, and said innocently, "Umm, I do believe I could learn to like this." He didn't respond this time, but as Mike was chuckling, she turned appreciatively to him. "So, Captain, tell me about the women you don't share. —Just how many are there?"

By mid-morning, Tom had grown weary of the continuing banter, and tuning it out, he gazed over the beach—which seemed wider now. Several groups of people had come out of hiding too: ladies with parasols out for a stroll; old men and young boys casting their fishing lines; swimmers bobbing in the surf; and still others, sprawled on blankets, doing nothing at all. Then at a good distance, he saw another pair; a tall girl, moving with graceful, gliding steps, while her shorter companion, wrapped in a long shawl, hopped along at her side. ...Mandria and Lucy? The realization brought him forward on the chair, remembering a promise to *talk more on the island.* And now, he was on his feet. "Mike, what do you say, we go down on the beach."

It wasn't posed as a question, and Mike easily followed Tom's honed gaze to its target. "Good idea. We've been here long enough. —*Just long enough, I'd say.*"

...*Bastard,* Tom threw his thought at the Captain—whose expression said he'd known Mandria would be here all along. ...*You're a damn good friend, but a bastard, just the same.* And, of course, the Irishman winked in complete understanding.

Going directly to the water's edge, the two men invented conversation while Nicole scampered about, collecting shells like a beautiful child. She had no idea her presence had become so important to Tom; or that he prayed she'd remember her manners in the next few minutes. ...If he could wait that long.

Deciding he couldn't, Tom positioned himself to face Mandria's approach, drinking in every possible detail. She wore a white peasant blouse and a yellow skirt, whose soft billows denied the existence of petticoat-stiffness beneath. Her waist, smartly cinched by a wide belt, flattered her curves in a way that made him ache to explore them without restriction. Her hair, in sunlight, a mellow, honey-oak color was gathered in casual bunches below each ear, where caressing curls blew softly about her shoulders. He wanted to do that—to softly caress those shoulders; blow his breath over her sun-kissed skin, after adding his own kind of heat to it. His quickened pulse was thoroughly enjoying each of her fluid steps; every supple sway of her hips; each graceful, effortless gesture of her hands. He wanted it all—her suppleness, bare-skinned and fluidly bent to a perfect fit against his body; her graceful hands, exploring him with as much deftness as he wanted to explore her. It was when she stopped, not ten feet away, looking both surprised and puzzled, that he decided there would be no passing this one up. He was going to insinuate himself into her life—and if possible, close-up and personal.

"...Nicole?" Mandria asked.

"It is Nico! —I told you it was!" Lucy scurried around. "I said, that looks just like Nico—and I was right!"

60

"Mandy! Lucy!" Nicole hurried to embrace them. "What a grand surprise! Mike promised Daddy he'd bring me by for a visit—but, here you are instead!"

"But what on earth are you doing at Tybee? I haven't seen you here in years," Mandria gave an exaggerated shrug of her shoulders. ...And Tom thought, one of these times, he had to be holding her against him when she did that, just to see what it felt like.

"I haven't either—not for years and years," Lucy agreed. "Not since we were all little girls."

"It has been a while," Nicole admitted. "But I'm enjoying it today. —See?" she showed off her soiled skirt and bare pink feet. "Oh, and come meet my new friends!" she led them forward, as Tom counted each century-long second. "Gentlemen, this is Miss Mandria Lucas and Miss Lucille Love."

"Lucy!" That one injected urgently. "It's Lucy Love, please? ...I just don't know why Mama picked such an ugly name for me—I really, really don't," she added, mostly to herself.

"Ladies, this is Captain Michael Herb and Mr. Thomas Scott—my newest admirer and friend," she looked between them with a smile that smacked of coquetry. "...Though, I can't seem to remember which is which," she finished, admiring her own wit.

Mike bowed, keeping his greetings brief, and then made it clear *he* was the admirer, by tucking Nicole's hand in the crook of his arm.

"I'm pleased to meet you, as well," Tom smiled at Mandria, who was every bit as beautiful at three feet away...but a little taller than he'd thought. "You too, Miss Love," he included Lucy. ...And wasn't she taller too? Instinctively, Tom glanced Mike's way, and finding he'd also gained height, he looked down to discover the watery sand on which he stood, had devoured his feet passed the ankles. "Well...I seem to have taken root," he remarked. Trying to move, he almost fell and the group burst into laughter all around.

"I've got you!" Lucy grabbed his arm, and in a new fit of chortles, held it cocked at a ridiculous angle above her head. "I won't let you fall, Mr. Scott—I've got you!" she peeked up at him.

Useless as it was, Tom was grateful for the assistance—and more grateful, from what he could tell, that Lucy did not remember it was him she'd seen that day in the square.

"Let's dig him up!" Nicole went to her knees with exuberance.

When Mandria followed, still laughing, Tom dug his toes in deeper. He'd stand here 'til sunset for this view of her neckline and the sound of that soft, throaty laughter.

"Hell, Tom," Mike grinned, seeing exactly what he was doing. "How can one man be so lucky? There you are, stuck in the sand—like a damn idiot—and *three* beautiful women rush to the rescue!"

Lucy went crimson in a titter of giggles. She may have objected to the language had it not been surrounded by such a nice compliment. Nicole was pleased with it too, and retained a hold on the Captain's hand when he helped her to stand.

"We idiots have our better moments," Tom replied, taking both of Mandria's hands, drawing her up and to his side. Very close to his side. He meant for her to feel his nearness and accustom herself to it.

Obviously, she did feel something. "…Thank you," she said, looking up—then up again. From his true height, the man seemed to tower above her. *…And doesn't he have the broadest shoulders?* she noted. Stepping back, but not exactly away, she turned to Nicole. "So, what are your plans for the day?" And now, she was rubbing at her hands, as if his grip had been too firm. It wasn't…and yet, the sensation of strength and warmth surrounded them still.

"I don't know," Nicole shrugged. "Do we have plans, Mike?"

"No, today we're gypsies!" he emoted eloquently—and with a flourish of hand gestures, "Barefoot and roving free; taking handouts, and anything else that comes our way!" Then placing a finger to his temple, as if the thought had just occurred, he asked. "Would you ladies care to join us?"

"Oh, Mandy let's!" Lucy was already removing her shoes. "Can we? —Oh, let's rove about too!"

Glancing at the suspect cause of her disjointed notions, Mandria found he'd closed the distance between them again and now wore a self-satisfied smile…on finely shaped lips. "I don't think so!" she answered

62

Lucy's question. As well as the one that hovered unasked. —*Enough!* her eyes said, shooting green shards straight at Tom. And the eyes looking back were the deep, deep blue of submerged undercurrents—and who knew what else in depths beyond that! Turning, to Nicole again, she said, "Listen, why don't you come to the house? Mama would love seeing you—and you're welcome to stay for lunch. Besides, you should get out of the sun for a while. You're not used to it, Nico, and your cheeks are already pink."

"Oh, you don't want to burn!" advised Lucy. "It hurts real bad! It really, really does!" she showed them her beet-red arms, thus revealing the need for a shawl on such a hot day.

"Oh, you poor dear thing!" Nicole's free hand flew to the warmth of her own cheek. And aghast, she made a wide-eyed plea to Mandria. "—No, I do not want to brown!"

"Then you're coming with me," Mandria insisted, and though she'd rather have bitten off her tongue, good manners deemed that she add, "…Your friends are welcome too." So now, she had two reasons for looking at the man again: to make certain he had not taken her polite invitation as encouragement; and to stop being polite, if he had dared to come any closer. He hadn't. …But he still wore that smile. And stood with his big arms crossed. Looking back at her. His eyes saying… oh, she didn't know! But it had to be why he seemed so amused—or whatever it was—and because she wasn't sure, it made her angry. "Yes, Nico," her tone took on sharpness. "Dealing with the sun, has been likened to dealing with a man: neither should ever be fully trusted."

Nicole cuddled closer to Mike. "Now, I've always enjoyed the *dealing* most of all," she smiled sweetly up at him.

"But, Miss Lucas is right," Tom stated, waiting as she turned and he'd captured her gaze again. "…Stay too long in the sun—or push a man too far—and both are apt to blister the tenderest places."

"Especially, this man," Mike growled, pretending to take great gobbling bites from Nicole's hand and arm

"My heavens!" squeaked Lucy, blushing as she disappeared beneath her wrap to a spill of giggles.

63

Mandria had been bested in the word match and was not pleased. "Well are you coming to lunch or aren't you?" she asked the group in general.

Tom answered again. "As the Captain said, today we're taking hand-outs—"

"And advantage of anyone who gets in your way?" she cut in.

"No, Mandy!" Lucy objected. "That's not how it went. It was anyone going our way. …Or was it everything out of the way? —Wait now, I'll get it right." And her eyes rolled upward, as if the answer was written beneath her lids.

Mandria could not suppress a smile of fondness for her confused little friend, never guessing the effect it had on Tom. He was close to snatching her to him for a good, long taste of that smile. "Never mind, Lucy," she said. "Let's go. Mother will be waiting."

As they started off, the men lagged a step behind, leaving the women to their chatter. There was much to appreciate from this vantage point too, and soon Tom and Mike were enjoying a silent chat of their own, punctuated with nods of approval and an occasional eyebrow lift of speculation: Nicole walked with a saucy bounce; Lucy hopped like a charming little bird; and Mandria moved with the timed rhythm of the sea. Nicole had the smallest waistline; what Lucy had was hard to tell beneath that shawl; and with each swaying step Mandria's hips begged to be touched.

Then the wind stiffened, and the men caught several glimpses of the pantalet ruffles at Nicole's knees before she batted down her dress with delightful dancing movements. Lucy's shawl and the dozen petticoats she must have worn, simply ballooned about her. And there was Mandria, who walked the wind as if she controlled it, never breaking her stride or bothering with her skirt at all. The protective wind seemed to know—as Tom suspected—that under that yellow skirt, nothing covered her legs but the golden kiss of the sun. He wanted to do that too, and the very thought cost him a groan…

# CHAPTER 6

"Here we go!" Lucy ran hippity-hop over the hot dune path, yelping a medley of oohs and ouches, while the shoes she'd forgotten to put back on, bounced along from the laces clenched in her fist. Mandria followed, keeping her easy gait as she ran. Mike, of course, carried Nicole, and Tom came fast on his heels, to gather with the rest on a brick walkway, leading to the Lucas beach house. As could be expected, it was nearly as large as the town residence, but here there was more warmth: a casualness in the wide second story porch that ran across a front corner and elbowed half way around the side facing the sea; charm in a lawn shaded by one of the giant, signature Live Oaks and beds planted with flowering, free-branched shrubs instead of clipped and molded hedges.

"Mother?" Mandria called as they entered a small foyer. "We have a surprise for you!" she led the way up a narrow stairway to the right. "Mama, where are you?"

"Out here, dear. Enjoying the breeze," an answer came from the porch.

"Guess what we found on the beach," Mandria continued across a well appointed sitting room and through a set of French doors.

"It's Nico!" Lucy flopped on a large hassock to fan her sore, hot feet. "See? It is. —Really, here she is!"

"Nicole," Evelyn Lucas rose to cuddle the girl. "You came after all. Your father said you might, and asked me to look out for you."

*…So Mandria's own mother was Mike's Leprechaun?* Tom glanced at the Captain, whose mouth entertained a smirk, in answer.

"But you didn't think I would, did you, Mamalyn?" Nicole hugged her back. "I've refused so many of your invitations, you didn't believe I'd come."

"I am surprised," Evelyn admitted. "I'll bet Mandy and Lucy were too. I'm afraid I didn't mention the possibility to them. But you're here now, and maybe you'll return more often?"

"Perhaps I will. —Now come meet my gentlemen friends!" And leading Evelyn to where they waited in the doorway, she slipped a hand into the crook of Mike's arm.

"Sirs, this is Mrs. Lucas; and Mamalyn, meet Captain Michael Herb. He and Daddy do business on the river, and he kindly brought us down on his sailing boat bright and early this morning."

"…Herb?" Evelyn paused over the name. "We know a Captain Dennis Herb at Lazaretto Creek. Are you kin of his?"

"Uncle Denny?" Mike was taken aback. "How did you come to know him?"

"Actually, through his pigeons," she answered. "Everyone down here uses his Carrier Service for sending messages back and forth to town."

"Oh, dear—Tom, I nearly forgot about you," Nicole took his arm with her other hand, neatly inserting herself between the men—and wasn't that just the most perfect spot to be? "So this, Mamalyn, is Mr. Thomas Scott from Athens. I heard Daddy say he is as rare a find as hens-teeth," she smiled at him sweetly. "And though I readily agree with that, Daddy says it's because he attended our University."

"Oh?" Evelyn laughed. "Are you visiting relatives in Savannah, Mr. Scott?"

"No, ma'am. I hope to make my home here. I like everything I've seen in the Low Country," he said, glancing at Mandria for a precisely emphatic moment. "And today, that's especially true," he finished with a smile for her mother. Then, he had the covert pleasure of watching Mandria raise a protective hand to her neckline and sink slowly onto a chair.

"Well, I wish you luck. —But where are my manners? Please, everyone, let's sit down for a chat," Evelyn invited.

The porch was furnished with several padded wicker chairs and divans. Where it elbowed, a pedaled swing hung from the ceiling on chains. Potted plants bloomed on each side table, and taking most of one corner was a rocking wicker chaise.

"Come on, Mike," Nicole tugged him along. "Let's sit in the swing." And grumbling playfully, he went.

Tom walked over to the chaise and rocked it a few times with his hand. "I've never seen a piece like this. It looks like a giant sugar scoop."

"You know it does!" Lucy exclaimed, as if a great mystery had been solved. "But it sits good, Mr. Scott, it really, really does. Try it and see."

So, stretching out on the chair, Tom was soon sighing his approval. "Yes, it *really, really* does," he chuckled.

"I can't get over your knowing my Uncle Denny," Mike said to Evelyn, as she settled back into her favorite rocker.

"Well, we do," Mandria began with a straightened posture. She had decided it wise to deny this man further knowledge that his words could effect her. ...And neither would his smile. ...Or deep blue eyes. ...Or those structured features the artist in her wanted to admire. But too bad: permission denied. "And Uncle Denny taught us to weave and cast our own hand nets," she finished, proud of her sensible decision.

"He even has you calling him Uncle?" Mike laughed. "That sly old sea-dog!"

"I know him too," added Lucy. "But I'm afraid of shrimp. They have such horrid, crawly, little legs—just like spiders, only fatter. And maybe thicker—and very much wetter!" she said assuredly.

"You ladies went casting for shrimp?" Mike still questioned. "You truly did?"

"Yes," laughed Evelyn, "and last time, Lucy caught the most! But she kept losing them—net and all. I'm afraid poor Dennis spent a good deal of time in the water that day, just fetching it out again."

"Now, that's all right, Lucy. We love you anyway," Mandria petted her friend. And smiled.

Lucy shuddered. "It's just those awful little legs, you see. I really think they're just horrid!" she sought agreement all around, but stopped to look at Tom, who looked at Mandria, and for some reason wore a really broad smile, as if he'd been given a coveted gift.

"Oh, and Mama, I've asked everyone to stay for lunch," Mandria said then.

"Of course they're staying," Evelyn rose. "I'll just go have extra places set." And she left, humming a little tune.

Meanwhile, Lucy had made a new discovery. "Do you know what, Mr. Scott? With you in it, that chair doesn't look so big. Why, you fill it from end to end and side to side. —Really, you do!"

"I...well, thank you. I think," Tom chuckled. Yet, because Lucy had drawn attention his way, Mandria was now sizing his fit in the chair too, and he caught himself tempted by a ridiculous urge to flex a few muscles.

"You're welcome," Lucy continued. "But I still don't understand something. My brother, Dan, attended University too, and when he'd come home on holiday, Mama worried so about his coloring. Pasty, she called it. She said he spent too much time poring over books and what he really needed was sunshine and home cooked meals."

"...Yes, I guess we all do," Tom offered, unsure of what point she hoped to make.

"Lucy, being perfectly honest," Nicole injected, "before Dan went off to college, he was getting quite—well, pudgy. I think he looks better today than he ever has."

"So do I!" Lucy vowed. "He has a sweetheart now, so she must think it too. But you know my Mama—and Papa's no better. They think Dan is pasty, and I'm too thin. The only one who pleases them is my little sister, Sabrina, and all she does is practice the piano and eat, and sleep, and eat some more. —Oh, anyway, to make a long story short," she paused for a much needed breath, "Mr. Scott was also a scholar, but he doesn't look pasty in the least. So, why is that, do you think?"

"I know!" the Captain leapt in with glee. "He is at-his-best *after* dark, so that's when he carried his heaviest...study-loads? And of

68

course, he spent his days lolling in the sun, where a bevy of beauties awaited with spoon fed delights—of the home cooked variety, you can be certain."

"Michael, you are such a tease!" Nicole swatted him, laughing along with the others.

With a residue of mirth still playing about his mouth, Tom leaned his head into the chair cushion, his eyes sliding closed, as he asked the powers-that-be, what he'd done to win the friendship of a lunatic.

And Mandria took full advantage, allowing her gaze to ride the muscle of Tom's thigh; travel to a lean waist; the breadth of shoulders and chest; to gauge the probable strength of his arms—all of which proved Lucy's observation astute, in spite of her round-about way of getting there. Why would a scholar have this muscular build? Seeking answers, she made the thigh to shoulder trek again, but slowly, this time, seeking flaws—that, in truth, didn't seem to be there. ... *Well, no one is perfect!* she thought. Certain she'd missed a slack jaw or bad teeth maybe, she raised her eyes to his face, and hers instantly flamed with color. He was staring right back at her, and never had she seen more smugness in an expression—bracketed, of course, by a firm jaw! Then he had the nerve to smile—baring wide even teeth—and thoroughly enjoying her humiliation! Snatching a guitar from the next chair and raking her nails over the strings, she wished more than anything in this world, she could smash it over his insufferable head!

"Do play something, Mandy," urged Nicole. "I love hearing you play."

"Oh yes, she does play well," Lucy added. "She really and truly does!"

Mandria sent a scathing look at Tom and when he let go of a chuckle, she all but attacked the guitar, lending a full measure of her frustration to a fiery flamenco tune.

"Bravo!" applauded Mike at the finish. "Wonderful, Miss Lucas! —Bravo!"

Lucy and Nicole added like praises, and then, though quietly said, but with the impact of a battering ram, so did Tom. "Indeed, pretty lady. Beautiful, indeed." And their eyes met, green ice dueling with blue flame.

As there is no polite way of ending a staring bout with any grace whatsoever, Mandria slowly turned, replaced the guitar on a chair, and remained with her back to Tom, pretending interest in what Lucy was saying. But she had to wonder if he was capable of understanding the subtleness of her snub. Oh well, it gave her time to plot the next volley…

What Tom understood was that he now stared at her shapely little rear and those hips that still begged touching, cinched and neatly packaged beneath her wide belt. Not so slowly then, he rose, crossed the porch, and while looking out to sea, hands grasped hard to the guard rail, asked a stupid question, to which he'd known the answer since grade school. "Mike, how many hours lapse between tides?" … But hell, he had to do something—Mandria was enough to excite a damned eunuch!

"Anyone care for lemonade?" Evelyn returned, carrying a tray of tinkling glasses.

"I do!" Lucy ran to help. "I'll pass it for you, Mamalyn. —Did you hear Mandy playing? It's been so long since she did and I told them she played well. —Didn't I Nico?" she went on and on, spiking each serving with words. "You heard me, Captain Herb? Don't you think she played well, Mr. Scott?"

"Absolutely, Miss Love," Tom turned to accept the offered glass, and resting back on the guard rail, he forced his eyes to remain on Lucy and not go flying off in search of Mandria. It was then he noticed that Lucy had quite a lovely figure. In fact, he'd have to credit her with the fullest bosom he'd seen in quite some time. …*Interesting how I could have missed that*, he mused.

"Lucy, please stop," Mandria pled. "They've heard enough on my behalf. Do give Captain Herb and Mr. Scott some peace." Yet she had to wonder…*So why hasn't he looked at me again?* She was so ready to spear his impertinence with some really fine barbs she'd chosen from her mental collection box. …But he did have to look at her first—or say something from which she could launch an attack…

"Well, I've heard enough of this stuffy formality," Evelyn claimed her rocker again. "Wouldn't we all be more comfortable without so many Misters and Misses out here? I know I would."

"Now there's a lady I could love," said the Captain. "Ma'am, please call me Mike."

"Very well, Mike," she smiled. "So now we have Mike and Nico; Mandy and Lucy; —and what do you prefer among friends, Mr. Scott?"

"Tom," he answered, amazed that Sam Lucas could treat this woman with anything less than adoration.

"Now, Mamalyn—fair is fair!" Lucy announced. "They have to call you Mamalyn too. Everyone does—even Mandy sometimes. Yes, sir, to one and all, Mamalyn it is!"

"If they'd care to, that's fine," Evelyn went on to explain. "After Nico's mother passed, she spent a good deal of time at our house. She would hear Mandy call me Mama, while Sam and Ransom used Evelyn. So, clever tyke that she was, Nico just combined the two and I've been Mamalyn to most of my family and friends ever since."

"Mamalyn, Mandy and *Lucille*—Mandy and *Lucille*," Mike chanted, as if committing the names to memory.

"It's Lucy!" she hastened the correction again. "Oh, I just know that's the ugliest name in the whole wide world! Say it slow and listen: *Looo-seeel!* —Now doesn't that sound like a sick cow?"

"Oh, Lucy, I had forgotten the fun you can be," Nicole laughed.

But Mandria hardly smiled. As the banter resumed, she found herself in a quandary. Tom still stood at ease, leaning on the guard rail now, and still had not looked her way another time. He was behaving as if she had wronged him in some way. ...Was that possible? Since seeing her father with his whore, she truly hadn't been capable of good judgment, much less civil behavior. She had managed a fragile kind of peace with her mother, but the plot for retaliation remained foremost in her mind, leaving no room for this nonsense.

...So, was her angst with Tom fair, when it was she caught examining him like a cut of meat at the Butcher's? No, but did it matter? ...No, because he wasn't awful enough or repulsive enough, or have anything Sam Lucas would covet enough to merit his hatred, and therefore, Tom could be of no possible use to her. Then he spoke to her mother, and like a magnet, Mandria's eyes were drawn right to him. ...Damn it all!

"Mamalyn, what is that cooking in there?" he asked. "It smells like cornbread."

"It is—along with beans, mustard greens and all the fixings. Down here, the servants just cook what they like, and we eat with the best of them—but enjoy it most, I do believe."

"There is a lady I could love too," Tom said to Mike. "Beautiful and she appreciates good food."

"Do you like pepper sauce, then?" Evelyn asked—and Mandria could have sworn to seeing a gentle blush on her cheeks.

"Yes Ma'am, I do," he replied.

"Good! I have some I've been waiting to try. —Mandy, go tell Old Jed to send up a jar. He'll know the one I mean."

Mandria's exit was made with her exceptional way of moving, and when Tom had enjoyed the bother of that one more time, he realized what else bothered him. "…Old Jed," he repeated, turning to Nicole. "What about Jenny? Don't you think she might be hungry too?"

"If she's awake she is," Nicole examined a fingernail. "She stays hungry, I'm afraid."

"But where is Jenny?" Evelyn asked.

Nicole toyed with a shrug. "She wanted a nap, so we left her at the cabin, of course."

"Well, she shouldn't have to sit there alone," Evelyn started to rise. "I'll just go tell Mandy to fetch her."

"I'll tell her—I'm already up." As indeed, Tom was and through the French doors, where he stopped and turned back. "…If you'll point me in the right direction, Mamalyn?"

"The door facing the foot of the stairs," she answered, "And thank you for saving me steps, Tom."

Then, as he started across the sitting room, he heard Mike sing out, "Run rabbit; Run rabbit; run, run, run!" Tom could have throttled him for it, but decided it was good enough the Captain now had to face three puzzled ladies and explain his sudden burst into song—and the hell of it was, he'd do it!

Picking up the pace of his escape, Tom went down the stairway, through the named door, on through a wash room, around a corner, and straight into jolting collision with Mandria. This sent the pepper sauce jar she carried, smashing to the floor half way across the servant's dining room, and left her clinging in the support of his arms—which Tom considered a really nice place for her to be.

"Oh!" she yelped. "Oh my heavens!"

"Mandria, I'm sorry!" he sized her fit against him—and liked it. "Are you hurt?"

"No; …no, I'm fine. But remind me never to make you angry— or better yet," she righted herself, ready to step away, "to keep a safe distance between us."

But he hadn't released her, and she had to watch, from far too close, as a smile inched across his tempting mouth. "Well, that isn't the message I'm here to convey," he said with a perfect mix of humor and innuendo.

Until ten minutes ago, Mandria would have felt her hackles rise. Now, she was safely back on her chosen path—which made him harmless, so why not just show some patience until he went away? Still and all, she backed out of his grasp. "And what message would you have me receive?" she kept her tone pleasant, while watching as two giggling maids hurried in to clear away the broken jar.

"Actually, it's from your mother. She wants us to go for Jenny," he lied, not regretting it a whit.

"But where is Jenny?"

"Your mother's exact words. And quoting Nicole exactly, Jenny wanted a nap." Then he gave a nod. "In truth, I think she was closer to being ill. The trip down wasn't easy for her."

"The sea!" Mandria's eyes widened—and Tom thought, magnificently. "Jenny is frightened of the sea! Nico knows that and shouldn't have made her come. Any of the other servants would gladly have taken her place. —I swear, Nico can be so feather-brained sometime!"

"…Yes," he agreed. He did agree, too, with all she said and the conviction with which she said it. "Anyway, she's at the O'Rourke's cabin, so shall we leave?"

"I can go," Mandria tried putting him off. "There's no need to trouble yourself, Mr. Scott."

"Tom," his correction was immediate.

"…Tom," she conceded. "But really, I'm perfectly capable of driving the buggy over there."

"And if she is ill, are you perfectly capable of lifting Jenny into the buggy?" he asked. And before she could think of another objection, he pointed downward adding, "Besides, I'd like to have my boots before we sit down to eat."

Mandria looked at her own bare toes and relented. It wasn't long then, before they had hitched the buggy and with Mandria at the reins, were on their way. *…No pampered darling here*, Tom thought. *…No carrying this one over every dune you come to. …No letting me drive because of gender, either.* But he couldn't have been happier with that, as it gave him time to absorb her; time to sit back and resume setting his lures. What little conversation there was, she kept light and impersonal, and of necessity, mostly kept her eyes on the road. So, that is where he began.

It was Tom's turn now to take advantage, but she would not catch him at it. As the useless questions and answers passed between them, he allowed his gaze to linger on her profile in stages. Mentally he traced a finger down her pert little nose; the next time, over the shape of her mouth; the next, along her jaw; circled the shape of her ear; over her chin; down her throat; and then…

Once again, Mandria felt—well, something! Yet all she could attribute it to, was the close quarters she was presently sharing with a very attractive man. There: she admitted it. Tom Scott was probably the most attractive man she had yet to meet. She couldn't allow it to matter, but was still glad when they reached the cabin so quickly, where before they could alight, Jenny came waddling toward them carrying three pair of shoes. Tom was more than happy to lean across Mandria and retrieve them too. And speaking of close quarters? Once Jenny had struggled and puffed her way on to the buggy seat, Mandria was physically wedged against Tom, with no hope of keeping that coveted distance between them.

Tom found little wrong with the arrangement. As they rode along, every bump in the road almost put her in his lap—and wouldn't that be something with not much more than the cloth of his trousers and that of her yellow skirt separating them? Her breasts rose and fell as she tried for a decent breath…and he watched in fascination, having only to lower his eyes for the privilege. Her hair blew repeatedly across his cheek…and he inhaled the honeysuckle scent that stayed with her. He wanted to say something—anything—that would cause her to face him where their lips would be within inches of touching. But then he'd have to kiss her, and it would start that duel they'd been fighting on the porch all over again. No, best to keep quiet, because right now he didn't know what he might do if she kissed him back. Yet, he did know one thing for certain: he wanted Mandria. And he'd take her in whatever way she could be had…

On reaching the Lucas house, Mandria pulled the horse to a stop and somehow, managed to hop over Jenny to the ground. "Let me help you. —Come on, Jenny," she uttered, refusing to look beyond the woman.

"Thank you. You a nice little lady," Jenny said, starting for the kitchen—and Old Jed, who stood in the doorway with a welcoming smile.

"You are nice," Tom said after a moment.

Mandria turned to find he had not moved from the buggy. In truth, he still sat in a cornered posture, one arm across the back of the seat, emphasizing the space she'd been forced to occupy. Impulsively, she brushed at sensations along her side which refused to leave. At that, his smile broadened, his eyes watching her foolish action. …Had he been referring to the assistance offered Jenny, or the *niceness* of their physical contact? She could not decide, and it upset her. "Why?" she chose the safer option. "Jenny is a human being—or don't you subscribe to that theory?"

"Of course I do," he said admiring narrowed eyes that had taken on the frosty color of mint. He very much wanted to test her capacity for a more stimulating emotion; to see their color then, but for now, it was best to back off. Climbing down beside her, he continued. "It's a beautiful thing to care about people. Now, can we please go eat? I'm starving to death!"

75

Mandria allowed him to lead her in and up the stairway, but her mind remained on the buggy ride. ...Why, when there had been no help for having to squeeze three people into a seat for two, had she been so ready to blame him for the discomfiting moments to follow? A few steps into the sitting room, she turned to find him sitting on the top step, pulling on his boots. She returned, reaching him just as he stood again. "Wait, please. ...Listen, I don't know why I snapped at you just now. And I've done it more than once today. I just...well, I am sorry if I was rude."

"You weren't," he nodded. "But you have more important things to consider."

"What things?" she puzzled.

"Dinner, for now," he handed her Nicole's shoes and retained Mike's.

"And for later?" she felt compelled to ask.

"Us," he replied. "And when you're ready, we will discuss that."

For the life of her, Mandria could not find a word to say. Then her mother swept through, marshalling everyone toward the dining room, and the chance was lost.

"Come on now," Evelyn shooed them along. "Dinner is on the table!"

# CHAPTER 7

When all were seated, Evelyn looked around the group of young people at her table. She'd hardly seen her daughter's beautiful smile since that awful day at Sam's office, and had hoped the get-away to Tybee with Lucy for company would lighten her somber mood. It hadn't. Yet, with today's arrival of Nicole and these two handsome men, she was perking up a bit. It was her job then, as Mandria's mother to make the most of opportunity. "Well now," she said cheerfully, "would anyone care to say grace for us?"

"Be honored to, ma'am," Mike replied, bowing his head over prayerfully folded hands and waiting for the total attention of all present. When certain he had it, he began: "Good God, good meat; Good God, let's eat!"

Dismay was Evelyn's first reaction, but when all laughed with such enjoyment—including Mandria—she forgot everything else and laughed along with them. Then when the bowls, bread baskets and condiments had nearly completed their ritual trek around the table, she noticed that Mandria was now staring at Tom, her fork poised half way between plate and mouth. ...But then, so were the others, which caused her to look too.

Tom had taken two large wedges of cornbread, laid one open in the center of his plate and heavily buttered the other, where it now resided on the rim. He was ladling a pile of plump brown beans on half of the open piece, with enough juice to soak the wedge beneath. The other half received a matching mound of greens and juice. He spooned on a blanket of pepper sauce—from a jar that made it safely up the stairs, this time—laid tomato slices to the side, showered all with salt and pepper, squeezed lemon into his tea, and sat back to admire his masterpiece.

"Mamalyn, I haven't seen anything this good since leaving—" his voice trailed away. All present were staring at his plate. They had claimed ample portions too, but not compared to his. "Well, aren't you people hungry? —I am!" he tried to make light of his piggery

"Evidently, my manner-less friend," Mike observed sagely.

"Can you really eat all that?" asked Lucy. "You know, he's pretty big and I'll just bet he can!"

"Yeah, but that's quite a mountain range he built," Mike persisted. "It has to rival the ones he left up in Tennessee."

"Must be the salt air, Captain," Tom replied, wishing Mike would choke on the cornbread he'd just bitten into. "Isn't that what you said about big appetites down here?"

Nicole's laughter rankled. "He also said it makes you romantic. So, when can we expect to see your big appetite for that, my dear man?"

"All right, children—enough teasing," Evelyn intervened. "Tom, please enjoy your meal. I appreciate a hungry man at my table. There's plenty more here too, so let's all enjoy it?"

As easily as that, the meal progressed, and Tom decided he truly could come to love Evelyn Lucas. …But her daughter was unusually quiet, wasn't she? Evelyn was aware of it too, as told by the repeated glances sent Mandria's way. For though she appeared to be involved in the table banter—nodding, smiling slightly, even laughing occasionally—it was without saying much of anything. He wanted to believe her pensiveness stemmed from their discussion on the stairway. He had given her much to ponder…

Repeatedly—and a-pondering for certain—Mandria ran a fingertip around the rim of her glass. It had occurred to her that what she must do against her father could only be done from town, so why not grant herself a reprieve for this one day? Stealing a look at Tom, she wished, mightily, that it could be the likes of him she'd use in meeting her goal; that somewhere in his past, he'd committed the nefarious deeds to qualify. It dawned on her then, that maybe he had. What did she really know about him, other than the strong attraction he was capable of rousing in her? She stole a second look. He certainly was appealing, wasn't he? The casual mannerisms; the impact of his physical presence—well, she could ask a few questions, couldn't she? A third look said she would, and if her inquiry proved wishful thinking, then she'd only have lost a day spent with a very handsome man, who'd suggested an *us* between them…

As the meal came to a finish, Evelyn rose to pass a box of small dessert cakes, and on reaching Tom's place, she added a question to his serving. "Tell me, what position do you hope to find in Savannah? If you've had no luck, Sam has many interests here, and might be of help."

Mike made an awkward noise, which was promptly covered by a cough, and swallowed along with a gulp of tea.

"Thank you, Mamalyn," Tom spoke around the Captain's antics, "But Mr. O'Rourke is already arranging interviews for me."

"Yes, and to help Daddy get to know Tom better—which is so important—I just may have him to dinner," Nicole injected. "Along with you, Mike, of course."

"Well, Tom, if you've earned Ransom's notice, that's excellent," Evelyn said, returning to her seat. "His judgment can not be ques-tioned."

"Oh how true; how true," Lucy informed the table in general. "Last year, he gave my Mama's pickled okra first prize at the church fair. He really did!"

Mike wondered why he had to keep reminding Nicole he'd been promised dinner first. "And your father showed the good sense to join *me* in a profitable business venture," he boasted to impress his worth on the forgetful little minx.

"Which just goes to prove Mr. O'Rourke can make mistakes," Tom joked—and then wished he hadn't.

"Now just let me tell you ladies about this ridge-runner who dares to besmirch me," the Captain was off and racing side-by-side with the devil. "For all his learning, he'd never heard of a hushpuppy. He's plenty tough in a fight—saved my damned life, I'm admitting that much.

But he also drinks hard liquor, plays a mean hand of cards, sweet talks the ladies like you wouldn't believe—and with all that going for him, can you guess the profession he chose?"

Tom watched with interest as Mandria inched forward on her chair, listening closely. ...Now why was that?

"Well, look at him, ladies," Mike continued. "Can you believe he teaches? The man is a schoolteacher!"

"No!" chimed Nicole and Lucy in what sounded like horror.

"But that's wonderful," countered Evelyn. "There's nothing Savannah needs more than good, qualified teachers."

Yet Mandria, Tom noted, slunk to the back of her chair again, seeming...what? Disappointed?

"He doesn't look like any teacher I ever had," Lucy nodded. "Mine were either mean old ladies with pinch-nose glasses or skinny old men who perched on their desk stools with knobby knees sticking out—just like grasshopper legs!"

"Lucy, dear," Nicole looked at her, "I'm afraid you have a leg fetish."

"Well, I don't know about that," Lucy puzzled. "But I will admit to a few freckles here and there."

"Tom, where do your parents live?" Mandria asked of a sudden.

"My mother died in Athens many years ago," he replied. "And though you didn't ask, she too, was a teacher." "Then your father still lives in Tennessee?"

"No, he died before I...," he paused, realizing she'd caught Mike's reference to the mountains there, "—That is, he died before my brother was born in Athens."

"Oh my Lord!" Lucy exclaimed. "Do you know what they say about people who never saw their dead fathers? They say they have special powers for healing or reading minds!"

"Feathers," Nicole chided. "Who told you that, Lucy?"

"All the servants believe it," she insisted. "And last year one of *them* took a wart off my sister's thumb—her Middle C thumb, at that. The woman had Sabrina rub the wart with bacon, then told her to bury it where no one would know, and in two weeks, that wart was gone! Oh my, but I would like to meet your brother, Tom—I really would!"

He might have special powers too, that he doesn't even know about yet, and maybe I could help him find them!"

Mandria had returned to pondering, so Tom gave Lucy polite attention. "Maybe you will meet him. I hope to send for Allen soon. He is about your age, I'd say, and always ready to greet a pretty girl."

"Well, special powers or not," Evelyn smiled at Lucy's rosy hue, "you'll have to bring your brother by for supper, Tom. We'll give him a real Savannah welcome. Now then," she rose, "if all of you are full, why don't you find something to do while I have the table cleared."

"I had planned to do some crabbing," Mandria suggested. "The tide should be at dead low now. ...Is anyone interested?"

"Oh let's do!" Lucy clapped. "Crabs don't scare me at all—not even those big pinchers. ...I wonder why that is? Oh, anyway, did you ever catch one, Nico? It's fun!"

"Mike said he'd take sometime," Nicole answered. But not about to pass on that perfect little play on words, she turned to smile at him. "You do want to take me, don't you, Captain?"

"Absolutely, me-darlin'!" he laughed. "Mandy, do you have enough line and bait for all of us?"

"And stick nets and catch buckets—in the store room," she answered.

So, their plans made, they thanked their hostess, gathered the gear, and headed back to the beach...

The first thing Tom noticed was the vast expanse of exposed sand during a low tide. And the waves now, did little more than gently pat the shore, as had those along Back River. Atlantic, it seemed, had crawled into her own rocking chaise for a rest...

A true novice at this crabbing expedition, he watched as Mike and Mandria tied chunks of raw meat onto the weighted end of long cords, while the other end of each cord was tied to a stake. Nicole stood with fingers pressed to her lips in distaste, at the notion of handling raw meat, and Lucy—again wrapped in the shawl—scurried from one tide puddle to the next, peering secretively into each from several angles.

"Crab!" she screeched suddenly, leaping up and down, a veritable yo-yo of excitement and bouncing ringlets. "Come quick, Mandy! I see a crab! Hurry! Come get the crab!"

"Well, Lucy," Mandria laughed, "don't scare it to death." And taking a stick net and catch bucket, she went to fish it out, with Tom and Nicole on her heels. "Oh, it's a female," she said to Lucy. "We'll have to throw her back."

"Wait," Tom went to a knee for a closer look. "How can you possibly know this is a female?"

Mandria flipped the net, putting their unhappy captive on its back. "See how the breast plate fits together—the elongated design? Males have more of a straight line across there. Also, if there's an orange, spongy mass attached to her shell, that's an egg sac and means she is about to give birth."

Blushing profusely, Lucy looked quickly from Tom to the approaching Captain. "Mandy, I don't think you should speak of such things," she uttered a whispered caution. "I really, really don't!"

"Feathers, Lucy," Nicole disagreed. "How often does Mandy get to show off what she learns from all those books she reads? Besides," she added, with a sage look at the men, "it's always wise to know about the ways of Mother Nature."

Bemused, Mandria said, "I've yet to find a book solely dedicated to the mating habits of crabs, Nico—but I'll let you know if I do. What I have learned about it, I learned from observation, or else, from my—," she faltered badly. "Well, from my father—who could surely be called an expert on the ways-of-Mother-Nature" Then, biting back sarcasm not meant for anyone there, she took the net, turned quickly and walked toward the sea.

"Oh dear," Lucy uttered to herself, "and things were going so well today. Drat—just a big fat drat!"

Mike and Tom exchanged glances, and before Nicole could play inquisitor, Mike said, "Come on, ladies, or we'll miss the tide. Tom can wait for Mandy. —Let's go now! We'll set out the lines down the beach there." And with some reluctance from Lucy, he herded them away, slapping repeatedly against the catch bucket to keep them moving.

Tom sat down beside the tide pool and watched as Mandria returned the crab to the sea. She turned to see the Captain shooing her friends before him, and as he hoped, then looked to where he was. *Decision time*, he thought, as she continued to stand there…

*All right*, Mandria decided, *so evidently, this schoolteacher is the very nice man he appears to be. But I do still have questions; pieces of his puzzle I can't quite put together…* It would be her final attempt, though. She'd just endured a painful reminder of her father's betrayal and time for dawdling was fast running out…

When Mandria straightened her posture and started toward him, Tom released a breath he hadn't been aware of holding. This was good, because before reaching him, she had cost him several more. The breeze at her back, blew her skirt forward, again baring glimpses of long, tanned legs. It had Tom praying for a gale. Yet, right on cue, when she dropped to her knees before him, the wind ceased. …Damn it.

For some seconds, she sat looking him straight in the eye and he was truly enjoying that. Then she asked, "Tom, is Allen your half-brother?"

The question was so far from his train of thought it shook him. "I…well; —Well, I'll be damned."

"Then he is," she read the truth for herself. "At the table, you said—or started to say—your father died before you were born in Tennessee. Then you changed it saying he died before Allen was born in Athens. …Why the mystery? What are you hiding?"

Unwilling to break eye contact, he asked, "Have you no skeletons in your family closet, Mandria?"

"Yes, —oh, yes, I certainly do!" she assured him. "So, please know I'm not asking out of nosiness or idle curiosity. I can promise you I'm not."

"Do you suppose the others guessed as much?" It was a genuine concern. Mike knew his story, but he didn't care to have everyone knowing it.

"No. They had no reason to examine your words so closely."

"But you did?"

"Don't ask me to explain. Please don't," she looked now at the hands she had clenched in the folds of her skirt. "It's just that I have a really important decision to make and I need to know…some things," she finished, forcing her fingers to relax, one by one.

Tom would have liked nothing more at that moment, than pulling Mandria onto his lap and just holding her. God knew, he did want her—that hadn't lessened a whit—but somehow, helping her seemed just as important now. "…Lady," he warned, "mine isn't a pleasant tale."

Her answer was a nod, as she quickly scooted up to sit beside him, hugging her knees and waiting for him to begin.

"I was born in Tennessee, but claim Athens, because we moved there when I was a boy. And, yes, Allen is my half-brother, but he doesn't know it. That was my mother's decision, and I'm bound to honor it."

"A most unusual decision," she observed. "It had to be difficult too. …So, what brought it about?"

"A most difficult stepfather, who caused us to go into hiding. But that's enough about him—"

"No!" she insisted, placing a detaining hand on his arm. "I want to know how your mother was able to handle that. But first, where is your step-father now?"

"In truth, I don't know. He left—and good riddance—when I was eight or so. But every now and then, I still look over my shoulder for him. Never have broken that habit."

"Did he leave because of another woman?" Green embers ignited in her eyes.

"He had other women," Tom nodded.

"But did your mother know? —Did she tell him she knew?"

"She finally discovered the truth—a whole lot of truths. And toward the end, yes, I used to hear them argue about his women."

"I've never heard my parents argue," she said, drawing slender fingers through the sand, "—Even when they should. …Don't you find that incredible?"

"I think…too many arguments—or too few—can both mean trouble."

84

"Maybe so," she shrugged prettily. "But if your stepfather was the one who left, why did your mother have to go into hiding?"

Tom leaned back on an elbow. "Because all in one night, he whipped both of us with a belt and just before leaving, beat my mother senseless with his fists. But the main reason was that he... Well, Allen was born nine months later."

"In Athens," Mandria deducted, "Where she could safely raise you and her baby."

"That's pretty much it," he said.

"Well, your mother was a very brave woman. At least she stood up and fought back."

"Was she?" Tom had questioned this many times over. "By hiding—by remaining in that marriage—she condemned herself to a life alone. She was never free to look for happiness again."

"Well, sometimes, other things are just more important." And up came her chin.

"Like what?" he smiled, finding pleasure in her stubborn little gesture.

"Like freeing oneself from an oppressive situation," she rose to pace and lecture before him. "Like living without hypocrisy. Even taking revenge when it's so richly deserved!" And when her eyes narrowed to spit green splinters, Tom laughed. "—Just what do you find so amusing?" she bristled, hands flying to her hips. "Your mother did what she had to and made the best of it! She gave you and your brother a home and love—things every child should have!"

Tom rose to face her. And to bait her. "You were a much loved child. That's easy to see."

"...Oh?" she asked once confusion had replaced pique. "What makes you think so?"

"Your disappointment. You keep comparing my parents to yours and yours haven't come out ahead on the score card yet—especially your father—which brings us full circle, to the reason for your disappointment."

"That is none of your business, Tom Scott! —How dare you try and analyze me!" she stamped a foot.

85

"And your attitude is both unkind and unfair," he stepped toward her. He didn't stamp down with his foot, but did think about it. "You were clever enough to piece my story together—and what you didn't guess, I submitted for your analysis. Do give me credit for some sense, Mandria. I could not help making my own observations in return."

"And your findings, sir?" she asked crisply.

"*Sir* is fascinated with you, lady—and determined to know you better."

Twice, she tried to say something and finally came out with it. "…So, that's what you meant on the stairway? You want *us* to be better friends?"

"It's a place to start." When she raised wary eyes to his, he smiled, lifting a curl from her shoulder, brushed it over the tip of her nose. "…But it won't end there."

Mandria retrieved her errant tress, and looked down the beach toward the others. Then, she started away, saying with the smallest bit of a laugh, "Quoting the Captain, *He sweet talks the ladies like you wouldn't believe.*"

"Mandria, wait," he tried recapturing her attention. "We're not done with this."

"I know," she said, walking backward, as she spoke. "But I don't know yet, what to do about it—or you." And turning to continue on, she added. "Come on, then, let's see if they caught anything."

Did she just admit…? He stood watching that walk of hers, hesitating even to finish the question. But vowing it was one to which he would have an answer, he hurried to catch up.

"Mandy! —Yoo-hoo, Mandy!" Lucy waved. "Mandy, come see what a big class of crabs we have!"

"Class?" Mike grinned. "Lucy, do you mean school—as in school of fish?"

"Class, school, herd—whatever," she shrugged. "We have bunches; we really do!"

"Yeah, Tom," the Captain laughed, "come see the *class* of crabs we've *herded* into the damned bucket."

"Mike!" Nicole squealed. "I've got one—I caught another one!"

"Pull it in slow," he instructed, as stick net in hand, he followed her line into the water. "Real slow now." And standing so his shadow didn't fall over the feeding crab, he simply scooped it from the shallows. "It's a big one, Nico," he waded in to show her. "And look at the size of those damned claws. —Yum-yum!"

"Oh, this is such fun," Nicole smiled, as he added her catch to the bucket. "I'm so glad I came today."

Pleased, Mike wore his smugness like a badge, as he said to Tom, "Give it a try, old son. My line is staked over there."

Tom picked it up, but found himself at a loss. "Now what do I do?"

"Here, I'll show you," Mandria came to stand beside him. "You see, crabs have very small mouths, and must rip their food into bites. So, holding the line, like this," she placed his fingers and closed them, "when it starts feeding on the bait, you'll feel a strong tug."

"I do already," he gave her a teasing smile, for which she returned one she hadn't meant to part with.

"Mandy, you could take my line now," Nicole offered, wiping a hand to her brow. "I'd really like to rest for a time."

"You could use shade from the sun too," Mandria looked at her with concern. "Mike, would you go back to the store room and bring the big umbrella and a blanket or two?"

The Captain quickly returned, and soon they had Nicole in the shadow of the large awning. And over the next few hours, all took turns crabbing and sharing the shade spot. But when the tide began to rise again, they reeled in the lines and gathered to survey the day's catch.

"That will make a good supper," Mike said. "We'll build a fire and boil them after while."

"Boiled alive," Lucy observed. "Isn't that a funny description? It implies the crabs were dead to start with, and life is boiled into them. —Now, isn't that funny?"

"It is when you explain it," Tom chuckled, admiring the smile Lucy could always get from Mandria. ...Maybe, he could learn how to do that as well.

"But it's too early for supper now," Nicole said, covering Mike's foot with sand. "What can we do in the meantime?"

Inspired by the mound on the Captain's foot, Lucy said, "I know! Nico, lets build a sand castle. Remember the fun we used to have doing that?"

"Why, yes I do!" she replied, getting to her feet. "Let's do it, Lucy," Then she stopped. "…But we don't have shovels and pails."

"So, move down by the water," Mike suggested. "The sand is already watery there and easy to dig with your hands."

"You are just so smart," she cooed. "Does my prince want to help build his castle?"

"I'll pass on that one," he replied, basking in her compliment. "But I will come down and inspect it. If your work is good enough, maybe we'll let you bid on the contract to build Fort Pulaski." And he watched happily, as the pair went giggling and skipping toward the sea. "Well, Mandy," he said then, pulling his shirt off, and stretching out on a blanket, "if you don't mind, I'm going to get a bit of sun."

"Not at all. I like the sun too," she replied. And rolling to her stomach, on a second blanket, she tucked her skirt beneath her knees, propped her chin on folded arms and closed her eyes.

Sitting between the two, Tom appreciated the chance to look at Mandria without having to be clever about it. When a slight frown crossed her brow, he wondered if she was thinking about her father or their talk by the tide pool. He'd have given much to know. Then, with one foot at a time, she began to dig her toes in the sand. In turn, her hips shifted in subtle repetitions—and Tom thought he might incinerate. …*Damn it* ! he thought, going back on his elbows. In search of distraction, he looked at the rolling white picture-clouds overhead, but they only presented a parade of plump ladies tumbling from one erotic posture to another. Sitting up again, he looked out to sea—a sea that now held the color and sparkle of Mandria's eyes when she laughed. And, he greatly suspected the Amazon out there was laughing at him now too. Next he made a real effort to study the texture of the beach sand on which he sat, but when pressing a palm against the firm surface, he felt the vibration of her digging toes. …

88

*Well hell*, he sighed, going to the flat of his back and closing his eyes against sun glare. What was there left to try? As he knew them, the sky, the sea, and the earth about covered the realms of possibility...

# CHAPTER 8

"It's just so hot today," said Mandria. And opening his eyes, Tom sat up to find she stood before him, looking out to sea. "I think I'll go for a swim. ...Anyone care to join me?" Then, without waiting to see, she went toward Lucy and Nicole.

Mike sat up too, squinting at Tom, who watched her walk away. Granting himself a bit of a look also, he chuckled, "Well, my boy, can't you swim?" But he nearly choked on that laughter when Mandria stopped to speak to her friends. Taking the back hem of her skirt, she pulled it up between her thighs, tucking and folding everything neatly into the front of her belt, leaving a shapely portion of her legs bare. "...Damn!" the Captain uttered, shoving at Tom's shoulder. "What the hell are you waiting for? —Get out of that shirt and go!"

On her heels, Lucy was a-jabber, as Mandria waded into the sea. "You better watch out, Mandy!" she held out her own skirts, as if to shield the view. "Now, pull down that skirt! —Oh Mandy, they're going to see—and you know God doesn't love ugly!" But unable to swim, Lucy was forced to stop and administer her warnings from the shallows. And when Tom passed by without a shirt, they became more frantic. "Mandy, watch out! Yoo-hoo! Mandy, look behind you! Quick now—pull down that skirt!" Then, in growing agitation, she hurried back to Nicole. "Oh, poor Mandy! What am I going to do? I don't think she heard me! —Nico, what should I do?"

Nicole had been torn between watching Lucy's amusing, if puzzling antics, and the play of muscle across Tom's very nice torso. The muscles won. "Why must you do anything?" she shrugged. "I enjoy seeing—, well, I want my friends to have fun. They're just going for a swim, after all."

"I can see that! But for Mandy to go tucking up her skirt—I mean, that's a man out there!" she pointed. "And in Mandy's state; ...well, Nico, that is a really big, living breathing man!"

"Oh, he is, indeed," Nicole smiled in continued appreciation. Then, glancing to where Mike sat, minus his shirt too, she rose and left for a closer look. Perhaps, if she could gain his co-operation, she'd even allow him a kiss. Or two. Maybe more, because the Captain truly was very skilled at that...

Not to be deterred, Lucy meant to protect Mandria, even at a distance. "Now God just doesn't love ugly," she repeated forlornly. And sinking on top of their sandcastle, she drew the shawl close about her, shaded her eyes with a hand and dedicated herself to the rigors of guard duty.

Mandria stood chest deep in the sea. "Come out beyond the breakers. It's not rough once you do," she called to Tom.

So, marveling again at the power of the Atlantic, he fought his way through the waves, and sure enough, just past the crest line, the water swirled about him in a gentle, almost massaging way. "This is good," he decided. "I think I'll move in and live here."

Her smile appeared, dazzling him as much as ever. "I used to say that too. When I was little, I fancied myself the daughter of the sea, able to tell the waves when to come and go—and daring them to knock me down. Once, I even told Lucy I was born in an oyster shell, with a pearl for pillow," she laughed. "I'm afraid she believed it for years."

"I believe it now," he replied. "Lady, you're like a piece of this beautiful landscape. In truth, I've never met anyone who fit their surroundings so well."

The smile dissolved as she leaned back to float her legs close beneath the water's surface. "How was it again? *He sweet talks, …like you wouldn't believe?*" she said cynically.

Tom was really tired of hearing that. "You are the damnedest woman. —What do you have against an honest compliment?"

Mandria drug herself upright and stood looking at him indecisively. "…Do you want an honest answer?" she finally asked.

"I'd love one—I truly would."

"Well, that's why I was hoping you'd join me out here. Your kindness in sharing your story, has earned that much consideration," she hesitated then. "…The truth is, I'm a little afraid of you."

Now, Tom hesitated. "…Why? Have I done something—said something—to frighten you?

"No; —oh, please, no! You've been completely charming, Tom. No, I find no fault with the nice man you are," she said, wanting him to clearly understand her point.

"…If that was a compliment, I enjoy them," he nodded in confusion. "So why, then, do I frighten you?"

"Your intuitiveness, maybe? I'm not really sure," she shrugged. But he smiled, which meant he wasn't hearing her. "Please listen," she stood close enough to vie for serious attention. "I know you won't understand this, but there is something I must do and it's not a thing an honorable man would want associated with his name. I'm warning you away now, because it is important to me to see it through. Please, just believe that I'm not trying to hurt you. Rather, I'm trying very hard to avoid it."

A rush of anger when through Tom like none he could remember. This is what his effort to help her had reaped? Had Mandria been screening him for a possible lover, but found him unsuitable—*without fault; completely charming*—just too damned *nice*? "Look, you silly, little jackass," he drew her before him, and effectively blocked any view of this from shore. "You won't understand this either, but I know what you're planning and why."

"Let go of me!" she demanded, prying at the broad fingers grasping her arms. "You don't know anything!"

92

"Oh, but I do!" And in one swift motion, her hands were bound to her sides by arms that anchored her stance too close to his. "You saw your father with a whore; you want revenge; a lover he wouldn't approve. Doesn't that about cover it?"

Mandria's struggles ceased. "How—?" she stared in disbelief.

"Never mind how!" he made no effort to curb his irritation. "Now I'm going to tell you something—and it's nowhere close to the sweet talk you're so fond of assigning to me: I am not a damned bit nice, unless it suits me—and if it's trouble you're after, allow me the pleasure. I want you, lady, and I can be as crude as you'd like about it!" Then, sliding his hands deeper into the water, he fastened them on her rear, and lifted her snuggly against his body. When she froze, it angered him further, and now she was held to him with a hand across small of her back, the other at the nape of her neck, and that one had drawn her mouth within an inch of his. "Take a lover and you will be handled. Get used to it!" Then, giving no heed to a whimpered protest, he kissed her hungrily; wantonly; thoroughly; demanding submission. And he got it...

Mandria could not move on her own; could scarcely breathe; and was rapidly losing the ability to think. But overwhelming as that was, so was his sudden release. Arms akimbo, he just stood watching as she floundered, seeking the balance and footing to stand again. Only when she had, did he speak. "Would I serve your purpose now?" he asked coldly.

"No!" she swore. "Never, damn you—No!" And swimming around him, she headed for shore.

Lucy was right there when Mandria came out of the water, and already repeating her dire warnings as she hopped about, tugging the yellow skirt back to its proper length. But paying her little heed Mandria started for the dunes at a pace Lucy could not match. "I just don't know what came over you!" Lucy called after her. "I really, really don't!" Then realizing Tom stood close behind, she immediately supported her friend. "Mandy is so sweet. —Isn't she sweet? Mandy is just a real sweet person!"

"Yes, she is," he answered, watching their subject stomp furiously over the dune crest. "But couldn't you wring her neck sometimes, Lucy? ...I came close to it, I guess." And leaving her to trail behind, with a puzzled look on her small oval face, he started toward Mike and Nicole, who were also observing Mandria's flight. "Captain, would you step over here for a moment?" And his tone brought Mike in a hurry. "No questions," he said ramming arms into his shirt sleeves. "If Mandria returns make an excuse for my absence," he pulled on one boot, then the other. "I'll see you back at the cabin." And he walked away, buttoning his shirt—but heading in the wrong direction.

Mike started to point that out, but decided against it. If Tom had finally met a woman who could so befuddle him, why should he interfere? Besides, recalling Nicole's attentive caresses to his bare chest only minutes ago, the Captain could readily attest that a little disorientation was not necessarily a bad thing...

Tom tromped along the beach, as if he could mesh his thoughts into order beneath his heels. From the start, he'd known what Mandria was planning, so why had he reacted so strongly when she confirmed it? His body presented one answer, but his mind kept delving for another. ...What was it? What made him want to kiss her and strangle her at the same time?

But the eavesdropping Atlantic would not permit such intensity over another woman in her presence—not even the daughter of the sea. So using her most accomplished tricks she set out to recapture his attention for herself. Hissing softly, she danced and swayed for his pleasure. She coaxed him closer and cooled him with a misty spray. She buffeted breezy fingers over his hair, slowed his pace, and after a time, brought a semblance of ease to his mind. Yes, when it suited, Atlantic could even be soothing...

When Tom saw the tavern ahead, and realized he'd gone the wrong way, he decided it was time he had a drink. "Guess I would have circled the whole damned island!" he muttered going in. Buying ale, he returned to the table they'd previously used, gazed from the same window, and slowly settled into his thoughts. He remembered how gracefully Mandria had come walking down that beach—hell, how gracefully she did everything. She had a way of caressing inanimate objects, as a blind person might, to learn texture, content and purpose: the tautness of a guitar string; a tea droplet on the rim of her glass; the gentleness in her fingertips, when touching someone she cared for. —And oh, but he'd wished, more than once that day, she'd place those hands on him.

Then there were her eyes: in anger, they narrowed to glistening, green embers; clouded to a moss when she was attentive; and if amused, they held the sparkle of emeralds. His greatest wish, still, was to see their color when lit with the fires of passion. —Well, there was a thought worthy of ale by the gulp. Maybe two or three...

Behind Tom, the bar whore had lost all but two of her playmates now. The coin game forgotten, the men only wanted the service she was there to provide. But hoping to better her price, she swatted at their groping hands, and when nearly cornered, escaped a chair, to lift her skirts and flaunt the nudeness beneath.

Tom became involved when one of the men made a forward lunge that sent the whore darting in his direction. Clumsy as a cow, she threw her arms about his neck, and with both men now in pursuit, planted a mushy mouth to Tom's face, cackling a vow of eternal love in barter for her rescue. That notion was not well received by the approaching men, and uttering dark warnings, they pried her loose and hoisted her onto the surface of their own table. The woman conceded, and lay there smiling, as she drew down her blouse and lifted a breast to each for suckling. In response to their avid feeding, she moaned guttural suggestions and spread her legs wide in preparation of what her kneading fingers—even through the cloth of their trousers—were doing now to both men's already engorged testicles.

Tom quit the place while the ale would still stay down. Returning to the sea, he stood breathing in clean bursts of fresh breeze, and focused on setting a new route for the cabin. He had no wish to backtrack along the beach until settling accounts with himself, so making use of an island road, he by-passed the Lucas place before cutting through a dune to continue along the tide-swelling waters of Back River again.

Hands stuffed in his pockets, he tried once more to solve the mystery of his extraordinary attraction to this one particular girl. That she'd affected his life from the moment he saw her was absolutely true. That taking her would mean as little as it had with other women, was not. But why?

Rejection? …Perhaps. He'd seldom been turned down by a woman. He couldn't say he enjoyed it either—and especially not from one he found so damned appealing.

Desire? As Mike would put it, *Oh-hell-yes*! He'd liked the feel of her in his arms, though she wasn't there by choice. …But he wasn't an animal, like the ones he'd just seen in the tavern, and would never have forced her to more than that kiss.

Pride? …Probably so. He sure didn't relish the thought of losing her to the low-life she believed needed to exact her revenge. Now, that was something to ponder…

The answer was creeping closer, and pausing to sit on Mike's dinghy, he allowed it catch up. "…I've been saying it all day," he realized. "I want it all." So, there it was.

Nice and simple, right? Except that after their clash in the sea, likely Mandria would never speak to him again. Yet, topping the final dune, he saw a wagon pulled up to the cabin and it looked like the one he'd seen parked in the Lucas' yard. Was she down there? Damn, he hoped so, and just over a hundred yards separated him from knowing.

"Hello in the house," he said from the doorway. And there Mandria sat at the table, though not looking his way as the rest did.

"Hello yourself," said the Captain, ready to repeat the alibi he'd been asked to create. "Couldn't find any firewood, huh? Well we did—and you missed a damned fine supper."

"Hey there, Mister Tom," Jenny grinned crookedly. "Ah was scared you got lost!" She was laced tight on alcohol, and Tom guessed this was Old Jed's way of fortifying her for the return trip. "Where you

96

been, anyways?" she finished on a tremendous hiccup, which brought smiles from all but the one somberly tracing her finger over a design in the tablecloth.

"Yes, the crabs were really delicious—," Lucy started, stopped and settled for staring.

Rising from her chair, Nicole was now staring too. "Mike, you were right!" she declared. "Tom did go find a mysterious island woman!"

Jenny strained for focus. "God bless him!" she slapped her knee. "For sure—it for certain sure!"

And all the while, Mike stood grinning, arms folded at his chest. "Well, I wasn't serious about that, but damn if it wasn't a pretty good guess."

Tom felt as puzzled as Mandria looked when grazing him with an inquisitive glance. He was more puzzled when she turned to face him fully, her eyes hurling great, frozen green stalactites directly at him. "…Captain?" he asked, seeking sense he could trust, "What are they talking about?"

"The woman who left lip rouge on you," Lucy volunteered. "I can see it from here. Really I can! And it's a rather harsh color."

"Lip rouge?" Tom brushed a hand to his mouth.

"No—no, no, no!" Nicole came forward with a napkin from the picnic hamper. "There now, you wicked, wicked man," she wiped his cheek clean. "Good as new."

"Oh my God," Tom remembered. "The tavern trollop…"

"Why, Thomas Scott," Nicole leaned to wag a finger in his face. "Did you play her lewd little game after all?"

"What game?" Lucy asked. "Why was it lewd, Nico? Did you see it? But, no, you couldn't have seen it—not in a tavern!"

"Well, of course not, silly," Nicole turned to take Mike's arm. "But the Captain did tell me all about it. Didn't you Captain?"

"Then perhaps the Captain would tell us too," Mandria said in a semi-sweet tone. "We're so anxious to hear how Mr. Scott spent his *lewd* afternoon."

"Hell, Mandy," Mike goaded. "On this or any afternoon, Tom wouldn't have to settle for that harlot. And even if the lip rouge was hers, he didn't ask her to leave it there. Women just seem motivated to do that kind of thing around him. Believe me, I've seen it happen."

"Really," Mandria gifted Tom with an ice spear. "All that, and a teacher too? Yet, should his character come into question, not one who'd likely hold a position for long."

Tom spoke slowly and succinctly. "But wouldn't that mean I now meet even more of your requirements for that other position you're so anxious to fill?"

"Now, Mandy," Lucy fidgeted, "it's unfair to judge when you want to—; I mean, it's uncharitable, considering that you want—; that is, we all have problems. We really, really do! …Don't we?"

Mandria lowered her lashes and took a nice deep breath. She had come to this cabin for one reason, and one alone. After leaving the beach in a snit, she realized Tom had admitted knowledge of her father's doings—could know much more—and she wanted all the information she could get. So, she had come in peace; to arrange another meeting where she could persuade him to confide his sources to her. But he hadn't been there, and with all the teasing about where he probably was, she'd quickly succumbed to another snit. Then, that stupid smudge of lip rouge had activated her smart mouth and she'd just come within a gnat's breath of destroying any chance she had to question him at all. No, it would be best to leave right now; to calm the whirlwind of agitation infecting her brain; and put reasoning off for another day. "Yes, Lucy, we all do have problems—so, Mr. Scott, for a second time today, I apologize." And to stop him from responding, she rose quickly, claiming Jed had need of the wagon and urged Lucy through hurried farewells.

But if she'd hoped to leave without more from Tom, it wasn't going to happen. Ambling over to the doorway, he stood there waiting—right in the center of the doorway, blocking her exit.

Mandria's first impulse on seeing him there was to walk right over him. And it wasn't his size that stopped her, but eyes that… well, gobbled up her every step. He had no right to look at her this way, and she thought she'd made that clear. He just would not do! So, coming to an exasperated halt, she set her chin stubbornly and glared.

"Good-bye, Lucy. I really-really enjoyed meeting you," he said sincerely. "Mandria is lucky to have such a loyal friend."

"Thank you," she peeped and peeked from one of them to the other.

"Mandria, thank you for the meal," he smiled, and she felt depths of warmth all the way to her toes. "And I especially enjoyed our invigorating swim. Wouldn't mind doing that with you again. Anytime. So, if the mood strikes, lady, do remember: …I am available to you."

"Lucy," Mandria guided her in between them, to lessen the urge to beat fists upon his person, "please meet the master of innuendo."

"Really?" Lucy's eyes rounded. "Is that close to Savannah?"

And now, the idiot man was expecting her to share his amusement, which left Mandria biting hard on her lip. This just had not been one of her better days. "Never mind, now," she gently steered Lucy around him, managing it without incident. But when she tried to follow—and watching carefully to see that he didn't move—their bodies brushed anyway.

"Oh…," she said somewhere between a moan and a gasp, for brief as the contact was, it had pushed her right back into the ocean; into arms that claimed; eyes that tempted and coveted; and a mouth that proved no matter how many times she'd granted a kiss, she had never been kissed at all until that precise moment in time.

"Mandria?" he placed a steady hand beneath her elbow. "All else aside, I truly did enjoy the day here."

"Oh?" she repeated—and this time with sarcasm. Then, in spite of absolutely everything she could do to keep from adding more, out it came. "I'm certain your tavern trollop will be happy to hear so."

It had been a full five minutes since Mandria's departure, and leaning against the doorjamb, Tom still stood gazing down the road she'd taken. Jenny thought it sad because he seemed so alone, just lamenting and pining away. Following the dictates of a kind heart, she went to offer what comfort she could. "Mister Tom," she said at his back, "Miss Mandy got a real good soul. She take after her Mama, don't you know. …So what you reckon be wrong with the chile'?"

"Well, Jenny" he turned with a really warm smile that surprised her, "I keep looking, but I haven't found the first thing wrong with her yet—except that the little goose just admitted to liking me, and doesn't know it." And she had, because that parting shot was suspiciously close to jealousy. Jealous—hell yes she was—and over a tavern whore. It was enough to carry him to their next encounter. That and remembering her breathless little "Oh" when they'd brushed together in the doorway…

Much later, after escorting Nicole to her door, Mike returned to the Irish Mist with the family Police Captain in tow. "Thomas, Uncle Pat has come up with a bit of news," he said, pouring them each a drink. "Remember Kathleen Morgan from the Seafest?"

"I believe so," Tom played along. "Nice lady. What about her?"

"Well, seems her affair with the boss has taken a new twist," Mike said.

"Lucas suspects another man is involved," Patrick added. "And it's hopping mad he is."

"With Kathy?" Tom looked into his glass. "He hasn't harmed her, has he?"

"Not yet," Patrick nodded. "But the search for proof is on, don't you know. The sketchy description he got only said a man—tall and dark-haired—was seen leaving the Seafest late in the night. That's it. But he's still having Kathy watched from every corner, just laying in wait for the man ta return."

"So, whoever the bastard is," Mike said nonchalantly, "he'd do well to stay clear of Kathy. —Wouldn't you say, Uncle Pat?"

"That I would, lad; —that I would. Over the years, I seen more than a couple of fellows Sam and the boys took care of. There wasn't much left untouched, that's for truth and for sure."

There was nothing Tom could say to that. But Patrick Herb wasn't a fool. He kept tabs on the happenings in his city, and likely knew exactly to whom he spoke. So heedful of a timely caution, from both of the Herbs, vigilance moved up a notch on Tom's new agenda…

# CHAPTER 9

Tom and Mike went separate ways following Sunday Mass. The Irish Mist was to resume her usual schedule on Monday, and after two weeks in port, Mike had much to do in preparation. Tom spent the rest of his day in search of new living quarters.

At one place, an anxious mother paraded five homely daughters before him, while bragging about their domestic capabilities. That one he scratched from the list before reaching their bottom doorstep.

In another house, a plump matron of indeterminable years made him an astounding offer: a nice reduction in the rental fee if he'd warm her bed once a week. Her door hadn't fully closed behind him before this one was scratched off too.

Rooms above a wash-house that reeked of lye soap and bluing vats in spite of being closed on a Sunday, and rooms below a tavern that was open and noisy in spite of it being Sunday, were also scratched. He then visited, and soon departed, establishments that were either unclean or infested with vermin—or both. Scratch; scratch; scratch!

He gave up being choosy late in the afternoon and making his way back to Bay Street, took rooms in the first boarding house he came upon. For this night, at least, if the walls shook with noise; if fumes burned his eyes and nose; if the bed was chock full of bugs and unsightly women; they'd just have to move over. He was too damned tired to care. And still, before retiring, he had to return to the Irish Mist, deliver a thank-you bottle of good bourbon to the Captain—from which they shared a few drinks—and then he got to haul his belongings back up that bluff. Except for Mike's camaraderie, it was not a day he wanted to repeat anytime soon…

Luckily, in the days to follow, Tom found there was much to recommend staying on at Harrison House. The landlady kept the place spotless and quiet. The table she set served aplenty and was at least palatable. His accommodations, a second floor sitting room with a daybed and one adjoining bedroom, were adequate for him and Allen to live as comfortably as they ever had. Also, because his windows faced the front and were shaded by a porch he could access through a main hall doorway, when a breeze did decide to blow off the river, the rooms should stay fairly cool.

He had finished unpacking his cases now, and sat before a window, bare feet propped on the sill, thinking how pleased Allen would be having the drawers in a spare chest all to himself. They had not had such a luxury since their mother died. Then, he realized something that had a smile begging equal space with the cigar clenched in his teeth. What he'd done was establish a home…and damn, but he liked the sound of that.

At nine o'clock sharp Tuesday morning, Tom was sitting in Ransom O'Rourke's office, where he'd just handed the banker a savings record, a packet of stock certificates, and asked to have his accounts transferred from a bank in Athens. That took care of Item One on his new list.

Ransom ran a quick tally of the stock first, and then looked at Tom in surprise. "Do you mind if I ask what made you invest in a Rail Road? It's the most lucrative thing around, but we've had real problems convincing our investors of that."

"It wasn't a stroke of genius," Tom assured him. "I just worked for that particular company a few years ago, and when they offered employees a chance to buy in, I did."

"No, son. You reinvested and that took foresight. Railways will soon be a life line for the South, and the quicker we get one here, the better. Its innovative companies like this," he tapped a finger on Tom's packet, "that are bidding for a contract to push a line north too. South Carolina is way ahead of us on this one. That line you worked on between Augusta and Charleston, will take inland Georgia products to their ports, not ours. Right now, we are the 18th largest city in the country and it's because of the ports. But we won't stay there, unless we too, can provide ways of bringing business to Savannah. And, here we sit, still trying to generate enough interest to move forward." Then, looking through Tom's savings book, he again showed surprise. "And your dividends are nothing to sneeze at either. Tom, I'd say you've done well for yourself all the way round."

And now, for Item Two: "Sir, turn back to the first page, if you will. The initial entry is what I inherited from my father. I want half that amount put into a new account for my brother, Ethan Allen Joseph Scott. And I want it available to him on his eighteenth birthday, September 10th, of this year."

"I don't mean to pry," Ransom hesitated, "…but your brother wasn't left a share?"

The story Tom would tell Allen about this was feasible enough to use now too. "No, he wasn't. You see, my parents were from England, and the eldest son still inherits there. But I don't feel the system has merit, and mean to see him treated fairly."

Ransom nodded approval. "I'll have it done and ready for your signature as soon as the transfer of funds is complete. Let's just hope your brother shows your good sense in handling money."

"When you have the time, perhaps you could explain how much it would profit him to invest in your railroad endeavor for Savannah— and I'd certainly be interested when you start counting heads, sir. But Allen will first need to recover from the shock of this sudden windfall," Tom chuckled. "He has never known we had a penny to our names."

"You'll have to tell me that story sometime. Sounds damned interesting."

"One day," Tom pushed on to Item Three. "Now, sir, about those interviews?"

So, with Ransom's letter of recommendation in hand, he spent the next day in conference with the revamped board at Chatham Academy and walked away with a job. Then he went home to complete Item Four, which was to write a letter of his own:

*Dear Allen,*

*Come September, I'll be gainfully employed in the beautiful old city of Savannah. So, when your job ends at the Hice Farm, start packing! Enclosed you will find a draft to cover travel and enough to pay Susan for your keep. Please add my thank you to yours and tell her I will write soon with details about my teaching position.*

*You will like it here, little brother. The women are delightful, the food is delicious, and the landscape so very different. No mountains or hills—and no more long, snowy winters! The heat you will learn to endure. I won't attempt describing the Atlantic Ocean. It is just something you must see for yourself.*

*When you leave Athens, take the stage to Augusta. Go to the river docks and find a boat named the Irish Mist. My good friend, Captain Michael Herb, will welcome you aboard and bring you downriver to Savannah. He is in Augusta until Thursday of every week, so plan accordingly. You will arrive here on a Friday, and if I'm not there to meet you, our new address is #4 at the Harrison House on Bay Street. Mike can tell you the way and the landlady will know to let you in. Until then,*

*Your Big Brer,*
*Tom*

On Thursday Tom was back at the window again, where he pulled out his list and looked at the only remaining item: Mandria. He wondered when she'd return from Tybee and how he'd initiate contact when she did. Nicole would probably know when, but without Mike being present, he didn't want to be in that one's company. "Come home, pretty lady!" he said around a good back stretch. Sixteen miles separated him from courtship. For in spite of the bastard who sired her and her insane notion of retaliation—which could destroy everything special about her—he intended to court Mandria Lucas; to talk her out of her plot and into his arms. It was just something he needed to do for himself...

After a visit to the barber, the next afternoon, who should Tom spot in front of Harrison House, conversing with two old gentlemen on a bench at the curb, but Captain Michael Herb. "Well, speak of the devil," he extended a hand.

Mike reciprocated, flashing his fine Irish smile, and in usual fashion, went straight for completion of his own agenda. "Yeah, and guess where we're going tonight?"

"I have no idea," Tom laughed. "And as I wasn't sure I'd be staying on at Harrison House when you left, how did you know where to find me?"

"We're taking the O'Rourke's out to dinner!" the Captain declared in his one-track mind enthusiasm.

"So Ransom told you," Tom answered his own question. "Did he also tell you I was hired by Chatham Academy?"

"He did," Mike grinned happily. "Yeah, Tom, Ransom met my damn boat today and told me in person. —In fact, we sat around and talked for an hour or so."

"About me?" Tom couldn't resist, a fist pressed to his heart.

"Oh-hell no!" came wrapped in a jolly chuckle. "I'm not that pleased with you. No, we talked business—and about Nicole some too. Anyway, I knew you'd want to thank him for the recommendation letter, so on your behalf, I suggested dinner and by God, he accepted!"

"Sounds good. But I also owe you a great deal, Captain Herb. How about letting me pay for your evening as well."

"Listen, old son, you are my excuse for being with Nico tonight. That's enough thanks for me. —Hey, did you write to your brother yet?"

"Yes, and told him to find you in Augusta, as you suggested."

"Fine. Now speaking of Augusta, aren't you going to ask about my trip?"

"All right, let's see," Tom pretended seriousness. "How much did you win at the game tables?"

"$200.00."

"And how many maidens deflowered?"

"None, but I sheathed-up for a couple of seasoned blossoms—horny little thorns and all."

"And how drunk did you get in the process?"

"Very, —oh God, very, very!"

"Is there anything else, Captain?"

"Yes. Wear a suit tonight."

"Hmm," Tom mused as if his wardrobe permitted. "The black one? Or my black one?"

"Black—definitely. It's your color!"

"Matches my soul," Tom agreed.

"Oh-hell-yes!"

"So, what time do we start this gala evening?"

"Pick you up at six sharp."

"Want to come up and see the place?" Tom asked. "Have a drink maybe?"

"Later. I'm off to buy myself a new suit—something dashing and dark green, I'm thinking."

"To match your Irish green hide, of course."

"Oh-hell-yes-some-more!" Mike answered as he turned to leave.

"Good-bye, Captain," Tom called, starting up his doorsteps.

"Bye—be ready now. Six o'clock."

After both had gone their own ways, the two old men on the bench, looked at each other and laughed. "Oh-hell-yes!" one exclaimed. "Horny little thorns and all!"

"Oh-hell-yes-some-more!" replied the other.

And sharing a sigh and a wistful nod, they each wondered the same thought too. *...Ah, the days of youth! Where have they gone so quickly?*

The evening began with drinks in Ransom's study. The room was paneled in dark wood and everything in it, richly bound in burgundy leather: the chairs; desk and table tops; the precisely shelved books; planters; and even the whiskey decanters and glasses. But there was something out of place about the woman's portrait, in an elaborate gold frame, that hung over the fireplace, and Tom wondered why it wasn't included with others in the O'Rourke family that lined the entry hall.

"Nicole's mother?" he asked, knowing it was. They had the same hair, delicate features and build.

"Yes," Ransom said after gazing at the portrait for a long moment. "Yes, that was Deborah." There was both pain and affection in his manner, and it caused Tom to look at the portrait again.

"I can't believe how alike they are," Mike nodded. "You're lucky to have known two such beautiful women."

"Beautiful, yes," Ransom rose to pass a box of cigars. "Alike? … Well, in some ways, I suppose they are."

Tom knew then, there was a deeply personal reason for the portrait being in this room. It was among the things Ransom loved best and worried over most—as evidenced by his effort to change the subject.

"Do much hunting, either of you?" he went to a gun cabinet and brought back a musket. "We're gathering one this fall after the first good cold snap. Going after boar. Care to join us?"

"I would," Tom took the gun and looked it over. "This is a fine piece, sir. I hope my brother gets here with mine before you go. — Now, there is an avid hunter. Would you mind if he tags along too?"

"Not at all. —So, what about you, Mike?"

"Oh-hell-no!" he answered emphatically. "I'm more familiar with fishing lines and shrimp nets than firearms and—"

"Oh, come with us, Mike," Tom goaded. "If nothing else, we'll use you as lure. You could squeal like a piglet, couldn't you?"

"As I started to say," the Captain began, with a sparkle revving up in his eyes, "I just don't care to meet an animal with tusks like that—not if it's my skill with a gun that keeps them from ripping me apart. Nor would I utter a sound he might find offensive—or horny. No, not the first grunt or squeal; not even from the upper-most branches of the very tallest tree. And if I went, gentlemen, that is where I'd stay. Hell, I wouldn't even come down to eat or pee! So, no thank you, I'll just forgo the manly pleasure of your boar hunt."

"Damn, Michael!" Ransom was laughing enjoyably. "I must remember that speech and repeat it for Sebastian. He's heading the hunt, and I think you've met him already?"

"Sebastiano Rizza?" Mike asked. "Yes, I dropped him off up river to look over some property. —Iano is Italian and new to Savannah too," he said to Tom. "Real nice fellow."

"A very wealthy Italian," added Ransom. "He bought that property outright and is calling the hunt to rid the area of predators before clearing the planting fields."

"I hope this takes place over a weekend," Tom said, returning the musket to Ransom. "That will be my only free time once school begins."

"Oh it's sure to run through the weekend," Ransom relocked the gun in the cabinet, then leaned on the corner of his desk facing his guests.

"Tom, I still can't picture you in a classroom," Mike puffed on his cigar, "—leading a bunch of kids in song or drawing pretty pictures for Mama. You just don't fit the damn part."

"Well Captain," Tom settled back in his chair, "just as you're drawn to the river, I'm drawn to teaching. And Robert Bennett, the Headmaster at the Academy, seems to be an innovative thinker. It may take a few years to accomplish everything he wants, but I'm going to like being part of getting there. He sees a day when students will be divided, not only into age groups but separate rooms. Then, I could spend a portion of the day with each, teaching Mathematics on their age levels, while other teachers will do the same with their specialties. Starting this year, he is also enlisting aides to conduct additional classes in chorus, music and art, thereby making use of local talent for the student's benefit."

"Yes, and I hear Mandy is considering enlistment," added Ransom.

"…Really?" Tom asked in surprise. "…When did this come about?"

"The appeal has been out for weeks, but I understand from Evelyn she went by the school and picked up literature on the program today."

"I can't tell you how glad I am to hear this," Tom said. "I'd really like offering a word of encouragement that she follow through on it."

"You may get the chance," Ransom looked at his pocket watch. "That daughter of mine takes the longest damned time to dress!" he commented. "But anyway Tom, Mandy is upstairs with Nicole right now. —Mike, how about something more in your glass? It seems we're going to have time for it."

Tom did not hear a word of Mike's reply. Mandria was upstairs, perhaps just above his head. He glanced at the ceiling wondering what magic it would take to bring her crashing down on his lap. And then, what could he say to keep her there? But with no magic and fewer words, he settled for a close watch on the study door...

Finally, it opened. "Daddy?" Nicole knocked as she entered. "Are you ready?"

"Been ready, sweetheart," Ransom rose. And in one unbelievable movement, Mike sprang to his side while straightening his tie.

Tom stood too, looking through that gathering in the center of the room, and for an awful moment Mandria wasn't there. Then she appeared in the doorway, but stopped when hardly into the room. ... And damn, but she looked beautiful! The rustle of her skirts suggested the softness of silk and the deep olive color of the becoming dress, lent that same hue to her changeable eyes. She wore a pendant on a long gold chain, which he noticed only because of the tan cleavage cradling it. Her hair, swept slightly away from her face, cascaded in natural curls about her ears and shoulders. He had liked her walking barefoot in the wind and sand at Tybee, but this Mandria too, was breath taking. And his appreciative smile said so...

Mandria had thought about the weekend a thousand times and her feelings continued to see-saw erratically. But two facts had not changed: Tom was her only lead to what her father might be doing; and she had to maintain contact with him no matter what. ...Well, the talking kind of contact, anyway. He absolutely could not be allowed to touch her again, as it brought on bouts of an emotion she just did not want to deal with. So she'd come here tonight, as she'd gone to the cabin: to make peace; to greet him pleasantly; to remain unbothered in his presence. It would be as simple as that. …But looking through the same centered group as he, she wasn't prepared for the image he projected while standing in the edge of lamplight. To say he looked handsome in his suit, grossly understated the truth. He flattered it. He filled the cloth to exact and exciting proportions, while flickering light blended his dark visage in and out of shadows playing on the wall behind him; it then illuminated the stark white of his shirt, accentuated the Sapphire of his eyes and danced wantonly about his mouth. And Mandria was captivated, wanting to commission the picture to canvas. Someday—for amusement, of course—she might try…

Nicole was making her own ecstatic conclusions. Unaware of being looked through and not looked upon, she assumed Tom was finally seeing her for the beautiful, irresistible woman she knew herself to be. Those smoldering eyes certainly said so, didn't they? Well, it was about time. She knew Mike thought of her that way, but how lovely if she could have both men vying for her attention. Why, the possibility was enough to make a girl breathless…

"Nico," her father was saying, "would you and Mandy care for a drop of sweet sherry?"

"I would!" she bubbled enthusiastically. "…I mean, that would be lovely, Father," she finished more sedately and conducive of her siren self image.

"None for me, thank you, Uncle Ran," Mandria said, proud of the cordial air she portrayed. "I only came in to say good-night, and wish all of you a pleasant evening."

"Don't go," Tom started toward her. "I've just learned we may be associates this school year and…," he paused, close enough now to inhale her honeysuckle scent. "Why don't you join us tonight? We could discuss some ideas over dinner."

Mandria felt his nearness, and before he guessed that, she must firmly, but nicely, refuse what seemed entirely too much like a social engagement. "Thank you, but I couldn't. Maybe at another time, because I would like to speak to you about…things," she managed. "But tonight my attention is needed at home."

"Oh, that is too bad," Nicole did all possible to sound sincere. "I do wish you were free, Mandy. It makes me sad that you'll miss the fun."

"Well, we can't have my beautiful daughter sad," Ransom draped an arm about her shoulders. "Mandy, I happen to know your father is at one of his meetings and your mother is out for an evening of Whisk, so there's nothing keeping you at home. Just go fetch your bonnet—or whatever young ladies wear to go out these days—and we'll pick you up when we've finished our drinks."

"But I shouldn't—" she tried again to decline, only to hear Mike's insistence added.

"You have to come, Mandy. We owe you that for your hospitality last weekend. And, the *yeas* here far outnumber your *nay*."

"It's settled then," Tom drew her hand to his arm. "Come, lady, I'll walk you home." And with that, he led her out like the mute she'd suddenly become.

Nicole gave a sigh of disappointment, but salvaged her pride in the admiring expressions of her father and Mike. Tom would just have to remain a work in progress, until willing to admit his fascination with her—and she would see that happen. Meanwhile she was in dire need of adoration. "So, do you like my dress?" she asked both men. "My wonderful father let me buy it today, Captain—and I thought of your eyes when I saw the color…"

They were well into the square before Mandria found her voice. "It is not settled, you know," she uttered, removing her hand from Tom's arm. "But I do need to speak with you and I want a promise there'll be no repeat of your aggressive behavior of last Saturday."

She reminded him of a spitting kitten that he very much wanted to pet and would risk getting scratched to do it. "All right, I won't attack you over the dinner table. Promise I won't!" he laughed. "How's that?"

Pausing on the sidewalk, her glare said his humor was not appreciated. "I still have to cross this square," she pointed. "Do you think you can control your savage instincts that long?" And raising her chin, she turned to walk on.

"Stop right there!" he snagged her arm, bringing her back to face him. "You can not have this both ways, Mandria. You're angry with me for taking a kiss—one—but you are going to allow some bastard lover you care nothing for, to ravage you body and soul—and you won't be angry about it? Now which of us would you say has savage instincts?"

"How can you—of all people—dare to say that, when you practically ravaged me yourself?" she fired back, arms akimbo.

"One-more-time: think-lady!" each staccato word was accompanied by a tap of fingers against his temple. "You are too intelligent to miss the damn point. Yes, I did kiss you—with absolutely no encouragement from you—and look how you're reacting. But the sort you're seeking won't come from this side of town. If you expect him to believe what you're offering, you will have to show more encouragement than your beautiful smile or that cute little walk of yours. It will have to be direct; it will have to be vulgar; and then, *ravage* will be too nice a word for what happens next. You'll find yourself raped; forcefully, brutally, criminally raped!" he nodded. "…Mandria, you'd never survive it. The way you ran from me should have proven that to you."

His concern felt real. His damned words made sense too, and both were confusing her. "But my father deserves punishment—"

"Do you?" he interrupted. "Does your mother? Your father has hurt her enough. What you're planning will kill her. Why can't you see that?"

Mandria had no argument there, as she hadn't considered the effect on her mother at all. Nor, it would seem, some truly frightening consequences for herself. She would be forced now, to give that more thought too. Yet none of it answered what should be done about her father—and Tom knew something. "Not now, of course," she watched her own fingers play along the pendant chain, "but when you have time…would you mind talking with me about this again?"

"Not at all, Miss Lucas: anytime; anywhere."

She met his gaze then and Tom noted that even puzzlement enriched the color of her eyes. "I wish I understood you," she began. "My impression keeps changing almost hourly."

"Confusing, isn't it?" he said, as a lazy smile slid into place.

"Yes it is," she agreed. "A few minutes ago, I wanted to slap you. Now, I feel I owe you something and I don't know what it is—or even if I like you for making me admit that."

"You owe me nothing but your company on this beautiful evening," he assured her. "And as I hear the carriage coming, we'd best hurry to meet it. —Now smile, Mandria! Let's make some fun of this chance, shall we?"

They smiled at each other then, realizing the warmth of a first connection between them. —Almost the first, anyway. There had been the warmth of that kiss in the sea. Both knew this too, and Tom savored it. Mandria…well, looking back, it didn't seem quite as terrible now, did it…?

# CHAPTER 10

The O'Rourke carriage pulled to a stop in front of a long, one-storied building near the west end of the downtown business district. The place was a swarm with people of every description and station. Some carried in crates of produce, while others carried out replenished shopping baskets. Children and dogs played amid the commotion and none, it seemed, were above pilfering a tasty bite from wherever they could. It was clearly a market and Tom thought it odd they should be there. "…We're going in?" he asked as Ransom left the carriage.

"Indeed, we are," he answered, watching as Mike assisted Nicole to the ground. "City Market serves the best steak in town."

Once inside, Tom still saw only a market place. Fruit and vegetable stands lined one wall in a patch-quilt array of ripened colors. The vendors nearest him sold dairy products and baked goods. The far wall was stacked high with wine bottles, ale and whiskey casks. To the rear, potted and cut flowers bloomed in a dazzling tribute to the green thumbs of the city. Buyers and sellers bargained in their known noisy way and adding to the din, more children playing night tag as they ran between and around the stands.

Purchases were made as they started through the isles. "To go with supper," Mike explained, choosing a wedge of cheese and loaf of crusty bread. Ransom bought potatoes, spring onions and enough tomatoes for everyone. Mandria and Nicole selected dessert; slices of sponge cake, containers of sweetened cream, small baskets of strawberries and pecan halves roasted in salted butter. Tom purchased a bottle of wine, and because the rest insisted, a piece of aromatic fruit he'd been curious about.

"Bananas," Ransom said as Mandria peeled away the skin so he could enjoy one. "Come to us by boat all the way from South America."

Then, purchases in hand, they continued through a door nestled in the flower stands, and greeted by the delicious aroma of roasting meat, descended a flight of spiraling stairs. The basement restaurant there had tables and chairs of the wrought iron Tom had admired all over the city. The floors were sprinkled with wood shavings and the walls were a literal gallery for the sale of local art work, as each piece bore a price tag.

When seated, a smiling Negro woman approached and gave Mike a friendly pat on the back. "Lord-y me! There that Cappin' Mike! How doing, Cappin'?"

"Just fine, Victoria Audrey!" he returned her jovial manner. "But we sure are hungry. What you got for us back there?"

"'Bout got it all. New beef come in today," she said eyeing Tom curiously. "Listen, Ah know the O'Rourke family, here, and Miss Lucas—how you good folks doing? But who this with the pretty smile? Ah ain't seen him a-fore."

"Then allow me," Mike stood and made a to-do of it. "This is Miss Victoria Audrey Benway. She is famous for never forgetting a name or face. And if you're a friend—as I'm proud to be—she'll thicken your steak and keep your glass filled to the brim. Now, won't you, Victoria Audrey?" he hugged her shoulder affectionately.

"Sweet—just sweet as sugar cane," she hugged him back. "Now tell me bout this man a-fore Ah get a toothache from all that sugar-mouth."

"Yes ma'am," he conceded obediently. "This is Thomas Scott, a very good friend, who has come to teach in Savannah."

"Sure enough?" she grasped Tom's hand and shook his whole arm. "You teaches reading, lettering, ciphering—all that stuff?"

"Yes, I do," Tom answered, surprised at her enthusiasm, but glad for a positive reaction, no matter that it was only his second one ever.

"Well, Ah just be," she stood looking at him. "Had Ah the chance, Ah always thought Ah could learn them things. Ah sure did."

"I'm sure you could too," Tom smiled, but felt sadness for her yearning. It was wrong to deprive anyone of knowledge and worse yet, when it was wanted so badly.

"Now, Victoria Audrey," Mike said, "unless you're planning to take me home with you for supper—and you know how your man Noah is jealous of me—you'd best fetch that meat tray. Better be quick too, or I'm going to pass-out, right here before you!"

"All right—just all right," she laughed, gathering their purchases. "Ah see these things get fix-up for the serving too. It nice seeing you folks again—and big welcome, Mister Teacher-man."

Nicole then began teasing Mike about his familiarity with the woman, and as she was being quiet flirtatious about it, Ransom was able to observe the Captain's reaction. Thus far, Mike had given her tit-for-tat—which surprised him, considering the number of beaus she'd purposely left tied-tongued and red faced. Yes, in time, Captain Herb might prove more than a worthy business partner—if Nicole would learn to look beyond herself and see that. Her mother never had, and the hurt of it remained locked in his heart until this day...

As the meal progressed, Tom saw glimpses of the lady Mandria was bred to be: relaxed and enjoying; smiling and laughing; with a keen wit and dry sense of humor. And so very beautiful it made him ache to hold her close and keep all that she was to himself. Toward that end, when supper was finished and coffee was being prepared, he turned to her with question. "Mandria, are any of your paintings here?" It was quietly asked, as he didn't wish to involve, nor include, those still having dessert.

"I think so," she turned to see, her throaty tone matching his. "Yes, one or two are left over there." Then looking directly at him, her green, tip-tilted eyes curious, she smiled. And Tom felt a piece of his soul dissolve. "...But how did you know that I paint?" she asked.

"Nico mentioned it," he answered. "And, I noticed your signature on others. At the beach...mostly," he added. He'd go to his death before admitting he'd seen the ones in her father's lair at the Seafest.

"Oh? Did you have a favorite? I'd be glad to give it to you."

He rose then, drawing her up with him and excusing them from the table, led her in the direction she'd indicated. "Let's see these first," he requested.

"...I'm not that good," she said as they neared the canvasses. "But if you really want one of these, I'll have Victoria Audrey put it aside for you."

"If?" his choice was immediate. "This one, please. I must have this one."

"Well...it's not very good," she insisted, wondering what he found special in the seascape.

"Oh, but it is. You did this from the dune in front of the beach house," he pointed to the slope and curve of the path. "We did our crabbing here," he moved his finger down the beach. "And it was just about there," he drew to a stop in the painted water, "That I kissed you for the first time."

"Oh," she lowered her eyes as if that would keep him from seeing her blush. "Oh," she repeated.

"Just *oh*?" he stepped closer. "Nothing more to say?"

Mandria touched the rough wood of the frame, and nodded. "Tomorrow, I'm sure to think of a hundred things. ...But I just don't seem to be upset with you or anything else at the moment."

"Is that because I kept my promise not to attack you over the supper table?" he teased around a lifted eyebrow.

"Possibly," she laughed a bit.

"Well, remember that you still have to *cross-that-square* again tonight," he took the painting from the wall and handed it to her.

"And you will remember saying we could talk," she replied, placing the canvas in Victoria Audrey's keeping. But on turning, she was startled to find him at her back. "Oh," she splayed a hand on his chest. "...Tom, why do you do that? Last weekend, I thought I imagined it. But it kept happening then—and now, you're doing it again."

He looked down at her slender fingers, before raising his eyes to hers. "Maybe, I like being where you are. Or maybe, I want you where I am. Or maybe, I'll just stand here making excuses as long you keep touching me."

117

"Oh!" she hurriedly tried to remove her guilty appendage.

But Tom was already drawing that hand to the crook of his arm and leading her back to their table. Just before seating her though, he said, "You know, I've changed my mind about limited vocabularies. Sometimes two-letter words and a blush can say a hell of a lot." And Mandria couldn't help it, she laughed.

With their return to the O'Rourke's, good manners dictated they should all be asked in for refreshments, but Mandria declined, saying she'd forgotten to leave a note telling her whereabouts, and her mother would be home now and worried. And not in a million years, was Tom going to miss walking her *across-that-square*…

"I enjoyed the evening," she said after a time.

"And I hate for it to end," he agreed. "Must you go right in?"

"Well no," she paused on the walk to look at him. "You see, mother isn't really home yet…and if you can spare a few minutes, I want to ask you something."

"Take as long as you'd like," he led her to his favorite eavesdropping bench.

Gathering her nerve, along with her skirts, she began almost as soon as she was seated. "Tom, where did you meet my father?"

"I never have," he sat facing her, one hand resting on the seat back.

"Never?" she puzzled. "Then how did you know about his…his indiscretion? I mean, you're still new in Savannah and—" Up came her hands to flushed cheeks. "Dear Lord! Is it common knowledge? Does everyone know but his family?"

"You certainly are full of questions," he smiled.

"And I must have answers, Tom. One way or the other, something has to be done about this."

"So, we're not going to behave?" he toyed with a curl on her shoulder.

"I didn't say—"

"Because," he interrupted, "if you're not, then I certainly won't feel bound to."

"But that's not—"

"And if I failed earlier to convince you," he over rode her again, "my offer of availability still stands."

Mandria stared at him, unsure what he was up to, so she brushed his hand away from her hair. "Why do men do this?" she asked—then was afraid she knew. "You are trying to distract me because; —because you're shielding my father, aren't you?" she shifted to face him with the accusation, while in her eyes, green embers bespoke reawakened anger.

"No, I told you I don't even know him."

"Ha!" she retorted. "You're shielding him—as all men do for each other—so the favor can be returned! I thought you might be different, but you're no better than the man I was seeking!" she grasped his lapels. "And since you're just so *available*, why don't I start with you!" Mandria kissed him then, as hard as she could or dared. Yet to her utter dismay, Tom did not return that kiss in any way. "—Damn you!" she said against his mouth before pulling away. "I don't understand you—not at all!"

"Neither do I," he nodded, leaning to the back of the bench. "Right now, I'm wishing you were some two-bit whore. I'd have you and be done with it."

"But I encouraged that. You said I'd have to. I offered—"

"To start with me," he finished it. "...Well, maybe this time, that's not enough."

"I don't see why," she argued. "It seems a fair trade: another trophy for your wall, and a lesson in male morality for me."

Tom heaved a sigh, stretching his legs out before him and his arms along the top of the bench. ...Lord, but he hated having to argue her out of the exact position he wanted her in, but this had to be on terms they both could accept. "Lady, you are just not that kind of woman. You're not built for it, and as I told you before, you'd never handle the back-wash."

"What am I built for then? —And if you dare to say a lady," she wagged a finger in warning, "I'll hit you with something!"

"All right. Hopefully, you are built for me. But you'd have to come openly and willingly—because of me—and not because of anything to do with your father. Because, Miss Lucas, if I start with you, I may never want it to end. Lady, I could easily fall in love with you. —Too easily, damn it."

That caused Mandria to lean back beside him, uttering a sigh of her own. "…No, don't speak of love to me," she nodded. "Except in novels, I've never seen any good come from it. In truth, it's a game men play and usually at a woman's expense."

"Then you've never been in love?" he asked.

"No, and I live with the reason why. Father hasn't brought my mother much happiness. —And look at your poor mother's life. Even Uncle Ran, so trusting and forgiving in the name of love, while Aunt Deborah went from one… Well, let's just say, she and my father would have made a prize winning couple. So, no thank you, I don't believe in love."

"In other words, I could have had your body right here on this bench, but never your heart?"

"No! …Yes—no!" she stammered. "Oh, stop confusing me again. I just don't want to be hurt like mother and the rest—and that's why I thought my plan would work. A lover I cared nothing for, wouldn't leave me with a broken heart when it was time to send him on his way."

"So, he'd leave your heart in tact," Tom countered. "But what would he take in its stead? Mandria, you'd have no self respect, no pride, and no satisfaction in what you'd accomplished. Now isn't that a lot to give-up for a moment of vengeance?"

"But you'd want it if your step-father returned," she refuted. "You said you still look over your shoulder for him. You wouldn't allow him to treat you as he once did. No, you'd want to see him punished for it, wouldn't you?"

"Yes, I would," he nodded, and then laughed. "But my solution would not be rushing out to make love in retaliation. Surely you can see that wouldn't solve anything."

"…Then what would—for me, I mean?"

"Living your own life; saying, Father, go to hell. I have a chance to be happy and I'm taking it. …Lady, maybe I'm not the right man for you, but shouldn't you find out? Please? Just allow me to show you how it could be and how little you have to fear from that."

"Perhaps I'm naïve, but how?" she glanced at him with a skeptical tilt of her head "You've refused me once already."

"Not so. I only objected to your motivation."

"…Because of my father."

"Yes. Turn your back on him, Mandria. And you might begin by kissing me again and meaning it this time."

"Because of you," she still quoted him.

"Because of us," he corrected. "And I won't touch you uninvited," he raised his hands for her inspection, then placed them back along the bench. "This will be your experiment entirely."

Mandria sat forward, turning to look at those wide spread arms. "…Promise?" she asked hesitantly.

"Promise," he smiled. For all her encouragement, she was truly cautious about his kisses, and it pleased him immeasurably. "—I promise!" he swore with a chuckle.

Mandria was not really sure she believed that, but leaned toward him with a testing brush of her lips against his. When he made no unexpected moves, she returned allowing a feather-light kiss to remain a moment longer. The same pattern followed with the next ones: a kiss; retreat; a watchful pause; and a more lengthy return. And where Tom found this lack of urgency intriguing, she found it simply astounding. How could this be the same man she'd encountered in the sea? Recalling that unsettling event, of a sudden, she straightened for a look at those out-stretched arms yet another time. But they remained in place, giving her the courage to move closer beside him; to add tasting to testing; interest to experimentation…

Tom was allowing Mandria to explore his mouth at her own pace, because as she learned, he taught. He subtly matched her growing involvement and gently urged her on. And when she paused for a needed breath, but didn't move away to avail herself of it, he carefully introduced his tongue, barely tracing the curve of her lower lip.

Dizzily, Mandria wondered how she could have forgotten to breathe, and at the touch of his tongue, caught her breath again.

Others had tried to persuade her to this, but she'd found it repulsive, and quickly thereafter, smothering. ...Yet where was that feeling now? Perhaps negatives didn't apply to Tom. Or perhaps because he merely continued to trace her lip in that most tantalizing way and forced nothing more, she began to enjoy it. So much so, that on their own volition her hands slid up his chest to grasp his lapels again and draw herself closer.

Tom was not unaffected. He continued coaxing her participation now, by slowly withdrawing his own, which brought her even closer. But had the bench been less sturdy, it would have splintered beneath his grip. Would she also withdraw, or would she want more? Steeling himself anew, he fervently prayed for the latter...

Sensing Tom's retreat brought an impatient sigh from Mandria. So, she began to trace the shape of his mouth as he had hers, and discovered the sensation most pleasant. The artist in her rejoiced as she memorized the firm texture and masculine chisel of his mouth, while the woman within said there had to be more to this business of kissing—and, if so, why was he keeping it from her...?

Never had Tom endured a more exquisite form of torture. Several times, his hands lifted but returned to the bench as he struggled to remember his promise not to touch uninvited. He had promised—damn it—and all he could do now was concentrate on each word, letter by letter, while they slammed against his brain...

Mandria was beyond remembering anything. His mouth was all that existed: a portal; a gateway; a spillway, readily absorbing emotions bubbling inside her. Boldly then, she pushed her own tongue past his parted lips, challenging him to deny her. He could not. But it was a duel she was destined to lose, whereby the aggressor quickly and gladly became a most willing captive. "Hold me," she whispered against his mouth. "Tom, I want you to hold me!" she demanded, crushing his lapels yet again.

He smiled at her worried expression. Did she actually think he wouldn't? "Yes, ma'am," he stood, drawing her up too. "Oh yes, ma'am," his voice softened; his arms pressing her close against him.

Mandria listened to the hammering strength of his heartbeat and felt a sense of belonging. But there was more; something more powerful than she'd ever felt before. Tilting her head back, she raised expectant eyes to his. "Is it permitted to ask for another kiss too? — Like the last one?"

"Yes lady, it is permitted," he nodded, and cupping her face; rejoicing to discover a smoldering ash-green to be passion's color for her eyes, he slowly lowered his mouth to hers. Spontaneous combustion might best describe what happened then.

*Spontaneous combustion: the process of catching fire and burning as a result of heat generated by internal chemical action.*

Openly, Mandria met and responded, lowering Tom's combustion point considerably. Willingly, she yielded when his arms spontaneously locked her against him. And in the midst of this mutual, but mindless, meshing of bodies, mouths and tongues, his hands naturally wandered up her ribcage, where his thumbs found the sides of her full breasts.

"Mandria, look," he groaned, tearing his mouth from hers. "Damn it, please look!" the words felt ragged and sharp in his throat.

"At what?" she uttered, dazed and entirely beautiful.

"At my hands," he pressed home his point. "At how easily we came to this, even with buggies passing on the street and people awake in every house on the square."

"Oh!" she grasped his fingers. "Oh no!" she unconsciously hugged them to her—which was not helping his situation in the least. "Oh Tom, we can't!" she glanced anxiously about, still pressing his hands against her.

"No, we can't. —Damn it!" he gently dislodged her hold, to stand with arms folded snugly between them. "...But, lady, for both our sakes, you'd better decide how you feel. You still have a choice to make, and you'd best give it some serious thought."

"I know," she placed her hands on his forearms, but feeling them tighten further—remaining the barrier he meant them to be—was hard to endure.

"Then go home and do it," he insisted. "—And go now!"

His sternness was real and this hurt too. He was ready to be rid of her, and that had Mandria moving quickly away. But from the edge of the street, she turned to look back, needing to understand what had happened. "…Have I done something wrong?" she asked. "Why are you upset with me?"

From the shadowy place where he stood, she heard soft laughter. "No, pretty lady. It isn't your fault I find you irresistible. I'm just a mite upset with myself, that's all."

"Why?" she asked now.

"Because at the moment, I'm in need of that two-bit whore. But after holding you, that option is entirely ludicrous."

"Oh," she nodded, glad he couldn't see the pleasure and relief his words brought her. "…So when will I see you again?"

"Whenever you wish. I'm at the Harrison House on Bay Street, #4, should you care to contact me."

"On Bay Street," she lingered, even at a distance. "…Tom, I really enjoyed—well, everything."

"As did I."

"But what I'm trying to say is I enjoyed our…experiment too. And I'm not bit sorry about any of it." Then turning quickly, she hurried across the street.

"…Neither am I, Mandria," Tom said once she was safely behind her door. But following a hefty sigh, a one-sided conversation ensued. "…You're glad you sent her away, aren't you, Thomas? And do you even know why? Because that is one lady you don't want on a park bench; or swimming away from you in the sea. Admit it: you want her in your own bed—and with you making sure she doesn't want to leave it." Then, as he felt like an idiot talking to himself in a darkened square, he turned and walked toward home…

124

# CHAPTER 11

Tom was better than half way to Bay Street when he remembered Mandria's painting. So altering his course for City Market, he covered the detour at a spirited pace, hoping to get there before closing. He did, but just as he neared the bottom of the spiral stairs to the restaurant, his presence was rudely challenged.

"Out of the way!" barked an angry man, his stiffened forearm shoving Tom into the railing. Clinging for balance, he looked upward, only to glimpse the shine of a boot heel and the flare of a cape tail disappearing around the curve. The encounter was more surprise than anything and yet, an inexplicable shudder passed through him.

"*Signore?*" said another from below. "Do you have *una ferita*—uh, injury?"

"No, I'm all right," Tom turned to see a handsome, dark-featured man, perhaps a decade older than himself. "But that poor bastard wasn't. Wonder who he was?"

"That, *mio amico*, was Samuel Lucas and I fear you caught the brunt of his anger for me."

"I'll be damned," Tom looked up the stairwell again. "As close as that, and still I missed him."

"That I could have been so fortunate. But come, let me be assured you are well," he extended his hand. "I am Sebastiano Rizza. May I offer *una bevanda*—uh, a drink?"

"Thomas Scott," he reciprocated. "But I should buy your drink, Mr. Rizza. I was invited to your hunt earlier tonight."

"*Molto bene*!" he said, leading the way to his table and calling for another glass as they sat down. "You are a true shot?"

"True enough, though it has been some months since—"

"Why, here's the Teacher-man again!" Victoria Audrey brought an interruption along with a fresh glass. "Mister Scott, ain't that right? So what you doing back so soon?"

"I forgot my painting," Tom answered. "Would you get it for me before Miss Lucas discovers my negligence?"

"Lord-y, I clean forgot it myself!" she hurried away, all a-chatter. "But Ah'll get it for you. Ah sure will."

"…Did she say you are a teacher?" Rizza asked, moving his unfinished dinner plate aside and filling their glasses.

"Yes," Tom replied, expecting the usual reaction.

But Victoria Audrey had returned. "Here you are!" she smiled. "Here's your pretty picture."

"Thank you," Tom nodded, his eyes going to a particular spot in the painted water. "Now, don't let me leave it again, Victoria Audrey. I wouldn't slight this lady's feelings for the world."

"And Ah wouldn't slight yours neither," she lingered. "…But Ah got a question Ah just busting to ask!"

"Then I think you should ask it," he faced her politely.

"Well, Ah ain't got much money, but if Ah pays what Ah could… do you think you could learn me to read?" And nervously folding her hands, she continued. "Ah free-black, Mister Scott, and free-blacks should get some learning. Ain't no school for us, but we could learn. …You done said you think so too."

Tom hated moments like this, when he was forced to admit he could thank Bob Trott for anything. But having been treated no better than a slave child himself—having walked in those same oppressed shoes—he was thankful his decision came easily. "I'd be happy to teach you, Victoria Audrey. Just give me a month or so to settle into my job and we can set up a schedule to suit both of us. All right?"

"Oh sir," she said gratefully. "Thank you so much! Ah'll be waiting to hear when you ready." And she left, dabbing a tear on the edge of her apron.

"*Signore*," Rizza lifted his glass. "*Cin-cin!* You are the—uh…other side of the coin, I think."

"How is that?" Tom smiled.

"Oh, day and night; good and evil; Thomas Scott and Sam Lucas; …and somewhere between, both his *figlia e amante*—uh, his daughter and mistress."

The smile was gone. "And what do you know of them?" Tom held the Italian's gaze.

"Enough to see you walk the thin wire," he replied. "*Per favore*, I tell you why Lucas is *arrabbiato*—angry. He says a dark-complexioned man, *straniero* to Savannah, is seen leaving his *amante* late in the night. He hears from her sons, they meet a man of this look and he talks alone to their *madre* in the *ristorante* last week. They say also, he is a teacher. Then he hears his daughter and such a man come to dinner here. He comes also, as you saw, but too late. Now, *Signore* Scott, you have just received Miss Lucas' painting. May I assume this is Sam's daughter, and you were with her, here, *stasera*—uh, this evening?"

"Yes, I was," Tom admitted, seeing no use in denial, but reason for a healthy swig from his glass.

"And you spoke with his *amante* last week?"

"Again, yes. But why would Lucas be angry with you for any of this?"

"Let us consider his evidence: Would you not say we are of *piu o meno*—uh, approximately the same *generale* description? And if seen in the night, would it not be hard to tell who is who? Also he knows, once I was *un professore a Roma*."

Tom nodded. "And you're also new to Savannah and happened to in here when he came looking tonight."

"*Si*. And I too, have been to the Seafest and often speak with *Signora* Morgan," Rizza paused to refill their drinks. "…But you do not deny involvement as I did to Sam."

"No, I'm the one he wants. And guilty of all he suspects. But, I'm sorry you were caught in the middle. …I'll make certain he learns you were unjustly accused," he added, wondering how.

"But no—no, no, *mio amico*!" laughed the Italian. "I have seen both these *belle donne* and had opportunity been mine, I would indeed be the man he seeks! So: as I said, considering both sides of this coin, I now choose *un amicizia* with you—uh, friendship. ...That is, if you could use another *amico*?"

"Sir, my name is Tom. And I heard Ransom O'Rourke and my good friend, Captain Herb, refer to you as Iano. Would you mind if we start from there? Because I think you should know details before involving yourself; and because I'd feel better calling you Iano, when asking your confidence about all of this."

"*Molto bene*, Tom," Rizza agreed. "As the *padre* in confession, my lips will be sealed."

Settling back in the chair, Tom began with Kathy's story, which so distressed the Italian that he rode the front edge of his seat by the time it was finished.

"*Madre di Dio*!" he declared. "This should not be. Lucas takes unfair advantage!"

"I agree. And I'm afraid our affair is what brought Kathy to this. Lucas may regularly cheat on his wife and lovers, but he seems to have a real problem with it happening to him."

"But she did come to you willingly? If so, he has no right to stand between you."

"Iano...I wish had an answer for Kathy. She is a beautiful, gentle woman with much to offer a man and truly deserves better from life."

"...But you do not love her."

"No and neither does she love me. I think I just came along at a point where she had to rebel against all that was being forced on her. But if Lucas can prove our affair, his treatment of her will grow even worse. As I told you, he holds her husband's debts over her head and can have home and children taken any time he wants."

"Could not her *debito* be paid? I would be happy to do this."

"As would I. But why should Lucas make a settlement when he has Kathy exactly where he wants her? Also, he would consider any offer of money as proof of an affair, and his reaction then, could be violent. He was close to that tonight, wouldn't you say?"

"*Si*—*si*, you are right," Rizza bridged his fingers in thought. "So, it becomes our job to deny this *bastardo* proof of an affair at all costs."

128

Tom lifted his glass. "I return your Salute, Iano. Any ideas on how to go about that?"

"*Sono Italiano, signore!* We invent *l'opera* because of our *passione* for drama," Iano laughed. "So: I think it best if we both remain suspect to Lucas. But, if this is to work, you should not *visitare* Kathy for a time. Do you see?"

"My interest is only that of a friend now," Tom assured him. "We each had reason for ending the affair."

"*Bene*, this too, is a point in our favor. Lucas can not discover what no longer happens. But *primo*, we must show our interest does not center on his *amante*. We must be seen often with other women, and he will begin to doubt his information."

"Even if the lady holding my interest is his daughter?"

"It is more than casual, this interest?"

"I'm afraid so," Tom confessed. "Much more."

Rizza nodded. "You do more than walk the thin wire. *Amico*, you cling by your *denti*—tooths...uh, teeth! Lucas would be much against this, no?"

"Probably, but I'm going to see her anyway."

"Now you speak with your heart, but not your head."

"Not entirely, Iano," Tom looked down at his painting again. "Lucas could yet cause Mandria's ruin as surely as he is causing Kathy's."

"His own daughter? —How could this be?"

"Because for the first time in her gently-reared life, she saw her father for the bastard he is and was bitterly disillusioned by it. What she planned in retaliation...well, I am not going to let it happen. Not to her."

"So, she comes to you with her *problemi*? You have gained her— uh, confidence?"

"I'm giving it one hell of a try," Tom nodded. "And I think I'm making progress with that beautiful, hard-headed, irresistible, green-eyed woman."

"This means much to you?" Iano smiled.

"Very much indeed," he met the Italian's gaze to stress that.

129

After a moment of thought, Iano nodded again and came forward to rest his elbows on the table. "Then, let us *cospirare* and devil takes Samuel Lucas. So: now our best attack is one of unity. Lucas seeks one man and we give him two—always two together: stopping often at the Seafest for *beve e mangiare*—uh, a meal. He will wonder why we are not fearful to be there and which of us he should watch closest. And, if Kathy shows no interest—which surely she will not—then as I said before, he will start to doubt his information. Perhaps it was a prowler seen in the night; perhaps your conversation was—as her sons had to report it—between parent and a teacher of her *bambini*. —*Si,* we can cause *il bastardo* great confusion with this boldness. Do you agree?"

"Only if he doesn't shoot us on sight," Tom chuckled.

"As I pointed out to Sam, at this very table, where would such a trail of blood end? He can not kill every dark-haired *straniero* in Savannah! No, he must be sure and we will hide the truth beneath his *naso*—nose. So: shall we go? We have our next *bevanda* at the Seafest and give the spies something to tell."

"Now?" Tom hesitated. "…Tonight?"

"*Adesso—si, adesso!* It is never too early or too late to champion a lady's cause," said Iano, leaving money on the table for their drinks and his forgotten supper. So with Mandria's painting under his arm, Tom followed him out, neither guessing how soon their plan would be drastically changed…

The late crowd at the Seafest milled noisily about the bar and restaurant rooms. Vying for the best chance of catching sight of Kathy, Tom and Iano took seats at the bar and ordered drinks. But she didn't seem to be there and it wasn't long before Iano voiced a sensation. "…Thomas, do you feel *il occhi*—uh, the eyes? Someone watches us."

"It's that party-of-eight by the stairway door," Tom directed attention to a mirrored wall behind the bar. "Some of those men were in here the day I spoke to Kathy and her sons. But Iano… there's something else. See how their table is blocking that door? I think they're guarding it."

Rizza studied the reflection for a moment and nodded. "They hear something too. Look how they lean to the door to listen. And laugh. ...I fear what happens here is not good for Kathy."

"And it's my damned fault!" Tom rose to his feet. "I'm going up the side way to check this out."

"*Fermi*!" warned the Italian. "Some of the jackals rise too. It won't help if they follow. *Rapidanente*, give me something from your *tasca* and sit down."

"From my what?" Tom asked in frustration.

"Pocket—your pocket. Then sit! *Adesso!*"

Tom did and the men sat too. "Iano, will you try?" he asked, really starting to worry. "If they follow, I'll ask you to—to bring that plate of cheese down the bar. If not, the stairway in on the right of the building."

"Si," Rizza nodded, but his luck was no better, and bringing the decoy plate, he returned to his seat as well.

"Iano, I know there are eight of them, but damn it, we have to do something!" Tom insisted. "There has to be a way to see if Kathy needs help."

And as if by providence, the way wandered in through the front door. "Thomas! Sebastian!" Mike clapped each on a shoulder and reached between to raid the cheese plate. "Well, move down, one of you and I'll buy us all a drink."

As one, Tom and Iano turned to face him and their grave expressions had Mike swallowing the cheese in a choking lump. "What the hell—"

"Shut up and listen!" Tom insisted. "Iano and I are under the watch of that group behind me, but we think Lucas has Kathy on the grill upstairs. How fast can you get up the side way for some eavesdropping?" And at that precise moment, a thud was heard from the ceiling.

"I'm gone," nodded the Captain.

"Well, be ready, Mike," Tom snagged his sleeve. "If they follow you too, we may have to take this whole damn place apart. You've evened the odds now, and I'm saying we can do it."

131

The Irishman backed away, with a proclamation. "I said I'd buy the next the round, damn it!" he declared loudly. "Order it up while I go pee. —Then hell, we might have to drink the bar dry!" And laughing jovially, he went out. Unfollowed.

The wait seemed endless, but in reality, Mike was gone only minutes. And though he approached with his usual swagger, Tom could see that he struggled with the pretense. "He's hitting her, Tom. Says he'll beat a confession from her," the Captain uttered, grasping Tom's glass and draining it. "Going to get worse too. If she doesn't talk, he's threatening to turn that whole pack of bastards on her at once—God damn his soul!" he swore, finishing Iano's drink too. "And look at them. Hell, they can't wait to be called up those stairs!"

"*Mio Dio!*" Rizza murmured. "What do we do?"

"A diversion," said Tom. "Think, Mike. You're good at this sort of thing."

That twinkle appeared in the Captain's eye as drew a cigar from his pocket. "A fire? In the outside kitchen, perhaps?"

"*Si!*" Iano agreed and reaching for a bar lamp, saw to it Mike's cigar was well lit. "Set the flame, *Capitano*, —then have my carriage wait around the corner. We'll meet you there with the lady."

Mike rose, wobbling dramatically. "Sorry, gentlemen," he expounded. "Can't hold down another damn drop!" And staggering away, he enhanced one of his finer performances with loud hacking coughs and gagging noises. But once outside, Captain Michael Leonard Herb rounded the building with a cockiness that promised sure trouble. Maybe six minutes later, he was climbing into Iano's fine carriage and ordering the driver around the corner. And there he sat, feet propped comfortably on the opposite seat, studying Mandria's painting, while puffing on the remains of his cigar and waiting for bedlam to begin.

It wasn't long in coming. The dry leaves Mike had heaped into the kindling box next to the back door of the kitchen, ignited instantly. The rosin soaked lighter wood followed quickly, and when the grease soaked walls exploded into flame, the hysterical cooks ran screaming into the restaurant. The sated diners and sotted bar-patrons, treating the whole thing as a lark, crowded into the yard and placed bets on how quickly the structure would burn. In panic, the closest neighbors, concerned the fire would spread, ran frantically to and from wells, splashing their own homes with untold buckets of water while yelling and pleading for any assistance. Dogs barked; babies cried; and soon a horde of curious passers-by were abandoning their buggies and wagons to join the crowd gathered in the back yard. Those unattended horses, frightened by the thickening scent of smoke, drug empty vehicles along the street and over near-by lawns and shrubs, which, in turn, brought these property owners into the throng, angrily seeking restitution from the careless horse owners. When the fire wagon finally arrived, it could get no closer than the street because of the heavy congestion, and on seeing that, Mike allowed a smile. A chuckle followed when he heard Sam Lucas bellow and roar from the back yard as well, because the Captain knew there was nothing the man and all his underlings put together, could do to restore the order needed to save the kitchen, and therefore the business.

Neither could Sam spare anyone during the disaster to watch Mike's co-harts, though Iano did keep a close eye on them while Tom went above-stairs for Kathy. Quickly rolling her unconscious body in a sheet, he lifted her to his shoulder like a carpet, and they exited the front door hardly noticed amid the hubbub. But still Iano watched to make certain no one followed or seemed unduly curious until Kathy was safely inside his carriage.

"That bastard!" Mike exclaimed when light fell across Kathy's blood-smeared features. "Look what he did! —Why don't we just beat the hell out of Lucas? He deserves a dose of his own God damned medicine!"

"Pace, Capitano—have peace," cautioned Iano. "It is best that you take her now, to a place of safety."

"Me?" he glanced at Tom, who stood staring at Kathy. "Aren't you coming too?"

"No, *mio amico*. Tom and I still have work to do. We throw Lucas off our trail, if we are seen here—by him—after Kathy is found missing."

"Well, there are plenty of places to hide aboard the Irish Mist," Mike suggested, realizing that Tom was still staring at Kathy's battered features and hadn't uttered the first word. "—What do you think?"

133

he placed a hand on his shoulder. And as Tom slowly looked Mike's way, the blue flint blaze in his eyes made the Captain very glad this man called him friend.

"Stop by her house and pick up her sons," Tom said then. "Sam Lucas will not use them to threaten her again."

"*Si*, Tom is right," Iano agreed. "Go, Michael. We must return to be seen." And when the carriage pulled away, but Tom hadn't moved from the spot where he stood, Iano looked at him and said, "…You are feeling *multo* anger. Are you not?"

"Yes, Iano. I am very angry."

"But not a *buffoon* as well. You would not do combat with Lucas now, and ruin Kathy's chance *di scapare*…uh, of escape."

After a moment, Tom expelled a long breath and turned to start back, the Italian at his side. "No, that wasn't the problem. It's…well, something similar happened to my mother and I guess I'll always be angry I was too young to stop it."

"We are all helpless to change the past," Iano nodded. "But we can help Kathy find *un meglio futuro*…uh, a better future. —That is, after we win time to plan it from Lucas. Come, we have our own *opera* to perform this evening."

"Let's do it then," Tom said. "Anyway, I'm long overdue seeing the bastard for myself." So, making their way to the back yard, through a crowd that hadn't thinned one whit, they found room on the rear stoop and stood enough above the others to be easily noticed. This also gave them an excellent view of the scene.

The firemen were doing their best, but from the heat and intensity of the flames, there was not going to be anything to salvage of the kitchen, which left them little to work on but containment. Of course, Sam Lucas was not accepting that, as evidenced by the harassment his men were doling out while following the firemen about the yard. Also to be heard, were shouts of encouragement from those who'd bet on an early time of total destruction, and hoots from those choosing later times. Bedlam, indeed…

"There is Sam Lucas," Iano pointed toward the front of the crowd.

But Tom didn't get the clear look he wanted, because he and Iano had been spotted too and the hirelings eagerly feeding this information to Lucas, closed ranks about him in a macabre sort of dance involving much head bobbing, finger pointing and the very worst job of pretending-not-to-stare, Tom had ever witnessed. Still, Lucas knew exactly where they were, though he didn't deem it necessary to look for himself. And that was a little eerie. But observing what he could, the only thing Tom could find that distinguished Sam Lucas from others, was the shoulder length mane of silver hair that Mike had spoken about. Especially here, where the glow from the fire shown through it, making his whole head appear to be in flames. Now, that was really eerie and Tom didn't wonder at the shiver wiggling up his spine.

"*Il divertimento commincia,*" Iano uttered. "—Uh, the fun begins." And both watched as one man broke from the pack around Lucas and went hurrying toward the side stairway. "Come, Thomas," Iano hopped to the ground, "it is almost time for *aria bella.*" Standing now in the path that same man would take on return, they waylaid him. "*Mi scusi!*" said the Italian, as Tom clothes-lined him from a dead run to a dead stop. "We do not wish to *disturbare il Signore en guesta sera difficile—*"

"Huh?" asked the man, in befuddlement.

"He said," Tom put it simply for the simpleton, "tell Mr. Lucas his friends over here are sorry for his loss. Can you remember that?"

The hireling looked at each of them, nodded once and ran on, anxious to report all of his important news.

"*Grazie,*" Iano chuckled. "It would seem between the tenor and the baritone, we are *finito qui'.* Let us go now. We have been seen, but detainment would not be desirable." So melting into the crowd again, they left...

"Damn!" was Mike's greeting from the upper deck of the Irish Mist as Tom and Iano started up the stairs. "What took you so long? Hell, I thought Lucas might be roasting you over a fire that I set!"

"And a grand one it was," Tom chuckled. "But only a temporary puff of smoke in the scheme of things. Where is Kathy?"

"Here in my cabin for now," he answered, still pacing in agitation. "Her maid is with her—I had to bring the damn maid too, Tom. She wouldn't stay behind!"

"*Ed i figli?*" asked Iano. "Uh, the sons?"

"Uncle Pat has them in the next cabin down. Those kids were really scared being pulled out of bed that way—and when they saw their mother… God, I'm still shaking!"

"*Poveri bambini,*" Iano sympathized. "Are they still so upset?"

"Oh-hell-yes! But at least they've stopped crying. Uncle Pat must be doing something right in there."

"I met the oldest ones," Tom moved away. "I'll speak with them, while you two see if Kathy is awake." And opening the door Mike had indicated, he saw Patrick Herb in a chair, with a pair of sleeping twins on his lap. On the edge of the bed, with Rob glued to his side, Jamie held another sleeping child.

"Come in, lad," Patrick said softly. "How goes it with Kathleen?"

"We'll speak with her in a moment," Tom replied, sitting next to Jamie and Rob. "Boys, you remember me, don't you? We met—"

"Who did that to my mother?" Jamie demanded, causing the little boy on his lap to stir and Rob to shrink further behind his shoulder.

Again, Tom was reminded of his own childhood anger. "Jamie," he said gently, "…the important thing is not letting it happen again. Don't you agree?"

"Well…yes sir," he answered and Rob nodded.

"All right then. I want you to know she is with friends here—and she's safe—so don't worry about that. As her oldest two sons," his eyes met and included young Rob, "I know she relies on you and she'd want you to help Captain Pat keep your brothers quiet and orderly. That's really important in assuring your mother's safety right now. Will you do it?"

"Yes sir," Jamie repeated and Rob's nod was repeated too.

"Thomas," Patrick said, "I've only ta ask, and there could be a squad of officers down here."

136

"And I'd like to see that," Tom confessed. "But wouldn't…our friend find it suspicious?"

"Did you not hear the news?" the family twinkle danced in Patrick's eyes. "A band of French thieves made a second attempt on me nephew's cargo. It is the duty of the force ta see it proper protected right ta the minute of departure Monday morning. Might not sound like much, but it will buy some thinking space, don't you know."

Tom smiled. "You've been doing more with your time than baby tending, haven't you?"

"And the wee lad on me right leg has done more than sleep. Would you mind then, slipping a few extra nappies beneath him?"

"Thanks, Captain Pat," Tom obliged, before turning to leave. "Your idea is probably the sanest one we've had all night." …*And damn, if that wasn't the truth,* he thought while heading to Mike's cabin. They had made many snap decisions over the past hours and were lucky any had worked—luckier yet, they were all still alive—and that evidently, God made allowances for well-meaning fools.

Mike and Iano stood at the foot of the bed, both wincing as the maid bathed a gash on Kathy's cheek. Her eyes were swollen nearly shut, her lower lip was split and dark bruises were already appearing nearly everywhere else. But she was conscious and stretched a hand toward Tom as he entered and the maid exited.

"My true friend," she said in a tearful voice. "You said you'd come."

Tom sat next to her, cradling her hand. "Kathy…do you plan to press charges against Sam Lucas?" He knew she wouldn't, but the question had to be asked so the decision would be her own.

"No, Tom. It would mean a public trial and I won't put my boys through the circus that would become."

"All right. But you are not going back to him. Next time, he could kill you. Where would your boys be then?"

"I know," she nodded as fresh tears slid past her lashes. "He could have tonight, but I still wasn't going to tell him your name."

"Kathy, don't—"

"I didn't admit to anything and still he kept hitting me and hitting me!"

"Stop! Stop dwelling on it," he brushed a hand over her hair. "…
The boys are here too. Did you know?"

"Yes, they told me," she tried to bring Mike and Iano into focus.
"How can I ever thank you—all of you?"

"By agreeing to our decisions," Tom answered. "We're going to
hide you out for a while. And the boys. Do you have objections to
that now?"

"Not anymore," she nodded, then caught her breath on a sob. "Did
you know I spent my wedding night in this room? I was so happy
then—so much in love."

"Treasure your memories, Kathy." Tom rose to stand with his
friends as the maid reentered the cabin with a fresh bowl of rinse water
and salves Mike had offered. "We'll see you have more time for it."
And as they turned to leave, he noted that neither of Kathy's other
two champions was doing a very good job of keeping the tear-sheen
from their eyes.

The wheelhouse door had hardly closed, when the Captain fairly
exploded. "Never—not ever—have I been so God damned fucking
mad! Did you see Kathy? —And the maid said her ribs are black and
fucking blue too! I'm telling you, Sam Lucas needs killing! That bastard!
—That God damn son of a whoring bitch needs killing!"

Rizza took the liberty of pouring them each a drink. "Michael,
your anger is wasted on him and does Kathy little good. Instead, let
us assist this unfortunate family. Place your energy there, as this is a
serious *responsabilita*, deserving of careful thought."

"Yeah, well…," Mike tried reining in his fury, but still gave the
door frame a good whack.

"I agree with you, Iano," Tom sank on a chair at Mike's table.
"But it will take time we don't have—unless we can buy some more
from the offer Captain Pat made. Mike, he suggested putting the Irish
Mist under police protection until Monday and even came up with a
damned believable excuse. What do you think? Would Lucas cross
through a police guard to come aboard?"

"Oh-hell-no—he wouldn't dare!" Mike grinned for the first time
in hours. "After what he did to Kathy, he can't afford trouble with the

police, because he doesn't know she won't be pressing charges. And, I'd feel a damned sight better having them here too. My crew would back me, but hell, they wouldn't stand a chance against Sam's boys. Yeah," he chuckled, "I'm liking Uncle Pat's idea a lot!"

"Well, we still have a part to play in keeping her safe," said Tom. "We need to be readily seen tomorrow—including you, Captain Herb. They know you were with us at the Seafest and Lucas wants some of you anyway."

"I wish he'd try for it!" Mike vowed. "I'm still in the mood to work on his God damned ass!"

"*Nulla*—Michael, do *nulla* against this man alone," Iano drained his glass and set it aside. "He and his men work as *iene*…uh, hyenas. They would rip you apart and fight for the pieces."

"Remember that, you hard-headed Irishman," added Tom. "I think we have Kathy's escape covered for now, but we need to insure our own safety too if we're to help her. And that means tomorrow, we go about our business as publicly and innocently as possible. They will be watching and we can't do anything to show we were involved with her disappearance."

"*Si,*" Iano said, heading for the door. "And as I have always *multo* fondness for *bambini*, I go introduce me to your *Zio* Patrick *e* stay while he gets *la polizia* into place."

"…Damn good man, that one," Mike said when Iano had gone. Then after giving a stretch to his tensed back muscles, he continued. "You know Tom, Uncle Pat also wanted Kathy to press charges. So I had to tell him all the things Sam holds over her and point out that even if he was convicted of battery, it wouldn't free her of debts owed by her husband. Hell, even from prison—and out of pure spite—he'd see her lose everything just for daring to go against him. And his conviction has a damned big 'if' behind it too. Sam has the money and has bought off juries before. Plus, there are those who'd say Kathy got what she deserved for sleeping with a married man. I think the only reason Uncle Pat agreed to go along with us now, is he's hoping for a resolution that keeps Lucas from ever touching her again—legally or physically."

"I'm hoping for that too," Tom looked from a window. "But Lucas will have his hounds on the street by dawn, so we'd best be moving her and the boys to a less travelled corridor don't you think?"

When this was accomplished and the Police guard in place, the three men lit cigars and climbed the bluff road, where they stood surveying the streets and bay area. It was nearing midnight and thankfully, all was found peacefully quiet.

"Well," Mike heaved a great sigh, "shall we call it a night?"

"A hell of a night, I'd say," Tom nodded.

"Si, and after well-earned sleep, we bring our thoughts together," added Iano. "So: where do we meet *domani*—uh, tomorrow?"

"Where else?" Mike offered lightly. "The center of Broughton Street, at damned high noon!"

"You jest, but that isn't a bad idea," said Tom. "If Lucas wants us followed, let's make it easy. Is there a tavern near the center of town, Mike?"

"Sure. The London Pub."

"*Molto bene*," Rizza signaled for his carriage. "The London Pub at *domani's* noon. —Tom, may I offer a ride home?"

"You're on my doorstep now," he nodded toward Harrison House. "And where are you staying, Iano, in case we need you?"

"I have a suite at the DeSoto, to which I now go," he boarded, remembering to return Tom's painting. "So: it is business as usual *domani*. We do not wish to upset Samuel Lucas, do we?"

Mike clenched the cigar in his teeth and grinned. "Oh-hell-yes!" he chuckled, which brought two really stern glances his way. "...Oh-hell-no?" he faked meekness.

"Oh-hell-no!" chimed Iano and Tom.

And so ended a very long day for them all...

# CHAPTER 12

Morning dawned to staggered rumbles of thunder as thick dark clouds gathered over the marsh and moved in to cloak Savannah in gloomy light. The city was in for a day-long deluge. For some, relief from the heat would be welcomed. For a few, the turbulence would but spawn greater storms...

Sam Lucas was livid; —had been for most of the night. His fury burned in red rimmed eyes, betraying a lack of sleep. It flared his nostrils, detailing the depth of unresolved frustration. Kathy had not been found. —Yet! When reported missing, he'd first sent a man to her home to see if, somehow, she had dragged herself over there. Sam was still in the yard, fuming over his loss of a profitable business, when the man returned saying he couldn't get anyone to answer the door. Cursing a blue streak, he sent the idiot back with instructions to break down the God damned door, and bring Kathy to him immediately! Sam was forced to leave the fire scene when he realized it would now be up to him to collect the night's receipts—the last bit of profit he'd take from these tills, God damn it—and that's when his man returned again, saying everyone living in Kathy's house was missing too. Then Sam knew. She had been abducted, just when he felt she was close to breaking; taken, while he stood less than 50 yards away, in front of a fire—that now smelled of arson—and at the cost of his God damned kitchen! He also knew the culprits—two by name, one by description—and though late in starting, he led the frigging search party himself. But at the DeSoto, the desk clerk, Rizza's driver and two bellhops vowed the Italian had "retired to his rooms alone—yes, sir, quite alone!" And not even offers of money changed their story one bit.

Then they went to the river. Sam preferred finding Kathy with Herb anyway. By God, he'd take her back and Herb's fucking life too! Yet, on reaching the docks, they were met by a swarm of uniformed officers and told in official terms, that the guard had been posted by the city because of a new rash of robbery attempts on the cargo stacks and that he and his party would be wise to seek another route to their destination.

Gritting his teeth until his jaw muscles ached, Sam was left with the task of locating the third and most mysterious of his antagonizers. His men agreed, this was the one who'd spoken "real secret-like" to Kathy in the Seafest bar; the "teacher" according to her sons. But when questioned, even under duress, Kathy had not—or hell, would not—give his name or residence. And neither, it seemed, could anyone else. All he could do then was assign tails for the two conspirators he knew and an extra to take up the trail of the third if and when the three met up again. Shortly thereafter, he'd have each of them tortured until one confessed Kathy's whereabouts—and should his men kill any or all of the bastards in the process, all the better!

So there was his situation after chasing uselessly about the city like a mad man. He had a God damned score to settle and no one with whom to settle it! No one, that is, but Mandria and by God, he meant to test her loyalty right now!

Startled from slumber by the crash of her door against the wall, Mandria was slow to realize it came from within the room and not from the echoing sky. Aware then, of heavy footsteps, she turned in the covers to focus on the man approaching her bed. "...Father?" she asked sleepily. "What is it? —What's wrong?"

"Nothing better be wrong, little miss!" he barked, barely keeping it civil. "Get out of that damned bed and come to my study. —Now! I have questions to ask of your behavior last night!" Then, with a turn on his heel and the flare of his cape, he stomped from the room as abruptly as he had come.

Mandria sought explanation and a robe in the same moment. ... *Someone must have seen us in the square*, she thought. *...They saw us when Tom—when I allowed his hands...* And unable to finish that even to herself, she hurried down the stairs, her heart keeping time with the thunder-beats. ...How would she ever explain what had happened? Tom had stopped it from going too far—not she. Tom had sent her home when she hadn't wanted to leave. And after wrestling with that truth for most of the night, she was no closer to understanding it. How then, could anyone else?

"Come in here and close the damned door!" Sam shot her an accusing glance. And because she seemed intimidated enough to obey without question, he decided to temper his tone; to play her for the information he sought. "...Here. Have some coffee and wake up. —Damn, but you look a fright, Mandy! You could have, at least, brushed your hair."

Confused by this, Mandria accepted the steaming cup, while glancing at the mantle clock. "Well, Father, it's not yet eight o'clock in the morning. I didn't rest well and you gave me no time for preening."

"You didn't rest well," he repeated, watching her cross to the windows. "I don't wonder at that after your little escapade."

Mandria gazed into the outside gloom as she sipped the rich black brew. The wind was rising, along with her culpable feelings—though she did manage to keep her voice steady. "What escapade?"

"Don't play innocent with me!" he slammed his hand on the desk, causing her to start. "You were seen with a man last night and I want his God damned name!"

Furthering her discomfort, a flash of lightening illuminated the area in the square where she and Tom had kissed and he'd... Her cup rattled its way back into the saucer. "Why?" she murmured, stalling the inevitable.

"Because I'm your father and I asked you, missy!" he explained the obvious. *...Why couldn't she just cooperate?* But, censoring his tone again, he said, "It's dark as hell in this room. Turn up the lamp, Mandy, and sit down here. You are going to tell your father all about this, I'll promise you that."

143

…*My father*, thought Mandria scanning her cowered reflection in the glass panes. …*My self-righteous, two-faced, lying, cheating father!* She began to straighten, as if just awakening fully. …What right did he have to make her feel guilty when his sin was worse? None—and damn if she'd let him do it! So, raising her chin, she adjusted the wick and sat before his desk. "Now then, Father," she said softly, "I came down stairs; I turned up your lamp: and I'll stay until I've finished this coffee—all as ordered. But I don't appreciate being spoken to as a child. I am of age. I can see any man I want—and as you should know by now, refuse to marry the ones you want—so, what is this all about?"

"Well now," Sam sneered. "I see your new friend has taught you disrespect—along with other scandalous behavior, I'm sure."

"And what about your own lack of respect?"

"Just what in the hell does that mean?" he said derisively, his eyes mirroring the fierceness of a lightening flash.

"It means, don't you trust me, Father? —As much as I've always trusted you…so…very…much?" She kept her tone sweet, but wondered how.

Lucas wearily rubbed his temples and sank back in his chair. "This is getting us nowhere. Neither of us could ever bully the other. We're too much alike, daughter."

"Know thy father, know thyself," she smiled slightly, before sipping her coffee. "And that doesn't say much for either of us, does it?"

"Enough of this—enough!" Sam cautioned. "I haven't the time or patience for deciphering your simpering moods. Now, as politely—and respectfully—as I can ask, would you kindly tell me who you dined with at City Market last night?"

Mandria hesitated. This wasn't about the incident in the square at all. She felt unbelievably relieved and anxious now, to defend her… her—Oh, she didn't know what to call Tom. A more-or-less friend, who'd touched her both emotionally and physically? Well, he had and her last words to him were that she wasn't sorry about it. She still wasn't. "Father, why you'd think I'm ashamed of this, I don't know," she leaned to place her cup on his desk. "I had dinner with Tom—Mister Thomas Scott—and then came home. Is that scandalous enough for you?"

144

After a pause, Mandria found unbearably long, Sam muttered, "Impossible." And ignoring her attempt at sarcasm, added, "And this…Scott is a teacher? —What was his name again—his full name?"

"I don't know Tom's full name, but yes, he is a teacher. —And you said you knew nothing about him."

"Maybe more than I'd care to," he paused thoughtfully again. "The point is, what do you know? —Where he lives, for instance? And he isn't from Savannah, so what do you know of his background?"

"Yes, I know where he lives and that he came here from Athens—"

"Georgia?" he injected.

"That's where the University is," she nodded. "…Why? Is there another Athens?"

"Several," he uttered, drumming his fingers, pensively.

"Oh?" she looked at him curiously, wondering what difference any of this made.

So was Sam, and he had to find out. "Mandy, you know that I traveled a great deal when you were small—now stop changing the damn subject! What else do you know about the man?"

"That I find him attractive. And honest. And very much a gentleman. That I am going to see him again—and that Uncle Ran approves of Tom, though you apparently don't."

"Ransom? —Ransom knows this—this teacher?"

"Yes. Uncle Ran helped him find a position and supper last night was Tom's way of saying thank you."

"Wait! Just a minute here: you're saying Ransom was with the two of you? It wasn't reported to me that way."

"Then ask the rest of our party," she shrugged. "Nico was there and so was Michael Herb."

"Herb!" he shot to his feet. "Ransom surely didn't allow it! —And how could you be seen in company with that riff-raff?"

Mandria blinked as much in surprise as from the lightening glow that bounced about the room. "…Now what could you possibly have against Mike?"

"He is a no-account, daughter! He comes from nothing and I assure you, he'll die with less!" he finished, tossing down a letter opener, he hadn't been aware of holding.

"Father…really," she chided.

"Well I don't like the bastard and never have!" Sam paced to the mantle and back. "And if Herb and Scott are that friendly, I'm thinking even less of your teacher and more of my own suspicions!"

"What suspicions?" she pressed him. "Tom is entirely reputable—and so is Mike, by the way. Mother liked both of them too."

"Oh? And where did your dear mother meet them?"

"At Tybee. They and Nico, spent a Saturday with us and—"

"God damn it, girl!" Sam bristled, wagging a finger in warning. "Too much is happening behind my back without this! I will not have Herb under any roof of mine—nor Scott! Do you understand me?"

"Father?" she said in amazement. "No, I don't understand! You're making Tom and Mike sound like criminals!"

"I think they are!" he retorted. "Someone set fire to the Seafest kitchen last night!"

Mandria could not help laughing. "And you think they did it?"

"I do and I have reason for making the connection, my wide-eyed girl. —Do you know a Sebastian Rizza?"

"No, but you are wrong about Tom. I've never met a kinder, more considerate man in my life."

"Well, I'll give the bastard credit for one thing," Sam flopped onto his desk chair in disgust. "He is damned good with women. Kathleen Morgan was even more adamant and protective than you are. —But then, they are more to each other than mere dinner companions."

The first huge drops of rain tapped at the windows like clucking tongues. "What?" Mandria tried not to ask. "…What are you saying?"

"Damn it, I'm telling you Scott and Kathy are involved—they're lovers!" Sam grew outraged about it all over again. "And that fire was a deliberate act to cover her escape!" he added more than he meant to reveal.

"Escape? —From what, Father? You're not making any sense!" Mandria hated the frantic edge on her voice; hated this whole conversation and the worsening storm that shut her in with the dizzying effect of lamp light on rain sheeted glass panes.

"Well hell," he backtracked, "you're aware Kathy owes me a great deal of money—and everyone knows I'm allowing her to work it off—but how am I to collect when she's gone off to be with Scott?"

Mandria nodded, still trying to digest these accusations. "You're saying she is living with him now; —right now?"

"Exactly! And I won't be cheated of my due—not for a tawdry affair; and not at the cost of valuable property. Now, God damn it, give me an address so I can stop them from leaving town together!"

"But what proof have you?" she heard her voice quiver—hating that too. "Why have you singled-out Tom for blame?"

Her persistence was really starting to wear on his temper, but he had no other choice but prying information from Mandria anyway he could. "For one thing, he fits the description I was given of the man Kathy has been sneaking in at all hours. And Scott was observed in deep, whispered conversation with her just a week ago. Plus, as I told you, he was at the Seafest when she disappeared."

"None of that proves an affair—"

"No?" he interrupted. "Then why did he go to the Seafest last night? If he dined with you, it certainly wasn't for the damned menu! No, by God, he and his friends went to collect their bitch—like a pack of dogs go after a bitch in heat! Everybody gets a turn at it!"

Mandria was starting to feel cold, as if the storm had dropped the temperature outside, and was slowly sucking the warmth from the inside walls too. "I don't believe you," she said snuggling deeper in her robe. "Uncle Ran wouldn't befriend such a man and—and Mama has always trusted his judgment about people."

Sam laughed, and it wasn't a pleasant or a pleased sound. "Your mother is about as naïve as they come—and what does Ransom know about life? He stays locked away, licking his wounds, half the time. It's made him susceptible to people of questionable worth."

"But Tom's worth isn't questionable," she defended in desperation. "His mother was well-educated in England. She came here, married and taught school in Tennessee. They moved to Athens when Tom was still a child, and she taught there too, until she died. That left Tom to raise his little brother alone—and still, he managed to finish the University. With all that on his plate…well, I just think you are accusing the wrong man!"

A violent roll of thunder shook the room with what seemed endless repetitions, while Mandria looked at her father, who looked back but was not seeing her at all. "Tom Scott…has a younger brother?" Sam said at last.

"Yes, and he's already sent for Allen. Tom wants to make a home in Savannah for him. Now does that sound like a man who'd stoop to the things you've described?"

"How old?" he ignored her question. "—And what did you call him? Adam?"

"No, it's Allen—Allen Scott—and he'll soon be 18. …But why do you ask?"

Sam only nodded in silence.

"…Father?" she tried anew.

"What—what do you want?" he said irritably.

"I asked what difference it made about Allen."

"None! —I'm certain of it. And yet…" his voice trailed away.

"And yet what?" she waited again. When he still didn't respond, she was forced to raise her voice. "Father! Please say something!"

Instead, Sam rose from the desk and went to pour himself a drink while she watched in puzzlement.

"Isn't it early in the day for that?" she asked and was ignored once more. Out of patience, she rose to her feet. "What is wrong with you?" she demanded. "You are behaving very strangely!"

Sam spared Mandria only a brief glance as he returned to his desk. "Listen…I've just thought of some things that need tending. Let's drop this for now, shall we?"

"We certainly will not! You've made damning accusations against Tom and I won't give up his friendship because of some idle bit of gossip—not when he has been such a gentleman!"

"Which shows your utter stupidity!" Sam lashed out. "It suited his purpose to act the gentleman because you were his God damned alibi for the evening—just part of the plan for spiriting away his mistress! And God knows what else he has in mind..."

"Do you think if you spew your filth enough times I'll believe you?" she fought back the tears welling inside. "Well, I will not!"

"Keep seeing Scott and you'll find out the hard way," he retorted. "After he has you stripped and bedded, he'll return to his sweet little Kathy—who is far better suited and trained to his tastes than you could ever be!"

"I won't listen to this!" Mandria started turning away. "I just won't!"

But Sam quickly reached over his desk and snared her wrist. "You will listen!" he threatened. "I won't allow you to sully the Lucas name!"

"The Lucas Name?" she spat. "And what have you done to sanctify the Lucas name? Less than nothing—nothing at all!"

"Explain yourself, Missy!" his grip tightened painfully. "I am your father and I'm trying to save you from disgracing yourself and your family!"

Mandria was too angry now for tears and though her wrist hurt terribly, she leaned closer, meeting him eye to eye. "All right, Father," she hissed in defiance. "Let's say you were successful. Let's say I'm so grateful for being *saved* that from here on, I will live by your standards. You said we're alike. I'll show you how much—in every bed, with every bastard, in Savannah!"

Sam slapped her. Hard. Then he watched in furious silence as she slowly straightened her posture and started for the door. "And just when may I expect your apology?" he demanded tersely.

Pausing in the opened portal, Mandria looked back. "Never," she said softly. "But I do want to thank you. At least there is truth between us now. What more could a daughter ask?" And she left, quietly closing the door.

"Hard headed chit!" Sam muttered. But that was the last thought he gave to their confrontation as he sank on his desk chair and into his rioting thoughts. ...*So the whimpering bastard grew up after all—and became a teacher, like his damned straight-laced mother. That figures; it just bloody well figures he'd choose the least masculine way to go. And God only knows why, but that gentle, polite type does attract many women—like*

*Kathy and my daughter too, God damn his soul! Should have made sure he drowned in that river when I had the fucking chance! Guess I'll just shoot him now—and preferably, sometime today.*

*…But the boy—the brother?* Now that he could take the time, he tore back through the years and then, as he hadn't for quite a while, forward for those requisite nine months. *…So if his birthday is in September, then…*

Sam stood, none too steadily, and returned to the whiskey tray for a refill. He could not jump to any conclusions here. It was too important. *…But why else would Margaret have moved and called the boy 'Scott' instead of 'Trott', if not to hide him from his real father? …Could his son—his own flesh and blood son—be on the way to Savannah even now?* "Oh, damn!" he halted abruptly, as a second thought occurred. *…Can't afford to touch Tom until after Allen arrives. If he's dead, it would leave Allen no reason to stay on here.*

Yet, he was at once beset with more worries. *…Would Tom recognize him as Bob Trott? —Or did he know already?* Sam's eyes narrowed menacingly. *…Kathy, the alliance with Herb, the fire, —even Mandy? Had the spineless bastard planned all this from the start?* But his caroming thoughts were now tripping over one another. *…No, after keeping the boy hidden—even naming him Scott—Tom wouldn't knowingly bring my son right to me.* "My son," he said aloud. *How long he'd yearned to say those God damned words!*

Sinking in the desk chair again, he sat rolling his glass between his hands while considering options. *…Tom was a mere child when I left, so maybe he wouldn't know me looking as I do now. If not, then until I've won favor with Allen, Tom continues to live. And should he know me, by chance, there has to be something he wants enough to bargain for—like Kathy, perhaps? But all depends on what he has in mind and the sooner I know, the sooner I can plan the rest.* "So…the first order of business is to locate him and find out," he uttered, while sliding open a desk drawer. "And just in case…" he removed a small revolver, checked the load, and slipped it into his cape pocket. Then fastening it about his shoulders again, he went out to the stairway.

"Mandria!" he called in his most authoritative tone. He'd neglected to get Tom Scott's address—and was it any wonder with what he'd just learned? "Come down here for a moment!" he added, trying to devise a quick way of getting it from his stubborn daughter.

"She…she's gone, sir," said a servant from the dining room. "Didn't eat nothing either. Just dress and went right out in that rain."

"What?" Sam went to glare at the woman over the table. "God damn it—where did she go?"

"Ah don't know!" was the frightened reply. "Miss Evelyn on the way down for breakfast. You going to eat too, sir?"

"Damn!" Lucas spun and raced for the carriage house. He knew where Mandria was headed and his confrontation with Scott had to happen before hers. "Damn!" he repeated as the rain beat down upon him. "God damn it!" he raged at the gloomy sky, for still he was without a destination…

The morning had been less hectic for Tom. Awakened by the grumbling thunder, he dressed early and went out to greet his favorite kind of day. At 9 o'clock, he was scheduled for an appointment with the Headmaster and later was to meet Mike and Iano, but for now, time was his and he chose to share it with a blustering breeze that smelled of rain and heralded the approaching storm. Yet, in the midst of his pleasant stroll, arose a nagging worry. He was alone when he'd expected one of Sam's minions trailing behind. During his stay at the Academy, it was the same. He glanced from a window several times, but the quiet before the storm revealed no one lurking about the grounds. And though early, as he made his way to the London Pub through the first swollen droplets of rain, still he went alone. On arrival, however, he found Rizza with the problem in reverse. Two of Sam's men sat at the far end of the bar and with Tom's entry, they began to mumble between themselves.

"*Come stai, mio amico?*" Iano lapsed into his native tongue, his eyes remaining watchful of the men. "*Che ora fa? Il mio orologio non funziona bene.*"

"I am your friend," Tom smiled, taking a stool beside him. "I caught that much, Iano."

"...*Scusi?*" Rizza turned to face him.

"I said your Italian is excellent this morning," Tom chuckled, signaling the barkeep for the same kind of ale Iano was having.

"*Perdona mi*, I forget when I feel unease," he looked at the men again. "Michael is late, is he not?"

"Not yet. I noticed the Police are still in place on the docks. Likely, he just ducked out of the rain somewhere. It's really starting down now."

"*Si*," Rizza tried concealing his thoughts behind a smile. But when a violent thunder clap rattled the windows, it also loosened his tongue. "One of us has *un problema*, Thomas. Were you not followed here?"

"No," he nodded.

"But this makes no sense!" said Iano. "What could it mean?"

"Damn if I know," he pointed to the entry. "But here comes the Irishman. Let's see how many he has wagging-their-tails-behind-them." So both watched as a somewhat befuddled man entered a few steps after the Captain and with the subtlety of a nail drawn to a magnet, joined his comrades down the bar.

"Sorry I'm late," Mike grinned, hanging his dripping slicker over a bar stool. "Just couldn't resist playing with the bastard a little. Had to double back and find him a couple of times, but I think I finally got the stupid jackass soaked to the skin. You know, every man should one—"

"*E quello il problema*," Rizza injected. "You have *uno*; I *due;* and Tom *zero*! It must mean they could not find him in the night—could not check the company he keeps. ...Lucas can not be happy with this."

"Damn," Mike turned to Tom. "That puts you at the top of his gift list, doesn't it?"

"It's where I belong," he shrugged. "But there are three of us and three of them here now, so I don't see that it matters much about last night."

"Your nobility is damned sickening, you know that? —And suicidal." Mike looked to Iano now. "So what do we do about this?"

"Perhaps accompany Tom to his home? Should Sam attempt to force his way in—"

"He won't," Tom countered. "It's like the shell and pea game, Iano. Lucas knows we're hiding Kathy or we wouldn't have our new friends over there. But if he openly accuses one of us and guesses wrong, it would serve to warn the other two and Kathy's location could be changed. He doesn't want to play Hide-and-Seek; he wants Kathy. So he'll just move more cautiously."

"…You're saying, now that he's found you too, he'll check your place for her on the sly—and Iano's as well?" Mike asked.

"Yes, Captain, if he hasn't already been in Iano's quarters this morning. But the process of elimination will lead him right to the Irish Mist. So, considering that and all else, we come to the purpose of this meeting, don't we?"

And as the rains poured down in earnest, they discussed the pros and cons of several solutions, deciding finally, that Iano's was best. He said he was expecting a great procession of materials and equipment to arrive at his up-river estate; that the storage sheds were built and a team of security guards already in place, but that someone responsible was needed to receive the goods, see them correctly logged, stored and dispensed without waste. He added that if Kathy wanted the position, he'd allow her the use of the main farm cottage and pay her a fair salary. "Kathy *i bambini* would have much *pace e sallievo*—uh, peace and comfort, and will also be guarded well by my people," Rizza finished

"Yeah, and I pass Iano's landing going and coming every week, so Kathy could signal me if she needs anything," added Mike. "I'll drop them off there on Monday too—and just to be safe, I won't accept more passengers than I've already booked. That way, Lucas can't put anyone on board at the last minute."

"*Si,* and I will also go, to see them safely settled," Iano nodded. "Sam can find nothing unusual in this—you, *Capitano*, on your river run; and I, on a weekly tour of my property."

"So, why am I being omitted from this?" Tom asked, realizing he had been.

"Hell, Tom," Mike grinned. "Don't you listen when you talk? You just told us how to pull this off. It's because Sam couldn't find you last night, that today you get to play lure for his hunting party."

"Si, you detain his process of elimination," added Iano. "You lead him to your *porta* and keep him waiting for a chance to check your rooms. When you do not go out, he will be very sure he knows why: the lovely Mrs. Morgan."

"And by not leaving your place for a full day, you'll have bought Kathy's way safely out of Savannah," Mike concluded.

Tom looked from one of them to the other and laughed. "You know, sometimes my cleverness is astounding, isn't it?"

At the far end of the bar, Sam's men strained ears that could hear nothing over the dark angry torrents of rain outside; and eyes which saw nothing inside but three friends enjoying each other's company over drinks. Such a report would not be well received by their boss. Still, they had located the teacher and could hope to gain favor for that…

# CHAPTER 13

When Tom left the Pub—and this time with one of Sam's hirelings in tow—he took advantage of a lull in the storm and went by City Market. If he had to remain inside his rooms until Monday, he would need food staples. In truth, he was also looking forward to a good long nap, because other than the time spent with Mandria, Friday had been one crisis right after the next. As a result, throughout the night, his logical mind kept waking him to point out the illogical risks they had taken. So, yes, he was tired and could use some sleep.

But his shopping done, the most pressing problem now, was going to be getting everything home in the middle of a new downpour. With the packages wrapped in his suit coat, he went dashing around corners and beneath every available awning in a rain so dense, he couldn't tell if he was still being followed. If not, there wasn't much he could do until the storm subsided. Then, as Mike had, he might have to go find the man and lead him back to Harrison House in keeping with their plan. For the present, however, he was getting thoroughly drenched, and as he next expected an ark to come floating down the street, he was making every effort to reach home ahead of the flood crest.

Mrs. Harrison handed him a towel as he entered her front hall and after a few pleasantries, she bustled off toward the back of the house as Tom went up the stairway.

But on reaching the second floor, the smile he'd shared with the landlady instantly vanished. His door was standing ajar. Quietly approaching it, he scanned what he could of his quarters through the narrow opening, but saw nothing more ominous than the eerie glow of storm light. …Perhaps Lucas had already been here, and finding nothing, was gathering in force on Mike or Iano. But even as the notion raised the hair on the nape of his neck, reason smoothed it down. Iano had no more to show than he did, and Mike was certainly safe, thanks to Captain Pat. …Or maybe, as Iano had warned, that pack of hyenas waited inside to pick his bones just for the hell of it. Cautiously, then, he swung the door open and keeping his back against the frame, slid around it into the room. Honing his senses, he checked every corner, but all seemed in order. There was no muffled breathing or movement other than his own. Still, after locking the door securely, he lit every lamp there and welcomed the shadow-banishing light.

Much relieved, he pulled the window drapes and speculated while stripping off his wet clothing, that the cleaning woman simply forgot to shut his door. Going to the bedroom in search of dry things and another towel, he noted while returning to the coziness of lamplight, that his bed was unmade. …*Damn, but the woman was in a hurry*! he thought, ruffling his hair dry with the towel. At the table, he spared a fond glance at Mandria's painting, while removing the market purchases from his rumpled jacket. Then he shook it out and hung it on the back of a chair with his other wet clothes. Removing the dampened wrappings from his bundles, he cut a wedge of cheese, poured a glass of wine, and cheated on supper as he dressed. The air-cooling deluge outside continued, making dry trousers feel good on his legs. But the food tasted better, so abandoning his shirt, he sat down for more, wondering idly, what a meal at three in the afternoon might be called. Brunch was between breakfast and lunch, so what came between then and supper? "I am tired," he muttered. "My mind has been reduced to drivel."

That was quickly remedied. As he started to break open a crusty loaf of bread, a noise jolted him back to alertness. Turning in the chair, he looked over the room another time. —There: he heard it again! … And it came from the bedroom. *Fool*! he admonished himself. Why hadn't he thought to check that room too? …But he'd just come from the dimness in there, so why hadn't advantage been taken of his naked vulnerability? This was a puzzle in need of an immediate solution.

So taking a lamp, and armed with the bread loaf he wasn't conscious of carrying, he returned to the bedroom door. A breeze fluttered the drapes, but checking the window, he found it opened no further than he'd left it that morning. The drawers and wardrobe door stood open too, as he'd left them only minutes ago. And kneeling beside the bed, he found nothing ready to rush at him from beneath it. But there was the sound again—and it came from atop the bed!

Rising quickly, he reached for the tumbled covers, only to discover the bread loaf clenched in his hand. —*Hell of a weapon*! he thought, tossing it aside in exasperation.

Holding the lamp in striking position, with one swift motion, he flung the covers to the foot of the bed. And now, surprise kept him frozen in place, the lamp still poised for attack. "Mandria?" he finally managed that single word. He felt incapable of more—certain she'd vanish if he breathed or blinked or spoke again. Then, he mutely watched as she rolled from her stomach to her back, inadvertently hiking her chemise high along her right thigh, while the thin, twisted garment tried, but didn't quite contain, nor conceal, the fullness of her breasts. And her gloriously mussed hair, tumbled about her shoulders as she sat up and began tugging her way toward modesty. But she had not looked at him once and did all else amid a constant stream of tears, punctuated with muted little sobs. This was the sound he'd heard, and it was finally dawning on him that she was deeply distressed.

Placing the lamp on a side table, he sat on the edge of the bed, wanting to comfort her, but not sure she wanted him to. "…Mandria," he began again, "what is it? What do you want here?" And when she turned her face further away, still crying, he nodded at his hopeless stupidity. "Hell, that's not what I wanted to say. I'm just surprised—and delighted…to find you here—in my bed…of all places in this world…" He was babbling, he knew it, and couldn't seem to stop—until Mandria suddenly came forward and closed her arms about his neck.

"Hold me," she sobbed. "Please…hold me?"

157

Tom put his arms around her in a state of numbness. But that lasted about a second, because there wasn't much separating his bare chest from her thinly covered breasts. And making matters worse, her crying caused them to heave against him. ...Or was that making it better?

"We're alone here, aren't we?" she wept, drawing herself even closer. And Tom thought, ...*No; no, this is definitely better.* "You weren't using me," she went on. "We're alone and you weren't using me!"

How he was supposed to make sense of that with her nuzzled up to his body, Tom didn't know. Yet her tone said this was important, so forcing himself back, just far enough to meet her eyes, he asked, "Using you how?"

But instead of answering, she cupped his face in her hands and spoke around and between gently repeated kisses. "I saw you, Tom... naked and so beautiful! ...I woke up...and saw you come in here. ...I wanted you. ...In spite of Father; ...all he said; —Oh, and I still want you!" And now, without tears, her kiss lingered warm and hungry on his mouth.

Tom decided then and there, he must be dreaming, until he opened his eyes and saw that she was expecting him to say something. He was determined there would not be a repeat of babbling and settled, somehow, on mild inanity. "If that's the case, I'd be happy to strip off again," he grinned.

She didn't. Instead, she eased back into the pillows and said, "Then do it."

Not since his teens had Tom felt awkward about disrobing before a woman. Now he did, and was quite unsettled about it. Why couldn't he simply comply with her request; share her very exciting mood? There was nothing he wanted to do more; nothing was keeping him from it; ...except himself. Heaving a ragged sigh, he leaned into the other pillow propping his weight on an elbow. "Lady," he began, "do you know what the hell you're doing? Damn it, you need to be sure of that; —sure you know your feelings now, better than you did last night."

"I know a lot I didn't know then," she watched her fingers move across the width of his shoulder. "Father said I was your alibi to cover an affair with Kathleen Morgan; that you took her from the Seafest last night; and that, by today, she'd be living here with you. He said you only wanted to bed me and then you'd go back to her because she is more appealing to you. ...So, I'm here to find out which of you is the liar. It's really as simple as that."

"Simple?" Tom collapsed beside her. "Lady, I've never heard anything less simple in my entire life!"

"It can be," she turned to face him. "Let me ask the same question you did: ...Tom, do you mind that I came? Do you want me to be here?"

"More than anything! But Mandria, you've been told some outright lies, some half-truths—and you're drowning in them. I don't want to mislead you. Maybe if I explained—"

"No!" she objected, putting fingers over his mouth. "Don't you see? I've heard all I can stand! Kathy isn't here, so maybe I was meant to be. I have to belong somewhere; to something; or... someone," she said, fitting herself along his side. "Tom, please," she whispered now. "Just make love to me?"

She was trembling and close...so damned close! "Lady, you aren't playing fair," he told her. "I haven't much resistance where you're concerned anyway, and you're making mush of my arguments with a request like that. I just can't fight you this way."

"Then don't," she offered her mouth. "Oh, please don't?"

Tom knew his noble efforts were beaten. He was too tired for logic; too hungry for her to question it further. And as he accepted the warmth of her kiss, he also accepted a truth: never had he wanted a woman more. With all her problems; in spite of the lies and deceptions yet to be sorted out, still he wanted her. He even admitted their relationship stood little chance if things weren't resolved to her satisfaction. But that would have to wait. Now, he was going to have her...

The rain seemed to intensify, to fill the room with its pulse beat, as Tom laid his palm on Mandria's cheek. "Lady, I have dreamed of this since the first time I saw you," he told her.

"Have you?" she smiled too easily; too brightly.

And as he knew they would, her eyes revealed multi-faceted emotions: she was hesitant and expectant; confused and determined; afraid of what he would do and yet, he was what she wanted. Surely, whether she realized it or not, she needed to know his feelings too. "Last night, we said that we each had thinking to do," he nuzzled his way down the slender curve of her throat. "I did mine, Miss Lucas," he continued across her shoulder. "And I've decided I might as well fall in love with you," he started back toward her other shoulder. "May I ask what you decided?"

"Tom…" she began. "Tom, I—" and she stopped again.

"You what?" he urged, savoring each staccato kiss he was placing at the neckline of her shift.

"Don't talk," she shuddered lightly. "Don't stop, but don't talk now."

"Oh, we will talk, pretty lady," he drew down her shoulder straps, exposing the swell of her breasts where the skin was pale and untouched by the sun's golden rays. And watching her the whole time, he enjoyed a smile when color rose in her cheeks and she closed her eyes, rather than witness her own disrobement. "Who is it you're hiding from in there?" he gently kissed each of her eye lids. "It's a lot more fun out here, anytime you want to join me." Gentle too, were the hands which caressed her nearly nude breasts; the cheek he laid upon them; the lips trailing a wandering path from tan skin to pale.

Mandria did open her eyes then, amazed that the shame she'd dreaded had not materialized; that she was, in fact, watching what he did and liking it. Now, she couldn't see enough; feel enough. …*Does he know my nipples truly ache for his touch?* she wondered. … *Would it be all right to tell him?*

Tom's efforts had been studied and deliberately paced, as hard as it was to keep them so. Her skin was sweet with the fragrance of wild honeysuckle and he, nearly wild for the sweetness that was her. But he'd seen Mandria open her eyes; sensed her curiosity; her pleasure— and her impatience. It had been worth every second getting her to this point. And now, it was time for more. Peeling the material away, his appreciative gaze lingered on the pert and alert nipples that stood sharply defined to greet him. "You are just so damned beautiful," he murmured. And lowering his mouth to them, his teasing was both tender and undisciplined at once.

Inhaling deeply—unevenly—Mandria closed her arms about Tom's head and he was happily smothered in her. She offered no resistance as he deftly worked her breasts, but neither was she passive. Relishing each new sensation, she encouraged more, arching herself to allow him fuller play. And play he did, until even the restriction of her gauzy chemise between them became unbearable for him.

Taking them both upward and to their knees, he began loosening the garment, while plying her mouth with kisses; moving it to her waist; anticipating and then feeling her breasts joggling freely against him; sliding chemise and all else he found, over her hips; past her knees; and finally—finally—flinging everything away...

And he never guessed that right along with her pretty, thin garment, went a lot of Mandria's bravado. This was real. She was naked; being snuggly held against the most handsome, half naked man she'd ever seen; and she wanted to be here. But...

"I said you were made for me," Tom said against her hair. "See how well you fit all the nooks and crannies?"

"I do seem to," she nodded, and at feeling his manhood stir against her, she leaned her forehead on his chest, hoping to conceal a flush of excitement.

"No lady," he lifted her chin. "Please don't hide. I want to see what you think of this." And, she managed to keep her face lifted to his, though her eyes refused to stay open. As his hands moved from her shoulders, down her ribcage, and over her hips, Tom couldn't have been more pleased with her shapeliness; the silky texture of her skin or her expression of wonder, even with her eyes closed. "I do believe you could learn to like being stroked," he chuckled.

"Yes," she uttered. "I think so too."

"And this?" he molded his hands to her buttocks.

"Y—yes," she nodded, eyes still closed.

"And especially this," he brought her against the proof of his swelling desire for her.

Then her eyes opened. "Oh," she made his favorite sound, and immediately burrowed her face in his chest again.

"Oh-hell-yes!" he said next to her ear, then toppling backwards onto the bed, he landed with her length stretched down his body. There he kissed her repeatedly, his hands roving freely from bosom, to back, to buttocks, and Mandria readily accepted his familiarizing touches. …Until he rolled her to the bed and began a leisurely exploration of her lower abdomen.

She tensed, clasping that hand in hers. "Tom," she uttered, studying the size and shape of his fingers, "…please wait."

"I'm in no hurry," he kissed her cheeks, her nose and her mouth, wishing again she'd meet his eyes. But she didn't, so he waited for her to speak. When she didn't do that either, he resorted to teasing. "What is it, lady?" he asked. "Ready to quit so soon?"

"No," she squeezed his hand tighter. "It's not that at all. I just—I want to say something…" Yet she didn't.

"And?" he encouraged—and felt encouraged when her eyes made an upward move.

But instead of stopping when they reached his, they now rested, along with her hand, on his hair.

"And," she watched as she smoothed his tousled curls, "Tom, I haven't—that is, you're the first. …I thought you should know."

"I do know," he brought that hand to his lips, hoping to catch her eyes should they follow.

Maddeningly, Mandria's gaze went to his mouth, where she traced her fingers over the shape of it. "But today—now," she continued awkwardly. "Please don't expect too much. It…it might take time for me to do this well."

"Oh no, it won't!" he laughed incredulously. And deciding to put an end to her elusiveness, he placed both of her hands over his eyes, and held them there.

"…Tom?" she puzzled. "What are you doing?"

"Trying to get you to look at me, damn it!" he grinned. And splaying her fingers, he peered between them. "There now: what were you saying?"

"Oh for heaven's sake!" she giggled at the ridiculous picture he made. "I'm sorry to seem so nervous," she propped on his chest. "Maybe that's why I couldn't look at you."

"It is, but everyone has nervous habits. Iano forgets English; Mike curses," he shrugged. "You look away."

"What do you do?" she questioned.

"I don't know," he ran a thumb across her lower lip.

"Then I'll watch you and find out," her eyes widened attractively.

"That, pretty lady, is only the second-best offer I've had today," he said around a great, dramatic sigh.

"And the first-best offer?" she said with her lips against his.

"Half price on a loaf of day-old bread at City Market," he pecked her mouth with kisses. "Now, can we please get back to the business of making love?"

Mandria held his face in her hands, and this time her gaze didn't waver. "Only if you understand. Tom, it's important that I please you—important to me. ...So, how will I know if I did?"

"Your novels didn't tell you?" he chuckled.

"No, but I know you could," she said earnestly. "So far, am I doing my part right? Is there something I should—or shouldn't—be doing more?"

"Lady," he rested his forehead on hers, "you are exactly as I hoped you'd be—a bit talkative at the moment—but I couldn't be more pleased. Truly, you've nothing to worry about."

"It's just that I couldn't bear disappointing you—not along with everything else. I don't want this to go wrong too. It just can't go wrong! ...And I think maybe I talk when I'm nervous too."

Tom rolled to the edge of the bed with a grin and stood up. "Then if I'm ever to shut you up, I'll have to provide a distraction." And removing his trousers, he straightened to face her. "Will this do?"

It would, indeed, do. Now, Mandria sat absolutely still and stared at him in total silence.

"One other thing," he added, coming closer. "Lady, making love—being in love—is a giving experience. And as all your concerns were about pleasing me, there's no room here for disappointment. But..."

he held his hands out to her, "the giving should be mutual. Now come here and let me show you that it is."

Mandria rose to her knees, put her hands in his and blinked at the close-up size of his naked body. "Will I be able to…" her eyes dipped downward, "to…hold that?" And she did not even attempt to hide this blush.

"Down to the hilt," he answered, gathering her against him with an accompanying chuckle.

But now she was pushing away to look between them again. And this time, she made a whispered request. "May I touch you?"

"Please—please do!" Tom gave his greatest approval. "You should know my body as well as I intend to know yours."

Sitting back on her heels, Mandria stared at what stood proudly before her. But only once did she try to reach out her hand. Then she threw herself back into his arms and holding on tightly she said, "I can't! I want to, but I can't because I heard… I mean, it's said—Oh, Tom, will it hurt terribly?"

"Lady, trust me," he cupped her face. "I'll show a world of patience. If you can trust me to do that, it will be minimal. And when the time comes, you may even welcome it."

Mandria gazed into Tom's eyes, touched by the caring words. Then he was kissing her so soundly, she couldn't remember what had frightened her. She couldn't even remember the question she'd asked, or how they'd gotten back down on the bed where, still kissing her, he played with the tips of her nipples; ran an open hand down the flat plane of her belly; over the crown of tan hair below; and on to sample the warmth of her inner thighs.

Tom thought he'd never tasted anything better than the breathless sigh she shared with his mouth just then. And searching for the patience he'd promised, he laid his face on her breasts, and concentrated on keeping his touch light and teasing as he dabbled with the folds and lips of her vagina…and especially with the sensitive little nub that would so activate pleasurable feelings for her. "You have a damn fine body," he murmured around the nipple he was tonguing.

"You have a damn fine touch," she pressed her cheek against his dark hair. And as his leisurely exploration continued, the more inquisitive Mandria became about his body too. Where Tom seemed to relish manipulating her softest, most hidden areas, she liked—indeed, clung to the feel of his taut, muscular frame. He was something solid; something with the strength to shield her from things that hurt. ... And finding her hand at the pit of his stomach, she also found herself possessed by a rush of boldness. "Tom, I have to touch you now," she announced. "—I really must!"

Going to his back, Tom bit down on laughter, pulled her close, and teased at her ear. "Lady, you don't need to give notice or ask permission. Please, touch me anywhere, anytime you want to." And borrowing a line from Mike, he added, "In the middle of Broughton Street at high noon, if you'd like. I'd love it!"

Mandria smiled at the picture that conjured up, but titillation soon replaced amusement. He was doing wicked things to her ear, and it was driving her nearly mad with shivery, spiraling currents of pleasure. She could even feel it throb in her nipples, and now in a new place he'd been touching between her thighs.

"Well?" he urged, guiding her hand down his body. "Go ahead. Play the brazen vixen for me." At first, she left her hand exactly where he'd placed it and Tom smiled at that. He was learning to gauge her reactions well: hesitance first; a moment of decision; and soon to follow sweet, sweet acceptance. A touch of his thumb to her rapid-fire pulse, proved her interest. But this time, he intended to satisfy more than curiosity. This time, he would bring her sensual nature to the surface and see that she acknowledged not only its worthy existence, but his ability to deal with it. So, he set about plundering her ears, her mouth, both breasts, and back to each, again and again; testing, tempting, waiting...until slowly, her fingers spread and closed around him.

Both of them felt that jolting first bloom of passion. He, because she sought the texture, content and purpose of his manhood as he knew she would do it: delicately, with wonderful ever curious, ever caressing fingertips. She, because he seemed to be everywhere at once—no longer gentle, but moving gloriously over her flesh with the hands of a sculptor and the mouth of a satyr; molding her into a desired and desiring woman.

"I'm not afraid," she whispered into his mouth. "Tom, I want you—and I'm not afraid anymore!" And prompted by ancient instinct, she was trying to work her way beneath him.

"Almost, lady," he murmured, silencing her with a deep, probing kiss. "You're almost there." And holding her fast to his experience, he continued the exquisite coaxing of her being and senses until she was fairly writhing; until her response became aggressive; her body moist and open to his aggression.

Now, she could accept him easily, as he'd promised. And yet, as he turned himself in position, he waited there between her thighs, not only to appreciate the searing ash-green of her expectant, impassioned eyes, but to steel his waning patience for a final test: for Mandria Lucas, daughter of the sea, the green eyed, tan haired beauty, whose skin smelled of honeysuckle—and all else that she was, had to enjoy the feel of him; to encourage his approach to that fragile wall within her and welcome him into the depths beyond. So, proceeding by mere degrees, forcing nothing, he slowly entered her threshold and was pleased to find it honeyed. Demanding nothing, he allowed her body to direct him, moving forward only as she made room for him to do it. And soon, his objective was reached. Again he waited, muscles a-coil, his kiss clearly relating the struggle he endured for her sake...

Mandria knew, then, what she had to do. With one small, hardly audible cry, she raised her own hips, pushed hard against him and took the man she wanted deep within. To the hilt. And so it began: the slow, calculated thrusts of experienced flesh, curbing violation of the new; the subtle pauses and varied position shifts, that led her ever closer to the crest. Oh, how she wanted this and her body was saying so in everyway it could...

Tom had never experienced such an overpowering, absolute sense of oneness. It surged between them like a living thing! Nor had he been made more acutely aware of a woman stressing her wish to join with a man; of fevered hands pressing into his spine and buttocks; the silken flesh of thighs and arms binding him to her; of cushioning breasts; of ravishing kisses and a tongue which encouraged—indeed, pointedly simulated—the total mating of cock and cunt; of body and spirit; of matter over mind. And seeing her find this pleasure, adrift on her mounting swell of passion, was causing one in him which promised to be monumental. Gladly then, he abandoned thought and freed the forces that drove their bodies, joining her on the suspended curl of that rapturous wave; mounting the crest her equal; and with the volatile impact of a mystical explosion, held her to him as they slid smoothly over the top...

It was over. ...And yet, as Tom looked at Mandria, he knew it would never be for him. Eyes closed, she seemed content lying so quietly in his arms. But was she? He'd done his damnedest to make it so—and she had come. Even now, he was absorbing those throbs of pulsating proof—coveting each as it beat against his deeply sheathed flesh. How he wished they would never cease! ...Still, what was she thinking and feeling? Tom had to know. "Lady," he rested his forehead on hers, "tell me your thoughts."

"I have none," she uttered, moving not at all.

"None?" he cupped her face, hoping she'd open her eyes and let him search truth from their depths. "None good or bad?"

"No," she nodded, pointing a single finger toward the ceiling. "I'm still up there somewhere and I'm not coming down."

"Oh," he grinned, much pleased with her reply—and with himself, he admitted smugly. "Well," he rolled to his side, taking her with him, "I guess you know, after being with you, the two-bit-whores of the city just lost all my business."

She stilled and with widened eyes asked, "...Does this make me a whore too?"

"Good God, Mandria—no!" he tightened his arms about her. "That was just a bad joke and I'm sorry for it. I only meant that you are very, very desirable. But you are a lady—my own beautiful lady and I love you beyond all reason..." He paused there to look at her. "Or am I still not allowed to say that?"

Mandria rose on her elbow above him. "But what kind of love do you have for me?"

"What kind do you want?" he looked back at her because it seemed important to.

"Will you want to…to be with me again?"

"Yes!" he exclaimed, reaching for her. "How could you ever doubt that?"

But she stopped him, wedging her hand against his chest. "As mistress or wife, Tom? And it's your turn to be truthful. …I have to know where I stand with you."

"As both, then" he shrugged. "And you can name the order."

"But you could want me?" she watched him play with a lock of her hair. "—Only me?"

"Well, you know how that goes," he said offhandedly. "In time, I'll want others." And when she glanced at him with something close to pain in her eyes, he relented. "Little ones, love! Beautiful little daughters with sea green eyes like their mother."

"Oh," she let go of a breath and smiled. "And what of sons? Would a tall, broad-shouldered dozen be enough?"

"Breast babies every one," he patted her appropriately. "With a jealous father the whole time they're nursing. —I suppose you noticed I was never properly weaned?"

Again, Mandria's eyes betrayed her dazzling smile, and he knew another question was coming. "…Then, can I ask a personal favor?"

"As long as it's intimately personal—yes!" he casually laced his fingers behind his head. "I've a great fondness for that sort of thing between us."

"All right then: Mister Thomas…" she paused, her lips parting in realization. "Dear Lord. I've been to bed with a man and I don't even know his full name!"

"You'd be amazed at how often that happens," he laughed. "But lady, you've only to look at your beautiful body. My name is branded everywhere. —See?" he traced a finger down her arm. "It says Thomas Phillip Scott from stem to stern. And it's done in the boldest print on that sassy bottom of yours."

"In that case, it shouldn't be too difficult to answer my question," she held his hand against her. "So: …Mister Thomas Phillip Scott, will you please—dear God, please—marry me?"

"No," he said, and his gaze never wavered.

"…But why?" she questioned. "You told me to be brazen. Doesn't that include marriage proposals?"

"Of course, but I still can't marry you. You have never said you love me—and lady, I need to be loved."

"Then I'll love you," she nodded. "…In fact, I already do."

"No, you don't."

"I do too," she argued. "I love you very much."

"You do not," he insisted.

"Tom?" she grasped his face in exasperation. "I do so love you. Truly I do!"

"Ha! I know your type well. You are just after a name for your dozen sons and green-eyed daughters—and you expect me to take in the lot of you! Bag and baggage! Kit and caboodle!"

"Oh—you!" she swatted him. "You are a tease! —An awful tease! I think you are serious half the time!"

"And I'm hungry the other half. Come on, love, we can talk over supper." And swinging to the edge of the bed, he paused to look back at her. "You know, it seems I've said that to you before—and where are your clothes, by the way?"

"Drying on the other side of your wardrobe," she followed to sit beside him. "But wait: you didn't answer my question and I am not leaving this room until you do."

But as he started to speak, a sharp rap at his door interrupted.

"Who could it be?" Mandria whispered in the silence that followed.

Again, the rapping started, became more insistent and Tom slipped into his trousers, knowing—sensing—trouble. "Come lock this bedroom door behind me," he whispered back. "And lady, no matter what happens, you are to stay put and remain absolutely quiet." Then lifting her chin in his hand and holding her gaze he added, "Promise it; —swear it, on the love you say you have for me."

"…All right, Tom," she nodded, "I promise."

But keeping that promise proved the most difficult thing Mandria had ever done…

# CHAPTER 14

Tom waited until the door lock snapped behind him. Then sliding arms into his shirt sleeves and mussing the day-bed covers in passing, he continued across the room as the knocking resumed. "Yes?" he said, opening the door, and pretending a yawn, as if he'd just been awakened.

"...Mister Scott?" came a hesitant query. "Hell, I must have the wrong damned room!" But glancing at the number on the door, the man nodded and looked at Tom again. "Are you Scott—Thomas Scott?"

"Yes sir. May I help you?"

"It seems you are the only one who can," was the reply. And slipping a hand into his pocket, he aimed a lethal question. "Don't you know me?" he smiled. "...You really should."

Bits and pieces surfaced in Tom's mind. He heard Kathy saying, *"The smile was still on his lips, but his eyes were as cold as death."* The rain soaked hair plastered to this man's head wasn't so easily recognized either, but it did appear gray and shoulder length. He remembered the whirl of a cape on the stairway; a caped figure profiled against firelight; and here was that cape again. Tom knew him, all right—and mostly because of the hand still in his pocket. "Sam Lucas," he uttered. "So we finally meet."

Sam's expression became a mixture of relief and displeasure. Tom had not recognized him as Bob Trott, which meant he could live as long as he was useful as a conduit. ...But what had happened to the Tom of yesterday? This attitude of confident reserve was not expected and it went well with the bastard's tall, rugged looks. "May I come in?" he managed a cordial tone. "I believe even you would prefer keeping this conversation behind closed doors. —That is, unless you have a reason for refusing to let me in?"

Tom thought that one over for a moment. If he refused, Lucas would be certain Kathy was hiding here, just as they'd wanted him to. But it would be Mandria caught leaving now and that just could not be allowed. Besides, he was more than a little curious to know what brought the man to his door alone, armed, and in the middle of a storm. So, stepping aside, he motioned him in with a sweep of an arm. And as Sam entered, and paused to survey the room, Tom glanced at another closed door. From here on, every word would be monitored and any judgments made were perhaps better done from the warmth of his bed. In any case, this was going to be a real, if cruel, test for Mandria…

"I see you were enjoying a nap. Good day for it," Sam looked first toward the day-bed, then to the table. "Have you anything stronger than wine? This will be rather difficult for me."

"How so?" Tom asked, as he studied the thin man ruffling his hair dry on one of Mrs. Harrison's towels. He was smaller in statue than Tom would have imagined; edgy; a mite too obliging; …and somehow, oddly familiar. But then, didn't he know too much about Sam Lucas for it to seem otherwise?

"Well, I find myself in a sticky situation." Sam settled on a chair at the table. "I know you think I'm here about Kathy, but it's Mandy I'm looking for. Have you seen her today? —Have you an idea where she might be?"

Tom chose his words. "I was out all morning and didn't see her then. But if you've conferred with your men, you know that already. Have you checked with Nico or Lucy? They might know her whereabouts."

"No, I have not!" Sam retorted in response to the audacity just shown to him. But immediately, he toned down his sharpness. "…Listen, may I have that drink now?"

"Certainly," Tom nodded, seeing the pretense for what it was. Lucas was thoroughly upset.

And as he crossed the room to retrieve a bottle from a tray on the bachelor's chest, Sam took a turn at nodding while scanning the breadth and muscular tone of the man he had come to manipulate. ... And what was it about those eyes that caused him to feel Tom was not looking at him, but through him? Private anger biled in his throat. He had come on a mission, and he'd see it through. But first, to soothe his pride, he'd cause Tom a good sweat. Oh yes, he'd knuckle the bastard under, as he'd always been able to do. Brawn did not mean he'd also developed brains, now did it?

Tom poured them each a drink, and handed one to Sam. Then straddling the other chair backwards, he sat facing his visitor with less than two feet separating them. "How did you find me?" he asked, slowly buttoning his shirt. "I wasn't followed from City Market."

Again, with the infuriating impudence! But this time Sam did manage a smile of sorts. "Ransom gave me your address, when I finally remembered he might have it. But I haven't found you yet, Mister Scott. —Not until we've found common ground on which to talk. Now, I could ask any number of incriminating questions: like how you came by my daughter's painting here; or why you think I'd want you followed. But I would prefer that we ante-up and lay our cards right on the table."

"So deal," Tom shrugged.

"Very well. Here is my hand: I believe you are having an affair with my damned mistress; I believe you and your friends set fire to the Seafest kitchen and abetted her escape; I also believe you're seeing my daughter—and that you know God damn well, I wouldn't approve." Then having made his speech, Sam looked at Tom for signs of guilt or admission, but saw neither. "...Any comments?" he asked, much perturbed.

"No," Tom answered, feeling sorry for Mandria. The test had certainly begun.

"Denials, then?" Sam added.

"Not yet," he replied in the same noncommittal manner.

Sam heaved a frustrated sigh. Tom was not bending as should have by now. "Well, damn it, Scott, you must have something to say!"

172

"All right," Tom's eyes held a granite edge. "Do you intend to use the pistol you pointed at me earlier?"

Sam laughed in utter surprise. "You're damned direct, aren't you? —And observant, by God! It leads me to think you've been in similar situations before."

"Not quite," Tom dared another glance toward the bedroom door. "No, never one quite like this. However, I want you to know something. We are evenly armed now. If you reach for the gun again, I'm close enough to stop you. And I would not hesitate in turning it on you. …Now, why are you here, Sam Lucas? I'm sure you have more on your mind than accusations."

Sam lowered his eyes to conceal the agony of holding his temper. Tom was still necessary if he hoped to meet Allen and cultivate a relationship with his own damn son. With that in mind—and none too easily—he forced himself to search for another approach. "Mister Scott—Tom," he feigned a distraught expression, "you see a desperate man before you, but I'm not here to shoot you. Indeed, if you are guilty of the things I named, I want your damned help." And he gulped at his drink, pleased that Tom finally seemed at a loss. "Shall I explain?" he asked with some satisfaction.

"Yes. —Hell yes!" Tom nodded, propping his chin on his hand. "Your logic has escaped me completely."

"Some questions then: what are your feelings for Mandy? —How involved is that relationship?"

"I've the highest regard for her, and deep respect—"

"No more?" Sam injected. "Nothing…intimate as yet?"

"You have already expressed disapproval, —Sam," he made a point of returning the man's use of first names. "If there was more, would you really expect me to admit it? —And to her loving father?"

"Well, you'd best remember that Mandria is my daughter!" Sam shot back. "I won't have her used as you used our little Kathy!"

"No woman should be used as Kathy was, Lucas," Tom countered. "She was never your mistress by choice—"

"God damn it—that's enough!" Sam bristled, smacking his hand on the table. "Such knowledge is most condemning!"

173

"Then condemn the whole city," Tom shrugged. "I heard the story my first night in Savannah."

"Still…your passionate interest prompts another question: What would you do to see Kathy free of me for good?"

"Almost anything," Tom replied truthfully.

"So Kathy is the one you care for?"

"If it was, would you expect me to admit that either?" Tom paused to sip his drink. "We seem to be going in circles here, Sam. Is this leading anywhere or not?"

"It's simple enough. Only the guilty man and I know how stimulating Kathy can be. Also, considering the lengths he went to last night, he must want more of her. And that being so, the guilty man would want to see her free from servicing me further. …Can you imagine how warm her bed would be for the man who accomplished that?"

"Damn," Tom uttered. "You're offering a trade. What in God's name could you want so badly?"

"My daughter's future happiness, of course," he stated as if it should be obvious.

"Then you're saying you would release Kathy if I stop seeing Mandria. —Is that it?"

"On the contrary!" Sam laughed, enjoying Tom's confusion. "Mandy wants your company. And if it takes that to bring her home safely, then by God, she'll have it—no matter the cost to me."

A thousand questions ran through Tom's mind, but he could not bring one past his lips until he knew what the hell was going on. "…This has got to be the strangest conversation in history," he nodded. "Now you're saying that I can have Kathy, only if I'll—what? Keep company with Mandria too?"

"Exactly—with strict limitations, of course. But you handle women well enough to pull it off. I've learned that damned much about you."

"Well, I've learned something about you too, Sam Lucas.," Tom retorted. "I won't hand you nails while you build my coffin—not just to prove my prowess with women."

"What could you mean?" Sam asked innocently.

174

"I mean there has to be a catch. No man is that generous with his mistress—much less his own daughter! Why would you trust me with Mandria if you think I'm guilty of the rest?"

"I don't trust you, Scott—and I'd gladly kill you—but I'm forced by difficult circumstances to bargain instead," he reapplied his distraught expression. "You see, I had a terrible row with my daughter this morning and made the sad mistake of telling her about you and Kathy. And quite frankly, her reaction—her quite hysterical reaction—scared the God damn hell out of me! Not only did she manage to blame me, but she made threats that have had me combing the streets for her, in spite of this storm—and deathly afraid of what I might find or have caused her to do!"

"…I still don't understand the role you expect me to play," Tom puzzled.

"I'm certain you already know Mandy is smitten with you. She listens when you speak; believes in your honesty—child that she is. You have to restore her faith in you before it's too late. Convince her I was wrong; that there never was an affair with Kathy—or that you ended it when you met her. I don't really care how you handle this, as long as you regain her trust."

"To what purpose? Mandria isn't a child. She is a beautiful, intelligent lady who wouldn't be so easily fooled." And Tom hoped she knew he meant that.

"You fooled her once; you'll do it again if you want Kathy for yourself. Don't you see? Mandy means more to me than a dozen like Kathy—or anything I might otherwise hold against you. …Tom, you said yourself that she is a lady. Help me keep it that way. Between us, couldn't we manage one decent act in our sordid lives?"

How could the man speak lovingly of his daughter in one breath and trade Kathy, body and soul, in the next? What was decent in that? No, Lucas was up to something far more devious and no good for anyone concerned. …Still, if bargaining with him meant seeing Mandria freely and helping Kathy at the same time, why not? It would be the grandest double-cross of the century and no one deserved it more than Sam Lucas. Surely, Mandria could appreciate this—and perhaps it would satisfy her thirst for revenge to so out-maneuver her father. "…Very well, you have a deal," he nodded. "But I have questions too, and one condition to make."

Sam came forward on the chair, congratulating himself. "Anything! Ask what you wish."

"All right. What if I had chosen Mandria over Kathy? You obviously don't expect her infatuation to last and wouldn't allow it to anyway."

"Yes, because I know the truth about you, don't I? I knew you'd have to prefer Kathy. Mandy may be a lady, but she is also a bit of a prude. Oh, she's the perfect daughter for a man of my position, but could never abandon herself to carnal pleasures—as Kathy has been trained to do so well."

"…And you want nothing out of this?" Tom suppressed anger. "Only to ensure your daughter's reputation?"

"That and the time only you can buy me," Sam's thoughts turned to Allen. "Time to regain the love and respect of my child; to become the father I should have been for all these years."

"That's a noble speech," Tom commented dryly.

"Don't be coy, Scott!" Sam retorted. "You're getting plenty from this—a hell of lot more than you deserve!"

"I suppose I am," Tom agreed paradoxically. "I won't deny that."

"Well, get on with it then. You said there was a condition?"

"Yes. I want a signed receipt—here and now—saying I paid Kathy's debts in full."

Sam was so taken aback he didn't even raise his voice. "You God damn bastard," he uttered. "If I gave you that, what would keep you from flaunting Kathy in my face all over town? As much as I love my daughter, I wouldn't stand for it, Scott."

"Aren't you forgetting something?" Tom asked. "According to your own proposal, Mandria is the one I'd be flaunting. …You do realize that, don't you?"

Sam smiled slightly, and it felt good. Tom was stepping right into place, closing the gap between father and son. "You're right," he conceded. "Mandy would want to prove me wrong; she'd want me to see you together; —to accept you as she does."

176

"Then if you'll write my receipt, we'll call this a bargain," Tom rose to his feet. "You see, I believe I know where Mandria might be—and from what you've said here, I think it's imperative that I speak to her right away."

"But you will send her home to me."

"As we agreed."

"Well, as long as you remember the terms," Sam rose too. "Kathy for you; Mandy for me."

"That does seem to say it all," Tom ushered him to a small desk and laid out paper, pen and ink well.

"There is one last detail which occurs to me," Sam said as he seated himself. "A matter of equal protection? I intend to keep a signed copy of this for myself."

Tom looked at him while calculating angles. "To show Mandria should her interest in me become more than you'd like."

"By God, you continue to surprise me!" Sam admitted. "Who knows? Stranger friendships have come about."

"Equally armed; equally protected," Tom dipped the quill and handed it over. "There can be no truer friendship for us."

Sam gave a hardy laugh as he set the pen to work. "I couldn't have said that a damned bit better—not one damned bit!"

So their bargaining done, their papers signed and each believing he had bested the other, Sam took his leave. There was even a lightness in his step as he headed down the stairway. But the coldness was still in his eyes and Tom was fully aware of it.

However, this was not the time for pondering Sam Lucas' motives. Tom went to the bedroom door and stood praying for some kind of guidance, but none seemed to be forthcoming. "...Mandria? Come out here, please." There was no response. "Mandria, ...please?" he knocked lightly. "I want to explain. It's not what it seemed."

"...In a moment. I...I'm dressing now." And the anguish in her voice went through him like a knife blade.

Tom leaned his head against the door and sighed at the irony of his situation. He was single, healthy and very much in love with the beauty locked in his bedroom. And if that wasn't crazy enough, to get her to love him back after this, all he had to do was convince her that what she heard so clearly was not what was said at all, but a word game where lying scored higher than truth and sanity was severely penalized. Then, if she accepted that—understood when he still didn't—he would tell her about the elephants scheduled to fly over Savannah on the third Sunday of November. And he had asked what came between lunch and supper? Today's answer would have to be total lunacy!

He went to the table, poured a drink and downed a healthy portion of it, before stretching out on the day-bed to await his beautiful lady. "Too much," he said, and indeed, quite a lot—good and bad—had happened in the last few days. "Too much," he repeated; too much, with too little rest in between. His head fairly spun with unanswered and unanswerable questions: Would Mandria even listen to him now? What had Sam Lucas really wanted? Even with the signed receipt, was it safe for Kathy to remain in Savannah? Had he relied too heavily on Mandria's declaration of love? Surely, if he weren't so tired, the answers would come more easily. Surely, if he could just close his eyes for a moment...

Mandria was desolate—stunned almost senseless by the things she'd heard. But that wasn't punishment enough. Oh no, while they traded back and forth out there, she was locked in a room with Tom's bed. ...And that sheet, stained with her own blood. Even now, she couldn't take her eyes from it. Such a small stain, yet it represented everything she'd lost, and her virginity seemed the least important. *Another trophy*, she remembered saying to Tom. Well, there it was, upon the appropriate canvas too, and hardly dry before he'd traded her away. *And a lesson for me*, she finished with a nod of certainty.

She went to the washstand and splashed her face with water. ...*I have to clear my head*, she thought. *I have to get out of this room and find a place to think. —Or else I'm going to start screaming and I'll never stop!* she muffled a sob against her fist. The question was how? Then

178

she recalled something from her morning trip up the stairs, and quietly opening the window, she crawled onto the porch and looked to see if the hall door was still open. It was, and now she only had to pass Tom's sitting room window to make her get-away.

But this was not Mandria's day for simple procedures. A sudden breeze parted the drapes, and she found herself gazing at Tom where he slept on the day-bed. Betrayed by her father and her lover—bartered for between them—this seemed the final blow. How could he sleep so peacefully when her heart was breaking? Didn't he know, even now, she wanted to curl up beside him? ...*But you chose Kathy*, she thought. *Oh Tom, why? —Why?* And when the question nearly became verbal, she moved quickly away. There was no sense babbling hysterically on the man's porch. —Hadn't she shamed herself enough already?

# CHAPTER 15

Mandria crossed Bay Street, entered the bluff-top park and wandered aimlessly along the pathways. It was almost dusk now, the rains were gone and the river below reflected the last sparkling rays of late afternoon sunlight. The moment seemed symbolic to her. In Tom's arms, she'd known sparkling moments too. But they would never happen again; dusk had come to stay in her life, for she felt suspended in nothingness.

She tried to hold back the tears and when that failed, she hid in a bank of azaleas and tried to keep from sobbing aloud—but dear God, how she hurt! The whole thing had been so degrading; so humiliating; …so deserved? She had thrown herself at Tom—crawled right into his bed. And worse, she'd begged him to marry her, when all along, it was Kathy he wanted. The thought stung like poisoned dart.

Then, from some dark place in her soul, resentment began to surface. Tom wasn't exactly blameless for her behavior. She had asked him not to speak of love, but he persisted, making her believe the beautiful lies he whispered in her ear; …into her mouth; against her breast… It was so unnecessary, a cruel act, done to increase her willingness and heighten his pursuit. *A game men play*, she had described it so aptly.

"Oh damn it!" she winced, thinking now of the casual way he had bargained with her father. …Yet, there was another maddening thing. Sam Lucas giving up what was apparently his pet mistress out of fatherly love was about as touching as a festering boil. And how she had suffered by comparison! Kathy was the *stimulating* one who enjoyed *carnal pleasures*, according to her sire. Tom had put *intelligent and high regard* on her side of the tally—to which her damnable father added *prude*.

"Well, damn them both!" she swore as resentment turned to anger, and that immediately pushed reason aside with a violent shove. She had said she wouldn't be used in the name of love—which only whetted Tom's appetite for the challenge of getting her to bed. But maybe, just maybe, the *giving and patient* teacher had taught her more than he knew. Thanks to him, morals were no longer a draw-back. Thanks to him, she knew exactly how to foil that bargain with her father—and keep both those bastards from getting what they wanted from it!

Mandria rose to her feet. No one was going to talk her out of this, or anything else, ever again. "Flaunt me all over town, will they?" she uttered. And going to the edge of the bluff, she searched the docks for the Irish Mist. "Captain Michael Herb," she spoke to the lantern glow in the window of a cabin behind the wheelhouse, "you are about to have a visitor."

It was nearly night now and Mandria found footing on the steep cobblestone drive slow-going. But because of it, she was more aware of the noise from the tavern row just ahead. It was a strange mixture: half-slurred voices, mingled with music and spiced with vulgarities; laughter too, yet not laughter—more a thinly veiled cry of loneliness or despair. It was odd that she understood this; …but then, didn't she feel the same way? On reaching the corner, she paused to get her bearings and it was then that a group of sailors in front of the next building caught her attention.

"Open wide!" one yelled, looking upward. "Come on, lady-bugs, show us them tits!"

And Mandria eased back against the building even more.

"Damned right!" joined another sailor. "You'll not sucker us 'til we've seen what's to suckle!" he laughed raucously at his own wit.

Mandria's ears rang, but she couldn't resist looking toward a balcony where one black and two white women stood pulling up their blouses; handling their own breasts; making them shake and joggle for that cheering pack below.

"All right, babies, come to mama! —Come on, you pussy fucking bastards!" said one. "Let's see what you can do with these!"

"Yeah, and maybe we find something to suck on too!" called the Negress. "Like that idea, don't you now? —How about that?"

"Hey, how you want it?" added the third woman. "Soft and warm or wild and fiery? Just name it, big man. Yeah, you!" she pointed. "The one with the pretty red hair and that nice fat bulge in your fucking pants!"

"Oh God, oh God, oh God!" Mandria whispered, turning her face to the wall. She was trembling and for a time couldn't seem to stop. But when she dared to look again, the street was quiet and the sailors were gone. ...But for how long? That was the question.

She glanced toward the Irish Mist. It was, perhaps, thirty yards away, yet she wondered if her legs were steady enough to carry her. The shadows seemed so much safer. ...What if she tripped on the cobblestones? What if someone—like those sailors—spotted her and gave chase? *You will be raped...* Tom had said. *He won't come from your part of town.* But hesitancy vanished with the squeak of a hinge, when a side door opened directly behind her.

Mandria was off like a shot—dashing across River Street, unto the dock and ducking behind a cotton bale before looking back. But no dreaded pursuer was in sight, though she did hear uneven footsteps moving up the bluff road. Nevertheless, she gave a long, shuddering sigh of relief, only to have it catch in her throat when a hand grasped her arm.

"Hold on there!" said a deep, male voice. "What are you doing around here?"

"Wh...who are you?" she barely managed, as she straightened. "Let go of me, please?"

"Not just yet," he answered, firmly leading her from the hiding place. "Come into the light and let's have a good look at you."

"...Police?" she breathed again, on seeing his uniform. "You're a policeman!"

"Yes. So what and who are you?" he asked sternly.

Mandria swallowed her fear. "Mike—I came to see Michael Herb."

"Oh?" he smiled too wisely.

Guessing his thoughts, she nodded around a blush. …But why should she care what he thought? He was right.

"Well, yonder's the gangway," he motioned grandly. "Just give me some notice when you leave. Wouldn't want to mistake you for a thief again."

Moving quickly away, Mandria made her way onto the boat and up the stairs, only to pause interminably before the cabin door. "Mike?" she called at last. "Michael, may I speak with you?" she tapped lightly. "It's Mandria."

"…Mandy?" Mike answered hoarsely from within. "Just a moment; —Mandy Lucas?"

"Yes," Mandria leaned her head against the frame. "May I come in…please?"

"I'm coming—just a moment," he repeated. And after a bit of shuffling, the door opened. "…Sorry for the delay," he said, with the most puzzled expression she had ever seen. "You caught me napping," he finished.

"You too?" she brushed past him, only to rush about the room. "Mike, I have to talk to you. You are the first one I thought of and I need your help."

"Whoa now, Mandy!" he rubbed groggily at his eyes. "Light somewhere, will you? You're making me dizzy!"

Mandria sat, but on the very edge of a chair, and said nothing more as she stared at her clenched hands.

"Now, what are you doing down here?" Mike asked with folded arms. "Don't you know it's dangerous?"

"Dangerous?" she laughed. "Even when you've no more to lose? Oh Mike, if you only knew! If Tom knew—or gave a damn!" And now she was crying. "But father would care—and I wish he were in hell!"

Mike knew something had happened and every conceivable thing went through his mind. "Mandy, where is Tom? And your father; where is he? —Is Tom all right?"

"Certainly!" she sobbed. "As I said, he is napping too. And father is likely scouring the city for a new mistress. You'd think Tom would be anxious to tell Kathy the good news—but no, he's asleep, damn him! And my mother? Mother sits properly at home knowing nothing. —Not a damn sorry thing!"

"…I'm afraid you lost me somewhere," Mike nodded, going to the whiskey cabinet. "You look like you could use a drink, though. Want one?"

"Yes!" she turned on the chair and wiped at her stubborn tears. "Maybe that is exactly what I need. Maybe a good drink will give me the courage for what happens now."

Mike handed over a brandy and sat facing her on the edge of his bed. "…And what is that? I think you're here to tell me."

Mandria downed the liquid and flinched. "I am," she replied, gazing at the empty glass. "I must, so you'll understand my proposal. Mike, I know my father detests you…and I want to know how strongly you value Tom's friendship."

"I see," Mike nodded, and immediately changed his mind. "—No, damn it, I don't see! Why can't women just say what's on their minds? Mandy, what is it you want?"

"I—another drink," she held out her glass.

Mike sighed and got to his feet. "Very well. But then I want some reasonable answers—straightforward and simply put." And when the Captain turned from the whiskey cabinet with her drink, she was standing right before him.

"This is as straight as I can put it," she looked him in the eye. "Mike, would you take me to bed? That bed," she pointed. "Right now?"

"Damn…," he uttered.

"I asked you a question," she moved closer. "That wasn't much of an answer."

"Mandy?" he managed, when able to close his mouth. "You are Tom's lady and—"

"The hell I am!" she pried the brandy glass from his hand. "I belong to no one. So, do you want me or not?" And finishing this drink, without flinching, she refilled the glass for herself with a much more generous portion than he'd given her.

"But why me? Tom would gladly—"

"Tom has Kathy!" she spat. "He bargained and bartered and bought her from Father—in exchange for me!"

Mike nodded. "...You can't mean that Sam and Tom actually met and talked; —not about Kathy!"

"Well, they did, less than an hour ago," she insisted. Then she straightened and downed more of her drink, before setting it aside with purpose. "You know, Captain, I saw something outside. Maybe I'll show you." And she began to unbutton her dress. "Would you care to inspect me? Shall I bare my breasts and joggle them for you?"

"God damn it, stop!" Mike grabbed her hands. "Now Mandy, you stop that and tell me exactly what happened!"

"Oh, shut up!" she pressed her bosom against the hands holding hers. "I've got to know this can happen because of me. —Me, Michael! Not Kathy, but me!"

Mike freed himself and moved a safe distance away, where he watched her lift the brandy to her mouth another time. "Mandy, any man with eyes in his head would enjoy you," he began. "But I couldn't take you if my life depended on it. —Damn it, Tom is my friend and no matter what you believe, I know how he feels. He wants you and that's a fact."

"Yes, to play with and listen to his lies," she banged down an empty glass. "Well, never again. And answer me this: if he and Father can share the same woman, why not he and his best friend? That only seems fair."

"Fair to whom?" Mike argued. "There is a limit to sharing in the best of friendships. I'd no more touch Tom's woman than he would mine. —No ma'am! What kind of man would I be stabbing him in the back with you?"

"Is the stab in my back less painful because I'm a woman?" she asked coldly. "Well, the hell with that! —The hell with all of you!" And crossing the room, she flung open the door and went out.

She was half-way down the stairs by the time Mike reached the door. "Mandy? he called. "Where are you going?"

"To find someone else!" she yelled back. "—Anyone else! I seem to be in *the right part of town* for it!"

185

"Wait a minute!" he demanded. "At least button up your dress!"

Feeling the brandy-fire, Mandria turned at the foot of the gangway, hands on hips. "Why the hell bother? It's all coming off soon enough!" she yelled angrily. And spotting the grinning Policeman, she yelled at him too. "Well, damn it, was that enough notice for you?" Then looking across the street, she went directly toward the nearest, noisiest tavern.

Mike knew what he had to do and was already tucking shirt-tails as he searched about for a missing shoe…

The Boar's Head was packed and the Captain mulled through the crowd, looking this way and that, before spotting Mandria toward the rear where a crowd had gathered to a watch a Greek dancer. The dark, plump woman encouraged her audience to clap along with the slow, easy rhythm of her steps and Mandria joined in at once, moving to the front of the group, where because of her fine looks and disheveled appearance, those inquiring male glances began. *Who was she? Was she with anyone?* That is when Mike worked his way up behind her, to answer every question with some strong expressions of his own. But now Mandria was involved with the dance steps and watching the Greek woman's feet, began to move her own in imitation. Hop, step, kick; Hop, step, kick…

And the ogling eyes returned—very pointedly, to her unbuttoned bodice. Mike knew he had to stem this interest quickly, so putting one arm across her shoulders and the other about the woman next to him, he joined them all in the dance.

After a curious first glance, Mandria tossed her head in laughter. "Welcome, *Tom's good friend*!" And latching on to a man next to her too, soon the traditional dance circle was formed, where the music slowly grew faster. On and on it went, even faster, until the strong winded were all that remained, while the rest stood back to wheeze and howl their encouragement. It was a glorious, boisterous experience for Mandria, who even took her turn alone in the center of the circle. She was dancing well too—better than the Greek, by the amount of applause she was receiving. And all that very nice attention truly made her feel warmly accepted by everyone. Mike, of course, knew better. She was admired, but they respected his *claim* just a little more. Few wished to cross the feisty Captain of the Irish Mist, and that's the way he wanted it.

When the dance finally ended, Mandria turned back to Mike. "Well, I don't know about you, but I want another brandy. It shouldn't be too hard finding someone to buy it for me now, do you think?" her glance encompassed all those grinning men about her.

"Come along, colleen," he steered her toward a table. "If its brandy you want, you'll damn well have it. —Among other things."

"...My goodness," she said coyly. "Has the *good friend* decided to *share* after all?"

"He is being tempted," Mike replied.

"Wonderful!" she exclaimed. "Can I have that brandy now?"

"All right," he paused for a moment. "...But button your dress, will you? Starting a riot in here is an altogether different thing than sharing with Tom."

"Do not mention his name again!" she pounded a fist on the table. "—And I'll tell you about the damn buttons! I will fasten one for every drink you put in front of me. And I won't argue the point. I am making my own rules tonight—and for the rest of my damned life!"

"I see," he nodded, making a quick count. Five buttons meant five drinks, and with what she'd already had, that should just about put her under the table.

"Well, shall we get on with it?" she suggested. "Why don't you just buy a whole tray of drinks?"

"I'll do that very thing," Mike rose to his feet. "But for God's sake, Mandy, don't you move while I'm gone. —And stop looking so beautiful! You'll have every damn stud in the room coming over here."

"A compliment?" she laughed sarcastically. "So the Captain also *plays-the-game* well. —Go now; go get my brandy—lots and lots of it!"

But the order Mike gave at the bar was a strange one. "Five brandies, a pitcher of ale and a few minutes of your time will earn you an extra two dollars," he said to the hired girl. "Are you interested?"

"A few minutes?" she grinned lewdly. "You are a quickie-dick ain't you, lover?"

"I—oh hell," he grinned back. "I need a message delivered. —For now," he baited.

"Oh hell is right," she pretended a pout. "I've far lovelier ways of earning your money—if you take my meaning?"

"I'll bet you do too," he brushed a finger on the tip of her freckled nose. "Now, go to Harrison House; just across Bay Street; second floor; number four. Tell Mister Scott to get his damn ass down here. Tell him it's about his lady and Mike said to hurry! Have you got all that?"

"She the one?" the girl nodded toward Mandria as she placed his order on a tray. "This Scott is coming for her?"

"He damn-well better; —he has to!" Mike answered, checking to see that Mandria was staying put.

"Then you will be needing company after all!" the girl's face brightened.

"Only if you bring my friend," he tucked money into the neckline of her blouse. "Now hurry yourself, wench—and don't come back without him!"

"You have just threaded yourself for a fine screw job," she giggled. "I'll bring that man if it means a butt-fucking all the way down the bluff!" And with that, she slipped from a side door and was gone...

Not that a mere oak door would have stopped him, but Mike was glad the thing stood open when Tom entered the Boar's Head. Anger blazed from his eyes as he searched over the room for Mandria. And spotting her, he started in their direction with a stride which brooked no interference. Never had the Captain seen anyone more furious. If she dared to argue with him now—or repeat the proposals she'd made aboard the Irish Mist—Tom would likely cuff her and haul her out by the hair. So, feeling a moment of real concern, Mike dared to wave him off, hoping their friendship granted that privilege. It did, but just barely, for Tom came to stop only a step behind Mandria's chair and stood looking at Mike for a reason. He was no less angry, but Mike thought he should hear the pain in her brandied words. Then if Tom felt she needed a cuffing…well, she did.

Mandria had finished all her drinks and giggled because she couldn't manipulate her last two dress buttons. "Damn—well, damn it, Mike, what's the difference? You're only going to pop-open-again-them anyway. …Or something like that," she shrugged.

As did Mike, when Tom peered over her shoulder at the state of her bodice and back at him with folded arms and a raised eyebrow.

"Come on, Mike, I want to dance now. It keeps me from thinking about Father and that damn Mister Bastard Scott!" But rising too quickly, Mandria grasped the table and sat down again with a bump. "Captain?" her eyes widened. "Is it an earthquake? What's wrong with this stupid room?"

"Nothing," he chuckled, and noted that Tom wasn't amused in the least. "…But maybe we should dance, Mandy, or that brandy is going to hit your head harder than it just did your bottom. Come along now," he drew her up by the hands. "Time to move around a bit, missy."

"Don't call me that!" she glared. "Father calls me that when he tries to bully me. —And I loathe the word!" Then, something close to moan escaped her. "But he was right about T…Tom—damn it! Mike, I am really and truly hurting. Did you know that?"

"So a dance is just the thing you need," he led her back to the forming circle and joined them in. But he kept an eye on Tom too, who now stood with his hands braced on the back of Mandria's chair, obviously counting the number of empty glasses at her place. Then, he lowered his head for several moments, straightened, took a deep breath, and to Mike's eternal relief, came their way with his usual easy gait. For a time, he only observed the dance, but soon joined the circle across from Mandria, and his eyes never left her again…

Though woozy, Mandria still managed to capture most of the tempo. And when the rhythm grew faster and the circle smaller, she laughed gaily, proud that she and Mike, the Greek and her partner were the only remaining participants. But now, Mike was pleading fatigue and for some reason, dragging the other woman off the floor with him, even over that one's loud protests. She laughed again when the woman kicked Mike in the shins.

Then, the Greek's partner was plunging her back into the accelerated pace of the dance, but with a difference. Instead of standing beside or in front of her, he stood behind, holding her hands to the sides as they went through the basic steps. And at the completion of each series, he would turn her out, only to twirl her back against his chest, where, with one strong arm clamping her against him, he'd set them into a spiraling turn. At first, Mandria was eager to incorporate these new steps with those she'd already learned. Yet, as the tempo grew even faster and those body hugging spins longer, she began to feel uncomfortable on many levels. She was glad to blame the brandy for the missed steps, her inability to focus her vision, and the dizziness after the whirling spins, …but why did she seem to crave the feel of these arms; to fit all the *nooks and crannies* each time her body touched his? And now, they were into another spin, faster and longer than the others; the momentum rocking her head back, helping her find Sapphire eyes while the universe spun crazily by. "…Tom?" she asked as his blurred image loomed suspended in motion. "Please be Tom!" she cried softly.

At that, Tom brought them to an abrupt halt. He watched as her head rolled unsteadily. He felt her knees buckle and knew she would have fallen but for the arm holding her against him. Then, to the delight of all who watched, he lifted her chin and kissed her quite thoroughly just before she slipped effortlessly from consciousness.

"More!" the crowd cheered, unaware or uncaring of her condition as Tom scooped her into his arms. "Come on, man—show us more!"

"Not on your life," he stated in a tone that left little doubt the show was finished. "A carriage, Captain," he added, following the path Mike was already clearing. "I am going to prove something to this stubborn girl once and for all, damn it!" he continued once they were outside. "Will you help me?"

"Oh-hell-yes!" Mike chuckled, hailing a cabbie and hurrying to open the door.

Tom climbed in, but paused to watch when Mandria stirred and opened glazed eyes. Then, she sighed, snuggled closer against his chest and closed them again. "Get in, Captain. I'll tell you my plan as we go. —And just how in the hell this all came about."

As the carriage started up the bluff road, Mike's voice raised echoes along the cobblestones. "Damn, Tom! I'll do it—hell, you know I will, if that's what you want. But—well, damn Tom!"

# CHAPTER 16

It was afternoon before Mandria moved her head on the pillow. "Oh," she groaned, wondering why so simple a thing brought discomfort. An attempt at turning in the covers in search of a more comfortable position, led to the discovery that her whole body was resisting the effort. "What on earth?" she muttered dryly. Too dryly. Her mouth and tongue felt as brittle as a sun-baked sponge. Next, she tried lifting her eyelids, but bright, needle-sharp sunlight definitely discouraged that.

...*Have I been stricken with some disease?* she wondered. ...*Could I be in a hospital?* And as her hearing seemed the only of her senses functioning properly, she listened for the hushed, efficiently hurried movements of the medical staff. But beyond her own breathing and something that squeaked in the wind outside, all was quiet. "Well, where am I then?" she shielded her eyes and forced them open again, only to find nothing familiar about the room—and what was that incessant squeak? Lifting her head for a glance at the window, she saw a sign, swinging in the breeze on rusty hinges…and it read Skidaway Inn. "Oh my God!" she bolted upright and immediately suffered for it. "My head; —oh my head; my head," she went reeling back to the pillow, certain her brain had torn itself loose by the roots. Yet, in doing so, it released a gushing flood of memory: making love to Tom; her father's fateful visit; horrid humiliation; heart wrenching pain; terrible anger. And then, brief flashes of more: Mike; brandy; buttons; a tavern; more brandy… "Then what?" she whispered. Looking at the sign again—recalling the clandestine stories connected with the place—she

192

knew *what*! And now, panic was mingling with a cold sweat that had the sheet clinging to her skin.

"To my skin?" she shrieked, lifting the covers. She was naked:—naked, in a tumbled bed, while her clothes lay scattered about the floor; ...naked, except for a ridiculous bit of ribbon knotted on her finger that she was noticing now, for the first time. "A poor joke if this is supposed to remind me of anything," she nodded. "Mandria the mindless; —the mindless whore!" she added, wanting to cry. But the tears wouldn't come and she had to wonder if she was in shock or just beyond caring. For the moment, all she knew, for certain, was that her head ached frightfully.

Sighing in resignation, Mandria sat up cautiously and swung her legs over the edge of the bed. "I will remember everything; —and who brought me here!" she said with determination. "I've come too far to stop now." Yet she did stop and moaned painfully as her weight pressed downward. Just how getting drunk—or doing what she evidently did do in this bed—could cause her feet to be sore, was quite beyond her reasoning powers. "That is stupid—just plain stupid!" she decreed. But as she hobbled about, gathering her clothes and dressing, she came to a halt. "Dancing—I was dancing with Mike; with a lot of people and...Tom? Was he there too?" She waited for the memory to clear, but it faded even as she spoke. "Oh, I don't know!" she lamented. "I was dancing; someone kissed me; and I ended up here. ...But with whom—and where is he now?"

Almost in answer to that question, Mandria spotted an envelope propped on the dresser, with her name written across it. But once she'd retrieved it, new doubts assailed her. Did she really want to read a confirmation of her deed? No, but she had to if she expected to deal with the situation. So taking the envelope to a chair by the window, she broke the seal, removed a note and found money tucked in the folded page. "...Twenty dollars," she counted numbly. "I—I was paid for the use of my body..."

Fighting a wave of nausea, Mandria just sat there staring at the wind-swayed limbs of the trees across the road. She had always found solace in the gentle, green sighs of the huge Live Oaks, but now, her staunch friends were hissing in scorn; whispering her sins on the breeze. *Mandria, the slut,* they cried. *So evil—just like her father. No better; no better at all.*

"Worse!" she added—and Tom had warned her about this. Where was the satisfaction she thought she'd feel? Where was everything she'd always valued about herself?

*All gone,* clicked the leaves. *Gone, evil girl—evil, wicked girl!*

"Do stop!" she begged. "What can I do about it now? —What is left I can do?"

But the trees were silent. Sunlight had broken through a cloud to banish the wind and censor the gossiping leaves. "That I could so easily banish my problem," she looked pointedly at the note in her hand. And only because it was necessary, she read the missive:

> *Thank you, dear one,*
>
> *From here on, determination and repetition will constitute the order of my life. For I am determined to enjoy our new closeness again and again—if possible, into the middle of the next century!*
>
> *Wish I had thought to bring more money, but then, who could have guessed the evening would end as it did? Anyway, spend it as you wish—perhaps for some thin, lacy thing to wear for me? And knowing your sensuous nature now, I do look forward to viewing your selection when next we meet.*
>
> *Meanwhile, the dining room is open downstairs. Will you join me there?*

"How can I join you?" Mandria asked the letter. "Am I supposed to approach every man in the room and say, *Pardon me, did I sleep with you last night?*" Her eyes flew over the words again, but there was no clue; not the slightest hint of the writer's identity.

"Damn it—damn, damn, damn!" she rose to pace in utter frustration. And it didn't help when another problem presented itself, front and center.

Now, she genuinely dreaded her father's reaction to all of this. He would literally explode—spewing his hypocritical wrath—if she went home with no excuse for being gone overnight. No, she couldn't return without a story and once she'd thought of one, some way of backing it up! ...But how had things gotten so turned around? Yesterday, she'd wanted to defy him; wanted him to know she had too. Today, she wanted nothing less. Today, she only wanted peace of mind and time to sort out the mess she'd made of her life.

...Time and peace. Wasn't that what she'd always found at Marsh Haven? It wasn't far to the country house from here—and she could stay until her father discovered her whereabouts on his own. Why, it might take days for him to think of looking at Marsh Haven and surely—surely—by then, she would know what she was going to do. The idea was so appealing, Mandria flung open the door, rushed down the stairway and out the front door, oblivious to all but her objective. And while impatiently pacing the yard, waiting for the smirking stable boy to return with a buggy, she noticed the ribbon still tied to her finger. Revulsion caused her to pull at it frantically; to throw it down and grind it beneath her heel. And once in the buggy, when the boy dared to say she *must have enjoyed a jolly good stay at the inn*, embarrassment and anger caused her to throw the money left for her into his face and set the horse off at a dead run...

From a dining room window, Tom watched the boy scramble after the money dancing on the dervishes of Mandria's hasty departure. He wasn't sure where she was running or why, but he was prepared for it. Finishing his last sip of coffee, he went out to the saddled horse waiting at the hitching post, mounted and followed after her.

For almost half an hour, he kept back, trailing her by the wheel tracks left in a road still muddy from yesterday's storm. When he had to rein sharply to allow the empty buggy to pass going in the opposite direction, he knew she had either reached, or was close to, her destination. Keeping a close eye on the surroundings, as well as her foot prints leading him down a side road, he soon came to an ancient stone archway, into which the words Marsh Haven had been etched. Below, looking much like an afterthought, hung a small wooden sign reading S. T. Lucas. And one of the massive wrought iron gates stood open just wide enough for her to have slipped through.

Pushing it wider, he kept the horse to a walk as they went along a straight drive canopied-over by River Elms. Then, at the far end, just starting up the steps of a columned house, he spotted Mandria. Pulling the horse into the tree line, he watched as she was warmly greeted and hugged by an older Negro woman and led inside. Then, for a time, he studied the grounds. In the casual manner of the beach house, they too were beautifully landscaped and as quiet as the vast savanna that came to the very edge of the back lawn. A deep tidal stream cut through the side yard on the right, and beyond that laid well tended growing fields. Tom knew she would be safe here. She would stay, and perhaps for the present, that was best. So, turning the horse, he returned to the main road and set out for Savannah. There was, after all, much left to do...

"But your room ain't ready!" Hassie said as Mandria started up the stairway. "We wasn't expecting you and there's no sheets on the bed; no dusting been done—"

"I said it doesn't matter," Mandria kept going. "All I want is a bath—and maybe something to eat," she added. ...When had she eaten last? She couldn't remember taking a bite since supper at City Market on Friday night. And what was today? ...Sunday?

"Well, the bath water will take a time to heat, but stuff still warm in the serving kitchen if you wants to eat now," Hassie suggested.

Mandria stopped and came back down. "Then I guess I'll eat," she shrugged. And as she followed her former Nanny through the house, she wondered how she could have been so unaware of her gnawing emptiness until now. ...*But then, hopping from bed to bed wouldn't leave time for much else, would it? Two men on the same day; —two, for Savannah's new twenty dollar whore…*

It was hard, but she managed a cordial greeting for the staff before helping herself from bowls along the servant's table and it was only Hassie's protest that kept her from sitting to wolf down the food on the spot. Hassie wanted Mandria in the formal dining room, to which she objected, until plate in hand, Hassie deposited her at a table on the rear veranda—and still, she received a disapproving snort as Hassie left.

Mandria just sighed and began to eat. It wasn't long, though, before her eyes were drawn to the marsh fanning outward below the slightly elevated spot where she was. *…It's like sitting on the chin of a giant*, she mused, *and looking down his long, reedy beard. …So, the sea would have to be a woman, teasing at his whiskers with warm salty kisses. … Both would want dominance and because neither could have it, they'd seldom be content. … Yet the affair continues, century after century; …a loving, but hateful, battle of wills…* It struck her, then, there was something of her relationship with Tom in the parable and that she would have to discover why it bothered her so.

But for now, Hassie was calling from the bedroom window. "The bath water's ready. Ah put in the last of the honeysuckle drops too, so bring more from town, girl."

Mandria hurried up the stairway, knowing a bath would not cleanse her soul or soothe the ache in her heart, but she was desperately anxious to feel clean on the outside again. Yet, as she sank into the warm fragrant water, even this small pleasure was overshadowed by guilt. "*Determination and repetition*—hell!" she spoke to the writer of the note, on finding the soles of her feet to be the least of her tender spots, devil take him!

"Damnation and retribution would be more like it," she uttered. And she just kept making mistakes. She knew now, that she should have gone to the inn dining room to see if anyone there looked even vaguely familiar. That might have prepared her a little more should they meet in Savannah. As it stood now, she didn't know what to expect. It could be any man—well, any with a nice hand-writing ability. Would she have to run over-town collecting samples from every male on the streets to learn the identity of her lover? Now, there was another brilliant idea! Finishing her bath, she dressed in the fresh skirt and blouse Hassie had laid out. Then, brush in hand, she went to the vanity mirror, hoping to bring some kind of order to her hair and thoughts as well. When both resisted taming and Mandria was close to slinging the brush to the floor, the door opened.

"Ah brought you up a cup of tea," Hassie smiled her way in.

"Well…thank you," Mandria settled on the window seat, determined to stifle her unhappy mood. "Yes, thank you very much, Hassie."

"No need for that," she handed over the steaming cup. "You lets me do precious little for you these days. It's good to feel needed ever so and again." And with that, she moved busily about, getting out fresh bed linens and gathering Mandria's soiled clothes and bath towels.

"It's not that I don't need you," Mandria tried making conversation. "But I can take care of myself," she cringed at the falseness of the words. "—And Hassie, please stop fussing with this room!"

"Humph! Ah don't know where you get them notions. Ah raised you up to be a lady—a real fine lady. Where you get these in-de-pen-dent notions 'bout taking care of yourself?" And pulling a dust rag from her pocket, she continued undaunted.

Mandria watched as Hassie lifted the note from her lover and dusted under that too. "A…fine lady?" she stared at the envelope. "No, Hassie, that's gone now. …All gone. I'm an evil, wicked girl. … The trees told me so."

"The trees?" Hassie stopped to look at her. "Mandy-chile', what you saying? What's bothering you? Hassie knows something ain't right! And another thing: how you gets here? Ah know you ain't walked from Savannah, but there wasn't no buggy, no luggage—no nothing!"

"Well…," Mandria hedged. "Well, Hassie, I had this fight with Father, so I went out and…I did what I thought was the right thing and then…well, everything just went crazy!" And in spite of a valiant effort to keep from it, she burst into tears.

Immediately, Hassie was beside Mandria, cuddling her in comforting arms. "Now, now, honey," she soothed. "You just cry it out—cry it all out. Hassie's here; been here since you was a sweet little baby. Ain't nothing going to turn out bad for my Mandy-chile'. You always been such a good girl; —so fair and kind to everybody 'round."

"I wasn't kind to myself, Hassie," she sobbed. "And I'm not good; not any more!"

"Yes, you are!" Hassie smoothed her hair. "If you was bad, you wouldn't be hurting 'bout it so. Now tell me what the trouble is. We make it better. We find a way to do that."

"Oh, how I wish we could, but I've committed too many sins! And when Father finds out about last night...," she shuddered. "I can't take any more of his two-faced reprimands!"

"So, what happened last night?" Hassie got right to the point.

"I don't know!" she exclaimed, crying harder. "I mean, I do know, but I don't!"

"...Chile'?" Hassie eased her back enough to meet her eyes. "You calm down now, and talk sensible. What you trying to say?"

"I...I drank too much and today, I—oh Hassie, I woke up naked and alone at the Skidaway Inn! And he paid me; —he left money!" she snubbed. "I was so frightened. I didn't know where to go, or what to do...so I came out here."

"Ain't that just like a man?" Hassie threw up her hands. "Black, white or purple, they all the same: full-growed, sweet-talking studs by night; and guilty little boys running home with the sunrise! —Who was it, child? Who this bastard be?"

"I just don't know," Mandria answered softly. "I was too drunk to remember."

"Oh, my poor lamb!" Hassie declared. "Just a innocent lamb led to the sacrifice—"

"No, Hassie—no!" Mandria rose to pace. "Don't make excuses for me. I brought this on myself. I was trying to get drunk; trying to find nerve enough to out-wit my father and Tom—" she drew in a breath, hoping to retrieve a name she said without meaning to.

But Hassie heard. "So who this Tom?

"Just...a man," Mandria shrugged.

199

"Oh?" Hassie gave her a sage look. "When a woman say *just-a-man* the way you did, she usually means *the man*. …Anyways, you had a fight with him too?"

"No, but we would have fought!" she answered as her pacing accelerated. "And maybe we should have fought, but no—I had to tend to the business of getting myself into worse trouble!"

"Girl, you going to walk holes in the carpet, 'less you stop!" Hassie snagged Mandria's skirt and sat her down again on the window seat. "You wound tighter than a clock. Now tell me this: does your Mama know the state of things?"

Mandria pressed fingers to her still aching temples. "No, she doesn't know much of anything. …But I guess she is worried that I didn't come home. I should go to her—but Hassie, I can't! Father would demand answers I don't have…so what am I to do?"

"You won't have to explain nothing to your Daddy, because we just say you been here since yesterday and couldn't get home for the storm. Ain't none of us at Marsh Haven wouldn't swear to it for you."

"…But I wouldn't ask you to lie," Mandria said meekly.

"Then we'll just call it a little fib. —Ain't you done good turns enough for us? Remember when your Daddy was fixing to sell me off to that man from Charleston? It was you and Miss Evelyn what defended my old bones and had me sent out here instead. And it was your doing, not two weeks later, had my man moved to join me. Then there was what you done for Verna Lou, Debbie Lyn and Cindy Anne—"

"Hassie stop!" Mandria interrupted. "Don't make me out a saint—I know better, don't I?"

"Then just admit your mistake and quit hurting so hard," she retorted. "Ain't a borned-soul don't make mistakes and need help sometimes. You letting disappointment bow your head, when you should be holding it up to see how you going to start over new. You got the stuff to do it—and Ah'm showing you the way. Ain't nobody has to know 'bout last night that you don't want to tell, Mandy-chile'. And 'bout your Mama? If you ain't ready to go home, she'd likely appreciate a little letter so she knows you're safe. You write it and my man Jake can take it to her today."

Mandria hugged Hassie dearly. "Thank you," she said softly. "Now if Father will stay in town and leave me alone, maybe I could learn to live with the rest. ...Maybe."

"Then go write your letter," Hassie grinned. "—But do it someplace else. Ah means to fix your bed and straighten this room up nice. Go—shoo, girl! Get out my way!"

And Mandria went. In the study, it took her several tries to get her message just right: to say only enough to comfort her mother and cool her father's temper. Then, when Jake was on his way to deliver it, she returned to the rear veranda for a breath of air. Her favorite time of day was approaching—her quiet time—when the sun grew swollen with orange, snagged on the tree tops and spilled its color over everything. Even the savanna was changing—deepening from green-gold to fieriness. Then yard-frogs, katydids and crickets began to serenade the cooling air; and adding to the chorus, birds flocked in from everywhere to rest in the elms by the tidal stream. And the bark of those elms, reflecting in the stream, looked metallic, as did the Spanish moss draping nearly every tree around in twilight lace.

Mandria sat down again, to enjoy the transition more fully. For the sake of her sanity, she needed to forget the harshness of reality for while. ...Or maybe just to look at her problems while their edges were softened in this glowing light. If she could only find some far-reaching purpose for all that had happened, she might be able to start over. "What was it I thought of earlier?" she uttered. "Oh yes, I was sitting on the chin of a giant..."

Like the sea, had she demanded too much of Tom? She'd been so involved with her own sense of justice; her burning need for retaliation—and so much so, she had not once considered the needs of others. And Tom, every bit as dominant as the gold bearded giant, had to resent her attitude. Hadn't he even said so? ... *You've got to come because of me and not because of your father.* But she ignored his warning—gone to his bed, still spouting vengeful words—and for that received exactly what she deserved: an affair she would not forget; an impossible dream that would never know fulfillment or bring contentment. ...Was it any wonder he had chosen Kathy? "No," she admitted, "and somehow I've got to accept that…"

But over the next few days, she learned she had set an impossible task for herself. Whether walking the growing fields, helping Hassie about the house, or simply gazing over the marsh, Tom was never far from her thoughts. …So why was that? Wasn't she looking for a way without him?

Another time, she'd been for a swim in the tide stream, and while lying on the dock to dry, was reminded of their day at Tybee, and how from the first, Tom was able stir curious, exciting emotions in her that she had not understood. Now she did. Now she had loved and hated him; clung to and run from him. Yet, his presence—or possession—remained and she was very much afraid its real name was love. What use was there denying it here in the bright revealing sunlight? In spite of everything, she was still in love with the man. She admitted something else too. "I don't want to give him up, damn it, Kathy! Just…damn," she sighed. For what could she possibly do about it?

The following morning, direction appeared. Mandria had taken a blanket and her sketch pad to the side lawn, hoping to capture the lines of a sprawling oak that covered a great portion of the area. But the tree was soon forgotten, for there on the pad was a face, framed with thick dark hair, high cheekbones and a wide, firm jaw—Tom's face. The eyes she had to draw looking aside, or she'd have gotten no further. His eyes just made her feel too many things. But there was his nose and that chiseled mouth… She paused, remembering his mouth in the softness of a smile; the sternness of anger; the throes of passion…lips parting, descending, drawing her in, giving life to her own passions… "*Oh Tom—please be Tom,*" the words seemed to come from nowhere and yet, were stunningly familiar. She knew she had said them and that they had been important to her. But to whom was she speaking? …Her phantom lover, perhaps?

"Stop it, Mandria!" she exclaimed when tears threatened. "Don't think about him. Just solve one problem at a time." As was her custom, when the sketch was finished, she propped it before her, ready to be her own critic and make corrections. Yet the moments passed and she could find no changes she wanted to make. It was good—by far, the best piece she'd ever done. She even knew why. "Because the others came from beauty I saw with my eyes. But this—oh, this comes from the heart." And for some time, she sat gazing at the sketch deep in thought.

"All right, Thomas Phillip Scott," she said then. "You dealt with father. Now you are going to deal with me. And I can't discuss it with you from here."

So there it was—what she had wanted all along—a reason for seeing Tom again. And what of her unknown lover? Well, if she ever heard from the man again, it didn't mean she owed him any consideration. Twenty dollars worth was quite enough, thank you very much. Yes, it was time to go home—home to Savannah and as much of Tom for herself as she could possibly salvage…

# CHAPTER 17

"Whoopee!" Old Jed sang out when Mandria pulled the buggy to a stop before the carriage house. "Mandy-chile', Ah thought you wasn't going to make that last turn! Swears to God, you had three wheels hiked in the air!"

"I'm sorry," she said climbing down. Then, noticing the snorting, sweaty horse she felt ashamed and went to comfort and apologize to him too.

"You run him all the way from Marsh Haven like that?" Jed asked as he finished unhitching the harnesses to lead the horse on a cool-down walk.

"No, Jed," she followed along beside him. "It's just that the closer I got to T—town," she corrected hastily, aghast at what she'd nearly said. "…What happened the first night I was away? Was Mama terribly upset? …And was Father?"

"He did him some hollering," Jed nodded. "Don't know what calmed him neither. But Ah wasn't calmed; —not 'til Jake brought your letter and we had us a talk. Had to have his word on it, you were all right."

"Thank you," she replied, touched by his caring. "…Is Father at home today?"

"No, but your mama is. —She resting-up though. Likely, she missed you too much to sleep proper. Likely, mamas don't never stop fretting 'bout their young. One day, you'll learn that for yourself."

"I know," she nodded, starting for the house. "I'll go up and see her now." And as she went, Mandria thought about Old Jed and loved him all the more for what he said. He had expressed concern, then gently scolded her for being a thoughtless daughter—and he'd done both so simply and in far more fatherly tones than she'd ever heard from Sam Lucas.

When Mandria saw that her mother was sleeping peacefully, she couldn't bear to wake her. So easing the door shut, she went to her own room, resigned to waiting for whatever would happen next. At this point, nothing much was going to surprise her. ...Except for the envelope among the things in her correspondence tray. Hesitantly, she pulled another from her pocket and compared the script. They were identical, of course, and now the closeness of the room was nearly overwhelming. The man knew where she lived! In a frenzy, she lifted every window sash as wide as it would go and batted aside any curtains that might inhibit air-flow. And once seated at her desk, she still found several deep breaths necessary before attempting an opening ceremony:

*My Dearest,*

*Forgive the ramblings of a mad man, but your image and the memory of our time together haunts me night and day. I miss you sorely and long to hear you say the same. Can we meet? —And please, make it soon!*

"Oh Lord," she uttered apprehensively. "He's beginning to sound insistent!" But there wasn't a clue to the writer's identity yet, which meant she couldn't even send a note of discouragement. She just prayed her silence would have the same affect. Surely—surely it would! So, placing both notes in a desk drawer, she locked them out of sight; out of her life. ...Or so she thought.

"Mandy?" Evelyn rushed in with an embrace for her daughter. "You're home—oh, I'm so glad you're home!"

Mandria returned and welcomed the warmth. "I didn't mean to worry you, Mama. Can you ever forgive me?"

"Sweetheart, there's nothing to forgive," Evelyn said as they settled on the edge of the bed. "I know about the quarrel with your father and after the vicious things he said about your friends, it's understandable that you needed to distance yourself from everyone involved. I'm just glad you made it to Marsh Haven safely in all that rain."

Her mother believed the quarrel caused her to leave. "…So, Father told you about it?" Mandria was compelled to ask.

"Yes dear—and I've wonderful news for you. He has discovered his information was false and all is forgiven! Tom, especially, has been most gracious about it. So what do you think of that?" Mandria rose and went to a window. She would love saying what she thought: that Kathy's name had yet to be mentioned; that the *gracious* Mr. Scott was role-playing in order to claim the woman; and that she didn't know enough four letter words to express her feelings about the damned bargain making all this possible. Instead, she muttered some inanity praising the wonder of it all.

"Yes, so your misery was for nothing—and I must say, Tom is most intuitive about you. He said you only needed time to sort through your feelings and then you'd come home. —And here you are!"

"Wait," Mandria nodded in confusion. "You've spoken to Tom about this?"

"It's really quite odd, but we keep bumping into each other almost daily and I can't tell you what a comfort he has been." Then Evelyn smiled. "Mandy, in my opinion, he would like spending a lot more time with you."

Mandria began to pace. That Tom was preparing to *flaunt the prude* she might understand, but he had no right to involve her poor, gullible mother. That wasn't part of anyone's agreement. "Oh, he is just so—so *intuitive!*" she settled for her mother's word, but had wanted to scream *Infuriating!* And she was going to tell him so, just as soon as she could devise a way of *bumping-into-him* herself.

"As we agree on that, shall we ask him for dinner tonight?" Evelyn asked now. "Tom assured me he'd come when you returned home."

That brought Mandria up short, struck by the irony of it.

"But first, sweetheart, your attitude toward your father is important here too. I'm sure he has apologized to Tom already, because it was Tom who encouraged him to tell me about your argument. So can you forgive your father too? We wouldn't want Tom to walk in on a family squabble, would we?"

*...And the irony just keeps growing!* Mandria realized. Now, everyone was steering her along a path she'd already chosen. She wasn't going to change her mind either. ...But shouldn't there have been at least one voice of dissent?

"Mandy?" Evelyn urged, reaching to grasp her daughter's hands. "You do like Tom...don't you?"

A nod was all Mandria was capable of communicating.

"Good!" Evelyn rose, already marshalling her resources. "Now, I'll send Jed with a note letting your father know you're home and what the plans are. Then, Jed can take another to Tom—for what: dinner at six o'clock, maybe? And, while I get things started here, would you do me a great favor? I ordered a burnt-caramel cake from Gottlib's that would be a perfect dessert, so be a dear and go after it." Then she was gone, humming a tune as she always did when taking charge of things.

"...Yes ma'am," Mandria said to the empty room and wondered what happened to her mother's decisiveness when it came to her father. Nevertheless, her own aims would be served by this dinner and though it was a little early, she left on her mother's errand, heading north toward Broughton Street, the river breeze, and people. She wanted people around her now: busy disinterested shoppers who wouldn't mind that she walked among them, listened to their prattle, or nodded in greeting to a passing stranger. It was her way of knowing an everyday world still existed and that not all lives were as complicated as hers had become. Then, she came face-to-face with Mike and Nicole.

"Mandy!" Nicole launched a bounce-the-topic conversation. "I'm so glad you're back. —Look, there's Rebecca Fralix, Brittany Spell and Caroline Clamp. Wave, everyone—Hello! Hello, there!" and turning her back on the smiling ladies, she went on. "What a fine day this is. Mike came in early and here you are too," she looked between them with a teasing smile. "You know, if you hadn't come from opposite directions, I might be jealous? —Oh, anyway, we've just come from Levy's, Mandy. Their Fall fashions are in and some are very nice—if you're selective, of course. I bought two bonnets and a pair of shoes. —And unmentionables," she added in a loud whisper, "which, I must tell you, Mike took a peek at. Isn't he just deliciously disgraceful?" she giggled.

Mandria glanced at the grinning Captain, who stood clutching Nicole's many bundles. …But was that a grin or a smirk? She couldn't help comparing his expression to a cat with bird feathers hanging from its mouth. And she paled remembering a possible reason. "…Mike," she nodded, afraid to say more.

He wasn't. "I must confess, Mandy, I've seen more roses in your cheeks. Have you been ill? —Nothing that kept you in bed, was it?"

"Yes, Mandy, now that he mentions it," added Nicole, "you don't look well at all."

"No, I—I'm fine!" Mandria cut into the Captain with a sharp look. "But I do thank you for caring enough to mention it."

"Yeah, old care-and-*share*," he laughed jovially. "That's what my closest friends call me."

"And Daddy will call us late," said Nicole, tugging on Mike's arm. "We'd best leave if we're still stopping for lemonade before meeting him. Oh, —Mandy, do want to come too?"

"No, thank you," she watched Mike for reaction. "Tom is coming for dinner and I'm just out to pick up dessert."

"Really?" the Captain smiled, and this time…proudly? "Well, you have a real pleasant evening," he said as Nicole pulled him away. "And hey to Tom for me!"

Mandria watched as they crossed the street to a sidewalk café before continuing to the bake shop. "Well, that was a lot of fun," she muttered. Everything and nothing could have been read into Mike's words. …Was he her second lover? She had asked him to be and he had joined her for drinks and dancing, but that was still all she could remember—which was not brightening her already hectic day. Damn it…

Cake box in hand now, Mandria decided to forgo the stroll she had been looking forward to and return home. Then, not a half-block further, from the far side of the street, she was greeted and bowed to most grandly by a group of young gallants who seemed particularly anxious to acknowledge her passing. ...*Now what was that all about?* she wondered. ...*What if it was one of them? —What if he has spread-the-word, to put it nicely?* And her pace quickened. "Now I have to remember! —I will remember!" she vowed. "I can't go around suspecting every man alive!" And with each step, the security of her room was becoming more and more appealing.

But she wasn't to reach it. As she crossed her home-square, Ransom O'Rourke left a group of friends to approach her. "Mandy?" he called. "Just a moment, my dear. I must speak with you."

"Yes, Uncle Ran?" she tried to sound pleasant; tried not to breathe as if he'd stopped her nearly at a run.

"...Uh, have you seen Nico lately?" he asked. "She and Mike were to meet me over half-hour ago."

"Yes, I saw them," she nodded. "They stopped for lemonade, but I'm sure they'll come straight along."

"Good; good," Ransom hesitated. "...And you, Mandy? Are you well?"

"I-am-fine!" she affirmed. "—Uncle Ran, do I look ill? You are the third one today to ask me that."

"Listen, I don't mean to press you," he stepped closer, "but I heard about your flight to Marsh Haven and I've been quite concerned."

"You have?" she took half a step backwards.

"Well of course," he nodded. "You mean a lot to me, my dear. And you should know that by now."

A weakness crept into Mandria's knees as she imagined the very worst. And now, Ransom's friends had them surrounded.

"That was down-right rude of you, Ran!" began Mister Embrey, head of the Planter's Association. "Did it never occur to you that we might enjoy being in on this?"

"Indeed yes!" added Mister Horton from the Cotton Exchange. "Especially as we were just discussing Miss Mandy's many talents. — And her lovely person," he added charmingly.

At that point, Mandria thought she might faint.

"And as Ransom has done nothing but brag about you," grinned Mister Gurley from the Georgia Gazette, "say you'll give our proposition serious consideration. We would be ever so grateful—and would gladly adhere to any stipulations you'd care to make."

"Gentlemen; gentlemen!" Ransom placed an arm about her rigid shoulders. "I'm afraid your enthusiasm has overwhelmed the lady—and rightly so," he chuckled. "You see, I haven't asked her yet! And, before we make such a request, don't you think she should know all who would ask this of her? Sebastian, kindly step forward."

As he did, Mandria stepped backward again. She did not know this man…so why did he seem familiar to her?

"This is Mandria Lucas," Ransom introduced, "and, Mandy, this is Mister Sebastian Rizza, the newest member of our elite little group—and according to the ladies, a most welcomed addition to Savannah."

"*Grazie*," Iano smiled as he lifted her cold hand to his lips. "But I met the lovely…uh, *signorina* a few evenings ago. It was much too brief an encounter, however, and I would enjoy changing this. Still, it is good seeing you again, *bella donna*."

"…Thank you," Mandria uttered. And then, she was wondering if this could be the man she'd danced with and mistaken for Tom. The one who kissed her and… what?

"Well?" urged Mister Embrey. "Now will you ask her, Ransom? Or must we put it to her ourselves?"

"Mandy, do try to overlook their eagerness," Ransom nodded. "But I have all but assured them you'd be receptive to this."

Mandria looked about the hovering group of men and wanted to scream—especially at the Italian, who now wore the same too-knowing smile that Mike had. But she seemed to be frozen in place and not one sound could she make.

"Come, Mandy," pled Mister Horton, "say you'll decorate the Harvest Ball for us."

"Yes, with your artistic touch, that hall would be turned into something special," added Mister Gurley.

"And," said Mister Embrey, "your efforts would greatly contribute to our success. You know the proceeds are donated to Bethesda for orphan support—a project your father supports, by the way."

"Gentlemen!" Ransom interrupted again. "Do allow her some breathing room! I'm sure Mandy will consider our request and give us an answer in a day or two. Won't you, my dear?"

"Yes; —oh, yes!" she nodded in great relief. "I will, in a day or two."

"Very well, we can ask no more," Ransom said to the others. "And now, my friends, I see my daughter and Mike coming with someone else I want you to meet. —Thomas?" he called. "Come and join us."

Mandria stood frozen in place—again—certain that never had another living soul experienced this many emotional upheavals in so short a time. And now her mind and body were fighting a war of opposing directives: her mind said to stay put, while her feet itched for flight; her mind insisted she stick with her plan and her heart just wanted to cry. Then Tom touched her and she knew she wasn't going anywhere. It had only been a hand beneath her elbow; a brief greeting; a silent hello, before shaking hands with the Italian, whom he seemed to know. And though presently giving polite attention to Ransom, he remained at her side—close, as was his want. But hers too, damn him...

"Thomas Scott," Ransom was saying, "this is Claude Embrey, Bill Gurley and Adolph Horton. I thought you'd enjoy meeting more of the friends going for the hunt at Sebastian's place. —And don't say I didn't warn you about Gurley. He is a terrible shot and likely, we'd all be safer putting him up a tree with Mike."

"Oh, I'm still not going," Mike grinned over the bundles he continued to carry for Nicole. "But if I did, I'd sooner face the boar than Gurley with a loaded gun!"

"Bill Gurley—from the Gazette?" Tom asked over a handshake and a chuckle.

"Guilty on both counts," he laughed too. "From the Gazette and a really bad marksman!"

211

"Not so bad with a pen, though," Tom said. "I've enjoyed your articles on Savannah. In fact, I plan to use them in a history class I've agreed to teach this year."

"An extremely intelligent young man," Gurley nodded to Ransom. "Already I count him as a friend."

"I thought you'd approve," Ransom replied. "—And Tom, since this seems a day for begging favors, I've one to ask of you. We, here, have asked Mandy to decorate for the Harvest Ball. Might you persuade her to say yes? It's rumored you have a slight influence with the lady."

"Well, she is a bit stubborn," Tom met Mandria's eyes, pausing for one eternal second. "…It could take thunder and lightning to move her in the right direction."

Mandria's lips parted in surprise. However deftly, wasn't he referring to the storm last Saturday—the one she'd forded to reach his room; —his bed? "I…I didn't say I wouldn't help," she managed a response, as one was obviously expected. "I just want to think about it first."

"See what I mean?" Tom smiled, looking about the group. "Gentlemen, this could take time—and my undivided attention," he added, moving even closer; placing her hand on his arm; covering it with his.

"Somehow," grinned the Captain, "I believe you could suffer through that, Tom."

So there Mandria stood, enduring a blush while the others laughed; wishing she were better at clever replies as their chit-chat continued; and knowing, for propriety's sake, she should remove her hand. … But there was such warmth in Tom's touch and now, he was tracing a line back and forth across one of her fingers. Of course, it was an idle gesture. Of course, he must never know it made her want to snuggle closer, and think of deeds no where close to proper.

Then he took the cake box strings from her other hand, which she'd totally forgotten she still held. "Lady, shouldn't we be leaving?" he asked. "Your mother said to come around six…?"

"Oh yes," she nodded. "You do have an ag—I mean, an engagement to keep," she stammered badly. But she had tried to say *agreement*, and that would have been grand! From what deranged part of her brain had this sprung? She was the one intending to make this work to her benefit—yes, she was! So straightening, returning to purpose, she managed to make pleasant farewells before Tom led her toward home.

"So," he began, as they strolled along, "how was your stay at Marsh Haven? I must say, you look rested—and more beautiful than ever."

"Well, you are the first person I've met today who thinks so," she commented. "But thank you."

"And I'm glad you sent word to your mother," he continued. "She was really worried for a time."

"You said she would be," Mandria murmured. "I should have listened—to that much, at least."

"…Meaning what?"

"Nothing, really," she shrugged. "It's…well, so much has happened and I feel differently about a lot of things now."

"What things, Mandria?" he asked pointedly and without releasing her gaze.

There. —There in his eyes was the look she hadn't been able to put into her sketch. It went through her defenses—her heart—and every time, left her mute.

His laugh drew her eyes to his mouth and a smile that said she didn't know what… "Not ready to talk about it yet?" he asked. "Never mind, then. For now." And opening her front door, he ushered her inside.

"Hey there, Mister Tom," Jed greeted, relieving him of the cake box. "Miss Evelyn and Mister Sam in the front parlor, should you care to join them. —And Mandy-chile', your mama been looking high and low for you! She said you won't never be dressed in time for dinner."

"Then I'll have to prove her wrong, won't I, Jed?" Mandria moved toward the stairs. And going up, she prayed above all things that she wouldn't trip and fall clumsily to her knees, because without looking, she knew Tom watched her every step of the way…

Changing into a presentable dinner dress and a quick casual arrangement of her hair, proved easy enough, but Mandria lingered at her vanity anyway. She was not displeased with the way her first meeting with Tom had gone. He had even suggested they had things left to say between them and somehow, she'd find a time and place for that. It was her father she dreaded seeing now. She had promised her mother there would not be a scene in front of their guest, but what attitude would her father assume? Which should she? From long experience, she'd learned never to count on Sam Lucas for anything but having his way—including the choice of what man she should marry. ... Or was that his true reason for entering this bargain with Tom? Was he *saving* her because he'd come up with another profitable business arrangement to be sealed by her acceptance of yet another selected bridegroom? A repulsive shudder brought her to her feet for a final check of her appearance and a renewed vow never to marry if that was her only route to the altar. But she had dawdled long enough, so with a deep breath, she mentally braced for the battle of wits to come and descended the stairs...

# CHAPTER 18

"Good evening, everyone!" Mandria swept into the parlor, smiling beautifully. "Sorry to be late, but as Tom can tell you, Uncle Ran and his friends had me cornered," she leaned to kiss her Mother's cheek, and then turned to stand before her sire, who along with Tom, had risen at her entrance. "...Father?" she said and left her greeting at that. It was he who suggested the bargain which brought Tom here tonight, so let him grovel a bit for her cooperation, false it was on both their parts.

"Glad you made it home," Sam said and when she continued to stand there, smiling, he was forced to continue. "All right, daughter, you want your pound of flesh, so here it is: I made some wrong conclusions," he lied and she knew it. "I've apologized to Tom already," he lied again, and she was sure of it. "Will you forgive me?" he took her hand and it took all she had to allow it. "Can I hope for as much understanding from my only daughter?"

"Oh, I do understand, Father," Mandria then withdrew her hand, but stayed long enough for a placating pat to his arm, "—more than you could possibly imagine. But the time for casting stones has long passed," she began a slow and graceful traverse about the room. "I haven't the energy for it—or the right, I'm certain. As Hassie told me," and this she imparted to Tom, "everyone makes mistakes. Yet we must go on; grow wiser because of them; and start over with renewed strength." When he nodded and made no effort to hide a smile, it gave her pause. ...Was he agreeing with her? ...Or laughing as he remembered that for all her platitudes, she had crawled right into his bed, eager to make those mistakes? "Well, what are your thoughts on the matter, Mister Scott?" she demanded an answer one way or the other, but tucked it behind her own smile.

"I think…" he held her eyes, "I'd enjoy knowing Hassie. —And what shade of green your gown is."

"It's—I…well, it's mint," she stammered hopelessly.

"Mint," his smile warmed even more—and she felt it. "You know, green has always been a favorite color, and lady, you truly do it justice."

Mandria's cheeks flamed to rosiness. Then Sam smiled too. After he'd used Tom to get to his son, he might have to kill him, but he wasn't above admitting the bastard was a God damned wizard with women. —And just look at that: on Mandria's behalf, Evelyn was fanning a blush from her cheeks as well. …Amazing.

But Mandria was far from pleased. Tom knew she was aware of his reason for being here, so she did not have to tolerate easy dismissal or meaningless flattery—and perhaps he should learn that right now! "Father, our guest needs his drink freshened," she moved across the room with purpose now. "And while you are about it, I would enjoy a sherry—as would Mother, I'm sure."

"Oh…uh, I, —yes, thank you?" Evelyn agreed. Sort of.

"Certainly," Sam moved affably to comply.

"Do sit down," Mandria motioned Tom back to his chair as she lowered herself on a sofa with a decorous spread of her skirts. "And tell us, Tom, are you enjoying your new life in Savannah?"

Tom looked at her for a second, and then, instead of the chair she'd indicated, he came to the sofa and sat beside her. Mandria's blush this time was real, for again, he was much too close. "To tell you the truth," he began, "I'm finding life a bit unsettled just now—too many loose ends to deal with,"

"Quite hectic, I'm sure," she shrugged prettily. "Moving, unpacking, learning new names and places. —Quite hectic."

"That's part of it," he nodded, "but not all."

"What else could you mean?" she gave him a semi-sweet smile, while accepting a glass from her father and scooting against the far sofa arm in the same motion. "Savannah is known for its hospitality—and as you've a knack for charming all-sorts-of-people, surely your needs have been well-tended?"

"The people here are hospitable," he agreed, taking the drink now offered to him. "And I've made many new friends. —One in the most extraordinary place. Would you believe, right in the middle of that storm we had last week—"

"Oh please!" Mandria made a strong objection. But that was his second reference to their disastrous affair and she had to consider if cruelty prompted it. "I mean, it was such a miserable day and time for all of us. —Wasn't it father? A day unfit for man or beast…and yet, plenty of both were lurking about."

Sam glanced at Evelyn as he reclaimed his chair, but she didn't seem to understand Mandria's point any better than he. Why he expected it of her irritated him. Evelyn always had been a numb-head.

"Ah, but what a day for staying in bed," Tom leaned to the back of the sofa with a pleasurable sigh—while Mandria tried to keep from choking on the sip she'd just taken. "And not feeling a bit guilty about it," he finished sending her one of those melting smiles.

Mandria could only stab at him with an icy green glare—for the present—but, how dare he say such a thing! Damn him for feeling no guilt! And damn that smile too!

"Well, I agree with Tom," Evelyn nodded over her sherry. "I did a bit of napping myself that day. It was so nice and cool—and that is a rarity during the summers here."

"Since when do you need an excuse to nap, Evelyn?" Sam's chuckle had an acid edge. "You sleep more than anyone I know."

"But that makes you a lucky man, Father," Mandria leapt to her mother's defense. "Your wife, at least, has a clear conscience. …I wonder how many husbands could make that claim."

"Especially those husbands who don't sleep more than three or four hours a night," Evelyn laughed, favoring Sam with a nod and the sweetest of smiles.

"Humph!" Sam retorted in annoyance. "Very amusing, my dears. But should either of you bore our guest with your quaint sense of humor?"

"On the contrary," said Tom. "I enjoy humor every bit as much as beauty—and as these ladies are blessed with both, I can only thank you, Sam," he raised his glass to the women, "for allowing me to share their company this evening."

"Goodness, what a pretty speech," Mandria commented. "You must be swamped with all kinds of invitations, Tom! But if you aren't careful, our ladies will come to believe that only the prospect of taking your fill—at table—inspires such eloquence." The flowery denial she expected didn't come and glancing at Tom, she found his expression quizzical. It was bookended by the ones of confusion worn by her parents. "Oh dear," she rose to move about the room again, but stopped to rest her hands on the back of Evelyn's chair. "Please forgive my morbid behavior," she apologized to all. "I don't know—maybe it's the heat."

"Humph!" Sam repeated, going to fix himself another drink. He'd earned it for not administering the tongue lashing Mandria deserved. But she simply had to fall into line because she, through Tom, remained his quickest route to Allen.

Evelyn reached to pat her daughter's hand. "Well, I think you could be right, dear. Somehow, I've grown tired of summer this year too and wish autumn would hurry and come."

"Speaking of which," Tom prompted a change in subject, "I hear there is to be a Harvest Ball?"

"Yes, the last Friday in October," Evelyn replied. "It's quite an event in Savannah too—an annual sounding-board for social announcements; engagements, births, elopements, anniversaries—the like. And it has become a game among the populace just keeping their secrets until the night of the ball."

Looking Mandria's way now Tom asked, "And what must one do to wrangle an invitation?".

"Why?" she asked curiously. "Have you an announcement to make?"

He chuckled, and to Mandria, it truly sounded...well, wicked. "Oh, I could think of one or two. But my brother will be here by then and a ball might be just the place for meeting new friends."

218

"Indeed it would!" Sam seized opportunity by the gonads. "Just plan to include yourself and Allen in our party. —When does the boy arrive, by the way?"

"…Late August or early September," Tom answered after a moment. …Why did it bother him for Sam to use Allen's name so easily? …And thinking back, he couldn't recall ever using it to Sam. Odd thing, that. He'd have to ask Mandria if she'd mentioned his brother to her father.

"Wait a moment," Mandria lowered herself on a chair beside Evelyn, "Tom may have others he'd want to include. —A certain lady, perhaps?" she asked, unable to stop herself.

"I certainly do," he looked directly at her. "Lucy," he took his time with a nod. "Do you think she would accompany Allen to the ball?"

"What a lovely idea," Evelyn approved. "Lucy would enjoy that—don't you agree, Mandy? She has already said she wanted to meet Tom's brother."

"I'm sure she would," Mandria answered vaguely.

"Well, that was easy enough," Sam said with great satisfaction.

"You are still being hasty, Father," Mandria tried to re-enter her question. "Tom must have others to invite—"

"As will your dear mother," Sam waved aside her notion "Our pre-ball gathering is always a large one, so what difference would a few extra guests make?" But he didn't care if all of Savannah came to his doorstep, as long as Allen was among them.

"Pardon the intrusion," Jed stood rigid with ceremony in the doorway. "Dinner is served."

"Thank you, Jed," Evelyn rose to await her husband's escort. "Mandy, bring Tom along and we'll see what Cook has been up to all afternoon."

"Shall we?" Tom already stood before her with a pro-offered arm.

But as they followed, Mandria managed to slow their pace for a private word with him. "I would appreciate a list of those you want included for our party," she explained, determined to hear him name the woman he intended to squire that evening. "It's our custom to meet here before the ball and as refreshments are served, we'll need to know how many to prepare for and then—"

"Lady," he interrupted, and his gaze seemed to devour her. "You know all my friends. But I would prefer attending your gathering, here and at the ball, as a party of two—you and I—with the whole dance floor and all the music to ourselves."

"Well…," And her voice failed when she realized he was not attempting a compliment, but living up to terms already stated. Of course Kathy couldn't attend. Her father had expressly forbidden having Tom's affair with his former mistress thrown in his face. "Never mind," she uttered, looking away from the devastating warmth of his smile—and how she wished he'd stop playing with her fingers again! "Just never mind," she sighed.

They were entering the dining room so Tom wasn't able to question her response. Nor were they alone again for the remainder of the evening. The four of them dined, chatted a while longer over coffee and said good night at the door. It was all very pleasant. But neither Tom nor Mandria slept well that night…

"Miss Mandy?" the voice came softly as morning air. "Miss Mandy, you ought to be waking now. …Please?"

Mandria opened her eyes to see the new maid standing over her. Barely in her teens, the thin girl was nervous and still unsure of her duties—which Mandria knew to be her fault. "Yes?" she asked. "What is it, Joleen?"

"This here letter came for you a while back. Your mama say to let you sleep, but now its near-on-to noon. …Did I do wrong to wake you?"

Mandria focused on the envelope and nearly snatched it from the girl as she sat up. "No, I'm glad you woke me. Thank you," she sat staring at the thing.

Pride beamed on Joleen's small face. "Can Ah do something else? —Want me to draw your bath water?"

"Not now," Mandria's attention remained on the envelope. "Thank you anyway."

Still the girl lingered. "Then Ah'll lay out your clothes."

"No, I just want—"

"Ah know! You want breakfast on a tray?"

"No—no, no, no!" Mandria said impatiently, and then had to look at Joleen's crestfallen expression. "Oh dear," she lamented. "Please, I'm not upset with you. It's something else entirely. I appreciate your wanting to be helpful—truly, I do—but I must read this letter, and that's all I want to do now."

"But Ah must can do something," Joleen uttered softly. "Ah must can."

Mandria sighed in defeat. "All right, then. Bring me a cup tea."

"Yes ma'am, Miss Mandy!" she exclaimed and smiling brightly, she left.

Nodding, Mandria watched her go. She had vowed never to own a personal slave, which didn't stop her father from giving her one anyway. But she hadn't called on the girl for much of anything, and just let her do what she liked about the house. Joleen, however, preferred serving Mandria and her endearing eagerness made it hard to stick to principal. *What else?* she thought. *...How many more rules can I break?* she sighed again while opening the latest note.

*Dear Illusive Lady,*

*To say I found yesterday's meeting disturbing is far from the truth. —I haven't had a peaceful moment since! And why do my notes still go unanswered? Truly, aren't you playing the game to extremes? A look, some small gesture of recognition—a written reply—would not give us away.*

*Please, won't you consider my feelings in this?*

"Then I did see him yesterday!" Mandria began an immediate mental list: Mike; any among the young gallants who'd bowed to her on the street; Ransom—unthinkable as that was—; his friends in the square, including the Italian with the familiar face and name.

"All right, I've narrowed it down to these few—and can stop suspecting the entire male population of Savannah—but how do I find out which one?" It dawned on her then, that it made no difference. As long as Tom remained a question in her life, the rest simply made no difference at all. "So, maybe I should state my position and get this thing settled. —Today!" she tried bolstering her courage. "I went to his room once. What would I lose by going again? Besides, anything is better than sitting here reading these notes and talking to myself."

"Beg your pardon, Miss Mandy?" Joleen came with the tea. "You speaking to me?"

"No," Mandria gave a startled laugh, "I was just…sitting-here-talking-to-myself!" And she laughed all the way to the desk, where she added this note to the others in her locked drawer, then back to crawl into bed again.

"Miss Mandy?" Joleen giggled along with her. "Are you all right?"

"Yes, I'm fine. Really," Mandria dabbed at her eyes before accepting the tray. "I'm just really happy about a decision I made."

"Now that's good!" Joleen laced her fingers behind her and rocked up on her toes. "Cause if you're happy, then Ah can be too!"

"…Joleen, why did you say that?" Mandria looked at her curiously. "Your feelings shouldn't depend on my moods. —Here," she patted the bed. "Sit down while I finish my tea. I want you to tell me things that truly make you happy."

Joleen sidled closer and ran timid fingers over a square of the rose satin bed spread. "Ah do think a bed like this would make me very glad. Then Ah wouldn't need no potion. Ah could have that Willie Luther then, Ah bet-ya. He be my man for sure."

"Your man? …But you can't be more than thirteen or so—"

"Ah fifteen, ma'am," she straightened proudly, "and full growed to the way between men and womens."

"Then you're wiser than I am," Mandria nodded. "But who is this Willie Luther?"

"Oh Miss Mandy," her smile appeared, bright as a sunbeam, "he's the new stable boy over to the O'Rourke's—and he drive for Miss Nico some too. But do Ah see him, my heart just want to bust, 'cause he so fine in my eye!"

"Then what was the talk of potions? Doesn't he feel the same about you?"

The smile faded and Joleen assumed a pouting posture. "He did. —Ah know he did! But them kitchen mammies won't let him be. Don't give him no rest; —no time for me."

"I'm not sure I understand—?"

"It a game them witches play with all the new men on the square, Miss Mandy. They calls it Breaking-Them-In and the men—well, they ain't got no sense above the waist no ways. Can't see they the ones being used by a bunch of old women can't get a man no other way. Feed them and fuck them—that's what they does: feed them and fuck them!"

"...You can't be serious," Mandria responded incredulously.

"But Ah am! —Done something 'bout it too! Ah paid visit to my own witch and she got me a love potion brewing for that Willie Luther. Then he'll look back to me. He'll do that, Ah'll bet-ya!"

"Oh Joleen," Mandria nodded, "potions and witches? I think you're wasting your time," she handed back the tray and moved to the edge of the bed.

"Ha! You don't know my witch," Joleen insisted. "She first-class— from Defauskie Island!"

"Well, don't say I didn't warn you," Mandria rose to select a day-dress from her wardrobe. "Now run along, my dear. I'll be leaving as soon I'm ready."

"All right, but you'll see 'bout my witch. She good!" Joleen grinned as she went out the door with the tray. "Oh," she called back, "Your mama wants to see you!"

As Mandria bathed and dressed, she shamed herself for belittling Joleen's beliefs. Her own hadn't proved so successful, had they? "And who knows?" she laughed a little, "Maybe I should pay a visit to that first-class Defauskie Island witch..."

# CHAPTER 19

Tom sat at his desk, surrounded by several school texts. He was taking notes, trying to create a study schedule for the coming year. He hadn't particularly wanted to begin the project today, but was searching for a quieter subject than Mandria to occupy his mind and finally, it had worked. He was so involved that he paid little attention to the footsteps in the hall. In fact, it was several minutes longer, before he looked up and listened. Someone was pacing back and forth outside his door: six steps one way; a turn; and steps going in the other direction. So, taking curiosity by the knob, he opened the door and looked out.

"Mandria?" he said as she turned to face him. "What are you doing out here?"

"Just...walking," she shrugged prettily.

"Really?" he folded his arms, grinned and looked up and down the walls. "I must try that sometime. I've never paid notice to the scenic view in this hallway."

"Tom Scott, don't you dare make fun of me!" she hissed, coming to wag a finger in his face. "I didn't like it last night and I don't like it now!" she glanced about for assurance her voice hadn't carried.

"Lady, I've never made fun of you," he nodded defensively. "And I'm sorry if you thought so, but—"

"Oh, never mind," she interrupted. "May I come in?"

"Please do," he made way for her.

Almost as soon as she'd passed him, Mandria turned with a question she couldn't ask the previous night. "Tell me, how is Kathy?"

Tom closed the door, paused, and locked it before turning to face her. And Mandria wanted to rip out her tongue because the silence between them was deafening.

"Why did you ask that?" he held her gaze. "Why?" he repeated, coming toward her.

"I wish I hadn't," she managed. "It just seemed…polite."

"And why do we need politeness?" he pulled her almost, but not quite against him.

Mandria lowered her eyes. "Well, it's better than nothing."

"Nothing?" he lifted her face in his hands. "Nothing, Mandria?" he kissed the edges of her mouth. "Nothing at all?" And seeing she wasn't interested in replying, he kissed her deeply, tenderly, with all the feeling he could convey.

She shuddered when he moved on to the curve of her throat. "Tom, I'm…wait! We have to settle some things first."

"All right," he teased at her ear now, "as long as this comes second."

"I'm serious. I've made enough mistakes."

"I don't understand a damn thing you're saying," he was back for another taste of her mouth. "We made no mistakes, lady. It was perfect between us—every wonderful moment; every wonderful—"

"Don't do that!" she pulled away and went to the window. "Don't lie to me. There has to honesty between us or I'll never get through this."

Tom nodded in confusion. "I thought I knew why you came. I thought you were through with pretending."

"Pretending?" green fire danced in her eyes. "I didn't pretend to hear what was said in this very room," she started toward him. "I didn't pretend to hurt. It hurt like hell!"

"But surely, you understand—"

"No! I'll never understand that. How—*how*—could you deal with my father while I lay naked in your bed?"

"Mandria, I am not the one who ran from an explanation," he said impatiently. "And straight to Mike with the damnedest proposition!"

"You know?" she halted abruptly, her hands pressed to warm cheeks. "…About the tavern and, and, and—?"

"Even to the number of drinks you had—you're damned right I know!" he retorted. But because she seemed so stricken, his reply lacked the sharpness he fully meant to imply.

"And afterwards?" she uttered, hardly above a whisper. "Do…do you know who I left with?"

Tom stared at her. "…Are you saying you don't?"

Mandria paled considerably as she lowered herself on the edge of the day-bed. "That's exactly it. I don't know."

"Well, I'll be damned," he nodded, realizing this explained much he'd found puzzling. It hadn't been him from whom she'd run, but the unknown. "So…what do you remember?" he proceeded carefully, because now he, too, was dealing with unknowns.

"Nothing. But the worst happened," she said close to tears. "And he left money. I am now a paid w…whore!"

"No—Mandria, no," he sat beside her. "Don't say that—don't even think it!" he slid an arm about her shoulders. "That isn't—"

"But it's true! And maybe it was for the best," she straightened, shrugging away his touch. "That's why I came today. Tom, if you don't hate me too much—or even if you do—you'll do exactly as I say now or…or I'll make you regret it."

Tom leaned to the back of the cushions and rubbed a hand across his forehead. Her tone seemed as rigid and unyielding as her arrow straight spine. Curiosity made him want to know why. "Lady, I'm feeling a lot of things at the moment, but hatred isn't one of them."

"Good," she glanced at him over her shoulder. "That should make things a little easier, I guess."

Instinctively—and because she sounded a bit forlorn—Tom pulled her back against him, locking his arms across her belly. "So what would you have me do?" he nuzzled the nape of her neck. "I hope it's something we do well together."

"Tom, stop!" she freed herself, rose and quickly returned to the window. "I can't think when you do that," she nodded. But feeling braver from across the room, she continued. "You made a bargain with Father. So, you are going to make one with me too—whether you want to or not."

"I see," he stretched his long legs out before him, crossed his arms and grinned. "Let's hear it then, lady."

"Well, as I understand it, you're to...to keep company with me; to flaunt me before my father?"

"Yes, but—"

"And in return, Kathy will belong to you?"

"That's what was said, but Mandria—"

"No buts, Tom! If you expect my cooperation—which you must have to get Kathy—my price is this: you will make love to me whenever I demand it of you."

"Mandria?" Tom said in abject surprise. "—What game are you playing now?"

"None. I swear to you that I'm serious."

"You can't be! No one makes love on demand—and certainly not us!"

"No? Prostitutes do it everyday. And you managed it the first time I came here. You made love to me when you really wanted Kathy."

"Damn it, I did not!" he came to his feet.

"Oh that's right," she began to pace, hoping to discourage his violation of the space between them. "You did that *before* you knew you could buy her from Father. But never mind. I found our time together more than pleasurable—and I will again. So, if you and Father can take your lovers and trade them all around, then you and I can too. And it seems I've already started my collection—for the grand sum of $20!"

Tom was growing very angry, very fast. "Let me get this straight," he glared at her. "We're to keep our damned lovers; see each other too—when you *demand* it—and a *pleasurable time* is all the hell you want from me?"

"Stop it!" she stomped a foot. "That is how I got into this awful mess—letting you twist my words; believing your pretty lies!"

"You beautiful little idiot—I did not lie to you!"

Now Mandria was angry too and came at him hands on hips, her voice dripping venom. "Why do you insist on denying the truth? I am not deaf or stupid—or anyone's beautiful-little-idiot! Did you or did you not have an affair with Kathleen Morgan?"

"Yes! But it ended before I met you."

"Come now. Can't you be more original? Those were almost Father's exact words of instruction to you."

"Mandria, I'm telling you nothing happened the way you think. —Nothing!"

"Oh?" she taunted with the sweetness of a smile. "And how many *ways* are there, Mister Scott?"

"…Lady, you are close to finding out," he replied in a tone that should have warned her to back off.

Instead, she jabbed him in the chest, emphasizing each of her points. "Exactly the reason I came to you, sir. You are an excellent teacher and I wish to learn more; all those *ways*—without the lies; without the useless endearments; and just for my own personal enjoyment. Truly, I won't monopolize you. You and Kathy can spend all the time you wish together. —After you have accommodated me!"

The words had barely passed Mandria's lips when Tom snatched her bodily from the floor. "All right, damn you! I promised crudeness once. Let's see how long you play at this!" And tossing her on the day-bed, he immediately penned her there and covered her startled mouth with a bruising kiss. Strong, determined hands roamed her body and a sharp gasp ensued when gruff fingers closed on her breast to administer the squeeze he did not dare around her throat.

But Mandria didn't try to restrain him and when the kiss ended, she looked at Tom with heated, tear-bright eyes. "W…wouldn't it be easier if I undressed first?" she breathed.

"Yes," he answered coldly. And sitting up, he pushed her feet to the floor.

"Then I will," she rose and started for the bedroom.

"Oh no, Mandria—not in there!" he said sternly. …*How could she think of defiling what they'd shared in that bedroom? And how would he now explain his objection?* "I would enjoy watching you disrobe. Take your clothes off right where you stand."

"Here?" she turned to face him. "…In the middle of the floor?"

"You said you weren't deaf," he folded his arms across his chest. "If you're so determined to become a $20.00 whore, then act like one. —As your *teacher* I insist."

Mandria could feel her face warm as she began to unfasten her dress. "...Does Kathy disrobe before you?" she asked, pulling her arms from the sleeves and lifting the garment over her head.

"She has on occasion," he answered curtly. "Then again, she enjoyed undressing me."

"Do you want me to undress you too?" she asked, keeping the dress against her as she stepped out of her slippers and under things. "As Kathy does...on occasion?"

"I want you to drop the damn dress and show yourself," he returned. "And I don't want you to say Kathy's name another time!"

His words stung and she lowered her eyes as she deeded her clothing to the floor. She wasn't to mention the woman Tom preferred. ... *But why does he?* she mused, glancing over her nudity. *Is my body so unattractive?* She wasn't vain, but she could find nothing drastically wrong with her form. ...Except for the red streaks on her breast where he'd handled her harshly. But those would soon fade, wouldn't they? And raising a hand, she brushed at them, as if to wipe away the flaws.

Tom made a sound—a moan—that seemed to emanate from deep in his chest. And looking up, Mandria was surprised to see him standing; coming toward her; and staring, very pointedly at those same offensive marks. She could not guess his thoughts, but his expression remained as stern as before, and when he reached for her breast again, she trembled.

"Don't!" he pled hoarsely, his hand freezing in mid-air. "...Mandria, don't shrink from me—don't!"

So, closing her eyes, knowing he would touch her and she would let him, she waited. But there was only tenderness in his caress; no anger. ... *Why?* she wondered searching the mellowed blue of his eyes as he drew her against him. She wanted to understand. *Why would he care about a temporary blemish when he's broken my heart?* And now, his arms tightened possessively about her; his face was buried in her hair; and he whispered her name as if his own heart was breaking. *Why? —Why?*

Then it didn't seem to matter. She was pressing herself closer and that mattered; keeping his arms around her—that mattered too; and raising her hands to his face, she drew his mouth to hers—reveling in his immediate response—because that mattered most of all. She felt his yearning as his lips moved from her eyelids to nose, cheeks and back again to each before settling on her up-turned mouth. And she knew if she lived to be a hundred, she'd not regret the decision to broker this pocket of happiness for herself…

And it wasn't done. Now, he was lifting her; returning to the day-bed, where he laid her before kneeling on the floor at her side. He said nothing, just hovered there, gazing at her body. No words were needed when he brushed his lips against her throat, found his way to her breasts and tugged and tongued her nipples back to alertness. Yet, when Mandria tried to pull him closer, urging him to take a firmer hold, he caught her hands and holding them away, moved lower to caress her stomach, navel, her lower belly and upper thigh…

Dear God, how Tom did want her! How he yearned, as with no other, to taste her in all possible places and ways; to make her believe in his love by the sheer, unrestrained intimacy of such. …But was exposing her to this the wisest or kindest thing at the moment? The greater their intimacies, the more she'd feel degraded if she chose to reject him—which was still possible when the truth was revealed about the night she couldn't remember. So uttering a groan of denial— wondering if the passion he felt for her would ever be granted free rein—he reluctantly turned her onto her side…

Mandria's blood raced through her veins with a velocity that had her ears ringing. Half rising, she had reached for Tom a second time, wanting to draw him upward; to feel his weight upon her and the emptiness within filled. Then, she heard the deep, almost animal-hungry groan as he turned her toward the wall and began a trail of kisses over her hip, then ever so slowly, up the column of her spine. She became so overwhelmed by sensation—so completely stimulated—she did not even wonder how he'd managed to undress. It was wonder enough finding him naked and lying spooned against the length of her body from behind; hands, filled with her breasts; legs entangled with hers; her nether-lips caressing the sides of his straddled and hardened penis. "Tom?" she leaned her head back into his shoulder. "Now, please?" Surely, he wouldn't deny her again. It would take only a slight move and she could be welcoming the rhythmic magic of his body working within hers, even from this back to front position, if possible.

Then, it was happening. With sure hands, he had her hips shifted; positioned for his entry. Reaching between her thighs, he pressed just the head of his penis into the mouth of her vagina, massaging her against him there. On a smaller scale, the fingers of his other hand moved in imitation on her nipples and hot breath assisted his play-mating tongue at her ear, causing the start of a quiver that soon encompassed her entire being. She was nearly panting, wanting full impalement; craving his penetration to the point of going after it for herself.

Tom allowed her to do just that. Encouraged it, by lifting one of her legs back and over his hip, opening space for her to probe her own depths with however much of him she wished to use; to seek her own rhythm while he moved only in counterpoint and from as many angles as she wanted to try. ...Then she began to climax, her inner muscles tightening about him; her spasms starting that build toward eruption, and Tom was not going to miss sharing in that. Taking back the lead, he directed them toward the conclusion both desired, and it came with the ferocity of a volcano.

Their bodies still joined, Mandria had somehow ended face-up, her limbs spread-eagle and laying right on top of Tom, who held her there with both arms keeping her exactly as she was, because he hoped to make a point of that. "Lady," he said huskily, "I have some questions to ask, and only truth will do when we are this connected. All right?"

"All right," she nodded.

"Well, was that as soul-shattering for you as it was for me?"

"I'm afraid so," she nodded again.

"I'll tell you how much. I think when we get around to putting our souls back together, we'll find the pieces have become interchangeable, one with the other."

231

"That…that's a really beautiful thought," she admitted.

"Yes, so answer me this: Could you honestly share what we just did?" he placed a hand over their joined parts. "What we're still sharing, and not come to hate me or yourself?"

"I don't know," she replied softly. "But I'm going to try. I have to."

"Why?"

"Because of your choice in dealing with Father. And if you're trying to talk me out of it, don't you think it's a little late?"

"Yes," he nodded now. "But I meant why would you want me at such a cost to yourself?"

"Maybe I just don't want to give you up—not to Kathy or to any other woman."

"But why? I want a reason, Mandria—the real reason." And he pressed more firmly on their juncture point, reminding her that only truth would do.

Mandria did not want to answer; never wanted to cede back any hard-won advantage that had gotten her here. …But she was naked, sprawled on top of the man like some sacrificial virgin, their bodies joined and him effectively stressing the why of that, for God's sake. And because of it, she just wasn't capable of denying him anything. "Well," she uttered, really grateful to be facing the ceiling instead of having to see that her admission meant little. "Well, I seem to have fallen in love with you. And I don't want to be with anyone else… like this. It's really as simple as that."

After a giant sigh, Tom rolled her to his side and turned her face to his, so that she had to meet his eyes. "For once, you could be right. It can be simple if you will just remember to keep that love foremost in your mind."

"…I don't understand."

"I know, and Mandria, I have so much to explain—"

"Tom, no! …Please?" she hugged herself to him. "I've accepted your choice. I don't want to hear reasons. Once was more than enough."

"Lady, you are running scared—just as you did before. But you will hear me out, or there can be no bargain between us; …nothing."

Mandria sat up, needing at least a little space to pamper her pride. "Then say what you must. But I want you and I confessed my love. Isn't that enough for you lord over me?"

Tom swung himself to sit beside her. "Damn, you've got a wicked tongue," he commented, then became thoughtfully quiet.

And to Mandria, that silence felt like a wall she didn't want there. "Well, even the smallest animal will turn when it's cornered," she offered defensively. And suddenly feeling her nakedness, drew the spread across herself.

"I've done enough hunting to know that," Tom nodded, still pensive. Then with another sigh, he added, "Mandria, I just wish we could be alone somewhere; —anywhere with room enough to settle this."

"But we're alone here," she puzzled.

"Not as we need to be," he laced his fingers with hers, and leaned his head back on the wall. "No, for this we need time and space with no interruptions: room for talking—or shouting; …for loving too," he kissed the hand he still held and added, "Even for tears, if it comes to that."

"…Would it?" she asked softly. "Come to tears, I mean?"

"Only if you felt like shedding them," he answered, his eyes locking with hers. "And, lady, I'd do my damnedest to see that you didn't. But it would be honest and I want honesty between us more than you do. There is just something you need to know and I want my best chance for making you see my side of it."

Now Mandria became pensive. Wouldn't it be worth risking tears to have him to herself even for a little while? It might be for the first and the last time, but it was a temptation she couldn't resist. "…We could go to Tybee," she began and was truly surprised when it earned his full and expectant attention. "I mean, Mama asked this morning if I'd take the servants down for some cleaning while Jed installs the new storm shutters. …I know where Uncle Ran keeps the key to his cabin and I could meet you over there."

"When?" he sat facing her now. "When can we leave—and how do we get there?"

"The same way we always do," she answered. "The shrimp boats come and go daily from Thunderbolt. A ride can be purchased on any of them."

"Then I'm going this afternoon," he reached to the floor for his trousers and stepped into them. "When will you be there?" he looked now for his shirt.

Not understanding his eagerness, she nonetheless, was dressing herself as he did. "Tomorrow. It will take that long to pack and ready the servants. …But Tom?"

"Yes ma'am?" he said happily, sitting to pull on his boots.

Fully dressed now, Mandria felt brave enough to continue. "Well, won't Kathy be upset about this? …I would, if I were in her place."

Tom looked at her for a moment, then rose and gathered her close to his chest while deciding what to say. "I swear to you, I will answer any question you have when we are at Tybee. Can I ask your patience until then?"

"All right," she tilted her head back, wanting to see assurance in his eyes. What she saw instead, left her wanting a kiss. And he must have felt it too, because the hands cupping her face were drawing her lips to his.

"But speaking of places," he said right against her mouth, "stay in your own," his teasing tongue parted her lips, "and I do mean the one exactly where you are." Then he was kissing her with a thoroughness that had her vowing to see herself and the servants packed and gone in record time…

# CHAPTER 20

Mandria inhaled deeply as the sea breeze mussed her hair and gingerly whipped her skirt forward. She was anxious to join Tom at the O'Rourke cabin; ...and yet, as she moved along Back River, indecision slowed her pace. It wasn't the honesty he'd promised that disturbed her, or the knowledge that if things didn't go well, the memory of their time alone here, might have to last a lifetime. But she did feel a bit uneasy about the steps she'd taken to ensure the quality of it...

Already, she'd lost count of the lies told over the last day and a half, and it worried her only now, that she felt no guilt for any of them. It started when she'd gone home and casually mentioned that Tom would be spending time up-river, helping Sebastian Rizza survey a plot of land. Her mother said, "Why how very nice of him." Her father just shrugged indifferently. A little later, she planted the notion that she'd be going down river, offering to take the servants on to Tybee as her mother had asked, which gleaned a "Thank you, dear," from Evelyn and a second shrug from Sam. So began a frantic day of packing, her talk with Joleen and more lies.

When Mandria asked the girl if she'd like to go too, she was elated. "Miss Mandy," she played nervously with the hem of her apron, "do you still want to know the thing would make me happier in all the world?"

"All right," Mandria nodded, "what is it?"

"Well," Joleen stammered as she danced about the floor, "…well, Ah'm just going to tell you! —Right out loud!"

"Joleen, what is it, for heaven's sake?" Mandria smiled at her antics.

"Well," she took a breath and rushed on, "well—could you borrow Willie Luther and take him too?"

"…Borrow him?" Mandria laughed.

"Yes-um—yes ma'am!" Joleen was squeezing Mandria's hand now. "My witch done sent word. The potions are ripe and ready for dosing, Miss Mandy! Could I get that Willie Luther off to myself, Ah could win him back now, Ah bet-ya! There wouldn't be no more hurting bout that man no more! Please, Miss Mandy—please do this for me?"

That Mandria was equally excited over the prospect of being alone with Tom, greatly swayed her decision to help Joleen, but after a considerable pause, she added a request. "If I can arrange this, will you do me a favor in return? …You see, there is a man I'm hurting about too. And he's at Tybee now, waiting to see me."

"So you want some of my potion?" Joleen's smile grew wider and wiser.

Mandria shrugged. "I don't see where it would hurt. I just want to make our time together special. …Maybe something he wouldn't be able to forget."

"Oh, Miss Mandy, it will be!" she twirled in delight. "We going to have those men for our very own! —Fact is," she giggled, "they'll be so mad for us, we might need a potion to turn them off!"

"Not in a million years," Mandria nodded. "…But how do we get them to take it?"

"So easy," Joleen assured her with the wave of a hand. "What man you know going to refuse a cool swallow when he hot and tired? —Or a drink to relax on come the evening time?"

"That's all? Just mix it in something to drink?" Mandria asked, wanting to be sure.

Joleen's laughter sounded like bubbling syrup. "No ma'am, that ain't all! That's just the beginning, Miss Mandy—just the fire what start the kettle to boiling!"

So, here Mandria was, walking the river's edge, clasping a small vial in her pocket—trying to hold on to her nerve—and praying with every step, that Joleen knew what she was talking about…

"Mandria?" Tom called. And she turned to see him waving from some twenty yards out in water. "Hey, pretty lady, care to join me?"

"Maybe later," she answered as he swam toward her. "B…but I'm terribly thirsty. Have you anything to drink at the cabin?" And she noted that he swam with the same easiness that he walked. …*Isn't there anything the man doesn't do well?* she wondered

"As a matter of fact, I do," he said gaining a foothold in chest-deep water. "There is white wine—brandy too, if you want to go that route again." And as he waded toward her, the water line dropped below his waist.

"Tom?" her eyes widened and her grip on the vial tightened. "Are you naked?"

He stopped there and grinned at her. "As a matter of fact, no—but if you want me to be, these skivvies come off real easy."

"But even so," she glanced toward the dunes and houses beyond, "you aren't afraid of being seen?"

"We're very much alone on this end of the island, Mandria," he continued wading toward her. "Believe me, I checked that quite thoroughly."

But no more, she was certain, than she was checking him at the moment. That knee length underwear clung to the shape of his thighs—and the way it was molding him across the front… "I'll be right back!" she moved toward the dune path. "You do want a drink too, don't you?" she called from the crest.

"Not as much as I wanted to kiss you first," he answered. "But hurry back!"

And she did hurry, returning with a full glass in each hand, to find Tom lying on his back in the sand, eyes closed, the underwear still molded to him. She couldn't help it she just stood quietly beside him, ogling this near perfect male and imagining all sorts of potion-induced scenarios.

"You're spilling our drinks," Tom said, smiling up at her.

"Oh! —Oh, no!" Mandria corrected her balance. And being exceptionally careful of the glass in her right hand, she handed it to Tom before settling on her knees beside him.

"Good, I was hoping you'd choose the brandy," he sat up and took a sip.

"Why?" she asked, for lack of better to say and watched as he swallowed another.

"I'll tell you about it after while," he drank more. "Your trip down with the servants went all right?"

"Yes," she nodded, wondering what to expect. …How long would it take for the potion to work? How much would he have to drink of it first? Did it matter that she'd spilled some? She hoped not—if, indeed, it worked at all—she dearly hoped not.

"You're very quiet," Tom gazed at her, over the rim of his glass. "Do I make you uncomfortable being out here in my skivvies?"

Mandria drew courage from her own brandy before daring to answer. "No. You have a handsome body. I enjoy looking at you."

At that, he set his glass aside, rose to his knees in front of her, and reached for her blouse buttons. "Then you have to return the favor. I like looking at you too—more than anything I can think of. And lady, I'll take my hello kiss now too." Leaning toward her, he collected the boon, letting it last until her last button was undone.

Holding his wrists, Mandria glanced toward the dunes again. "You're sure we're alone out here?"

"I'm sure," he parted her blouse. "Damn, lady," he smiled, seeing that she wore no undergarments. "I believe you have your heart in this adventure," he fondled the fullness of her breasts.

"In every way," she handed him his glass again.

"And beneath your skirt?" he persisted. "Would your boldness allow you to go that far?"

"Finish your drink and I…I'll show you. But out there," she pointed to the river. "I was thinking about our first kiss…?"

"Offer accepted," he drained the glass, rose and extended a hand to her. Yet once standing, Mandria was pulled against him and caged in his arms. "Just a moment," he pecked at her mouth. "I feel a sudden need to kiss you, lady," he said against her lips. "Indulge me, please." And indeed, she did, silently blessing Joleen and her witch for this *sudden need* of his.

Hand in hand, Tom then led her into the moving water, where he stopped to watch when she was deep enough for it to lap at her breasts through the opened blouse. The heated eyes that he lifted to hers, drew her right into his arms again, while beneath her skirt, his hands gripped her bare buttocks. He turned her and with palms pressed flat to her belly—and she fairly tingling with anticipation—his hands did a slow downward slide until he could cup and hold her sex.

And then he spoke. And it was over, for his hands had returned to grasp her arms. "Mandria, I've so much to tell you," he said next to her ear. "You may not like some of it, but will you make me a promise?"

"All right," she sighed in disappointment. Evidently the potion had failed and she was doomed to suffer through his explanation with no magical moments to remember for either of them.

Tom turned her to face him again, vying for her strict attention. "Then promise you will hear me out. And that you won't leave this island until you have. If you're angry, take it out on me—but do it to my face. If you're happy, I want to share that too. If you're puzzled—as I am by parts of this—maybe we can work out some answers together. Now, is that asking too much?"

"No," she said softly. "But I hadn't planned to leave. I came here to be with you."

"And I to be with you," his arms tightened about her. "Lady, we do belong together. And for that reason, I want you to believe every word I'm about to say—starting with the fact that I love you more than anything on this earth."

Mandria straightened, her eyes instantly filled with tears, and never had Tom seen a more sorrowful expression. "Oh, what have I done?" she placed a hand on his cheek; his forehead; then a hand on each cheek. "Oh, I thought it would cause you to enjoy making love to me, but I never considered it could make you say things you don't mean. This is so much worse than the brandy, because I don't remember a thing. But you will remember everything, because you aren't the least bit drunk. Then you'll hate me—I just know you will. Oh, now I've ruined this whole thing!"

"Lady?" he puzzled. "What in the hell are you talking about?"

"It's the potion, Tom! I put a love potion in your drink, and it's making you think you love me—which is well and good for me, but I can't keep you drugged for the rest of your life!"

As her words registered, a smile skittered across Tom's mouth. Then, he began to chuckle and when that turned into great fits of laughter, Mandria was horrified! Could her witches brew be responsible for this terrible hysteria too?

"Tom—please," she tugged at his arm. "Please, let's get out of the water, all right?" And she led him to shore, though he kept laughing. "Come on—and say something. Scold me; send me away—anything— just please stop this laughing!"

But he couldn't. "A potion?" he yowled as they returned to their previous spot, where she encouraged him to sit again. "Mandria, did you really give me a love potion?" And with her guilty nod, he fell to his back and gave in to laughter again.

She hovered, wiping at his face and hair. "Oh, I'm so worried about you," she administered comforting pats. "There'll be no punishment cruel enough if I've harmed you with my meddling!"

Still laughing, Tom's arms went about her and in one motion, their positions were reversed. "You wonderful, confused, beautiful little fool," he smiled happily. "The only punishment you'll get will pleasure us both. In a very few minutes, I'm going to grind your pretty little ass into this sand—and if you choose to believe I'm under a spell, then go ahead. But I will enjoy it, because I always do with you. And I will say I love you—because damn it, Mandria, I do!"

"It...it's the potion," she warned, as he pulled her skirt up and out of his way.

"So you say," he went for maximum depth. "So shut up and humor me while it lasts," he said against her lips. "I love you, woman," he pounded the words and himself into her. "I love you; …I love you; …I love you!"

It was late afternoon when Mandria made her way toward the cabin again, and this time, carrying a covered plate of food for Tom. The sun would be setting in an hour or so and never had she seen it so brimming full of orange fire. It hung above the river like a gigantic ball, glorifying its own image in the rippling, changing reflections on the water. Knowing she, too, was bathed in the wonderful, warm color, Mandria glanced at her arms and the skin at the neckline of her peasant blouse. She felt she looked her best at this time of day, and hoped Tom would care to notice. Physical appeal might be her only remaining forte with him now.

Her pulse quickened when she thought of their earlier meeting on the riverbank. If ever a man seemed sincere in professing his love—in the making of it—Tom certainly had. Yet, now that he'd had time to recover from her trickery, how would she find him? Joleen had offered more of the potion, but in good conscience, Mandria couldn't accept it. Tom had a right to anger; a right to treat her coldly in protest of words said that he didn't feel; and worst of all, he had every right not to bother. She wouldn't blame him if he'd already left the cabin and returned to Savannah.

If he hadn't though, she owed him his moment of fury—as well as her promised attention to whatever he'd wanted to say. At least, she'd know his words were his own now. Tom had wanted to talk in the afterglow of their union and she'd begged him to wait for that very reason. He wasn't very happy about it, though had finally agreed. … But why had he seemed more upset by the delay than with what she'd done? She didn't think she'd ever truly understand him…

"Hey, lady," Tom greeted from the gazebo with an outstretched hand. And when she had accepted it, and given him the supper plate, he looked back toward the river. "It's going to be a beautiful sunset, don't you think?" he ate as they stood side by side.

"Yes. Yes, I do," she nodded; glad he didn't yet seem hostile. But she wasn't glad his shirt was unbuttoned. She needed a clear mind to face what was coming and here she was fighting an urge to place her hands on his bare chest. "I...uh, do my best thinking at this time of day. There are fewer distractions—usually."

"Exactly," he sat on the railing facing her, "And that is precisely what I've been doing out here: thinking about you."

"And?" she braced, unable to meet his eyes.

"And after your...delve into the occult, I'm more convinced than ever that I was right about you—and the decisions I've made over the last few weeks."

"Oh," she responded softly. "Well, I don't blame you. I want you to know that."

Tom gazed at her for a moment, and chuckled. "Lady, that is absolutely the last time you are going to misinterpret me." Then, draping an arm about her shoulders, he led her toward the cabin, taking the plate he'd finish later. She looked tastier anyway.

Mandria could not bring herself to question his statement. Whatever he had in mind now, at least things were still civil between them. And she kept her silence when he seated her at a table set with a bottle of sparkling white wine and two glasses.

"Did you settle your servants for the night?" he asked as he lit a lamp by the window, then joined her. And still, his expression gave no hint of his purpose.

"All but two of them," she decided to approach this awful subject herself. "Joleen and Willie Luther are younger than the rest...and right or wrong, I hadn't the heart to say no."

"No to what?" he turned his attention to the wine cork.

"Well, Joleen loves him so," she hesitated, "...and Willie Luther was dosed too."

"With your potion?" he looked up. "Was he?" he grinned.

"Yes," she nodded and it was a negative one. She was that confused with his response. "Wasn't I wrong for allowing it?"

"Mandria," he paused to consider her question, "I doubt if you could have stopped them. If they want to be together, they'll find a way in spite of you—or your potion," he added with a grin.

"But what of mutual consent?" she continued to pry at his opinion. "…Was it fair to Willie Luther?"

"If he enjoys it as much as I did—hell yes!" he chuckled, continuing to pry at the cork. "But then, Willie Luther doesn't have my reason. No man has ever had my reason."

"What does that mean?"

"We'll get to it shortly—as soon as I can loosen this damned thing!" he said in exasperation.

Mandria leaned her chin on her hands and sighed. "I've never been more puzzled in my life. I thought you'd be angry about this. I thought that was what you were saying in the gazebo."

"Do I look angry?" he kept at his task.

"…No," she nodded. And turning within herself she sought other explanations. "Maybe I'm just feeling guilty, at long last."

"What for?" he smiled as the cork finally popped free.

"Well…first, for lying to nearly everyone I know to get down here. I lied to my parents; I bribed Joleen out of a dose of her potion in exchange for bringing Willie; and to do that, I lied to Uncle Ran too. I said Jed wasn't well and needed help with the shutters. Then, there's what I did to you today—and that has to be a lie of omission. Tom, for the last day and a half, it's just been one lie after another."

"But you did it to be with me and I love that," he poured and handed her a full glass of wine. "So, let me ask you this: for all your worry, the lies and the guilt, would you do it again?"

Mandria shrugged. "Yes, a thousand times, God help me," she said rather sadly.

"He already has, lady," a smile crept across his mouth. "Now, since we were so completely distracted earlier today, may I begin this with a toast?" And he waited until she had raised her glass to his. "To those thousand times; to simpler times; and to a very productive year ahead—because, lady, you have until spring to give me one of those sons or green-eyed daughters we spoke about before."

Blushing hotly, Mandria lowered her glass untouched. "H…how could you wish for such a thing now?"

"Why not? he smiled. "I've a right to expect—"

"*You* have a right?" she injected. "What of the child's right—or mine? What could I tell him about his…, his…" And she paled as quickly as she had blushed, when faced with another possibility.

"His very proud father?" Tom finished it happily.

But Mandria nodded. "Have you forgotten I slept with another man?" she turned away. "I could be pregnant now—and I'd never know whose child I carried!"

"Mandria…" he reached for her hand, but she snatched it away.

"Both on the same night!" she anguished, covering her face with her hands. "Oh, God—don't let it happen! Don't!"

"Hey now!" Tom drew her up and into his arms. "Lady, truly, you're upset over nothing—"

"Nothing?" she looked at him in disbelief. "Oh, I see: one man's bastard is as good as another's. —Is that it?"

"Mandria would you kindly shut-up?" he clamped an arm about her waist and a hand over her mouth. "Damn if I know how this got so turned around. I was trying to tell you that we do have a right to our own children, because we—you and I—are married. That is what you did with those hours you can't remember. You are my wife—and there was not, is not and will not ever be another man in your life. You have been with me every time—and then, only the first was out of wedlock. So there; there is the truth of it."

She stared at him unable to breathe, though his hand was gone from her mouth. She heard what he said, but the words refused to penetrate, and she just continued to stare in silence.

"Well?" he finally said. "What say you, pretty lady?"

"Ev—it was you—everytime?" she spoke with great effort. "And we're married?"

"Very, very married," he kissed the tip of her nose.

"But—Kathy and your agreement with Father?" her eyes questioned.

"I almost lost you because of that," he said, reseating her. "And I promise we'll discuss them later. But for now, there are still things to settle between us, Mrs. Thomas Phillip Scott."

"Mrs. ...," Mandria uttered, pressing fingers to her temples. "Oh, I don't understand this. —It just can't be!"

"Here," he guided the wine glass to her lips. And when color returned to her cheeks, he continued. "I know you're confused, but before we get to details, it's only fair that you know something. ... Mandria, if you don't want this marriage, there is a way out for you."

"Then it isn't...valid?"

"Oh, yes ma'am," he said reaching into his watch pocket. "Valid, legal and binding," he placed a wide gold band on the table before her. "...I hope you'll take better care of this than the yellow ribbon I used in my haste."

Mandria could not take her eyes from the ring. She had considered the ribbon a joke, never suspecting the symbolic finger on which it was tied. Yet, there lay a wedding band to take its place and Tom kept saying she had a right to wear it. How she yearned to touch the cold precious metal and feel it grow warm on her hand; to believe the glimmer of hope that danced on its mellow surface. But try as she might, she could not think of single reason to feel hopeful. So, raising her eyes to Tom's she began her own search for the honesty he had promised, while the ring remained on the table. "A lot has happened between us, hasn't it?"

"Yes," he nodded. "Yes it has."

"And somehow...we've managed to be friends."

"Well, it does go a bit deeper, but what's your point?"

"That maybe it shouldn't...go deeper; that maybe you married me on impulse, because of some misplaced feeling of guilt...or pity."

"Listen, lady," he chuckled, "What I feel for you borders on cannibalism. I married you because I do love you—and you'd damn well better know that, or you'll never believe the rest of this story."

"...Then why did you offer me a way out?"

Tom leaned to the back of his chair and sighed, knowing her next reaction was likely to be explosive. "Because, in protecting my own

245

interest, I used you in ways you might find hard to forgive. Mandria, I allowed you to think terrible things about yourself—immoral things you needn't have suffered."

Mandria gazed at Tom and realized he'd done just that. "…You did, didn't you? I thought myself a whore—confessed that to you." Then she paused and he watched the dramatic color change in her eyes. "You even let me bribe you into sleeping with me—and all the while, we were married?"

"Yes, but—"

"Damn you!" she rose suddenly. "Thomas Scott, you made me act the fool—and you sent those frightful notes too. Oh! —No wonder you laughed about the love potion!"

"There is more to this—much more," he injected.

"Really?" she began to pace. "What else have I done to amuse you?"

"Lady, you have caused me nothing but sleepless nights and more worry than I thought I could handle."

"Things you'd expect from a child or a pet—but certainly not from a woman you wanted to marry!"

"Did marry," he corrected. "I did marry you."

"Am I supposed thank you after this?" she stomped her foot angrily. "Well, you can go to hell waiting. —In fact, you and Father can both go to hell! I won't be *saved* by either of you!" And turning abruptly, she headed for the door.

"Mandria, stop right there!" Tom ordered. And she stopped, hating the command he exercised so easily. "You made me a promise," he continued. "I expect you to honor it."

"What? —What promise?" she tossed the question over her shoulder.

"Not to leave this island until we settle this…one way or the other."

She faced him then, purely to emphasize the cool sweetness of her smile. "Why, Tom—darling—I wouldn't think of leaving. Somehow, I seem to be holding trumps—and you are not playing through me again. No, when I've figured out your game, I'll be back. You can count on it."

"All right," he nodded. "But, lady, the hand you've seen is from the board and it's weak. So don't go trumping aces until you know who your partner is."

"You?" she gave a bitter laugh. "And that's my only choice?"

"No," he answered. "Your father and Kathy are still playing too."

"Damn you!" she flung the door back. "Just damn you!" And she left the cabin.

Tom sat listening to her angry footsteps crunch down a shelled walkway. Then dropping his head back he made a sound somewhere between moan and growl of frustration…

# CHAPTER 21

Tom finished the wine in both glasses, re-corked the bottle and went in search of sturdier stuff. All the while, he kept telling himself that Mandria had reacted exactly as he knew she would; that it was normal for her to stomp away in a huff; that she just needed to be alone with her thoughts; that she'd promised to return and she would.

Almost immediately, she did. "Don't you say a word—not one word!" she wagged a finger as she crossed the room. And snatching the ring from the table, she held it before him. "This is mine, isn't it?"

Tom nodded yes.

"Well, I might just throw it in the ocean! —What do you think of that?"

Tom nodded no.

"And…and I might put it on and make you spend the rest of your damned life regretting it!"

Yes! Tom's pronounced nod said here.

"I should, you know. You deserve the very worst treatment I can think of."

She only got a shrug for this one.

"Well, you better remember that!" she snapped, stomping away again.

And Tom nodded again, wondering at the pleasure he'd found in such an odd conversation…

Two glasses of brandy and an hour later, Mandria called from the fast-fading twilight outside "Mister Scott, I wish to ask a question!"

So, going to the door, he started out.

"That's far enough!" she backed down the step. "You stay right there and tell me about the wedding. I seemed to have missed it, thanks to your manipulations."

"And about a barrel of brandy," he grinned, leaning casually—and maddeningly at ease—against the jamb. "Oh, sorry. Am I permitted words this time?"

"Just tell me and stop being funny! Was there a minister? Did we exchange vows? And witnesses:—were there reputable witnesses?"

"Yes, ma'am. Yes, to every question.

"Who witnessed it?" she demanded.

"Mike, Sebastian Rizza, …and a Miss Candace DeShoka."

"Oh," Mandria cringed, realizing now why Tom's friends had smiled at her so knowingly. "And Miss DeShoka is a good church-going woman?"

"I wouldn't know," he answered that one carefully. "But she was in church the last time I saw her."

"Well, did I stand on my own two feet during all this?" she asked now.

"You did. Though, I must say, brandy affects you strangely."

Hadn't she guessed that already? Not remembering your own wedding was about as strange as one could get. …Or was it? Glancing at Tom, who seemed anxious to provide an answer, she had to ask, "How?"

"Well, lady, you were just so obedient. But only to me," he said so smugly she wanted to hit him with something. "When the good Reverend asked all those important questions, you totally ignored him until I told you to answer. I'm afraid you treated our witnesses in much the same way. You wouldn't acknowledge their presence or accept their congratulations until I asked you to do so. You just seemed to prefer standing there; cuddled against my chest; wearing the most endearing and enchanted expression."

"I suppose you're proud of that story!" she folded her arms snuggly, as if this was all that held her together. "Now, tell me about the way out you offered."

Tom's smile faded—and that, at least, pleased her. "An annulment," he explained. "You could say I gave you no choice in the matter—which

I didn't. You could say I took unfair advantage of your condition—and I did. No court in the land would deny your petition on those grounds. …And, if you truly want an annulment, I won't contest it. But I'm still holding you to that promise to hear me out. Now, if you'll just come inside, I'd be happy to—"

"To what?" her hands flew to her hips. "Give me a *place* beneath you? Well, no thank you! I don't relish a life where you have a legal right to demand my body, so annulment sounds perfect to me. Then, as previously stated, *I* will make those demands and you will live with it or forfeit Kathy all together!" And the next sound she made was a surprised, "Oh!" For, with a hand beneath each arm, Tom lifted her right through the doorway.

"I said this would take room and time, but you've had enough of both," he muttered. Then pointing her back to a chair at the table, he added, "Sit!"

And Mandria sat, knowing from his expression and the set way he stood, there wasn't to be another choice.

"Now, you are going to listen," he sat across from her again. "And this time, if you even try to leave, so help me God, I'll turn you over my knee—as I should have when I found you in that damn tavern on River Street!"

Shrugging indifferently, Mandria turned her shoulder to him. … *Let him talk. Just let him!* she thought. He could talk all night, but she didn't have to listen. No, she was not going to hear another word!

"You did bring this on yourself, Mandria," Tom began. "It's your only flaw—this running away from anything you don't want to face. But if you hadn't been so anxious to escape the day your father came to my door, this whole situation could have been avoided."

"Oh, don't you wish you could avoid it!" she immediately forgot her vow of deafness. "It cost you your freedom, didn't it?"

"No," he replied, allowing her input. But his eyes still dared her to move from the chair. "We would have married eventually. It was bound to come to that. But it was your impulsive behavior, your hell-bent compulsion for retaliation—first against your father; then me—that left me no choice but taking matters in hand. Don't you see? I used the only way I had of stopping you; of forcing you to reconsider a love you doubted so greatly."

"And still do!" she lifted her chin stubbornly. "Because whenever you get your *way*, I end up naked, damn you! First, in your bed, where you promptly traded me away; and then, at the inn, where I woke up alone and frightened out of my mind—with an unsigned note and $20! Was that supposed to make me love you? No, you wanted me to think the worst—the absolute worst!"

"Damn it, lady, that's the last thing I wanted, but I did have to make allowances for it. Mandria, you were fairly well soused—but never alone, by the way. You spent your wedding night, with your husband. And yet, it was during those wonderful hours, that I realized you might not be thrilled to wake up in my arms."

"Oh, such an understatement," she injected icily.

"Exactly. Because you still believed that conversation with your father," he pointed out. "So, I had to think of one plan to cover three possibilities: that you'd want to find yourself married to me; that you wouldn't; or that you didn't recall a damn thing about it. And, that's why I left the notes unsigned.

If you were happy, they'd read as written—from husband to wife. If you were unhappy—in the sober light of day—you'd still have to see the love I tried to express. And I hoped you'd care enough to seek me out and discuss our situation—which I did think when you came by my rooms the other day. As for a memory lapse, yes, the notes were meant to scare the hell out of you—just little reminders of the unsavory, unwanted entanglements such behavior can cause. Lady, I would have done anything to keep you from trying that damn-fool stunt again." Then he nodded. "Of course, you did it again anyway, by coming to proposition me—which made me angry, but it sure as hell didn't keep me from crawling right back into bed with you, did it? So, answer this for me: If I had wanted Kathy, why would I go through all of this for you? Why bother? What sense would it make?"

"As much as anything else does today," Mandria uttered. "Wasn't winning back my confidence part of your agreement with Father?"

"And in the process, I was to keep my hands to myself. But did I? —Could I? No, I married you, hoping you'd see how little I thought of that agreement."

Mandria looked at Tom, while tapping her fingertips on the table. He did have a point there—damn him. "Then what about your affair with Kathy? If it was over, why did you bargain with Father at all?"

Tom really disliked doing Sam Lucas a favor, but Mandria didn't need to know the full extent of her father's brutality. Yet would even the part he could tell her be too much? There was no help for it now. He had to tell her something—and disconnect himself from Kathy at the same time—or risk that she wouldn't believe a single word he'd spoken so far. "If you'll think back, I said to your father that Kathy was not his mistress by choice. Mandria, he held her husband's debt over her head, threatening the loss of her home and children unless she submitted. Now, yes, we had a brief affair, but parted friends. So, when she wanted to break free of your father, we helped her get her sons and leave Savannah. I swear to you that was the only reason I agreed to those damned terms. We just needed time to get them safely away from here." He was quiet then, hoping for the best, as he sat watching her digest everything. And when she spoke, it surprised the hell out of him.

"I met Kathy a couple of times, when Mama and I took over some things for the children," she said with downcast eyes. "She is a beautiful woman, but not a strong one, in my opinion—which gives weight to how Father could take advantage of her."

"So…you believe me?"

"About my father—absolutely. And I should know. He has tried enough times to force me into marriages that profited him in one way or another. And that I dared refuse those repulsive offers, he took as a personal insult to him. So I can easily see him doing exactly what you said to Kathy."

"Let me ask this another way," Tom laid an open hand before her. "If you believe that, surely the rest is falling into place. …So do I get to keep my wife?" he asked hopefully.

"I don't know why you'd want to," she shrugged, tracing a finger across his palm. "With the father I have, degeneracy is likely to run in the family; —amoral degeneracy."

"Sorry, but that's the wrong excuse to use with me, lady," he laced his fingers with hers. "What if I had turned my back on Allen because of the father he had? No, ma'am, you have your mother's blood too—as Allen has my mother's—and in both cases, the good won out."

"But that's not true," she sighed. "Tom, from the day we met, my behavior has been…well, irrational at best, and far from decent."

"You can say the damnedest things," he nodded. "Now, if you're talking about your plan for getting even with your father that was irrational. However," he paused to enjoy the thought, "…I've no complaints, whatsoever, with your behavior towards me. Love, I could do with a bit of your indecency every damned day. —Even when you're trying to feed me witch's brew."

"Oh…!" she cringed, turning nearly backward in the chair. "Doesn't that just prove my point? —Oh, I still can't believe I did such a horrid thing!"

"Lady," he grinned inanely, "I don't happen to see it that way." And now he was chuckling. "…I mean, there was never a man in less need of a love potion," he struggled against a spate of laughter. "…And when you were so sure my mind had been affected," he stopped, clinching his teeth on the storm of mirth threatening to escape his control.

"Well, it was still just awful!" she turned half-toward him again. … Now what on earth was the matter with her? Why did she feel the urge to share his amusement? But in her heart, if she had already accepted everything he told her as truth, wouldn't that make it understandable? And to Mandria's amazement she realized she did believe him. Unbidden, then, the merest hint of a smile tugged at the corners of her mouth and in spite of all she could do, the ridiculous thing was spreading— even behind the hand she raised to the bridge of her nose in hopes of stifling it. Daring a peek at Tom was her final undoing, for suddenly they were both laughing helplessly. And it only worsened when he showed her the skinned knees he'd earned trying to convince her of his love in the gritty sand of the riverbank.

"Oh, lady, that will ever remain my favorite story," he said when he was finally able. "One I'll take great pleasure telling our sons one day."

"A humiliation I'll likely be spared," she replied, dabbing a gleeful mist from her lashes, "…as the making of sons usually requires closer contact than this."

"Much closer," he immediately hauled her onto his lap. "Much, much closer!" he locked her securely in his arms.

"I wish I could say something beautiful and poetic," she sighed happily. "But I do love you, Thomas Scott and I won't fight with you ever again; or question your motives; or doubt your judgment; or—"

"Mandria," he interrupted her litany, "I only wanted to change your name to mine, but never your temperament. Lady, I'd prefer stalking a lioness to leading a lamb on a string."

"But a lioness will scratch," she drew nails across his cheek. "And bite," she nipped his ear.

"I'll take my chances," he pecked at her mouth. "But could we please—*please*—continue this in the bedroom?"

Mandria rose to stand before him with a great show of dignity, "I am afraid not, sir! I am now a married woman, and I refuse to enter that bedroom without my wedding ring."

"Well?" he stood to tower above her. "Must I fetch it from the bottom of the sea?"

Mandria glanced down the front of her blouse, then saucily back at him. "No, it hasn't sunk as deep as that."

"Ah, but I still insist on retrieving it," he laughed, and took his time doing so. Then, placing it on her hand, he watched as she examined the fit and look of it on her finger.

"You know," she smiled beautifully, "I should have kept that yellow ribbon as a reminder of my mysterious lover. I do believe he will merit an entire chapter in my scandalous memoirs."

"It was supposed to remind you of our wedding, scandalous lady—as was my toying with your ring finger at every given opportunity. Did you even notice, or do I need more lessons in dropping subtle hints?"

I noticed, but didn't make the connection," she answered. "I just liked it that you wanted to touch me."

"Lady, you've no idea," he drew a finger across her lower lip. "I've dreamed of touching you in ways… Well, you are mine and I do plan to take full advantage."

"Please do," she hugged him too briefly. "And bring us some wine when you come?" Then lighting another lamp, she took it and hurried to the bedroom.

As Tom locked the doors and refilled their glasses, he knew he was grinning like a loon, but there wasn't much he cared to do about it. That did change a bit when he entered the bedroom though. Settling on the edge of the bed, he watched as Mandria finished undressing and found himself caught in a serious study of contrasts as lamplight flickered over her body. Her slender limbs and proud straight shoulders glowed with a golden warmth. The globes of her breasts, the taut skin of her belly and buttocks seemed pearlized and fragile. It was impossible to decide which was most desirable. "You know, I don't often brag, but I'm proud of myself for claiming you, Miss Lucas."

"And who, pray tell, is she?" Mandria loosened her hair and started toward him as it tumbled about her shoulders. "Doth my husband dream of another so soon? —Doth he, per chance, relish a simple Miss more than his wife?"

"Nay, my lady," he fell in with her banter as he handed her a glass. "Though yon fair and gentle Miss will ever kindle a spark within my breast, 'tis only my wife who ignites the inferno of my passion."

"And you'd damn-well better remember that," she smiled haughtily, pausing to sip her wine. "…You see, I've had my own dreams about us."

"Truly?" he placed his glass on a table and drew her between his knees. "Tell me your dreams. I hope they were wicked."

"Pretty much so," she replied, dipping her fingers into her wine and rubbing them over a nipple. "I do hope you enjoy the flavor," she repeated the process on the other one.

"How could I not?" he drew both to his mouth. "It has such… body," he chuckled.

"More?" she offered, tracing wine soaked fingers in ever expanding circles.

Tom watched as one crystal droplet slid from her cleavage over the plane of her belly and caught in her navel. In an instant, it pooled, shimmered, then spilled downward into the deep tan thicket of curls below. "Damn," he uttered, almost dizzy with craving. Never had he been so thirsty for a single drop of wine! …Why was she able to stir this particular hunger in him? He had to keep reminding himself that she was, in truth, no more than a fledgling and too much, too soon was not the way to go. They were married. Time was on his side. He could be patient, couldn't he? Certainly—as long as she kept the comfort these really nice breasts and tasty nipples readily available.

"Please get up," Mandria placed a kiss on his forehead. "Up. I claim the right to undress my husband."

"Yes ma'am," he said agreeably, glad that he never did get around to buttoning his shirt. And soon, those nipples were lightly searing his chest as she drew his shirt down his arms. That done, Mandria retreated a step, which both pleased and displeased him. He welcomed a moment's respite—needed it. But he also needed the feel of her against him. What he got, instead, was a beautiful naked woman, with closed eyes, proceeding to move slow, methodical hands across his entire upper torso.

"I think I would know your body in total darkness," Mandria smiled. "In a pitch-black room full of strangers, I could choose your body from the rest."

In his heart, Tom knew she meant this as a compliment, but in his head he was murdering strangers in a pitch black room. And for the first time in his entire life, he had to admit to jealousy, or possessiveness, or whatever the hell it was. "Try that, and I'll break some damn heads," he grumbled. "I'll come to you, lady. You won't have to grope in dark places to find me." And drawing her close, he enjoyed the kiss she had waiting, while between them, Mandria deftly loosened his trouser buttons.

He was still kissing her when she worked them and his skivvies over his hips, far enough down to bring her hands forward and fondle the so evident symbol of his manhood. Stroking the firmness of his penis, kneading the fullness below, she hoped to urge his enjoyment to greater heights. When his kiss became almost savage, she suspected she had.

She knew for certain, when Tom grasped her hands, keeping them away. "Mandria," he said raggedly, "You'd best climb into that bed."

Holding his face in her hands, kissing the edges of his mouth, she asked, "What was it you said to me? *Almost; you're almost there?*" Then she made a downward slide along his body, to her knees, where she continued to tug his clothing down his legs.

Tom could only expel a shudder. In his state, had she dallied midway in any form or fashion, he would have been lost; without a shred of fortitude or stamina to stay him.

With everything about his ankles now, she said, "Well, there does seem to be a problem here." She was sitting back on her heels, smiling up at him—around the protrusion in her line of sight. "You're not cooperating with my efforts to free you." That's when, on its own, his penis lifted toward her and she blithely brushed it aside to finish with, "And Tom, I can't lift you."

This time, Mandria was given no choice about going to the bed, and the tumbling passionate moments that followed were immensely pleasurable for her. Tom's wandering kisses fevered her flesh; his unquenchable hunger urging her responses way beyond the wildest of her romantic dreams. And yet, when he attempted penetration, she resisted.

"No—Tom, please?" she said anxiously. "Let's go for a swim. — Wouldn't you enjoy a moonlight swim?"

"Now?" he blinked. "...Right now?"

"Yes!" she answered. "I—I'm just not the least bit sleepy."

Tom gave his head a good shake, as a nod was not going to clear it. "Lady, I've no idea why you would be. If you are, then I'm doing something drastically wrong here."

"No, you're not!" she assured him. "I just don't want it to end so quickly. I mean, we do have most of the night left and—and I'm just not sleepy!"

"...You really don't remember our wedding night, do you?" he chuckled, rolling to his back. Then he sat her astraddle of him and pulled her forward for a kiss while managing her impalement from beneath.

"Tom, I asked you to wait!" she said in surprise; pushing against his chest; straightening to her tallest sitting posture…which somehow, increased the angle of his depth. It also sent shimmering waves of sensation up her spine, but she wasn't going to say so when she had a valid point to make. "Really, you could show some regard for my wishes about this."

"But your wishes seem quite obvious to me," he toyed with the tips of her tattle-tale nipples. And when she swatted at his fingers and tried to squirm beyond their reach, he clamped hands to her hips. "Mandria, if you don't keep still, it will be over too soon!" he warned.

"Well, didn't I just say that?" she expressed exasperation. "Tom, why don't you listen? You just never—"

"Hush!" he placed a finger across her busy mouth. "Now, where did you get the notion there was a one-time limit on this sort of thing?"

"…You mean there isn't?" she asked in renewed surprise, her eyes widening beautifully.

"No ma'am. Usually, once will suffice, but whenever the mood or the need arises, we're free to indulge as often as we please—and did on our wedding night. In fact, I think we may have set some damn kind of record!"

"Oh," she nodded and then struggled to pose a question. "Is that why…I mean, I don't want to sound stupid, but afterwards—the next day—is that why…well, I ached from head to toe!"

He was fondling her breasts again. And grinning. "Well, you did a lot of dancing, which would account for your toes. And the brandy would most certainly cause your head to ache. But I'll gladly take credit for anything in between." And making a slow and nearly complete withdrawal, he returned to stress his point, which had Mandria experiencing more of those spine tingling sensations.

"You would," her hands went to his chest seeking balance when he rose beneath her a second time. "But will it happen again tonight?"

"Which?" he kept nudging her from within. "The soreness or the repetitions? —And was that merely a question or a subtle request?"

"Both!" she answered from the core of her being, for even that slight forward tilt was offering a new set of feelings.

"So what's it to be? Do we swim or does Lady Godiva prefer riding her worthy steed?" And he provided a few emphatically persuasive thrusts.

"Oh!" she yelped, thrown forward, where she now braced on arms to either side of his head. "I don't think her steed tried bucking her off!"

"No, but then his knees weren't skinned all to hell," he said grasping her hips and setting a rhythm between them.

"Well," she shuddered, for involuntarily, her internal hold on his penis was tightening.

"Well what, my love?" he took advantage of her position shift, lifting his mouth to sample her swollen nipples. How could he not, when her breasts bobbled so invitingly close to his face? "Do we swim or ride?" he muttered happily, hands full of breasts, and a tongue trying to taste both nipples at the same time.

"Damn! —Oh, damn!" Mandria breathed. How was it possible to know such pleasure? His hands and mouth at her breasts; his driving movements within—all at once. ...Swimming: had she actually suggested swimming over this? Then, clasping her knees against his sides, she leaned into his arms, urging this steed to take his head...

# CHAPTER 22

It was nearing dawn when Tom pulled Mandria into the curve of his body and kissed his way across her shoulder. She sighed contentedly, refusing to abandon her dreamy state. And yet, the hand sliding up to span and caress her breasts and the voice at her ear were not guided by passion, as they had been throughout the night. "Love, I'm afraid it's time to get up," he said.

"It can't be," she protested groggily.

He kissed the slender column of her neck, but all too briefly. "I'd best get you home before the servants discover you missing."

"I am with my husband," she reminded him, as a smile tipped the corners of her mouth. "They will understand."

"Lady, listen…," he said with hesitance. "You can't tell them we're married. You can't tell anyone yet."

Mandria turned in his arms and saw his troubled expression. "You're serious," she decided. "So, why?"

"Because there are things that still bother me about your father's reason for offering that bargain. And letting him think its going as he wants is the quickest way of discovering what the hell he's up to."

"All right," she nodded. "I can see the sense in that."

"Thank you," he placed fingers along her cheek. "I just don't want you thinking I'm not willing to acknowledge my responsibility to you."

Mandria rolled to her back laughing. "After such a night, how could I doubt that? —Here;" she held a measuring hand above her head, "your responsibility to me was fulfilled up-to-here!"

"My pleasure," he reached for her airborne hand. Holding her close, he placed a kiss on her palm and closed her fingers over it. "Keep that with you today. It's redeemable on request and for you, the supply is endless. —Now, up, woman!" he swatted her nicely rounded bottom. "Let's see if we can find some coffee around here."

They did and put on a pot to boil, yet a futile attempt at dressing led them back to bed and it was only the smell of burning coffee that brought them out again. But there was even happiness in sharing a left over supper plate and a cup of bitterly scorched coffee, when both were flavored with teasing and laughter. Then as Tom walked Mandria home in the pinkness of pre-dawn light, they also shared moments of contented silence, punctuated with smiles and the sweetness of many kisses. And during the hours to come, resting in their separate beds—his ring now on a chain about her neck—they were still more together than apart...

Tom smiled down at Mandria from the cabin doorway. "Don't you look beautiful this afternoon? You know, if you weren't a married woman, I'd marry you myself."

"I'm flattered, sir," she bobbed him a curtsy, before handing him two ham biscuits wrapped in a napkin, "—though my husband wouldn't think much of your notion."

"Ah, but as long as I hold this," he exchanged the biscuits for a folded page that lay on the table, "you may have to deal with me anyway," And he waved it above her head.

"Oh?" she tried snatching for it, and missed. "So what is that— the deed to the family home? The title to my vast wealth in diamond mines? —Tom, what is it?"

"Only your marriage certificate," he still kept it beyond her reach. "Surrender, lady—yield—or I'll destroy the proof of your union with Thomas Scott!"

Mandria stopped and raising a theatrical hand to her brow, feigned a dramatic sigh. "So be it, you dastardly villain—take me, for I must see this proof."

"Quitter," Tom chuckled, handing it over before drawing her to him and teasing outrageously at her ear.

"Tom, please!" she scolded, but it was clear he had no intention of allowing her a moment's peace, so she managed to turn in his arms and hold him off with her back. "Well," she smiled, "that is my signature, so I guess it really is legal."

"And binding," he gave her a final squeeze, before sitting to eat his late lunch.

Mandria sat too. "It says we were married at Thunderbolt, Georgia, by a Reverend Anthony Wickliffe on the 25 th day of July, 1829. And the witnesses are listed too…," she paused, looking more closely. "Tom, how old was Miss De Shoka?"

"I've no idea," he answered as innocently as possible. They would have to be wed for many, many years before he'd admit to allowing Mike's last minute-choice of a prostitute as the female witness at their hurried ceremony. "…Why?" he had to ask.

"I don't know," she shrugged. "I was picturing her as elderly, but compared to Mike and Mr. Rizza's signatures, hers looks…well, almost childish."

"It's better than an X, Mandria," he said. And as he'd finished eating, he rose, and drew her up with him. "Now, put that aside and give me a proper kiss before we leave."

She was more than glad to do that and only afterwards did she realize what he'd said. "…We're leaving? Where are we going?"

"For a walk," he led her out. "And we'd best hurry along now."

"But why the hurry?" she asked as they climbed the dune path. "Its mid-afternoon and they're not expecting me to make an appearance at home until dark."

"Lady, the time of day has nothing to do with it," he grinned at her. "I just have some things I want to discuss with you, and unless we keep moving, I'll never get to it. I'll end up taking you to bed, because that happens every damn time I get near you."

"Oh," she nodded, and after a moment, her soft, throaty laughter followed. But before Tom could begin his topics, she introduced one of her own. "Can I ask you about Kathy?"

"As long as I have your assurance that truthful answers won't turn you against me again, ask what you'd like," he shrugged, lacing his fingers with hers as they walked.

"Well, were you in love with her?"

"No. Love was never in the picture—for either of us."

"But she had to feel something for you—a man who makes love the way you do? …Well, I mean, how is it possible to share that deep, beautiful closeness and feel nothing for it? What words passed between you, Tom? Surely there were terms of endearment; —of mutual concern about something! And to have it end in… in friendship? I don't think I could ever again call you just a friend."

"And I think you just explained why I love you," he brought her hand to his lips. "In spite of all your big plans to the contrary, you are incapable of making love without first being in love. Soused as you were in that tavern, just before you passed out, you looked at me and said, *Please be Tom*. And, though you don't remember the rest, it was my name you kept repeating; me you made love to and wanted throughout our wedding night."

Mandria hugged herself to him, fending off the urge to cry. "Thank you for telling me that," she said after a moment. "…Somehow, it makes me feel better about myself."

"You do the same for me, lady," he eased her back, to look into her eyes. "And that's as it should be: giving the best of ourselves to each other."

"Yes, though I can't help but feel sorry for Kathy now. To be treated so badly by my father and then, to lose you too? Oh, Tom, I hope she finds happiness—truly I do!" And impulsively, she was hugging him another time.

"So, can we talk about your father now—and that agreement?" he backed her away again. "But, lady, this is important and if you don't stop pawing me, it won't get very far."

"Oh, very well—for now," she smiled and taking his hand, they resumed walking. "Tom, can I tell you what I think—or rather, how much my eyes have been opened just because I know you love me?" And not waiting for him to answer, she went ahead. "Your reason for bargaining with Father was to free Kathy of any debt to him. And I even know why you did it—the real reason," she finished smugly.

"All right, Miss Smarty-pants," he chuckled. "What was the real reason?"

"Your mother," she said. "You didn't want Kathy to live in fear of Father coming after her again—always looking over her shoulder, as you had to do. So, what you couldn't do for your mother, you did for Kathy—and I believe, for yourself."

Tom stopped and looked at Mandria for several seconds. "…You could be right," he said then, "…Lady, I've needed you in my life for a very long time."

"No more than I've needed you in mine," she replied. "Unlike my father, you loved me and wanted nothing back for it."

They weren't touching, but may as well have been, as the warmth of understanding between them was nearly tangible and entirely pleasing.

"Well," Tom cleared his throat. "Well, back to your father," he got them moving again, though holding on to her hand now seemed a necessity. "Mandria, just as I had a reason for accepting his terms, he had to have another reason for setting them. Don't you see how strange it was? On Friday, my very existence provoked a… confrontation with Kathy. Yet, the next day he offered me his mistress—and the company of his daughter."

"You said as much to his face," she pointed out, "—expressed the same doubts."

"And he claimed it was done for your sake. …But do you believe that?"

"Hardly," she said with resentment. She had wasted so many years loving an unloving father.

"Then, what changed over-night? What caused him to go from murderous anger to coldly calculating?"

"Well, it didn't happen over-night," Mandria nodded. "We argued the next morning—Saturday morning—and believe me, he was angry then. He wanted to know who you were and where you lived, with no questions asked. And when I dared to defend you, he let me have it with both barrels. He said—well, you know what he said, because he said it to you too—except the part about your using our dinner engagement as an alibi for spiriting Kathy away."

"And there's a strange thing too," Tom said. "His version is out of time sequence. There is no way dinner at 7 o'clock could be an alibi for something that happened hours later. ...Why would he tell you differently?"

"To gain my co-operation. Tom, my father will say or do anything to get what he wants. That morning, it was you and he didn't care that his accusations were nearly killing me," she explained.

"But you didn't tell him where to find me, because he said Ransom O'Rourke did. ...So his attitude change occurred either during or after your argument," Tom puzzled. "Love, what else was said? Any scrap of information might give us a clue."

"I defended you. I even told him I admired you for raising your brother alone; and for wanting to make a home here for Allen. I said Mama and Uncle Ran approved of you too, and for a while he was so quiet, I hoped he was reconsidering his charges against you. Then I mentioned your friendship with Mike and he became even more vicious. But Tom, I was never hysterical—that wasn't so. He said some ugly things and when he held himself up as the moral protector of the family name, I did lose my temper. Father slapped me a good one for it, but that was only—"

"He what?" Tom stopped so abruptly, she was jerked backwards a step. "Sam hit you?"

Mandria's breath caught at the intensity of furious resentment in his eyes and in that single moment, she knew what a formidable enemy he would be. Paradoxically, she was also remembering tender moments, when his touch had been as light as a butterfly wing—and she treasured that about him even more. "Yes, Father slapped me, but then—"

"God damn it!" he finally exploded, grasping her shoulders. But again, even in anger, the strength of his hands on her was restrained. "Why didn't you tell me before now? No man is going to abuse you—especially Sam Lucas, and—well, I don't care if he is your father, damn it! Mandria—well, damn it, I won't stand for it!"

His concern was for her and because she cared as much for him, Mandria wanted to calm him. At the same time, in some secret corner of her mind, she stored a discovery: when truly upset, Tom's nervous habit was to pepper his sentences with the word *well*. "Listen to me," she cupped his face, feeling a steely tenseness beneath her palms. "Tom, please listen! I was hurt by what he said, not by what he did. I needed that slap—I did!" she insisted, when he wanted to object. "It drove me into your arms and for that, I would gladly thank him. …Really, it wasn't so painful," she lied, smiling tentatively. "See? No bruises. No anything. Please forget it. We have to think of our future now. Isn't that more important?"

Tom pressed her hands closer against his face and slowly—so slowly—she felt his anger ebb. "Yes, our future is important," he said at last, but now with such deadly control she had to wonder if he wasn't more dangerous this way. "…But Mandria, if Sam Lucas ever touches you again, I'll kill him. And that isn't a threat; it's a fact. This…beating thing just goes too deep."

"I know," she cuddled against his chest, listening for the hammer-hard beat of his heart. "I know, my husband."

A shuddering sigh went through Tom as he closed his arms about her, and for a time they were silent. "…I do tend to over-protect the people I love," he reasoned aloud. "Maybe because of the past—or maybe because my loved ones are so few. In your case, that urge is doubly strong, because I love you so damned much."

"Why, thank you so-damned-much," she kissed the edge of his mouth. "And as the feeling is so-damned-mutual, what could father really do to hurt us? We are married and he will just have to accept it."

"Still, I would like to know what he's up to first," he said as they walked on. "And until I do, I feel it would be much wiser—and safer—to keep it from him."

266

"So, we'll pretend to be courting?"

"Yes," Tom nodded. "Sam is not a patient man, so whatever he's hatching will come to light fairly soon."

"Well," she laughed, "we've done everything else backwards. Why not this too?"

"Meaning?" he smiled down at her.

"Meaning, that most couples do their courting before they marry. …And yet, this might be fun. No, I don't think I'm going to make a proper courtship easy for you. Instead, I'm going to flirt and tease and entice you at every opportunity."

"You do that already, pretty lady—just by breathing," he said. "I'm even fascinated by the way you sleep."

And now Mandria came to an abrupt halt. "…But will it be with you?" she asked. "We don't have to carry this pretense that far. Tom, I'm your wife and I won't let Father rob me of my—my right to be with you!"

"So you like that, do you?" he grinned, gazing at the rising sea and the fading sun light. "Lord, what am I to do with her? Her mind stays in the bedroom—always the bedroom!"

"But what bedroom?" she insisted.

"Mine, woman—or it damned well better be!" he teased.

"And when your brother comes?" she pointed out. "Oh, I can just hear it now: *Excuse me, Allen. I'll be back to talk with you when Tom is done with me.* And he'll say, *Go right ahead, Mandria, I'll just read a book or something.* I mean, even if you tell him we're married, won't that be rather…awkward?"

"Not *if* I tell him. Sweetheart, I can't wait to introduce Allen to his new sister. He will love you from the start, Mandria. …And about our meeting place? I've been working on that since the day after we married."

"You have?" she said in surprise. "…Tom, were you so sure things would work out with us?"

"Hell yes!" he pulled her into his side. "Aren't you, now that you know the truth?"

"I guess so," she nodded. "But as your wife, there's so much I should know and don't. Your birthday; your favorite foods—"

"Mandria, strangers can learn those things passing on the street," he stopped to insure her attention to his words. "You and I have learned and shared more important things already:—like how to get married and not know it; how to administer a love potion to an already besotted husband; and best of all, a healthy—but rabid—taste for amorous behavior. So, what's there to worry about?"

"Nothing!" she was laughing enjoyably, leaning back in his arms, to raise her arms skyward. "Nothing under God's big heaven!"

"Well, damn!" he frowned, setting her at arms length. "Must you always bring up that subject between us?"

"Tom?" she puzzled over his serious expression. "What subject? What did I say?"

"This one!" he brought her smartly against his growing erection. "Every time—you do this to me every damn time."

"Oh, my poor lamb," she rubbed against him. "Is it painful? Can we make it back to the cabin or must I lay my ass in the sand for grinding again?

"The only thing you must do, lady, is never—ever—change," he lifted her to him for a kiss, only to find she was very nearly right: his need was close to painful. "Come on, Mandria," he eased her along him to the ground, "we are going for a swim."

"*Now?*" she mimicked him from the previous night. "*Right now?*"

"Yes, and right here on this spot," he said leading her into the sea. "If you'll notice, this is where we had our first kiss. And I think I'll just go ahead and do now what I wanted to then. So don't even consider hitching up your skirt—though I would like to see how you do that sometime."

"You mean we're going to…in the water?"

"Yes ma'am, we sure are," he drew her to him for some below the surface clothing adjustments.

"But standing up? Tom, you're much taller, so how—?"

"Ah, but thank God for buoyancy," he laughed, floating her right into place. And as the sun took its final bow in the west, Atlantic watched all with a sigh of approval for the lovers at play in her undulating waves...

# CHAPTER 23

"Well, by damn," Sam rocked forward on his office desk chair. "The bastard finally comes." And looking down from his Factor's Walk window, he watched Tom cross River Street and head for the crowded boat landing. "You'd think he'd be more anxious," he muttered into his brandy snifter.

But Sam was the anxious one, and seat-weary from his two hour vigil. It was Friday, after all, and any moment now, the Irish Mist would come into view, bringing its most important passenger ever. "My son," Sam had uttered each time he looked up-river. "My son."

Glancing at Tom again, he smiled slightly and poured another drink. For nearly a month, Mandria's disposition had been as rosy as her sun-kissed cheeks, due, no doubt, to Tom's frequent visits. "Sweet," Sam said lightly. "That relationship is sweet enough to draw ants. *Father we are going for stroll; Father, we're going for a ride; Father, I've asked Tom to stay for supper again*," he said in snide imitation. "Sweet—and effective." Yes, he had to admit things were going well. Evelyn had even been helpful in that respect. She was delighted that Mandria was seeing so much of Tom and encouraged her to include him in more and more of their family functions, which suited Sam completely, as at one such occasion he learned the date of Allen's arrival. At another, that Allen's birthday was September 10th; his mother was named Margaret Scott, nee Morris, born in England. That was proof enough of Allen's parentage for Sam, because that staid schoolmarm would never have considered a lover. T'wouldn't have been proper.

"…But one day, Thomas Scott," his expression hardened, "you'll pay in full measure for Kathy. You may be the perfect God damned gentleman and keep our bloody bargain to the boring end, but Mandy's pristine ways are not enough for you to suffer. Then, if Kathy wants what I leave of you, she's welcomed to it—piece by fucking piece!" How Sam was enjoying those thoughts and would have continued to, had not the long, low moan of a boat whistle brought him to his feet. "At last!" he exclaimed, watching as the Irish Mist headed straight down the middle of the river. "Come on, Herb," he finished his drink in a gulp. "—Come on, you bastard, pour on the God damned steam!"

It seemed to take hours for the boat to dock; longer for the crowd to thin, and in trying to spot Allen for himself, Sam lost sight of Tom. "Damn!" he gripped the window sill in frustration. "Damn!" he kept repeating, as he scanned the people below. "I've missed him! God damn it, I missed seeing him!"

Then, the wheelhouse door opened, and Tom came out. Mike followed, pausing in the doorway to converse with someone still inside. Tom found the comment amusing and laughed.

Sam did not. "Well?" he said impatiently. "Well, Herb, out of the way! If my son is behind you, God damn it, move or I'll—" he stopped in mid-sentence, for there, at last, had to be Allen.

…*Taller than I am*, Sam settled on his chair again and into his thoughts while observing the boy. …*A bit lean, as I was at that age too, but taller and with shoulder width to spare.* …*God, he looks like Margaret. Same good features—finer than Tom's. But he did get my full head of black hair, by damn.* …*And, no use denying there is a marked resemblance to Tom too—even moves like him,*" he added distastefully. …*But maybe that's for the best. I'd be hard-put explaining the same resemblance to me—or to his half sister. He has my blood. That is what counts and by God I'll see it acknowledged somehow!* "So, go along with Tom, son," he uttered aloud, "and learn the city well. You should, you know. If I have my way, you'll own a damn big chunk of Savannah one day—as befits the Lucas son and heir."

Then Sam fell silent, content with just watching Allen, as he shook hands with Mike, picked up his baggage and went down the stairs on Tom's heels. He watched as they crossed the gangway and noted, again, how alike the brothers were in appearance and mannerisms. But as they started across River Street and Tom put an arm about Allen's shoulders in a moment of private greeting, Sam ground his teeth in deep-felt resentment. He had not considered a bond existing between the two. That could cause problems; snags in his plan to win Allen over.

Neither had Sam considered his own reaction to such a bond. And in the days to come, he would discover that envy was the cruelest of his soul's dark companions…

While climbing the bluff road, Tom hoisted two cloth-bound muskets to his shoulder and smiled, careful to look straight ahead. "So, Mike showed you around Augusta. How did you like it there, little brother?"

"Oh, fine," Allen answered, revealing a sheepish version of the same broad smile—and being even more careful to avoid eye contact. "One morning, we toured a mill near the river, where he had to pick up some cargo and I found that interesting. Then, there was an outdoor concert in the afternoon…," he hesitated. What more dare he to add?

"And for evenings at Delilah's, I trust you took precautions," Tom uttered.

It was neither a statement nor a question and Allen was decidedly at a loss. His lips parted, words formed, but no voice accompanied them.

Tom chuckled. "Mike gave me the same tour."

"He did?" Allen shifted his luggage uncomfortably. "…Then, you wouldn't disapprove if I said I did use precautions and enjoyed myself a hell of a lot?"

"I'd be disappointed…" Tom made a deliberate pause, "if you hadn't done both."

Allen expelled a rush of breath. "Hell, Tom! …So you really went to Delilah's too? That surprises me, you know. You've always been so serious about everything."

"Children learn by example," Tom shrugged, relieving his brother of a valise—and a good bit of tension.

272

"So what lesson should I take from your visit to a whorehouse?" Allen countered, hoping—for once—to put Tom in a corner.

"That I don't consider you a child any longer, obviously," he replied.

Surprised again, but pleased, Allen ventured another question. "Are there ladies in Savannah to equal Delilah's?"

"There are and I'm certain you'll find them."

"...But you won't point them out, or go with me, is that it?"

"I'm afraid not—not now," Tom grinned.

"Mike did and you had no objections," Allen puzzled. "Are you bothered because we're brothers?"

"That has nothing to do with it, Allen."

"Then why do I feel you've just sent me hunting with a pop-gun?" he asked in frustration.

"Hunt all you like, little brother—as long as the game is in season and you're protected. It wouldn't be sporting, otherwise. Or healthy."

"Lord," Allen muttered, "I think I understood you better when I thought you weren't human."

"Meaning what?" Tom directed him along a park path.

"Meaning everyone in Athens measured me by your yardstick. Teachers would say, *Study harder, Allen. Tom made better grades and you can too.* And the farmers—oh, Lord, they were worse! *Yeah, Allen, Tom cleared them fields almost single-handed. Never fooled around a bit. Gave me a full day's work for a full day's pay—now, git to it, boy!*"

"And you resented the comparison," Tom concluded.

"No, not really. But I did wonder if you ever had any fun. I wasn't having much trying to match your image."

"Allen, for every day's pay there was a night—and more often than not, a daughter to compensate her father's mean wages."

"Damn, Tom! —And your grades? You did date old Miss Rutledge for a time."

"Whoa, now. Don't get the wrong idea. I did work hard in those fields; I did earn my pay, as well as those grades—and I didn't really date Susan. Besides that, she's not old. She is a beautiful woman; a damn fine teacher; a good friend to both of us—and was our mother's

273

friend too. She took us in more than once; boarded you again, until I could get settled here and—"

"I know! —I know!" Allen injected. "Lord, I didn't mean to set you off. It's just that I had to live in her house and she stayed on my back about studying. I either had to keep my nose in a book or hear a lecture every night!" he said, as they crossed Bay Street.

"Yes, well, she badgered me too—right through college," Tom said with remembered fondness. "But it didn't hurt you, little brother. You finished in the top third of your class. You'll be grateful when you go back for college—"

"Hey, can't we talk about something else?" Allen insisted. "— Women! Now, I was really enjoying that subject, so tell me about the women of Savannah."

"In general or do you want specifics?" Tom laughed.

"Specifics—please!" Allen laughed too.

"Well, as soon as you've cleaned up a bit, we're going for an afternoon drink, where you will meet the most beautiful woman in the world."

"Then she must be yours," Allen sent him a knowing look. "Am I right?"

"Very much mine," Tom answered with deep satisfaction.

"And would she have a beautiful friend for me?"

"Many, you young scoundrel, but not for that purpose," he turned on the Harrison House doorstep to face his brother. "…Allen, she is my wife."

"Wife," Allen repeated numbly.

"And your sister now, by marriage."

Allen nodded, not knowing how to react. "…Tom, that's quite a bombshell. How long have you been married?"

"One month and six days," he grinned. "Want a minute count too?"

"But you haven't been here much longer than that!" Allen exclaimed, then wished he hadn't. "I mean…maybe I shouldn't have come. You're still a newly-wed and you don't need a kid-brother underfoot."

"I'll always need my kid-brother," Tom assured him.

"But your wife might resent it—and I do want her to like me."

"I'm glad to hear that. I was beginning to wonder if you were happy for me or not."

"Oh, of course I am!" Allen put down a case and extended a hand. "Damned happy, though I feel a bit foolish now. Imagine, asking a married man to show me to the wenches of Savannah!"

"Yes, you'll have to do without my company there," Tom smiled, reaching for the door. "But who needs-a-big-brother then, anyway?"

"Does my new sister live here?" Allen asked following Tom in. "And what's her name, by the way?"

"Mandria. But we haven't announced our marriage yet, so she still lives at home. Now, hurry little brother. I'll explain later, but we're to meet her in half an hour."

"My Lord," Allen nodded as they went up the stairway. "Now I have a sister who's still a secret. —Tom, what have you gotten yourself into?"

Deloras' was crowded, but when Tom and Allen arrived, Mandria had been seated and was enjoying a cup of tea. She watched them approach, her lips parting in a smile of greeting—and appreciation. She had married into a family of exceptionally handsome men.

After a lingering kiss to her cheek and a delightful whiff of her honeysuckle scent, Tom said proudly, "Allen, this is Mandria, my very beautiful wife. Mandria, my brother, Allen."

"Welcome to Savannah, Allen," she offered her hand. "...I hope I'm not too big a shock for you."

Allen made her a stiff formal bow. "Well, you are," he said without smiling.

"Then...you don't approve?" she searched his solemn expression, and retrieved her unaccepted hand.

"No, I don't." he nodded.

"Allen?" Tom said aghast.

"Well, I don't!" he insisted, then leaned close to Mandria and whispered aloud, "I think any man who would keep his claim on you a secret is a fool." And he kissed her cheek too.

"Oh," she laughed softly, while Tom expelled a pent breath. "I should have known: more of the Scott charm. I wonder if the city can withstand another siege."

"Cut a wide path, did he?" Allen glanced at his brother knowingly, then turned back to Mandria. "But if you are sample of the bounty, I sincerely hope my path can be just as wide."

"There," Tom laughed as they claimed chairs, "now you two are off in the right direction."

"We three," Mandria extended a hand to each. "We three Scotts. A brand new family—and a special one, too."

Allen's smile broadened. "Tom, I think she is wonderful! ...And I want you to know I'm glad to be here. I wasn't sure I'd fit into you new married life, but I couldn't ask for a prettier, sweeter sister."

"Well, now," said Tom. "Well, well, now." But he couldn't think of anything to add to one of the happiest moments he could remember.

"Does he often speak with such eloquence?" Allen winked at Mandria. "I do hope he managed his proposal better. I can hear it now: *Well, Mandria, —well, I think we should—well, well—get married.* Is that how it went, dear lady?"

"Not exactly," she laughed at his antics. "Actually, Tom didn't propose at all. We just happened to meet once too often and before-I-knew-it, we were married."

"Only way I could catch her," Tom smiled at her phrasing. "Had to pick-her-up and carry-her-off to the preacher," he returned.

"Yes, and then—" she faltered and grasped Tom's arm. "Father's here and he's coming this way!"

Tom stood, uttering a caution. "Remember, Allen. Not a word about us."

"Good afternoon!" Sam swooped Tom's hand in greeting. "And to you, daughter," he bent with a fatherly peck for her cheek, his eyes already fastened on Allen. "Tom, I'm on my way to a meeting near-by, but thought I'd stop in to meet your brother. ...And here, certainly, is the lad."

"Yes, Sam, this is Allen Scott," Tom introduced. "Allen, Sam Lucas, Mandria's father."

Sam's smile broadened. Allen's eyes were brown—a shade or two lighter than his own, but brown nonetheless, and not blue like Margaret's or brother Tom's.

"Happy to know you, sir," Allen extended a hand, wondering about the man's pensive gaze.

"Son...I'm happy to know you too," Sam moved a step closer. "Very happy indeed."

"Uh...won't you join us for a drink?" Tom asked for the sake of politeness, but hoped Sam would decline.

"If you'll permit me to buy them," Sam took a seat next to Allen, even as he spoke. "—Waiter!" he summonsed. "Here! —Over here and be damned quick about it!" And that his brusqueness embarrassed Mandria was duly noted by the Scotts. Once their orders were taken, however, he wore a genuinely pleased expression. Allen had wanted brandy—brandy, by God! Lucas blood was spiked with brandy! "Tell me, son," he said, "how was the trip from Athens?"

"Hot and dry, for the most part," Allen answered and then, for some unknown reason, decided to test his new-found acceptance into adulthood. "But thanks to Captain Herb, I had a really fine time in Augusta." There: he'd said it; Tom knew what he meant; and he'd yet to have his ears boxed. ...In fact, Tom seemed more interested in Sam's frown at the mention of Mike's name. So, being curious, Allen said it again. "Yeah, Mike and I became really fast friends." Then he wondered if he should have said that, because Sam's frown deepened and Tom hastened a change of subject.

"Listen, Sam, we're planning a tour of Savannah for Allen and of course, Mandria knows the usual points of interest, but I'd also like for him to see what they're doing out at Fort Pulaski. Do you know anyone who might get us in?"

"I certainly do. Lieutenant Robert E. Lee, one of the young engineers, who happens to purchase materials from me," he was all smiles again. "And I've another tour to suggest that a young man like this should find highly stimulating."

"Oh?" Allen laughed. "Can we speak of it front of a lady?"

"I should hope so!" Mandria looked at her father with widened eyes. As she remembered it, *stimulating* had been his term for a sexual encounter with Kathy. And Allen had given it the same connotation, hadn't he?

"The boy was merely jesting, missy," Sam gave her a look of irritation. "—Where is you sense of humor?"

"S…sorry," she lowered feathery lashes on rosied cheeks. Simultaneously, Tom caught her hand beneath the table for a comforting squeeze.

"You should be," Sam continued. "Your caustic primness has already cost you many a worthy suitor. —And I'm certain Tom would agree, old maids are the dreariest of God's creatures."

Allen cleared his throat, hiding a smirk behind his fist. Tom's expression remained unchanged, but flintiness appeared in his eyes, that told Mandria he had about reached his limit. So, she laughed. "Really, Father, now where is your sense of humor? I was merely jesting too."

"Yes, well, when you've shown Allen the local attractions, I'm sure he'd allow me to show him what really keeps this city alive." And turning to his son, he was charming again. "You see, I own interests in many businesses here; a lumber yard, real estate, an import company; warehouse storage on the river—and the whiskey kegs, I am now reminded by this waiter's damned tardy arrival!" he sneered at the man. But once served, he was civil again. "So, Allen, would you care to see my little empire?"

"That's kind of you, sir," he said in awe of these rapid mood changes. "Thank you."

"Too kind," Tom commented. He had not appreciated Sam's condescending tone with Mandria, nor did he like his doting on Allen any better. "We wouldn't want to intrude on your time. With so-many-interests, you can't have much to spare."

"Nonsense," Sam lifted an eyebrow. "I always have time for friends—and making new ones," he looked back to Allen. "I mean to help your brother feel at home here."

"Your generosity is sometimes unbelievable," Tom said with a near-smile, for now Mandria was squeezing his hand beneath the table. "—As well as those you choose to call friends," he added anyway.

"That is a mystery, isn't it?" Sam warmed to the word game. "Especially, when certain of those friends is little more than a thief who would take what is rightfully mine."

"Yes, and that can't be good for an empire," Tom jousted and Mandria squeezed his hand harder.

"True, but I can afford concessions," Sam nodded, "when I know that such a blackheart is forced to work in my interest to further his own."

"My Lord!" Allen exclaimed. "The world of business must be awfully complicated. It seems to me a thief of any kind should be prosecuted—not tolerated!"

"Allen," Mandria offered, "maybe they're saying it takes a thief to know one?"

"And a genius to keep him at bay," Tom concluded.

"…Well, all things still being *equal*, I'd have to agree," Sam added, but wondered which role Tom had assigned him. "Anyway, as I must leave, may I propose a toast now?" And once they'd raised their glasses, he continued. "To each of us; to new relationships and old; to closeness among the kindred here; and as Tom once summed it so aptly, *there can be no better friendship between us.*"

"Amen," Tom nodded. "We can all drink to that." Which they did, and Sam was soon off about his business.

"All right, Big Brer," Allen leaned to the back of his chair, "What was that all about?"

"Yes, was Father angry with you or not?" Mandria's question followed quickly.

"Not really," Tom smiled at their concerned expressions. "Just redrawing our battle lines. That happens now and again. It keeps us both on our toes."

"Well, I wish I hadn't told him we were meeting here," Mandria sighed. "Father has an absolute talent for ruining a happy occasion."

"But some of it was amusing," Allen grinned, "—like his warning that you'd be an old maid, *Mrs.* Scott? And Tom, wasn't he saying you *aren't* a worthy suitor for her?"

"Yes, that's exactly what he meant," Mandria replied. "He doesn't like Tom at all—and not to confuse you more—but he still arranged this courtship between us himself. Now aren't you impressed with the family your brother married into?"

"Still, that is why he came," Tom sipped his drink thoughtfully. "He meant to impress someone with his wealth and status. …You, Allen. It has to be you."

"Me? —Why me?"

"Damned if I know, little brother, but did he succeed? Were you impressed?"

"Now…he is Mandria's father," Allen hedged.

"And she knows him for what he is, so give us the truth."

"Well, his treatment of that poor waiter was a bit overbearing. But to answer your question, yes, I was impressed. Maybe it takes a certain bluntness to succeed in business—and he has every right to be proud of that."

"To the point of reciting his accomplishments for you? No, Allen, the man does nothing unless it earns him more power or money."

"And Father is usually so secretive about his affairs—of all kinds," Mandria said sardonically. "I can't remember a time when he offered to personally guide anyone through his projects, unless it was potential investor."

"That's a laugh—me, an investor?" Allen expounded. "I can't even pay for my next drink—which I'd really like to have, Tom. Then, I'd enjoy getting to know my new sister better—and to see her beautiful smile again."

"He's right, you know," Tom watched Mandria run a slender finger over the rim of her tea cup. "We shouldn't let Sam spoil our first day together. And, lady, I'd like seeing you smile too."

"All right," she straightened resolutely. "We just will not allow Father to ruin this for us." And she did smile, trying very hard to mean it…

It was later in the afternoon when the Scott brothers walked Mandria home and stayed for a pleasant visit with Evelyn. But on leaving, they'd hardly crossed into the square before Tom was assailed by questions.

"So, how many people know about your marriage?" Allen asked.

"Mike and one other friend. You'll meet him soon, too."

"That is one gorgeous lady you have, Brer—and also wonderfully nice."

"Thank you," Tom smiled. "Did myself proud there, didn't I?"

"And that's one fine house she lives in, too," he turned to look at the place again.

"…So?" Tom started them along a walk to the north.

"So what is wrong with marrying a beautiful girl and at least trying to get on with her rich father? You've obviously charmed Mrs. Lucas already."

"Now you sound like Mike," Tom sighed. "But Sam Lucas and I will never get along. Too much has happened for that."

"What?"

"Well…a woman, for one thing."

"Before Mandria—and as I'm certain you aren't speaking of her lovely mother, we leave the realm of respectable ladies. So, Old Sam goes a-prodding, does he?"

"Like a damned alley cat," Tom commented as they exited the square, still heading north. "Anyway, it's a long, involved story. Suffice it to say there are hard feelings because of things he forced on this woman. But, according to him, we came to an agreement for Mandria's sake."

"What's involved about that? Evidently, you relinquished your interest in favor of Mandria."

"I did exactly that. But Sam thinks I am seeing both women—and he set the damn terms."

Allen nodded. "I'm confused."

"You aren't alone, little brother," they turned east onto Broughton Street. "A loving father would not sanction his only daughter's association with the man who stole his mistress—not without one hell of a motive."

"…The *friend* he makes concessions for; the *thief* who must work in his interest," Allen cited Sam's words. "And Mandria knows this—the whole story?"

"Yes, I've kept nothing from her. —Well, one thing I did. She doesn't need to hear the extent of Sam's abuse to the other lady."

"But you stole his mistress, Tom. How can this end happily for you? Even if you discover his motive—even if you get yourself out of the middle, somehow—he's never going to except your marriage to his daughter."

"Allen, Mandria is mine—and I don't give a damn how he feels about it!" he said as they rounded a corner. "But when I tell him so, I'll be armed with more than honorable intentions. I'll have to tree him. There's no other way with a man as cunning and dangerous as Sam Lucas."

"And what happens if Mandria gets with-child beforehand?"

"Then you will become an uncle," Tom grinned, as they turned onto Bay Street now.

"Uncle to my dead brother's child—that's what I'd be!"

"Now who's being too serious?"

"But my Lord, Tom! I let you out of my sight for just over a month and you're in more trouble than I ever heard of! If Mandria wasn't so right for you, I'd kick your ass all the way back to Athens!"

"That's odd. I thought I raised you," Tom said around a raised eyebrow.

"You did, but you should have kept some of the sense you taught me and stayed away from the likes of Sam Lucas—and, especially, from his damned mistress!"

"The way you avoided the women at Delilah's so chastely?" he chuckled. "Can this be the same young stallion also wanting a run at the wenches here a few hours ago?"

"All right; all right!" Allen raised hands of surrender and laughed too. "So you're still the best ass-kicker. But I'm a close second, aren't I?"

"Close enough, little brother—and believe me, I appreciate the concern," he paused on the sidewalk before Harrison House. "Listen, let's go down for a drink with Mike before supper. Want to?"

"Suits me," Allen shrugged. "You know, I really like him, Tom. The Captain is a hell of a lot of fun!"

"He is that and more," Tom clapped his brother's shoulder as they started down the bluff road. "I can never repay the favors he has done me—and I owe him for one in particular. Would you believe he arranged every detail of my wedding?" And with the promise of an explanation and Allen still laughing, shortly thereafter they stood knocking at the Captain's cabin.

"Damn!" Mike grinned as he opened the door. "It's a damned invasion. —The Scots come seeking more Irish blood, no doubt?"

"I'll settle for Irish whiskey," Tom grinned back.

"Who wouldn't?" Mike ushered them in and went to fix drinks. "It had to be a thirst for decent whiskey that started the rebellion. Years of drinking that God-awful Scotch is what drove you highlanders to violence."

"And both Scotch and Irish will drive some of us to our knees," said Allen. "Mike, I'll stick with brandy if you don't mind."

"I meant to ask you about that, little brother," said Tom. "When did you out-grow a mug of ale?"

"After his first night in Augusta," Mike answered, handing out glasses, "when he tried every damn whiskey and liquor that exists."

"And did you remain standing?" Tom teased.

"Absolutely!" Allen vowed. "—But Lord, I was miserable come morning!" he quickly confessed, seeing Mike would have if he hadn't.

"And broke," Mike added something anyway. "I think little brother could use a few lessons from you, Tom. He paid dearly for his miserable fun."

"Then here's to experience," Tom raised his glass to Allen.

"And may the pickings stay easy and your prick stay hard," enjoined the Irishman, with a twinkle in his eye.

"Speaking of which," Allen said now, "Captain, since Tom has gotten himself all properly married, could you show me to the nearest collection of available ladies?"

"Glad to, but not tonight," he turned to Tom. "I have been asked—finally—to have dinner at Ransom O'Rourke's. And get this:—by the man himself! Can you believe that?"

"Certainly," Tom nodded. "Ransom knows good breeding stock when he sees it."

"Now that sounds interesting!" Allen injected.

"If you saw his daughter, you'd be even more interested," Mike chuckled. "Then I would politely break your damned jaw."

"Oh?" Allen looked at Tom. "Does friend Michael also have a serious side?"

"When it comes to Nicole O'Rourke, I'm afraid so," he answered, gazing at the toes of his boots.

"And I suppose she's another beauty, like Mandria," Allen sighed.

Mike grinned. "Let's just say both ladies would leave you with reason to envy us."

"It sure as hell does," Allen lamented. "I was counting on at least one of you showing me something special on my first night in Savannah."

"Well…that's still possible," Mike hesitated. "After dinner, I'm taking Nico to see the Turkish Dancer and you two could come with us."

"Can we, Tom?" Allen came forward on his chair. "So I could meet Mike's lady too?"

Tom didn't answer. He didn't even hear the question. "Captain, that's a rough place and could be dangerous—in more ways than one. …Should you expose Nicole to that?"

"I promised her we'd go, friend, and I won't disappoint her. But if you want the truth, I'd feel a damn site better about it, if you had my back," he admitted.

"Then we have to go!" declared Allen. "Tom, you even said you owe him a favor."

"I do but—"

"But nothing!" Mike folded his arms. "Whatever it's for, I'm calling in this favor, so be there at half passed nine. We'll come as soon as Nico can slip out of the house."

"Whoa now, Captain!" Tom rose to his feet. "That is not a wise decision. I'd hate like hell for you to mess yourself up with Ransom."

"Listen to him," Mike winked at Allen,. "—Him, who is so messed up with Sam."

"But Ransom likes you," Tom persisted. "Why push your luck when everything is already going your way?"

"Oh hell, Tom, what can go wrong in a couple of hours? We'll sit in a dark corner; she'll see the dancer; and I'll take her right home. Now, be a friend," he grinned, "and get the hell out so I can dress for dinner?"

"Yeah, don't doubt Mike's luck," Allen nudged Tom toward the door. "He's Irish!"

"Oh-hell-yes!" laughed the Captain. "And Old Fort Irish breeding stock to boot!"

Taking his doubts with him, Tom departed with Allen to find a quick supper. But during the meal, try as he might, he couldn't dismiss or reason away his apprehensions.

And Allen was aware of his brother's unsettled mood. "Tom," he said, "if it would make you feel better, why not ask Mandria to join us tonight?"

"Never—not in a place like that!" Tom retorted, then realized he'd been baited.

"Because Mandria is the lady she seems to be."

"Yes."

"And Nicole O'Rourke?"

"Allen…as far as I know, she is," Tom leaned to the back of his chair.

"Then what is bothering you, Brer? You haven't been the same since we left the Irish Mist."

"…Mike is, I guess," Tom said after a considered pause. "He is making a mistake that could cost him his dreams."

"That's a bit stuffy, isn't it? So he's taking his girl to a place you don't approve of, but what's the harm in an evening of fun now and then?"

"Nothing, but Mike wants to marry this girl and he wants it gut-deep. He is just risking a lot to satisfy one of her stupid little whims."

"You don't like her, do you?" Allen asked pointedly.

"I don't like what she could do to Mike."

"You mean, if they're caught in this place, her father would end their romance?"

"He wouldn't like it, but that's not the real problem."

"You told Mike it was."

"Because if his dreams are realized, he has to stay on the right side of Ransom's financial backing—the one argument I thought he might heed."

"Then it is the girl you object to, and Mike doesn't want to hear that, because he's in love with her," Allen guessed. "Right?"

"Yes and the sad part is, he means to do right by Nicole and Ransom both."

Now Allen paused. "…Tom, I've asked this question forty different ways. What about Nicole O'Rourke? Is Mike's love one-sided—is that it?"

"I'm afraid that it is. I don't think Nico has the least notion what being in love means, because to her, everything is a game. You can bet your socks it was her idea to sneak away from the house and if she is that willing to deceive her father—who worships her and denies her nothing—how long before she's deceiving Mike too?"

"Damn," uttered Allen.

"I want to be wrong, little brother, so once you've met her, I want your opinion. Maybe knowing she could cost Mike everything—well, maybe I've misjudged her."

"Lord," Allen nodded. "What if I agree with you? —What then?"

"Then stand by to help pick up the pieces, because that's all she'll leave of the Irishman."

"Lord," Allen repeated. "That scares the hell out of me."

"You're not alone," Tom left money for the tab. "But it's time now. Shall we go?"

As they started down to River Street again, Allen made an observation. "You know, on the surface, Savannah seems like such a peaceful old city. But underneath—damn, what a maze of intrigue!"

"Did I tell you too much, too soon, little brother? Are you still glad you came?"

"Yeah, I'm glad. —Somebody has to keep you out of trouble! I guess that's what makes us the special family Mandria talked about, huh?"

"It is," Tom cuffed an affectionate fist to Allen's jaw. "We-three-Scotts could take on the world and win every time."

"Then come on, world!" Allen danced about, sparring with the air. "Come on, you bastard, we're ready for you!" he pranced a circle around Tom. "Come on—do your worst!" he challenged a lamp post. "You're in for one hell of a surprise if you tangle with the Scotts!"

So they continued, both in better spirits. Would that it could have lasted...

# CHAPTER 24

The brothers arrived early at The Shipworm Tavern, so Tom took the liberty of choosing the most secluded table, in the darkest corner he could find, but still doubted it would be enough to conceal or constrain Nicole O'Rourke if she decided to act-up. And from the moment Mike led her through the door, she justified his latent misgivings. Yes, Nicole wore a hooded cloak, as Mike had insisted, but the garment was saffron yellow and made of a costly silk. *...About as inconspicuous as a damned daffodil in a dung pile,* Tom thought, rising with Allen as the couple approached the table.

"Hello again, little brother," said the Captain as he seated her.

"Hello," he replied, inhaling the scent of a heady, rose perfume. "This must be Nicole?" he reclaimed the chair, next to her.

"Indeed it is," Mike pulled in his own chair and circled an arm across the back of hers. "Nico, meet Allen Scott."

"The young man *always ready to impress a pretty girl?*" she laughed gaily.

"...Pardon me?" he asked, trying to see beyond the silken shadows of her hood.

"I was only quoting your brother," she waved delicate, lace-gloved fingers toward Tom...who still stood and obviously missed the hand she offered for his kiss of greeting. So, turning to Allen, with a lifted chin that revealed a glimpse of her pretty mouth, she held a hand out to him. "Come, Allen, let's become true friends, shall we?"

"Oh—yes, ma'am," he marveled at the small, finely boned fingers on his, as he readily raised them to his lips.

"Now then," Mike gently drew her back. "Is everyone ready for an evening of unusual entertainment?"

"Well, I'm not, Captain," Allen contended, flashing the Scott smile. "Not until I've given you a chance to make me feel cheated too. Tom did today, when I saw him with Mandria."

"Allen," Tom drawled, suspecting another display of youthful gallantry. "Talk about cutting wide—and deep—paths?" he added, taking a seat now too.

"But I want to see Nicole O'Rourke for myself, Brer," he persisted. "If the lady is only half as enchanting as her laughter—or a tenth as alluring as her smile—then Mike has captured a goddess!"

"Oh, how utterly marvelous," Nicole reached immediately for her hood. And Tom kept silent, knowing Allen was about to learn, the hard way, that this little goddess specialized in misperception.

"Nico!" Mike made a stern objection. "You did promise to keep that on."

"I know, dearest Captain," she turned her face up to his. "But the room is so warm and it's quite dark in this corner. Couldn't I remove it for just a few minutes?" And even as she spoke, the tilt of her head was causing the hood to begin a backward slide. "Please, Michael?" she cooed, brushing her lips to his.

Trying to make the decision his, Mike paused to consider it, but by then, the point was moot. "Only for a few minutes, Nico, and on it goes to stay when the show starts."

"Thank you, my handsome Captain," she kissed him again, her head already bare.

Allen stared as much in awe of her easy maneuvering of the strong-willed Irishman as her stunning, white-blonde beauty.

Nicole, of course, took his expression as her due and played upon it. "So do continue, Allen," she made him a dazzling smile. "I just adore compliments."

"I can't," he said truthfully. "You leave me quite speechless, Miss O'Rourke. And I've never met a woman who did that before."

"My heavens," her lilting voice expressed ready favor. "Now I know we'll be true friends, Allen—and Tom said we're about the same age too."

"…We are?" Allen asked and clearly in surprise.

"You find that hard to believe?" she came forward for a confidential murmur. "Just which of us did you think the elder: Nico, the wrinkled crone; or Allen, the crusty old codger?"

"But you misunderstand!" he declared, all too aware of her closeness; of the rasping scrape of Mike's chair; of his silent observing brother— who should have been coming to his rescue. "It's only that girls your age—our age, rather," he corrected, not meaning to imply she was juvenile. "Anyway, they aren't usually so confident—and poised!" he added, lest he'd made her sound too worldly now. "…And never have I met one so, very beautiful," he finished lamely, looking again at Tom, who still sat there like a great lump of clay, offering no assistance or guidance whatsoever.

Nicole laughed, pressing for further advantage. "What you really mean is you usually credit older women with the ability to render men speechless. Women of…experience, shall we say? But there are a few of us—a special few—who are born with the talent and most men do find that wholly devastating." Then with extraordinary smugness, she patted his hand. "You'll survive, Allen, though you will recall our first meeting more often than you want to admit."

"Nico, stop your teasing," Mike chided. "You're making Allen… uncomfortable." He could think of no better word than how he was feeling for the lad.

"Would you object if it was you I teased, Captain?" she leaned conveniently into the curve of his arm. "I could you know. And I'd see that you were more than uncomfortable."

"And you, little Nico, might find more than you could handle," Mike smiled his Irish smile, and lightly kissed her fingertips.

"You are such a devil," she laid her head on his shoulder. And while cuddled there, asked Allen, "So what else could we have in common? Many things, I would think."

Allen was determined not to fall victim again. "Well, we certainly value the same friendships," he looked the Captain in the eye.

"We surely do," she gazed now at Tom, who seemed to be studying the ceiling. And Nicole found his inattention unforgivably rude. If he couldn't at least be sociable, she'd just force him to do her bidding. "And now—Tom," she said emphatically, "since you look as if you need something to do, I would appreciate a nice cool drink."

To the company in general, Tom made a small to-do of a lengthy apology about his preoccupation, while avoiding acknowledgement of her request. He was not going to be the one to add alcohol to Nicole's fire—and he hoped Mike wouldn't either. Yet even as the thought passed, the Captain rose to his feet.

"Ale, all-around?" he asked, and received two affirmative nods before leaving.

A new thought had just occurred to Nicole. ...*Maybe Tom isn't purposely unresponsive; maybe he's just unhappy the other two have monopolized my attention—and maybe I should do something about that right away.* "Be a dear," she patted Allen's arm. "Catch Mike and tell him I'd prefer a sweet sherry."

With her fingers still caressing his arm, Allen watched her eyes slide over to Tom and remain there. "...Sweet sherry," he repeated, but thought *sweet revenge.* And ignoring Tom's negative nod, he too, rose and left the table.

"Well, this is long overdue," Nicole began immediately. "An intriguing statement, wouldn't you say?"

"A veritable understatement," Tom remarked, seriously considering a number of ways to throttle Allen.

"Why, thank you, Tom," she laughed. "I will take that as a compliment."

"Would you even consider taking it another way?" he uttered.

"No, because I know you find me attractive. —Why not admit it?"

Tom laughed now. Her outrageous vanity was just that comical. "And risk being rendered *speechless*? Surely, one *born to devastate* the male species needn't go begging for compliments."

"My-oh-my," she purred. "So you were listening and you're jealous because you weren't included. Well, it's good to know that it bothered you so much."

Was there no end to her assumptions? Maybe he could try changing the subject. "There are a lot of things I find bothersome—"

"Oh, so do I!" she interrupted, and this was followed by a swift move to the chair beside him. "Like the thing I saw in the stable tonight," she leaned to speak in confidence. "Even if they were only Negroes, it was so primeval—so soul stirring!"

Tom glanced at the agitated fingers clutched to his sleeve; at the undiluted excitement in her eyes, and decided she had found another subject on her own. Still, he was cautious. "…Am I supposed to guess what you saw, or do you plan to tell me?"

"Heaven forbid!" her eyes widened innocently. "It was too, too wicked and you'd never expect me to repeat such a thing. —Would you, Tom?" But it was more a dare than a question.

"*Heaven forbid,*" he quoted dryly. And knowing she wasn't finished, he leaned to the back of his chair, putting all the distance between them he could.

"Yes, being a lady does have restrictions," she sighed too sweetly. "…Of course, as you suggested, you could try guessing. I couldn't stop you from guessing."

"But as a gentleman, I shouldn't," he parried. "No, I wouldn't think of offending your delicate sensibilities."

"You rogue!" she jabbed him playfully. "You'd like nothing better. —I know I'm not wrong about you. You would have found my experience fascinating! Now, let me give you a clue. It was a person to person act and very—very—romantic in nature."

"Nicole," he said, suspicious of her direction, "I really don't care what you saw and I don't like guessing games."

"You mean you don't need them," she replied sagely. "All right, we'll forget about the stable—if you'll make some romantic suggestions of your own. …My reaction could surprise you," she made him a sloe-eyed finish.

"Then may I *suggest* that you stop this and behave yourself?" Tom asked seriously.

"And miss the chance to flirt with you?" she moved closer. "Tom, I enjoy romantic interludes—and the mystery of what might be. It can lead to acts of wonderful madness."

"Or terrible rage," he countered.

"Oh, come now," she traced fingers up his lapel. "You aren't angry with me."

"But Mike will be, if he finds you nearly in my lap."

"I know! And isn't it grand?" she actually laughed about it. "But should we meet on another evening—alone—well, it's something to think about, isn't it?"

The silence to follow was awkward; her eyes searching for a positive response and his remaining unreadable.

"...Do you care so little for Mike?" he finally asked.

"I care—of course I do. The Captain is a very handsome man. However...," she paused for emphasis, "we are not married or even engaged and until something of that nature occurs, I can have as many suitors as I wish." Then she was all smiles and laughter again. "Oh, do give in! When and where shall we meet?"

Tom had an answer he was more than willing to share, but first he intended to learn just how devious she was. Slowly, and also for emphasis, he moved forward in his chair. And his tone, when he decided to speak, was husky and conspiratorial. "So, how would you have this meeting go, Nicole: with or without Mike's knowledge?"

"Oh, without!" eagerness hissed from her whisper. "It will be our own secret affair."

"An interesting word...affair," he assessed her with a scorching gaze. "Should I take your meaning figuratively or literally?"

If his eyes had not held her in place, Nicole was sure she'd have magically floated away. Never had she been so jubilant; so sure of her beauty and ability to charm. For this one man, who had resisted her every effort, was attainable after all. "Why, darling, you'll just have to try me and see," she cooed provocatively.

An inviting smile crossed Tom mouth and to assure her complete attention, he lifted a silky, blonde curl from her shoulder, tested the texture and allowed it to sift from his fingers as he spoke. "Only if you'll do me a favor first. ...Will you, little Nico?"

"As I said; ...try me and see," she managed, feeling each hair fall back into place and wishing he'd follow after them. When he did, and was merely an inch away, she was so certain he meant to take a kiss that her breathing ceased.

Then, without moving; without the slightest change in his smoldering expression and using that same intimate voice, Tom said, "Kindly go straight to hell."

It took a moment for the message to register; another for her gasp of surprise. "What?" she recoiled to the back of her chair. "—What did you say to me?"

"Your hearing isn't bad," he assured her.

"W—well I never!" she stammered. "Thomas Scott, how could you lead me on that way? And to think you could so distort a simple offer of friendship!"

"What you offered, little girl, was nothing but trouble—and I seriously doubt if you have one real friend in Savannah."

"I do so!" she declared. "Mike is a very dear friend—and so are Mandy and Lucy! Why I have a lot of friends, who would never hurt me so cruelly!"

"But you'd have no qualms about hurting them," he countered. "Didn't you just offer to meet me behind Mike's back?"

"I wouldn't have!" she swore, only to reopen the question in the next breath. "And even so, a real gentleman would be discreet about it and Mike wouldn't be hurt at all."

"My God," Tom laughed, wondering if she actually believed her own logic.

"How dare you laugh at me!" she exclaimed angrily. "I am not just any woman, Tom Scott! Wealth does have its privileges and my wishes are never refused—not by any man!" There: now he knew she dealt from power; now let him laugh if he dared.

Tom didn't. He was too close to losing his temper to utter a single word.

Nicole, of course, took his silence for acquiescence, which greatly boosted her self assurance. And as long as he now accepted her position, she didn't mind explaining it further. "I will have what I want from life and always will. That's just the way it is."

"…And what—exactly—do you want?" he asked, more to test his control than from curiosity.

"The best of everything!" she said with a tilt of her proud little chin. "Fun, luxuries, men—especially, the admiration of Savannah's most eligible, handsome men. …And Tom, in spite of our little tiff, you still rank highly on my list."

"Men," he ignored all else. "But not man—as in Captain Michael Herb."

"Are we back to that?" she blessed him with a tolerant smile. "I'm not denying an attraction between us. Mike is fun to be with and he enjoys my company just as much—"

"More, Nicole," Tom injected. "Mike is serious about you."

"I—well, one of these days, I may feel the same thing for him. But for now, I intend to do as I please and see whomever I want."

"Then tell him so, damn it! —Be as honest with Mike as you're being with me."

"If I do," she sent him a look meant to melt all resistance, "then will you see me?"

"No," he answered almost pleasantly.

"And just why not?" her eyes flashed indignantly.

"I don't owe you an explanation," he shrugged.

"Is it Mandy?"

"That's none of your business," he said, wondering where in hell Mike was.

"Thomas Scott, I demand an answer!" she stated in a fresh rush of anger. "And if it's your loyalty to Mike, believe me I could destroy that with a snap of my fingers!"

"…Meaning?" She had his full attention now.

"Meaning I could tell Mike you've been trying to seduce me—and even if you denied it, just who do you think he'd believe?"

"Miss O'Rourke," Tom said slowly, and very softly, "you do that and I'll see your reputation ruined. I'm a far better liar than you and when I'm finished, Mike—nor any of your so-called gentlemen, will touch you on a God damned bet."

Nicole had never experienced anything as frightening as the dreadful blue-flamed inferno of those eyes, contrasted against such gently spoken words. It sent her to the back of the chair again, and this time, like a physical blow. And for reasons unknown, excited her beyond the telling. "You wouldn't. N...not really," she stammered, befuddled by her roiling emotions.

"*Try-me-and-see*," he quoted, but giving new connotation to her words. "I can always leave Savannah. Can you? Your wealth and privilege are here. But they won't do you a hell of a lot of good if your father disowns you. —And I wouldn't stop until he did."

"All right!" she pressed her palms to the table top. "...All right, Tom, I was only teasing," she attempted a smile that quivered badly. "Anyway, I don't know why you're so upset. I was just flirting with you—and all in the spirit of innocent fun."

Tom heaved a sigh. Already, she was excusing her own behavior. "Just have your fun with Mike tonight. He is risking a lot to show you a good time. ...Do not ruin it for him, Nicole O'Rourke." This was said as a rather bored sounding command and seeing her resentment, as well as the returning Captain, he smiled, adding, "You know the options, so the decision is now entirely yours."

"What decision is that?" Mike queried, placing three mugs of ale on the table. "What devil's work is he up to, Nico?"

She looked from Mike's laughing sky blue eyes into the living blue embers of Tom's direct gaze and drew her cloak about an involuntary shiver. "He wanted me to—to help Mandy do something," she answered, conceding a win to Tom. ...*But only for tonight,* she thought. And really, wasn't that all he'd asked? *Have your fun with Mike tonight.* Well, didn't that just leave all sorts of opportunities open for the future? Indeed, it did...

"So, where is that brother of mine?" Tom asked the Captain.

"He met up with part of my crew and stopped for a chat. —And Nico," he chuckled, "I'm sorry about your sherry, but that's not served here. It's ale and hard stuff for the like of these folk."

"Ale is fine," she made him a sugary smile. "It was a silly notion to begin with." There. Now she'd behaved as Tom wanted, but glancing his way for approval, she found him scanning the crowd, oblivious to her effort to please him. The man was absolutely infuriating!

"Well, the show is about to start. Last chance to back out, Nico; —sherry drinkers might take offense," Mike teased, while attempting to adjust her hood.

"Do stop—you're mussing my hair, Michael!" she irritably took the task over. "And I mean to see this dancer, so don't try talking me out of it again."

"…All right, then," he shrugged, baffled by her volatile mood. "You've been warned,"

Which was precisely true, for the look Tom sent her could only be interpreted as such. "Yes," she gentled again, "And that's why I'm here with you, my Captain. You care about the things that make me happy—unlike some heartless people I know."

Mike beamed her smile, but before he could reply, the room filled with bawdy applause and loud whistles. Nicole watched as the barkeep lit a row of lamps across the bar top and now, mingled with noise from the crowd gathering up there, she heard the beat of a drum and a strange whining flute. Soon, the crowd was clapping to the drum beat; soon the fluted tune built to a series of screeches; and from a gauzed-curtained alcove atop one end of the bar came the sound of tiny bells.

Ching, chinga-ling; Ching, chinga-ling;

Ching, chinga; Ching, chinga;

Ching, ching, chinga-ling…

Then silence fell, as the curtains parted to reveal the brown skinned Turkish dancer, swathed from neck to toe in lengths of jewel hued veiling. Her raven hair was pulled severely away from her face and plaited in a long pigtail, beginning on the crown of her head. She stood with arms arched gracefully above and attached to the posed fingers of each hand, were small, cymbal-shaped, brass discs. She was, in fact, totally posed, from the arrogant tilt of her chin to her arched spine and amply protruding breasts.

Ching, chinga-ling;

Ching, chinga-ling…

said the little cymbals Nicole had mistaken for bells, and the music resumed as the Turk glided slowly along the bar top. Every drum beat, each note from the flute had a purpose in her dance, for they helped draw the eye to one section of her body as she deftly removed a veil from another. And, when the last one fell away, she wore more body oil than costume. Hips, buttocks, belly, legs, bosom and arms—all glowed with an oily sheen. Patches of flesh colored netting did lie over her breasts, but in no way concealed them or restricted the gyrations of her dance. The bottom was a mere row of black fringe that shimmied along with her hip and stomach rolls, enhancing the illusion of nudity. And, as Mike had promised, Nicole saw the pea-sized ruby tucked in the hollow of her navel.

Then, the woman went to her knees and began a controlled backward arch amid all her many moving parts, until her shoulders touched the bar. And when the men at next table rose for a better look at what the fringe covered between those wide-spread thighs, Nicole rose too, not even hearing Mike ask her sit down.

The dancer righted herself then; rhythm of drum and flute accelerated; and she undulated her way toward a large wicker basket on the other end of the bar. In growing expectation, the thickening crowd swept after her—and Nicole was among them. Before Mike could stop her, she darted away, pushing and shoving through the forward pressing throng, until she reached a spot, right in front of that basket.

The beat of drum and flute was fevered now, building to a crescendo, as the Turk removed the basket lid, and bracing her legs, leaned head and shoulders into the opening.

A hush descended over those standing closest and Nicole rose on tip-toes in avid anticipation.

Ching, chinga-ling;

Ching, chinga-ling…

the wee cymbals sang in the stillness.

Ching, chinga;

Ching, chinga…

and the Turks' stomach muscles suddenly tightened under the stain of a sizable weight.

Ching, ching, chinga-ling…

she straightened slowly, while her arms moved in imitation of the huge snake now draped about her neck.

Ching, chinga-ling;

Ching, chinga-ling…

the dancer gave musical directives, leading the snake into a coil about her body from ankle to breast, where the serpents head rose and the pair indulged in touching tongues.

Ching, chinga;

Ching, chinga;

Ching, ching, chinga-ling…

her hands led the way and the snake slithered ever downward, squeezing just enough to seem it was feeling her breasts, the span of her waist, the plumpness of hip and thigh. Then, as the head reached the row of black fringe, it paused—as directed—hovering there to flick its tongue repeatedly.

The suggestion was enough to cause Nicole a rare bout of embarrassment. "Oh my!" she spun away—right into a male embrace, where she was held and hustled, none too gently, to the rear of the crowd.

"So, is this a ghost come to haunt me?" he slid back her hood. "Or has little Nico finally shed her cocoon?"

"…Uncle Sam?" she peered upward.

"Yes, indeed," his hands closed on her upper arms. "Your dear old friend and neighbor."

"Well, if you'll excuse me," she tried freeing herself, only to feel his grip tighten almost painfully.

"Now, now," he admonished. "You're not going anywhere until you've explained your presence here."

And Nicole just stood there, feeling the strength of his hands; playing it against the odd, taunting gleam in his eyes; and finding both…rather intriguing? "Uncle Sam," she attempted a smile of appeasement, "I only came to see the dancer."

"Obviously, my dear," he smiled back. "But not with your father's permission—and surely, not alone."

"Oh, I'm with friends. And really, Daddy knows—"

"Don't lie to me!" he gave her a good shake. "I stopped in to see Ransom, not an hour ago, and he said you'd gone to bed early!" Then his hold eased and his hands moved caressingly down her arms. "… What else do you do behind his back, Nico?"

"Damn it! No need in smothering her, Lucas!" Mike swore, drawing Nicole from the man's grasp, but adding a reprimand for her too. "— Why did you leave the table? That was a really stupid thing to do!"

But as the Captain led her away, it dawned on him that his troubles had just begun. It wasn't enough when that brick wall of people had allowed Nicole to pass, yet refused to budge for him; or his fright upon finally reaching the front of the crowd to find her gone; or fighting his way out again to see her in Sam's clutches. —No, none of that compared to the trouble following so close on their heels right now.

"I've got you, Herb! —By God, I've got you at last!" Sam laughed long and gleefully. "Ransom will nail your hide to the fucking bank door for this one! —Now, how will my story go? You encouraged his innocent daughter to deceive him. You brought her into this evil den of iniquity, plied her with liquor and salacious entertainment, while attempting to seduce her. —And I can truthfully say I found her wandering alone in a room full of hot, horny bastards. Oh, yes, Captain Herb, this time I have you by the God damned balls!" And Sam was so involved with his tirade, he failed to see Tom rise from the far side of the shadowy table.

"What you have, my friend," he smiled as Lucas turned to face him, "is exactly nothing. You'll make a complete ass of yourself if you go to Ransom with that story."

"Look—you stay out of this!" Sam pointed a finger in warning. "I am not about to let Herb off this hook!"

"Aren't you?" Tom asked, meeting Mike's eyes as he slid an arm about Nicole. "Thank you for returning my run-away lady, Captain. I missed her sorely," he said, placing a tender kiss on her forehead.

Sam's frown deepened and his irritation rose. "Scott, what in the hell are you trying to pull?"

"Why nothing at all," he nuzzled Nicole's cheek, hoping to conceal her stunned expression. "As I said, the lady is with me."

To this point, Nicole had paid little attention to the angry words around her. Tuning them out was a trick she'd learned as a child, when her parents did frequent battle. Later, it served her again when she was delegated the role of hostess for her widowed father, the only adolescent at many a boring dinner party. But she was paying attention now, her heart scampering wildly; her senses honed to exquisite peaks of awareness—and it had nothing to do with the continuing conversation, but everything to do with the feel of Tom's arms about her and the touch of his lips on her face. Here was the chance she had wanted—a chance to make him aware of her physically; to make him reconsider his hasty refusal to see her. So, she moved forward, securely locking her arms about his waist and herself to his chest. Wasn't it lovely, too, that all would be considered just a part of whatever it was they were arguing about?

"I see what you're doing!" Sam was saying. "But God damn it, Scott, I know you're lying!"

"Am I, Nicole?" Tom tried and failed to dislodge her. "Come now," he managed to force her shoulders back—which swung her lower body in closer. "Give Sam an answer, won't you?"

"If you'll kiss me," she answered sweetly, drawing a look of surprise from Sam and an indescribable one from the Irishman.

"But only one," Tom lowered his mouth a few tempting inches. "Any more and I couldn't stop," he added, remaining just beyond her reach. And as he hoped, she released her hold, rising on tip-toe to grasp at his lapels. It was a decidedly brief kiss, but effective on many levels, for Sam's expression said he found it real; Mike was doing a fairly good job of feigning disinterest; and best of all, Tom had been able to turn Nicole around and the arms corseting her ribcage now greatly restricted her breathing—and purposely so.

"I still think you're lying," Sam insisted, even as Nicole gave him more reason for doubt. She was actually pressing Tom's arms closer about her. "Mandy said Herb was courting Nicole. —And Ransom said he dined with them this very evening."

"Business," Mike said, his eyes glued to the tabletop. "Strictly business." …Nicole was playing-acting—of course she was—but he couldn't watch it.

He would have felt worse had he observed what Sam was at the moment. Slowly, and with more brazenness than he'd seen since her mother was alive, Nicole began to press and swivel against Tom's loins. "God damn it," he muttered, wondering if there was a woman in Savannah who wouldn't play the bitch for this man. "Neither of you bastards is out of this yet. Ransom will just hang you both—and let me help him!"

"He probably would," Tom smiled, because he'd managed to shift Nicole to his side—and if she tried to move, he swore to squeeze her until she fainted! "But after a full day under the…uh, prim and proper terms of our agreement? Surely, Sam—man to man—you can see the need for relief."

It was into this cozy scene that Allen returned. "…Tom?" he stared.

"So there you are little brother!" Tom hoped for a minor miracle. "Nicole and I were beginning to worry about you."

Allen nodded in confusion. "Well, here I am, but—"

"But you left your manners elsewhere. Didn't you notice that Sam has joined us?"

"I'm sorry, I didn't," Allen extended his hand. "Good evening, sir. It's good to see you again."

Sam now faced a huge dilemma. He wanted Michael Herb just where he had him—and he did have him, in spite of the garbage Tom was throwing in his path. …But with Allen involved too, could he afford to appear the villain in his own son's eyes? No, God damn it, he couldn't! So, searching mightily for self control, as he shook Allen's hand, he said, "It's…uh, good seeing you too, son. Quite the—uh, quite a show the Turk puts on, huh?"

"Indeed, it is," Allen watched as Tom grasped the hand Nicole started to run up his chest, but quickly lifted to his lips when Sam looked their way. "—So what kind of snake was that?" he asked attempting to draw Sam's attention away. …*But Lord*, he thought,

*Mike looks almost ill—and why is he staring at the table like that?* "The damn thing had to be ten or eleven feet long!"

"Boa, I believe," Sam nodded. "Native of South America. ...Leaves you to wonder how a Turk came up with it."

"Yes sir," Allen chuckled. "It certainly does."

"So, Sam," Tom said then, "if you're satisfied that the three of us have adequately protected this lady, I'd like to get her home before midnight. —And do you need a ride? You did mention something about seeing her father."

After an endless moment, Sam declined. "...No, I've changed my mind. For now. But Scott, you'd best see this is kept quiet as well. More people than Ransom would be upset—if you get my *prim and proper* meaning." Then, turning on his heel, he walked away into the crowd...

# CHAPTER 25

Tom placed Nicole's hand on his arm and led the way out, with Mike and Allen following behind. All were silent until boarding a cabbie carriage, where he literally plopped Nicole on the seat next to Mike and sat across from them.

"All right," Allen glanced from Mike's somber expression, to Nicole's look of miffed surprise, to the aggravation etched into Tom's demeanor, "…who is going to tell me what happened?"

"Tom saved our damned lives; that's what!" Mike exclaimed. "Hell, Allen, Sam was going to say he caught me trying to seduce Nico—and Tom stepped in and saved our damned lives!"

"No, I didn't—"

"Not alone, you didn't!" Nicole interrupted, still upset that Tom would hand her over so easily after all she done to entice him. …*Well then*, she decided, *it must time to for my favorite ploy: I'll just make him jealous.* "And Mike, I was so frightened having to pretend I wanted to be with Tom instead of you; —and listening while Uncle Sam said the scariest things about cocoons and ghosts!" she snuggled close. "Oh, do hold me, my Captain—as if you'll never let go!"

Mike obliged, but was too distracted to respond with the enthusiasm she wanted seen. "Why so quiet, Tom?" he asked over her head. "That usually means I missed something."

"I-don't-know!" Tom said in frustrated staccato. "When Sam came to the table, he was jubilant; then angry; then not. I just can't make any sense of the man!"

"I still say it was your quick thinking," Mike insisted. "You and Nico!" he added, when she jabbed him in the ribs—but not so much for forgetting to credit her, as his lack of fervor for her big performance.

"Captain, Lucas wasn't fooled." said Tom. "No, something else happened there; something I can't quite put my finger on…"

"Well, thank God for the outcome, no matter the reason," Mike nodded. "And I'll tell you this: we won't be sneaking off anywhere again—not ever!"

"…Michael?" Nicole sat up to look at him, all else forgotten. "You can't mean that. You said we'd go everywhere!"

The expectation in her eyes nearly killed the Irishman. "I'm so sorry, little Nico," he apologized, "But I can't be putting you in that kind of danger again."

"Then we'll just be more careful," she argued, nesting against his chest, "I'll keep my hood on at all times and stay as close to you as this."

"Why did you wander off?" he thought to ask. "That was so foolish and—"

"Driver, stop here!" Tom called as they turned onto Bay Street. "Mike, we'll be going home now—but do let me know who wins this argument, will you?"

"Good night, Nicole," Allen kissed her hand. "You're as beautiful as Mike claimed and then some. —Captain?" he added a smart salute, before joining Tom on the street.

"Thank you, Allen," she replied. "But Tom, I don't care what you say; I think we performed our Charade rather well together." And before the carriage even pulled away, she had resumed her pleading, hands cupped to Mike's face. "Dear Captain, you know how much these outings mean to me…"

Tom just nodded as he stood looking after them.

"So, you're at it again, huh?" Allen grinned as they started for Harrison House. "Out of my sight for less than an hour and you're back into trouble."

"And if you can tell me why I'm not now—why all of us aren't—I'd appreciate it." Tom muttered. "Sam has wanted something on Mike for longer than I've known him. And tonight he had it; —had Mike in the palm of his hand; and damn it, he simply…let go," he finished as they entered the front door.

"Well, if you don't believe it was your Charade, as Nico put it, then it must go back to that agreement to court Mandria," Allen said around a yawn.

"…Tired, little brother?" Tom asked while they climbed the stairway. "It has been a long first day here, hasn't it?"

"Pretty much," he agreed, following Tom into their rooms.

"Tell you what, then: I'm going to be up for a good while yet, so you take my bed for tonight. That way you can sleep late in the morning too."

"I'm for that, Brer," he started for the bedroom, but paused in the doorway. "Still want my opinion of Nicole?"

"Let's hear it," Tom nodded.

"She is very, very beautiful; a little cruel; a lot self-centered; … and she has a real liking for you. Without meaning to, brother Tom, you could be Mike's biggest rival. So, maybe you just dislike the girl for putting you in that position?" he finished around another yawn.

Seeing that, Tom thought better of keeping Allen awake with details of his confrontation with Nicole. "…Maybe so," he said instead, sitting to pull off his boots. "But go get some rest. We can talk later."

"Well, don't stay up too long. You told me often enough, there's no sense worrying over things you can't change. And I leave these words from your wise little brother: When the apple is ripe," he grinned tiredly, "the other shoe will hit the floor." Then, ducking the sock Tom threw, he went to bed.

Bare-foot, shirt-tails out and wearing the smile Allen could always win from him, Tom fixed a nightcap. But it would be a while before he could unwind enough from the night's events to sleep. Besides, he was half expecting a late night visitor…

A second drink was going down smoothly, when Tom heard a familiar rap at the door. Filling another glass, he unfastened the lock, handed it out and closed the door again. Then, with a hand on the knob, he patiently waited for the knocking to resume, before reopening it. "Oh, did you want come in too?" he asked.

"Yes, damn you," Mike chuckled, passing himself in. "And I'll also take another drink."

Tom crossed to the bedroom, looked in at his sleeping brother for a moment and quietly closed the door. "I thought you might, but grab a chair and let's take the bottle to the porch. No need in waking Allen just because we're still prowling about."

"He's a hell of a kid, Tom," Mike said while they lugged everything out to the porch. "And very much like my best friend."

"Thank you. He and Mandria hit it off today, too—just like blood kin. I'm really pleased about that," he said as they sat side by side, feet propped on the banister and the bottle on the floor between them. "—Hey, Captain," Tom added with a chuckle, "if we had cigars, this would be like sitting on the deck of the Irish Mist again, wouldn't it?"

"Which I just happen to have," Mike pulled two fresh smokes from his jacket and soon had both of them lit. "…So, do you think Sam might go to Ransom yet?" he asked a few puffs later.

"I really don't see how he could. With Nicole safely at home again, how would he back his story? And he has to know Ransom would not take kindly to unsupported tales about his daughter."

"But you still don't think Sam believed Nico was with you?"

"Not for a moment. And Mike, he has no love for either of us, so why make all those threats and then back off and do nothing?"

"Maybe it's the deal you two made; —maybe there's more to it than you know."

"That was Allen's thinking too," Tom nodded. "But what in hell do I have that he wants so badly? —And how many times will I ask myself the same damned question?"

"I can fix that," Mike suggested. "I'll just shoot the bastard—or challenge him to damned dual or something. With him dead, the rest of us would be put out of our misery."

307

"Captain, one would be murder and the other foolish," Tom grinned. "You can't shoot straight and I hardly think he'd settle for casting shrimp nets at ten paces."

"Yeah, well, I guess you're right," Mike replenished their drinks.

"Did you win the argument with Nico when you left here?" Tom asked then.

"…Sort of," the Irishman said with a nod.

"Captain, how do you *sort-of* win an argument?"

"By letting her think she did—but believe you me, I'm not taking her anywhere Ransom wouldn't. She's young, Tom, and hasn't been many places anyway, so she won't know the difference,"

"After seeing the Turk and that damned snake?" Tom questioned this logic. "You are doing the right thing, Mike…just be prepared for a possible rebellion. She may grow bored with anything less outrageous than tonight."

"Hell, not with the Captain of the Irish Mist around, she won't!" he finished off his drink and rose. "I come packed with all kinds of damned surprises. —And speaking of which, there is a place at Thunderbolt called The Pier that serves supper and has room there for dancing too. Want to go next weekend?"

"No, thank you," Tom said rising too.

"Oh. You have other plans?"

"No, Captain, I just don't care to dance with you. Mandria is more the type I'd choose to partner with."

"You know what I meant, damn you!" he laughed, heading for the hall. "And see if Mandy can scare up a date for Allen too. We'll go for an early supper on Saturday and just make an evening of it. But for now, I'm off to bed. —Night, Tom."

"Night, Mike," Tom watched him descend the stairs. Then, heaving a sigh, he carried everything back inside from the porch while making a decision he didn't like. He wasn't going to tell Mike about the conversation with Nicole. If he did, he'd lose the Irishman as a friend. It would be best to let her do her own damage—and after hearing that wish-list she spewed, it shouldn't be long in coming…

Morning sunlight spilled into the bedroom when Tom drew the curtains aside. "Allen?" he called, giving his brother's toe a thump. "Wake up; coffee is poured and waiting."

"Oh? What time is it?" Allen smiled, yawned and stretched all at once.

"Close to eight. A note from Mandria came asking us to be at the Lucas house by eleven o'clock. It seems she wants you to have a phaeton tour of the city. So, if you'd like breakfast, hop to it. Mrs. Harrison serves until nine thirty on weekends."

"I'm coming," Allen reached for his trousers.

"Sorry about the plan to sleep late, little brother," Tom added. "But school starts in a week and I won't have much free time for helping you get acclimated after that."

"Tom," Allen asked, buttoning his shirt as he followed to the sitting room table, "are you going to tell Mandria about last night?"

"Most of it, yes," he sat to sip on his coffee.

"But not everything, surely. …Nicole was all over you—and she did maneuver me away from the table. For whatever reason, I think she wanted to be alone with you."

"Subtle wasn't she?"

"Like a velvet sledge-hammer," Allen grinned, blowing steam from his own cup.

Tom laughed in agreement. "To answer your question, I won't tell Mandria enough to make her resent Nicole."

"Why not?" he asked around a tasty swallow.

"Because as long as Mike wants to see the girl, we'll all be thrown together and it's best that things remain friendly. And because Mandria and Nicole have been friends since childhood."

"Nicole wasn't concerned about that friendship last night—and if she knows nothing else, she should have known you and Mandria were dating at the very least."

"Allen, things happened so fast with Mandria and me, I don't know what Nicole thinks there is between us," Tom went to the mirror on the bachelor's chest and brushed his hair into place.

"Well boy, does she have a surprise coming," Allen said, slipping on his shoes.

"The point is Mandria needn't worry about it one damned bit," said Tom. "I'll handle Miss Nicole O'Rourke."

"That, big brother," Allen smirked, "may be exactly what she has in mind."

"And you, little brother," Tom grinned back, "better finish your damned coffee."

"I am—I'm drinking it!" he replied. "So, tell me about your job. How far is the school from here?"

"A few blocks, but there won't be much to tell until I've started. —Oh, but Mandria is doing some art classes there, so I'll get to see her even more often."

"…Which brings up something else we should discuss," Allen said hesitantly. "Tom, I don't want to embarrass her. I mean, you are married and she doesn't need me… well, when you two—oh, hell, do you know what I'm trying to say?"

"That you can't just *read-a-book-or-something,*" Tom smiled, remembering Mandria's worry over the same subject. "I'll let you know when to make yourself scarce, little brother, but it won't be a problem much longer. …You see, I'm buying a house—a real home, Allen, and Ransom thinks he can close the deal fairly soon: possibly in a week or two."

"Tom, that's great!" Allen nodded. "So your job must pay well to afford you a new home."

"*Our* new home. There is plenty of room there for you too, Allen."

"Yes, well, we'll see," Allen hedged, needing to say something more, but unsure of how. "This place seems pretty nice. I could stay on here… if I had a steady income."

"Oh? I had hoped you'd be entering the University come spring."

"I know that's what you want, Tom, but I'm not the student you were," Allen went on, eager to get this settled. "I'm not saying I'll never go back, but for now, I'm tired of school! I want to try my hand at something else—anything else—and you did too. Remember? You worked in a store, a mill, the railroad…"

"I know—I do remember!" Tom agreed. "And that is when I came to appreciate working my brain instead of breaking my back."

"Those damned farm chores would have done it too," Allen stood to tuck his shirttails. "So that's something else I don't want to do. I never want to see another farm! …Does that surprise you too?"

"No, at your age, I said the same. Though had Dad lived, it may have been different. Mama said he was really proud to be a farmer."

"Then I must be a throw-back to Mama's side of the family," Allen brushed his hair now. "Her fine English breeding must run stronger in me. Yeah, I think I was meant to be the Lord of a great manor—or at least, a spoiled rich man's son."

"Mad ravings, little brother," Tom waited by the opened door. "But you'd best remember those farm chores kept us together and our bellies full—kept us out of some orphanage too."

"I know," Allen paused beside his taller sibling. "And I'm grateful, but hell, that's behind us now, isn't it? There must be other things to try, right here in Savannah."

"So, you're ready for city life," Tom concluded, heading toward the stairs.

"Damn right! It has to beat *clearing-them-fields*. —And I'll tell you something else. City women smell better."

"They smell better?" Tom laughed.

"Hell, yes! I'll take perfume and powder over field dust and lye soap any day of the week. —And what is that Mandria wears? It really smells good."

"Had you *cleared-them-fields* properly, you would have pulled out a ton of the stuff, Allen. It's honeysuckle."

"It is honeysuckle!" he turned on the bottom step in realization. "And you have to admit something too, brother Tom. Surely you'd prefer wrestling with Mandria's kind of honeysuckle, than to wrestle one of those God-awful vines from the earth."

"Any time," Tom pointed Allen toward the dining room. "Any time at all."

"Morning to you, Mister Tom; Mister Allen," Jed displayed his fine, toothy greeting. "Come on in the house!"

"Good morning to you too, Jed," Tom returned. "Is Mandria ready to leave?"

"She been ready," he chuckled, leading them to the morning parlor. "But she's gone now to fetch Miss Lucy. Said you was to wait, 'cuz she'll be right back. Just sit down, please, and I'll tell Miss Evelyn you're here, like she asked me to."

When Jed left, Tom smiled at Allen. "Lucy huh? Well, little brother, the day could be more pleasant than you expected."

"Is she pretty?" Allen whispered. "—Is she, Tom?"

"I think she is," he nodded. "And quite…well, you'll see what I mean when you meet her—"

"Good morning!" Sam's voice boomed from the doorway. "Good to see you, Tom" he came, hand extended—and not a trace of the previous night's angst in his manner. "You too, son," he moved smoothly on to shake Allen's hand next. "Mandy tells me you're in for a day of sight-seeing."

"It seems that I am," Allen nodded.

"Good; …good," Sam stood looking at the boy with pride. "And don't forget my offer, when you have the time."

"I won't, sir. I'm most interested in the opportunities Savannah has to offer."

"And there are many. —Right, Tom?" Sam graced him with a brief glance, before returning to Allen.

"…Certainly," Tom answered, as that strange uneasiness returned to nag him.

"Good morning, all," Evelyn entered smiling. "Allen; Tom, please sit down. May I get you a cup of coffee?"

"Thank you, but we just finished breakfast," Tom said, scanning her attire. "You do look lovely today, Mamalyn. Are you going out? —We're not detaining you, are we?"

"Not at all," she replied. "I've a meeting to attend, but we've plenty of time for a visit—and an invitation. Would you and Allen care to join us for supper?"

"Yes, Allen, I'm sure you'd enjoy a good meal," Sam leapt right in. "My cooks are the best in captivity—and tonight, I've ordered a pork roast with all the trimmings."

"Tom?" Allen said hopefully. "That sounds mighty tempting."

"What does?" Mandria came in with Lucy on her heels.

"Supper," answered Evelyn. "We've asked them to stay—and you're invited too, Lucy."

"Thank you, Mamalyn," she bobbed a curtsy, while shyly peeking at Allen. Then giggling, she turned to Tom. "Hello again, Tom. How are you, Tom?"

"Fine, Lucy. And you, Lucy?" he teased.

"I'm fine too—I really, really am," she sneaked a second peek at his brother.

"Allen," Tom brought him forward, "This is Miss Lucille Love; Lucy, my brother, Allen Scott."

"Oh dear!" Lucy's eyes rolled upward. "There is that ugly thing again!"

"What?" Allen followed her gaze to search the ceiling. "Where? —What is it?"

"My name!" she exclaimed. "Nobody wants to meet anybody named Lucille!"

"Oh...," Allen nodded and then began to laugh. "Oh, but I do!" he took her hand. "In fact, I've never enjoyed an introduction more."

"My gracious," Lucy blushed as he raised her hand to his lips. "Oh—my goodness gracious!" she giggled again when he then stood smiling at her.

"...Mandria?" Tom sounded doubtful "What do you think? If we stay for supper, do you suppose they'll bicker and fight this way all evening?"

313

"Heaven knows," she feigned a sigh. "It is a shame they took such an instant disliking to one another."

"Now you two stop that," Evelyn smiled. "All of you just run along now, and we'll see you later this afternoon."

"And Allen," Sam injected, "as you're likely to spend as much time here as Tom or Lucy, you're to call me Sam. It's Sam and—and Mamalyn. Is that understood?"

"Yes sir," he answered, noting the curious look Evelyn gave her husband. "…If Mrs. Lucas doesn't mind."

"Of course not," she said warmly. "Now, shoo, all of you! Be gone and have fun!"

The two couples stood conversing in the carriage yard, waiting for the phaeton to be brought around and Sam watched all from the morning room window.

Evelyn came to stand beside him. "Sam, you've always hated my nickname," she said. "…So, why did you encourage Allen to use it?"

"Half of Savannah already does," he replied, his attention remaining outside. "Surely, you can't object to one more."

"No," she gazed from the window too. "You just made such a point of it—"

"Oh, for God's sake," he interrupted impatiently. "As you suggested, Evelyn, I was trying to make peace with Mandy. —Do you find that curious too?"

"Well, she does seem happy," Evelyn said softly. "Look at her, Sam—smiling and laughing."

"Um," he muttered dryly.

"Tom is good for our daughter," she continued. "I wouldn't be surprised if she ends up marrying him."

As the phaeton pulled away, Tom at the reins, Sam turned to look at his wife. "Don't bet on it. —And don't you be putting such notions in Mandy's head," he added, going to the coffee urn, but changed his mind when her questions persisted.

"Why not?" she puzzled. "I think Mandy is already in love with him."

"Damn it, woman, Tom Scott has neither the means nor the inclination to take a wife—and he could not have my daughter if he did!"

"You…you've only pretended to like him," she uttered in realization. "—Why, Sam?"

"To-make-peace-with-Mandy" he repeated the tiresome phrase, and started from the room. "Why the hell else?"

"Liar!" Evelyn stomped her foot. "Samuel T. Lucas, you are a liar! But whatever you're up to, it will not be at Mandy's expense—not this time!"

Sam stopped short and turned to face her. "You, madam, are my wife—even from your separate bedroom—and are bound to respect my decisions, if nothing else. So shut your God damned mouth and remember your place!"

"No, Sam, I will not let you ruin this for Mandy," she came toward him. "You cause her any problems now and you will answer for it!"

"And what does that mean?" he sneered. "Am I supposed to be afraid of your insipid threats?"

"You had better be," she said, arms akimbo. "Unbeknownst to you, I now hold controlling shares in my father's company. You merely run it—which means I get to name *my place*—and yours too!"

"Damn it, I've earned my keep!" he did all to cover the surprise of her revelation. "I've done well by you, Evelyn. While you sat here in your icy mansion, I have managed your investments and doubled the profits many times over!"

"How wonderful!" she laughed sarcastically. "You loved, honored and cherished my money! Thank you so much, you—you bastard!"

"Careful, my dear," he mocked. "Such passionate outbursts might thaw your chastity belt. After all, it has been—what? Six or seven months since I bedded you last?"

"Two years to be exact, and you—"

"Ah! And she keeps an *exact* count of my visits. Another glorious testimony to our burning love!" he ran a finger around the neckline

315

of her dress. "Well, perhaps it's time to bed you again, my dear little wife. It might improve your disposition."

"You can leave me and my disposition alone, Sam Lucas!" she slapped his hand away. "I get along very well without any of your improvements!"

"Now I do find that interesting," he patronized. "A modern day miracle!" he followed when she turned away. "Tell me, Evelyn, what do you do behind your locked door every night? Do you masturbate—or bribe your maids to bring you satisfaction? Is that why you have no need of a man?"

"Shut up!" she whirled to face him again. "Shut your vile, evil mouth! The man I need and love is around—and I'd rather be alone with only the thought of him, than open my door to you!"

"God damn you!" he bellowed, grasping her arms. "There's been someone else in your bed? —That's what you're saying, isn't it?"

Evelyn was so outraged—so disgusted—she was glad he'd misunderstood. "And he is in my heart every moment of every day and night!" she spat the words in his face.

"I want his name!" Sam shook her. "Damn you, I won't be cuckolded!"

"Let me go!" she cried. "You got what you wanted from this marriage. You doubled the profits, remember?"

"I said give-me-his-name!" Sam shook her more viciously. "Or by God, I'll beat it out of you!"

"Sam Lucas, if you don't take your hands off me right now, I'll give you a divorce!" she yelled right back. "And you will leave my house as you came—with nothing!"

He stopped and stared at her. "After such a confession, how dare you talk of putting me out? —On what grounds would you put me out?"

"Adultery," she answered, smoothing her dress into place. "I know about your love affairs—and can prove them with names and places."

"But you just admitted to the same damn thing!"

"Can you prove it? I can. —Would you like a sample of my evidence? The first of your conquests—after we married—was Ransom's wife. And to this day, he would kill you if he knew. Then there was Nancy Dillard, Eleanor Gregory and Mary Patton, in our own circle of friends. And who knows how many ambitious employees, paid harlots and slave women? Then—oh and then, last but not least—Kathleen Morgan, who should have killed you herself."

Sam was absolutely stunned. "…But, if you knew and could prove it…why have you kept silent?"

"For Mandy," she said simply. "—Only for Mandy, in hopes that her life would at least appear normal."

"And now that it's in the open?"

"Sam, I could care less who you sleep with," she patted her mussed hair. "But if you wish to continue this sham of a marriage and enjoy all the benefits you do now, I must insist on one thing. You will not interfere with Mandy and Tom's relationship. You break that rule and I'll slap you right into court—and strip you of every cent of my money in the settlement."

"Not if I can prove your affair, you won't." he countered with all the slyness he could muster.

"Try, if you must," she said sweetly. "Where you were careless, I've been extremely careful. You'll not find a single witness against me. But the ones I have against you are standing in line—and well paid for awaiting my summons. Sam, I even have a copy of the plans for your love-nest above the Seafest."

"Well, I could bribe witnesses to say whatever I want them to," he tried to express a confidence he was not feeling. "Yes, I could invent situations you couldn't explain. What would Mandy think of her dear mother then?"

"Husband, don't grasp at straws. Your affairs are whispered all over town. I have been pitied and sheltered for years—which has worked beautifully to my advantage."

"And if I catch you in the very act?"

"You haven't yet, but thank you for the warning. I'll be even more… discreet. Isn't that the favored word among us adulterers?"

"…Evelyn, you are a bitch," he nodded in amazement, "—A real God damned bitch."

317

"Why, Sam" she smiled, walking past him, "that is the nicest thing you ever said to me."

"Well?" he turned, following her into the hall. "What do we do now?"

"That is up to you," she paused before a mirror to put on her bonnet. "But I have you beaten, Sam, and you'd best weigh this decision very, very carefully."

"So where are you going?" he watched her move on toward the front door. "—To your lover?"

"No, to a meeting at the church," she answered, opening the door.

"The church?" he trailed after her again. "Now I do find that amusing. Isn't it a bit late to worry about your immortal soul?"

"It's not my soul I'm protecting," she turned on the porch to face him. "Just my pure and spotless reputation. Church work is beneficial to my cause. You see, Sam, I rather enjoy playing your game, but by my own rules. It's much safer."

Evelyn left him standing with his mouth open, while wondering where on earth she had found the words and the nerve to place him there. She knew he must be wondering the same thing after so many years of silence from her. And that her only lie was admitting an actual affair mattered not a whit. She felt wonderful!

Sam stomped down the hallway, not even seeing the servants scurry from sight. But they heard it all—every word—and knew it was best to avoid the man. When the study door slammed, however, they reappeared and the glances exchanged spoke volumes. There was real fear of the cruel Master, but deep pride for the Mistress…

"The God damned bitch!" Sam said, taking a bottle and glass to his desk, where he downed three straight shots before throwing himself into his chair. "Evelyn is a God damned bitch!" he said it again. But names would not change one simple fact. She had him by the throat and did not even know it. He couldn't claim Allen now, because she'd insist on an investigation and bigamy added to the rest of her knowledge, would topple his kingdom about his ears.

"All right, God damn it—all right! So I'll just go about it another way. But Allen will have the fortune he deserves as my heir—even if I have to kill Evelyn first!" Then he thought of Tom and Mandria and it galled to know his treasured agreement paper was now useless; that showing it to Mandria would further incur the wrath of his dear little wife. "I'll just find another way there too," he vowed, pouring a full glass of brandy this time. "And another woman is still the right wedge. But if not Kathy, who? …Nicole perhaps?" he paused, remembering her brazen behavior in the dimness of the Shipworm Tavern. …And come to think of it, maybe Tom was the reason she frequented the square between his office and Harrison House. He'd seen her there on several occasions and assumed she'd come to check on the return of the Irish Mist. But maybe not; maybe Nicole was hoping for a chance meeting with Tom? It was worth having her watched to see, at any rate…

Going further back in time, Sam remembered Deborah O'Rourke's unquenchable desires, and felt his penis stir in salute. "Now wouldn't that be the perfect answer? If Nico was only half the tramp—the nymphomaniac… Well, if so, her craving for Tom could be encouraged and of course, directed," he laughed, downing a goodly swallow. "Oh yes, my white blonde spider, I could spin you a web and even provide the victims." Then leaning to the back of his chair, Sam let his mind play with possibilities…

# CHAPTER 26

"Cotton, wrought-iron, timber, brick, ship-building and open waterways for import and export," Allen summed what he been shown of Savannah's wealth. "That and some brilliant business minds built this beautiful city."

"And were it not for the fever epidemics, rice would be on that list," Mandria told him from the front seat of the phaeton.

"…But what has one to do with the other?" he asked as Tom drove them back through town.

"Mosquitoes," offered Lucy. "They have Yellow Fever."

"Well, several of our physicians believe they carry it," Mandria explained. "And the watery rice fields were perfect breeding places for them. The death tolls were just too high to be argued with, so the crop was outlawed and the fields destroyed."

"Lord, but that must have ruined a lot of planters," he nodded.

"It did," Mandria turned sideways on the seat as she spoke, inadvertently pressing a knee against Tom's thigh. "And it caused a lot of hard feelings, Allen."

"Then—and now," Tom added, returning the pressure with a smile.

"Still, there is a lesson here in good business practice," Allen observed. "And Mandy, your father made it work well. He invested in many enterprises, so the failure of one couldn't possibly ruin him."

"Never put all your eggs in one basket," Lucy added wisely.

"Exactly," Allen grinned, admiring her clear blue eyes.

"Or your mosquitoes in one field," she continued because he kept smiling at her and she felt compelled to. "We still have mosquitoes, though. They're just the wrong kind. ...No, they're the right kind—not that any mosquito is much good. But you know that, of course."

"I think I do," Allen laughed enjoyably.

"Mandria, you'd best direct me!" Tom said hastily. "The street dead ends just ahead!"

"Oh, —turn right! Turn here, Tom!"

And as the phaeton, slid around a corner, Lucy slid right into Allen's arms. "Why, Miss Love!" he held her there. "Are you throwing yourself at me?"

"No—oh, no!" she looked up at him, blushing furiously. "You know that I wouldn't...well, no, you don't know me well enough to know what I'd do or wouldn't do," she babbled. "It's just that Tom took the corner so fast—and I didn't! But really, Allen, I'm really, really sorry."

"Now, you've hurt my feelings," he continued to hold and to tease her. "Now you're sorry you came."

"No, I'm glad to be here!" she insisted. "I just didn't mean to be here. —This close here. That's what I really mean."

"Well, I enjoyed it," he finally released her. "So much I think we should do it again. —Tom, would you mind?"

"No!" Lucy touched a hand to her hair and giggled. "Tom, don't you dare."

"Well, Allen, maybe we can arrange a few sharp turns on the way to Thunderbolt next Saturday evening," Tom offered. "What do you think, Mandria? Mike suggested we all go to supper at The Pier. Do you know the place? I especially wanted Allen to try Seafood. Is theirs good?"

"I was there for a dance, but never a meal," she answered. "What about you, Lucy? Your family dines out a lot. Have you eaten at The Pier?"

"No. Poppa won't venture much further than Hester's or Deloras'. He has the gout, you see," she explained to Allen, as Tom drew the horse to a stop in the Lucas carriage yard again. "He can't eat just everything, nor travel far when it's bad. It makes the swelling worse—and so do I, I'm afraid."

"You do?" he puzzled, turning from the ground to extend a hand to her. "…How could you worsen his gout, Lucy?"

"Well, I know you won't believe this," she accepted Allen's assistance and started from the phaeton, "But when I get excited, I trip over things—a lot!" And so saying, she missed her footing and fell into Allen's arms a second time.

"Lucy!" Mandria gasped. "Are you all right?"

"Of course she is," Allen flashed the Scott smile as he righted her. "Lucy was only proving a point—in her own delightful way."

"Poor Poppa didn't think I was so delightful this morning," Lucy confessed. "It was his sore, swollen toe I stepped on."

"Oh?" Allen asked as they followed behind Tom and Mandria. "Dare I hope the cause of your excitement was the prospect of coming to meet me?"

"Lucy, when you tire of his drivel, cuff him," Tom said over his shoulder. "There's no way of handling it gracefully—just cuff him a good one."

"Big brother, I'm hoping she doesn't do it gracefully," Allen returned. "Wonderful things happen to me when she doesn't. —And, if things still occur in threes, Lucy will be in my arms yet another time this evening!"

"Oh my stars," Lucy said, more pleased than she dared admit. And as they went into the Lucas house for supper, she secretly hoped if Allen was right about things happening in threes, that tripping over her father's foot didn't count.

…Supper: where Lucy and Allen discovered each other in accidental glances across a candle-lit table; where Tom and Mandria sought such moments and any excuse to repeat them; where Sam and Evelyn directed explicit stares when either was reminded of their morning quarrel. Supper at the Lucas home—a lull in the eye of yet another storm…

It took almost two weeks, but finally one of Sam's men brought him information of interest. "Bernie Brown?" he closed his office window on an early September breeze. "And Nico met him in Forsythe Park?"

"Yeah. He's a new one on her list, ain't he?" Harry pulled at his ill-fitting trousers.

"No, but an important one; —one she was forbidden to see. Did you hear what was said?"

"Well, she gave him a bunch of bull shit, about keeping their meetings secret. And he give her the same, swearing devotion and wanting another go at her."

"And?"

"And she let him steal a few kisses and feel of her tits some—you know, just enough to make him fucking hot?"

"So, while the Captain is away, little Nico wants to play," Sam chuckled, reaching for his wallet. "You keep those reports coming, Harry. I want every detail."

"Yeah, well see you, Mr. Lucas—Thursday, most likely, 'cause she's meeting Brown for supper Wednesday night at the Hideaway."

"Is she now?" Sam rose thoughtfully. "Tell you what: I think I'll just cover that one myself."

"B…but what will I do? I mean, I been on her closer than a tick, Mr. Lucas. So what will I do Wednesday night?"

"Well hell, Harry!" Sam vented. "Go fuck a damned knot-hole, for all I care. I'm giving you a night off—not a jail sentence!"

"I know, sir—I know!" Harry quivered. "I just wanted to see if he gets to her. But my money's still on Herb—ain't yours, Mr. Lucas?"

"No, my money is in your pocket because I pay you for facts—not your stupid speculations. And speaking of that, you've yet to bring me a report linking her to Scott."

"Boss, I told you before, I ain't seen her with Scott—not lessen they's all together; the same six of them—ever weekend. Now Scott, he danced with her once the night they went out to The Pier; and he walked her home once, but he was going to see your daughter and Miss Nico was just heading home too. …Or I think she was. She waited a long time outside the school, and when he come out, home's where she went. Anyways, I don't think they're seeing each other—not less he's sneaking into her bedroom, which I'd a seen—or out to her stable, maybe."

Sam ground his teeth. The man had the mentality of a gnat! "And what is going on in the stable, Harry?"

"Damn if I know," he shrugged. "I just seen her go out there more than a few times."

"Here's a thought: Why don't you just-go-out-there too?"

"Can't, sir—not as yet. There's a seven foot wall 'round that there courtyard—and a seventy pound dog inside. I can't get no closer than roosting in a tree across the street. In the square, don't you know? But I still don't think its Scott she's meeting. He don't pay her no attention at all."

"And you don't know Scott," Sam said acidly. "Women pay attention to him. Hell, he could fuck your God damned grandmother, Harry, and she'd thank him for it."

"Why would he want to, Mr. Lucas?" he puzzled. "My Granny is ugly as a toad—"

"Out!" Sam winged a book at the man, who beat a hasty retreat. "—And find out what's happening in that God damned stable!"

On Wednesday evening, Sam entered the Hideaway and sent for Mister Strickland, who on many occasions had provided him a private compartment and intimate dinners for two. Tonight, he'd made different arrangements; tonight, he'd asked to observe such a scene and Mister Strickland had been more than glad to oblige this valued customer. Sam was shown into the dim confines of a service hall, where a stool had been placed for his comfort while making use of a waiter's peephole into the booth where Bernie and Nicole had been seated…

"Did you enjoy the meal?" Bernie asked, refilling their glasses with a nut-colored sherry.

"Very much," Nicole smiled, running her fingers over the plush curve of the wide booth seat. "But I don't think the menu is the main attraction here."

"It isn't," he moved closer and nibbled at her ear. "It's the privacy."

"Yes," she sat forward, propping her elbows on the table to sip her drink. "You know, Bernie, this is very cozy—almost like being in a big, old curtained bed."

"I know," he too, came forward to caress the nape of her neck. "Nico, would you mind that I've thought constantly about the night your father caught us?"

"Of course I would," she declared, but invited his attention to her bare shoulder with a subtle shrug. "Your behavior was disgraceful... there in my courtyard."

"And here, in our *big-old-curtained-bed?*" he circled her waist from behind and pulled her snuggly against him. "Would you consider the same disgraceful here?"

Nicole laid her head back on Bernie's shoulder, offering a perfect view down her deeply-cut bodice as he inhaled the rose perfume she'd expertly applied there. "Bernie, you're holding me so tightly," she feigned several breathless breast heaves for his pleasure. "I feel quite dizzy—almost faint in your arms."

"As a beautiful woman should, in the arms of a virile man," he emoted. Then giving the table a dramatic push, he eased her downward on the seat. "As you should in my arms," he added, resting his knee on top of her thigh. "I was told once that we are a perfect match: the son of a wealthy planter; the daughter of a wealthy banker," he parted her lips with the tip of his tongue. "That's quality stuff, Nico—quality bred to breed quality. Don't you feel that urge between us? It's so strong—so good—and I mean to show that to you."

"I do feel...something," she uttered as he drew his knee upward and across her hip. "But Bernard, dearest, there is hardly room here for much of anything. ...Is there?"

"Oh, but there is," he slid easily on top of her, fitting himself into place. "You'd be surprised at how little room this takes." And lowering his mouth to hers, he raised his hands to her breasts, while further down, his hips moved in fine imitation against her…

Sam smiled at Nicole's eager response. And he watched as she performed an interesting feat. Allowing Bernie to play greedily at her breasts, handful by handful she inched her gown and petticoats upward. That done, her leg moved over the edge of the seat, allowing him to lay more directly in position—his trousered cock upon her pantalooned vagina. And never aware of her maneuver, Bernie went steadily on, grinding his way toward glory.

But she got there first and then it was over. Nicole suddenly wriggled free to huddle on the edge of the seat, shuddering, face in her hands.

"Nico?" Bernie groped. "Come back—damn it, please come back!"

"No, Bernie!" she answered firmly enough to keep him in place. "I'm sorry, but no. You're just so—so masterful! I can't trust myself around you." And for good measure, she conjured a pitiful little sob.

"…You're not going to cry, are you?" he all but whined. "You used to cry and it made me feel so awful!"

Even from where Sam was, he could sense Nicole's displeasure with his childish tone, but her own remained sweet. "We were younger then, Bernie. We're not now and one of these days, I won't be able to stop you in time. —Then, you'll surely hate me!"

"I'll never hate you—I've wanted you all of my life! Can't you see how much?" he winced, for his need was so keen, pulsations were visible through his bulging trousers.

"Oh, then I must go—I must!" Nicole rose quickly. "No, don't get up, dearest. Please? …We'll meet tomorrow and talk it all out. All right? We'll meet at Hester's for coffee—at ten!"

"…All right," he called, as the booth curtain swished closed behind her. "Damn it, I'll be there," he added in disappointment.

Still watching, Sam next saw Bernie stand, unfasten his trousers and masturbate. His contorted expressions were truly comical; his tenderness exaggerated as he cleansed with a linen dinner napkin. And when he straightened his clothing and went strutting through the restaurant as if he'd made his coveted conquest, Sam burst into laughter. "That puny little pup!" he said when he was able. …*And what a beautiful bitch Nico is,* he thought, *more like Deborah all the time; a bitch in need of a good hard cock. …Well, tomorrow morning, we will just have to discuss that very thing.* Then recalling Bernie's facial expressions again, he dissolved in a spate of laughter that left him weak and teary-eyed…

The next morning, Nicole arrived before Bernie and chose an alcove table nested in potted palms as their trysting place. Sam was close by and finished a breakfast plate and two cups of coffee, waiting for their meeting to end. As he expected, Bernie left first—and wearing a familiar expression.

Sam chuckled as he rose from his table, knowing the boy would likely repeat his handy performance before reaching home. But now, a cup in his own hand, he eased into Bernie's vacated chair. "Good morning, my dear," he smiled, as Nicole looked up in surprise, then glanced quickly after her departing beau. "Down town for some early shopping, are we?"

"Why…yes, Uncle Sam," she accepted the offered alibi and returned his smile. "As soon as I've finished my coffee."

"Ah, then let me guess where Ransom's money goes today," he paused. "…A blouse; a confection of lacy ruffles; none of which dares to conceal the delicate swell of a very lovely cleavage."

"No," her smile broadened. "…Would you care to guess again?"

"Petticoats, then—of such fullness and exquisite stitchery, milady might hope for a windy day and appreciative eyes to glimpse them."

"No, again!" she laughed gaily. "Dear Uncle Sam, you sound like a catalogue advertisement—only much more personal and exciting."

"And you do enjoy excitement, don't you, Nico? You have a talent for causing it, too, among your young swains."

"Only among the young ones?" she leaned closer. "Wouldn't a mature man find me worth a sigh and a backward glance? Or, at least, a fresh cup of coffee, shared in a secluded corner?"

"Excellent, my dear—excellent!" he laughed, standing to signal a waiter for refills.

"And of course, you are right," he continued when they were alone once more. "No matter his age, any male with cock and balls would enjoy your lovely presence."

"…Why Uncle Sam," her eyes registered surprise and interest in equal amounts, but she showed him mild effrontery. "Such language. —I am truly shocked."

"Are you? I think not. You spend much of your time courting cocks—and standing them at full attention."

"Really, Uncle Sam," she said a bit more firmly. "If my father heard—"

"That you sneaked off to join Captain Herb on the river front? Oh yes, I know the truth. And when Scott tried to cover the deception— when he held you in his arms—you were willing to go as far as he'd take it. You've also met Bernard Brown on several occasions. And last night, at the Hideaway, you played with sensation—experienced your own delights—without giving Bernie the benefit of a well-earned fuck."

"Oh!" she gasped. "Oh, how dare you say such things!" she whispered while trying to gather her belongings. "I will not listen to any more of these lies!"

But before she could rise, Sam had a firm grasp on the nape of her neck and when he brought her around to face him, his words held a biting edge. "If you don't sit still, this time I will take my information to your father. Then, my dear, being a very moral man, he will marry you off by nightfall. —And, I could persuade him to choose Bernie Brown as your bridegroom."

Nicole sat there, held by the neck, and stared at him for several seconds. "But I don't want to marry yet," she said softly. "And especially not Bernie."

"And well you shouldn't," he released her, to run fingers down the length of her arm, where they closed about her wrist. "Brown would deposit you at Hollow Oak, under the domineering eye of his mother, and you'd rarely see Savannah again. You'd spend your entire life breeding heirs. And would Bernie be at your side? Hardly! The wealthy planter's son would continue a life of luxury and privilege here in town, while you are wrapped in tissue like a Christmas ornament awaiting his pleasure."

"Well, Father wouldn't force me to marry him," she raised a proud little chin. "He doesn't even like Bernie!"

"No, but he'd assume you do—enough to disobey him and engage in these secret meetings. Ransom would rather see you safely wed, than dropping bastards at his door."

"Uncle Sam, you can't do this," she pouted. "Is there nothing I say to dissuade you?

"Indeed. You've only to hear me out," he took her purse and gloves from her hand and returned them to the table. "You see, little Nico, being a man of few morals, I don't condemn your behavior. I applaud it! There is a fire burning in you and I mean to see you use it; to enjoy it as much as you want."

"A—are you propositioning me?" she asked. "It feels like you are."

"I have a taste for unripened fruit," he admitted. "But what I want from you—and for you—has little to do with that. Communication, my dear—we must establish deep communication between us. We are kindred spirits, you and I. Spirits that crave lusty adventures and seek them out. Shall I describe the symptoms we share?" And as Sam spoke, he began to uncurl the tightly clinched fingers of her hand. "It's a hunger that flares in the pit of the stomach, spreading hot, tingling flame in every direction. —You are feeling it now, surging in the tips of your nipples. Excitement, Nico, that dries the mouth but leaves the body moist with molten need." And stressing his point, Sam lifted her open hand to his lips and lightly tongued the dampness of her palm.

Nicole trembled, trying to dispel his powerful effect on her senses. "You really shouldn't say these things," she uttered, but did not remove her hand. "Uncle Sam, in spite of what you might think, I'm still an innocent—a virgin."

"A bothersome condition, but easily remedied," he smiled. "You've considered it often or you wouldn't keep tempting your beaus to over ride your objections."

"Now, I do resent that," she straightened, but without anger. "I may tempt them, but I've no intention of becoming a common trollop."

"Little Nico," he chided, "there is nothing common about you! A poor woman is called a trollop, while a rich one—with your exceptional beauty—can do the identical things and is merely called adventuresome or spirited. You are a jewel; a diamond of fire and ice; destined to shine in a setting of 24 karat gold."

"A very pretty picture," she was back to pouting, "but not long ago, I told…well, someone, that wealth had its privilege and he scorned me!"

"And from what social structure did this man come? The lower class has always been jealous of uncensored privilege—afraid of it! So, they condemn us and hide behind their Sunday-go-to-meeting principals, because that's all they have. But you can't spend principals, Nico. They won't buy you a damn thing but self-denial. And you were not born to be denied anything."

"…Not even a lower-class-man, if I want him?"

"Not even that. Once you've learned to wield the power at your disposal, not even that."

"And you want to help me; —to see that I enjoy it," she gave him her wisest expression. "In exchange for what, dear Uncle?"

"I haven't decided," he chuckled. "But you'll pay the fee."

"My virginity—that *bothersome condition?*"

"Nicole," he placed fingers beneath her chin, "your destiny—everything you want—lies just beyond the confines of virginity. You've only to make the transition. It's not the great sin preachers would have you believe, but merely a decision to rule your own life. Claim your birthright—the right of the rich!" Sam urged, his hand moving again to the nape of her neck, where his thumb applied enough pressure to the pulse in her slender throat to be felt. "You were meant to know many lovers; to become the envy of trollops and superior to ladies of your own class. Deny that you want it all. Deny the excitement I can feel singing sweetly through your veins this very instant,"

Nicole opened her mouth to make that denial, but found he was right. The blood hammering against his thumb proved it. And she'd been impressed by his insight—his revelation of her most secret ambitions. She was also fascinated with the command in his touch and knew she could use the influence of such an ally. Wasn't it up to her, then, to secure it? "Dear Uncle Sam," she said with a smile playing at the corner of her lips. "I do believe we are kindred spirits. And as you have named my desires quite correctly, won't you tell me yours? Isn't your *taste for unripened fruit* behind all this? It is a fact that men your age lust after younger women."

Sam laughed. She was flirting with him, which meant he'd won Round One. "Of course we lust after you," he drew a finger from her ear to her mouth. "Though it more often happens in reverse, little Nico. Intelligent young females prefer men of my age. Experience and refined bedroom techniques bring them our way. Why you'd be amazed at the things a seasoned old cock can do with a sassy young cunt."

"Mercy!" Nicole said, enjoying herself shamelessly. "—And you still say you aren't propositioning me?"

"In time, perhaps I will. For now, I'm offering my confidence and assistance. As I've already said, I do applaud your romantic endeavors."

"Your assistance," she repeated coyly. "Now what could that mean?"

"Set me a task. —Any!" he exclaimed, keeping his tone amusing. "Is there some bauble you desire? A life taken? …One man you want brought under heel?"

Nicole looked at Sam and her smile wavered. "There is such a man. And you've already described my feeling for him. I did like his arms around me—and I would have gone as far as he'd take it."

"Tom Scott," he said with deep satisfaction. He'd just won Round Two.

"Yes, Uncle Sam—yes! He just keeps spurning my interest and it infuriates me beyond all reason! Oh—but Mandy is seeing him too, so I don't suppose you'd want to help me?"

"Perhaps not, if Mandy were the problem," Sam covered her hand with his. "But Scott keeps a mistress, so what does that tell you about Mandy's hold on him? She is merely a polite diversion."

"Then is it the mistress?" Nicole listened avidly. "Is he so attached to her?"

"She is only a whore," he shrugged, "and provides the service Mandy won't."

"So what is the problem? —Why does he refuse to take me seriously?"

"He does, Nico. I saw it that night on the riverfront. His interest was there or he'd never have come to your rescue; never dared to hold you right in front of Herb. They may be friends, but at that moment, protecting you meant the most to him."

"…I don't know," she said doubtfully. "All we seem to do is argue. And if I flirt with him—or anyone else—he lectures me."

"Because he is jealous."

"No, Tom Scott is stubborn! He says I belong with Mike and my wishes don't faze him in the least!"

"And how does Captain Herb treat your wishes?" he asked, hoping to make a point.

"Oh, Mike is wonderful and I do enjoy his attention—"

"But it isn't exciting, because he can't afford to offend your father," Sam offered.

"…Maybe so," she considered his words, just as he wanted. "Now, Mike and I have had our moments, but he hasn't tried… Well, maybe he is afraid of Daddy."

"And Scott knows this, Nico. You are safely protected by Herb; —just where he wants you, as long as you cling to childhood. And that is the real problem between you. Tom doesn't need another Mandy on his hands. Why should he trade one frozen virgin for another? As I do, he prefers a woman skilled in the art of making love. Therefore, as long as you hold out, so will he."

Nicole circled a hand through his arm. "If you could prove that to me; if I could see jealousy in his eyes or desire in his manner—"

"Consider it done!" Sam placed a finger over her parted lips. "But you must be patient and allow me to direct you, step by step."

"Dear Sam," she laughed, now hugging his arm against her bosom, "you've never met a more willing, obedient student. —So what would you have me do first?"

His reward for winning Round Three was playing with a white blonde ringlet. "Jealousy is a fast growing weed, little Nico, and we'll plant the first seeds at Allen's Birthday Dinner this Monday. As he will be the center of attention anyway, I think you should flirt with Allen—outrageously. Hell, flirt with me too. Use both of us, but ignore

Tom completely. He will be quite helpless with Mandy there; —unable to deliver a single lecture. And, while he must suffer his jealousy in silence, we will have the pleasure of watching it grow. After that, we'll find other ways of provoking Tom."

A seductive laugh bubbled from Nicole. "If it works, Uncle Sam, you may as well buy a polishing cloth, because this little *diamond of fire and ice* will be ready for a shining," she came forward to place a warm kiss on his cheek, and stayed to gaze into his eyes. "In fact, if all goes well, you will have earned a private viewing; —which I'll gladly grant should you care to call the morning after the party."

"Careful, my dear," he met her nose to nose. "I am not like Brown or Herb. I would not settle for dry-fucking your hot little honey-hole; —and neither, ever, would Scott."

"I know," she said, not backing off a whit. "But if I must learn new skills, shouldn't it be from *a master of experience and refined technique; —*one willing to direct me *step by step*? We'd have to begin very slowly, of course, but who can guess where it might lead?"

Sam knew she was flirting again—trying to ensnare him with promises she always made. He also knew a man of his intelligence shouldn't be impressed, but he was. So feeling more admiration than he wanted to admit, he conceded Round Four to her. "Little Nico," he nodded, "you are going to turn this whole damned city upside down. With your attitude, Scott hasn't a chance; —no man would."

"Not even Sam Lucas?" she persisted. "He has yet to accept my offer for a private viewing."

"I will consider it most carefully," he replied. "Meanwhile, there is Brown to keep you amused; —and the ever-gallant Captain Herb to get you through the weekends."

"A token then," she caressed his cheek again and blew warm breath in his ear. "From beauty to her beast; a promise to a *seasoned old cock from a sassy young…* Sam, what was that word you used?"

"Cunt, my dear—cunt!" he laughed.

"Lecherous Uncle Sam," she teased. "I'm so glad we had this chat. Aren't you?"

333

"More than you know," he rose and stood looking at her loveliness. It stirred him, as her mother had years ago, he reasoned. "I must leave now, my dear. But feel free to contact me if the need arises."

"The need?" she cooed, raising a hand for his departing kiss.

...And there was the other side of Deborah—need; wondrous need. "Good-bye, Nicole," he bowed in tribute over her hand before taking his leave.

But as Sam made his way out, he realized how deeply their meeting had affected him. "Damn little bitch," he steeled his posture and stride. For the disturbance in his loins could not be allowed to show, and as he had no intention of masturbating, he headed for the nearest brothel, wondering all the while, just how many Rounds he'd actually won from Nicole O'Rourke...

# CHAPTER 27

A llen hopped along the street, trying to fit a heel into his shoe. "Damn it, Tom, wait!" he called impatiently. "Where are we going at this ungodly hour—and aren't you late for work?"

"I told them I would be," Tom replied, but did not slow his pace. "Hurry now, Ransom is waiting at the bank!"

"But why?" Allen tucked a shirt-tail, his tone still grouchy. "It's my birthday; —you'd think a man could sleep late on his birthday!"

"A hangover?" Tom's glance held a tad of sternness. "Celebrating a bit early, weren't you?"

"Only from the stroke of eight," Allen attempted a grin and a swipe at his hair with the same lack of enthusiasm. "I had to go somewhere while your Mrs. was there and a tavern seemed as good a place as any. —But you still haven't explained why we're racing down the street at the crack of dawn!"

"It is not dawn. It's almost nine o'clock, and we'll just call this race your penalty for early celebration. —And Allen, the deed to the house is ready too. Now I can show the place to Mandria, at long, long last!" Tom laughed. "Damn, but I thought today would never come!"

"Thomas," Allen came to a determined halt on the bank steps, where he pressed gently on throbbing temples. "As dear as you are to me, why must I watch you sign a deed? And you certainly don't need me to show Mandy your house. Please, can't I just go home and crawl back into bed?"

"No, little brother. Precisely because it is your birthday, you can't," Tom urged him forward again. "I have a surprise for you; a gift from Mama and it's waiting inside if you'd care to open the door?"

Of a sudden, Allen felt revitalized and so curious he couldn't concentrate on much else. ...*A gift?* he thought as Ransom spoke his greetings and led them to his private office. ...*A memento, perhaps; —something Mama wanted me to have,* he decided as he watched and then witnessed Tom's deed signing with his own signature. ... *And Tom has kept this gift for me all these years...* He then noticed the Cheshire Cat grins worn by the other two as both looked at him now. But when handed an account book with his name on it and seeing the healthy balance inside, he nearly slipped into a mind-numbing trance. He heard Tom explain the origin of the money. He listened when Ransom cautioned him to guard it well—even managed a few intelligent questions when the banker suggested the same investments that were paying off well for Tom. And yet, he was truly dumbfounded and so full of questions, he could hardly contain them...

"Whoa, Tom!" he began, as soon as they were on the street again. "I know you have to get to school, but I think you owe me a few minutes here."

"...Yes, I guess I do," Tom nodded. "Come on, little brother," he led the way across the street and into a square, where he sat on a near-by bench. "So, you have questions?"

"Well, hell yes!" Allen stood before him. "Tom, if the money has been there all along...why was I never aware of it?"

"Because you were a child and children sometimes tell their secrets without really meaning to," Tom patiently explained. "Allen, some of our employers were pretty unscrupulous people; —willing to work us into the ground, but never to pay a fair wage. Had they known about the money, they'd have found ways of getting to it, believe me."

"But with money, we needn't have worked so hard—or so long, maybe. Our lives could have been so much easier! Damn it, Tom, why didn't you—"

"Spend it? Waste it, when we were surviving on our own?" Tom injected.

In near exasperation, Allen threw himself down beside Tom. "Hell yes, spend it, when surviving meant wearing the same winter coat for four years—until the sleeves came nearly to my elbows? And yours did too, so yes, why not spend it?"

"Allen, as you received a share on your eighteenth birthday, so did I," Tom stretched his legs out before him. "I was sixteen when Mama died and it took every back-breaking day of the next two years for me to realize why she set the inheritance terms as she did. I think Mama hoped—because of the hardships—we would learn to manage our lives, and our money, responsibly. Our *manhood money* is what she called it." And when Allen made no comment, he continued. "Don't you see? Mama knew a day like this would come. A day, for me, when having money meant affording the home I just bought. For you, little brother, it can mean whatever you want. There's a whole world out there, full of wonderful opportunities, and you worked as hard as I did learning what Mama thought we should know. Just remember what it was like to do without and never put yourself in that position again. If you're wise—and I believe you are—you'll make the money work for you now."

"Well, you needn't worry there," Allen blinked away a suspicious mistiness from his eyes. "I'm going to build my share into a damn fortune!"

"I hope you can," Tom nodded. "If that's your special dream, I hope you can."

"...And the first step is keeping my capital free from personal needs," he said mostly to himself. Then he was smiling, "Just like you did, Brer. So today I'll start looking for a job. ...But where should I start? After lounging on my royal ass these last few weeks, I don't know much about what jobs are available."

"You could try the ads in the paper," Tom stood, "but at seven o'clock tonight, your royal ass had better be at the Lucas house. Mamalyn is giving that dinner in your honor, birthday-boy."

"I know," Allen nodded. "Shall I meet you there or at home?"

"Meet me there. I promised some tutoring to Victoria Audrey after school and as I'm expecting a delivery wagon at the new house, I've arranged to meet her there. Then Allen," his smile broadened, "I'm meeting my lovely wife in town and taking her back for the grand tour!"

Allen was laughing as he rose to face his brother. "Well, maybe I should remind you that supper is at seven. Mandy is sure to like the house—which means she'll express gratitude; which means you'll get greedy; which means it could be midnight before you arrive!"

"That's a real good thought," Tom chuckled as he started away, "but we'll be there on time. So long, Allen, I'm off to finish out the school day."

"Tom?" Allen called after him, not caring who heard him while passing through the square. "Thanks for…well, for everything. And especially, for being such a damn good brother!"

"You're welcome," Tom called back, feeling very good about—well, *everything* as Allen just said…

Mandria opened the jeweler's box as soon as she climbed onto the seat of the rental buggy. "Do you think Allen will like it? See; I had it engraved just as we decided."

Tom inspected the pocket watch dutifully. "Yes love, that will do nicely—and I like the chain you selected. Did I give you enough money to cover everything?"

"You did," she smiled, then noticed their direction. "This isn't the way to Harrison House."

"I know," he said off-handedly.

"So, where are we going?" she gazed at him expectantly. "What I mean is…we are going to your room aren't we? —Soon? Tom, I've thought of nothing else all day," she confessed, blushing a luscious dusty rose.

"Is that a fact?" he held her eyes for a deeply felt moment. "Well, neither have I, pretty lady. But be truthful. Aren't you tired of the same routine; of meeting at my place every time? Let's go somewhere else. —Yes, let's be a little daring today."

"As long as it's not me you're tired of," she briefly leaned her head on his shoulder, but curiosity soon got the better of her. "Tom, where are we going?"

"How about…there?" he pulled the horse to the curb and pointed toward an empty house. "Come on, let's see if the place is open," he added, looping the reins through a hitching ring. "No one would find us in there."

"Oh, but Tom," she said as he lifted her down. "We can't just break into a house. It belongs to someone—see? The sign is gone from the porch and I remember seeing one a few weeks ago."

"Do you?" he asked, pleased that she liked the house enough to notice that.

"Yes, it's a lovely old home," she said as he led her around a corner and along a smooth tabby-walled fence, "So the new owners wouldn't want us poking about."

"Mandria," he unlatched an arched gate and ushered her through, "where is your sense of adventure?"

They were now standing in a cozy sized courtyard and in spite of her apprehensions, Mandria paused to look around. "This is nice, isn't it?" she said in a hushed voice next to his ear. "See the climbing roses all along the fence? And over there: camellias, azaleas and gardenias—and even a little fountain in the middle of the lily beds. It must be really beautiful here in the spring."

"I'm sure it is," he answered in like tone. "But I'm not sure why we're whispering."

"…Oh," she laughed at her silliness. "I don't know! It just seemed the right thing for a house breaking."

"And what, lady, would be the right thing for a house-warming?" he nuzzled the softness of her cheek. "Shall we do the new owner a favor and christen the place right here on the court-yard floor? I'll wager he'd like seeing that."

"You'd do it too!" she smiled enjoyably. "You'd have us naked and down on those icy flagstones—not caring that it's almost winter, and that we'd catch pneumonia."

"Well, all right, if you want to wait for warmer weather; —but I'm not forgetting the part about getting naked out here," he said, leading her across a veranda, up some steps and pretended surprise when a doorknob turned in his hand. "What have we here?" he asked as they entered a multi-windowed room that ran across the back of the house. "A sun porch?"

"In the winter, yes," she nodded. "And a sleeping porch in the summer. See the bed-post marks down the floor?"

"Ah, wall to wall beds; —and I'd have to try you on each one," he chuckled as they went into a small rectangular rear entry hall.

Still laughing at his notion, Mandria hurried through one of the matching archways in each corner. And Tom stopped, listening to the sound echoing through the emptiness. ...*House, hear the voice of your mistress*, he thought. ...*Help me keep her this happy...*

"Lucy won't be there tonight—did I tell you?" Mandria called. "Her Aunt Jerlene is very ill and Lucy went to stay with her on Wilmington Island for a while. But Nico was coming anyway, so she can be Allen's dinner companion."

"Wonderful," Tom muttered, following the sound of her voice as she approached the archway in the opposite corner.

"Well, the stairs go right up the center here—between these breezeways," she explained. "There are beautiful stained glass panels on either side of the front doors, as well as in the fan light above," she snagged his hand in passing and towed him toward a door to the left. "Now what's in here?" she opened it wide as they entered. "The study," she stood looking it the ceiling high shelves. "And what is this wood, Tom—cherry or walnut?"

"Black oak," he answered. "The mantle too—look, love, at the carving on this one."

"Yes, that is beautiful," she ran fingers along the intricate design, while glancing over the room a second time. "...Wouldn't leather-bound furniture, like Uncle Ran's, look nice in here? But I'd choose a lighter leather—a camel, maybe; and butternut for the walls for more contrast with this dark wood; and I'd put down a gold sculptured carpet to bring out the stripe in those drapes."

"And in here?" Tom went to slide back a tall set of pocket doors. "What would you put in the front parlor?"

"I've always loved these things and thought them so clever," Mandria stopped at the sliding doors. "When closed, you have two separate rooms—and that makes it easier to heat in the winter. But opened, just look, Tom, one huge room—large enough for a wonderful party."

"...A party," he said, draping an arm across her shoulders. "Do you know I have never given a party? I wonder if I'd make a good host?"

"Of course you would!" she laughed, finding his doubt absurd. "You do everything well, Mr. Scott."

"Thank you, Mrs. Scott," he smiled as they crossed the front hall to the dining room. "Still, I am lacking certain social graces, Mandria," he continued, while she went to inspect a butler's pantry and dumb-waiter to the basement kitchen. Then she was peeking into a morning room beyond that. "Suppose we were having a dinner party here. I'd have no idea what wines to offer—the proper ones, I mean." He was realizing there was more to establishing the home he'd wanted all his life than signing a deed.

"Well, as long as we're supposing," Mandria returned, pausing to admire another mantle piece, "let's suppose there is a wine cellar in the kitchen downstairs; that it's well-stocked and that our servants are so well-trained, they'd never bother you with such unimportant things."

Tom stuffed his hands in his pockets and nodded. "But they are important. ...I'd never want to embarrass you."

Now she stood before him, waiting for their eyes to meet. "Then let me quote something a very wise man told me once. He said, *Mandria, strangers can learn those things, passing on the street. But we've already learned more important things, like—*"

"A damned *healthy taste for amorous behavior!*" he finished it with a chuckle. Then lifting her feet from the floor, he whirled her around and about the empty dining room.

"Tom!" her laughter gurgled pleasantly past his ear. "Oh, do stop!" she clung tighter. "Please, please stop!"

So he did, as suddenly as he had that night at The Boar's Head. Then, watching her lean against him, in the same dizzy way, it seemed

341

natural to re-enact the next step as well, so cupping her face in his hands, he lowered his mouth to hers.

But Mandria would not faint this time. This time she welcomed him wholly. Indeed, she was no longer concerned that they stood in the center of an empty room in someone else's house. She was there because Tom wanted to be and she only wanted to be with him. Anywhere! On those precisely laid flagstones; this highly polished, wide-planked floor; on the beach; in the sea; in any bed; in wall-to-wall beds—anywhere, as long as he continued to love her so thoroughly.

"...Mandria," he uttered with effort, "we haven't seen the upstairs yet."

At that moment, she truly didn't care, but it was useless to argue when he'd already dragged her half-way up the wide staircase. Reaching the top, she commented on the open stair-well and black oak railings which gated the second level. Tom pointed out the doorways, saying a bedroom must occupy each corner of the house, and it pleased him when she wanted to see. He watched as she inspected the two at the rear; then steered her to the left side of the balcony and waited patiently for her peek into a third bedroom. He next opened the door to a second story front porch and brought the matching door on the rear to her attention, saying there must be a back porch above the sun room as well.

"Want to see the view?" he stepped onto the one before them. And propping against the railing, he held a hand out to her.

"...Do you think we should?" Mandria was whispering again. "What if someone spots us from the street?"

"Let them!" he laughed, and when she shuddered in the fast cooling air, he drew her close. "They'd only say, *Look, there are the proud new owners!*"

"Yes—unless they happen to know the new owners already," she argued. "Tom, really, I don't think we should—"And stopping in mid-sentence, she stared now, at the windows of the remaining, and yet to be explored, bedroom. "Oh!" her eyes widened. "There's a light in there! Oh dear—what will we say if they catch us out here?" And she leaned past him, to peer through the glass pane. "Tom, there is furniture in there—and a fire in the hearth!"

"Why, so there is. Come on then, let's have a closer look," he smiled at her earnestly whispered protest as he pulled her back inside and closed the porch door.

"No, Tom!" she kept trying to resist their forward movement. "We can't go in there! Please—we could be shot for burglars!" But her pleas went unheeded and now they stood in the warm, fire-lit room.

"Well, what have we here?" Tom went to a rickety table he'd dragged up from the basement. "Look, Mandria, two glasses—and the same white wine we enjoyed at Tybee. Isn't that good luck?"

"Put it down," she begged. "We shouldn't be in here. Please, Tom, I want to leave." And she gasped when the cork popped loudly from the bottle. "I...I don't understand what's come over you," she stayed rooted to her spot by the doorway. But she couldn't leave him here, so what was she going to do? "I'm so frightened, I'm shaking. Please, Tom, we have to go—now?"

"I thought you had given up worry," he poured a glass of wine and sipped it as he started toward her. "I thought you trusted me."

"I do trust you, but be reasonable," she was hugging her arms close. "I mean, if this beautiful room were mine—if I had put out wine and left a fire burning—I'd be returning to enjoy it with someone. Wouldn't you?"

"Yes," he nodded, pulling a curl to the front of her shoulder. "That is a fair assumption."

"...Then wouldn't you resent coming home to find strangers in your bedroom?"

"Well, hell yes!" he exclaimed. "—And that's a certainty!" he added, chuckling in spite of himself. She just looked so confused, eyes glued to the floor and unable to condone his insane behavior. "...Do you really think the room is beautiful? There isn't much in here yet."

"It's beautiful," she still spoke to the floor. "Now can we leave?"

Tom went back to the bed and sat on the edge facing her, ready to observe the moment of her full realization. "Now there are several pieces to match this, but I had no idea which you might want," he patted the mattress, "So I bought the only one that interested me." At that, she raised puzzled eyes to his, but seemed unable to do more.

"…Well?" he continued. "Is that all the reaction I'm going to get from you, lady?"

"That bed is yours?" she began. "Then…the house? —Tom, you bought this house?" When he nodded, she gave a squeal and ran straight at him, fists flying. "You are the new owner you kept referring to!" she pummeled his head and shoulders. "You are a terrible man for teasing me so, Thomas Phillip Scott! A terrible, horrible man!" she laughed as he wrestled her down to the bed. "A horrible…awful… man!" she managed while he found her lips again and again. Then he claimed her mouth in earnest and all he heard was her beautiful sigh.

"And now, Mrs. Scott," he paused to gaze at her, ever-fascinated by those changeable green eyes, "shall we undress? As I see it that should be the thing for christening the Master bedroom."

"Indeed, sir," she agreed. "Undressed it should be!" And so saying, they both soon were. "Tom, did you notice that every room has one of those wonderful mantle pieces?" she smiled, bringing full glasses of wine to the bed. "Not only that, the balcony and stair railings and doors are black oak too. —And the support columns in the front hall. Did you notice?"

"I'm noticing that you look beautiful by firelight," he said accepting his glass. "Does that count for anything?"

"Much," she looked over the length of his reclining body, and smiling drew a finger down his belly; then on to gauge the height of his interest. It was Tom's turn, at that point, to utter a sigh. "You know, we'll have beautiful children," she sat beside him to continue her caressing strokes. "…But sometimes, I wonder if we should have them. I love this and don't want to swap my—my immorality for motherhood."

Tom looked at her and started to laugh, but she seemed so serious, he didn't dare. "Would, uh…would you mind explaining that? I've never before heard motherhood likened to entering a nunnery. In fact, it would seem on the opposite end the scale to my way of thinking. —And what, pray tell, do you find immoral about yourself?"

"Well, it's normal for a man to want…sex," and she did not manage the word easily, "but Tom, I do too—and so much, I often feel guilty."

"Why, for God's sake?" he asked. "Lady, you felt guilty when you thought you'd taken a lover. Are you saying now, that marriage only gives you the legal right to feel the same damned way? Mandria, that is insane!"

"But I have no morals when it comes to you, Tom. I would do anything—commit any sin—to keep you in bed with me."

"Really?" he grinned wickedly. "Shall I make a few sinful suggestions?"

"Oh, don't tease me," she placed her glass on the table in distress. "The point is I'd be a terrible mother! I'd resent giving up this room; this bed—you—and I'd blame the children, I just know I would!"

"...Lady, every time I think I know what's going on in your head, you prove me wrong," Tom nodded. Then, placing his glass beside hers, he drew her on top of him and held her there, nose to nose with him. "Now: very slowly, what makes you think you're giving up this room, this bed or me? Where in the hell are you going? —And how could our children be blamed for it?"

"Well...it's usual to take separate bedrooms once children start coming," she explained. "Mother did and all her friends I can think of—though most have connecting doors to their husband's rooms, where Mama doesn't." Then she was pointing. "So, maybe we could cut a door through that wall and—"

"No. Absolutely not!" he said emphatically. "You, dear one, will never move out of my bed. And you've yet to explain why children make this practice usual."

"I don't know!" she admitted. "Maybe mothers need to be closer to the nursery; —or maybe they want to keep babies from disturbing their husband's sleep," she shrugged prettily.

"That's not good enough. If you want a door cut, it will be into a nursery, but not a separate bedroom for you. Lady, a crying baby would not disturb me nearly as much as you moving out of here."

"But we should try to raise our children properly!" she said now.

"Mandria, not everyone lives in a big house with nurseries and his and her rooms. Are you branding a family raised in a one-room cabin as improper—or immoral?"

"No…, of course I'm not," she mulled that over for a moment. "But the children in those cabins—especially the older ones—would have to know what their parents are doing in bed together. Wouldn't ours know too, if I stay in here?"

"Probably," he chuckled, fitting his hands to her rounded bottom. "Ours especially, I'd think."

"Oh, I'd just die if they did!" she hid beneath his chin. "They'd know how disgraceful their mother is; —that all she wants to do is make love to their father like a harlot!"

"Lord—oh, dear Lord, but I hope so," he ground her down upon him. "I do most sincerely hope so."

"Oh, but Tom!" she exclaimed.

"Oh, but Mandria!" he imitated, laughing as he turned her onto the bed, where he kissed her parted lips before propping on an elbow above her. "Now, my complicated, confused little wife: in the first place, we're not going to couple in front of our children, but they can only benefit from the closeness we do show them; —the real love we share. They will know they were born of that love and treasured all the more for it. And when they're grown, I can only hope they will seek the same kind of love for themselves—because of the example we set them. Secondly, Mrs. Scott, morals are standards of decent behavior for all but two people on this earth: a husband and a wife—like you and I. And between us, nothing—no act—is immoral as long as it pleases us both and deepens our closeness. …Do you understand what I'm saying to you?"

"That I'm not moving out of your bed?"

"No, you are not."

"That my children won't think I'm…perverted?" a smile tickled at her mouth.

"Well," he chuckled, leaving that open for question.

"That you think my upbringing was a bit too straight-laced," she added.

"Perhaps just a bit," he played with the chain holding his ring. "And yet, I am grateful for the training and manners that make you a lady. Most especially, I enjoy knowing that I, alone, can turn you into a fiery little bitch; that afterwards, cock-weary and happy beyond the telling, I can lay back and watch my lady reappear—like a butterfly, rising from the warmth of silken nest."

"Tom, make love to me," she circled her arms about his neck. "Fill my body the way you fill my mind with your beautiful thoughts."

"Ah—the bitch is restless tonight," he said, flipping her over. "Well, up on your knees, woman. It's time we christened this bed—and convention be damned!"

As indeed, it was. His insertions were slow and deliberately deep; the withdrawals, careful and nearly complete. And he kept to these leisurely thrusts, as if he wished to study the act; to trace every inch of her internal walls with the head of his penis. It was more intensity than Mandria could withstand—and inhibitions released, she was suddenly backing into his advances; her body opening to him. Tom would never know if the burst of warmth flowing about his insheathed member came first from her or himself, but it received his prompt and appreciative attention...

Once again, it was good between them, and Tom eased down on Mandria's back to better enjoy the pulsing after-waves lingering inside her. "I love the feel of that," he caressed the nape of her neck. "But then, there's nothing about you I don't love the feel of."

"I wish we weren't expected tonight, don't you?" she sighed half into a pillow.

"Yes, lady, but we are," he nodded, lifting his watch from the little table. "...Six thirty," he told her. "We'd best leave soon."

"I know," she turned on her side and watched as he put on his shirt. "Tom, thank you for buying the house. I've never been so surprised."

"You're welcome, pretty lady," he smiled contentedly and pulled on his trousers. "We'll be able to move in here soon. All right?"

"And meanwhile," she sat up, "we can start meeting here, can't we?"

"Of course," he answered, searching his pockets. "Here; —here is your key. Come and go as you like. It's your home, Mandria." Then, after a pause, he went on. "...I wish I could tell you to begin decorating it on a large scale, because I want to see your touch in every room. But with the cost of the house, you will have to start slowly—a few pieces

347

at a time—until Christmas, maybe. Then, my investments should balance things out again."

"Tom, are you short of money?" she rose to her knees. "I have money. I've quite a lot and—"

"No, love," he said firmly, while searching for a missing sock. "It may take longer, but I want to pay for everything here."

"Oh? …I thought you said this was my home too."

"And so it is," he located the sock, and sat to put it on.

"Then why can't I spend my money on my home?"

"Because I said you couldn't," he drew on his boots now.

"B…but that's not fair," her voice remained calm, yet her eyes flashed a warning Tom missed.

"Perhaps not," he busied himself banking the fire to nothing, "but that's the way it has to be."

"And of course, nothing else matters," she hurried off the bed to snatch up her own clothing. "You have spoken, and I am to obey."

Tom turned, surprised at her tone. "Hey now, lady…are you miffed with me?" he asked, starting toward her.

"Miffed is no where close to it," she retorted. And when he tried to draw her close, she wedged the armful of dress and petticoats between them. "Please don't wrinkle my gown!" she said then.

"Then move it out of my way," he said with a smile—which she wanted to slap from his face.

"No!" she tried to back away and felt his arms tighten. "Will you stop? I want to wear this dress tonight and you're ruining it!"

But Tom was not put off. Circling her waist in one arm, he took hold of the dress with his free hand. "I told you to move it. Now will you, or shall I rip it in half?"

"You wouldn't dare—I've nothing else to put on!"

"I don't give a damn," he replied and she felt a serious strain on the fabric.

"Oh—all right!" she released the bundle and watched as he flung it aside. In silence then, she accepted the hands lifting her mouth to his, but if he expected a response he wasn't getting it.

"...Mandria?" he drew back to look at her. "You are my wife. Kindly behave like you know it."

"Why?" she made him a peevish shrug. "You'll have what you want anyway. I'm not strong enough to stop you. But don't expect play-acting from me. I am very angry and I can not be loving and angry at the same time."

"Then stop being angry," he suggested, as if that were the simplest of all solutions.

"Give in, you mean! Submit to your bull-headed notions! Well, I certainly will not. —No, I want a voice in this matter!"

"Damn it, Mandria!" Tom's grip on her arms tightened as they stood glaring at each other. But neither was going to yield and both knew it. Slowly, then, he set her at arm's length and released her. "I will be Master of my own house," he said with a calmness that deepened her fury even more. Then turning away, he scooped up her clothing and tossed it to her. "And I won't have your father's money involved here—directly nor indirectly," he added.

"It's not Father's money—it's mine!" she tried shaking the wrinkles from her gown. "What a fine mess! My dress just looks terrible"

"Well, like your husband, it's the only one you have at the moment. You might try making the best of both situations. —But do hurry. It's quarter of seven."

"It's not quite the same," she irritably worked into her chemise. "I can change dresses at will."

"And husbands?" he watched her fasten a shower of petticoats at her waist. "Does your *will* mean that much to you?"

Mandria gave Tom a scathing look as she lifted the rumpled gown over her head and wriggled it into place. "Damn you, button this thing—and you might also button your mouth!" she snapped.

He did both and neither easily, for he was clearly as angry as she. And on leaving the house, they rode silently away in the chilled September darkness; a chill rivaled only by their own moods...

# CHAPTER 28

Nicole had looked forward to this party for days. It might be Allen's birthday, but she would be the star of the evening. Sam had promised it! She'd taken special care in dressing and when Allen arrived to escort her across the square, his approval was obvious. He scarcely took his eyes from her flawless perfection—or the plunging cut of her favorite flesh-colored gown. Yes, men always reacted to this dress and tonight her seductive appearance was all important. But on arrival at the Lucas', Sam had whisked Allen off to his study and she was left in the parlor to chat with Mamalyn, alone, because Tom and Mandria were late in coming. Growing decidedly restless, she excused herself and now stood in the entrance hall appraising her mirrored reflection again. Her hair and make-up were perfect, of course...and yet, on second glance, the gown seemed too pale. Pure excitement over things to come, had lent her complexion a heightened rosiness, destroying the flesh-on-flesh allure she coveted. And not even an extra dusting of powder was correcting it.

"I should have worn something else!" she muttered, remembering the rich lilac hue of the dress she purchased that morning, but forgetting that it lay in a heap with a half-dozen others she'd rejected when color mattered less than revealing the cleavage. "If I hurry home, maybe there's still time to change..." But she had tarried too long, for Tom and Mandria were arriving and she'd be forced to suffer through the evening in what was now deemed *this pale pink rag!*

"Goodness, but you're late," Nicole straightened, noting Tom's stiff, formal gestures as he helped Mandria remove her cloak. Then she watched the silent, angry brushing Mandria gave her gown. ... Her very rumpled gown. "What have you been doing all afternoon?" she added, and turning back to the mirror, thought better of her own appearance. ... *What is a pale color compared to Mandria's unsightliness?* she thought. *And if they have been arguing—which does seem the case— that would be grand too.* "Well?" she gave her hair a final pat. "Confess all—or was it something you dare not speak of in polite company?" she added sweetly.

Even wrapped in a smile, coyness was not welcomed by Tom at that moment and his reply was barely civil. "We were shopping for Allen's gift, Nicole—and waiting for the engraver to finish his tedious job. Anyway, it's only ten past seven."

Mandria drew the jeweler's box from her purse, but left her husband the gift of a whispered barb. "*Master of your house—and of ready answers, aren't you?*" And before he could do more than glare, she was going up the stairs. "Nicole," she said without looking back, "come and wrap this present for me. It seems I have a *change* to make before dinner."

"Of course," Nicole answered, but did not hurry to follow. Instead, she turned on the bottom step and gave Tom her most mysterious smile. "Did you have to ruffle her feathers as well as her gown?" she said in a hushed voice. "What happened, Tom? Did you forget which of your women you were with?"

Tom went to where she stood, hoping she'd continue to keep her voice level low. "What are suggesting, Nico?" he asked from the other side of the newel post.

"Why nothing," she said innocently. "But I know about your mistress."

"...Do you now?" he uttered.

"Yes, and for a man keeping company with Mandy, it's a logical solution," she assured him. "Tom, I've known her for years, and your advances are not the first she has spurned. Mandy has always been a bit prudish in these matters," she paused for a telling glance up the stairway. "—And obviously, she intends to remain so. What I don't understand is why you continue this hopeless pursuit. If your mistress doesn't satisfy your needs, then perhaps you should look for a different kind of woman: one who would give you social standing in the parlor and more passion in the bedroom than a common whore could muster."

For a spoiled, self-centered girl, Nicole had presented a precisely stated case and it occurred to Tom that she'd been coached; that her knowledge—even some of her phrasing—belonged to Sam Lucas. Who, but Sam, believed he was keeping Kathy as a mistress? Who, but Sam, had ever called Mandria *prudish*? The hair at the nape of his neck prickled uncomfortably as he considered such an unholy alliance. "…And who," he asked cautiously, "would this one woman be?"

"Oh no, Tom, I'm not about to subject myself to another of your horrid lectures," she said sagely. "For now, I only want you to admit the truth. Just say there's nothing between you and Mandy and that your mistress is hardly filling the void."

Now, here was a curious dilemma: if he denied having a mistress, through Nicole, it would reach Sam, who must believe this for a while yet. Confirmation, on the other hand, would surely be gloated to his angry wife—and in no more time than it took Nicole to climb the stairs. The *master of ready answers* nodded mutely, knowing how Mandria would enjoy seeing him at such a loss. Appreciative of the irony, and because there seemed nothing better to do, he laughed.

"Stop that!" Nicole hissed, reverting to more typical behavior. "How dare you treat this so cavalierly—not to mention me!"

"Cavalierly?" he laughed again, and this time because it upset her giving him the advantage. "Let me assure you, Nico, from the day we met, I have never made such a mistake."

"Well, that's better," she straightened, confidently. "It's about time you paid me a real compliment."

"But did I?" he asked, pleasantly.

"You did—you just did and you know it! Now don't spoil it. I want to hear all about this mistress."

"Don't you ever stop?" he smiled. "I've no wish to lessen myself in your esteem. Surely, you wouldn't trust a man who gossips about the women in his life."

"Feathers!" she retorted. "The truth, Tom, or—or you will regret it before the evening is done."

"That should prove interesting," he replied. "Though I hardly think Sam will thank you for warning me. But then," he leaned close to whisper, "if you don't mention it to him, I won't."

"Sam?" her lips parted in surprise. "...I don't know what you could mean."

"Come now, can't you be as honest as you'd have me be?"

"You think you're so clever," she began to back up the steps. "You are just trying to confuse me. Well, it won't work, Tom. —You'll see!" And turning on her heel, she fled upward.

"Dear God, what next?" he sighed, starting for the front parlor. There was no telling what Nicole might say to Mandria now—as if that one wasn't upset enough already. And he couldn't do a damn thing about it.

"Good evening, Tom," Evelyn greeted. "Come in—and help yourself to coffee or a drink, will you?" She, too, was busily wrapping a birthday gift.

"Thank you," he said, pouring a much needed brandy. "Has Allen arrived yet?"

"He's in the study," she answered. "Sam wanted to show him an article about slave-runners, I believe. Those stories have caused the South a lot of unrest lately."

"Yes," Tom uttered, going to stand by the fire.

When he said nothing more, Evelyn looked up from her task to find him staring blankly into the flames. "...Tom, would you like to join Allen?"

"No thank you," he smiled briefly. "I'd rather talk to you," he hesitated. "...In fact, I need to talk to you, Mamalyn."

"What is it, Tom?" she joined him at once. "Is something wrong?"

"Nothing serious," he assured her. "A disagreement."

"Between you and Sam?" her eyes narrowed, much like her daughter's.

"Between Mandria and myself. —Now, I'm not asking you to take sides or listen to complaints. It's just that I don't know how to argue with her! Mamalyn, all of my life, in virtually every circumstance, I've been able to hold my own. If I didn't agree with someone, I said so and backed my argument with sane, logical reasoning. But your daughter—your very beautiful daughter—baffles me completely. All my logic and reasoning may as well be set to music. I tell you, arguing with her is like butting heads with a damned goat!"

"Oh, Tom," Evelyn laughed, giving his arm a sympathetic pat. "Let me tell you a secret about Mandy. She will defend her point of view and argue, nose to nose, for as long as you care to stand there. But all the while, she is listening to what you say and once she cools down a bit—weighs one side against the other—she usually does the right thing. And if she was wrong, she won't be too proud to say so. …I'll tell you something else too. Usually, disagreements are not altogether a bad thing. Sometimes, they're a healthy way of clearing the air. Then, if the people involved really care for one another, they can compromise their differences."

"If they really care," Tom repeated, turning to face Evelyn. "… You know that I'm in love with her, don't you, Mamalyn? I hope you don't object too much."

"No, because you are right for Mandy," she smiled warmly. "And you couldn't have come into her life at a better time. …I was truly worried about her for a while," she lowered her eyes, "but you gave her stability, Tom, and I'll always be grateful for that."

"No, I'm the grateful one," Tom took her hand. "To you, for having such wonderful, hard-headed, mule-stubborn daughter—who happens to love me back, in spite of herself."

"A credit to her intelligence," Evelyn straightened pridefully—and this gesture, too, was so like Mandria, Tom chuckled. "Well, it's good to hear you laugh again," she smiled. "After all, we are here for a party!"

"Yes ma'am, we are," he responded. "—Though I've one more request. Would you keep my amorous confession between us for a while?"

"I won't tell a soul—if I may request something in return," she leaned to speak confidentially. "Tom, please—*please*—patch this quarrel with Mandy soon. When you two are not on good terms, she is almost impossible to live with!"

"It can't happen soon enough," he said, placing an affectionate kiss on her cheek.

"Well, just look at that!" Nicole exclaimed from the doorway. "Mandy, I do believe Tom is now flirting with your mother!" And as the two young women came to join them by the fire, she continued. "*Don't you ever stop*, Tom? How many ladies does it take to please you?" And once more, her taunts were wrapped in innocent smiles.

"Nico, do behave," Evelyn chided. "Pay her no mind, Tom—none at all."

"Oh, he won't, Mama," Mandria offered. "Tom is stone-deaf when it suits his purpose," she added with a snappish swish of plum velvet skirts.

Tom simply turned away on the pretext of escorting Evelyn back to the sofa and changed the subject. "Tell me, Mamalyn, how go the plans for the Harvest Ball? I heard from Mandria you were made ticket chairman this week."

"Yes, and they're selling very well," Evelyn replied, noting the ire his easy dismissal caused her daughter. But before she could even attempt smoothing things over, Nicole was off on a tangent of her own.

"Oh, Mandy, did I tell you? I ordered my ball gown today!" she said with much excitement. "You will just love it—everyone will! It has these darling little cape sleeves, skirts out to here," she measured with a graceful twirl, "and its blue; a lovely, rich turquoise blue!"

"What, pray tell is *lovely, rich and turquoise blue*?" asked Sam, as he and Allen entered the room.

"My new ball gown, of course!" Nicole hurried to greet them. "And both of you must promise me a dance, here and now."

"Most assuredly," Allen was quick to agree with Sam's nod. "I'd be honored to claim you for a dance, Nico."

"I knew I could count on you, Allen, dear," she kissed his cheek coquettishly. Then, standing between the two men, a hand tucked in each of their arms, she turned mocking eyes on Tom. "And what of the elder Mister Scott? Will he turn me about the dance floor—or about his finger, as he's done so wickedly tonight with Mandy and Mamalyn?"

"By God!" Sam approved—but with feigned sternness. "Wickedly, you say?"

"Well, what else is one to assume?" Nicole replied. "Only moments ago, we caught him kissing Mamalyn in this very room—and heaven knows what spell he cast over Mandy. She was quite...*undone* when they arrived, but still so enchanted she hadn't a word of disapproval about his flirting with her mother so openly."

"So, Scott, must I demand satisfaction? —Have you no defense against this sharp-eyed little minx?"

Tom heard Allen's intake of breath; saw the color stain on Evelyn's cheeks; the green shards Mandria was sending at Nicole, as all stood in awe that those veiled suggestions could have been taken seriously. But Tom knew better. Sam was good at disguising anger in a smile, but had much to learn about hiding pleasure, for those usually stone cold eyes now held a rare, but genuine sparkle. "Sam," he said seriously, "your greatest satisfaction in life must surely be in knowing your wife and daughter are the true ladies here; —genuine ladies, who would never embarrass you or themselves. Not even in the guise of humor. ...As for you, *Miss Minx*," he smiled now, at Nicole, "I had every intention of asking for a dance. You needn't resort to petty libel to fill your prom card."

"Why, I did no such thing!" her color deepened over the double slap he'd just dealt her—and she was glad Sam was there to see the contemptible way Tom could treat her.

"Then let my apology equal the sincerity of your denial," he made her a slight bow before turning to Evelyn again. "Back to our discussion, Mamalyn, I'm told we're to meet here first and proceed to the ball in a group?"

"'Tis the custom," she nodded. "—Mandy, how many in our party so far?"

"Well, twenty one, counting Uncle Ran," Mandria sent another quizzical glance at Nicole, "Twenty three, if Nico and her escort decide to join us."

"But of course, they will join us," Sam soothed her hand with encouraging pats. "The belle of the ball could hardly travel in lesser company."

"Thank you, dear Uncle," she still pouted. "Captain Herb and I will be most happy to join the party here—expressly because you have asked us to."

As one, Tom, Mandria and Allen looked at Sam, wondering if he could stand the gaff.

"…Michael Herb?" his voice reflected surprise. "You're going to the ball—*our ball*—with Captain Michael Herb?"

Naturally, Nicole had forgotten her pique in favor of new excitement. "Yes—oh, yes, Uncle Sam—and how that man can dance!" she turned gaily before him. "Why, with my new gown and the escort of that handsome Irishman, I'll be the envy of every woman there! —Isn't that wonderful?"

Sam swallowed his ready reply on seeing the expectant lift of Tom's eyebrow. "Indeed," he uttered instead. But resentment rattled in his chest like phlegm while he vowed to hasten the time when Nicole would destroy Mandria's infatuation with this man. …And, he decided just then, with a few twists in the plot, she could also set Tom and Mike at each other's throats. That would get both of the bastards out of his life—and his home—forever. "Really, Nico, it is wonderful," he added with a smile—which broadened as Tom's expression grew perplexed.

"Isn't it just!" Nicole giggled. "Mandy, you're getting a new gown too, aren't you?"

"I don't know," she shrugged. "For some reason, I haven't thought about it this year."

"But you're doing the decorations."

"Yes—"

"And Tom is escorting you?"

"Well—yes!" Mandria said, wondering why it seemed important to stress that.

"Then you'd better get one," she advised. "Tom must know your entire wardrobe by now. A new gown might stimulate his interest—add a new...*wrinkle*, so to say?"

Mandria looked first at Tom and could tell he was as aware as she of Nicole's second reference to the state of her apparel upon their arrival.

"Well of course you'll have a new gown, Mandy," Evelyn injected, watching her daughter's eyes slide from Tom to Nicole. And narrow. "Mrs. Amos has been pestering me for weeks to send you over. The material you chose several months ago has arrived and its lovely—just the color of your hair. She has found the perfect trim, too: a deep chocolate lace studded with seed pearls."

"Really," Mandria said, wondering how the resident flirt—and life long friend—had become so attuned to what Tom needed to see. "Well, I think I'll visit Mrs. Amos first thing tomorrow morning," she said with decision. ...*Oh, yes, this ball gown is going to be daring enough to stir the interest of a damned rock—as well as my errant husband,* she thought. ...*And one thing more: if Nicole dares to mention my rumpled dress again, that new wrinkle is going to come from a slap, right to her pretty blonde mouth!*

"The dinner is served," Old Jed made his favorite announcement. And sojourning to the dining room, they enjoyed an excellent meal in relative calm. Afterwards, the table was cleared and coffee served; a rich, black coffee laced with almond liqueur and topped with thick dollops of sweetened whipped cream.

"Allen, I hope you like cake," Evelyn tinkled a crystal bell beside her cup. "Cook has outdone herself on this one."

"So she has!" he exclaimed as a servant carried it in. "Look, Tom—chocolate! One of my favorite weaknesses!"

"Is that before, or after, beautiful women?" Nicole purred.

"Before and after," he eyed the dark, gooey wedge of cake passing his way. "I've a ravenous appetite for both!" And savoring a bite, he sighed in appreciation.

"Somehow, son, I knew you would," Sam chuckled, certain Allen's appetites were inherited from him. "Tell me, have you met many of Savannah's young women?"

"A few. But as Tom said, none holds a candle to the ladies here; —or to Lucy," he said with true charm. Then Allen paused to look at Sam. "...Nevertheless, courting does present a problem you might help me solve, sir."

"How so?" Sam came forward on the chair. His son was asking a favor and nothing could have pleased him more—except the fork that stopped half-way between plate and mouth as Tom paused to listen too.

"Well, Mr. Lucas—Sam—courting is expensive and as I hope to do my fair share, its time I found employment."

"Little brother," Tom entered a polite objection. "You know what a busy man Sam is—"

"Don't be ridiculous!" Lucas cut him off. "Allen, what kind of work do you want?"

"Anything! I'm willing to do any job—though I do favor accounting. I'm very good with numbers, sir."

"Are you now?" Sam took further pride in a second inherited trait. "As it happens, I'm in need of a bookkeeper at one of the river front warehouses. Come to my office in the morning and we'll talk terms."

"I will—and thank you, sir!" Allen grinned, took another large bite of his cake and turned to Tom. "What a day this has been, big brother. If I believed in charms, I'd swear one was working for me!"

"Oh, you've guessed my secret," Nicole declared. "And I thought my magic so cleverly disguised."

"So, it's you I'm indebted to?" Allen teased back in high spirits. "Well, fairy-lady, as I'm in such a good mood—and wouldn't want my luck to sour—I hereby offer repayment. You were kind enough to stand in for Lucy tonight and I know you are at loose ends until Mike returns on Fridays, so I'll buy you lunch from my first pay envelope. Is that acceptable?"

"It will do," she said to Allen. "For now," she added, catching Tom's negative nod. "And I will hold you to it, Allen," she leaned toward him, to better display her inviting self.

"Good," he said, seeing Tom's lowered eyes and tight lip-line. "... Very good," he repeated noting, in contrast, the pleased smiles worn by both Nicole and Sam and the quizzical ones of Mamalyn and Mandria.

But Sam was more than pleased. He was close to leaping from his chair and turning a jig about the floor! It had come to him like divine revelation:—as Mandria glanced suspiciously at Nicole; as Allen smiled charmingly at her; as Nicole's eyes slid slowly and repeatedly over Tom. Yes, Sam would wedge his protégé between Tom and Mandria; then between Tom and Mike; and finally, between Tom and Allen! And what better place to start than their luncheon engagement? … Which meant Nicole's indoctrination had to begin immediately—by morning if possible…And hadn't she asked him to call for a *viewing*? "Yes, uh—Allen, I've just remembered an early appointment," Sam said then. "Could you come to my office tomorrow afternoon—at two, perhaps?"

"Yes, sir. I'll be there at two o'clock sharp," he answered, as Old Jed placed several gaily wrapped gifts before him.

"That's fine," Sam nodded, his mind racing forward again. … First thing in the morning, he would fire one of the bookkeepers and make room for his son where he belonged—in *his* employ and under *his* supervision. From there, he could guide Allen's steps in many directions. And the second thing on the morning agenda would be paying Nicole that visit… But Allen was opening his gifts now and as he read the inscription on a gold pocket watch, Sam's attention returned to the company at hand.

"*From your special family*," he said. Then the boy looked at Tom with an expression Sam found hard to bear. "…You've given me enough already, Brer. I didn't expect more—not after the gift I received this morning."

"Yes, well, Mandria had her heart set on buying that chain and I more or less felt obligated to attach something to it," Tom joshed with him.

"And wasn't Tom just the smartest thing to figure that out?" Nicole laughed. "Was his other gift that ingenious, Allen? What did he give you this morning?"

"…A book," Allen replied cleverly. "And a first edition, at that."

"But the watch inscription," Sam nodded. "I thought Tom was your only family."

"Special family is a term Mandy inspired," Allen winked at his new sister-in-law. "It means Tom has managed to be—or provide—all the family I've ever needed."

"Humph!" Sam retorted. "Endearing, Mandy—quite endearing, I'm sure."

Allen opened Lucy's gift next. It was a gold, egg-shaped watch fob and Allen laughed when explaining the confusing note enclosed. *"So you'll keep the mosquitoes and eggs separated in the basket—and remember the day we met."*

Nicole's present was a monogrammed ascot and along with accepting Allen's thanks, she extracted a promise. "You must wear it to our luncheon."

*"From Sam and Mamalyn,"* Allen now read the card tucked inside small velvet box. And looking beneath it, he gasped in surprise. "A stickpin—a diamond stickpin!"

"How beautiful!" exclaimed Nicole, coming forward to examine it more closely. "Oh, yes, this is truly elegant. And think how grand it will look on my ascot, so you must promise to wear both for our engagement. —It is just so beautiful!"

"Sam chose it for you, Allen," Evelyn sounded almost apologetic. "I hope it's not…too much for a young man's taste."

"Of course it isn't, Evelyn!" Sam said in true irritation. "It's a handsome piece!"

"And expensive," Tom uttered in bewilderment.

"That depends on one's circumstances and connections, doesn't it?" Sam replied. "It hardly cost me a thing." But it had. The stickpin was one of Sam's own—a reward he'd purchased for himself, all those years ago, when over the objections of her lawyers, Evelyn finally allowed him to run her father's company. Yet he'd never found an occasion to wear it, nor a reason to explain its existence, so it had lain in limbo among his private possessions, gathering dust like an heirloom. And that was his exact thought when he came across it again: here was an heirloom, to be passed from father to son. He had only to put it in a new box and have it presented as a birthday gift. …Now, if Tom and Evelyn would just shut-up and let him enjoy his parental offering!

361

"Still, sir," added Allen, "after the wonderful dinner—and that cake! …Well, you needn't have spent another cent on me."

"Nonsense, boy!" Sam gave a laugh. "What is money for if you can't spend it?"

Mandria's tone was pleasant, but her message wasn't. "Father, just today, I heard from someone who would not agree with you on that."

"Then your someone is either a fool or a beggar," he retorted, "And certainly not worthy of the company here."

"Indeed," Nicole concurred. "Generous spending is expected of our class."

"And I know someone who must agree with you, Nicole," Tom countered. "But can you explain to me why you feel it's expected?"

"…Of course, Tom," she smiled, greatly pleased that he was truly seeking her opinion. Maybe Sam was right! She had seen real displeasure on his handsome face when the date was made with Allen. *Could jealousy be prompting this new attitude?* "You see, it is we who keep those marvelous little down-town shops in business, because the poor, very obviously, can't afford to buy much. And we greatly enrich the lives of our little people in other ways too. It's through us that they are allowed a glimpse of the latest fashions—modeled in the flesh, as they say; through us, they are given an inspiring example of culture and good taste. Oh, yes, Tom, they do look forward to our doings—and our spending—as much as we."

Tom heard Evelyn's sad sounding sigh and it spurred him on. "So what about your home—the house where you live—do these *little people* expect the same inspiration from that as well?" And now, Mandria's sigh was heard, though it signaled exasperation.

"Naturally!" Nicole laughed, feeling elated with her newly-found importance to Tom. "They pass by the wagonloads to point out the O'Rourke house—and this one too, I'm sure. Why, Savannah is full of beautiful, richly decorated homes and the whole city is proud of them."

"Tom, this is not fair!" Mandria suddenly exclaimed. "There is no comparison here and you know it!" Then, realizing what she'd done, she blushed. "I…I am sorry," she tried to explain. "It's just that Tom and I had a small disagreement and—well, it has nothing to do with anyone here, and I didn't mean to involve you."

"But none of us would mind," Sam chuckled. "And as Tom so actively sought Nicole's advice, perhaps you have earned an outside opinion too."

"Yes—oh, yes!" Nicole leapt in. "I'd love a good debate. Let's choose up sides and have a grand one!"

"No, we will not," Evelyn rose, smiling sweetly. "We will finish our coffee around the pianoforte. It's still Allen's birthday and I won't see it spoiled by a silly little spat."

"Spoiled?" Allen hurried to offer his arm. "Mamalyn, nothing could spoil this incredible day. And I thank you, one and all, for the feast, the gifts and the friendships, that grow dearer to me each day."

Only because Sam wanted to promote that friendship more than he wanted to pick at Tom and Mandria, he smiled cordially, escorted Nicole to the parlor and willingly joined in a merry songfest. Tom and Mandria were obliged to follow, but as neither felt the least bit inclined to sing, they stood before the fire, pretending to listen with painted smiles on their faces.

Finally, on the pretext of turning to place his cup on a table, Tom uttered, "Mandria, I don't want this thing to drag on any longer."

"Well, neither do I," she replied as softly. "But I see no way of ending it as long as you refuse to hear my side."

"All right, damn it, I'll listen. —But I won't like it!"

"When?"

"Well, tomorrow, I suppose—"

"Tonight!" she insisted. "Tonight or I won't sleep a wink."

"But...how? —Where?"

"Where it began. I'll meet you at the new house when everyone here is asleep."

"You-will-not!" he whispered a stern warning and felt his painted smile crack. "I won't have you wandering the streets at night."

"Tom, we must talk this out," she raised her chin stubbornly. "So I'm coming."

"No. I will pick you up," he corrected with stubbornness of his own, "At the carriage house gate, just after midnight."

It was precisely midnight when Mandria closed the wooden gate behind her. It was a few seconds later that Harry, the tree sitter, saw a buggy pull away from the dark side of the Lucas house. Then, a series of things happened at the O'Rourke's, demanding his attention. First, he saw Nicole slip across the courtyard and into the stable—and tonight the hound wasn't with her. Next, the side street door to the stable opened and a young Negro girl sprinted across the square in a fit of sobbing. Harry had seen her do that before and watched as she disappeared into the shadows. Then Bernie Brown came sneaking around the corner, knocked lightly on the same door and was quickly admitted.

Harry sat there for several minutes, scratching mosquito bites and trying to assemble the significance of all he'd seen. The buggy leaving the Lucas place could have been his boss going to see one of his women. The little colored gal didn't seem to fit into it anywhere. …But Bernie Brown alone in the stable with Nicole O'Rourke could mean…"Well, God damn," he snickered, scrambling down from his perch. "Think I'll just go have me a look!" So crossing the street, he hoisted himself to the top of the courtyard wall and walked it tight-rope fashion until reaching an open hay loft…

# CHAPTER 29

"Were your parents asleep?" Tom asked, tucking a robe across Mandria's lap.

"Yes," she nodded, blowing warm breath on her hands. "...Did Allen enjoy his party?"

"Yes," he nodded back, clucking the horse into motion. Then as they had made all the small talk either cared to, they rode for a time in silence. And when Tom did speak again, it came suddenly. "—Mandria, listen. I don't think this meeting tonight is wise."

"Why not? You said you didn't want it this way between us."

"I don't. But I've a lot on my mind and it wouldn't be fair if you're expecting me to see your side of any argument objectively—not tonight."

"Why? What's on your mind that's more important than us?"

"Not more important, just...well, when things happen that I can't explain, it bothers me. —Like that luncheon engagement Allen made with Nicole; her intentional jabs at everyone; Sam's costly gift and the convenient job opening for Allen—neither of which, he could be swayed from accepting, though we argued about it all the way home."

"Oh? So, now you think our money will taint Allen too?"

"Something sure as hell has!" Tom retorted sharply. "He defended your father most valiantly. Allen said Sam has always treated him courteously, kindly and with genuine interest."

"...My father?" This gave her pause.

"Yes—and damn it, he's right. For weeks now, it's been happening right in front of my eyes and for whatever reason, Sam Lucas has been making a rather determined bid for my brother's friendship."

"But why? …Tom, that is very strange."

"So was the whole damn evening, Mandria," he nodded. "It was like being at a masquerade. You and I were fighting—and nearly everyone else was preoccupied with their own hostilities, it seemed to me."

"Not Nicole," she turned to watch his reaction. "She felt no hostility towards you." And when he made no comment, she went on. "Tom, do you find her attractive? She certainly finds you so."

"I've never encouraged her, if that's what you're asking."

"I didn't ask that. Do you find her attractive?"

"Physically, yes. But I don't like her very much."

"Well, she likes you. Nicole watches you, too—and if I've noticed it, I know you have. Why if you weren't married you'd—"

"But I *am* married and all of this is beyond the point! …Or maybe it isn't. Maybe it proves we shouldn't do this. I'm telling you, we're both too edgy to settle anything tonight."

"Oh, does it bother you to talk about Nicole?"

"No, damn it!" he snapped. Then, determined to remain calm, he began again. "Lady, do try to understand. If we can sit here, bickering about that girl, who has nothing to do with our quarrel, how can we hope to sort out the real issues? We can't—not while we're looking for others to blame."

Mandria was silent for a moment. "Thank you for saying *we*. But I'm the one who started this nonsense about Nico and I'm sorry. … Anyway, we're here now," she said as Tom stopped before the carriage house. "Please, I want to go in; —I really feel we should."

"Where it began," he sat there, still hesitant about the whole idea.

"Yes, Tom—yes!" she climbed down impatiently. "Now get me a lamp and I'll go up and stoke the fire while you shelter the horse. There is no use freezing when we do have a warm place to talk—and hopefully, to end this fighting."

Tom was still not convinced, but found and lit a candle stub for her, then watched as she marched staunchly through the courtyard. "Lady," he uttered, "I pray you're right…"

It should have been a brief walk for Mandria, but while retracing earlier steps, she kept remembering things—like the warmth of Tom's words as they stood looking over the garden shrubs.

"…Shall we christen the place right here on the courtyard floor? I'd wager the new owner would enjoy seeing that…"

And on entering the sleeping porch, she heard him again. "…*Wall-to-wall beds—and I'd have to try you on each one…*"

Mandria sighed and moved on through the narrow breezeway toward the front hall. "…*I've never given a party*," his voice echoed from the front parlor. "…*I wonder if I'd make a good host?*" "…*I'd never want to embarrass you…*"

"…*Amorous behavior*!" added the dining room and she could almost hear their laughter as he whisked her up and spun about the floor.

Mandria felt a tightness grip her throat and was blinking away tears as she hurried up the stairway. But memory, nor the house, was done with her yet.

"…*If you want a doorway cut, it will be into a nursery…*" she heard while passing the empty, waiting bedrooms. "…*But you, dear one, will never move out of my bed…*"

And now, she stood looking at that bed, unable to hold back tears or memories.

"…Several pieces to match this; …bought the only one that interested me; …damn, you look beautiful by firelight; …Shall I make a few sinful suggestions? …I alone can turn you into a fiery little bitch; …afterwards, happy beyond the telling; …convention be damned! … be damned! … damned!"

"Oh, God, what have I done?" she stifled a sob against her fist. Tom had been so proud of the house; so anxious for her approval. Why had she ruined this special day in his life? "Money!" she snatched up the poker and angrily prodded the glowing logs. "We argued over money!" she continued, fueling the grate as well as her evaluation. No amount of money could buy the love he lavished on her so freely.

How dare she try to exchange that fortune for the price of a few sticks of furniture! "I've been so stupid," she sighed, standing back from the roaring flame. "How will I ever make it up to him?" Then, looking at the bed again, she smiled and began to undress in a frenzy…

When Tom came in, he saw that Mandria lay covered to the nose. "Did you catch a chill?" he asked, hoping to stall the unpleasantness of reopening their battle.

"Must have," she answered cozily.

And as Tom went toward the fire, to warm his hands, he thought she looked cozy too, cuddled beneath Mrs. Harrison's borrowed quilt. He also thought of the warmth she was meant to bring all the nights ahead of them and for no particular reason, asked about the coming season."…How cold does it get in Savannah? —Does it snow here?"

"We have flurries once in a great while, but it rarely sticks to the ground," she watched as he removed his coat and turned back to the fire. "…Why do you ask?" There was something distant in his attitude that disturbed her.

"We had a lot of snow in Athens—more in Tennessee. Sometime, I wish…" And his voice trailed into nothingness.

Mandria swallowed hard. What did he wish? That he'd never left those places? Never met and married her? Had she pushed him that far? "—Tom, please, I'm still cold," she said. "…Would you mind lying next to me?"

"All right," he replied with less enthusiasm than she wanted to hear. But removing his boots, he stretched out beside her and idly played with a lock of her hair when she nestled her head on his shoulder. He remained preoccupied, however, and Mandria couldn't bear it—nor could she stand the quilt separating them.

"I'm still cold," she manufactured a shiver. "Get under the cover, will you?"

Tom did, but on feeling her nakedness against him, he became so still, she could hardly feel him breathe.

"Thank you. That's much better," she urged herself onward. "Everything will be better now. You'll see," she nuzzled his neck, leaving a trail of kisses to his ear. "Love me, Tom. Our feud can't mean more to you than this."

"Mandria, don't!" he sat up abruptly. "Don't use your body as a weapon against me. —I can't believe you'd try winning this way!"

"...But I'm not," she came forward too. "Why would you think such a terrible thing?"

"Why?" he said irritably. "Haven't we been arguing all night? Didn't you insist on being heard; —on having your way? You were damned well going after it too!"

"Oh!" she fumed, rolling from the opposite side of the bed. "Oh!" she repeated, stamping both feet in anger. And going to her knees, she disappeared from view.

Tom could hear her rummaging beneath the bed and leaning from his side, he peered at her. "Now what in the hell are you doing?" he questioned.

"Getting my clothes, if you don't mind!" she continued her grappling. "I hid them—hoping to surprise you! But I'm the one who got the surprise! You—you cad!" And hurling a shoe, she caught him squarely on the jaw. But before Mandria had time to appreciate that lucky, caroming shot, Tom had swung across the bed and was hauling her up by the waist. "Let go of me!" she stormed. "Let me be! I want to go home!"

"Well, you're not!" he came right back, and turning her to face him, pinned her there. "Now I'm sorry your scheme didn't work, but you're not winning that way," he went on in a quieter, but far more threatening tone. "—And, you will not throw things at me ever again! Do you understand that?"

Mandria was too angry now to heed him. "I understand all right!" she struggled to free herself. "I know what you think of me! Let me go—damn you—let go!" And when prying at his fingers proved useless, she kicked at his shins and stomped on his toes.

"Damn it, Mandria!" he bristled, then determined to subdue her tantrum, he tossed her on the bed and immediately fell across her.

"Get away!" Get off of me!" she fought all the harder.

"Enough! —Damn you, that is enough!" Tom commanded and holding her wrists, he pressed his full weight upon her. "Stop fighting me!" his face loomed above hers. "Stop!"

"I won't!" she continued with the fury of a feral cat. "You don't want me here! You think I tricked you; —that I used my body to trick you!"

"I said stop!" his grip on her wrists tightened. "Mandria, stop your wiggling... and stretching...and..." Suddenly his mouth consumed hers with a searing kiss. In the next instant and still kissing her, he released one wrist and ran a hand down the length of her torso, before loosening his trousers, spreading her unwilling thighs and making a lunging entrance.

Mandria gasped into his mouth as he probed unprimed flesh. ... And yet, it wasn't altogether unpleasant and grew less so with each successive thrust, but she would not allow herself to respond. Oh no, Tom was going to pay dearly for this one. How she would scorn him! How she would shame him for committing this painful; ...sweet; ... wonderful; ...ravage?

But such was not to be. As suddenly as it had started, it ended. Tom rolled away, laying flat on his belly now, his face turned from her. Mandria heard his ragged breathing and keeping very still, because she didn't know what else to do, she watched a long violent shudder wreak his body. ...But what made him withdraw? What cooled his raging ardor at such a crucial moment?

"I'll drive you home," he said in a dead sounding voice. "We'll leave as soon as you're ready." And without looking at her, he rose from the bed, adjusted his clothing, pulled on his boots and stood looking from a window as he shrugged into his jacket.

Mandria felt as though she might suffocate from the intensity of her confusion. Moments ago, she had been so very angry with Tom and now, more than anything on earth, she wanted to hold him. What sense did that make?

In her own defense, she had tried to make up with him and had her motives misjudged. ...But what had she done about that? Explained—told him the remorse she felt for wanting her way about the money? Oh no! She had allowed her pride free rein and reasoning was chased right out the door…

In his defense, Tom tried to warn her about this meeting; told her he was unsettled by events of the evening and was in no mood to think rationally. …And instead of listening, she had insisted on having her own way again. *Her* needs, *her* right to be heard—*her* damned pride—the all important thing. This was the belligerent attitude she had shown him since they quarreled and having no knowledge of her change of heart, wasn't it understandable that he could misjudge her naked offering?

Remembering his shudder, she wondered if that was his way of expelling the demon she had become to his soul. Looking at him now, it was likely, for he stood immobile and withdrawn, like a statue of cold, shadowed marble. …Lost to her forever?

"Oh God, no!" she uttered, as tears welled in her eyes. Why was she an expert at retrospect and such a failure at all else? It was bad enough to lose him, but knowing it was her own fault was unbearable! And now she was crying in earnest…

Tom clinched his fists at the sound, wishing himself in hell. Returning to the bed, drawn there by horrible guilt, he stood looking at her body. Reddened skin—the marks of his hands—rode her wrists and inner thighs and he damned himself anew. "Mandria, please. …I said I'd drive you home," he managed finally. "…Do you need help in dressing?"

"No," she answered, certain he wanted to be rid of her. And wiping uselessly at tears that wouldn't stop, she went on, "B…but I would like to know what you're thinking right now; —how you honestly feel."

"Well, disgusted; …rotten; —disappointed," he replied to his own version of her question. "And deeply sorry about…well, everything. There's no more I can say."

His words sounded so final Mandria panicked and rising to huddle against the headboard, it shone in her eyes. "It…it's over then?" she drew the quilt across her nakedness "…Is that what you're saying?" she swiped at her tears again.

Her frightened expression cut Tom like a knife, and turning away, he sank on the edge of the bed. "Get dressed, please. And yes, it's over. ...So there's no need to cower from me. I won't touch you again."

"But you can't just walk away from this!" she nodded frantically. "Too much has happened!"

"All right, then," he lowered his head in resignation. "When you run out of names... Well, I can suggest a few more."

"Names?" she puzzled, gazing at the breadth of his shoulders and the curls that lay close on the nape of his neck. If only she didn't want to touch him so badly. "I haven't any names to call you. But I do want you to know something. Tom, I wasn't trying to trick you into anything—"

"Don't! ...Please, don't do this," he interrupted. "If you're trying to make me feel worse, it isn't necessary."

"I'm not trying to do that either," she said defensively. "I only wanted to make peace with you. Instead I lost my temper...but you did too...and then—"

"And then I raped you!" he finished it. "Just like my God damned step father—I raped my own wife!"

Mandria was completely stunned. He was acting out of shame and not for any of the reasons she had feared. "B...But it wasn't the same," she uttered, for her heart was beating so hard and so fast, it greatly restricted her voice. "And you didn't rape me; —you did *not* rape me!" she exclaimed as her tears magically vanished.

"Well, I know that I did!" he insisted. "I saw the marks; I heard you cry out. Mandria...well, I must be losing my mind! —I'd have to be to ever hurt you."

Mandria rose—drawn to him—where she turned his face to her. "Now, you are going to listen to me, Tom: You are my husband; —my lover! I respond to your touch, be it gentle or not. It's something I can't help any more than breathing."

"But you didn't respond. I heard your cry and forced you to it anyway!"

"It was anger you heard," she replied, knowing that was mostly true. "And if I seemed unresponsive, that was done in anger too. But you did not rape me. —Hush now!" she rested fingertips on his lips when he wanted to object. "Was it an act of violence, Tom? —Did you set out to do physical harm or demean me?"

"Dear God—no!" he vowed.

"So it happened because—angry or not—you can't help responding to me either. We were a little close there—rubbing together—and me without a stitch on…? Well, that's never failed to get your attention before," she said with a tiny hopeful smile.

"But afterwards…why were you weeping so bitterly when I came over here?"

"Because—damn it—you stopped in the middle of what you were doing and I thought…" she paused, lowering her head to his shoulder. "Well, I thought a lot of things—all of them stupid and wrong, as usual. But if you don't soon put your arms around me, I'll start to wonder again."

Gently, then, Tom pulled her to him and held her close against his heart. "…I love you," he began awkwardly. "It hardly seems enough to say, but…well, I do love you, Mandria, and somehow I'll—well, I'll make this up to you."

"*Well* just make me one promise," she nuzzled the curve of his neck and smiled. She was his wife and should have remembered his nervous habit. The *well*-peppered sentences had been there to give her clues to the depth of his feelings. Would she ever learn to listen beyond his words? Yes, she would—she swore to!

"Anything," he nodded. "What promise do you want of me?"

"No matter the circumstance, promise you won't ever—*ever*—allow me to fight you off. Tom, I don't seem to have a grain of sense unless I'm beneath you."

Tom chuckled and the tension he felt simply melted away. "Gladly," he agreed. "And damned if I want to hear another word about Mike and his Irish luck. I mean, most women are governed by their hearts, but mine draws wisdom from the depths of her pretty little—"

Mandria squealed, flinging herself against the pillows. "Thomas Scott, don't you say it! Just take off your clothes and get into this bed—now!" But he was already doing so.

373

And yet, once beside her and both knew it was right between them again, Tom uttered a sigh of contented discontent. "Lady, do you know what I'd enjoy most right now?"

Mandria raised herself on an elbow and gave him a skeptical look. "Are you about to make one of those sinful suggestions?"

"I just might," he smiled. "But once—just this once—I would like to spend a whole night with you, like a peaceful, old married couple with all the time in the world for each other."

"Well, not *too* old or *too* peaceful, I hope," she ran teasing fingers down his belly.

"That, my love, would not be possible with you around—as you're about find out if your hand goes much lower."

Which, of course, it did. "You prove your point quite well, Mr. Scott," she laughed. "So, I've decided to grant your wish and stay the night."

"Without being discovered?" he drew back to look at her.

"Yes, because everyone at home saw me retire; my bed already looks slept in; and should they check in the morning, they'll think I've gone for an early walk—which I often do. Or I'll tell them I went to see Mrs. Amos for those dress fittings—and I am going, first thing tomorrow."

"Let's chance it then—dare we?" And he sounded so hopeful, she wouldn't have left at gunpoint.

"Yes—yes, we will!" she pressed her cheek to his.

And he winced. "You toss a wicked shoe," he explained. "Remind me to keep my musket out of your clutches, lady."

"All right; —all right," she moved back to the other pillow and taking his hand, she gently traced the shape of his large, strong fingers. "…Tom," she began hesitantly, "I'm sorry I ruined your day. I do love this house and I'll say nothing more about the money."

Tom brought her hand to his lips. "Did you know your mother is a wonderful lady? She said when two people care for each other, they'll find ways of compromising their differences—and that's what we'll do about this."

Mandria's lips parted in surprise. "You told Mama about our argument?"

"Not in detail. But I did tell her I love you—which she took remarkably well."

"I'll just bet she did," Mandria rose on her elbow again. "Tom, Mama has had you picked out for me since that first day at Tybee."

"Oh?" he rose to meet her nose to nose. "Am I the victim, then, of two scheming females?"

"Of course. Mama staked you out… and I wiggled the bait," she said, joggling her breasts against him.

"Minx! Vixen! Witch!" he wrestled her down. "Siren! Huntress! Temptress!" he reveled in the sound of her laughter. And when both were finally exhausted, they lay close, gazing into the cheery fire.

"…How?" Mandria asked after a time. "How can we compromise? I can't think of a way."

"Right now, I can't either—and I'm not going to try. Please, love, you've no idea how long this day has been for me. I don't want to think about anything but holding you."

"Very well—if I can say one more thing?"

"Say it; —say it! I may nibble on your ears, but I won't bite off your head."

"Well, maybe there isn't a way. If not, I want you to know that I'm very thrifty—and creative, if I must say so myself. I love to hunt for bargains and I've never bought anything because it came from a certain shop—or because I felt it was *expected*, as Nico put it so badly. Tom, I really am very practical. I'll use the money you decide on and I'll make you proud of this house—and of me."

"Because you're just so practical," he laughed, pulling her closer. "Well, I'm already proud of you, lady, and jealous of anything or anyone who might intrude on my happiness. …And that is what started this argument to begin with…" he finished pensively.

"No, it isn't. It was me, wanting to use my stupid money. And it is mine, Tom—inherited from Mama's side."

"Mandria," he paused again, "…I hope I can put this into words. I have just realized the truth of the matter myself. …You've never been cold or hungry or alone, have you? You've never envied a friend new gloves and been too proud to ask for the old ones. —Or as Allen

375

pointed out, worn a coat for so long the sleeves only reached your elbows? I lived that way for a lot of years. Working hard—summer and winter—doing everything I could to keep Allen and myself together. Then I found you: a beautiful girl with tan hair and green eyes, who made me forget the past and look for a happy future. Don't you see? Again, my first impulse was to protect my prize—to shut off every outside influence and so…" his voice faded as his thoughts aligned in rapid clarity. "I was wrong," he said, looking at her. "I shouldn't have smothered you so closely."

"But I like the way you smother me," she smiled, propping her chin on his chest. "And I want to protect our relationship as much as you. The money is not that important."

"Yes, it is. If I expected you to reject everything money has given you, you'd have to return the clothes on your back; your jewelry; even your hair ribbons—and that is absurd. I love you for what you are, just the way you are, and all of those things are a part of who you are—including the money. You said you have some of your own, so use it the way you want. Spend it on the house—or save it for our children—just enjoy it as long as it lasts. But there, I do draw the line. When your own money is gone, you will have to live on what I can provide. We won't be penniless—budgeted, maybe—but can you do it? …Does my compromise suit you?"

"Yes; —Oh yes, Tom!" she hugged him ferociously. "But I'll still be practical—you'll see!" And fairly trembling with excitement, she sat up as her eyes flew over the room, mentally measuring wall spaces, window widths and lengths. "Oh, Tom, I can hardly wait to begin!"

"Me either." he chuckled, pulling her down and against him. "But come, pretty lady, do begin with me…"

# CHAPTER 30

"Yes, sir—yes, I am sure!" Harry insisted. "I ain't lying, Mr. Lucas. I seen Nicole O'Rourke and Bernie Brown in the hay. Naked, she was, and him a-feeling her pussy and tasting her tits—I seen it all!"

"All right, Harry; —calm down, God damn it!" Sam exclaimed. "I'm not accusing you of lying. I'm just surprised that she met him right after the dinner last night—and right under her father's nose."

"He wasn't home," Harry nodded. "Goes out ever' Monday night— or has since I been watching the place."

"...Ransom's poker night," Sam remembered an arrangement he'd once had with Deborah for Mondays. "But you say they didn't couple; that Nicole is still holding him off."

"Far as I know—which ain't to say she don't get her jollies," Harry snickered. "I tell you, boss, that little girl is something else. Brown, he left kind of doubled over, if you get my drift—had me going too. Had to beat old Peter down a-fore I could leave that loft!"

"Yes," Sam grimaced, "she does seem to have that effect on a lot of men. But is that all now—nothing more to tell?"

"Well, one thing. I keep seeing this skinny colored gal come from the stable and go running 'cross the square—and most times she's a-bawling."

"So?"

"So, nothing," Harry shrugged. "You just asked what all I seen. Seen a buggy too—"

377

"Hell, Harry, stick to important things, will you?" Sam said impatiently, for the more he thought about Nicole and Bernie, the more it disturbed him. Bringing the boy that close to the house was risking too much. Had Ransom caught them, she would, indeed, be married off, or sent on an extended cruise somewhere—and neither suited Sam's purpose. No, earlier today, he had created a place for Allen in the warehouse directly below his office and now, having already decided it was time to set other wheels into motion, he sent Harry with a message for Granny Geeter. Then from a locked desk drawer, he removed three small envelopes. The first was marked with a Z, and Zombie Powder granted easiest access and control; the next, marked B, was Bella Donna and good for release of inhibition; the last, a C, was Cocaine and this brought on euphoria at its best. As he pocketed all three and left to pay a promised visit, he wondered which he would end up using. But not knowing had always been the intriguing part of this particular diversion...

Cup and saucer in hand, Nicole received Sam in the morning room, a comfy place, full of plump, embroidered cushions and defused sunlight. "Why Uncle Sam—do come in," she greeted. Then, uttering a word of instruction to Jenny, she closed the door in the woman's face. Turning, she stood there smiling; allowing him to appreciate the revealing cut of her silk, whisper thin dressing gown. "Would you care for some?" she toyed with words. "...Hot cocoa, Uncle Sam?" she added, lowering herself gracefully on the over-stuffed sofa.

"Not just now," he replied, settling beside her. She wanted to flirt. He wanted a lot of things. But he knew he must proceed by degrees, for discipline was what she detested most, yet had to learn quickest. "...I stopped by to congratulate you, my dear," he began. "Your performance last night was superb—and wrangling that lunch invitation from Allen was a stroke of female genius. I tell you, Tom was green with envy!"

"Yes," she agreed. "So, I would say you completed your promised task, Uncle," she sipped cocoa. "But almost too well. I think Mandy also suspected Tom's true feelings. ...So tell me, how will we handle her when he starts calling on me instead?"

Sam smiled with satisfaction. So she hadn't forgotten their talk, as she was apt to do in favor of a more current interest—which meant she still expected his assistance. Now, he would see if see intended to pay the price. "More importantly, Nico, how would you have handled being caught naked, in the hay with Bernie late last night? Really, my dear, that was most dangerous."

Nicole laughed in surprise. "How do you manage to learn these things? —Do you spy on me, Uncle Sam?"

"My knowledge is merely routine. I'm a rich man today because I know what goes on in Savannah—and take advantage of the right opportunities."

"And what opportunity do I afford you?" she asked sweetly.

"Pleasure. You are purely a personal pleasure. ...But I'm wondering now, if you are worth the risk."

Her smile wavered. "What do you mean? —You promised to help me get to Tom."

"I promised to guide you—and would never have told you to bring Bernie right to your father's house."

"But Daddy wasn't here! And you're the one who told me to amuse myself. Besides, I needed to see Bernie," she made him a pretty pout. "Having to look at Tom all evening—wanting his kiss, his touch, until it hurt—"

"And Bernie eased the pain," Sam uttered, bored with her dramatics.

"A little bit," she replied. "Surely my kindred spirit can understand that?"

Recalling the visit she had forced him to make to a brothel, Sam understood all to well. "Still," he nodded, "for your own safety, you should meet elsewhere."

"Where, Sam—a public inn? I would never lower myself to that!"

"Of course not. But there is The Tabby House on St. Julian Street. It is run by the same people who run The Club and caters to a select group of people. If you were to take a suite—"

"Move? —Out of this house?" she said, appalled. "No, Uncle Sam, I won't live anywhere but here—I belong here!" she banged the cup to its saucer.

Sam dug deep for patience. "…Little Nico, I did not say to move out. I said you should take rooms there too. It is a very private place where you could safely entertain as much as you like."

"But I wouldn't have the least notion how to go about something like that," she gave him a truthful reply.

"Why do think I'm here? I'll take you and see that your accommodations are suitable. Now, if you'd care to get dressed we'll leave—and be sure to wear something that won't draw attention."

"But Uncle Sam," she stalled, "…I promised you a viewing today," she took his hand in both of hers; held it nestled against her breast. "And I was so looking forward to it." As she obviously was, because Sam could see the hardened tips of her nipples beneath the thin robe. "Come now, collect your reward," she leaned toward him. "I am very curious about the pleasures you could teach me.…*Step-by-step?*"

Sam brushed his knuckles across those pert little nipples, but instead of the fondling she expected, he tightened his hold on her tender flesh. She flinched, but did not pull away—which pleased him in the extreme. "Haven't you heard a word I said? Do you now expect to play naughty games inside your father's house too?"

"Why not?" she whispered. "Daddy is out of town for the day; I've already locked the door and ordered the servants to their quarters. —So why not here?"

"Your cleverness astounds me," he nodded, wondering why it should. Hadn't he been on this sofa before with her equally clever mother? Easing his hold, he traced a finger across the twin protrusions of those silk-clad nipples. The idea was tempting. Not many men could boast of dallying with mother and daughter in the same cozy cushions. But he was not the daring young hellion he'd been in the past and could ill afford to gamble with securing his son's future. "However," he continued, rising to his feet, "if I am to guide, you had best learn to follow. My buggy is around the corner, Nico. I'll wait exactly ten minutes. If you don't come, I'll consider our association ended. If you do come, wear a hat with dark veils, a dark coat and come through the alley gate." With that, he turned and left while she was still too shocked to say anything…

Nicole was both frightened and irritated, but in the allotted time, she was sitting in Sam's buggy, wearing the recommended coat and hat. "Really, Sam!" she began as they pulled away. "I do not like being rushed—and I'm not even sure I approve of this notion of yours!"

"Oh—shall I take you back? You can continue meeting your playmate in the stable dung—until you're caught. But you'd have to forget about Tom when you're forced to marry Bernie."

"Forget him?" she asked as if the notion were absurd. "Oh no, I won't! I mean to hear Tom take back every unkind word he ever said to me! —I'm going to own that man body and soul…"

Sam nodded in resignation as she went on and on. But if talking about Scott made her ride into promiscuity easier for him, he would tolerate it. After all, St. Julian Street wasn't that far away. "May I ask something—purely out of curiosity?" he injected when she finally paused for a breath.

"What is it?" she shrugged, still miffed with him.

"Well, what is it about Tom Scott that fascinates so many women? He's not rich. His looks are not handsome in the classic sense—Allen has better features. And it can't be his out-going personality, because he says very little unless spoken to—or provoked. Neither does he show any burning ambition or drive. The man is only a school teacher, for God's sake, and seems a rather cold fish to me."

Nicole gave him a wistful sigh. "I don't know, Uncle Sam. There is just something magnetic about him—even hypnotic. A woman can sense his presence in a room before she has seen him. When she does see him, she knows she wanted to. And if Tom looks back—as he did once at me aboard the Irish Mist—well, if I hadn't been sitting already, I would have fallen!"

"It's eye contact then? As they say in novels, he undresses women with his eyes?"

"Not at all!" she said emphatically. "It goes deeper—beyond the flesh. Sam, he could make the pulse rise in a stone cold statue—if it was female," she added with a breathless giggle.

"Fascinating," he remarked, wishing he'd never encouraged this conversation, for the trip to St Julian Street had never seemed longer.

They approached The Tabby House from an alley and as Sam pulled into a walled stable-yard, he realized Nicole had been silent for several moments. But he'd not allow her to balk now, so he brought out his mentoring manners. "Remember, Nico," he said while assisting her down and solicitously adjusting her veils, "this is a most exclusive place. You'll be able to come and go at will; and as long as you protect your identity as carefully as this, no one will question who you are."

"But what about you?" she asked as they started up the back steps. "You're sure to be recognized."

"I should hope so," he laughed. "I own the building."

"Sam, it's not a whore house is it?" she stopped. "I'd die if one of those creatures tried to speak with me!"

"Nico, would I subject you to anything so vulgar?" he chided. "The tenants here are of our own class. You have socialized with 90% of them; —laughed, danced or sung with all. But you won't do so here. The Tabby House is quieter than a church. Granny Geeter insists on it."

"And who is Granny Geeter?" she asked as they entered a long, velvet-papered hall.

"Well, the property manager, so to say," he paused to knock lightly on a door. "And before she answers, you'd best think of another name to use here."

"If she is some gaudy, offensive Madam, Sam, I'm leaving!" she whispered with distain.

But Granny opened the door dispelling that notion quickly. Tiny in statue and well advanced in years, the old woman's skin still held a rosiness about her cheeks. Fine gray hair crowned her head and she wore it fashionably styled. Her lavender dress was quality-made, as was the lace cascading from her sleeves and high collared neckline. Crystal blue eyes, alert and sparkling, warmed her features as much as her cheery smile. She truly looked like a Granny and Nicole wondered if she knitted and baked cookies too.

"Well, Sam," she gently patted his arm. "Good to see you again. Please, won't you come in? The young lady's suite is ready and all that remains is the paperwork." Then making her way to a desk beside the glowing hearth, she motioned Nicole to a nearby chair. Putting on her wire-rimmed spectacles, she slowly thumbed through a ledger, dipped a pen in the inkwell and tapped it more times than seemed necessary. At last, she turned her attention to Nicole. "Now, my dear, your name please?"

"Deborah" she answered, the choice bringing a smile to Sam's lips. "Deborah Scott" she finished and Sam closed his mouth on a garbled oath as he lowered himself on a chair facing Nicole.

"...Deborah...Scott," Granny pronounced each syllable as she wrote it. "And what instructions do you wish to leave?"

"Instructions?" Nicole looked to Sam for guidance.

"Yes, Miss Scott," Granny continued, "There is maid service if you want it. A choice of wines, liqueurs, coffee, tea, chocolate, pastries and cold-cuts—all available on request, or with notice, delivered to the suite before your arrival."

"I see," Nicole nodded, the bit now firmly in her teeth. "Maid service is a must and I'll expect clean linens daily. I want an assortment of liqueurs; a good sweet sherry; and brandy—Sam's favorite, of course. Also, I'll need a competent hairdresser on occasion and bath water drawn—preferably, soon after my arrivals. Is this possible too?"

"Certainly—yes!" Granny smiled, scribbling as fast as she could, which wasn't fast at all. Finishing that, she searched interminably through the desk drawers for a key, finding it, finally, in her pocket.

Nicole was growing impatient with the woman's dawdling, as well as insufferably hot with the smothering veils about her face. So rising she moved away from the fire and about the room, fanning herself with her purse.

Granny watched and then looked at Sam over the rims of her glasses. "You'd best be careful of this one," she murmured confidentially. "The young lady knows what she wants and seems most anxious to have it."

"Indeed," Sam answered in like tone, "And will have it, very soon now."

"I'm certain of that, Sam Lucas," Granny rose with a tinkling laugh. "Now, Miss Scott, if you'll follow me, I'll show you to the suite."

As they went down the hallway, Granny's tone was hushed, her words keeping pace with her mincing footsteps. "Should you stay the night, Miss Scott, I will gladly waken you at whatever time you wish. You've only to stop by and tell me. Also, there is a pull-cord in the room that will summon a servant. They are available 24 hours a day, 7 days a week. There is no extra fee for the services we offer, as the rental covers it all. Payment is due the first of each month—and yours, of course, will be prorated this time. A few days prior to the first, I'll slip a reminder under your door. —This one; Suite D," she stopped. Then turning the key in the lock, she gave it to Nicole along with her best Granny smile. "Welcome, my dear. Enjoy yourself now." And winking at Sam as she passed, she went about her business.

Sam followed Nicole in closing the door behind him. He watched as she dropped her hat, coat and purse on a chair, and looked over the small, but nicely furnished sitting room. "Is the suite suitable?" he asked. "The bedroom is beyond, in that curtained alcove, if you'd care to see it."

"Suitable—compared to what?" she answered the first part of his dialogue, and ignored the last. "Sam my room at home is twice the size! —And what will it cost to keep this place? You neglected to mention that!" she sat abruptly on the sofa, folding her arms belligerently.

Sam ambled over to a waiting tea-cart. Time to calm her nerves and get on with the indoctrination. "You should be comparing the comfort here to wallowing in horse dung," he said, preparing her a very special cup of tea, laced with today's choice of…envelope Z. "Nico, the rental fee is only $50.00 a month—a fraction of what you spend now, on clothing," he handed her the steaming drink and watched as she sipped some. "Denying yourself one new outfit a month will allow the money for this."

"I'll do no such thing!" she stated. "Meeting Bernie is not that important. No, I won't give up anything for him," she drank more.

"And what would you give up to have Tom here?" he asked, pouring himself a brandy. "Won't you need a place like this once I've taught you how to seduce him?"

Nicole paused to consider that and drained her cup as she looked over the room a second time. Then she smiled. "You are a very smart man, Sam Lucas. It's the perfect place! And now, I want to see that bedroom," she rose and started for the alcove.

*...And I will fix you a second cup*, he thought, returning to the cart. "While you're in there, Nico," he called now, "I'd like that private viewing you promised, so surprise me with all you think I should see."

She stopped and looked back at him. "As I am putting myself... in your hands," she said teasingly, "I suppose it is time for my first lesson. But remember, Sam, it must go slowly: *step-by-step*," she added, going through the curtains.

Sam nodded. She was inordinately fond of that stupid phrase and he wondered what she thought was in store. He had little doubt she'd return nude, for she'd gone that far with Brown. He chuckled then, dropping a few extra grains in her fresh cup of tea. He suspected that she felt he'd be equally awed by her beauty and therefore as easily controlled as her young beau. *...Poor white-blonde spider*, he mused. *It's my web you're playing in now...*

"Sam, the bedchamber is lovely," she called. "Blue is my color, you know."

"I do know," he replied. "Some in Savannah call you the Blue Lady."

"Do they?" she asked, much impressed with this bit of information.

"Yes, your mother was called by the same title—and you do look so much like her."

"Unfortunately," Nicole remarked. "You know, I've always been jealous of the time Daddy spends staring at her portrait. But I don't think Mother and I would have gotten along well at all."

"That is for sure," Sam muttered. Deborah had resented the ties of motherhood and left the care and feeding of her daughter to the servants. Yes, Deborah sought more erotic pleasures and much of the time, that meant being in bed with him…

"Well, Sam?" Nicole came toward him, naked, slowly trailing the sheer partition curtains through her fingers. "What do you think?" she turned gracefully, as the curtains whispered back into place. "With this to work with—and your instructions—we should be able to tempt Tom beyond resistance, shouldn't we?"

"Indeed," he smiled, his eyes touching the tautness of her belly and thighs; the tiny waist; the globular shape of firm, young breasts. "Now, come have seat. I've fixed you a fresh cup of tea."

Surprised, and a bit insulted, her hands flew to her hips. "A cup of tea? Sam, you can't be serious! —What romantic lesson am I to learn from that?"

Sam replied in patiently measured words. "You look most fetching with your breasts bobbling about and your pussy silks begging for a good drubbing, but do-as-I-say. We are going to share an intimate conversation—very intimate, Nicole. I mean to learn your preferences in physical pleasures. And you must learn to be comfortable wearing nothing, even while enjoying a mundane cup of tea. Lesson number one, remember? Step-by-step?" he added her favorite enticement, as he handed her the cup and went to freshen his brandy.

Nicole sat, but as his back was to her, she posed herself on the sofa, shifting about until satisfied with the picture she presented—a beautiful nude, sipping on her *mundane* cup of tea. —*One certainly worthy of being painted by some great artist*, she thought.

Sam nodded appreciatively as he came to sit beside her. Time was all that was needed now. "And so we begin," he took a leisurely sip of brandy. "You must be totally honest with me, if you expect to derive the utmost from physical pleasures. Remember that, my dear."

"I will," she shrugged. …The tea was hot and sweet and tasted like nectar on her tongue. It was just so soothing…

"Good," he replied, and for several moments more, he let his eyes feast on her body, knowing this pleased her. But seeing the anticipation in her eyes, he merely returned for another leisurely sip from his glass.

So Nicole did the same from her cup. …And wasn't it odd that being nude could add such intrigue to tea-time? Just thinking about it, caused her skin to tingle delightfully. It wouldn't be long before Sam had to touch her…and what would happen then?

"You can prove your honesty by telling me about each of your beaus—and I want to hear every detail of what passed between you. Romantically, of course."

"Why, Uncle Sam, I do believe you're trying to embarrass me." And finishing her tea, she casually set the cup aside. She could be as off-handed and unruffled as he.

"You are sitting here—stark naked—babbling about embarrassment?" he said sharply. "I do have a reason for these questions, Nicole—but if you want to act the fool, we'll forget the whole God damned thing."

"No, —I'm sorry, Sam. I misunderstood," she was clutching his arm against her. …And the fabric of his jacket felt strange on her inquisitive nipples. "Dear Uncle Sam, don't be angry," she watched herself rub against his sleeve again. …Why had she never noticed the expensive weave of his clothes before? She could see the quality of the cloth, right there in the tightly knitted, precisely lined threads… "My first little-girl romance was cousin Perry. We spent most of a summer playing with each other—and I do mean physically. My favorite thing then was pretending sleep so he could touch me wherever. His favorite was getting away with it," she shrugged. "Kind of silly, huh?"

"So, tell me about Captain Herb," Sam encouraged. "Has he tried to make love to you?"

Nicole laughed warmly, resting her forehead against Sam's shoulder. "There were times when I thought he would—and I gave him every reason to try—but it seems I can't tempt my Captain. …Not yet, anyway."

Sam already knew Mike's objective, but was truly surprised at his self-discipline. This girl had to mean quite a lot to him—in which case, Sam considered it poetic justice that he would have her first. "And Bernard Brown?" he continued. "How hard was he to tempt?"

Nicole looked into Sam's eyes and suddenly, she was plunging deep and naked into pools of deep brown-gold water. Down she went… deeper…only to surface from the bottom, somehow in time to answer. "Bernie touches me," she replied. "Here," she drew a hand over the skin of her breasts. "All over," she added, watching her fingers move over her hip. …Her skin was just very smooth today. Why didn't Sam touch her beautiful smooth skin…?

"With his hands?" Sam baited. "His mouth too—he sucks your tits?"

"Yes. That feels best," she nodded. …It was so easy to talk with Sam. His voice was soft; so gentle…

"Come now," he drew her onto his lap. "You said Bernie touches you here," he lifted her breasts on his hands. "I can see why. You have the most delicate nipples—all pink, and puckered for tasting." And watching for reaction, he repeatedly traced thumbs back and forth over the sensitive tips.

Nicole looked on in fascination as her nipples hardened even more and rose under his touch. Back and forth, and her pulse reacted to the stimulation. …And yet, she remained detached, an observer of her own self from some high perch near the ceiling. Back and forth, until Sam lowered his mouth, fusing body and mind with a warm, moist tongue. "Yes, Sam," she murmured. "You do that better than Bernie. …What else do you do better?"

The comparison irked, but he decided against a snide remark. After all, the carefully measured powder grains were working beautifully. She was now keenly aware of anything that touched her skin; sensually aroused by his every move, and truthful to a fault. "Does the boy kiss you here?" he tongued his way up the slender column of her throat. "Or here," he reamed her ear, extracting the expected quivers.

But Sam, being Sam, that comparison to Brown galled him yet and she would be punished for it. With one hand clasped at the back of her head, he circled an arm about her rib cage in a tight hug, while parting her lips and forcing his tongue deep into her mouth. He now controlled her breathing. Exhaling, he felt his own breath flow through her nostrils. Inhaling, he tightened the arm about her, drew the air from her lungs and held it, even against her struggles. Then, he released her entirely and watched as she fell spraddle-legged and gasping into the sofa pillows.

"Yes, you'll be an excellent protégé," he lowered his eyes to the parted thighs lying across his own. And stroking her there, he posed his next question. "Here, little Nico; what does young Bernie do for you here? You have let him pretend to fuck you. Was a good sweat his only reward? Did he never expose his cock for you? —Have you not wanted to touch his bare flesh too?"

Nicole was still trying to catch her breath. She had never experienced a kiss so entirely consuming; —wasn't sure she wanted to again, either. ...And yet, as she lay where she fell, in a most unlady-like posture, Sam was exciting her anew with sensitive questions and lazy, coaxing strokes on her sex. "...I've only touched him through his clothes," she answered, and for some reason, felt compelled to part her legs wider.

Sam smiled at that. "What about his fingers, then?" he gently manipulated the silent lips she had just opened for him. "Has Brown done this?"

"Yes," she nodded.

"And inside too?" he pressed in a thumb.

"Oh, don't Sam," she placed an unrestraining hand on his. "The other felt...so much better."

"Only because you haven't yet learned to release your own juices," he replied, continuing the play with his fingers. "But there are other ways. Tell me, has Brown tongued you here?"

"No," she whispered. "...But I've seen it done. ...Two of the slaves..." And her flushed complexion told him much.

"You found it exciting to watch; —erotically exciting," he said.

"So much!" she answered, moving against his hand, and unaware that she was.

"You must never be ashamed of your desires. Nor should you deny the need to experiment. So that will be my gift to you—my first lesson. If you'd like, I will tongue you out."

Nicole's eyes were glazed as they widened, but she understood and nodded her approval. She watched then, as Sam stood to remove his jacket and wondered why he seemed so far away. But now he was back, lifting her in his arms, moving toward the bedchamber and talking softly against her ear.

"Shall I tell you what to expect?" he murmured. "You will come for me, Nico. You'll fill my mouth with the proof of your pleasure. And I mean to pleasure you greatly."

"Yes," the word hissed from her lips. And as he laid her on the blue velvet spread, she felt her senses floating away again. "Dear Uncle Sam, my wonderful mentor," she said drowsily.

Of course, Sam made some adjustments to his trousers while spreading her legs to lie between them and plant nibbling little kisses on her lower belly. Then, nuzzling her forest of white-blonde maidenhair, he snaked his tongue through her tenderest flesh, pausing to capture her silent lips in greeting. He heard her moan as he warmed her virgin tunnel with spittle and staggered lengths of a practiced tongue. Satisfied that he'd prepped his entry portal sufficiently, he returned to those nether-lips, seeking the button protrusion that keyed her passion and tongue-massaged it unceasingly, waiting patiently for her hips to rise on their own to meet his mouth.

"Oh Sam," she breathed, reveling in the sound and feel of his sweet, wet love-making. And now, she was drifting again; upward; lifted from the hips; wanting—needing—his open mouth to devour her there as his kiss had on the sofa. Then a pleasant buoyancy engulfed her; a rushing outflow of her own making; a tingling over-flow that he seemed to crave. And while his tongue returned again and again, lapping the pleasure from her body, she relaxed, closing her eyes in a drug-induced sleep…

Very slowly, Sam rose above her and eased forward on his knees. Her spread-eagle thighs; her body so open and moist; her mind in the grasp of his powders—all were causing the searing heat in his loins. And keeping his weight on knees and palms, with one quick thrust, he was in. Nicole was no longer a virgin and the only objection she made was a groggily whimpered sigh. Nonetheless, he kept his embedded penis still, concentrating now, on her ear. Soon his efforts would rouse her body in spite of her numbed little mind. And when he felt her tighten about his ready cock, he urged her to take part in what was to come. "Fuck me, Little Nico," he whispered warm breaths in her ear. "…That's it," he guided her to and away. "There, you're getting the idea. Come on, you're doing just fine." For her hips were moving on their own now; seeking deeper involvement while she moaned for something she could not even name. "God damned little bitch," Sam muttered. "I know what you want—and by God, I want it more!" So, joining in her frenzy, he gave himself over to passion…

# CHAPTER 31

Sam rolled from the edge of the bed. Going to the wash stand, he poured a basin of water, cleaning the virgin's blood and cum from himself. That done, he adjusted his clothes and with basin in hand, returned to Nicole, who still lay as he left her. He cleansed her too, carefully, until no trace of their love-making remained. Then, he ordered and very much enjoyed, a lunch of cheeses, sliced beef and buns, washing all down with brandy. But Sam was not finished with Nicole. The drug she was sleeping off had given him easy access to her body. There was work needed now on her mind. So, removing all his clothes, he returned to the bed chamber again.

"Sit up, Nico," he prodded her. "We are not yet done."

"Oh Sam," she cooed, stretching dreamily and cat-like before him. "That was so lovely."

"But not yet done," he repeated. "Now, damn it, open your eyes and sit up. You've slept long enough."

Nicole dragged herself up, but seeing him naked, she froze. "Wh— what are you doing in here like that?" she tried to sound stern. "… What are you going to do?" she ended on a whine.

"My dear child, that is rather a stupid question," he retorted. "And yet it is not. Let me ask it: what are *you* going to do? You have experienced a small sample of the pleasure a man can bring to a woman; —just one of the pleasures you hope to know from Tom Scott. But let me assure you, little Nico, he will expect something in return. … Are you ready to learn how to give it?"

392

"No, Sam, I hadn't planned—that is, not today," she gave his erection a curious glance. "It's much too soon."

"Bull shit!" he retorted. "If you think Tom will lick your sweet little pussy and stop at that, you've already lost him. He needs a real woman—not a teasing, selfish bitch!"

"I know—Sam, I know that!" her eyes returned to his penis, which seemed to be pointing at her. "And I want your help, no matter what I must suffer."

"Well, you needn't make it sound like torture," he snickered. "Believe me, Nico, there is nothing ahead of you but pleasure—more than you ever imagined."

"But I don't know what to do," she shrugged, raising a hand to point back at his penis and then feeling drawn to rest her fingertip on the tip of it.

"The hell you don't!" he smiled. "That is good, hard cock, Nico. Feel it—learn that your hands are valuable tools. And remember, the better you use them, the better your final reward."

Nicole nodded, already intrigued with how different a man's body was. Tracing the shape and length of him with inquisitive fingers, she marveled at the spastic reactions her touch could evoke. And now, she had discovered two bulbs of flesh tucked below that rudely pointing cock. Lifting them on her palms, she probed their mysterious fullness, noting the feel of their tightly ribbed skin. ...*Why*, she wondered, still wading in the dregs of Sam's persuasive powders, *do men keep this hidden? They should go nude so that women can acquaint themselves freely and study them closely. ...More closely, even, than this?*

"Good," Sam uttered huskily. "Very good, little Nico." And his expression as he looked down into her eyes was so blatantly carnal that she experienced a shudder of raw, sweet excitement.

Yes, this was good. She liked watching his swollen cock sway and straightened before her. It reminded her of that large snake used by the Turkish dancer. ...Could she, perhaps, entice this one to slide seductively over her skin? Maybe hands weren't enough. So rising taller, she offered it breasts, guiding her serpent through the hills and valleys and back again over the peaks. ...The urge grew stronger. Nicole held the blind, velvet-skinned head and pressed a nipple into its tiny mouth. …Lust sang dizzily through her blood and she knew what she had to do next. Lowering her mouth, she flicked her tongue over its mouth, just as the dancer had done to her snake, and when this didn't seem enough either, and Sam urged her closer, she begin to feed on him, as he had on her. Then his body stiffened; then she tasted a saltiness on her tongue; then a marvelous moisture filled her own loins and her greedy feeding intensified. Oh yes, this was good too…

It had taken Sam months and large doses of his miracle powders to bring Kathy to this. But Deborah's daughter, had done it on her first small dose. And though unaware of it, she was close to saving the virginity she thought she still had. That, Sam could not allow. Shoving her backwards, he stepped between her legs, lifted her hips and spent little time on the burial.

Nicole gasped, fully expecting pain. But there was none—only a rich, sweet feeling of fullness. Her eyes widened at the wonder of that, and a smile touched her lips as she stared up at him, savoring the feel of their very intimate connection.

"You will have Tom Scott," Sam stroked her breasts. "You're good at this—that damn good." Gradually sliding his hands down her body, he began to caress her at the point of their union. "Taste me in this mouth too," he manipulated her flesh, flattening those nether-lips closer about him. "Touch me from within," he constricted his embedded penis. "Answer me, Nico—I want to feel you touch me from inside."

Her body responded on its own, her contractions rubbing against his. "I do feel you, Sam", she whispered. "Deeper—make it go deeper." Sam obliged, pushing further into her young snug-fitting vagina.

Again, it pleased him to think of the plum he'd stolen from Captain Herb. It pleased him even more when she parted her legs wider for him; wanting him—Sam Lucas—deep inside her. "The ultimate bitch," he made his first serious thrust. "Obey me, Nico," he readied for the next. "Wrap your legs about my hips and lift to meet me—hunt for it; move with my cock and fuck me."

"Yes! Anything; —yes!" she urged him on, ready now to greet his descent. "Sam," she hissed out the word, "don't stop again—don't!"

And Sam did not. He rode her into the mattress, enjoying the moans of her first—well, her first remembered flight into the world of tactile pleasures. When it was done, she lay panting before him, her legs hanging loosely over the edge of the bed, an arm draped gracefully across her eyes.

"You did well, little Nico," Sam rubbed his palm into her wetness. "An excellent start." In response, she smiled, but remained unmoving. "Excellent indeed," he went to the sitting room and cleaned himself a second time. Then, with a wash cloth, a sea sponge and a fresh basin of vinegar-infused water, he returned. "Scoot up a bit, my dear," he patted her inner thigh, "and spread your legs again."

"Not now," she murmured, rolling to her side. "I want to rest."

"Do as I said!" he whacked her bottom sharply.

She did, with a yelp and an angry glare. "Really, Sam! I don't think—"

"You certainly don't think! Do you want to find yourself pregnant?" he interrupted. "Now spread your legs, God damn it—and pay attention!"

Still miffed, Nicole nonetheless complied and Sam settled on the bed to bathe her.

"Granny makes certain there is always a cruet of vinegar in each suite, so be certain to mix it into your cleansing water. Use it, preferably, soon after your lover fills you—while your body is open and easy to manipulate."

"Why?" she rose on her elbows, forgetting her pique in favor of watching—and the nice feelings resulting from his gentle rubbing motions on her highly sensitized folds.

"To soak up and wash out his seed," he answered, as he slowly began to stuff the dripping wet wash cloth into her yielding vagina. "And to keep you from having his bastards."

"Or yours?" she asked coyly, experiencing tingles that seemed to start upward from the soles of her feet.

"I am sterile, Nicole," he continued his task. "I will fill you with nothing but pleasure. But see and learn to do this for yourself. Also, for extra protection, you might want to cut a wedge of this sea sponge, soak it in pure vinegar and insert it before making love."

"Nothing but pleasure," she repeated the part that interested her most. "There must be a great demand for your kind of loving, dear Uncle Sam. —And so much more for me to learn and experience from you?"

"Indeed," he nodded, as he slowly withdrew the cloth. "Much, much more," he slid a finger into her and testing his work, found it satisfactory. "Remember, too, if this fails, and you find yourself in trouble, Granny knows the right people to cure the problem—but that does cost extra, of course. However, for now you are fine and ready to enjoy whatever pleases you."

"You certainly did," Nicole rose on her knees to wrap arms about his head and hold it against her breasts. The tingling had now reached the point of throbbing. "Play with me, Sam," she pressed a nipple to his mouth. "I love the feel of your tongue."

What she got was the feel of his teeth. Her breed—and a second generation nymphomaniac, at that—could fuck a man to death! Sam meant to dampen her enthusiasm and not only did he bite, but rammed the width and length of three fingers, twistingly, into her over eager cunt.

Nicole just sighed, for the passage was already honeyed. "See? I did learn something," she tongued his ear. "I learned to release my juices for you," she kept at it relentlessly. "Bite harder if you want—anything to waken your beautiful cock," she reached and gave it a frightful squeeze. "Take me, Sam—I want you to take me hard and mean!"

In spite of himself—and cursing her for it—Sam was responding to her demands. But he was supposed to be the master; the one who would take her at will. And now, the master was grasping her breasts, going from one to the other, fastening his whole mouth to her nipples in tight, hot suctions.

"Do it, Sam!" she breathed, grinding her wetness against his belly. "I want to be fucked now!"

Shoving her gruffly to her back again, Sam entered her too-willing flesh. "Hard and mean, Nico?" he whispered, rising on hands and knees over her. "So it shall be!" And with his full body weight behind each heavy lunge, he moved her up the bed a few inches at a time. It mattered little if she was uncomfortable—less if she climaxed. She had to learn he controlled that and everything else, God damn her! When it was done, he drove that point home with a final lunge that jarred her against the headboard. Then he rolled to sit on the edge of the bed, awaiting her expected complaints.

Her arms came around his neck from behind. "A little rough on the lungs and skull, but most satisfactory," she uttered.

...*Oh shit*! he thought in exasperation—and a state of near exhaustion. *The little bitch enjoyed it! And why do women insist on clinging after sex? It's like having a snail attached to the flesh.* Loosening her hold, he rose from the bed, pushed the alcove curtain aside and began to dress.

"And where are you going?" she asked.

"I have a two o'clock appointment with Allen. —Remember?" he asked stepping into his trousers.

"Yes—but you *are* coming back," she spread her legs invitingly. "So I'll just wait for you, right here."

"My dear Nico," he corrected, sliding into his shirt. "I do appreciate the offer—and the tempting view of your warm little pussy—but I am a business man and have a full day ahead."

"But what about me?" she demanded, sitting up. "Sam, I want you to come back!"

"And I will let you know when I'm free to do so," he insisted, adjusting his tie in a mirror. "Meanwhile, you can go home if you'd like—just don't forget to wear the hat. Or, you might want to go shopping and pick up a few things for your new suite."

"Like what?" she pouted.

"Toiletries, perfumes—something lighter than you're wearing now, if you don't mind a request. Oh, and lingerie, my dear. You'll need little else here," he shrugged into his suit coat.

"I still wish you'd come back," she flung herself against the pillows in a peevish gesture.

"Not today," he said firmly. "…Listen, I know you have a new toy and that you want to play with it, so why don't you? Brown would come and there's no reason now for putting him off. Surprise him, Nico. Raise that nice young cock and fuck it to a God damned nub."

"Well, I just might!" she snapped. "If that's all you care about seeing me, I just might. —And how dare you insult my perfume. It's very expensive!"

"Little Nico," he chided. "It was only a small request. And of course, I plan to see you again—nothing could keep me from fulfilling your dream. Oh yes, Tom Scott will share your bed. That's a promise from me to you. Meanwhile, but toward the same end, you need to experience being with another man—several, if you'd like. Consider that an assignment. I want you to make a study of the things men find pleasing. Then, when we do meet again, you can show me all you've discovered—and, of course, I'll have something new and exciting for you to try too."

"…Well, when you put it that way," she smiled, enjoying the notion.

"I just did," he turned to leave. "Oh, and when Allen asks you for lunch, stall him. I want to arrange something special—something Tom will object to most profoundly."

"Yes, Uncle Sam," Nicole said and when the door closed, she rolled from the bed giggling, as she yanked the pull cord. "First a bath—and then Bernie!" she decided. …But how would she get him to come? She certainly couldn't sign her name to a request that he join her at The Tabby House--and he'd have no idea who Deborah Scott was.

So, while awaiting her bath water, she set loose her devious mind. As Sam had said, she was *a diamond of fire and ice*, destined to shine, and surely she could solve this one small problem. Yes, because this little diamond was now free to choose her own polishers too. "—As well as my own perfume!" she pouted, but only for a moment. "…And Bernie adores my perfume; …so a scented note should bring him running!" she said, going to search her purse; hoping, that despite her hurried morning, she'd remembered to tuck her vial of scent inside. And there it was! Oh, this was going to be fun…

Two weeks passed and Sam met frequently with Nicole—his practices becoming perversely erotic; her involvement, with the aid of his powders, even more avid. His purpose, naturally, was two-fold. While sating his own jaded tastes, he was convincing Nicole that his special techniques brought on her frenzied responses—the same responses she'd get from Tom, once she'd mastered his instructions. He knew she believed him when she complained that Bernie's greatest talent as a lover was an ability to remount and ride on command—pleasing, to be sure—but nowhere near the dreamy heights to which Sam led her. And he was amused by the notion of Bernie sweating over Nicole in all his youthful exuberance. But Sam had no interest in, or need to become a marathon man when drugs allowed better results and made Nicole easier to cope with...

Harry reported in on a Wednesday and was wise enough to leave Sam's name unmentioned when reporting Nicole's movements. "Yes sir, she's got herself a regular routine now. —You could set a fucking clock by her comings and goings. Friday night to Sunday, she's with Herb—though he still gets her home on time and only lingers over their kissing at the door. Monday mornings, she meets Brown at Granny's—and this week, he come on Tuesday, too."

"I see," Sam nodded. "And during the weekend, she and Herb still socialize with my daughter, Miss Love and the Scott brothers."

"Yes, sir—The Usual Six, I calls them."

"Good," Sam nodded again. "Now think carefully, Harry. Has Nico's behavior changed in any way: does she invite Captain Herb's attention more than she did—or pursue Tom Scott more actively?"

"Well...that's hard to say, 'cause she's always been kind of flirty. She does manage to get herself next to Scott right regular, but your daughter ain't no dummy. I seen her step right between them time and again, just smiling sweet as you please. And Herb, he don't bore her none. Fact is, I still think he could fuck her a good one, would he try."

Sam smiled at that. Mike wouldn't be able to satisfy Nico now, anymore than Brown, but would have the intelligence and experience to know it. ...*And when he continues to fail and she lands in bed with Tom,* Sam savored the thought, *the Captain's frustration and disappointment will turn to rage! ...But for now, it's time for Nico to spin her web a little closer to home and her next victim is going to be Allen...*

"Mr. Lucas?" Harry was saying. "You ain't answered my last question. What you want I should do about that business in the O'Rourke stable?"

"What business?" Sam's attention sharpened. "Is Brown still hanging around there?"

"Not as I can tell, no sir."

"Then what in the hell are you talking about?" Sam said in exasperation.

"Only that she still goes out there most nights; —late like, when her Daddy's done in bed."

"But why would she?" Sam wondered, coming forward on his chair. "Is she meeting someone else? Could a man come by another door—in another way?"

"Could, I guess, but I ain't seen nobody," Harry shrugged, "—'Cepting that same little colored gal, a bawling her eyes out."

"Well get your ass back in that loft!" Sam demanded. "Harry, you find out what's going on!"

"I can't, Mr. Lucas!" Harry cowered in his chair. "That hound ain't been pent but the onest. He's always with her and ready to give out a warning."

"Well get rid of it!" Sam chopped his words. "Poison the God damned dog!"

Harry was appalled. "He's a hunting dog! —A man sets store by his hunting dog!" But the expression on Sam's face now made Harry sorry he'd dared to speak. "...Sir, they's valuable...Mr. Lucas; ...sir," he finished meekly.

"Don't give me that shit!" Sam pounded a fist on his desk. "Get rid of the fucking dog, Harry! And that is a God damned order!"

"Yes, sir! I'm—I will, sir! Right away!" Harry stammered, backing out of the door. "I'll do it right away!"

The next morning, Ransom's dog went missing. He sent servants searching in all directions, but all returned to say he hadn't been found…

Sam was on hand when Allen received his weekly pay envelope. "Well son," he asked pleasantly, "how does it feel to have a jingle in your pocket?"

"Most comfortable!" Allen replied. "And I hope you're satisfied with my work, Mr. Lucas."

"It's Sam and I'm very satisfied," he nodded. "In fact, I have something to talk over with you. Come along—I've just opened a fresh bottle in my office, if you'd care for a drink while we discuss it."

"…Yes, sir, but I've only time for one," Allen followed Sam in and took a seat before his desk. "You see, I'm taking Lucy to her sister's music recital—"

"And you can't keep the lady waiting," Sam chuckled as he poured and served their drinks. "But that brings another lady to my mind—as it should to yours."

"Who is that?" Allen enjoyed a sip of very fine brandy.

"Nicole, of course," he sat facing him across the desk. "You did offer to buy her a meal and she will hold you to it, son; —ascot, stickpin and all!" he said jovially.

"I haven't forgotten," Allen laughed. "And I have asked her twice already, but she wasn't free. I'll ask again, though, I'm hard to discourage when it comes to a beautiful woman."

"Well then, I've a favor to ask," Sam began. "Here; —I want you to accept this card." And when Allen set his glass on the desk to take it, Sam poured him a second drink. "That will admit you to my private club. Take Nicole there for supper this coming Monday. I'm sure she will be quite impressed."

401

So was Allen. "If this is the place off of Johnson Square, I'd hardly be able to afford their prices."

"It's to be my treat. I pay a yearly fee and entertaining guests is just one of the privileges."

"But—The Club!" Allen said, retrieving his drink.

"Not such an original name," Sam said amiably, "but for numerous reasons, it's the very best club in Savannah."

Allen looked at Sam. "…Which means I'd have little business being there."

"Not so. Business is exactly the reason I want you to go. …Allen, you are a bright, capable young man and I do see a future for you in this company. But climbing the ladder takes more than luck and a keen mind. You must be accepted socially, which means knowing the right people; being seen where they congregate. And as Nicole O'Rourke is not without prominence either, taking her to The Club would be a definite step in that direction. You see, son, if this goes well, I'll be asking you to return with some of my clients when I'm too busy—and that, too, will boost your reputation in the business community."

"…But what about Lucy? I wouldn't want her to get the wrong idea. Sam, I had planned on asking her to join us for lunch."

"It's only for one evening; just so those clients of mine who frequent the place will learn who you are—and recognize you when I send you among them on business. …So, if you feel Lucy won't understand, don't tell her. In fact, don't tell Nico either. Let her be surprised by your destination. She'll love it! Yes, son, as I see it, an evening spent with one of Savannah's most beautiful women—in the company of Savannah's richest people—could be very beneficial to your career. … Now, what objection could you possibly have to that?"

Allen took another sip, savoring the offer as much as the excellent brandy. "Sam, I don't know what to say. If you knew how much I want to accept this… Sir, I do intend to be successful—and rich one day, if I'm lucky. But…well, not to sound stupid or unappreciative, but why should you want to help me?"

Sam sat back in his chair and heaved a sorrowful sigh. "I'm sure Tom told you that we got off to a rather bad start—not that I blame him, mind you. I'm afraid it was entirely my fault. But to this day he mistrusts me and because of that, so does Mandy. ...But Allen, Tom is not a father. He can not understand how far a father will go to bring about a true reconciliation with his own flesh and blood."

"So you're doing this for Mandy?"

"For my child, yes," Sam answered his own way. "If Tom sees that I've helped his brother—treated you fairly—surely he'll reconsider my worth and realize I really have changed. Whereby, Mandy will too."

"I see," Allen sat looking at the card; knowing Tom would not feel the sympathy he did for the man. ...But wasn't Sam making an honest effort to mend the rift between himself, his daughter and Tom? Wasn't it his duty, then—because he loved them both—to help? Besides, he wanted this chance to make something of his life and couldn't think of a gracious way of refusing. So, he didn't. "Thank you, Sam" he rose to extend his hand. "I will accept your offer and try very hard to prove your faith in me." This of course, left Sam feeling almost jubilant...

And, while crossing the bluff-top park, Allen made another decision: He wasn't going to tell anyone about this. Tom would only try to talk him out of it; Mandy would agree with Tom; and Lucy would be hurt unnecessarily. Yes, and it was only for one evening, just as Sam said. With that, Allen hurried toward the Love's house, unaware he'd been maneuvered by a blend of brandy, inexperience and the careful prodding of a devious sire...

# CHAPTER 32

---

Sam sat reading the Sunday newspaper this late afternoon. Evelyn was also in the parlor, working her needle point, with quick, deft fingers. It was quite the domestic scene, complete with a cheery fire in the marbled hearth and two steaming cups on the coffee table between them. But in truth, had it not been for the occasional turn of a page or snip of the scissors, each could have easily forgotten the other's presence.

"Mother?" Mandria called from the front hall. "Mama, where are you?"

"In the parlor, dear," Evelyn answered, her smile immediate when Mandria entered with Lucy and Nicole close behind. And on catching the scent of Nicole's heavy perfume, Sam lowered the paper, to nod a greeting to all.

"Well, you girls are home early," Evelyn said. "—And look at your rosy cheeks! Is it that cold out today?"

"Too cold for a very long ride," Lucy assured her. "And it's so windy too!" she fussed with her ringlets. "It really, really is."

"Mama, we want to know if you're still going to Tybee next weekend." Mandria asked.

"Yes, to close the house for the winter," Evelyn replied.

"Then we'd like to go too, if you don't mind. The ball is only a few weeks away and I want to gather some things for decorating."

"Yes, we're going to help Mandy, you see," added Lucy. "—Aren't we, Nico?"

"To be sure," she answered, moving somewhat aside, in hopes of catching Sam's eye. Even in the presence of his wife and daughter, he owed her at least one admiring glance or lusty expression, now didn't he?

"How very nice of you both," Evelyn said to her daughter's friends. "And of course you can go. I'll make travel arrangements while I'm in town tomorrow."

But Mandria wasn't finished. "Mama, Tom wants to take Allen down too—for his first look at the sea? But if that would be too many houseguests, Nico said they could stay at the cabin."

"Certainly not. We've plenty of room and I'd enjoy playing chaperone."

"And you, Father?" Mandria turned to observe his reaction. "Have you no objections to our house party?"

Sam looked from his daughter to Nicole—whose inviting smile, he ignored. ...*By the weekend, Allen would already be her newest, besotted conquest and recalling those long stretches of beach and the sand dunes so often used by lovers*, he chuckled over the thought, ...*Yes, should Allen and Nicole avail themselves; and should she make Tom aware that they had, there would be no end of trouble between the Scott brothers.* "Why should I object?" he chuckled again. "You forget that I was young once too, Mandy."

"Then why don't you come with us, Uncle Sam?" Nicole still sought his attention. "You'd make a most interesting chaperone," she purred.

"Thank you, my dear, but I must decline," he said pleasantly. "Business, you see."

"And Mama, you needn't bother with travel arrangements," Mandria continued. "Captain Herb has offered to take us aboard the Irish Mist—for which we must also extend the hospitality of our home to him." Then facing Sam again, she added, "Shouldn't we, Father?"

Sam felt as if he'd taken a punch to the stomach. Mandria knew he couldn't admit the Irishman into one residence and refuse to in another—not with Nicole standing before him, believing she and Mike had been *expressly asked* here on Ball night. But, God damn it, having Herb at the beach too, was going to disrupt everything!

"Well why wouldn't Mike be welcome?" Evelyn rose. "Of course he is. —And now that we've settled that, you young ladies are coming with me. I'm going to put cream on your cheeks or your skin will be dry and rough."

Sam watched the women depart—Nicole wearing a peevish pout of neglect—and thought Evelyn's last words better described the taste in his mouth: *dry and rough.* …So when had Mandria become so clever? She had tricked him; backed him right out on a ledge and left him bound and gagged. …Maybe Harry was right; maybe she did suspect Nicole was after Tom—in which case she'd make certain Mike was along to keep Nico occupied. Then, he leaned his head back on the chair and smiled. What Mandria didn't know was that his protégé could probably take on both Scotts and the Captain—individually or as a group, should the notion strike. …But he hadn't introduced her to that yet. Oh well, there was time before the weekend and she was, delightfully, a quick study…

On Monday evening, promptly at seven o'clock, Allen called for Nicole. But Sam saw her a few hours earlier to convey his instructions—in bed, of course, as that was where she was most co-operative. She was told to make certain Allen became enamored of her. This, he assured her, would set the tone for the weekend at Tybee, because with both Allen and Mike paying court to her, Tom would be pushed a step closer to declaring his own interest. So, her head filled with Sam's promises, lightly dusted with his powders, Nicole greeted Allen at the door with a sigh in her voice and a lingering kiss to his cheek…

To say The Club was an elegant place, greatly understated fact. Allen had never seen such grandeur; had never imagined its existence. This was the best—for the best—and the proof glowed in a collage of polished reflections. Every button and buckle on the staff's livery gleamed; every door knob, floor board and window pane invited inspection; even the candlesticks, cutlery and china along an enormous buffet in the main dining room boasted of careful attention. And glancing upward, he was all but mesmerized by the intricate design of twinkling, cut-glass chandeliers.

The gentlemen, he noted, mulled about from one group to the next and never had there been a better display of fine clothing than they wore. But oddly, the ladies among them seemed on exhibit. Bejeweled, coiffured and dressed in the most outrageous fashions, each seemed determined to out-do her sister in the matter of daring necklines. Still, there was a refined quietness about the place and voice levels rarely rose above a pleasant hum.

As they were led up a short flight of stairs, Allen wished that his boot heels didn't sound so loud against the marble steps and for the first time, the diamond stickpin he wore in Nicole's ascot became important. It didn't escape his notice when several inquisitive and approving glances came their way, though. He felt proud of that from such company; prouder, still, that Nicole was by far, the most beautiful female present.

It had not occurred to Allen to question their destination, but finding that they were to occupy a small private dining cubicle, he did wonder if it was proper. When the host-waiter left, he decided he'd better ask Nicole's opinion, but she didn't give him the chance...

Nicole had made her entrance superbly, moving through the gathering of her peers like a haughty princess. Looking neither left nor right, her composure had been absolute. But in truth, she had been making a quick count; pairing lovers; taking in details of every gown and item of jewelry. These were Savannah's most expensive ladies—the kept women of the city's wealthiest men. And this place this very private club—was surely the only place they were allowed in assembly.

"Allen! —Oh, Allen, did you see them all?" she began as soon as the waiter had closed their door. "Did you see their dyed hair and rouged cheeks; their scandalous gowns—and oh, the jewels! Do you suppose they ask for jewels? I would, I think. Jewels never lose value, though I wouldn't wear them all at once—like badges or medals for so many good performances!" she said excitedly.

"...So they were actresses?" Allen asked, while seating her—and noting that Nicole's neckline bordered the subtle side of scandalous too. But as he took his own chair and heard ridicule in her laughter, he realized she laughed at him and why. "…Nico? You can not mean—uh, those women aren't—"

"They're whores!" she finished it for him. "Well-paid and very select, to be sure, but whores just the same!"

"Oh," he nodded, his color deepening. "I—I'm so sorry. Would you like to leave?"

"Heavens no!" she declared. "Allen Scott, I would refuse to leave! In fact, I must thank you for this surprise. It will be my grandest adventure yet!" And reaching across the small table, she took his hand. "I'm glad you are sharing it with me. Let's make the most of it, Allen. After dinner, we'll just have to go down and mingle. —Maybe, we'll even pick up a few juicy bits of gossip!"

Allen laughed in spite of himself. Her exuberant mood seemed to be catching.

The waiter returned then, bringing champagne and a tasty tray of hors d'oeuvres. Not long after, he brought their dinner and a hearty red wine. When the meal was done, Allen was presented a decanter of good brandy and Nicole one of her favorite sweet sherry. So, as the hour progressed and the drinks went down, just as Sam planned it, both became less awed by their surroundings and more at ease with each other.

"You know what?" Allen made an astute observation. "I think the gentlemen down stairs were jealous of me—jealous, by damn! They had to wonder, *What could such a goddess see in him?*"

"Then shall I tell you what the women thought of you?" she asked warmly.

"Yes! —Hell, yes! Tell me something good, Nico."

"Well, first they looked you over…," she paused to do so herself. "And liking what they saw, they hated me immediately. They wondered how it was between us—if you are a capable lover. So, I answered their questions with my most serene and contented expressions. —In the affirmative, of course!"

"You didn't," his smile broadened. "—Did you?"

Before she could reply, the waiter returned. "Would monsieur and mademoiselle care to view this evening's entertainment?" he asked with ever-averted eyes.

Allen and Nicole shared a shrug and a prickling of curiosity. "But of course!" Allen answered authoritatively.

"You may join the others in the main dining salon or view it from here, as you wish."

Another glance was exchanged—and smiles, as both were in a mood to challenge the offer. "From here," they chimed, daring him to prove it possible.

But it was done. The waiter simply drew aside the drapes behind their table and they found themselves overlooking the room below from a private windowed box. Raising the windows, he then bowed his way out, closing the door again, while they sat watching the downstairs diners turning their chairs to face a small stage at the far end of the room.

"Well," Allen laughed, refilling their glasses. "What do you suppose is in store for us next? Damn, but the evening has been fun, hasn't it? Just one surprise after another."

"And it's not over yet," she moved her chair next to his; —so they both faced the stage, Allen assumed. But looking into his rich, nut-brown eyes, whose color rivaled her own, she continued. "I'd really like to kiss you now. Would you mind?"

Allen laughed, believing the request to be in jest. But drawing his mouth to hers, she was indeed kissing him—overwhelmingly so—almost smothering the air from his lungs. "My God!" he gasped, breaking free. "My God—Nico?"

"So sorry," her response was interwoven with silken laughter. "I didn't mean to frighten you, dear thing."

"Y—you didn't frighten me," he replied. "You only...well, surprised me."

"But you did say it was that kind of evening, didn't you?" she purred sweetly.

Allen's reply was lost in a gulp of his drink when polite applause greeted the man stepping from the stage wings below.

409

"Ladies and Gentlemen," he began, "what you are about to see has been banned from public theatres in seven states. —Banned! Labeled obscene!" he portrayed dramatic disbelief, followed by an even more dramatic pause. "…We do not happen to agree with that narrow-minded view. As the great museums of the world display the Masters with pride, so do we—and in faithful, detailed reproduction. For your pleasure then; your cultural appreciation, the Club presents a living tableau dedicated to Venus—goddess of spring, bloom, beauty and love!" he finished with a flourish, as the curtains parted slowly to reveal a huge gilded frame.

"The Birth of Venus, by Sandro Botticelli," they were told. And this living Venus was every bit as nude as her canvas counterpart.

Allen glanced quickly at Nicole, certain she'd take offense, but found her totally enthralled; studying the scene so intently, it led his own eyes back to the stage. There, against a sea-scape background, Venus stood delicately balanced in a large, pearly shell, a tress of her hip length hair drawn demurely across her nudity. To the left, with arms and legs entwined, two painted wind gods hovered in mid-air, puffing gentle breezes toward their Venus. A living handmaiden stood on her right, gracefully posed and ready to serve her mistress. Allen knew his interpretation was shallow and though the announcer was giving a more detailed account, his attention kept returning to Venus—to the apex of her legs, to bare breasts, the curve of her thigh, the mystery in her motionless features. …*So much for the cultural aspect,* he thought as the curtains closed. And draining his glass, he reached to refill it.

"Allen," Nicole said softly, "I'll have another sherry too."

"Certainly," he nodded. And when the curtains parted a second time, they were holding hands.

"Sleeping Venus, by Giorgione," said the moderator. This nude appeared to recline in a lush green pasture, eyes closed, one hand resting upon her maidenhair.

"Oh, now isn't that sad?" whispered Nicole.

Allen couldn't fathom her reasoning, as he found the portrayal pleasing…stirring even. "How so?" he whispered back.

"She is so alone. And so lonely, look what she has resorted to."

410

"Uh, I don't—I mean, maybe that isn't the case at all," he stammered.

"Isn't it?" she circled his arm, holding it close against her. "Then what is she about to do there; —to herself; …with her own hand?"

"Nico, behave yourself, damn it," he laughed. And tilting her chin upward, he pecked a kiss on her pretty mouth.

"So now we present Venus and Cupid, by Diego Rodriguez de Silva Velázquez," they were informed. And Allen and Nicole looked away from each other reluctantly.

Venus now lay with her back to the audience, gazing at her reflection in a small standing mirror, held in position by a cherub. It was a lovely scene in all but one respect. The cherub, meant to be a chubby, angelic faced child, was portrayed, of necessity, by an elfin sized dwarf, who was visibly aroused by his Venus.

"What do you suppose is bothering that little man?" Nicole asked when the curtains closed.

"The same damn thing that's bothering me," Allen chuckled, resting his forehead against hers. "—And you aren't even nude." Then he kissed her again and as Nicole let him have the lead this time, they were still kissing when the curtains opened a fourth time.

"Toilet of Venus by Francis Boucher—favorite artist of Madame Pompadour," it was decreed. This Venus lounged upon a chaise, attended by three dwarf/cherubs. One arranged her hair; a second—the aroused one—stood adoringly at her elbow; while the third selected a string of pearls for her from the cup of a sea shell.

"Madame Pomp-a-dour!" Nicole giggled, refilling their glasses herself as the curtains closed. Then, nesting herself in the crook of his arm, she asked, "Allen, would you like to see me nude?"

Allen happened to be gazing at her nearly exposed breasts at the moment. Not that he meant to, exactly, but she did have a talent for presenting them in a most convenient way. "…Well," he swallowed dryly, which called for a soothing sip of brandy, "I wouldn't close my eyes—or stand idly by like that bastard dwarf." And his answer seemed to call for a deeper kiss.

"Venus and Adonis, by Titian," said the announcer. With her back to the audience again, Venus sat spraddle-legged upon a bench, her

411

arms wrapped about the waist of her handsome lover. Standing at the end of the bench, supposedly happy for the couple, was the horny dwarf—who was happy, indeed, to ogle what Venus' spread legs put just at his eye level.

"Could I trust you that much?" Nicole used her most innocent voice, while bringing Allen's hand to her breast. "Could you touch me—bring pleasure to us both—and have as much will power as that dwarf?"

"…Nicole," Allen's voice quaked. "Nico, you are just so beautiful!" And when their lips met in a fevered kiss, his hand slid easily into her dress to toy with a hardened nipple.

"Mars and Venus, by Paolo Veronese," declared the man below. In full battle gear, Mars, god of war, sat in a garden setting with Venus before him, one of her legs draped casually across his knee. Together, the famed couple watched in amusement as a cherub tied a swatch of cloth about Venus' dangling ankle.

Sam Lucas watched in amusement too. Not the stage performance, but the one taking place in the box directly across from the darkened one in which he sat. For wrapped in a tight embrace, Allen and Nicole were slowly sinking from their chairs, onto the floor and out of view. "And one day, son," he murmured victoriously, "you'll thank me for doctoring her sherry." After all, his son deserved no less from the bitch than he demanded for himself…

That same evening brought the conclusion of many days of busyness for Mandria. It all began when she purchased some used furniture from the back room of a junk shop near Oglethorpe Barracks. Tom was sure that was where it belonged when he saw it sitting in the front parlor layered in dusty grime and sadly worn upholstery. But Mandria insisted the lines were classically stylish and the cushions and construction solid. She then called upon Mrs. Amos, who sent over two of her assistants to work on the bolts of slate-blue upholstery velvet Mandria had waiting. And while they recovered cushions, Mandria re-stained, waxed and re-waxed the wood trim on the furniture pieces as well as several small service tables. Then on discovering a pair of ornately carved side chairs in a closet beneath the stairs, she promptly hauled them out and process began anew, only these were recovered in a muted plum brocade, which was also used to make throw pillows and tie backs for the almond-hued drapes left by the previous owners.

Tom felt useless among the chattering women and at first, tried to stay out of the way. But he did admire Mandria's energetic drive, because when she worked, it seemed the others tried to keep pace. He suspected it might be infectious when Victoria Audrey deserted one of her after school lessons in favor of joining the group. He was sure of it, when he began to hang about the doorway, hoping to be called upon for help. But he wasn't and finally admitted to a twinge of jealousy. He missed being the center of Mandria's attention.

Now, thankfully, the work was completed. Tom and Mandria were alone again and much elated about the evening ahead, as they were going to arrange their old-new furniture in the parlor and had just finished unrolling a large carpet which had blocked the front hall for days. She had chosen a design of twirling, green-leafed stems, interspersed with blossoms of slate blue, muted plum and almond that brought the whole color scheme together in a way even Tom could appreciate. In fact, he had found the room pleasing in each of the half-dozen ways Mandria had already wanted to try it. Not that he minded lifting furniture all around the parlor and back again, but this was September twenty-fifth, their second month's anniversary—which she seemed too busy to notice—and he was rather hoping for a celebration before taking her home.

Yet, when Tom suggested they had done enough and insisted the room looked perfect, she began telling him how much the right paintings would add to the décor; pointing out where they should go; and assuring him she intended using some of her own to cut expenses. When he mentioned the fading light and the hour, she avowed that several well placed lamps would lessen the gloom and that she would look for some on the morrow. Finally, he just took her in his arms, even as she talked of fern baskets, dried sea oats and violets for the bay window, and giving her no time to say more, presented a dinner ring, wished her a happy anniversary and made love to her in the center of their nice new carpet…

Much later, after retiring to his bed on Bay Street, Tom remembered a request Mandria had made and rose to search through a storage trunk in the sitting room. It was at this point that Allen came home.

"Oh! I'm…I didn't expect to find you awake," he stammered. And Tom knew at once, that something was amiss.

"I was hunting for these portraits of Mother and Dad," he replied, turning up a lamp. "Mandria wants to frame them for hanging in the new house."

"Yes. That's nice—a real nice gesture," Allen said. Silence followed, as Tom stood looking at his brother, who appeared to be making an in-depth study of his boot toes.

"Well, what's the problem, Allen?" Tom finally asked. "You may as well spit it out."

Allen exhaled raggedly and lowered himself on a chair at the table. "In a word: Nicole. …I saw her tonight, Tom."

"And?" he shrugged, showing little surprise. "Who was she with?"

How Allen dreaded Tom's next reaction, but there was no avoiding it now. "Me," he answered. "I took her to dinner…and came within an inch of seducing her."

"Damn it, Allen!" Tom exclaimed and the reproach in his eyes was all Allen expected it to be. "You can not get involved with that girl! What in hell were you thinking? You had to know better! There's Mike to consider and—"

"I know! —Tom, I know! And I won't be seeing her again," he fought off a shudder. "I don't want to see her again."

"…Then why did you in the first place?" Tom tempered his tone, seeing that more had happened and Allen was upset about it.

"Well, I promised to. At my birthday dinner, remember?"

"That is a sorry excuse—and very much beside the point. Allen, you just said you tried to seduce her!"

"But I didn't plan to; —I didn't leave here with anything like that in mind! It's only…well, we drank too much—saw too much—and then, things seemed to happen so fast! It was supposed to be an evening of fun; an evening important to my career—and it sounded just that simple when Sam explained it."

"Sam?" Tom sat across from Allen. He had to sit. His knees had all but buckled. "—Sam Lucas arranged your evening with Nicole?"

"Sort of. He had us admitted to his club and I'm certain he arranged the special treatment we received. But no, Tom, I can't let you blame Sam for what happened. I just drank too damned much!"

"Listen, maybe you'd better tell me about this from the beginning; —from when Sam explained it," Tom insisted.

Which Allen did, even to the parts he found shameful and disturbing. "…So, it continued that way: the passionate kisses; both of our hands where ever they wanted to be—even on the ride home; at her front door; and in the stable, where she asked me to wait while she told her father goodnight."

"And you did? —You met her there?" Tom's voice held more than a note of disbelief. It all but said, *Allen, you stupid jackass!*

"Tom, I'm not God! When she came to the stable, all she wore was a night robe and then she was all over me: arms, legs, lips, breasts—so hell yes, I was going to make love to her. Would have too, except for two things that happened. And you should appreciate this, because while I held her, the name she called was not mine or even Mike's… but yours."

Tom nodded, feeling thoroughly uncomfortable with Allen's revelation. None of this was his doing, but Nicole was involving him just the same. "…And what was the second thing you spoke of?"

"Well, the first started to sober me and that's when I saw the colored boy. Tom, she had a colored boy at the door—as a look out, you know—but damn it, he could see what we were doing! …And she didn't seem to care," he shuddered again. "But it bothered the hell out of me."

415

Tom didn't wonder at that. "…And this is when you left?"

"Yes, and I don't even remember the excuse I gave, but she was furious—called me names ladies shouldn't even know! …And I just tucked my tail and ran, feeling less like a man than I ever want to feel again."

"You did the right thing, little brother. It took more of a man to leave than to stay."

Allen rubbed his throbbing temples. He wasn't sure he believed that, but was glad his brother said it.

"…Do you know what I think?" Tom observed after a moment of drumming fingertips on the tabletop.

"That I'm seven kinds of a fool, most likely."

"Three kinds, maybe," Tom gave him half a smile. "No, I think Sam Lucas is finally making a move. I think he wanted you to bed Nicole—planned on it. Look how carefully he set this up: a private room; drink in abundance; provocative entertainment; —Nicole? Hell, he didn't leave out a thing."

"Tom, that is absurd!" Allen argued. "Sam didn't force me to drink so much—I did it! What you're suggesting is diabolical and even if I had bedded Nico, what would Sam gain by that?"

"If you had, Allen, consider the damage—the bitterness—just in our own circle of friends. I'd be caught between you and Mike—trying to keep him from killing you; Lucy would never speak to you again; Ransom, I wont even attempt to describe; and Nicole…well, likely she'd be nipping at everyone's heels, stirring all the trouble she could—and still could do that very thing. Don't you see? For whatever reason, this was a definite effort to destroy all of our friendships."

Allen's nod was negative. "I just don't believe it was Sam's fault. Tom, he is a powerful, rich man. Why should he fear anything from us?"

"You continue to defend him?" Tom asked in amazement.

"And you to condemn him! You're not being fair to Nico, either. Granted, she has a thing for you; granted, I didn't like what happened in that stable. But maybe it wouldn't have if I had been sober enough to control how much she drank. No, Brer, the real blame is mine, not Sam's…and poor Nicole nearly paid the price for my mistake."

"Now, that is just too much!" Tom said in exasperation. "Allen, are you blind as well as deaf? You won't hear a word against Sam, but damn it, you do have eyes. *Poor Nico*—hell! *Who* invited you to the stable? *Who* was sober enough to go in, tell her father good night and sneak out half-naked again? *Who* didn't care that a stable boy watched—and *who* cursed you for leaving? No, you were led down that garden path, little brother, and Nico knew the route just a little too well."

"Meaning what?"

"Meaning you were the victim—more seduced than seducer."

"…But if that were true, what does it say about Nico?"

"Nothing Mike would want to hear—nor you, evidently, because I think she and Sam may have planned this together."

"You're right, I don't want to hear it!" Allen rose hastily, but shakily, from the table. "I feel bad enough already and your melodramatics are only making it worse. …Good night, Tom. Maybe we can talk tomorrow when my head quits hurting and you're in a more reasonable mood." And with that, he fell face first onto the day-bed.

"Good night, then," Tom started for the bedroom, but paused in the doorway to add, "…I'll make you a bet, Allen."

"How's that?" he muttered into his pillow.

"I'll bet you a dollar Sam will ask questions about your evening with Nico."

"Since he arranged it, would that be so unusual?"

"No, but the questions could be. I'd appreciate knowing how personal they get. Do we have a bet?"

"Tom, that's the silliest thing I ever heard. Now, for the last time, good night!"

With a nod, Tom turned toward the bed, but just stood there looking at it. …Why wasn't he in his own bed, with his own wife, in his own house? No, he wasn't anxious to crawl into this torture rack—which was what it became when his mind wouldn't let him rest. And tonight, he was destined to spend hours toying through Sam's puzzle box of mysterious motives…

❦

417

Sam was up and away from the house before eight o'clock the next morning—and never had he felt more alive! He could not wait to hear the results of Allen's evening with Nicole and his first stop was made at Harry's ramshackle residence.

"M…Mr. Lucas!" he rubbed at sleep-crusted eyes. "Come on in, sir. I'll just put on some coffee—"

"Forget it, Harry," Sam stepped over the dog tied to a porch column; turned to give it second look; then shrugged. "This isn't a social call. What report do you have for me?"

Harry was half afraid to speak, but in case the boss hadn't noticed, he pointed to the hound. "…Well, sir, I got rid of the dog, like you tolt me. But he's fitting in here real good—"

"Damn it, man—that's last week's news! What about last night?"

"Oh, I followed them home from The Club—just like you said to—and they loved it up pretty good all the way. At the front door too. Then when she went in, young Scott dismissed the carriage and made his way round to the stable door—"

"God damn her!" Sam began to pace Harry's porch. "She's going to get caught there yet! Why would she risk it? —The hard-headed bitch!"

"…Yes, sir," Harry nodded. "…You want I should go on now?"

"What? —Oh, yes, do go on!" Sam snapped. "What did you see?"

"Well, I seen her come out the back door and head for the stable and then something kind of strange. You know, being a careful man and all, I always peer into the courtyard gate 'afore climbing the wall, but there was a colored boy standing in the stable doorway, so I knowed I couldn't find out nothing by that route—"

"Harry!" Sam interrupted. "What did you fucking see?"

"Nothing. —But I knowed this was important to you, so I went round to the alley door. —The one the Scott boy used, you know? But it was locked, so all I could do then was listen—"

"And? —And?" Sam vowed if Harry didn't soon get to the point, he was going to be wearing that stolen hound stuffed up his God damned ass!

"And I heared them loving it up again—sounded pretty hot and heavy too. Then it just quit and she went to talking real mean at him;

followed him right to the door, calling him names and such—and I just did get ducked behind a bush in time when he come out! She relocked the door then, but I went back and listened some more. She was still cussing loud as she dared—and whipping on something or somebody. But I didn't hear whatever it was cry out or whinny or nothing—and she must of kept at it a good ten minutes. Now...that's all I got to report. That's all what happened, sir."

Sam left in a huff. His plan could not have gone wrong. —It couldn't! Perhaps Allen had just made a quick lay of Nicole and taken his leave. —And with those powders heating her blood, of course she'd be frustrated and angry. That's what happened. It had to be! At any rate, Sam was going to find out, so of necessity, he'd regained his composure by the time he reached the river.

"Good morning," he smiled broadly as he entered the warehouse office. "Hard at work already, son?"

"Yes, sir," Allen attempted a cheerful expression. But his head still throbbed, his stomach felt queasy and now, he was remembering some stupid bet Tom had proposed.

"Good lad," Sam nodded. "—Say, how did your evening go? Did they treat you well at The Club?"

"Yes, sir, we were well received by everyone there—and thank you again for the opportunity," he managed a smile, but felt compelled to go on when Sam continued to stand there grinning at him. "Everything was first-rate; the food, the service, the brandy—"

"And Nicole? —Did you find Nicole first-rate too?"

"...Of course, sir," Allen said, feeling the hair on his neck prickle, and trying not to look as guilty as he felt. "Nicole is a beautiful young woman—"

"Not to mention a budding nymphomaniac," Sam said in a confidential tone and laughed when Allen's lips parted in surprise. "So tell me, son—just between us—did she lead you on a bit, or is she granting more exceptional favors now?"

Allen raised a hand to the bridge of his nose, hoping to conceal the rush of color he could feel on his face. ...*Why is Tom always right?* he thought...*And how do I answer this question?* "I...uh, we sort of…" he stammered as the full impact of Sam's word's registered. "A nymphomaniac? …Sir, why would you say such a thing?"

"I can because I've known one or two myself. And from what I hear about town, Nico is showing those tendencies more and more. Tom suspects it. I've seen the way he looks at her; watches her—and not long ago, he was seeing her on the sly, as I recall it."

Suddenly Allen wondered. …*Is this the thing his brother sensed about Nicole and had not wanted to name? —No, it's just too awful to think about!* "Sir, a lot of girls will tease a man more than they should, but that doesn't mean they're—I mean, I've heard some pretty sad stories—"

"If you heard they can't get enough cock and will do almost anything in their quest for satisfaction, then you heard right. —God, but their appetites are glorious!"

Allen could feel bile rising in his throat. Lord, how he wished Tom was here to handle this. "But…I hope you don't think—I mean, let me assure you, sir, Nico went home the lady she left."

"Do you think I'd blame you if she hadn't?" Sam was growing irritated again. *Why wouldn't the boy just admit the truth?* "Listen, Allen, I still get an ache deep in my loins when I think of the eager little cunt that I knew. For me—and the legions she hosted—there will never be an equal. It's a once in a life time experience, and any man who would pass it by is a God damned fool!"

When Allen stared at him, nodding negatively, Sam turned and left, afraid he might have said too much—which did nothing to improve his mood. Allen had spent entirely too many years under the influence of his half brother, who, himself, had been drilled in the corseted ways of that English schoolmarm. But the boy was his son too, and entitled to boast of a juicy conquest, damn it all! Oh, how he looked forward to the day when Allen would take his rightful place among the gentry and learn the free-spirited ways of his father! …Meanwhile, perhaps he'd left him with things to think about—to lust after—as the weekend grew nearer.

Indeed, Allen had a gracious plenty to occupy his mind. And the gist of it was that his respect for Tom was greatly reinforced, while his opinion of Sam underwent a drastic reformation…

# CHAPTER 33

From the riverfront, Sam went by the O'Rourke's hoping Nicole would be awake by then and have better news for him. But Jenny told him she had left for the morning, which sent him to St. Julian Street, cursing her for causing him so much trouble. Granny Geeter confirmed her presence, saying Nicole had ordered a breakfast tray—for two—only a short while ago. So, scribbling a quick note, he had it delivered and impatiently cooled his heels in Granny's office until he saw Bernie hurry off down the street—and that one did not seem in the best of humors. Neither was Sam, but if he expected to stay in control of Nicole, she could never know she had the power to un-nerve him.

"Really, Sam!" she snapped as soon as she opened her door. "How dare you intrude! Bernie was really upset at having to leave—and he was just at the point where I wanted him!"

"Poor little Nico," he soothed. But an attempt to fondle her through a filmy, night-blue negligee was met with a swat of rejection, which further irked him, because without the aid of his powders, she could be fucking difficult. Taking a deep breath, as she paced before him, he tried again. "…Nico, Brown is merely a pass-time and you know it. Now, it's important that we talk about last night. —And about Tom Scott," he added, cursing inwardly when she stopped at the mention of that name. "So," he took in a second calming breath, "fix me a cup of coffee—and join me, won't you?" he asked while lowering himself on the sofa.

Nicole did pour them coffee, but took a chair facing him to better portray her snit.

"…I saw Allen a while back. He called you a beautiful, enchanting lady," Sam said.

"Oh *did* he now," she replied sounding bored. And that was followed by a bang of her cup to the saucer.

"What is it, Nico?" Sam kept his inquiry simple. "Didn't you enjoy your outing at The Club?"

"I enjoyed the entertainment," she answered shortly.

"But?" he encouraged.

"But Allen was a huge disappointment. He left at a crucial moment between us—and thanks to you, the same damned thing has happened this morning!" she pouted.

Sam could not believe what he was hearing. "Nico, Bernie will return and you can fuck him all afternoon, if it pleases you, but your conquest of Allen is important in the scheme for capturing Tom—"

"I know that!" she injected. "And Allen will not escape my anger when next we meet. It's the lady's privilege to halt such things—not the gentleman's! Sam, it made me look positively cheap!"

"Maybe it was the stable straw matted in your hair that made you look cheap," he offered. "Nico, why did you risk going there—and while your father was at home?"

"…I really don't know, Sam," she leaned to the back of the chair, with a sad sounding sigh. "I mean, Allen did excite me—almost as much as you do. We were both ready for it too, and…well, the stable was just the closest place, I suppose."

Sam had to accept that much as truth. He was the one who fed her those powdered grains of impatience. "But what could have caused him to leave before the deed was done?"

"I don't know that either, but he did. And my humiliation didn't end there—oh, no!" she was back to sulking. "Willie Luther saw my distress and when he dared to smile about it that was just the last straw! I whipped him a good one, Sam—let me tell you, I did! Then I made him masturbate before me and crushed his seed in the dirt—the uppity bastard!"

Sam Lucas was not often left speechless, but for a moment, he could only stare at the girl. "…May I ask, why Willie Luther was there at all?" he managed finally.

"Because, as you've already pointed out, Daddy was at home," she replied as if he were stupid. "Someone had to keep watch."

"But…why a young, black buck? Couldn't you have taken a maid or a—a dog?" he kicked himself mentally.

"There isn't much difference, is there?" she shrugged. "Besides, I nearly have Willie Luther trained."

"Trained?" Sam asked, conquering a second bout of muteness. "…For what?"

"Why all sorts of things!" she laughed for the first time. And typical of Nicole, she was ready to forget all but her own delights. "You know, Sam, you really need to join me sometime. Willie and his little bitch put on quite a show—and I can make them do almost anything, in any position."

*Well that solved a mystery, didn't it?* And Sam chuckled, as he said, "My dear, you have revealed a jaded taste I find delightful, but shall we discuss the week-end now?"

Her pout returned immediately. "I think I'm upset about that most of all. I was so looking forward to having both Mike and Allen dance attendance on me; —to throwing it in Tom's face until he became so jealous he'd—"

"It's not too late, Nico" he disrupted her fantasy. "It's only Tuesday, and we could set Allen up again—"

"Oh, no, Sam!" she rose for an agitated pace. "You can't expect me to go through such humiliation again! Unlike you, I have lost my taste for unripened fruit. I haven't the time or the patience for tutoring boys!"

"All right then, we'll get to Tom another way," he stood, gliding her to a stop—and it irked him anew that it was the mention of that name which gained her attention for him. And more. For when he stroked her body, she allowed it, though her expression clearly said she awaited further mention of Tom. "My dear, have you considered that a boy might not run home and tell big brother what he tried and failed to do? —Especially since the young lady involved is supposed to be the sweetheart of his brother's best friend."

"So?" she asked, drawing both of his hands to her breasts now.

"So a few well placed words would make Tom think something did happen between you and Allen. And if reminders of your encounter were whispered in Allen's ear over the weekend, how would he behave? He would feel guilty—may even look guilty—and Tom would draw the conclusion we wanted him to anyway."

"But so would Mike. He isn't stupid, Sam."

"Well, obviously, you can't pit the Scott's against each other in front of Herb, but you could distract your Captain as you do it best," he shrugged. "In fact, if he were to become your lover too and Tom sees that you have spread your wings at last—as well as your pretty thighs—how appealing would he find Mandy then?"

"Now, I do like the notion of testing that Irishman," a smile crossed Nicole's lips as she nodded agreement. "Yes, I could still make Tom believe that both men are dancing attendance; …and Lord knows what might happen between those tall, secluded sand dunes—or even at the cabin…"

"Or in this suite," Sam rewarded himself with a taste of her ear.

"Which is legally mine until next May," she laughed. "Aren't you proud of me, Uncle Sam? I talked Bernie into giving me the money—and now, I won't have to sacrifice a penny of my allowance!"

"My, but you have learned the ground rules quickly," he remarked.

"Yes, but you owe me something too, my dear man," she ran a hand gaugingly over his trousered penis. "After last night's fiasco and your visit here that spoiled my plans for the morning?"

"Nico, it is yet morning," he chuckled. But he still had some prep-work for her to consider should the opportunity arise at Tybee. "Now, I have a wager to propose," he said, going to fix them a drink.

"Oh? What sort of wager?" she released the sash at her waist and stepped easily from her thin little gown.

"You said that Allen excited you. I'm willing to wager that of the two brothers, he would be the better lover."

"Then you'd lose," she laughed coyly. "—And how would you know such a thing? Do you spy on their intimate moments too?"

"No, but I recognized your passionate needs, didn't I?" he tapped his powder into her glass as she preened before a mirror. "I have listened to both of them talk and let me assure you, Allen's passions are closely akin to my own—inherited, so to say, from a long line of lusty sires." And how he did enjoy his own bit of fantasizing.

"Brothers do share the same sire, Sam," she intruded. "But you'd still lose. Speaking as a woman who has kissed them both—and Tom, much too briefly—Tom received the lion's share of that inheritance."

The unfavorable comment about Allen—and it wasn't her first of the day—galled Sam so deeply he stirred more than a few extra grains into her sherry. Nicole might suffer a hangover for the rest of the day, but he would benefit from her punishment. Besides, he was weary of playing the patient advisor and had earned something special from her. "Well, little Nico," he came to hand her the glass, "Have we a wager or not?"

"I haven't heard the terms yet," she sipped deeply, while fondling him again.

"The terms will be pleasurable, whoever wins," he clinked his glass to hers, thereby encouraging her to drink more. "It will be a new adventure for you in the art of love-making, inspired by your enjoyment of watching Willie Luther and his bitch. So, if I win the wager, I will have another woman join us in bed; if you do, a second man."

Nicole ran her tongue over lips that felt dry and now she was gulping at her drink, as anticipation burst into bloom. "And the loser can only watch?" she rubbed against him. "Or is the adventure to be shared by all?"

"Shared to the fullest," he leaned to plant kisses along her throat; to feel the rapid pulse beneath his probing mouth and tongue. "Imagine it, Nico," he guided the glass to her mouth and kept it there as he murmured enticements. "Warm lips tugging at each of your nipples; four hands caressing your silky flesh; two sturdy cocks throbbing to fill you; and two tongues working their magic everywhere."

"Yes; —oh, yes, Sam! Look how I'm quivering. Yes, we must have this wager."

And Sam meant to keep her quivering, so as he led her toward the bed, he encouraged more eroticism. "Now, if I win, tell me what would await?"

"Well…four breasts to fondle and four nipples to tease with your wonderful tongue," she began as he laid her down. "Four hands to stroke and straighten your swollen cock," she watched it appear as he stripped away his clothes. "Two mouths to tongue and suckle it; and two cunts, eager to mix their juices with yours," she spread her legs in invitation as he approached.

"Yes, a brand new adventure for you either way," he mounted her, enjoying the ease of it. "And the possibilities are endless, little Nico. Imagine the lovers you could enjoy all at once: Tom filling your warm little pussy; Herb tenderly licking your nipples; while your suck the juice from Allen…?" he thrust about in her honeyed passage.

"Sam?" she said then. "Let's not wait on that silly wager. Could Granny send us someone to practice with now?"

"Granny could," he said, pleasantly surprised at her ready acceptance. "So which would you prefer; —a man or a woman?" he asked reaching for the summons cord.

"Two more men, please. But as I'm unsure about their personal habits, I'd rather have you in my mouth, if you don't mind."

With that, Sam pulled the cord more vigorously. The morning would not be a total disappointment after all…

At a little past two, the following afternoon, Nicole entered the square across from her home and found a bench in a sunny spot. It was brisk out, but the air felt good, as she was still suffering the dregs of a headache. Jenny said her mother had suffered them too and suggested several of Deborah's remedies, but nothing had helped much.

Nor had a boring visit from Bernie, who'd dared to come right to the house that morning, spouting a marriage proposal. She'd sent him away without an answer, of course, but after her new experience with Sam, knew just how to handle that. Bernard Brown—of *The* Brown family—would be appalled when she had a second woman join them in bed on St. Julian Street. Then the proposals would stop. "But not his visits," she laughed to herself.

Meanwhile, she had thought about Sam's advice for the weekend and decided an early start was called for. Soon, Tom would be passing, on his way to see Mandria as he did every day after school. But today she intended to give him something new to ponder. So, here she waited as comfortably as her poor head and wonderfully sore genitals and nipples would allow…

Across the street, Sam had come home for some papers he'd left in his study, when he happened to glance from the window and saw Tom coming through the square. Snarling, he was ready to leave by a rear door—anything to avoid having to greet the man and pretend he was glad Mandria had this particular suitor. Then he saw Nicole. And giving the surrounding greenery a quick scanning, he muttered, "Harry, if you miss a God damned word of this, I'll beat your fucking ass!"

"Good afternoon, Tom Scott," Nicole said. "How are you today?"

"Fine, thank you," he responded before realizing who had spoken to him. "…And you?" he added, making the unwelcomed discovery.

"I'm fine too," she rose, stepping directly into his path. "Especially after the evening I spent with your handsome brother."

"Oh?" Tom asked a little surprised that she'd mention it.

Nicole read his reaction her own way. "So he didn't tell you," she wagged a tattling finger in his face. "Well, maybe neither of us recognized Allen for what he truly is."

"And that is?"

"An avid romantic! I was quite taken with his…persuasive boldness," she laughed. "Yes, Allen is one Scott male who knows how to handle a woman. —And I'd say, with just a bit more experience, he'll rival you as a lover."

"…Nicole, I have no idea what you're suggesting," Tom nodded.

"That Allen knows what a real woman wants and was at least accommodating," she smiled, enjoying his continued confusion.

"But you're not claiming he seduced you; —at least it doesn't sound as if you're making that accusation."

"Well, it was the other way around, actually," she ran teasing fingers along his lapel. "I expect he'll deny the whole thing, though. He was just so embarrassed, you see, not being able to go the full distance? But in time, I'll show him the finer points. …If I must."

None too gently, Tom seized her wrist, to lift her hand away from his coat. "I don't know what you hope to gain by this, but don't try involving my brother."

Nicole could feel her pulse beat beneath the strength of his grasp. Surely, he felt it too: his flesh on hers; a promise of things to come. "On one condition," she said moving closer. "Take his place, Tom, and I won't sleep with Allen ever again."

There just wasn't anything Tom dared say to that. He believed Allen had told him the truth, but what if he hadn't? Until he was absolutely sure of where things stood—as angry as it made him to do so—it was best to say nothing. Stepping around her then, he walked toward the Lucas house with the ring of her laughter trailing behind. It was like kindling being tossed on a barely banked fire…

Sam found it hard to remain patient while Old Jed admitted Tom to the front hall; harder still, to keep a solemn expression as he stepped from the study to summon the bastard, for he couldn't wait to stir the embers dancing in those dark blue eyes.

"Spreading yourself a bit thin, aren't you?" Sam began, motioning him to a chair before his desk.

"How is that?" Tom snapped and remained standing.

"Well, I saw you arguing with Nico just now," Sam closed the door, then leisurely took to his desk chair. "Mandy may have too. Her room does face the square, after all—and I don't think she should know about your entanglements. That wasn't part of our agreement."

"Damn it…," Tom started, stopped to load and lock, then leveled his aim on Sam's purpose. "Is that all you called me in here for?"

"Yes; —and sorry, I didn't mean to upset you. …More," Sam said innocently. "It's just that your involvement with Nico is too obvious and I did warn you about that on the riverfront, did I not? …Though, I must say," he chuckled, "I do envy you this genuinely rare experi-ence."

There seemed to be an epidemic of strange behavior among his adversaries on this fine early October afternoon. "Do you, now?" Tom had to ask.

"Hell yes!" he expounded. "She is really out to capture you—the little bitch. But Tom, she is a born trouble-maker: she had you jumping hoops out there; Herb and Brown are still jockeying for position; —and now Allen, too, if I've guessed right."

Tom nodded. "…Sam, there's no guess work here. You arranged Allen's evening with Nicole, but it won't happen again."

"Only to get her off my back! —Man, she's a nympho, just like her mother," he said, surprising Tom yet again. Allen had told him what was said at the warehouse, but this was a novel twist. "She has offered herself to me repeatedly," Sam continued, "—and I don't deny being tempted to take her. But I have too many business connections with Ransom to become involved with his daughter. So, I saw no harm in passing her on to a younger man, with the energy and stay-power to deal with—with her little problem, shall we say?"

"But…well, damn," Tom repeated. "I still don't want Allen connected to any of this and I mean to see that he isn't. —Which is what I just told Nicole, if you're wondering."

"Well, if it's not already too late, handle it as you see fit," Sam shrugged as he rose and started for the door. "But for God's sake, don't send her my way again. In fact," he paused, a hand on the knob, "… as she does seem to have her eyes on you, you'd do us all a favor if you'd fuck the little bitch silly. Just keep it from Mandy," he added the aside, as he opened the door to usher Tom out; and to thoroughly enjoy his look of muted astonishment…

That evening, when Allen came in from work, Tom was waiting. "One question:—and little brother, I need the truth, if you've ever told it, so look me in the eye when you answer. Did you have sexual relations with Nicole?"

"No, I did not," Allen replied as straight-forwardly as Tom could have hoped for. "It was damn close, just as I said, but no, Brer, I didn't. …So, what's happened to make you question that?" And after Tom related his conversations with Nicole and Sam, Allen voiced confusion. "…But if you're right—if they're collaborating—why would Sam betray his own partner by telling that story about her again? True or not, if it's repeated many more times, people will start to believe it—and he said he heard it around town. So what if Mike hears it too?"

"Allen, betrayal is likely Sam Lucas' middle name. But if Mike hasn't heard the story by supper on Friday night, then word is not on the street—and I don't think it is. What I find more interesting is their unity in promoting the idea of an affair between you and Nicole. Both wanted me to believe it, but surely Nico wouldn't want Mike to. What sense would that make?"

"I keep remembering what you said about her nipping at everybody's heels—which will put a real damper on supper, as well as the trip to Tybee. And damn it, Tom, I was looking forward to that!"

"Well, I think we'd both be wise to avoid being alone with her for a single second; —and if I were you, I'd prepare Lucy beforehand. Nico will likely make some pretty outrageous taunts."

"But how? What can I say about an evening spent with Nico that Lucy wouldn't find hurtful?"

"I never thought I'd encourage you to be less than honest, but this time I am," Tom answered. "Just tell Lucy what Sam told you: that it was a business engagement. Then you might say how boring you found it and that you hope Sam doesn't ask you to stand-in for him again. Keep it light; mention Nico's presence there only as something in passing, with no details—and no guilty looks—or she will know there is more than you're telling. Then, little brother," Tom nodded, "no matter what Nicole says to the contrary, deny; deny; deny."

"Well, I won't enjoy doing this to Lucy," Allen sighed, "but I guess you're right. —Again!" he nodded too.

Sam met with Nicole at The Tabby House on Thursday morning and came away with mixed feelings about the weekend house party. She had to remain focused; a constant irritant between the Scott brothers and he had drilled her relentlessly until she could repeat his instructions by heart. Yet when she again expressed delight at the prospect of luring Herb into her web—as Sam, himself, had suggested, God damn it—he felt more resentment than he knew he should. He reasoned it was because she had a job to do. He reasoned that her enjoyment of Herb in the interim would take attention from the business at hand. But in spite of all his reasoning, when they made love, he purposely kept her dosage of powder light. By Monday then, in spite of what she did with Herb, frustration would bring her looking for him again. Yes, deep frustration and sexual disappointment—as well as a bout of withdrawals—that she already believed only he could alleviate.

Late into the night, however, when the demons that drove Sam Lucas were somewhat asleep, he had to wonder. ...Was it possible he could still experience jealousy? If so, he had to deter it. Nicole was his pawn—his route to securing his son's future and loyalty. Nothing could stand in the way of that. No mere woman was worth the risk...

The Usual Six met for dinner on Friday and Tom and Allen shared moments of confusion caused, of course, by Nicole O'Rourke. From start to finish, she did little more than gaze lovingly into Mike's eyes, monopolizing his time and conversation, which so surprised the Scotts, neither could help watching her openly. And reading this her own way, Nicole could not have been more pleased...

Later, the ladies were returned to the Lucas house for the night, as Evelyn had promised Mike to have the entire entourage at the river in time to catch the morning tide. Midnight found them retired to Mandria's room, but as none were sleepy, they sent down for a pot of hot chocolate to enjoy while they chatted. Joleen brought it, served them dutifully—and in absolute silence—leaving as soon as she had.

"…Mandy," Lucy asked, "what is the matter with Joleen? It's not like her to be so unfriendly."

"No, it isn't," Mandria nodded agreement. "Something is bothering her—and I tried talking to her about it today, but she just wouldn't say what it is."

"Well, I will," laughed Nicole. "They breed like cattle, you know. Joleen thinks she's pregnant."

"Pregnant?" Lucy exhaled the word aloud, only to inhale it back in whispered horror. "*—Pregnant?*"

"Nico, …how would you know that?" Mandria questioned in surprise.

"Because I heard Jenny talking," she lied, but couldn't resist adding truth to it. "And because I saw her in the stable with Willie Luther. They've been meeting there for months."

"You mean they actually…in—in your stable?" Lucy stammered. "With the horses watching and all?"

"Yes, Lucy, horses—and all," Nicole answered coyly. And taking Mandria's lowered eyes as offended modesty, she smiled. It was just this immature outlook that would cause her to lose Tom—and perhaps by the weekend.

In truth, Mandria was feeling guilty. She knew Joleen loved Willie Luther and should have given her wiser council; paid closer attention to the trouble she was headed for. And because she hadn't, Joleen was now afraid to ask her help. But something would have to be done…

"Mandy; …Nico," Lucy said timidly, "…do either of you know what a man looks like when that—that mating urge is upon him?"

"Why, Lucille Love!" Nicole gave an excellent portrayal of shock. "What are you accusing us of?"

Mandria quickly hid her smile in a sip from her cup, as she had a definite fondness for seeing Tom that way.

"From pictures!" Lucy was frantic to explain. "I meant from picture-books or museums or…or—"

"Paintings by the great masters?" Nicole recalled a recent night's entertainment. She could also have mentioned cousin Perry, Sam, Bernie, Allen and whoever those two men were that Granny sent by.

"Yes, paintings too!" Lucy nodded. "And why is it they all show women from top to bottom, but cover the men with leaves or something? I've only found one museum statue that didn't. —The new one, down town, with his hands on that fat marble lady's bosom and fanny? But still, I couldn't see more than a kind of bulge and I've looked at him from every angle: standing and sitting; —even bending, when nobody was looking."

Mandria couldn't help it; she just started laughing—which greatly surprised Nicole. "Oh, Lucy, what did you hope to see? —What do you think happens to a man when that mating urge is upon him?"

"Well, Mama says they sort of grow and become rather starched. ...Or was it stretched? No, I believe Mama did say starched."

"Oh my Lord," Nicole was now laughing too.

"Well—well anyway, Mama said it's dangerous for a young lady to be near when it happens," Lucy insisted, wondering what her friends found funny. "So maybe Joleen just didn't realize she was in danger until it was too late."

"Now that is too much!" Nicole declared. "Of course she knew, Lucy!"

"But how? I've never been able to tell—and it seems to me, that would be a very wise thing to know. It really would," she looked from one friend to the other.

"Believe it or not, Lucy," Nicole said, "I happen to agree with you. And when Daddy wouldn't answer my questions about men, I took matters into my own hands. Yes, I hid in the stable and watched the whole thing between Joleen and Willie from start to finish."

"Nico...how could you?" Mandria uttered.

"She didn't! —I know she didn't!" Lucy chimed in. "...Did you, Nico?"

"I most certainly did," Nicole insisted. "I watched and I learned. They are only slaves, after all."

"Oh, Nico, what was it like?" Lucy climbed to her knees. "What did they do?"

"Well, they began by petting and kissing—his hands roaming into her dress and over her little bottom—"

"Nico, please," Mandria objected. "I hardly think this is… Well, it isn't very nice."

"But I want to know!" Lucy said. "Oh please, Mandy, I should know. It might save me from getting…*pregnant!*" she whispered the word again.

"And you should be curious yourself, with a man like Tom around," Nicole sent Mandria a look. "That is, if the relationship is serious."

"But you're missing the entire point," Mandria suggested. "Joleen and Willie are really in love and it just seems wrong to treat their intimacy with such indifference."

"You mean it is un-lady like, don't you?" Nicole's voice had an edge on it. But her feelings about intimacy were not indifferent. They were highly intense—a fact Tom Scott would soon come to appreciate.

"No, that's not the point either," Mandria continued. "I'm just very fond of Joleen and it makes me uncomfortable to hear you speak of her this way."

"Oh feathers!" Nicole exclaimed. "Mandy, I've heard you called prudish and straight-laced before, but I've never believed it more than now. What is wrong with three friends privately discussing a subject that interests every *normal* woman on earth?"

"Will you two stop arguing?" Lucy's arms flew akimbo. "Hush now! Mandy, I am old enough to hear this—really I am. So, please, Nico, what happened next?"

Needing no further encouragement, Nicole launched into descriptives. "Well, they stripped off naked and began to pet again: first, standing close, body against body; and then as they rolled about in the hay laughing and sighing when something felt really good. Why, they were feeling and kissing each other all over—and all the while Willie's penis kept growing. What had started as a bulge, as you put it, —well, it grew and stiffened and—"

"That is enough!" Mandria said sternly. Nicole was enjoying her dissertation far too much and Lucy looked as if she'd swallowed a bug.

But Nicole would not be stopped. "Yes, oh, Lucy, it was this long—and thick as the neck of a dipping gourd! And when Joleen parted her legs, he rammed it into her over and over—and dear God, I thought she would faint from the pleasure! Then guess what happened?"

Mandria was now on her knees, and determined to be heard. "Nicole O'Rourke! If you say another word, I'll—I'll *ram* this pillow right down your throat!" she threatened, weapon in hand.

"Oh, very well," Nicole shrugged. "Neither of you could stand hearing the rest anyway. You'd think it too carnal; —too Negro for refined White tastes."

"...But you're White," Lucy found her voice again. "Why didn't you find it offensive?"

"Because I have an open mind," she glanced accusingly at Mandria. "I don't want to be stupid about men. I will use my knowledge—and I'll have the man I go after."

"You mean you'd actually...well, encourage a response like Willie Luther's?" Lucy asked now. "Deliberately?"

"I would; —and I have," Nicole answered sagely. "Temptation is a woman's most powerful weapon, if she knows how to use it. Tell me, Lucy, have you never teased Allen until a hot, hungry look came over his face? —Until he just had to crush you in his arms and smother you with kisses?"

"No! —Good heavens, no!" Lucy vowed. "I'd be scared to even if I knew how!"

"And you, Mandy?" Nicole asked sweetly. "Tom is a handsome, virile man. Surely, you've had to restrain him a number of times."

"No, Nico," Mandria smiled, enjoying the truth of her answer. "I never have and I'm sure, I never will."

"How very sad," Nicole nodded. "—And how very boring it must be for the both of you."

"You know, I'm glad Allen doesn't make hungry faces at me," Lucy said mostly to herself. "I'd probably laugh and just ruin the entire moment."

Mandria laughed then—and it wasn't over the picture Lucy had painted. "Boring?" she lay back against the headboard. "Tom—boring?"

her laughter grew. "No, Nico, our relationship may be many things, but it will never—*ever*—be boring."

"Oh? Would you care to explain that further—since you find my notions so amusing?"

"No; no I wouldn't," Mandria nodded, swiping a gleeful mist from her eyes. "I haven't your flair for description. What I do have is Tom's devotion and we don't need to provoke our feelings. We just enjoy being together, even when there's only time to share a cup of coffee."

Lucy sighed. "How beautiful. Really, Mandy, that is so beautiful."

"And about as exciting as a sewing bee," added Nicole. "But Tom will tire of that, Mandy. A man wants more than sharing coffee. They need passion—and when someone takes Tom from you, don't say you weren't warned."

"Now there you go again!" Lucy wagged a finger of reprimand. "Each advising the other; each thinking her way is best. Well, why don't you both listen to me for once? Why don't you stop arguing and find your own separate ways of being happy—with your own self, I mean. That's who you live with the most: your own self!"

Mandria and Nicole looked from Lucy to each other. "...She's right, you know," Mandria smiled. "But far too smug about it," she lifted her pillow again. "Shall we teach her a lesson, Nico?"

"But of course!" Nicole joined in and both buffeted Lucy to the tune of her giggling squeals...

Later, as all drifted toward sleep, Lucy asked a question, and her voice sounded small in the darkness of the room. "Mandy, will they marry?"

"...Who?" Mandria replied as softly.

"Joleen and Willie Luther. Will the baby have a name or will it be a...a bastard?"

"There's no need to whisper. I'm not asleep either," Nicole spoke up. "And marriage isn't important for them, Lucy. Besides, it would only cause a lot of useless problems."

"How?" Mandria had to ask.

"Well, if they married, they'd have to belong to one household or the other. Daddy and Uncle Sam would have that to decide and then they'd haggle over prices. As it is, Uncle Sam will gain a new slave baby and all Daddy will lose is the stud-fee," she laughed. "—Which he'd certainly collect if Willie Luther was one of his hunting hounds."

Lucy's giggle was one of politeness, but she wasn't smiling. Mandria bit her lower lip, vowing to see the couple marry—even if she had to buy Willie Luther herself. And with that notion, another began to emerge. ...*I'll ask Tom about it*, she thought, raising a hand to touch the wedding ring beneath her night dress.

Then as there was nothing more to be said, each silently weighed her own thoughts on the right of things—not just for Joleen and Willie, but in the society where they lived. And Nicole fell asleep long before Mandria or Lucy...

# CHAPTER 34

With the coming of autumn, the marsh had taken on the color and hollow reed sound of wheat fields. But today, their impressive spances were obscured in a mantle of fog, leaving only the reeds closest to the riverbank visible to those aboard the Irish Mist. It was just as well, for Allen was more interested in avoiding Nicole than admiring the view. And she had been in rare form from the moment they boarded. Looking Mike in the eye had been enough of a chore on Friday evening, but he felt truly miserable today when she prompted the Captain to add his thanks for her evening of *fun* at The Club. And Lord, was he thankful he'd followed Tom's advice and told Lucy beforehand. She had seemed a little surprised, but so far had not treated him any differently—though that made him miserable too—so he vowed to repay her understanding with devoted attention. This did not suit Nicole at all and seeking to draw Allen's eyes back to her, her comments became increasingly riddled with teasing innuendo. Finally, escorting Lucy, he left the wheelhouse on the pretext of showing her around the boat. They were standing now, by the paddlewheel and while he explained the mechanics of the churning marvel, she listened, pretending to comprehend every word. Allen knew that she didn't, but much preferred her gentle good manners to Nicole's biting sauciness…

Tom and Mandria had remained on deck after boarding and waited along the rail with the Lucas servants, hoping the sun would appear and burn away the fog. But the hour was still early and when

438

Mandria began to quake from the cold, they decided to go in search of the hot tea Mamalyn had promised. However, tea was not the only thing brewing as they gathered at the wheelhouse table.

"Tom, do you remember our trip to Tybee together?" Nicole began, taking the chair to his left. "Mike and I were just telling Mamalyn how much you enjoyed your first look at the sea."

"It was a memorable trip," he made a point of smiling at Mandria, who was sitting on his right. "Most memorable," he added when she returned his smile.

"It was for me too," Nicole playfully petted his arm. "Remember the fun we had getting ashore? Mandy, he was holding me quite snuggly in his arms but I just knew I was going to fall in the water. Believe you me, I clung to Tom as long and as hard as I possibly could!"

"How frightened you must have been," Mandria said innocently enough. But both Tom and Evelyn caught the nuance behind her words.

"Yes, we had more trouble out of you than Jenny," Tom said, then issued a subtle warning. "We're not in for more of the same today— now, are we?"

"Was that a request?" she laughed and hugging his arm now, she tossed her next taunt to the Captain, who stood in place at the wheel. "Mike, your good friend just asked to hold me in his arms again!"

"Here, Nico," Evelyn brought a full cup and waited for her to take it. "Enjoy it while it's warm, dear."

Tom smiled. As sweetly as that, Evelyn had given Nicole something else to do with her hands.

"Not to worry, me-darlin'," Mike answered, his vigilant eyes on the river. "We'll be putting in at Lazaretto Creek today. Uncle Denny has a deep-water pier—which means, little Nico, that you may walk ashore as daintily as you came aboard in Savannah. Then we can use his mule and wagon to haul us across the island. —So how's that for service, Mamalyn?"

"Excellent," she approved, while filling the rest of their cups. "It will be good to visit with Dennis again, too. How is he, Mike? Have you seen much of him since summer?"

Tom didn't catch Mike's reply. It was lost in the feel of a persistent pressure along his left leg. Yet, glancing at Nicole, he found her sitting primly erect, her fingers still laced about her cup and for all intents, listening to the ensuing conversation. Looking Mandria's way now, he saw that she studied Nicole with slightly narrowed eyes. Then, as if guided by an instinct known only to females, she circled a hand through his arm and snuggled her own knee against his right leg. It was, of course, an impossible situation: left and right, Tom felt repulsion and desire; aggravation and stimulation; Nicole and Mandria. ...*Damn*, he thought, and excusing himself to Mandria, he went to stand beside Mike at the wheel, staging an interest in the Captain's ability to navigate the foggy river. In truth, he just wanted time—and definitely the room—to think. If this was an example of Nicole's intended behavior, the weekend would be a disaster. He considered calling her aside for another lecture, but knew she'd consider it an invitation—and hell no, he wasn't falling into that trap! For a time, he wished Mike would go ahead and bed her. That would keep her occupied, but wouldn't be a good thing for Mike in the long run. So, nodding an admonition to himself, Tom admitted a loss for answers. What he should have considered, as the boat moved ever closer to the bosom of Atlantic and the arms of destiny, was trusting his premonition...

Looping the sand bars off of Cock Spur Island, Mike headed into the Lazaretto channel announcing their arrival with a series of blasts from the boat whistle. Then gliding in next to the dock, they waited for Mike's skeleton crew to tie up and lower the ramp. "Uncle Denny!" he called to the man coming along a rough plank pier. "Get your Irish hide on down here!"

The man stopped to wave, and when he smiled, Tom saw naught but an ancient version of Mike. His clothing was faded from long exposure to salt water and sun; his skin leathered and bronzed from the same. Instead of the Captain's hat, Mike always wore, a black knit cap crowned his thatch of unruly gray-white hair. And when he spoke, his brogue was pure, sweet Irish, thicker even, than his brother Patrick's.

"Michael, lad," he said as they embraced. "Sure-en Oi'm glad ta see ya," And Tom marveled again at how alike they were in statue and their wicked way of grinning.

When introductions and greetings had been exchanged, and while Jed and the servants saw to loading the wagon, they headed for a house, which Tom found truly impressive. It was built right on the edge of the creek bank, and the end extending above the water, rested on tall poles. The shrubs hugging the foundation on the yard side, were neatly clipped and lined off with painted white rocks, as was a walk-way leading to a row of pigeon coops at the rear of the property.

"Oi put pot ta fire when I heared yer whistle," he said as they entered, where he hurried to tend his perking coffee. "Set yer-selves down ta table, now—and Michael, get the mugs, if ya would."

This time, Tom put Mandria between himself and Nicole as they gathered about a round table. Then, more at ease, he looked over the one-room dwelling. It was small, but every accommodation was present and in neat order. The floor boards had never seen paint or stain, but nonetheless wore a mellow glow from wear and countless scrubbings. On the far wall were two half beds with a sea chest at the foot of each, and the bed blankets were stretched tight and uniformly tucked at the corners. Closer to where they sat was a keg-table separating two old, but comfortably stuffed chairs. A bible lay open on the table, next to a whale lamp and on the wall above, hung a crucifix. Behind the dining area, stood a fireplace, a sink well and an open cupboard in which dishes and grocery supplies were precisely stacked and aligned.

Coffee served, Dennis looked at each of the lovely women there and nodded. "Tell me, Mrs. Lucas, how is it ya've come ta know the likes of me nephew?"

"Yeah, I asked her the same thing about you," Mike chuckled.

"He certainly did," Evelyn agreed. "But we met Mike through Nicole. And they met, I believe, because Mike and her father do business."

"Then he must be Ransom O'Rourke?" Dennis turned to Nicole for a smiling nod. "Oh ya must remember me ta him. He's a old, old friend and such a fine man."

"Isn't that funny?" Lucy said then. "I think its funny how everybody knows everybody else and nobody knows anybody does."

"Oi'd say ya have spun us a puzzle, lass," Dennis laughed along with the others.

"Is that your shrimp boat anchored across the creek?" asked Allen munching a cookie from a tin Evelyn had brought in.

"Aye. When the pigeons brought word Michael were sailing his great smoke puffing monster downriver, Oi put me lady out of its reach."

"Your lady?" Tom smiled.

"The pigeons?" Allen asked simultaneously. "Then, they're carrier pigeons. I read about them in the paper."

"Your lady," Tom repeated, looking toward the shrimp boat now.

"Sure-en ya can see her," Dennis looked too. "See the cut of her: double full of bosom; cinched in tight down the sides; and just look at the tilt of her nose! Aye, she's a proud one, me Emma B."

"Oh, now I see her too," Mandria made a graceful sweep of her hand toward the rigging. "She's wearing stick combs in her hair and shrimp net mantillas draped about her shoulders."

"Now isn't that the most romantic thing?" Lucy sighed. "Nico, isn't that romantic?"

But all Nicole could see was an awkward looking boat that had to smell of dead fish. "Well, I can think of more romantic things. … Can't you, Allen?" she added, sending him a sloe-eyed glance.

"Listen, it never hurts to keep one's mind on a higher plane," Allen retorted, surprising Tom. "Which is exactly why I enjoy Lucy's company so much," he finished with kiss to her cheek that brought out a blush and a titter of giggles. Tom laughed too. Was this the same young man who'd scampered to the farthest end of the Irish Mist to avoid Nicole?

"Well, you got your wish there, little brother," Mike grinned. "Lucy's mind operates on the airiest, loftiest—and most charming— plane I've yet to encounter." And as Lucy's blush resurfaced, Nicole had to swat the Captain for daring to compliment a female other than herself.

And Mandria wondered....*Does Nico now covet Allen's attention too? For weeks, she has been pressing hard for Tom's—and still is, judging from her behavior in the wheelhouse. ...Am I the only one who sees that?*

"Tell me, Dennis," Evelyn asked. "Does Mike get his nautical knowledge from you?"

"Well, he spent summers with me as a lad, so Oi suppose he learned a bit. But he had more a eye for females than fishes—the young devil did. Oi had me hands full keeping him at work, off the beach—and away from Defauskie Island."

"No, Michael!" Lucy gasped. "Why would you go over there? They do strange things over there—like drinking chicken blood and putting hexes on people—just like they did in Africa!"

"But that sounds like witchcraft or voodoo," Allen said, turning to the Captain. "Meet any witches, Mike?"

"A few," he flashed a wicked smile. "And sampled my share of their brew."

"No!" Lucy's eyes grew round. "You could have been hexed—or given a love potion! Did you think of that? Why, you could have fallen in love with a person you didn't want to love!"

"Well, I didn't, did I?" he looked at Nicole, while Tom and Mandria dared each other not to laugh—and both lost the moment their eyes met.

"I'm sorry," Mandria explained. "It's just that we know a story about a wife who gave her husband a love potion and then refused to believe a word the poor amorous man had to say! It was really quite amusing."

"But did it work?" asked Nicole. "Do love potions truly work?"

"If we told you, it would spoil the story's ending," Tom said lightly. "Besides, I want to hear more about Defauskie Island. Is it true no white men live there?"

"Very few," Lucy stated. "And those who don't come in peace have met with some very bad treatment!"

"That's mostly true, Oi suppose," Dennis nodded.

"But how did Negroes come to live there?" asked Allen. "Are they runaways—and if so, why hasn't the law brought them back?"

"'Cause they're not runaways, but castaways," explained Dennis. "And there's no record of where they was bound when the ship went down. None was reported overdue from Charleston ta Jacksonville; and nobody come forward a wanting his cargo. So them that survived the wreck, swum ashore and there they've been ever since."

"But missing or not, the market for slaves is a profitable one," Allen said. "You'd think a band of traders, if no one else, would try to recapture them."

"Hell, they have tried," Mike answered now. "Several times—and some of the local gentry in South Carolina even got in on it, treating the whole thing like a fox hunt. But every time, they were chased right off the island. Remember, Allen, these Negroes were never tamed, so to say. They were warriors among their tribes; —warriors, who learned to distrust white men from the moment they were chained and tossed into the black hold of that slave ship."

"Yes, but now-a-days, nobody wants ta be rid of them," Dennis continued. "They proved ta be very good farmers, and keep Savannah in fresh fruit and vegetables near the year round."

"Surely, you've seen them on the streets," added Evelyn. "The men with their pushcarts; the women balancing those huge vegetable baskets on their heads?"

"And I love the Gullah!" Lucy exclaimed. "Especially early in the morning before I'm even awake. It sounds so dreamy echoing up and down the streets."

"All right," Allen laughed, "what's Gullah?"

"Their language," Lucy replied, and raising hands to her mouth, she managed a fairly good imitation. "Budder beens! Oh, good frash budder beens! Fie pow a half-dime; tan pow a dime! Ah got good frash budder beens! Buy ma budder beens now!"

"Yes, I've heard them," Tom said, reaching for a cookie before Allen ate them all. "And didn't someone tell me they row their goods into town every week?"

"There and back, if they can't catch a ride on one of the fish or shrimp boats," Mike rose to point from a window. "It's still foggy, but you can see Defauskie from this end of Tybee. It's off the Carolina coast, just inside the mouth of the river there."

"You know an odd thing they do?" Evelyn offered. "At the end of the week, they take the money they've earned to the banks and have it changed into as many nickels as can be spared. No one knows why, but it seems they value that particular coin."

"Aye, there's not much known of their ways," said Dennis. "And they're not so anxious to be sharing their secrets. On clear nights, when Oi see their little witch fires a burning, Oi'm just as happy not knowing what they're up ta, Oi'm saying."

"But Mike knows," Nicole said with curious admiration. "He went there and dared to sample the brew."

"Aye, and he'll end a part of it, one of these days—the main ingredient of witch's brew!" Dennis grinned.

"But not a love potion, Captain Denny," Tom chuckled. "Mike would likely become a cure for hangovers."

"Or baldness!" added Allen "Or bunions; or—"

"Enough from the Scotts!" Mike said jovially. "Anyway, the wagon is loaded and we can be leaving now."

Before they did, Evelyn invited Dennis to join them for supper and Mike felt a gratitude he found hard to express, so he hurried to assist her climb into the wagon. But this uncle had always seemed a lonely man, having little contact with people other than his crew and rare holiday visits to see his brother in Savannah. Mike decided then, as Tom had before, that Sam Lucas did not deserve this lovely woman…

It was still early in the day when the three couples left the Lucas beach home, each carrying a burlap sack for gathering the things Mandria wanted for her Ball theme.

"My God!" Allen skidded to a halt as they topped the dunes. "… Oh my dear God!" he repeated in opened-mouthed amazement. Atlantic had made her expected impression once again. And Tom smiled, noting that the autumn sea did seem darker—fiercer—just as

Mandria told him it would. "That is a lot of water!" Allen still stared. "It's scary too…"

"Not in the summertime," Lucy assured him. "Not to say there isn't just as much of it, but it's so refreshing when you need to cool off in a hurry."

"Lucy, you don't mean you'd try to swim out there?" Allen pointed in disbelief.

"No, any deeper than my ankles, and I'd sink to the bottom," she answered. "But when the temperature gets really hot, you'll be wading right in with the rest of us. You will, Allen—really!"

"Wading?" Nicole said slyly. "Tom and Mandy did more than that. Remember how worried you were when they went swimming, Lucy? And Mandy, you never did tell what made you stomp away in a huff. —Did Tom get fresh? I mean, one minute you were splashing about like a pair of courting dolphins and then—"

"Tom? —A dolphin?" Mike laughed. "No, Nico, I'd say he's more of an octopus!"

"Yes!" Tom stalked Mandria, playfully. "With eight hungry arms to fill!" And as they rollicked their way down to the beach, all but Nicole was ready to enjoy the day ahead.

Jealousy gnawed at her mind and as they moved southward, searching for coral, conch shells and interesting pieces of drift wood, she decided Mandria needed to feel the same way. Yes, Sam would approve of that. And when spotting the sea-side tavern ahead, she was certain she'd discovered a way to make it happen. "Why look over there!" she pointed. "Remember that place, Mike? Tom bought me my first ale there—while you and I watched his trollop entertain four of her other lovers."

"Four lovers?" Lucy craned her neck, as if she might see them.

"Yes, but I could tell right away the whore wanted Tom the most—even before he did anything about it."

"Really?" Mandria looked at Tom sternly. And winked. "So what did he do-about-it, Nico?"

"Nothing at first—which just proves how clever he is. Tom hardly looked her way—or not so you'd notice. But she was staring at him like a starving wolf! Yes, Mandy, what she meant to have from him was perfectly clear."

"…Well, I didn't see any of that," Mike nodded.

"You wouldn't," she cooed. "Your eyes were on me."

*…There's lot Mike hasn't seen lately*, Allen thought. And though he felt sorry for Tom at the moment, he hoped Nicole would continue to ignore him as she had for the last few hours.

"Anyway, I actually believed Tom wasn't interested in what she had to offer. Yet, he *did* return there—*alone*—and when we saw him next, *her* lip rouge was smeared all over his face. So tell us, Tom, after Mandy rejected your advances—that first time, I mean—did you dally just to spite her; or was it for personal gratification; —or was it little of both?"

"Or was it none of the above? I guess you'll never know," Tom said, wishing Nicole would give it a rest.

"But I will know!" Mandria took a firm grip on Tom's arm. "March, Mr. Scott! We are going to gather the sea oats while they get the shells—and you *will* tell me all about your wicked ways with tavern trollops! Yes, sir—indeed you will!" And as they started toward the sand dunes, Nicole took a certain pride in the way Mandria kept poking him in the back.

"…Oh, dear," Lucy murmured. "Was Mandy really mad? I think she was—I really, really do!"

Allen nodded, not knowing what to make of it. He'd seen Mandria wink at Tom when this started, but she didn't appear to be amused now.

"Nico," Mike issued a gentle reprimand, "you didn't have to remind Mandy of that. And none of it was true. …But damn, the things that can set a woman off."

"Well I was only teasing," Nicole said innocently, watching as Mandria poked Tom again just as they disappeared over a dune crest. "Now, don't worry. Things will work out just they should," she smiled happily.

But time passed at a snail's pace for Nicole. Tom and Mandria had not yet returned and the shell hunt was taking the rest of them further down the beach than she wanted to go. She had spotted them once more and watched as Mandria stooped to snip the long stemmed reeds and handed them up to Tom for bundling, but from this distance, it was impossible to know their moods. And not knowing was driving her mad!

"Mike?" Allen came a sudden halt. "Look what I found! —What the hell is this?"

"It's a horseshoe crab," Mike answered, freeing the dome shaped shell from the sand. "Do you think Mandy could use this, Lucy?"

"I don't know how," she nodded. "It's big enough for a punch bowl—but yuk! Who would want to drink from that ugly thing? … Still, Mandy does come up with more ideas than I can, so what do you think, Nico? Would Mandy want a horse's crab shoe?"

"Its horseshoe crab, Lucy dear," Nicole was smiling again, "Yes, I think I'll just run up there and ask Mandy if she wants it." And she did, indeed, run before anyone could raise an objection.

Choosing the spot where she'd last seen them, Nicole went between two dunes, almost tripping on a pile of scattered sea oats. But the pair she sought wasn't there and she wasn't going to call to them, because she intended to do a little spying. So, cursing the sand that filled her shoes, she started for the top of a taller dune, hoping to spot them from there. As she climbed, she passed a second pile of broken reeds, which made no more impression on her busy mind than had the first. She was panting when she reached the crest, but for once, her efforts were rewarded. For on the back of the next dune, she saw Mandria trying to get a string beneath a stack of freshly cut sea oats. Then Tom appeared and defeating her purpose, he used the toe of his boot to nudge the reeds into a mat-shaped configuration.

"Tom!" Mandria looked up at him, arms akimbo. "Will you stop that? We'll never finish at this rate!"

"Depends on what you're talking about," he stepped toward her. "One or two more times and you might let me finish what I've been trying to."

"No, you won't!" she rose to meet him nose to nose. "They'll be coming to find us any minute now."

"Then we'd best get on with it, hadn't we?" he caught her waist.

448

"Tom, don't!" she pushed against his chest. "You can't hope to ruin every bundle!"

"I can hope for it," he easily lowered them both to the reed mattress.

"But we'll have to...; start all over again!" she protested while he kissed her repeatedly. "The cutting...; the binding...; the—Tom, please leave me be! ...We'll have stripped the dunes...; and won't have a decent...; sheave to show!"

"Mandria," he paused to look down at her, "Do shut up." And holding her still beneath him, he kissed her into full participation.

Then, they began to whisper, things Nicole could not hear. But she heard their laughter as they rose, and went arm-in-arm around the side of their dune. She felt the sting of own tears now and fought the urge to scream, as she scrambled to the bottom of her dune again. ... *Why? —Why is Mandria able to extract this behavior from Tom when I can't? Why does he even want to kiss her when Mandria does nothing but discourage it? Well, she isn't going to have him—damn her!* Oh, how she wanted to scream that aloud, and stumbling to her knees, she had to press a fist to her mouth to keep from it. And as if she weren't hurting enough, she had landed on one of their broken sea oat beds, which worsened her silent rage; brought her to her feet to stomp and trample the reeds; to kick and crush and scatter them in every direction!

Mike came up the dune path just as she launched that attack and rushing forward, he grasped her by the arms. "Nico! —Nicole, what is it? What in the world are you doing?"

Nicole was not sure she could trust herself to speak without revealing her anguish, so she just stood staring into Mike's concerned eyes.

"Poor little Nico," he gathered her to him. "What frightened you so badly? Was it a snake or a mouse or—"

"Yes!" she latched onto his sleeves and his explanation. "But not a mouse—a rat! Two filthy rats!"

"Well, I'm surprised you had the nerve to go after them," he smiled, wiping at her tears. "And I doubt they escaped unharmed. That was one hell of an assault!"

Nicole suddenly hugged herself to him, deciding in that instant that Mike *would be* her next lover. She had been hurt and so deserved consolation. And not just soon, but today—preferably, within the hour. "Mike, I want you to kiss me. Right now, please!"

"Glad to, ma'am," he obliged, readily responding to her warm, eager mouth. ...Too readily, he realized, for he was quickly losing control of that kiss. "Whoa, Nico," he nodded, easing her back a step. "I...uh, believe we'd better go find the others."

"No, that's not where we're going," she grasped his hand, and towed him along. "I have something to do and Michael, I will need you with me."

As they came onto the beach, the other two couples stood at the water's edge—and Nicole noted sourly, Tom and Mandria had managed to secure several bundles of undamaged reeds. No matter. She had a seduction on her mind—oh, yes, she had been tolerant of Mike's will power quite long enough. "Mandy?" she called, waving them down. "Listen, there isn't much left to do here, so we could be spared for a while, couldn't we?"

"Certainly," she nodded. "But where are you going?"

"Well, Daddy asked me to check on the cabin too. You know—bring in the rockers; things like that?"

"Oh?" Mandria's eyebrow lifted in question.

"Yes, and with Mike's help, it won't take long."

"Then we'll come give you a hand," Mandria offered sweetly.

"That won't be necessary!" Nicole insisted. "Truly, we can manage alone."

"But I'm only trying to return a favor," Mandria's smile remained constant. "Don't you think I've noticed how *very* hard you've worked today—at everything?"

"Mandy, I said we could manage," Nicole's tone took on an edge. "Honestly, there just isn't that much to do!"

"Very well, then," Mandria laughed, for she'd been watching Tom and Mike look from speaker to speaker with synchronized head swings, while trying to determine the point of the conversation. "But we will come over in a couple of hours, if that's all right with you. Mama is fixing us a picnic basket now, but it's too nippy to eat on the beach.

So, Mike, would you mind building a fire—and maybe putting on a pot of coffee?"

"Sounds good to me," he agreed, where Nicole would not have. "I'd love cuddling this lady before an open fire."

"Oh, all right!" Nicole said in exasperation, and without another word, she started away with the Captain in tow once again.

"…Mandria," Tom looked after them, "what the hell was that about?"

"Nothing," she laughed, checking to see that Allen and Lucy remained engaged with their own conversation. "But Uncle Ran came down to close the cabin last week, so Nico was just arranging some time alone with Mike."

"But you weren't making it easy for her, were you?" he asked, combining their bundles and lifting them to his shoulder.

"No," she smiled mischievously, "—though I am glad to have her out of my hair for a while."

"Why? I thought you handled her teasing rather well; —and arranged some alone time for us in the dunes too."

"Then call it cattiness, if you wish. But, Tom, I'm not blind. Nico has been flirting with you and Allen all morning long. And it's more than teasing, as you put it. She means to start real trouble. Now I don't know why she's doing it—or why Mike can't see that she is, but I had to pay her back just a little."

"You are catty—a real she-cat!" he chuckled. "Yes, I may have to de-claw you before the weekend is over."

"Dare you," she whipped her skirt against his leg. "I dare you!" she challenged, finishing with a feline hiss. And had Allen and Lucy not been coming along behind them, Mandria would have found herself on yet another bed of sea oats…

# CHAPTER 35

By the time Mike and Nicole had rounded the point, her scheme for the too-honorable Captain was in place. "Mike, do you remember our first walk beside Back River?" she began.

"I always will. You looked so damned beautiful that day—with your wet skirts clinging and your hair blowing free in the wind."

"Beautiful?" she laughed. "You just described a ragamuffin!"

"No, you were my gypsy and a sea-witch, remember? Anyway, you couldn't be a ragamuffin if you tried. I've never seen you look less than scrumptious—and that's a damned fact."

"Well, thank you," she smiled in genuine appreciation. ...*Bernie nor Sam ever has time for pretty compliments*, she thought. ... *Yes, Mike should make a most interesting lover.* "Do you remember the kiss you almost gave me—kneeling in the water there? Remember that?"

"But I did kiss you. I've never forgotten a single one of our kisses."

"A peck—you only gave me a peck and then dribbled water on my nose. ...Why, Mike? I wanted a passionate kiss, and we've had some since."

"There must have been a reason," Mike shrugged. "Maybe because Tom was with us? I really don't recall the reason."

"Tom isn't here now," she came to a halt, "and I still want that kiss."

"Oh-hell-yes!" he reached for her.

"Oh-hell-no!" she danced about. "You'll have to catch me—and as you said then—pierce my gypsy ear, so I'll be your woman forever and ever!" And as Mike gave chase, she made sure to dart in and out of the river's edge, soaking her shoes; splashing icy water onto her skirts; and splashing him too. This done, she allowed Mike to claim his prize, seeing to it that he lingered over the task. "…Mike," she said then, "I think we'd better go build that fire. I'm soaked and it seems to be getting colder."

Of course, Mike was feeling pretty heated at the moment, but hurried her through the dunes to the cabin and after unlocking the door, turned to see Nicole's precisely timed shiver. "I'll get the fire started," he said with concern. "You'd better take off those wet shoes though—and whatever else that needs drying. Go on, now," he nudged her toward the bedroom. "And, Nico, wrap yourself in a blanket before you catch a chill."

"Yes, Mike," she obeyed, enjoying a private smile. It was splendidly easy to manipulate men—which was fast becoming her favorite pass-time. …Wasn't it nice, too, that the drapes were all drawn? And door would also be locked again, as soon as she could convince Mike to do that.

Bundled in a quilt, Nicole returned to find Mike kneeling on the raised hearth. He looked up and smiled as she placed her shoes close to the fire. And while he put the coffee pot on the hook and swung the arm over the heat, she purposely arrayed her under things along the mantle, leaving her dress draped over a dining chair. …*This will be fun*, she thought, looking over a room she had never liked before. *Fun, to make love in front of bright, warm fire.*

"Nico, are you still cold?" Mike asked. "Shall I bring you a chair up by the hearth?"

"Please do," she staged another shiver. "I suppose it was stupid of me; —getting so wet in weather like this."

"Yes, but a hell of a lot fun, wasn't it?" And once she was seated, Mike lowered himself on the hearth facing her. That way, he wouldn't have to look at those pretty, frilly things hanging over his head.

"Oh, dear," she pointed. "Your boots are all wet too!"

"Yeah, well, they are a bit soggy," he nodded.

"And your trousers?" she ran a hand along his thigh. "Why, Michael Herb, you're wetter than I was—so maybe you should take your clothes off too."

"And maybe I shouldn't," he laughed. "No, Nico, you're still the beautiful, tempting lady I met on the trip from Augusta—and I'm still determined not to frighten you away."

"Still a very cold lady," she pouted, forced to try another tactic. So stretching her legs toward the fire, she made sure they were bare to the knee as she settled them close beside his hip. "My toes are so numb they hurt—and my fingers feel as if they might snap off."

"Here. Let me rub them," Mike reached for her hand and avoided the sight of her slender calves and ankles. "This should start the blood flowing again."

"Michael," she gazed at his head of dark, sand-auburn hair, as he blew warm breaths on her fingers, "…have you been in love before?"

"Before what?" he smiled, teasingly.

"Well, I know you must have made love to a lot of women, but were you in love with any of them?"

"I don't know," he shrugged. "I suppose I thought I was a time or two."

"What happened?"

"Oh, first one thing, then another. Why?" he asked, curious about her direction.

"Because I need to know something," she said, remembering what she'd seen and felt in the dunes. "When you make love, do you want the woman to give in right away or pretend to fight you off? —And would you rather she matched your passion, or held herself aloof?"

"Damn, Nico," he chuckled. "What kind of questions are these?"

"Important ones!" she insisted. "I want to know the kind of woman you prefer. And if you've ever wanted me?"

"Well, there isn't another woman like you: a crazy little blonde, who never behaves the way I expect; who excites me beyond endurance—and then asks if I want her."

"But could you love me? —Mike, will you ever fall in love with me?"

"Nico…I already have," he admitted. "And I want you so much it scares the hell out of me."

"Oh," she lowered her eyes demurely, while allowing the spread to slip from a bare shoulder. Hearing his intake of a breath, she quickly added in her sweetest tone, "Do you want to make love to me now?"

"Of course I do, damn it!" he rose to pull the perking pot from the fire. And how glad he was for any excuse to look away from the tempting picture she made. But as he straightened; saw that he faced those lacy under things again; he had to force his body into compliance with his mind. "...Nico, you are not like the rest. You deserve the proper circumstances. If it's to be for us, I'm willing to wait for that." And nodding, more to convince himself than her, he took the coffee pot with him to search for cups—proving how befuddled he was. Now, he'd have the pot, two cups and two saucers to carry back.

"Are you saying that if we made love here—right here, on the floor before the fire—that you wouldn't love me any longer?"

"No, I'm not saying that at all," he started back, keeping a careful eye on everything he was trying to balance. "I'm just saying...I'm— Damn," he came to a near calamitous halt. For Nicole had dropped the quilt and stood nude before him. "Damn!" he repeated, unable to keep his eyes from the firelight playing over her fair skin. "Damn it, Nico?" And this was more a plea for mercy.

"Come, my Captain," she held arms out to him.

"Nico, we can't do this," he fumbled everything down on the table. "It's not sensible. The others will be here soon—damn it—so it's just not sensible!"

"Michael," she purred, repeating Tom's words to Mandria. "Do shut up." And knowing his eyes never left her, she knelt on the floor and slowly spread the quilt, then lay upon it, to lift arms to him a second time.

"Damn," he said, yet again. "I'll just be damned."

"No doubt we both will be," she coaxed. "Lock the door—please, my handsome Captain?"

Mike did that in a daze and returned to kneel beside her; to look at her perfect loveliness. "Beautiful," he murmured, "As delicate and fragile as a porcelain figurine. Too fragile for the likes of me, little Nico."

455

"But feel my cheek," she pressed his hand to its warmth. "The things you make me feel are not delicate. —Or my heart," she slid his hand downward and into place. "What is fragile in the rapid-fire beat your closeness causes me?" Then satisfied with his adoring expression, she made him a sad sounding sob, complete with two crystal tears—as befitted his description of her. "…But Mike, I do have a small imperfection and I'm so afraid of disappointing you!"

"What imperfection?" he asked huskily. "No, Nico, you have the most beautiful body I'll ever hope to see."

"It… its inside," she pressed his hand closer on her breasts, and made her voice quiver, "It's the reason I've never let myself fall in love. —Oh, Mike, I am a virgin, but I've no way to prove it. When I was barely thirteen, I fell from a horse and…and I bled! The doctor said I had ruptured myself and—and oh, do you hate me? Are you terribly disappointed? Please don't hate me!"

"Nico—no, I could never hate you!" he gathered her close. "It wasn't your fault. Please don't cry. It doesn't matter. —Really, it just doesn't matter."

"Thank you—oh, thank you," she smiled smugly against his shoulder. "And Mike, I want you too," she cupped his face. "I want to be your woman—not some frightened child afraid of love since that terrible, terrible accident."

"Yes, woman—yes, you will be mine," he laughed, kissing her quickly. Then he rose to strip away his clothes—which Nicole very much enjoyed, as he had a fine, muscled body and a large nicely swollen cock. It was all she could do to keep from fondling it, but she was supposed to be a stupid virgin, all aquiver with anticipation and ignorant of the things men liked.

Mike crawled up her body and covered it with his own. "Nico," he said when they were nose to nose, "our friends will be here soon and we haven't time now for the careful build-up you deserve—"

"I don't care; I don't care!" she squirmed herself into more direct genital contact with him. "I want you inside me, Mike—for as long as we have. Please, I want to know what it feels like!"

As the head of his penis was already seeking entrance, it just seemed the most natural and beautiful thing Mike had ever experienced to simply slide right into her depths. He shuddered it affected him so. "Nico," he sought her eyes, "I fully intend to marry you. I want you to know that. But for now, I'm going to ride you, and if I'm not done when the others get here—well, they can go to hell waiting."

"Irish bastard," she smiled, coaxing him deeper. "I haven't said I'd marry you."

"You will say it—bitch," he teased back. "Damn, Nico, you move your ass like you've done this for years!"

"For years to come," she said against his mouth. "Promise, Mike—promise it!"

"I do—Oh-hell-yes, I do!" he said most sincerely.

"I am a bitch, Captain," she greeted his first serious thrusts. "In my heart, I've always known it."

"You're my bitch now—my little Irish bitch," he watched as she stiffened and caught her breath.

"More—yes, Mike, more!" she breathed passionately. "Help me—please help me!" And Mike made every effort to do so...

Mike and Nicole were cuddled on the sofa drinking coffee when the others arrived. No one noticed that they held hands without once letting go. Tom and Allen were only glad Nicole was quieter than usual. And Mandria and Lucy found nothing unusual about laying out their lunch without an offer of help from her. For Nicole, this was typical behavior.

At one point, Mandria was tempted to seek a bit of vengeance. Yes, she would have enjoyed mentioning the wrinkled state of Nicole's dress—*repeatedly*—as Nicole had done to her at Allen's dinner. And had two pair of shoes not sat drying on the hearth, she would have. ...But Nicole did deserve it, and Mandria hadn't changed her mind on that!

So it was that in spite of Sam's careful tutoring or his emotion altering powders, Nicole spent the remainder of the weekend in avid pursuit of her Captain. Mike, of course, was elated; listening in admiration as she invented multiple excuses for being alone with him. And in each instance, he marveled that her passion had not ebbed a whit; that she was ever eager to receive him, caring little for the preliminaries, time or room denied them.

…Oh, yes, Tom should have trusted his premonition: especially the one he'd had about Deborah Nicole O'Rourke all along…

On Monday morning, Nicole had her usual session with Bernie, but compared to Mike's fiery love making, the experience was less than rewarding. Besides, her head had begun to ache during the night and the nagging pain was still with her. Later and feeling worse, she met with Sam. But when she admitted ignoring the Scotts—as well as every one of his instructions—in favor of wooing Mike, a terrible quarrel erupted.

Sam watched as Nicole continually rubbed at her temples. She had been without his powder for nearly three days now and he was so angry, he decided to let her suffer. In fact, when the argument escalated and she ordered him from her suite, vowing never to speak to him again, he went home, packed a bag and left for Charleston. Yes, a full week of withdrawals would serve Nicole right. Besides, there was a lady in that distant port city he'd been meaning to call on for quite some time…

Nicole did, indeed, suffer. She went straight home to her bed and wasn't able to leave it again until Thursday. Ransom was most concerned and twice called in a doctor, who only prescribed a series of foul tasting tonics, which did nothing for the grueling headaches and chills but nauseate her. Just as they had his wife, Deborah…

Slowly then, the strange illness subsided and though Nicole was able to function, she found herself unbearably restless. Bernie was not worth considering for the attention she was certain she needed. She was still too angry with Sam to go begging—became even angrier on hearing he'd left town—and Mike wouldn't come in until the following afternoon, which irritated her all the more. It just wasn't fair that there was a perfect solution to her problem somewhere on that damn river! So, for the rest of the day, she prowled the house like a caged animal, snapping at her father and the servants until one and all scurried from her presence.

As soon as Ransom returned to the bank after lunch on Friday, Nicole was not long in leaving the house too. On horseback, she flew, leaving Harry, the tree sitter, agape and with no way to follow. On she went, west along the river road out of town. If she hurried, she could reach the landing some ten miles away, where the Irish Mist made a final stop before docking in Savannah.

Needless to say, the Captain was surprised to see Nicole. There was a breathlessness about her; a state of agitation that caused her eyes to seem over-bright. "Nico?" he took her arm as she rushed into the wheelhouse. "What is it? —Is something wrong in Savannah?"

"Yes, Captain, there is," she stated for the benefit of the helmsman. Then drawing Mike aside, she continued in confidence. "You're not there—that's what's wrong. I've missed you and just couldn't wait to see you. Let's go to your cabin—let's go now!"

"Of course, Miss O'Rourke," he also said for the helmsman's ear. "We'll tend to this immediately. I had no idea it was so important. What you want in is my cabin. Come; I'll fetch it out for you."

As they went toward the interior entrance, Nicole giggled. "Bastard! —*Fetch it out*, will you?" she whispered.

"Yes; —oh-hell-yes!" he replied, ushering her through the portal, then locking both doors.

"Bastard," she repeated as he turned to face her. "Bastard Irishman."

"Bitch," he responded. "Beautiful Irish bitch."

They stood for several seconds, looking but not touching. Then, Nicole began to unfasten her riding skirt and when she stepped out of it, the lower part of her body was nude. "How long before we reach Savannah?" she asked, loosening her jacket. And when it came off too, she wore only her tall topped riding boots.

"Too soon," Mike uttered, feasting on her slim, pale body. "But I will have to be in the wheelhouse before we dock."

"You won't before I get what I came for, Captain," she sat on the edge of his bed. "Now, take off your clothes."

"Bitch," he chuckled. "Horny little bitch," he began stripping to her nodded approval. But when he started toward her, she went back on her elbows, lifted a leg and wedged a foot in his belly.

"Help me off with these boots, will you?" And while he stood holding her heel in his hand, she spread wide her other leg, displaying herself for his viewing.

"Damn," Mike breathed, venting his mounting excitement. And turning away with reluctance, he straddled her leg to work the boot free.

"Now the other one," she commanded. And as the second boot came off, she raised that bare foot higher between his legs, fondling his scrotum and the base of his penis with her toes before drawing her foot backward and out. "Face me now, Michael Herb," she continued. "I mean to study you closely." So Mike turned, wondering at the brisk, unromantic tone of her voice. The assumption grew when she began to poke at his erection with a touch that seemed almost clinical.

"Mike," she said finally, "can I tell you about something I saw?"

"Of course," he nodded, wishing she'd end her examination, for now her grip was more suited to softening oranges.

"Well, I saw two of the slaves together. A man and a woman; —as we are man and woman," she raised her eyes to his. "They used their mouths. …Do you know what I mean?" she added, moistening her lips with her tongue.

Clinical—he'd thought her mood clinical? "Nicole," he trembled and grasping her grasping hands, brought them to his lips.

"Would you want that for us?" she climbed to her knees before him. "You've only to ask. Mike, I'd do anything to please you."

"Nico—oh, Nico," he lifted her onto the bed and held her close. "I could never ask that—not of you, my beautiful lady. It's so touching that you'd care for my pleasure, but you'll see. Once we're married, you'll see. I'll be content just keeping you that way—and that will bring me more pleasure than anything."

"Will it Mike?" She opened her legs to him. "Will marriage make me enjoy this even more? Then will I know fulfillment?"

"That's the second promise I'll make you," he whispered, mounting her eager, undulating body. "A solemn promise!" he swore as her passion infected his whole being.

Her need for him was so urgent—always so wonderfully urgent—and fighting his own need was not easy. But he didn't give in to the mindless response his body demanded and when it was done, the experience left him unwilling to release her, yet gasping so for breath, he was certain he'd never summon the strength to rise in search of his clothes. So for a time, he just lay there holding her against his sated body...until he felt her hand return to the stump of his throbbing penis. "Nico," he drew that hand to his lips again, "...am I still invited for supper tonight?" It was a useless question, but all he could think of in the way of dissuasion.

"Certainly," she returned her hand to fondle his most interesting appendage anyway. "And then, you're leaving early."

"...Why?" he puzzled.

"Because, Mike, you are going to meet me in the square and we're coming back here to do this again—and again—until I learn all there is to know about it."

"I can't see where you've missed much," he chuckled, responding to her suggestion and her touch more readily than he would have thought possible. "And as you've just lit fire to me shillelagh again, I'm supposing I'll have to flog you with it anew, little Irish bitch." So saying, he remounted confident of depleting her amazing store of energy...

Mike departed the O'Rourke residence before nine that evening and Harry, the tree sitter heaved a bored sigh. It had been a very slow week. Nicole hadn't left the house in days—other than the horse-back ride she'd taken earlier in the afternoon. She was gone for three or four hours too—time to screw somebody a good one, he was sure—but luckily for him, the boss wasn't returning until Monday and would

461

never know he'd missed an assignment. So when the lights went out in Nicole's bedroom, Harry decided something else. If Sam Lucas could take a week's vacation, he could take a night off…maybe two. He left the square then, thinking how long it had been since he'd spent a full night in his own bed. Harry would have been surprised to learn that some thirty minutes later, Nicole met the Captain directly beneath his post of duty and did not return home for several hours more.

Saturday morning, Harry was still sleeping when Nicole left her house again. She had stolen Mike's cabin key the night before and letting herself in, she quietly undressed and slipped into bed beside him. It was noon before she went home. And Harry still slept in his bed…

A rare twinge of conscience brought Harry back to work Saturday evening. He followed when the Usual Six met for supper at Hester's—and even he was surprised at Nicole's new affection for Mike. …But it was the Captain's attitude he found puzzling. He wondered if the illness Nicole had suffered might be catching, for Herb didn't look at all well. Harry was certain he must be ailing when he and Nicole left early. So, not bothering to follow—surmising that Herb would take her home, then surely take to his bed—Harry rewarded himself by spending all day Sunday just as he pleased. And Mike did, indeed, take to his bed, for Nicole was not returned home until well past midnight. Sunday morning, Mike awoke to find her in his cabin again.

Sighing deeply, he threw back the covers and gave himself over to her. But afterwards, somehow feeling they needed to go, he insisted they attend an early Mass…

# CHAPTER 36

"I have put this off long enough," Mandria muttered, hurrying home after church. Yes, while her mother played hostess at a Sunday coffee in the rectory and her father not due until tomorrow, this was the perfect time to speak with Joleen. "And by heavens, if I have to lock her in a room, she is going talk to me!"

And that was precisely what Mandria ended up doing. She had called the girl upstairs, but when she began to question her reason for going to the O'Rourke stable, Joleen bolted for the door in tears. Mandria barely caught her. "Now," she turned, showing the frightened girl the door key. "It's locked, Joleen, and it will stay locked until you stop this silliness—and your crying—and tell me what is bothering you."

"B—but ain't nothing to tell, Miss Mandy!" she fell to her knees, cowering on the floor. "Please, Miss Mandy, ain't nothing to say!"

"Oh, Joleen," Mandria knelt before her. "I am trying to help you, —truly I am." And lifting the girl's face in her hands, she continued. "Maybe it would be easier if I go first: I heard you are pregnant and that Willie Luther is the father. I am not angry about it; —nor am I shaming you, if that's why you're afraid. In fact, if you want to marry Willie, I'm determined to see you do it."

Joleen was snubbing badly when she straightened. And sitting back on her heels she faced Mandria while dabbing at teary eyes. "...Miss Mandy, Ah thanks you for caring bout me; —from the bottom of my heart, Ah do. But Willie, he ain't going to marry with me. Him under

463

a spell and ain't no potion going to work against this witch! He done told me, if Ah don't like things as is, he just have to screw somebody else, cause that what she wants to see. And anyways, Ah scared of crossing her myself. Ah wants to, Miss Mandy, cause sometimes Ah feel so shamed, Ah just wants to go off and die!"

"…Joleen," Mandria nodded, "I don't understand what you're saying. Is Willie Luther in love with someone else; —someone you're afraid of? And surely, you aren't ashamed of your baby."

"No, it not my baby," she pressed small, thin hands protectively on her belly. "Baby's only thing of Willie what's mine. But Ah can't tell you no more. That witch, she done promised to see me dead if Ah talk—me and Willie both!"

"Well, there must be something I can do," Mandria nodded, "—some way I can help you?"

"…Miss Mandy, just one way out for me and that to leave here; to get where that witch don't have no power on me."

"And Willie Luther? If he were to leave, would her power cease over him too?"

"Maybe; maybe not," Joleen shrugged pitifully. "But I don't hold no hope for him leaving. Ah just got to worry bout my baby now. Ah got to find me some peace, Miss Mandy, or it going to kill me and this chile' 'fore she can."

"Well, would Marsh Haven be all right? You'd be safe there with Hassie and the others. And we're driving out there today, if you want to go."

"To stay? —For good?" Joleen questioned.

"Perhaps—or until I've worked out another plan I have. So, do you want to go, Joleen?"

"Yes—yes, ma'am, Ah has to!" the girl was crying again. Then coming forward, she threw her arms about Mandria. "And thank you again for caring. Somehow, Ah'll pay back your kindness. Ah do that, Ah bet-ya…"

Harry wasn't the only one to notice Mike's haggard appearance. That afternoon, in the O'Rourke's parlor, Ransom made a polite inquiry about his health. Nicole glanced at the Captain when the question was asked, but her expression portrayed impatience more than anything else. Would her father ever finish the boring business matter that was disrupting her afternoon plans? After all, she and Mike had precious few hours before he left for Augusta and she intended to spend them back in his bed.

But concern for Mike also brought unexpected visitors to the O'Rourke's. "Captain, we haven't seen much of you and Nico this weekend," Tom smiled as Mandria passed him a cup of coffee. "So we've come with an invitation."

"…Yes," Mandria looked from Mike to Tom, and her smile was one of concession. She hadn't wanted to do this; there were other matters she needed settled today; but Tom was right. Mike did seem depressed and perhaps needed the company of friends. "Yes, we wondered if you and Nico would care to join us for a drive out to Marsh Haven."

"Thank you, but not today," Nicole said sweetly. "It's much too cold out; and Daddy and Mike haven't finished their business yet either."

"Yes, we have—and it's not *that* cold, Nico," Mike injected, and the fray on his voice did not escape Tom's notice. "…Please, I'd really like to go."

"Ransom?" Tom asked when Nicole seemed ready to refuse again. "Is Mike free to leave?"

"Yes, he is," Ransom answered. "And frankly, I think some fresh country air might do him good."

Then Tom made a rather deliberate bid for Nicole's cooperation and got it. "Not that your pretty cheeks need more roses, but we'd certainly enjoy having you along too," he said engagingly.

Mandria smothered a sigh in her cup as she watched Nicole's reaction to that calculated compliment. Bedazzled, she nodded consent while the pout on her lips dissolved into a seductive smile. The smile Tom returned said more than Nicole could see. It said Mike's well-being was worth this small deception, and begrudgingly, Mandria had to agree. So they were soon on their way, bundled snugly in the Lucas carriage with Old Jed at the reins. And beside him, Joleen sat stiff and mute as a statue…

However, had Joleen stood on her head and jabbered like a magpie, Nicole wouldn't have noticed. She was far too busy testing her smiles and cleverest comments on the man sitting across from her. Tom had finally paid her a genuine compliment and she was determined to hear another from him. Why, who knew what other surprises this day might hold? And the more enthused she became with the notion, the more she fondled the Captain beneath the large quilted lap robe which covered them nearly to their noses.

It was not a happy experience for Mike. He was literally at the mercy of that roving hand and short of making a scene, or forcibly holding her wrist immobile, there wasn't much he could do. On reaching Marsh Haven, he discovered an added problem. He could not let Tom and Mandria see such an obvious protrusion in his trousers, so assisting Nicole down from the opposite side of the carriage, he kept it between them. "…Mandy," he searched desperately for excuses, "you and Tom go ahead. I've seen the house and I think we'll walk down by the creek for a while."

"Oh?" Mandria asked curiously. "…When did you see Marsh Haven?"

"Mike, no," Nicole injected a complaint. "I'd rather go inside too."

Then Old Jed pulled the carriage away and Mike quickly drew Nicole before him, circling her waist from behind. "I was here for your sixteenth birthday, Mandy," he began. But now Nicole had discovered his ruse and was pressing her bottom against his embarrassing erection.

"Were you?" Mandria nodded in puzzlement. "I don't remember that. How could I forget meeting you?"

Mike was growing really angry with Nicole's squirming. "I wasn't a guest!" he retorted. "I only delivered the damn cake!" And with that, he turned them both and started away.

"Oh," Mandria uttered and then called after him. "You should have been invited. We could have been friends that much longer."

Mike stopped, realizing he must have sounded brash and that she thought it was directed at her. "Oh hell, Mandy," he said over the top of Nicole's head, "then I'd probably have you and Nico to deal with—and where would that leave Tom? Listen: we'll join you shortly, so go ahead out of the cold."

Tom had been a silent observer to all this and he nodded as Mike grasped Nicole's hand and towed her along at a determined pace. There was definitely something wrong and because of Nicole's all too familiar behavior—reminiscent of their night on the riverfront—he was afraid he knew what it was. Of course, there was nothing he could do to help, but it worried him and to the extent that little would be remembered of Mandria's introduction of the servants or her tour of the house…

Determined was a good description of the pace Mike set. Across the front yard they went; around the corner of the house; down the long sloping lawn on the side; stopping at the creek only because it was there. "Nico!" he turned on her then. "Don't you ever do that to me again!"

Nicole hadn't wanted to leave Tom's company and she certainly did not appreciate being yanked over the grounds at break-neck speed. …But Tom wasn't yet ready to give more than compliments and the rise in Mike's trousers said he was. All she had to do, then, was baffle the heat of his temper into a flame of passion, wasn't it? "Captain, whatever are you talking about?" she asked innocently, circling her arms about his waist; straddling his leg; holding it between her thighs.

"You know what!" he muffed an attempt to dislodge her. "Damn it, would you please stop that and listen to what I'm saying?"

"Oh, very well!" she spun away. "I won't bother you again; —not if you're going to fuss because I enjoy touching you!"

A long sigh escaped Mike. "Nico, I want you to enjoy that. But there must be a difference in our public and private behavior. And you know I'm right about this."

"Well, we're alone out here," she turned immediately back into his arms. "I want you, Mike. I need you so much!"

"But how—and where, for God's sake? We can't very well go in and ask to borrow a damn bedroom!"

"No, but a real lover would know about the boat house; a real lover would have me there—and later tonight, a real lover would meet me aboard the Irish Mist and have me there too."

"Oh hell," Mike almost groaned. But grasping her hand again, he strode toward the boat house with one purpose in mind. "This time, I'll quiet you—or know the damned reason why!" And behind him, Nicole only smiled…

Tom and Mandria had reached the study, where she closed the door for a private chat. "While we have a moment, I need your consent on something. It's why I asked you to drive out here today and once you've heard that, I need for you to do me a great favor. First, Tom, I want to tell Hassie about our marriage, if it's all right with you."

"Would that be wise?" he questioned. "The more people who know, the harder the secret will be to keep. …Lady, have you lost patience with me? Is that it?"

"Of course not," she assured him with a hug. "But don't you agree that we could use all the eyes and ears we can get in staying a step ahead of Father? Tom, telling Hassie about us will put her squarely in our camp—and you just have no idea how helpful that could be."

"All right, I'm listening," he settled them on a small leather settee.

"Well, Hassie is the eldest—and the leader—among our family of coloreds. What she says is law and she could have every word Father utters about us reported to her. We, in turn, would hear it from Hassie."

"No, love," he nodded. "Hassie might give the order, but I'd feel responsible if Sam were to catch and punish anyone for spying on him."

"I promise you, he will never know it. Tom, my father doesn't even see the servants. As long as they do their duties and tend his needs, they're invisible to him. I've heard him discuss the most private family and business matters when the room was full of servants. That is why the coloreds are so knowledgeable about the houses they serve. And at the Gathering, Hassie can learn what her friends have heard about Father all around the city and report that to us also."

"…How?" Tom asked, curious now. "And what is a Gathering?"

"Why, that is just the highlight of their Sunday service. You see, after church, they *gather* for a social—or dinner on the ground—and more importantly, to sit in The Circle, if they have a bit of gossip to share. You know, things like which lady is getting dentures; who dyes her hair or is in a family way? But here is where it gets interesting. If a place in taken in The Circle, it means there is a secret and when Hassie sits there, but remains silent, this means she is there to *out-mystery* the rest and a really serious guessing game begins. They understand that her secret—which would be about us—is too sacred to tell, so they'll watch her expressions for clues as they repeat every scrap of gossip they've heard about my family. And as that would have to involve my dear father, Hassie could learn some important things for us."

"Well, she might at that," he agreed. "So, how do you know about this?"

"Because when I was little, I'd sometimes go to church with Hassie and I loved every minute of it—especially The Circle. But Mama quit letting me go when I came home and announced to Uncle Ran that Aunt Deborah was having a baby before she'd told him so," Mandria laughed. "…Anyway, Hassie will be hunting us down soon, so may I tell her?" she rose to stand before him.

"If you think it would help," he rose too, and pulled her to him to nibble at her ear. "Now, what was the great favor you wanted? —What dragon must I slay for my lady?"

"None," she tilted her face to his; to grasp his lapels; as if he might miss that she was ready to do battle for this request. "I want you to buy something for me, as my agent and using my money. Now, I know we've talked about this and agreed not to own slaves, but this is a special case and no matter what it costs, I want you to buy Willie Luther."

It would never cease to amaze Tom that her every mood and gesture pleased him. "Well, you must have a reason," he smiled. "Let's hear it."

Then he had the pleasure of watching her determination slide right into uncertainty about his reaction, as proven by her repeated peeks at him as she spoke. "You see, I am going to have Willie Luther marry Joleen. Then, if you'd like, we can set them both free. —Or maybe hire them to live and work in our home. Now, that's even a better idea!"

"Sweetheart," Tom had to point out, "Willie Luther won't be free if he's forced to marry. He'd just be exchanging one form of slavery for another,"

"But Joleen is pregnant by him—and not at all well!" Mandria's eyes flashed with emerald insistence. "She has been crying and sulking about the house for weeks and it's not healthy for her condition. —There's another thing, too. She is deathly afraid of someone; so afraid she was willing to come out here to stay. She swears Willie Luther is under a spell and can't leave. Now, I know she is overly fascinated with that sort of thing, but whatever happened in the O'Rourke stable, has her terrified!"

Tom suddenly felt leery. Nicole, then Allen and now Joleen—all with disturbing tales about that stable? Maybe there was more to Mandria's concern than even she knew. "Listen, let me do this: let me talk with Willie Luther first. If he is willing to marry Joleen, then I'll speak to Ransom about a purchase. …But lady, let's not mention this to Nicole, all right?"

Mandria only had time for nod of agreement before Hassie knocked and came in to join them. "Done with your house tour, Mandy-chile'?" Then she honed in on Tom. "This the one, ain't it? This *just a man* you didn't want to talk about when you come before."

"Yes, Hassie," Mandria laughed, "and as you said then, he did turn out to be *the man*. —Oh, before I forget, I'm leaving Joleen here and I want you to take special care of her. She…well, she'll tell you why later. Now, can we share a wonderful secret with you?"

"You always has," she turned proud, sparkling eyes on Tom. "Her my baby. Ah seen to her birthing, Mr. Tom. Ah hold her even 'fore her mama did and Ah loves her like my own. So?" she looked back to Mandria. "What this secret you got?"

"If you recall, I told you about the night I drank too much and the awful thing—"

"Hush, now!" Hassie snapped, her head making a meaningful nod toward Tom. "That best put aside, don't you know."

"But Hassie, I was with Tom! We were married that night and I just didn't have the sense to remember it!"

"Married?" she came to hug Mandria. "You been married all along? —And to him?"

"Yes, Hassie; —yes!" Mandria laughed. And noting her husband's smile, she circled an arm about his waist, hugging him too, which left Tom with the pair against his chest, so he just hugged them both. "Hassie, I love this man so much it's scary—wonderful scary," Mandria finished

"Ah can see that you do," Hassie pulled away to look from one to the other. "You makes a handsome couple, Ah got to say that. You going to take good care of my Mandy-chile, now ain't you, Mr. Tom?"

"Yes, ma'am, you have my word on it," he answered sincerely.

"And your mama?" Hassie asked Mandria. "Ah bet her proud 'bout this too!"

"She would be, if she knew," Mandria faced the woman again. "Hassie, Mama approves of Tom whole-heartedly. ...But Father doesn't and you've seen the kind of husband he wants for me. He would not respect my choice or give us any peace. So, until we're ready to announce this marriage, it's really important that we stay aware of his knowledge about us. ...Will you help us keep abreast of that? And keep our secret?"

"You knows better than to ask!" Hassie retorted indignantly. Then with a wide grin, she hugged Mandria again. "Married! —My baby done married! —And Sunday? Now ain't we going to have a time at The Gathering? Listen now; go on to the parlor while Ah brings in some coffee and my special pe-can pie! Yes, siree—now we got some real celebrating to do!" she chuckled hurrying away.

"Put out extra," Mandria called. "Nico and Captain Herb will be in after while."

471

"Sure will, Mandy-chile. But Lord, how we going to strut next Sunday! Lord knows we will!" her voice echoed down the hall.

"…Mandria," Tom asked as they crossed over to the parlor, "she does realize we can't really celebrate now; —that Nico doesn't know about this either?"

"You still don't understand, do you?" she smiled as they settled on another sofa before a cheery fire. "Trust me, you'd have better luck getting words from a mute, than our secret from Hassie," she laid her head on his shoulder, then pulled away to search his eyes. "…Tom, you don't feel enslaved by our marriage, do you?"

"Lady, you would have more right to that feeling than me," he replied. "I saw it done without your consent—remember?"

"No, I still don't," she kissed him. "But I am not complaining," she added, cuddling against his shoulder again. "I guess I just want Joleen to be as happy as this."

"You know, in a way, I could envy that pair," Tom day-dreamed aloud. "I wish we were in living in our home and having a baby of our own."

"Well, it isn't spring," Mandria uttered as a warm smile crossed her lips. "You did say I had until spring, sir."

"Yes, I did," he lifted her mouth to his. "And meanwhile, I will continue my efforts to make both things happen. Now, kiss me again, pretty lady—again and again."

A seductive laugh from the doorway interrupted that request, as hands on hips, Nicole sauntered into the room. "Careful," she said silkily. "I was just given a sit-down about petting in public. …And, evidently, there is a price to be paid for it," she aimed this at Mike, who was sinking into a chair wearing a truly perplexed expression. "But he could be right on one point, Mandy," she continued, prowling about the room. "Why, if you weren't my dearest friend, just think of what I could tell about you and Tom petting on that sofa?"

Mandria laughed in the throaty way Tom so enjoyed, but he sensed the undercurrent of her displeasure with Nicole. "Well, maybe you'd do me a service telling your stories, Nico. Maybe that would force

Mr. Scott to declare his true feelings. For *me*," she stressed. "Men are just so slow about these things—don't you agree?"

Nicole was still staring in surprise when Hassie brought in a huge silver tray. "Coffee ready," she announced. "Coffee and this good old pe-can pie!"

Nicole's second surprise came when they started back to Savannah. Almost immediately, Mike dozed off in the corner of the seat, which not only left her bored, but aware of something vital. "Wait—where is Joleen?" she glanced toward the house. "Do you expect her walk home from here?"

"Of course not," Mandria assured her. "I meant to leave Joleen. She could use some rest and Hassie will see that she gets it."

"But...surely, you'll need her in town!"

"I'll manage, Nico—really. I am capable of dressing and feeding myself."

"Well, you'd better go back and get her. Your father won't approve if you pamper his slaves. Why, you'll spoil her and she won't be good for—for anything!"

"In the first place, Joleen doesn't belong to Father, but to me," Mandria stood her ground. "In the second place, you were the one who told me how she was feeling and why. Nico, she isn't well and it won't spoil her, to take better care of her health."

"It's still a mistake," Nicole pouted. "And how long do you plan to let her stay? I mean, Willie Luther will miss her; —and you're the one who told me they were in love!"

"And then you said...," Mandria recalled a remark about stud fees. "Oh, never mind. Joleen is staying and that's that." Then as Nicole folded her arms in a huff, Mandria turned to Tom. "The favor I asked? Kindly tend to it—*tomorrow*, please?"

That evening, Nicole received yet another surprise. Mike didn't come to call as she'd expected. So when Ransom retired, she had Willie Luther drive her down to the Irish Mist, but the Captain wasn't there either. She waited on deck for a full half-hour and when he still hadn't returned, she was in quite a state: cursing his inconsideration; herself for loosing his stolen cabin key; Mandria for daring to interrupt her favorite pass-time; and the quarrel with Sam, which had lasted quite long enough. Yes, Mandria had said he'd be returning tomorrow, so she would go to his office with a peace offering—and then back to Savannah Joleen would come! Meanwhile, she re-entered the carriage, ordered Willie to take her to St. Julian Street and from there, he was sent to deliver a note to the Brown's Sunday house…

In the night shaded square above the riverfront, Mike had watched Nicole come and go. Then, finding a bench in deeper shadow, he sat mulling his thoughts for a long while. And as he did, he idly turned his cabin key through his fingers…

# CHAPTER 37

Nicole strolled into Sam's office around noon the following day and removed her coat. "Well," he said from behind his desk, "does the mountain come to Mohammed?"

"I wouldn't know anything about that," she shrugged nonchalantly. "But I'm here because I've missed you." And smiling, she closed and locked the door.

"Obviously," he chuckled. "Evelyn told me you'd been ill," he watched as she came to his side of the desk and perched on it facing him. "How are you feeling now?"

"Bored," she sighed. "Restless. And at the moment, very upset."

"Why is that, my dear?" he kept his probe simple. "Hasn't Bernie given you long enough rides?"

"Sam, Bernie is such a child," she grimaced, "and I hate being drooled on by children of any age."

"And Herb? You can't find his attention boring already."

"No, Mike is a different breed altogether," she nodded. "—Though I am miffed with him at the moment too."

"Oh? And why is that?" he tried to keep his enjoyment over this news from his tone.

Nicole leaned on an elbow before him to better display her cleavage. "Well, at first it was truly wonderful between us. In fact, during one or two exceptional moments, I was tempted to forget our plans for Tom."

"…But?" Sam leashed the panic that had started to creep into his throat.

"But yesterday, when Mike knew I wanted to see him, he wasn't there for me," she pouted. "I just don't know what to make of it. It's like trying to work a puzzle, only to find vital pieces missing."

"You do know why, Nico," he said coming forward on his chair, to take up a quill and run the feathered end along her neckline. "You are still in love with Tom Scott and you know nothing would be missing with him."

"I know what I've seen lately, too," she watched the feather move over the swell of one breast now; then the other. "I've seen Tom kissing Mandy and he enjoys it."

"It may appear that way, but Mandy, like her dear mother before her, is an unyielding little cunt. And take it from a man who knows, that is hell to live with."

"Don't speak so crudely of Mamalyn," she leaned toward him, wanting more from the feather. "She is very dear to me."

"So dear you sleep with her husband?" he chuckled.

"Well, I'm not trying to steal you or anything," she laughed too. "But I do enjoy borrowing now and again. ...And Sam, it has been over a week," she finished on a seductive note.

He knew what she expected in the close quarters of his office, but she wouldn't get it. Without the magic of his powders, she'd find him lacking too and he would not allow that control to slip from his grasp. ...However, she had now unbuttoned her blouse and he could torment her a bit longer; prep her for the evening ahead. So, playing it safe, instead of his hand, he continued with the feather back and forth across her nipples. And suddenly, with amazing agility, she was on his lap, breathless and her skin feeling hot to the touch; breasts bare; skirt hiked and legs open.

"More," she demanded. "Dear God, I've missed the pleasure you give me!"

It took a moment, but Sam had to quell the stirring in his loins. "There are many kinds of pleasure, Nicole. Shall I demonstrate?" And her nod was eager and immediate. "There is the tantalizing kind of this feather," he ran it over her lips. "The stimulation of touch," he rolled a nipple between finger and thumb. Then she watched his hand go under her skirt. "But there is another," his fingers danced lightly over the tenderness of her woman's flesh. "If dealt by a master, it can bring the most exquisite pleasure of all: Pain," he whispered, his fingers tightening cruelly.

"Stop!" she flinched. "Damn it, you're hurting me—stop!"

Satisfied he had discouraged her lust for the moment, Sam plopped her back on the desk and rose. "No more than you've hurt me, Nico. I'm expecting a client in a very few minutes and must greet him with a fair-sized erection because of your ill-timed visit. We can meet at The Tabby House later, if you'd like, but there just isn't time now for the fucking you deserve."

Nicole had been gauging that erection and absolutely could not bring herself to pass it up. "All right, I'll wait my turn," she reached and grabbed him now. "But Sam, I have to have something to get me through the day!" And she franticly worked at his trouser buttons.

"God damn you!" he felt himself respond to her intention even more. Then she was off the desk, he was backed into it, his penis exposed and in her mouth. "God damn you!" he repeated, grasping her head and pulling her closer. "If you want it that bad, you will drink every drop! —All of it, do you hear me, bitch!"

Nicole certainly took that as consent and when she released Sam, he was lying flat on his back, on his own desk, gasping for air. "Now, dear Uncle Sam," she came to caress his cheek, neatly attired once more. "I would suggest you make yourself presentable too. It just wouldn't do for that client to see you this way," she gathered coat and purse. "So: I'm off to buy a new negligee especially for you. Have you a favorite color?" And when his only response was a groan, she smiled. "What's that you said: thin, low-cut and easily removed? For shame, Sam!" she laughed, going to the door. And when she opened it, he went scrambling for cover behind his desk. "Dear, Uncle Sam," she said sweetly, going out and closing the door again.

Sam sat there for a few minutes, uncertain if he was happy with how that had gone. Nicole could not be allowed to disarm him so easily. ...And yet, that was one hell of a head job; which meant she was definitely ready to resume their relationship; and that meant his powders would soon reestablish his dominance over her. There was something to smile about. But it faded as he looked to see what was causing a stinging sensation along his penis. "God damn!" he swore, finding his flesh scored with tooth marks. "The damned little cannibal!" Then he felt the hair on his neck prickle as he recalled his own words about pain. *If dealt by a master, it can bring the most exquisite pleasure of all.* The question was who had been the master in this instance? The answer did not please Sam in the least…

Luckily, for Joleen and Willie Luther, Nicole had again become so involved with herself, she'd forgotten her original reason for going to see Sam. Luckily, too, Harry had followed when Nicole went into town, for it was during Tom's lunch hour from school that he went by the O'Rourke stable to speak with Willie Luther. And that one displayed a complete gauntlet of emotions. At first, he was as close-mouthed and sullen as Joleen had been with Mandria. When Tom happened to mention Joleen's pregnancy, it became shock that kept him silent. Then, anger set in and he cursed that same unnamed witch, vowing to make things right if it cost his life. So Tom suggested Mandria's solution instead and he wept openly, pleading for any help. Tom promised it, going immediately to see Ransom at the bank.

"Sir," he began, "first, let me thank you for allowing Allen and myself to become investors in your railroad venture. According to the paper, they're to start work on it early next year."

"Yes, they will. And because of it, I see good things for Savannah's future—as well as profit for those of us willing to invest in her."

"It's good to hear that," Tom nodded. "Now, to the purpose of my visit: …Sir, I think you know Mandria for a fair-minded young lady—and a sentimental one, too."

"Yes; yes I do," Ransom replied. "Evelyn's daughter would have to be."

"Well, she has this notion in her head and I find it impossible to argue with her romantic way of reasoning."

"Romantic, you say?" Ransom chuckled. "So, let's hear it. I assume you're here to tell me about it."

"I am," Tom laughed too. "You see, she is very fond of her little maid, Joleen. But the girl seems to be pregnant and Mandria is determined to see her marry the father of the child."

"A true-life shotgun wedding, huh?"

"No, sir, the boy loves Joleen; —wants to wed her. The problem is you own him."

"And Mandy wants to buy him so they can marry and live happily ever after," Ransom nodded in understanding. "So which of my coloreds is it?"

"Willie Luther. —And Mandria thinks I am the one who should own the pair! Sir, I have shown her my new home, and she has graciously agreed to guide my choice of décor. But she says when it is ready for occupancy, I will need good reliable servants too."

"She is certainly right there," Ransom agreed. "And a settled, married couple would look after the place better than a whole staff with nothing in common."

"Then you'd sell Willie to me?" he asked hopefully.

"Well, if Mandy is willing to give up her maid in the name of true love, who am I to stand in the way? ...Of course, Nico does use him as a driver, but in truth, he isn't very good; —too young and inexperienced. Still..." he hesitated again.

And fearing Ransom wanted to ask Nicole's consent, Tom dug into the Captain's bag of tricks—which meant when the truth is too plain embroider the edges with a few decorative fibs. "Ransom, would you believe Mike shares your concern for Nico's safety? Not long ago, we happened upon a lady who was stranded because her driver couldn't replace a broken wheel. Mike said at the time he wouldn't want to see Nico left helpless, on a dark stretch of road, as that poor woman was. And another thing—"

"You don't need another!" Ransom halted him. "I'm convinced, Tom:—Willie Luther is yours! Come by here for the papers after school today and collect him from the house whenever you'd like. I paid two hundred for the boy, but as I've done precious little to see him trained for anything useful, I'll sell for the same price. Done?"

"And done," Tom extended his hand, knowing that with their handshake the bargain was sealed no matter what objection Nicole might raise later. That settled, Tom continued. "…Sir, one more favor; and it won't cost nor earn you a cent?"

"Yes?" the banker asked curiously.

"Well, I would appreciate it if you'd continue to keep it to yourself that I've bought a house—as well as the news that I'm staffing it. This is another of Mandria's schemes," he made a put-upon sigh, knowing he was already a yard deep in embroidered fibs. "It seems she thinks I should finish the place completely and then throw a grand house-warming party for half the damn city! Ransom, she is so intent on keeping this under wraps—well, she hasn't even told her parents what she's planning. And frankly, I'm beginning to feel as nervous as a debutante, but there is no dissuading her."

Ransom looked at Tom as a smile spread over his mouth. "Young man, you can complain all you like, but you are enjoying every minute of Mandy's romantic ways, now aren't you?"

"Yes, sir," Tom admitted. "That's the God's-honest truth." …*And how good it feels to use it again*! he thought.

While making his way back toward the O'Rourke's to collect Willie, Tom had to wonder though. …Why did he feel so certain Nicole would object to this sale? Maybe because there had been something…base in having Willie present for her rendezvous with Allen; something… grasping that she'd named the boy a reason for bringing Joleen home during yesterday's argument with Mandria? And it had been Nicole who told Mandria about Joleen's pregnancy to begin with. So how did she know—and what more had been said between the two women that would cause Mandria to add urgency to her repeated request for this purchase? He would have to ask her about it. Meanwhile, she would be at the house now, working on her latest project and able to explain all Willie needed to know about the place. And if he hurried, there might even be time for a kiss or two from his beautiful wife before returning to school…

It was during supper that evening that Nicole heard what her father had done. "How could you?" she banged her fork to the plate. "Willie Luther is *my* driver—and you must buy him back!"

"I'm sorry, Nicole," Ransom nodded. "I've already accepted money and turned over a bill of sale."

"Who's money? —Who bought Willie? I'll speak to the man myself."

"I am not at liberty to say, my dear, as I handle his affairs and he requested anonymity."

"B—but what will I do without Willie Luther to entertain…me?" distress tripped her tongue. "I mean, he was just so amusing and kept me laughing as we drove about Savannah. Oh, Daddy, I'll miss that so—*please*, get him back for me!"

"You wouldn't be amused if you were stranded in a broken carriage, Nico. I'll get you another driver; someone strong enough to look after you and the carriage should there be a mishap."

"And meantime, just what am I supposed to do for a driver?" she rose angrily. "Daddy, I was planning to go out this evening, but without a driver—Oh, damn it, you have ruined everything!"

"Nicole!" Ransom bristled now. "Watch your language! —You will not speak so again!"

"I certainly wont—because I never want to talk to you again!" she ran crying from the room "—And damn you too!"

"Deborah Nicole O'Rourke!" Ransom stormed up the stairs behind her. And when she slammed the bedroom door in his face, he jerked it open, removed the key and locked her inside. "Now, you will stay in there until you learn to keep a civil tongue in your mouth!" he yelled. "You will not be going out tonight, either—or any other night—until you do!" And with that, he ordered the servants away from her door and left for his poker game.

Needless to say, Nicole had a blue-screaming fit, but nevertheless spent a miserable evening at home. Sam fared no better as he waited, powder in pocket, alone at the Tabby House, wondering what had happened.

*Poor little Nico, with a brand new negligee and no one to wear it for;*
*Poor little Nico, with no where to go—not even the stable any more…*

On Wednesday, the 17th of October, Mandria drove out to Marsh Haven to pick up Joleen and Hassie. It was a day and date Joleen would certainly remember, for it was her wedding day.

"How Ah look, Miss Mandy?" she giggled, climbing into the buggy. "Willie Luther, he'll like my dress, Ah bet-ya!"

"Oh, I know he will," Mandria agreed. "Joleen, you do look so beautiful!"

"Done told her that near a hundred times," Hassie chided good naturedly. "So what time this wedding be, Mandy-chile'?"

"Four o'clock," she smiled. "But Joleen, would you like to see your new home first? And maybe spend a few minutes with Willie Luther?"

Joleen's eyes widened. "Ain't we going to live with you?" Then fearfully, she rushed on. "Miss Mandy, you ain't sold me! —We ain't got to live to the O'Rourke's, do we?"

"No, I wouldn't sell you," she patted the girl's arm. "Now, I know Hassie has explained my story to you, as I asked. So, you and Willie will be living at my husband's home, Joleen. —And wait until you see what those men have done! They have been cleaning and painting and moving furniture into your quarters all week. And there is even room for a nursery…," Mandria paused. For now that she'd managed to bring the conversation to where she wanted it, she didn't know how to proceed. After all, Hassie had always been as sharp as a tack. "So, when will you need it, Joleen? —How far along are you?"

"Was four months last week," she smiled happily.

"Well, no one would guess," Mandria smiled back, before returning her eyes to the road. "Hassie, when will Joleen really start to show?"

"Way her built, she be popping-out any day now and likely, she carry it all to the front," she chuckled. "Going to look like this skinny gal done swallowed a big old watermelon!"

"And…when did you know you were pregnant, Joleen—the symptoms, I mean?"

"Well, first thing, my bosoms got sore; —and then, Miss Mandy, I got me some bosoms where I ain't never had much!" she stated. "But when Ah miss my curse three times running, Ah knew for sure. Was sick to the stomach for a spell, too. Glad that over now, Ah bet-ya!"

"Oh," Mandria nodded in puzzlement. "…Hassie, is it always like that; —the sickness too?"

"Not always," she answered sagely. "So how far along you be, Mandy-chile'?"

"I…I'm—why, Hassie!" Mandria fumbled for words and finding none had to laugh. "Well, coming up on three months, I think."

Joleen squealed in delight. "Oh, Miss Mandy! We going to have our babies together—in the same house—and they can play and grow up right next to each other!"

"Mister Tom know?" Hassie joined in with a happy smile. "You told him he going to be a new Daddy?"

"Not yet. I'd rather wait until I'm sure," Mandria nodded. "Mama said when she first married, some irregularities caused her to think she was pregnant when she wasn't. So, no, I don't want to disappoint Tom if that's what this is."

"Well, if it prove real, your wedding have to be told, in spite of your Daddy's objections," Hassie said while giving Mandria a measuring glance. "Course, way you built, might be a while 'fore you showing. Was for your Mama, too. Last couple of months only time folks could guess she carrying."

Mandria sighed. "If there is a child, wouldn't Father have to accept my husband? Surely, he wouldn't harm the father of his own grandchild."

"No telling what that man might do," Hassie said bluntly. "But you best be telling your Mama, girl—and soon. She stronger than you know and going to be your best defense against Mr. Sam."

"…Well, as I said, I'm not sure yet, so let's keep this quiet until I am," Mandria replied, wondering how she and Hassie could see her mother so differently. There could be no gentler, sweeter soul than

Evelyn Lucas...but strong? Able or even willing to stand up to her father? Mandria had yet to see it, sad to say...

Tom and Mandria watched from the vestibule while the Reverend George Cuthbertson gave final instructions to the wedding party. From the corner of her eye, Mandria had seen Tom smiling more than once, but catching him at it was another matter. When she did look his way, he only wore the expression most men did for weddings: one of quiet resignation. "What on earth is the matter with you?" she finally whispered. "You are up to something; I can feel it!"

"Well, I had hoped to surprise you," he whispered back, "but Allen got the day off too, and he's bringing your mother to this wedding."

"How nice. Mama has always liked Joleen," she replied while considering his answer. "...But that is hardly a reason for you to be grinning like a loon—and there! You're doing it again!"

"Yes, love, I suppose I am," he chuckled. "But damn it all, I'm just that happy. Mandria, I moved my things over to the house last night—as did Allen, I'm glad to say. He was quite impressed with your front parlor and the start you've made on the morning room. And when he learned I already had two servants? Well, he said once, he was meant to be lord of a manor and I guess he figures this is close enough. Anyway, he wanted to pay rent, and when I wouldn't hear of it, we agreed—with your approval—that he could buy the furniture for his room instead. Which he has already claimed, by the way. He is camping out in the rear, right bedroom, if that's all right with you."

"Well, of course it is. Really, that is wonderful news!" she reached for his hand, hoping her envy for them both didn't show.

But Tom knew her better. "No, lady, it won't be wonderful until you live there too," he nodded. "So, I've decided that Mamalyn should see the house today too. She knows I love you, Mandria, and I want to show her I have something of value to offer her daughter. Then, I might just—"

"Oh, but Tom!" Mandria's eyes widened beautifully. "Some of my clothes are—oh, no! I think I left a robe on the bed and she gave it to me last Christmas!"

"Don't worry. I put everything in your wardrobe; —even your hairbrush and perfume."

"What wardrobe?" she puzzled. "Tom, there isn't one in the whole house yet."

"Isn't there?" he teased. "You seemed fond of the one beneath the bed, as I recall; —the one with room enough to bounce a shoe off my head?"

"Oh," her laughter was soft and melodic. "Anyway, I'm very pleased. Mama will be more impressed with you than ever."

"I'm counting on that, pretty lady. ...Though one bed and one and a half furnished rooms isn't much to show."

"It will be enough," Mandria assured him. ...*Or it might be too much*, she thought as a tiny concern crossed her mind. But there wasn't time now to fret over it, because Allen had arrived with her mother, and the ceremony was starting...

# CHAPTER 38

Tom drove one of the buggies that pulled to the curb before his home and Old Jed, who'd been Willie's best man, drove the other. But no one moved from either until Tom had explained the unscheduled stop to Evelyn and they heard her say, with approval, "Oh, how wonderful! I knew the Badgetts, and always admired this place!"

Then, as they all began alighting, all smiling now, and heading in their own directions, Mandria launched into her explanation, because the more she considered it, the larger that tiny concern had grown. "Mama, Tom has asked me to advise him on decorating the house. So, come along, I'd like your opinion on what's been done so far." And taking her mother's hand, they started for the door. "Would you like to help me finish the project? We'd have the run of the place while Tom and Allen are at work—and plenty of help from Joleen and Willie Luther too. Oh, do say you will. It would be such fun for us!"

"…Joleen and Willie are to live here?" Evelyn asked as they entered. And wondering what his wife was about, Tom tethered the horse and with Allen close behind, hurried to catch up.

"So now Tom owns them both and we—that is, *he* doesn't feel it's anyone else's business, so please don't mention their whereabouts," Mandria was saying as the brothers entered the parlor. "Besides, as Uncle Ran told Tom, a married couple will look after things better—and I think so too. Don't you?"

"Yes, dear, I do," Evelyn answered as she looked over the room. "Mandy, this is lovely. And I would have guessed you had a hand in it. All your favorite colors are here. ...And your favorite paintings?" she turned questioning eyes on her daughter. "I'm really surprised you'd part with them."

"Yes, well, I did," Mandria gave Tom a look that said no matter how fast you talk, or how many subjects you introduce in the way of distraction, there were just some things a girl could not hide from her mother.

Evelyn easily followed that silent exchange and turned away to enjoy a smile. Those two were so in love and trying so hard not to be obvious about it, she just had to tease them a little more. "But Mandy, did Tom approve your color scheme? I seem to recall he has a definite fondness for green."

"Yes, and I'm planning—I mean, Tom has asked that the master bedroom be done in greens. But I'd really feel more...well, comfortable if you'd help me with that," she tried to say all expected of a single woman who would dare enter a forbidden chamber.

"And I'd feel better if you ladies would sit down," Allen grinned. "Then I could too."

"If you're tired of standing, Allen, for heaven's sake, sit!" Evelyn laughed. "Now, Mandy, I want to see the rest of the house and hear what you're planning."

"Mamalyn, we just moved in last night," Tom said. "There's not much upstairs yet, but a bed and a mountain of luggage, but please, look all you'd like."

And the ladies were off at once, chattering from room to room; arranging imaginary furniture; deciding on colors or ideas; and promptly changing their minds, which brought a smile to Tom's lips.

"What has you so amused?" Allen asked as Tom sat on the other end of the sofa.

"I'm wondering how my wife will explain the fibs she just told, once I've sprung the next surprise," Tom chuckled. "And I'm enjoying the sound of women in the house. ...Allen, do you remember the way Mama and Susan used to talk and laugh when they baked and cleaned on Saturdays? I always enjoyed hearing that. It was the time Mama seemed happiest."

"I remember the baking," Allen nodded. "The house smelled like fresh bread and cookies."

"And cinnamon buns," Tom added with a fond sigh for a past memory he wished he could taste again. But now the ladies were returning and now it was time to deal with the future.

Toward that end, he suggested they go down and join the wedding celebration, as it was from there he wished to proceed. On reaching the bottom of the basement stairs, they found Jed and Hassie ready to make a toast—and much to Jed's chagrin, the bottle sitting in plain view among plates of pastries and fruit, was from Sam's private stock of a most expensive cognac. He made a move to snatch it from the table, and received a swat from Hassie.

"Fool!" she admonished her brother. "You think Miss Evelyn don't know—or she cares? This here a special occasion, so get some more cups and we all have a drink for this sweet little couple. —Ain't that right, Miss Evelyn?"

"Yes, indeed!" Evelyn agreed. And after several toasts, all were soon gathered about the large kitchen table.

Then reaching into a pocket, Tom withdrew three folded papers. "Joleen and Willie Luther," he began, "I hope you'll be happy here and stay in my home for many years. But not because you must. So, my wedding gift is your freedom and here are your papers," he pushed two of the documents toward them.

Silence followed and Tom wondered at the different reactions around him. Allen seemed the most perplexed; Jed sat with lowered eyes; Joleen and Willie Luther looked repeatedly from each other to Hassie. And Hassie and Evelyn looked back at him in oddly conflicting ways. His mother-in-law's eyes were misty—which he'd expected from Hassie. Instead, Hassie's were skeptical. Only Mandria gave unquestioned approval, circling a hand through his arm.

"Can Ah see them papers?" Hassie finally asked. "Ah reads, Mr. Tom. Miss Evelyn teach me a long time back."

"Of course," he consented. "They're in order, Hassie. I can assure you of that."

The old woman scanned the documents for several minutes before flattening them on the table before her. "May be in order, but ain't fair to you or this couple. ...Mr. Tom, it not wise to give childrens so much candy all at once—and that's what you done here. Now, don't get me wrong. Ah admires your gesture and hopes for a day everbody be free. But Joleen and Willie got to earn this gift or it won't mean a son-na-ma-gum. They got to be indentured to you—like white folks was when they come here a hundred years ago. No sir, they can't just live free under your roof and eat your food for nothing."

"But I'd pay them a salary," Tom injected.

"Won't do," she argued. "Not 'til they has a right to take it. Don't you see, Mr. Tom? They still have to stay because they feel indebted for what you done. No, sir, if you wants them here because they wants it too, then they can't owe you nothing. That's only way this going to work."

"Well...what do you suggest?" Tom asked.

"Like I said, indenture them. Set your salary and let them work off the money you paid for them. Then these papers going to mean something. Then they can stay because they choose to. Then they can take their pay, just like white folks do, and it be honest and right for everbody."

Tom nodded. "Hassie, I said to Mandria once, that you must be a wise lady—and you truly are. So we'll handle this as you've suggested."

"Oh, Willie!" Joleen squealed, hugging her new husband. "We going to be free blacks! Free—and then that witch can't never bother us again!"

"Tom," Evelyn reached to pat his hand, "thank you for letting me be here today. Your home will surely be a happy one."

"And complete very soon now," he caught her hand, turned it palm up and placed the third document there. "Mamalyn, there are reasons you didn't know about this and I'll do my damnedest to explain them."

All watched as Evelyn unfolded the page and gasped. "Mandy!" she exclaimed, hugging her daughter. "Oh, how wonderful! I am so happy about this!"

"…But why?" Mandria said in bewilderment. "What is that paper?"

"Only your marriage certificate—that's all!" Evelyn said tearfully. "Sweetheart, why did you keep this from me? Surely you know I approve of Tom."

Then Mandria was crying too and hugging her mother back. "Oh, Mama, I am glad you know—truly, I am." And turning to Tom, he received a swat on the shoulder. "But you, Mr. Scott! No wonder you've been grinning all day! You are just full of yourself, aren't you?" This, of course, was followed by a hug for him too.

"Well, Jed," Allen grinned, "I think it's time for some new toasts. We seem to have two brides and two grooms among us!"

"And lots to talk about, appears to me," Hassie sent Mandria one of those looks. "Like the little discussion we had on the way to town this morning?"

"Oh, no, Hassie—not yet!" Mandria hastened to quiet her. But seeing that Tom was curious and knowing her sudden blush required explanation, she called upon feminine logic and stared back at him accusingly. "After what this man put me through today, I owe him a surprise—and he will not hear of it until I'm certain of each little detail."

"So," Jed raised his glass. "To both brides and both grooms; long lives and early blooms!" And when Joleen rubbed her already budding belly, all enjoyed a laugh. Jed then brought out a mouth organ and played a tune which soon had the wedding couple dancing about the red tiled floor while the rest clapped in accompaniment.

But Tom had not forgotten his promise of an explanation, though he did regret having to return to the serious amid so much gaiety. "… Mamalyn," he began, "Lord knows, I'm tired of asking this, but only a few people know about our marriage and it has to remain that way for a while yet."

"Then it must be because of Sam," she said without hesitation, which drew a look of wonderment from Mandria.

"Well, I did have a run-in with him," Tom confessed.

490

"If you are talking about the dust-up over Kathleen Morgan, I know about it, Tom. Just yesterday, I saw the paper saying you had paid off her debts. And though I don't understand what prompted Sam to release her—or how you became involved—I'm glad you helped the poor woman!" Evelyn said surprising everyone now, but Jed and Hassie. They had been her informants for years. "But you are right to be cautious," she continued. "Sam has admitted to me that he dislikes you and no matter what he says to the contrary, don't trust him. —No, don't ever trust Sam Lucas."

"Believe me, I don't," Tom nodded and because Mandria still looked at her mother in something akin to shock, he covered her hand with his own, before relating the terms Sam set for their agreement. "So if he learns that I double-crossed him—and married his daughter, too—Kathy becomes fair-game again, and it wouldn't be that difficult to learn where she's hiding. Retaliation against her would be cruel and done for spite, because that's just how he operates. Now, here's the thing—and I don't mean to make light of what Kathy would suffer—but hers is not the only life he has been trying to manipulate. And for whatever reason, I seem to be the linchpin. ...Mamalyn, that's not a comfortable feeling. One by one, he has involved himself with everyone I know in Savannah—and has made some pretty concerted efforts to destroy friendships. So if he knew about us, what in heaven's name would he try against our marriage?"

"Nothing you've said surprises me, Tom," she nodded, "And until you discover his game, your secret is safe with me. But just so I'm fully informed, who does know about the two of you?"

"Only Mike and Iano Rizza, at first." And this was smiled at Mandria, as a teasing reminder that even she hadn't known. "But the list seems to keep growing," he indicated everyone there.

"Done told the rest of my crew, too," Hassie said. "And done heard something back. More whispering going on to the O'Rourke's than that 'bout Joleen and Willie Luther."

"You ain't going to talk about that, Hassie?" Joleen's eyes went round. "Talk about something nice. —It's my wedding day!" And turning, she buried her face on Willie's shoulder.

"Yes, it is," Tom rose, holding Mandria's hand. "And I think the rest of us should return to the parlor so these newly-weds can celebrate properly."

"Thank you, Mr. Tom," Willie Luther said as they filed up the stairway. "Hopes to make you proud of me and mine."

"You're more than welcome," Tom called back, but anxious to know what Hassie had learned, he hurried to join the others…

"Them poor childrens," she muttered, perching on a side chair next to Jed. "They done suffered things decent folks don't do to their dogs. Now, don't go asking me what, 'cause it ain't fitting and could get people harmed—'specially them two downstairs."

"Then what can you tell us?" Tom asked.

"Couple of things: Jenny say the house being watched; say they seen this man hanging about the square; seen him follow after Miss Nico too. And Miss Nico been romancing young Mr. Brown in the stable 'til a few weeks ago. Then he stop coming at night and come one morning asking her to marry with him, but she put him off. Other thing is she had two house visits from Mr. Sam. First time, after he leave, she meet him in the alley wearing a hat full of veils and they ride off in a buggy. Second time he come, she wasn't home and he acts real upset about something."

"Well, what on earth could that have been about?" Evelyn asked, not liking the answer experience had taught her to expect from her husband. …*But not Nicole—not Ransom's wife and daughter too!* she lamented. "It…it just sounds very strange," she uttered, with a nod of denial.

"It be strange, Miss Evelyn," Hassie insisted, revealing as much as she dared. Sad to say, coloreds had been hung for speaking truth about white folk's depravities. "Ah knows things and Ah telling you all, that girl ain't up to no good. Way Ah sees it, she and Mr. Sam two of a kind—and that can't mean nothing but misery."

Having had nearly the identical thought, Tom turned to Mandria. "Aside from Joleen's pregnancy, what made you determined to see her marry? The day we rode home from Marsh Haven, it seemed to me, that you and Nico may have had words about it."

"We did," Mandria shrugged. "…I guess I just didn't appreciate her remarks."

"Which were?" Tom urged, reading her reluctance correctly.

"Well, she made some crude reference to Uncle Ran losing a stud-fee for Willie Luther to service Joleen—and that was after she'd vividly described hiding in the stable to watch them."

"Oh!" Evelyn fanned her cheeks, as Tom and Allen exchanged a glance. "Oh, how could she! —And then dare to tell it? The girl needs a good, hard paddling!"

"Ah's telling you, Miss Nico got evil in her—real bad evil," Hassie repeated her warning a second time.

"Well, Bernie Brown isn't the only one she met in that stable. She met me there too," Allen spoke up. "And, that time, she had Willie stationed at the door as a look-out—"

"Now don't misunderstand," Tom said to the wide-eyed ladies. "Nothing improper happened. Allen was only making a point—in his own tactless way," he finished with a look at his brother.

"Tactless or not," Allen countered, "there is no use denying facts if we're ever to solve this puzzle. And the part I don't understand, is why Nico is romancing anyone else when it's you she wants, Tom. I heard her say it—and Willie Luther probably did too."

With that, all but Hassie's eyes turned to Tom. "Willie heard," she said simply. And now, all but a pair of tilted green eyes swung to Hassie.

But it was Mandria who had more to say, while gazing at Tom with suspicion. "Now that I think about it, Nico seemed awfully anxious to name reasons why it would never work between us; —and how certain she was of what it would take to hold your attention. She asked questions too; —things that were none of her damned business!"

"Dear, your angst with Nico is understandable, but you can stop looking at your husband that way," Evelyn laughed—and Tom could

493

have hugged her. "He is not responsible for anything Nico says and certainly not for her deplorable behavior."

"You're right, of course," Mandria sighed, wondering at how threatened she'd felt.

But Hassie didn't wonder. Emotional upheaval was one of the clearer signs at this stage of a pregnancy.

"So why are we even discussing Nico?" Mandria went on. "It's Father who stands in our way, now isn't it?"

"And yet, there is no separating that pair from our problems," Tom said, noting Hassie's nod of approval and deciding that it might be wise to watch her reactions more closely. "I'm afraid Allen and I have reason to believe Sam is encouraging Nico's attitude; that through her, he means to accomplish his ends."

"Well, at least that would explain their odd association," Evelyn said. Anything was more acceptable than her first notion. But the eyes Hassie cut toward Evelyn then said, *Quit grasping at smoke!*

"Tom, please," Mandria rose and began to pace. "Why do you believe this?"

"Because they have both said things—used identical words, in fact. And because Hassie has just confirmed at least one meeting between them."

"But what was it they said?" she persisted, clearly growing upset again.

"Well...nothing flattering to you."

"I'll say!" added Allen. "Nico keeps suggesting herself as your replacement, Mandy—and Sam said after a day under *your proper thumb*, Tom should take Nico and—"

"Allen?" Tom interrupted. "That's enough, don't you think?"

"What you're saying then," Mandria turned away, "is that my own father...; that he will never accept my husband or my..." And she burst into tears.

As one, Tom and Evelyn rose and went to her. "Oh, Mandy," Evelyn held her daughter close, "it doesn't matter what Sam will or won't accept. If we present a united front, neither he nor Nico will succeed. And why you'd care what he thinks, I don't know. Look at the number of times he tried forcing you into loveless marriages. Dear, go to the husband you do love. He is standing right behind you and I believe he wants a turn at holding you—in spite of your crazy family."

"Oh," Mandria sighed, burying herself in Tom's welcoming embrace. "Mama is right. I don't why I'm behaving this way." And over her head, Tom looked gratefully at Evelyn. She was truly becoming very special to him.

"Well, welcome to this crazy family, Tom," she smiled. "—My side of it anyway."

"Thank you, Mamalyn," he chuckled. "As Mandria tells it, you stalked me for her and she only wiggled the bait. But in truth, I married her only because you were taken."

"Oh, for heaven sake," Evelyn laughed too and looking at her lapel watch, she turned to the others. "Shall we go, Jed and Hassie? It's nearly seven o'clock—"

"Is it that late?" Allen jumped to his feet. "I'm supposed to pick Lucy up at seven! —I'm taking the buggy, Tom. Bye, now; it sure was interesting!" And he was gone.

"It good Ah stay the night in town, Miss Evelyn," Hassie said as Mandria showed them out. "Come morning, Ah just see what else being said round the square."

"And Ah might just have me another talk with that Jenny," Jed nodded with a wide smile.

"That's fine," Evelyn paused on the porch, allowing the pair to start for the Lucas carriage. "Now, Mandy, don't be too late," she kissed her cheek. "…And may I assume you'll be more comfortable in that Master bedroom than you led me to believe?"

"Yes, Mama," she laughed. "It was just a little fib—but I really do want you to help me decorate the house. You will, won't you?"

"Dear, I haven't stopped thinking about it!" Evelyn waved as she went down the steps. "Remember: not too late. We don't want to rouse your father's curiosity."

"I'll remember," she watched them pull away with a final wave. Then going in, she closed the door and turned to find Tom standing by the stairway with a plate of assorted tidbits from the party and a bottle of white wine tucked beneath his arm.

"Upstairs, lady," he said, pinching off a hunk of cheese.

"Yes, sir," she smiled, demanding half of his bite. "Tom, wasn't Mama wonderful? She was so happy for us. I only wish…" she paused, nodding wistfully.

"That your father would accept us that way?" he put an arm about her as they went. "I wish so too. But for me, it's enough that your mother is supportive—and love, it may have to be enough for you too."

"I know—really, I do," she said as they rounded the landing. "But how is it, Mr. Scott, that you always know what I'm thinking?" she tried for a better mood.

"Because I'm one of *them*; and Lucy said *them* have powers for healing and reading minds," he teased.

"Well, I have powers too," she declared, closing their bedroom door behind her. "Want to see what I can do?"

Tom adored her mischievous expression and putting aside the plate and bottle, he faced her. "Yes—oh-hell-yes! I'm always ready to see-what-you-can-do."

"Then watch my hands," she began in a slow droning voice. "Never let them out of your sight," she started toward him slowly. "The hands, Tom," she pressed her body to his. "You must keep your eyes on my hands," she rubbed against him seductively. "They have yet to touch you, but the power still exists," she rose along him on tip-toes and whispered against his mouth. "Rise! —Rise, oh, sleeping monster!" And she grabbed for the proof his trousers held so snugly. "See?" she laughed. "I told you I had powers."

"So you did," he gave her a quick kiss. "But I demand satisfaction," he turned her about to unfasten her dress. "A rematch: your powers against mine."

"And is that to be the dueling ground?" she pointed toward the bed.

"'Tis the usual one," he nodded, as he began undressing too.

"And will you name a Second?" she asked, leaving her clothes where they fell.

"Hell no! I believe I can handle this alone," he said as his clothes went the same route.

"But I want seconds, sir," she faced him, arms akimbo. "And thirds and fourths—"

"Then get to that bed, lady!" he whacked her bottom playfully. "Get; get; get!" he shooed her.

And she went, squealing happily; diving into the covers; burying her face in the pillows when he gave chase.

But instead of pouncing, as she expected, Tom knelt over her, caressing the nape of her neck. "I love you, Mandria," he said, tracing lips and tongue over her proud shoulders. "I need you with me all the time; every day and every night."

"I know. That's my dream too," she agreed. "And we have Mama on our side now too, so it's getting closer, isn't it?"

"Yes, love," he moved down her spine. "My love," he added, teasing at her hips and buttocks in the same tantalizing way. "God help me, I can't get enough of you!" he laughed, gently biting the back of her thigh. And when she yelped and wanted to squirm away, he held her still, proceeding as before, down the slender length of one leg and back up the other. Reaching her hip again, he rested his chin there and paused, trying to formulate a question he'd wanted to ask forever. "...Mandria," he began hesitantly, "how do you feel about...uh, oral stimulation?"

"I think it felt good—all shivery and tingling," she sighed. "I had no idea the back of my legs were so sensitive."

"No, lady," he chuckled. "I meant more than that."

She was silent for an eternal second, before he felt her tense. "Oh," she uttered. "...I don't know. ...Would you like it?"

"Very much—but only with you," he answered. "And only if you enjoyed it too."

"Then you've never...; I mean, with other women...; you haven't?"

"No," he answered the question she couldn't phrase. "Mandria, I haven't needed that intimacy with another woman."

"But you've admitted knowing all kinds. Whores do it, —isn't that fairly common?"

"I didn't say I hadn't experienced it. I said I haven't done it myself. And that is because I've never loved a woman the way I love you. I want you, wife, and I can't bear the thought that any part of you is beyond my reach," he pressed a kiss to her hip. "Lady...please?"

The way Tom worded his request—not to mention that final plea—had Mandria remembering something he'd said the night they christened their bed: *Nothing—no act—is immoral between husband and wife, as long as it pleases them both and deepens their closeness.* So, turning over to face him, she smiled timidly. "It seems, husband, I can't deny you much either," she ran a hand over his head of dark hair. "And I want our intimacies to be special for you. I'll always want that."

"Mandria," he lowered his cheek to her tan-haired mount. And after yet another pause, he laughed. "Well, damn! Now that I can, I feel as awkward as a stripling lad."

"Then you know how I felt our first time," she offered, nervously. "And that turned out all right, didn't it?"

"Oh-hell-yes!" he nodded, loving the feel of her against his face. "But as we're both new at this, it may take some practice."

"Well," she tried to think of something helpful to say, "...that's what we did with the other and I think we do that wonderfully."

"And it can't be so different," he nuzzled his mouth a bit lower. "What you enjoy from my hands—the sensitive spots..." he allowed time to seek them out. "Surely, they would be the same," he murmured, feeling the warmth of passion envelope his own body.

"That's...reasonable," a tremble inserted itself between her words.

"Yes," he smiled, tasting and testing each treasured piece of flesh... until she trembled again. Then he knew why. Then he knew how. Then he felt his confidence return, as he returned to repeat his loving assault again and again on the very pulse of her female being. ... And then, he had only to control his own passion, for it raged in his loins like molten lava. But when her hips started an involuntary rise to greet his mouth and he felt a matching rise within himself, Tom literally scrambled up Mandria's body to mount her. And holding her still beneath his weight—wanting to stay the eminent eruption—he rained kisses on her face and mouth, hoping to vent the deep internal pressures in them both...

Mandria was beyond being helpful. She had learned new words to the love song he'd etched on her soul: *Tom*, went the lyrics as she encouraged his reason for ensheathement; *Tom*, went the verse as arms and thighs locked him to her; *Tom*, soared the melody as she arched, wanting to touch all of him with all of her; *Tom*, her eyes pled for accompaniment. "Oh, Tom—yes!" sighed her lips. And relenting, he joined in, enjoying her song all the more when played in duet...

Later, they sat cross-legged on the bed with the food plate and wine bottle between them. "I enjoyed that," Tom smiled, feeding her a piece of sticky-bun. "Thank you, pretty lady."

"Ha!" she exclaimed, smiling back. "So you'd never done that before. Well, Mr. Scott, I don't believe you. So what do you say to that?"

"I say I've never loved you so much. —But just why don't you believe me?"

"Because you did it too damn well," she chose a piece of cheese and popped it in her mouth. "And there is likely a string of women, from here to Athens, saying the same."

"I can assure you there isn't!" he feigned indignity. "Besides, I wasn't all that pleased with my part in this."

"...Why on earth not?" she asked, trying to fathom a reason and couldn't.

"I don't know," he shrugged. "I just feel that we haven't explored it enough; that there are feelings in you I've yet to tap."

"You can't be serious," she giggled, drinking a sip of wine from the bottle. "Tom, how could you doubt the things you make me feel? —Must I wail and moan at the top of my lungs to prove my pleasure?"

"Dear God, please don't!" he nodded emphatically. "I once knew a girl who did that. She sounded as if she were in mortal agony—and I'll tell you, it wilted all desire to nothing. Then she did yell; —really yelled at me."

"Is that one of your stripling-lad stories?" she asked, handing him the wine.

"I'm afraid so," he took a drink too.

"Then, let me assure you, you have learned how to please women quite well since."

"What I learned, Mrs. Scott, was to be selective. And from there, I learned the kind of woman—not women—I needed in my life permanently."

"Me," she said smugly and leaned toward him for a kiss.

"You," he reciprocated and finished the last bite on the plate.

"In spite of what Nico wants," she continued with a smile that didn't reach her eyes.

"You're jealous of her?" Tom questioned. "Please, lady, don't be."

"No—truly I'm not. You've never given me reason to be," she nodded. "It's just that she is beautiful—you've even said you think so. But Tom, she has always had every damn thing she wanted—including more beaus than you can shake a stick at. And knowing she wants you too is not a comforting thought."

"Sweetheart," he laughed, "in the first place, most of Nico's beaus are those stripling lads we talked about. All but Mike—and damn, I wish he could see her from my point of view, which isn't at all flattering. In the second place, I'm very much involved with you and will be for the rest of my life—especially after tonight. Which means, in the third place, pretty lady, I do mean for us to repeat that—and often."

"Oh, well," she sighed, "I suppose I could suffer through it—and often."

"With no loud moans and wails?" he teased.

"With *repetition and determination* at my side—and all over me—who knows to what heights I might soar?" she said on a dramatic sigh.

"Sassy mouth," he laughed, drawing her close for a hug.

"Smarty pants," she retorted, "—And what you carry in them is too," she hugged him back, wondering again if the time would ever come when she didn't have to leave Tom and return to her father's house. And that made her wonder what it was Sam Lucas and Nicole O'Rourke hoped to accomplish together. Surely, with these strong arms about her and the help of her mother and friends, they wouldn't succeed. Surely, they wouldn't…

# CHAPTER 39

Friday, on St. Julian Street, Nicole paced about the sitting room in agitation. "I'm telling you, I've had all the disappointment I'm going to take, Sam! First, Mandy sends Joleen away; then Father sells Willie Luther; *dares* to lock me in for the night; —and now, my ball gown doesn't fit! I cannot imagine a worse week than this has been. I mean, who did the woman think she was making that gown for? It was long enough to fit my new driver and big enough inside for three of me!"

"Heaven forbid," he commented, dutifully stirring their second round of drinks. She had done nothing for days now, but repeat a growing list of complaints. "...So, how is your new driver working out?" he asked, hoping for a change of subject.

"He drives, Sam. That's all I can say for the stupid oaf!"

"But if you miss your entertainment so much, couldn't you train him too; —as you did Willie Luther?"

"And just who would I train him with? He and rest of our servants are too old. —And I've no wish to see the mating of wrinkled walruses! Sam, Joleen and Willie were young and their bodies moved together with a supple beauty. —Oh, damn Mandria anyway! She has done nothing for months but mess up my life!"

"Because of Tom," Sam encouraged both the thought in her mind and the drink to her lips.

"Yes, it does all seem to revolve around him, doesn't it?" she added one more complaint. "And Sam, I don't see where we're making any progress there at all. I get so exasperated with that man, I sometimes want to shoot him dead!"

"Not to rub salt in a wound, little Nico, but you slowed our progress by dallying with your Captain that weekend at Tybee instead of driving a wedge between the Scott brothers—as you were instructed to do," he lied, because he could not express resentment of her admitted fondness for the Irishman's love-making. "But don't be disheartened," he drew down the shoulder strap of her new and now not-so-neglected-negligee. "In fact, I find what you've just said most interesting. Tell me: when I deliver Tom Scott to your bed, would it really matter what condition he's in?"

Nicole paused to finish her drink and smiled. "Well, I'd want him alive, Sam, and able to make love to me."

"Of course," he lightly stroked the breast he'd bared. "And he will be more than willing. That, I can guarantee."

"He'd better be," she breathed. And as his drug, his touch and visions of his promises infected her mind, she handed Sam her glass and wiggled free of her gown,

"…Anxious, my dear?" he laughed, following her toward the bed alcove.

"Yes, but mostly short of time," she stretched out before him, presenting her tempting, lithe body. "It is Friday, Sam, and I should bathe before meeting Mike. I don't believe he'd appreciate the scent of another man on my skin—nor *mixing with his juices,* as you once put it so deliciously."

Sam had started undressing, but curiosity gave him pause. "Which begs a question: How did your Captain take finding you aren't a virgin?"

"Very well, actually, because I told him—in tears, of course—that I had fallen from a horse and ruptured my poor, little, virgin pussy," she said with a certain pride.

"The idiot," Sam nodded in begrudging admiration. "…Nico, I could almost feel sorry for him."

"Wouldn't you rather feel me instead?" she spread her thighs and patted the patch of white-blonde hair between. "Come, Sam. Give me a good ride—something to last through the weekend?"

"Impossible, little Nico—not as much as you like it," he replied, mounting her. "And by the way, if Herb's ineptness leaves you wanting, I'll be close by. I don't mind mixing juices with any man. Or pleasing his woman when he can't."

"Dear Uncle Sam," Nicole raised her hips to meet that thrusting descent she so craved. "You are just so wonderfully unselfish..."

All week, Mike had tried to reason with himself; to accept Nicole's enthusiasm for their new relationship; to believe he was the luckiest bastard alive to have such a beautiful, passionate woman waiting for him in Savannah. She was his lady—brought to womanhood by him— and just the memory of her sweet awakening was enough reason to avoid the whores of Augusta. Then he had to laugh, admitting it was Wednesday before he was able to look at other women anyway—and even then he had no urge to bed one. He was that much in love, he kept thinking. Yes, he was that ready to marry and settle down. And by Friday, he was ready to do something about it too...

After an enjoyable dinner with Ransom, Mike and Nicole returned to his cabin, where he fixed them an Irish Cream as he watched her undress. "Nico, I want to discuss a really important matter with you," he began as she started toward him.

"Oh? Are you going to apologize for not being here last Sunday night?" she sipped her drink. "Really, Mike, when you didn't call, you had to know I'd come to see why. And when you weren't here either, it kept me angry with you for most of the week."

"It was business, Nico," he lied, still unable to explain his behavior, even to himself. "Anyway, it's not likely to happen again; —especially after we've had this talk."

"Can't it wait?" she put her glass aside to unbutton his shirt. "Conversation is not what I had in mind for us."

"That is what I want to talk about:—us."

"So, we'll do that, but first…" she unfastened his trousers and slid her hands deep within. "First, you must give me what I've done without for five…lonely…days."

"Nico," he tried to dissuade her. "…Please, this is important."

"No, Captain, nothing is more important to me than having you. —Now!" she insisted. And capturing his mouth, her kiss and her body demanded appeasement…

So it went for the rest of the evening and again from Saturday morning until noon—and still, Mike had not asked the question he wanted to so desperately. … *Why?* he kept asking himself. And the only answer he could surmise and accept was this: Marriage was a sacred, lifetime commitment. Therefore, it was vital that Nicole's decision be one of serious consideration and not made in a frenzied moment of passion. *Patience,* he repeated again and again—that's all he needed. And the right time and place…

That evening at dusk, Mike called for Nicole and they joined their friends in a carriage, ready to enjoy their weekly get-together. Mike noted her serene smile and quiet attitude as she rode close beside him and hoped the sterling effort he'd put into their morning was the reason…

It wasn't. Nicole had spent the afternoon with Sam. And to ensure that his love-making would not be unfavorably compared to the Captain's, he added just a few grains of Belladonna to her usual mixture. He would then have the new wine and Mike only the dregs. For soon, Nicole's languid mood would be replaced with nausea…

All were aware of her passive manner as they gathered about a table at The Market. Mike kept smiling—yes, if her present mood continued, he'd be able to make his proposal this very night! Lucy worried. Nicole had barely picked at her food, and there was a flu thing going around, she said. Allen could have cared less. To his mind, no one deserved a good ailment more than Nicole. Tom was just plain uncomfortable. It was his leg Nicole kept nudging beneath the table, as she had on the Irish Mist. Mandria wasn't cognizant of this, but in spite of Nicole's tame mouth, she'd seen her play this game before, placing herself between two handsome men and taking every opportunity to touch them both: a pat to the hand; a squeeze to the arm; a touch on the cheek—touch, touch, touch! So, pulling her lacy shawl close, Mandria asked Tom to swap chairs, saying a draft had chilled her shoulders. The look she received from Nicole was chilling, indeed, but the warmth and gratitude in Tom's eyes equaled it rather nicely. It was then, Mandria decided, when her marriage was told, she would save the pleasure of informing Nicole for herself. Meanwhile, the smile she sent Miss O'Rourke was as benevolent as she cared to make it...

At that very moment, Nicole felt the first flutter of pain in her stomach, for which she readily blamed Mandria. *How dare she interfere with the duel flirtation I had going with Tom and Mike?* she fumed. And her condition worsened as she pouted her way through dessert. Finally then, fearing she might truly be catching something, she asked Mike to take her home, which he did, with great disappointment. It seemed he must remain patient a while longer...

Come morning, however, Nicole felt better and celebrated the quick recovery by staying home from Mass to pamper herself on tea and toast before a warm fire. And it wasn't ten minutes after her father's departure for church that Mike arrived.

"I just saw Ransom," he began, sitting beside her. "He said you were better, but I had to come see for myself."

"And miss hearing Mass?" she teased, running fingers up his thigh. "Shame on you, Captain."

"Nico, please don't start," he rose abruptly, only to sit right back down. And holding both of her hands in his, he continued. "For two days now, I've been trying to ask you to marry me. Nico, we can not keep on this way. We have been to bed more times in the last three weekends than most married couples could squeeze into three months—and I mean if they were together day and night! I'm afraid I'll get you pregnant at the rate we're going and I don't want anyone to think you had to marry me!" he paused for a breath. "… So will you?"

Nicole opened her mouth to speak, but couldn't. Mike had mentioned marriage often and she had assumed it was done in the heat of the moment. Yet, he looked quite serious and she wondered just how to answer him. Bernie's proposal had been an irritation she had remedied, but Mike's presented a real problem. If she refused him, it would surely end their relationship, thereby severing her closest tie to Tom. Besides, she wasn't ready to give Mike up any more than Bernie—and certainly, not Sam.

"Captain," she groped for words, "you do me a great honor. … But marriage is a most serious step."

"I know that; —I'm so glad you realize it too," he raised her fingers to his lips. "And damn, but I didn't mean to blurt out my proposal so unromantically! Please, all I want from you now is consideration. Take all the time you need to think it over; to consider the life I could offer you. Nico, you must know how much I love you—and you'd never lack my attention or the price of anything that pleases you. But…" he hesitated, "just as you said, I would be gone five lonely days each week, and we'd have to be content with making it up on weekends."

"As we do now," she observed.

"Oh-hell-yes—more than we do now! Then I'd have a right to bed you." And he laughed, happy to finally discover a reason for something that had plagued him. Then as any good Catholic, he had to confess; to cleanse his soul. "…Nico, I wasn't away on business last Sunday night. I was in the square on Bay Street and I watched you come and go. I wanted to meet you—to make love to you—and now I know why I couldn't. I was feeling guilty for taking advantage of your trust—of your truly beautiful need to be with me in spite of the possible consequences for yourself. I just couldn't face you. And by damn, if anyone had dared to say Michael Leonard Herb would ever hide from a beautiful woman, I'd have been the first to laugh!"

"And I'd have been she second," she nodded in wonder. "...But you don't expect my answer right away? You'll give me time—and meanwhile, we can still see each other as often as possible?"

"Yes, little Nico—yes!" he hugged her close. "I won't be hiding now that our feelings are in the open."

"Well, you can just prove that by taking me to your cabin right away," she toyed playfully with his trouser buttons, "where you had best take advantage of my trust and anything else you happen upon. In fact, you owe me the rest of your day—and maybe, right up until midnight..."

It was well past midnight when Tom heard a rap at his door. Allen had long since retired to the make-do pallet in his room; and Mandria knew better than to come over so late. ...Besides, he remembered, reaching for the knob, she had her own key.

"Thomas!" Mike grinned as the door opened. "I need to talk—come with me, will you? It...it's personal and I wouldn't want this overheard."

"Well, good evening to you too, Captain Herb," Tom chuckled, pulling him inside to close the door. "Now, Allen has been asleep upstairs for some time and the newly-weds downstairs don't know other people exist in the world. So if you want to talk, I have a perfectly beautiful parlor, a bottle and all the privacy you could ask. —Shall we?" he lifted an arm in that direction.

"I guess you're wondering what could be so important at this hour," the Captain said as soon as the doors to the parlor closed.

"No, I was thinking it's about time you came to see my home. Mandria is doing a fine job here, don't you think?"

"What? —Oh, yeah, Tom," he nodded, but noticed little as he began to pace. "Listen, I have this...this problem and it's going to drive me mad!"

"I see," Tom said, not seeing at all. "...Well, are you going to tell me what it is before or after you've walked a path in my carpet?"

"Yeah, but most men would welcome my situation, so maybe the problem lies in me. It could be, Tom, don't you see that?"

"Not exactly," Tom answered truthfully.

"It could be my health. —Maybe I should see a damn doctor!"

"Aren't you feeling well?" Tom grew even more puzzled.

"Oh-hell-yes—as long as I'm in Augusta! But you're a married man. Has anything like this ever happened to you?"

"Damn it, Mike," Tom laughed. "Anything like what?"

Mike stopped and stood staring from a window as he answered. "It's…Nico and me, and I want to know if it's normal… Well, day and night; night and day; every weekend—all weekend? And right now, I am thoroughly disgusted with myself again!"

Tom took in a deep breath and went to fix them a drink. He needed one now as badly as Mike. "…I don't think you're talking about the number of events on her social calendar, are you?" he ventured, handing the Captain a glass.

"Hell, I wish I was! At the moment, I'd welcome anything that didn't land us in bed every damn hour on the hour!"

"Oh," Tom nodded, lowering himself on the sofa.

"Well?" Mike came to join him. "Have you?"

"Have I what?" Tom shrugged. "I still don't know what you're asking."

"Hell, there is just no easy way of putting this," Mike leaned back, watching the toes of his boots this time. "…Tom, has any woman—and Mandy, in particular—I mean, have you ever been at a point where… Well, damn it, where you were just fucked out?"

Tom rose to retrieve the bottle and refill their glasses. He had a feeling it should remain within easy reach. "Why Mandria in particular?" he asked curiously.

"Because you love her—as I love Nico. And because today, Sunday, October 21st, I asked her to marry me."

The smile that had been on Tom's lips slid into his glass as he gulped down a swallow. "…What did she say?" he managed to keep the dread from his tone.

"That she'd consider it…and that's good with me, Tom, because I want her to be absolutely sure. But after tonight—hell, I wouldn't blame her for refusing me," he paused. "…I mean, she was there and all ready, but damn it, I—I couldn't! Do you believe that? I just could not do it another time!"

Tom nodded, choosing his words by careful phrases. "Well, it happens, …once in a while, …to every man, …I'm sure."

"But two weekends in a row? Last Sunday night, I hid from her rather than admit what is happening to me. That took real guts, huh?" he asked, finishing off his drink and pouring another. "And I thought I knew the reason, until it happened again tonight—which was after we'd made a half-way commitment to each other. So, now I have to admit the truth. Tom, there is something wrong with me. I couldn't satisfy Nico—and damn, but she was upset!"

"Which didn't help your problem in the least, did it?"

"Well…no, but she has a right to expect better from the man who asked to marry her."

Tom took another deep breath. "Does she, Mike? Day and night; hour on the hour; every weekend; all weekend? No man could keep that pace and not pay a toll."

"Then it has happened to you and Mandy? You never did answer that."

"Captain…how do I word this? My wife is a very passionate creature and has never failed to arouse me. But her needs aren't as—as overwhelming as those you've described."

"Just because it's still so new to her, Tom—and you have to remember how that was. Hell, I tried to screw anything female and standing on two legs! She'll settle down; we all do. Now, if I can only keep her until that happens—but I'm off to a God-awful start!"

"…And what if she doesn't settle down? Mike, for the sake of argument, just suppose she doesn't? Would you really marry a woman with a problem of that sort? If so, you are in for more misery than you're feeling now."

"Such as?" Mike poured yet another drink.

"Well, if she wants more than one normal, healthy man can give…?" he left the question dangling. Then deciding the Captain needed to see at least a glimpse of truth, he continued. "And Mike, Nicole O'Rourke is up to something right now."

Mike looked away and Tom saw his knuckles whiten as his grasp tightened on his glass. "All right, what bit of gossip have I missed?"

"It isn't gossip. Now for starters, she has been out with Bernie Brown again. Allen has seen them together a couple of times. And for a while there, she was meeting him in her stable late at night."

"So? She came to me as a virgin. What does that prove?"

"Nothing, but there is more, if you want to hear it."

"By all means, Tom," he retorted. "Don't let me stop you."

"…Captain, if you are angry, I'm sorry. But were you teetering on the edge of a cliff, I'd try to pull you back—and I don't see this any differently. I've only kept quiet this long because I know you love the girl. Now there is more to tell and what you do with the information— how serious you consider this—is up to you. At least you won't be blind to it. And remember, Mike, you came to my house; asking my advice—and you're drinking my damned whiskey too. So for the sake of a friendship I really value, would you kindly just hear me out?"

"…Those poor little school kids," the Captain nodded, accepting the sit-down as gracefully as he could. Besides, he valued their friendship too. "Get on with it, will you?" he poured both of them a drink now.

"Well, she asked me to meet her alone—and if that were your only worry, I'd never have brought this up. But after the dinner engagement with Allen, she stopped me in the square and tried to convince me she had slept with him. Of course it was a lie, but she does so damned many things like that—suggestive little things—and Mike, that isn't even the dangerous part. You see, I'm not certain how much of her behavior is hers and how much is dictated, because lately, Sam Lucas has become her mentor."

"God damn," the Captain uttered, sinking to the back of the sofa. "And?"

"And I'm still gathering information on that. She has met with him once, for certain—the morning after Allen's birthday dinner, according to what Hassie learned. But they've talked more, because just before that dinner, she said she knew I kept a mistress—and who but Sam believes I do? Mike, it was Sam who arranged the evening between Nico and Allen—and saw to it both had way too much to drink—hoping, I believe, that a seduction would take place."

"But why, for God's sake?"

"As I told my brother, can you think of a better way of severing each and every one of our friendships?"

"That God damned bastard!" Mike came forward again. "Using an innocent, gullible girl to get at us! And what about Brown—how does he fit into this?"

"Frankly, I don't see that he does," Tom answered.

"Then, you're suggesting she sees him because she wants to—and against her father's orders?"

"Captain, I am not suggesting anything—nor would I presume to guess Nico's motives. I am only telling you the facts—and it is a fact she is seeing Brown and that she's conferring with Sam Lucas."

"Well, I'll find out why. —By damn, I'll just ask Nico what this is all about!"

"In turn, she will tell Sam we are aware of the alliance," Tom braced for Mike's next reaction. "…And he is playing her false too. Sam said to me that Nicole has made sexual advances to him."

"God damn! —The God damned filthy mouthed bastard!" the Captain rose to pace again. "I'll kill him! I'll kill Sam Lucas for this! Tom, you know he's lying—using her for his own ends and then spreading filth behind her back! Hell, I told you she was a virgin—and I'll believe that as long as I live!"

There was a huge inconsistency in Mike's statement and Tom couldn't let it pass. "…Friend, once again, what you believe has little to do with fact. Either there was some proof or there wasn't."

Mike stopped and sat down again. "There wasn't," he admitted after a time. "But she explained why, Tom. She fell from a damn horse and things like that do happen! Anyway, she was in tears over it and I know she was sincere—damn it, I know she was! …Besides, when you really love a woman—and I do love her—virginity is not so important."

"If she is faithful to you, no," Tom nodded, refilling his glass.

Mike did the same and drained his. Then for a time, they sat in silence. "…Tom, Nico is a flirt and a tease," Mike said at last. "She always has been and will be. But I still believe she was an innocent when she came to me; and that the problem between us now is because sex is so new to her. Yet, I believe everything you've told me too. Sam Lucas is behind her strange behavior. He has put her up to doing these things and we have to stop him before he ruins her reputation. …Haven't you any idea what he's after?"

"None. And I've tried for months to guess," Tom sighed. "I have so much at stake here, Mike. My wife is under his roof instead of mine—and I'm getting damned tired of waiting for him to show his hand."

"…Then why don't you force him to do it? Hell, you have the lever. Announce your marriage and let's see what he does."

"He'd go right after Kathy—just as he vowed to her he would. He'd hunt her to the ground, purely for revenge—and this time, he could just finish the job and kill her. How do I claim happiness at the cost of her life? —Or condemn her sons to a life as orphans when I lived it and know the hardships so very well?"

"Old Sam might have gone after Kathleen Morgan," Mike grinned, "but he wouldn't dare lift a finger against Mrs. Sebastiano Rizza. I stopped by Iano's place coming in and he told me they were married last week."

"Well, I'll be damned," Tom smiled. "—Good for them! And Iano liked the boys too. He'll be a great Dad for them, don't you think?"

"Yes, I do," Mike agreed. "Iano also said they would be announcing it at the Harvest Ball next Friday. And, Tom, if you did the same, what could Sam do about anything then? He would have to stand there in front of half the city and accept both things or expose his true self."

"…Speaking of pure revenge!" Tom laughed as he warmed to the idea. "Damn, Mike, have another drink! I haven't felt this good in ages—and by God, I'm going to celebrate! A toast then: to you, Captain Michael Leonard Herb; the best damn friend a man ever had. May your life be as happy as you've made mine tonight."

And with that, they proceeded to get most wonderfully smashed…

# CHAPTER 40

Eleven o'clock Monday morning found Mandria collapsed at the bottom of the stairway in tears—great sobbing tears of utter frustration. And beside her, crying just as hard because she knew no better way of expressing her sympathy, sat Joleen.

It had started early that morning when Mandria went to the clothiers to pick up the material she had selected for a bedspread and drapes. Mistakenly, a clerk had returned her order to the shelves and it took almost an hour to locate everything again. Next, she stopped by Mrs. Amos' shop to collect the seamstresses she'd used before and found they were not available. "The Ball," Mrs. Amos apologized, "has to take precedence and all my ladies are needed here." Mandria pled her case to no avail, but finally the woman did recommend the Alexander sisters. "Three old maids," she said, "who do excellent work but are offered few assignments because of their crankiness." Nonetheless, Mandria was determined to see the job done and drove to their home—which, of course, was half-way across Savannah. She would hire them, drop them at the house and be on her way to begin the Ball decorations.

But Tina, Gaila and Mia Alexander, as Mandria soon discovered, deserved their reputation. First, the sisters could not agree on what to charge and argued not only among themselves, but with every suggestion Mandria made. Then, when the price was set, they balked about starting that day and negotiations had to begin anew. Only when Mandria offered a doubled fee did they get their sewing baskets and their persons into the buggy, where she had to listen to them bicker over absolutely everything on the ride back.

It didn't end there. The Alexander's were deposited in the Master bedroom with yards of a new-leaf green fringe, bolts of deep forest green velvet, one of sheer light green and all the accompanying threads, pins and hooks, which they spread out in every direction and then proceeded to argue about where to begin. That was still going on when a delivery wagon arrived, a day early, with a dresser, chest, wardrobe and two marble-topped tables for the same bedroom, and what resulted was near chaos. The sisters threatened to quit if disturbed and made to refold and reroll all that material and the movers threatened to leave the furniture in the yard if the Alexander's weren't removed from their way. And topping it all, the store had forgotten to send the carpet, which had to go down first, anyway.

It took Mandria nearly a half-hour to calm the tempest, but finally the ladies were persuaded to go down to the parlor for a cup of tea and Willie went for the carpet while Mandria picked everything up from the bedroom floor. Willie Luther returned quickly enough, but even so, Mandria had to run upstairs and down checking on furniture placement and seeing that the restless sisters remained put.

"Miss Mandy!" Joleen had yelled frantically from the parlor door three times already. "—Miss Mandy, they going to leave! Do something—do it quick!"

"Well, it's early, but offer them lunch!" she called back once. "Get them more tea!" she said next. And the third time, Joleen was told to give them a bottle of sweet sherry, in hopes it might also sweeten their dispositions. But when the movers left, Mandria opened the parlor doors and found, instead, that the sisters were not only tipsy but more argumentative than ever.

"Take them home!" she said to Willie Luther over the squabbling women. "—Just get them out of my house and take them home!" Then came the flood of tears and Joleen's not so helpful sympathy.

Both were still sobbing when Evelyn arrived. "Mandy, what on earth?" she hurried to sit on the other side of her daughter. "What

514

happened, dear? —Please tell me." And when Mandria had poured out her distressing tale, Evelyn hugged her close and laughed.

"Sweetheart, learning to manage a household does take time—and even then, we all have days like this. But dry your eyes now, and go powder your nose. When Willie returns, we are going out to Marsh Haven to pick up my wedding gift for you and Tom!"

"At Marsh Haven?" Mandria snubbed. "What could it be?"

"Furniture, for one thing. The attic is full and you are welcome to anything you'd like. Grandma's lovely dining room suite is up there, and it had twelve chairs, as I remember—"

"And Grandpa's big roll-top desk!" Mandria exclaimed. "Oh, Mama, it would look so nice in Tom's study."

"I know!" Evelyn laughed again. "There is enough to fill this whole house—if you don't think Tom would object to using it?"

"He won't—he can't! Oh, I just won't let him object!" excitement brought Mandria to her feet. "Besides, it's from you—from your side of the family. And he won't care that it's used because nearly everything here already is. Why, only the bedroom furniture is new…" she paused. And reminded of her disappointment over the bedspread and drapes, she stomped a foot. "Drat those old biddies anyway! I wanted the bedroom completely finished when Tom came home today, because I still have the Ball decorations to do this week."

"Mandria—today?" Evelyn declared. "Dear, had the Alexander's been fairies, with magic needles, they'd never have finished that soon!"

"Oh," she nodded. "…Would they have finished by Thursday? The 25th is our third month's anniversary and this time, I wanted to surprise him."

"Well, I don't know if they could have, but Hassie and her crew of women can. —And that is the other part of my gift. Mandy, I want you to bring Hassie and Jake back to stay as long as they're needed. Hassie will put this house in order and teach Joleen how to keep it that way, while Jake does the same for Willie Luther."

"Mama, what a wonderful idea!" Mandria grew excited again. "Joleen, you'd like Hassie's help, wouldn't you?"

"Yes ma'am! —Oh, yes, Miss Mandy! Her might could teach me to cook better too—and Willie appreciate that, Ah bet-ya! Last night, he call me to the kitchen and when Ah start down the hall, he roll my corn bread to meet me. It hard like a rock! Didn't even bust when it hit the wall—just turn whang-whang round like a plate and not one crumb drop off!"

They had a good laugh at that and as Willie had just come in, Mandria and Evelyn soon had him driving them to Marsh Haven, arriving about noon. By three o'clock, they were on the way back with two wagon loads of furniture, Hassie, Jake and a crew of hand picked seamstresses. And Hassie had even managed to slip two cradles aboard the rear wagon…

When Tom came in from school, Joleen greeted him with the story of Mandria's day and by the time she'd finished, he, too, was in tears—of laughter. He was still laughing as he went up to change clothes. Yes, Willie and Jake would need help unloading, because if he knew his wife, she had all but emptied those attics. …*And it's good the house will look more like a home*, he thought while approving the new bedroom pieces, *because though Mandria isn't aware of it, in four days' time, she'll be moving in too.*

Then he nodded, acknowledging that he wouldn't be seeing much of his wife once she got back today. He hadn't when she became involved in her other projects—and now, she would be bringing a whole house full of stuff. Lord no, he wouldn't see her until each item had found a place. "Oh well," he rubbed the fleeting remains of last night's hang-over from his temples, "the busier she stays, the less chance she'll discover what I'm up to." But as he started down the stairs, he realized he'd have to have Evelyn's help for what he wanted to do… For now though, the wagons were arriving and putting the thought aside, he hurried out to the front porch.

"Hey, lady?" he called. "I've invited some friends over this evening. Do you know them by chance? —The Alexander sisters?"

"Thomas Scott, you didn't!" she rose from the wagon seat, arms akimbo. As quickly, she realized he was teasing and started to laugh. So did the entire group, who'd just heard the story retold to Hassie and soon all laughed so uproariously, the neighbors on both sides came to peek from their windows...

Knowing Mandria to be safely occupied somewhere between Ball and house decorations, Tom used his lunch period on Tuesday for a visit with Evelyn. He told her what was to happen at the Ball, why it could finally come about and warned that Sam's reaction might not be what any of them would wish. The last, she listened to solemnly and with understanding, yet her joy soon bubbled forth in dozens of elated questions. Tom patiently answered until he found an opening to make his request for her help. "...Mamalyn, she should have had a grand wedding with all the trimmings. I know you wanted that for your daughter."

"Well, big weddings are nice. Mine was truly beautiful," Evelyn nodded. "But they don't guarantee happiness, Tom. One look at my marriage should tell you that. No, Mandy is happy with you and I'm certain she wouldn't change anything that brought you together. The thought would never enter her mind."

"But it's something I want for her too; something I can do to partially make up for the wedding she missed having. ...Mamalyn, when I make our announcement at the Ball—while you and all her friends are there to see—I want to put my ring on her finger, as I would have in a church ceremony."

"Oh, I wish you would, Tom," she smiled her approval. "That would be such a lovely gesture."

"Yes, ma'am, but impossible unless I have your help," he replied. "She wears my ring on a chain and—well, could you steal it back for me?"

"...I'm not sure I could," Evelyn hesitated, "Tom, when she showed it to me, she said she'd never taken it off—not once."

"She hasn't as far as I know either," he nodded too. "So do you think my plan impractical? Too romantic, perhaps?"

"Yes, but that's why I love it!" she laughed. "Just let me think about this and if there is a way, I'll get that ring to you."

"Thank you," he rose to leave. "I'll be waiting to hear from you, Mamalyn."

And he did, sooner than he expected, and not about the ring. When Tom exited the school that afternoon, Evelyn was waiting at the curb in her buggy. "Here," she handed him the reins, "you drive, while I tell you what I've thought of all on my own!"

"Yes ma'am," he chuckled, setting the horse in motion. "May I ask where we're going?"

"To the printers on West Broad Street—and you needn't stay. I just wanted you to know what I'm doing and why. Tom, I know a way to keep Sam from ruining the night for Mandy:—At-Home Announcements! Formal, printed At-Home Announcements, that give the date and location of the wedding, plus your new address—and I will have them distributed at the Ball while you are telling the news!"

"…But how would this restrain Sam?"

"Because, the cards will read, *Mr. and Mrs. Samuel T. Lucas proudly announce the marriage of their daughter…* Don't you see? Publicly, Sam will not be able to claim surprise or deceit because the cards will say he knew and approved beforehand!"

"And he'd never admit in front of all those people that he'd been so royally duped," Tom concluded, pulling the buggy to a stop before the print shop.

"Exactly," Evelyn smiled. "And for that one special evening, Sam Lucas will wear my muzzle, because I intend to give him one of these announcements myself—at *just* the right time—and he'll know I was the mastermind behind the whole thing."

"Is that…wise?" Tom had to ask as he helped Evelyn to the sidewalk. "What if he—well, I wouldn't want you harmed in any way."

"Tom, I'm not afraid of the man. He knows better than to bite the hand that puts money in his wallet. Besides," she laughed, "it would please me to zing Sam a good one. I have owed it to him for years!"

"…Mamalyn, I realize we're standing on a public street," Tom nodded, "but I have a tremendous urge to hug you. May I?"

"Please do," she lifted her arms, "Son," she added sweetly.

Later, Evelyn also visited the Society Editor at the Gazette. A write-up of Mandria's wedding announcement would appear in the Sunday edition. Lastly, she went to the bank, removed a jewel case from the vault, and of course, stopped to enjoy a chat with Ransom. On the ride home, she laughed pleasurably over all she'd accomplished. "No, this won't be as grand as a formal wedding; —by glory, it's going to be better!"

As Tom had predicted, it was Thursday and he hadn't seen much of his wife for most of the week. She had even taken leave from her art classes and spent mornings through the lunch hour working on the Ball decorations with Lucy and Nicole—when the latter felt inclined to show up. Then for the rest of the afternoon until well after dark, she was queen-bee among her hive of helpers at the house, buzzing from room to room, and from one project to the next. And when he drove her back to the Lucas' each night, she was so exhausted, she would usually doze off against his shoulder. Trying to find extra patience, Tom had comforted himself by counting down the days.

"Just one more now; —one and she'll be moving in to stay," he said while walking toward the home they were soon to share. And thinking again about her recent whirlwind of activity, he was reminded of a term his mother had used. The *nesting urge* and he wondered if his wife might be experiencing that. It occurred, according to his mother, just before the onset of a woman's monthly cycle and was signaled by a great burst of energy, usually directed at putting the house—or nest—in order. They had been married three months today and three times he'd seen the symptoms: Once when she became involved with the parlor; next with the morning room; and again now. Yes, and each time, she'd kept herself busily unavailable to him. "The little sneak," he grinned going up the front steps. How like her to let that time pass without having to mention it or refuse him.

On entering the house, though, the first thing he noticed was the absence of the hive. He looked into the parlor and finding no one, crossed to the dining room, where he stopped to admire it. The oblong table, the scrolled side boards and all twelve chairs gleamed with coats of fresh wax. The new chair covers, done in a burgundy brocade, picked up that color in a new oval carpet, a floral centerpiece and the rims that banded the bone china and crystal displayed in the curved windowed cabinets. Tom thought then, that Mandria's grandmother could not have been any prouder of her things than he was.

From there, he went through to the morning room with its comfortable green pin-striped, over-stuffed furniture and knew that, come spring, it would be a favorite place for viewing the flowers in the courtyard—with the wife he still hadn't found. So moving on to the study, he had to stop again to admire his personal favorite of the pieces Mandria had brought in: the big roll-top desk. He noted too, the almond colored drapes, a smaller carpet of multi-green leaves and a gaming table she'd placed in the center of it. "Well," he mused, "gold stripes are out and leaves are in. …Probably, so the rooms coordinate when the pocket doors are open to the front parlor." He liked the change, though, and knew he'd enjoy this room. The shelves were still empty, but there were boxes beneath them and he assumed they held books to take care of that. Then glancing above the mantle, he saw the seascape Mandria had given him and it cost him a smile. He guessed it always would.

"Mandria?" he now called down the kitchen stairs. "Are you there?"

"She upstairs!" Hassie called back. "—Up to something too!"

"Be careful, Mr. Tom!" added Joleen with a giggle. "You in for it, Ah bet-ya!"

"Now what?" he muttered, taking the steps in twos. He'd likely arrived just in time to move more furniture. So going directly to the other front bedroom, because that's where she'd been working last, he didn't find her, but this room, at least, seemed to be finished too. Done in lavenders, and furnished with her grandmother's mammoth four-poster bed, a matching shift robe and a truly beautiful triple-mirrored vanity, Mandria already referred to this as the guest room.

As he turned away, he noted that Allen's door stood open, and curious to see what had been chosen for his brother, he went to look. A large sleigh-bed, had replaced the pitiful floor pallet. The lamp on a table top desk shared lighting duty with a comfortable easy chair next to it, creating a cozy reading or work area. A handsome oval mirrored bachelor's chest held a neatly arranged accumulation of Allen's toiletries. More of his possessions adorned the bedside tables and hanging from a wardrobe door was a mended shirt on which he'd asked to have a button replaced. The bedspread was a patch quilt design of blue, brown and gold squares and Tom smiled looking at the windows. "Well, there are my gold striped drapes," he nodded. It amazed him how Mandria could change things all around, nearly as often as she changed her mind and still manage the right results.

"Mandria?" he called yet again, going now toward the other back bedroom, which was still a shoulder-high jumble of furniture, boxes, trunks, bolts of cloth and he really didn't know what else. And here, he decided, was where he'd find her, wanting him to lug something out again, yet going in, he discovered she wasn't there either. ...But what was it he'd just seen behind that mountain of stuff? "Ah-ha!" he chuckled, unearthing a cradle. "I guess this is to be the nursery. ...And just about there," he mentally measured the front wall, "is where I must cut that new doorway. When the time comes," he added wishfully.

"Mandria?" he called, moving on toward the Master bedroom. But noticing that the door was closed, he paused before it, thinking maybe she'd finally worked herself out and was taking a well-earned nap. ... Yet, hadn't Hassie and Joleen said differently; —that she needed his help or something to that effect? At any rate, he eased the door open quietly and peered into the room.

"Do come in, Mr. Scott," Mandria's reflection smiled at him from an oval floor-standing mirror, where she stood brushing her long honey-tan hair. And all she wore was her thin, loosely sashed little robe and the chain holding his ring. "Well?" she gestured gracefully. "How does the Master of the house like his newly finished Master bedroom?"

"With you in it, mostly," he replied, leaning against the door as he closed it.

"The perfect answer once again," she came to kiss him hello. And the scent of her freshly bathed self, plus her honeysuckle, wreaked its usual titillation on his senses. "But seriously, are you pleased?" she went on. "We finished everything yesterday, but I didn't want you to see it all put together until today. So do you like it?"

"Lady, it has been days, and if you think I'm taking my eyes off of you for a second, you're mistaken," he smiled down at her.

"Well, happy one-fourth of a year's anniversary anyway, Tom," she kissed him again. "Now, the bath water is still hot. Shall I scrub your back for you?"

"Why, hell yes," he laughed, allowing her to lead him to a tub by the fire. And when she had him undressed, she proceeded to fondle him with her body and wonderfully caressing hands.

"So, husband," she finally murmured, "if you will get into that tub now, I'll get us some wine." And waiting until she had turned away, Tom retrieved something from his coat pocket before complying with her request. "Here we are," she returned to give him a glass. "To us," she added, kneeling beside the tub.

"To us," he repeated and touching his glass to hers, they shared a sip, a smile and a kiss.

"Now will you look at the room?" she pled. "It's my gift to you and I want to know if you like it."

So, mostly to tease her, he took an exaggerated amount of time to scrutinize her offering, but in truth, he was much impressed. The carpet she'd chosen was an oriental tableau, depicting maidens in brilliantly hued costumes dancing through a green, multi-flowered meadow. Green velvet drapes were tied back with strips of a paler green fringe and sunlight was reduced to a minty glow through the light, almost white-green sheers beneath. A tailored bedspread of the deeper hued velvet was also edged in the paler fringe and where it lay invitingly turned back, he could see that the pillow cases and top sheet were bordered with wide green lace. More of her paintings hung above the bedside tables, while lamps with fragile Tiffany glass shades and small

522

potted plants sat on the white marble tops. Bracketing the fireplace, where he was, sat two wing-back chairs, covered in the green of the fringe, and between them was the rickety table he'd dragged up from the cellar. It had been repaired, refinished and now held a tray of cut glass decanters and glasses. Yes, along with the rest of the new furniture pieces, the room was tastefully complete. It amazed him anew that he'd lived with the carpet and most everything else for several days and hadn't noticed how beautiful they were until she had added her finishing touches. "Thank you, pretty lady," he smiled at her hopeful expression. "The Master of the Master bedroom is very—*very*—pleased. In fact, I've just given myself a tour of the place and you've done a wonderful job all around. I am really proud of our home."

"So am I, Tom," she reached for the bath sponge. "There's more to do yet, but I wouldn't swap this house for the finest mansion in Savannah; —not the finest."

Tom leaned forward as she began to scrub his shoulders. "I had a visit with your mother the other day and she said you'd feel the same way about the wedding we had. …Do you, Mandria? Or do you regret not having the big ceremony most girls want?"

"Hardly," she remarked. "It's very romantic sleeping with a man I don't remember marrying. Maybe it's that air of mystery that keeps me attracted to you."

"Now, just a minute, lady," he chuckled, leaning back to look at her. "I have *something* to do with that. My experienced knowledge of the female anatomy is what keeps you attracted—that and my ability to provoke great fits of purple passion."

"Idiot," she giggled, tossing the sponge at his chest. "Tom, you are such an idiot!"

"When it comes to you, I certainly am," he nodded. "I mean, what sane man would get into a tub of warm, sudsy water wearing his wife's anniversary present?"

"…But I undressed you myself," she puzzled. "You aren't wearing anything."

"I know," he agreed, "and that left but one place to hang the gold bracelet I bought for you to wear to the Ball tomorrow night."

Mandria's eyes widened magnificently. "Tom, you didn't put it there? —Yes, you did," she immediately changed her mind. "That's exactly the thing you would do!"

"So? Do you want your present or not?" he asked smugly. "I once offered to fetch your ring from the sea—and as I see it, it's your turn to go fishing."

"Experienced knowledge, huh?" she snaked her hand across the water. "Provoker of great fits of purple passion, huh?" the hand dove and her fingers closed about him.

"Careful, love!" he exclaimed. "The monster down there is really hungry for a taste of you!"

"Ha!" she retorted, slowly twisting the bracelet about her finger— and him. "I'm not afraid. I lead this creature about on a golden chain. Monster indeed!" And rising to her feet, she drew her hand upward and Tom too, as he had no choice but to go.

"Mandria!" he laughed in astonishment. "You haven't finished that nursery in there. If you hope to use it, you'd best not strangle the source."

"Poor darling," she cooed, untangling the leash from the neck of her creature. "Poor thing," she bestowed a pat to its head, then a kiss to his lips. And handing Tom a towel, she started for the bed admiring the new bracelet she'd already fastened to her wrist. "Thank you, Tom," she said without looking back. "This is very beautiful."

"It certainly is," he stood watching the graceful sway of her hips, the stretch of her slender limbs as the crawled on the bed to sit crossed legged facing him. Her smile, which had always captivated him and her eyes, seeming even greener against the green spread, brought a smile to his mouth and a gnawing anticipation to his soul. *One-more-day—only one now*, he thought. And morning, noon and night he would find her here, in this room, where she most certainly did belong...

"Mr. Scott, are you going to stand there and drip dry?" she asked. "Surely, you can think of *something* better to do. —Or must I make sinful suggestions to you now?"

"Oh, God—please do!" he chuckled, stepping from the tub to towel himself. "So what would you say to persuade me to your bed, lady?" he asked curiously.

"That I wish to do my own experiment today," she ran fingers through her hair, and mussed it into great flowing tangles. "That I want to play the whore for you," she slid from her robe, rose on all fours and rocked forward and back while her full breasts kept their own rhythm. "And the pat I gave that monster pointing at me—right now—was a promise of things to come."

"Damn!" Tom flung the towel aside and joined her. "One," he said, bringing her body hard against his. "The magic number is one, lady. —Remember it!" And as he claimed her mouth, all thought of meaning melted from her ability to care.

But her stated intention hadn't. Pushing herself away from his embrace, she knelt over him and began a nibbling, tasting descent of his body: teasing at his button size breast nipples and actually feeling them harden; on to his navel, where her tongue lingered in the depression; then to the dark forest of hair below, to play about the edges while watching the creature who resided in the center grow taller, tantalizing her as much as she tantalized him. "Oh, Tom," she murmured, leaning to place kiss on that velvet skinned head.

It was softer there, than her own lips, and enjoying the sensation, she brushed them against it again and again. The skin along the rest of his proud erection was not so silky soft, and yet, she needed to feel her lips and fingers here too. So just as she'd done to his body, she descended tasting, kissing, nibbling down one side and up the other. On reaching the head again, she circled it with her tongue, luring it toward the recess of her mouth with each coaxing repetition. When she finally made her capture, she heard Tom's surrendering sigh, but sensed he was pleased with her victory. And like any victor, she could not help celebrating; dabbling even more playfully with the spoils...

Mandria, however, did not expect the reaction this caused in Tom. In an instant, she was virtually yanked from her knees, thrown to her back and covered, inside and out, by a most determined man. Passion burned in his eyes and when his mouth met hers, she was certain they had never shared such a kiss before. Then his passion became hers; his need hers; his assault on her senses no more desirous than hers upon him. It was purely a glorious experience from start to climax.

Afterwards, as they still lay in the stunned grasp of each other's arms, Mandria knew Tom had been right. There was more to be explored and feelings yet to be tapped—in both of them. She was tempted at that point, to tell him she might be pregnant and suspected it had happened their first time together. She smiled then, thinking of the wagging tongues and months counted on busy fingers that would cause. But Mandria was counting days for now, and if she could only wait another week, when the time for her third missed cycle was well and truly passed, then her gift for Tom would be one of certainty…

# CHAPTER 41

It was just after noon on Friday, when Lucy and Mandria turned in the doorway of the ballroom for a final look at their work. Each window sill held a small, fan-shaped palmetto frond, clipped and centered behind a conch shell cornucopia filled with sea-oat tips, nuts, crab apples, persimmons and fall flowers. Several more of these arrangements had been placed along the refreshment tables. There too, reigning supreme, because it had been slightly elevated, was the horse shoe crab shell, into which a large glass punch bowl had been placed. It was ringed by others and all spaces in between were filled with an assortment of shells. Other autumn hues were displayed against shrimp net swags draped here and there about the walls—a harvested collection from land and sea, including starfish, gourds, hedge apples, sea-sponges, sand dollars, bunches of dried red and yellow corn and sea ferns. A riser had been placed at one end of the room for the orchestra and behind it, hung sheets, dyed a light blue, on which Mandria had painted white puffy clouds and a line of sea gulls in flight. Across the base of the riser, they had banked slanted trays of sand, interspersed with ridges of long-stemmed sea-oats, creating the impression that the orchestra would play from atop a dune. At the opposite end of the room, hung sheets dyed night blue, in front of which they had nestled a potted palm forest and one taller Palmetto tree. On this background Mandria had painted a full harvest moon that appeared to be shining through the Palmetto fronds, as she had touched them with paths of the moon's yellow-gold paint.

"Well, I'm pleased with it, Lucy. Are you?" Mandria asked.

"Yes, I really, really am," she nodded. "I just wonder why Nico didn't come today?"

"On the day of the Ball?" Mandria asked incredulously. "Likely, she has been preening for hours already."

"I guess so," Lucy shrugged. "But it must be worth it. Nico always looks so beautiful. Her dance card was filled days ago. —All the men want a dance with Nico,"

"She does have an allure about her," Mandria touched the ring beneath her blouse protectively. "Anyway, if we want our share of those dances, we'd best go home and do some preening of our own." And as they left, Mandria realized she had every intention of doing just that. She wanted to look her most beautiful, as Nicole surely would too…

Friday was also payday, but instead of making his usual deposit, Allen made a withdrawal. Tom still wouldn't allow him to pay rent, though Mandria had furnished his room from her raid on the attics of Marsh Haven. For days then, he'd searched for a way to repay them and finally found it. The owner of an Import Shop on Broughton Street was waiting now for his money and within the hour, a tall English made Grandfather clock and two mirrors in heavy gold frames would be delivered to the house in his name. As Allen saw it, if he was going to feel like part of the household and yet be denied a share of the expenses, then he could certainly contribute to the beauty of the place. He just hoped Mandria approved of his tastes…

"Allen?" Tom called stepping from the bedroom as the mellow gongs of the new clock drifted up the stairs. "It's seven o'clock. Are you about ready?"

Allen stepped from his room too and the brothers faced each other across the balconied stairwell, both wearing dark formal suits;

both adjusting ties; and both nodding approval of the other's dashing appearance. "It's still a bit early, Tom. I don't pick Lucy up for another half-hour yet."

"All right, then we've time for a drink—and I do seem to need one."

"Why so?" Allen asked as they met at the head of the stairs. "From what you've told me, you and Mamalyn have everything under control."

"I know," Tom replied as they went down. "But it's never safe to feel too sure when Sam Lucas is involved. —And by the way," he paused before the grandfather clock in the front hall, "thank you again, little brother. This is one thing Mandria won't have me lugging from room to room and back again."

"So, where do you think she'll hang the mirrors?" Allen asked as they entered the parlor.

"Who knows?" Tom shrugged, pouring and serving their brandy. "But tonight she comes home for good and by tomorrow, she'll have me hanging them someplace. —Oh damn, I'm jittery!" he said. "You'd think I was really a bridegroom instead of an old married man of three months and a day."

"Mandy is the one I'm concerned about," Allen nodded. "Hell, she won't faint or anything, will she?"

"Lord, I hope not—and yet, staying low to the floor might be the wisest thing if Sam decides to start shooting."

"Tom, you are nervous!" Allen chuckled. "Now, why would he take a gun to a formal Ball?"

"He wouldn't, I guess. But damn it, he had one the first time I met him; —had it aimed at me too."

"All right, Brer, if it will make you feel better, I'll manage to be standing next to Sam when you make your announcement. —Mike could be too, you know."

"I doubt that!" Tom laughed now. "In fact, having Mike in the Lucas house beforehand will make Sam more ill-tempered than usual."

"Well, you could call the whole thing off," Allen finished his drink. "But somehow, I know you won't. If Sam pointed a cannon I don't think it would keep you from claiming your wife tonight."

"No, Allen, it wouldn't," Tom smiled in agreement. "…Hell, I just worry too much; —I've always worried too much. So come along, little brother, it's time we started this very special evening." And finishing his drink too, they were on their way…

Evelyn moved through the front parlor and over to the dining room, stopping here and there to swap pleasantries with her guests. All of their party was present, except for Nicole and Mike. But that was to be expected, as Nico adored a grand entrance. Tonight, however, she would have a hard time outshining Mandria. And eyes beaming with pride, Evelyn looked her daughter's way again.

The ball gown was so very flattering to Mandria's willowy figure. The tan silk fabric clung to her waist and hip line across the front, while the a-line cut of the close fitting skirt draped into a slight bustle effect behind. The bodice had a wide flounce collar of the fragile chocolate lace glimmering with seed-pearls. It began at the edge of her shoulders, fell over her upper arms; and front and back, followed the swooping deep vee-cut of the neckline. Her hair, so nearly the color of the dress silk, was swept softly up on the sides and away from the nape of her neck, only to fall in natural curls from the back of her head—a style which certainly did compliment Grandmother's emerald necklace and earrings. But Evelyn nodded, convincing Mandria of that had not been an easy task…

Earlier, while Mandria was dressing, Evelyn had taken the jewel case to her room. "Listen, Mandy, I brought these home from the vault thinking I'd wear them tonight, but as you can see, the onyx looks perfect with my gown. Then, I thought how the emeralds would enhance your eyes, so why don't you wear them instead?"

Tempted, Mandria's fingers touched the beautiful stones, but returned to the ring concealed in her gown. "Thank you, Mama, but I think I'll just wear my chain."

So Evelyn resorted to a ploy no female could ignore. "Well, maybe Nico will come early and we'll ask her opinion. —Now that young lady certainly knows how to dress to her own best advantage. Likely, she is prepared to dazzle absolutely every man coming tonight. Anyway, Mandy, think about the emeralds," she finished, leaving them with her.

After a few minutes, Evelyn passed Mandria's door and saw her looking thoughtfully at the jewels. Going to the end of the hall, she turned, counted to twenty and retraced her steps passed Mandria's door. This time her daughter was holding the emeralds, comparing their color to the color of her eyes in the mirror—and Evelyn paused to watch. Then to her delight, up went Mandria's hair; off came the chain; and on went the emeralds. Later, Evelyn went in and took Tom's ring from the chain tucked into Mandria's jewel box...

Now the problem was getting Tom's attention long enough to deliver it to him, but so far, he hadn't been able to take his eyes from her daughter. Evelyn smiled at his bewitched expression—and right in the middle of Caroline Littlejohn's dissertation on the pains and woes of her latest ailment. Then Mike and Nicole arrived and she smiled yet again when neither Sam's stiff formal greeting, nor his menacing looks, did anything to dampen the Captain's high spirits. ...But she really had to start listening to the woman still talking beside her or, without meaning to, she'd hurt the poor thing's feelings.

Indeed, Mike was in high spirits. Nicole had forgiven his poor performance and accepted his peace-offering of an aqua marine ring, that matched her dress; and which she wore tonight—on her left hand ring finger. It tickled him that the little tease was having a grand time coyly avoiding straight answers from the curious. But he was happiest about the revelations soon to be made at the Ball, because as Sam Lucas' plans dissolved before him, so would his interest in using

Nicole to accomplish them. Oh-hell-yes, he felt good! And as they made their way around the room, he also had the fun of winning acceptance among Sam's friends. The ladies were treated to gracious compliments; their husbands, who were already aware of the Captain's growing success story, were further impressed by his knowledge and glowing admiration for their own achievements. And many wondered at Sam's dislike for the charming young Captain of the Irish Mist…

"Thomas!" Mike called, leading his beautiful Nicole in that direction now. And stepping close, he uttered, "I can feel Sam's daggers in my back as we speak—and damn, ain't it wonderful!"

"But the evening is young, Captain," Tom replied in like tone. "You haven't a chance of keeping his attention, as much as it pleases you."

"Why, Mandy!" Nicole was saying, waving her ringed hand in another bid for notice, "How pretty you look…though I'm sure I'll never get used to that style. I know it's the latest, but I do so enjoy fuller skirts—and all the petticoats I can wear. It's just much more feminine. Don't you think?"

"I think," Mandria made a real effort to curb her tongue and ignored the hand that continued to wave in her face, "I like your gown too, Nico. It's so…blue."

In spite of Mandria's pleasant expression, Tom hastened to intervene. "Ladies, I must say you both look extremely lovely tonight. —Don't you agree, Captain?"

"Oh-hell-yes!" he grinned. "And before I forget, you must promise me a dance, Mandy."

Mandria opened her mouth to accept, but Nicole spoke up again. "Of course she'll dance with you, Mike—and that's only fair, as Tom begged one from me just weeks and weeks ago."

"And I will collect it, Nico," Tom cut in before Mandria could.

"Oh, I'm certain you will," Nicole swatted him playfully with her tiny ivory fan. "You have always been crazy about me—and don't even try to deny it!" she laughed gaily, as Mike led her to where Allen and Lucy stood talking to a group of young people.

Tom turned to his wife and chuckled. "Her gown is so…blue?" he teased.

"Well, it is, isn't it?" she replied and the emeralds were far out-shown by the green fire dancing in her eyes. "And that's as nice as I could be about it."

"Why?" he dared to look after Nicole, who was waving her hand beneath a new set of noses, "Her dress is pretty with all those little sparkly things at the hem there."

"Tom, it's not the gown; —it has nothing to do with the damned gown," she sighed. "And why were you so quick to claim that dance with her?"

"I don't want to dance with her, lady. I only jumped in there to keep you from saying something you might have regretted. —And you were going to say it," he smiled. "Admit it now, weren't you?"

"Well...yes," she confessed, laughing softly. "But Tom, you did not *beg* her for a dance. How can she say such outrageous things and get away with it every single time?"

"I've no idea," he nodded. "I am just eternally grateful that governing her behavior is no concern of mine."

A mischievous sparkle appeared in Mandria's eyes as she looked up at him now. "Mr. Scott, are you saying that Nico would present a challenge to your powers of purple persuasion?"

"Mrs. Scott," he countered, "if I even had that in mind, tonight it would be quite impossible. You look so gorgeous, I'm wondering how I will get through a single dance and keep a proper distance between us."

"If you do," she made him one of her dazzling smiles, "I'll never forgive you. Besides—"

"Tom; Mandy, it's time we were leaving for the Ball," Evelyn stopped beside them. "—But Mandy, would you mind getting me a fresh handkerchief? Caroline splashed a drink on her sleeve and I soiled this one helping to dab it dry."

"Certainly, Mama," Mandria turned and before she had left the room, Evelyn extended a closed hand to Tom...

533

The crowded, music-filled ball room made it easy to avoid closer contact with Sam Lucas than an occasional sighting as he pompously politicked his way through the most elite of the attendees—even to dancing with their wives, while leaving Evelyn, the true aristocrat, to her own devices. And though this was standard behavior for the pair, Tom made it a point to partner her in a dance or two while Mandria danced with friends. He saw that Ransom was doing the same and made a mental note to offer his thanks.

Not long after, as he and Mandria were dancing again, Tom became aware of hushed whispers and heads turning toward the door. But it was seeing Sam's dark expression that caused him to look too. The Rizza's had arrived. Coming to a halt in mid-step, he explained as briefly as possible. "Lady, Kathy and Iano were married last week and are here to announce it. That could be very good for our own situation, so come with me to greet them, will you? It looks as if they could use a kind word. …Please?"

Glancing about the room, Mandria saw that he was right. "Let's go then," she nodded. "—But oh, dear God, Tom, look at Father! They won't speak to him, will they?"

"Let's see that they don't," he answered. "Come, love, there go Mike and Nico too—and your mother, Lord bless her." Then as Allen and Lucy danced by, Tom asked for their accompaniment also.

"Kathy; Iano," Mike was saying as they gathered about the couple, "it's good to see you both. —But Nico, have you met Kathy; Kathleen Morgan?"

"No, I have not," she said crisply. "However, I believe I've heard her name mentioned around and about."

"Well, of course you have, Nico," Evelyn took Kathy's hands in hers. "I've told you many times how fond I am of her. Kathy, you do look so lovely tonight! —And how are your beautiful little sons?"

"They…they're fine," Kathy gave Evelyn a grateful smile. "Thank God, Mrs. Lucas, we are all well and happy now."

"My name is Evelyn, dear, and it's high time you used it. —Iano," she extended a hand to him also, "will you be staying in Savannah a while? You've been missed at our socials."

"*Grazie, bella donna,*" he bowed. "We will be here a few days, awaiting *un nave*...uh, a sailing ship to arrive."

"Oh, good," Mandria joined in. "Then Kathy can join us somewhere for lunch, can't she, Mama? Lucy, you must come too; and you, Nico. Yes, we'll just have ourselves a ladies day out."

"Sorry, but I will not be free," Nicole said then. "Now, if you'll excuse me for a moment, Captain, I see my father and I must speak with him." And she left the group to their abhorrent introductions and disgustingly friendly greetings.

"Ransom, how can you defend the man?" Sam was saying as Nicole approached. "Where does he get the gall to bring that woman among us?"

"I could not agree more," Nicole injected. "Daddy, I was mortified having to stand anywhere near the common thing! —And believe you me, Mike is going to regret putting me through that!"

"Nicole!" Ransom said sharply. "Kindly keep your voice to a whisper. —And you, Sam, had best do the same. Sebastian Rizza may be new to Savannah, but he is not without friends, substantial wealth and influence. Yes, and by the growing number of our peers going to greet him, the man is very well-liked. It is none of our business whom he chooses to escort, nor have we the right to censure him in public. ...And you, my friend," he looked Sam in the eye, "have less right than any, in this particular case."

"But Daddy, I've even heard it said each of her sons has a different father, so you can't condone this?" Nicole still argued. "—Just look at poor Mrs. Benway. She is about to swoon from embarrassment!"

Ransom exhaled in exasperation. "Nico, Amy Benway can swoon at-will and does whenever she wants attention. But at least her protest is not verbal and I am warning you both, it would be wise to keep silent. Now, if you'll excuse me, I'm going to welcome Iano—and Mrs. Morgan—myself."

Nicole stared after her father in astonishment. "Sam, I can not believe Daddy would do this. Look—he is actually kissing that woman's hand!"

"Humph!" Sam snorted. "I don't know what Tom Scott is up to, but I see his hand in this. Remember I told you he keeps a mistress? Well, my dear, you are looking at her."

"Kathleen Morgan?" Nicole's eyes widened as she turned to study Kathy more closely. "Does Mandy know about Tom and that whore?"

"I told her myself, but she didn't believe me."

"And still doesn't from the way she's fawning over the bitch," Nicole sneered. "Sam, how can she be such a fool? …But then, who would have thought a pale little mouse like that could attract Tom?"

"Humph!" Sam repeated. "Her skin may be overly fair, but take it from one who knows, when coaxed, that red hair is rooted in fire."

"So Sam," Nicole said slyly, "the gossip about the two of you is true?"

"It was true," he said bitterly. "But at least I still have the decency to resent the presence of even a former mistress in the same room with my wife and daughter. —And look what Scott's doing now: standing there between Mandy and Kathy—flaunting both in my damned face!"

"And mine, Sam. —Don't forget that. Oh, there must be some way to set those two stupid women at each other!"

"Leaving Tom to you, of course," he said dryly.

"Yes, dear Uncle, to *me!*" she insisted. "You've already promised him to me and I expect you to deliver."

Sam chuckled nastily at that. "Well, at the moment, my hands seem to be tied. Yours aren't, however. If you were to rejoin your Captain, not only would it please him—and your father—but you might find a chance to tweak a few noses. But do remember to be discreet?"

"Yes…," Nicole said thoughtfully. "And don't worry, Sam, I'll stop by, from time to time, and keep you informed." So making her way back, she arrived just as Tom led Kathy, Allen led Evelyn and Mike led Lucy onto the dance floor. And while the others continued to chat, she sidled up beside Mandria, who stood watching two of the dancers with special pride. "Listen, Mandy," she whispered, "as your dearest friend, I need to warn you about the woman with Tom."

"Oh?" Mandria smiled pleasantly. "Is that what you and Father were discussing?"

"Well, he is worried about you. What father wouldn't be when his daughter could be hurt so badly?"

"By whom, Nico?" Mandria asked innocently.

"Mandy, don't be dense!" she hissed. "I mean, there Tom is—cavorting with his mistress—while you stand here alone and looking the fool. Why, everyone here is staring and feeling sorry for you!"

"Oh, surely not everyone," Mandria glanced over the room. "There—look at Mrs. Moody. She's not wearing her glasses and we both know she can't see a thing without them."

"...Mandy, are you deliberately missing the point?" Nicole said in exasperation. "I'm telling you, Tom is sleeping with that whore!"

"Well, yes, he did do that," Mandria nodded, yet said no more as she looked to the dance floor again.

"Don't you care?" Nicole persisted. "Not even when she has him in her clutches right now—and at your expense?"

"Your concern is so touching, but absolutely unnecessary," Mandria graced her with yet another smile. "Kathy is not here to hurt me."

"Fool! Mandy, you are such a fool! If you insist on being so blind and so stupid, you deserve to lose Tom—and you will, I promise it!"

"But not to Kathy," Mandria replied. "...Now is there someone else I should worry about?" she pretended to ponder, tapping a finger to her lips. "—Maybe, someone who has mentioned my impending loss twice in the last month or so?"

"Nico, me-darlin'!" Mike joined them just then. "Come along, my dances are long overdue!"

"...Yes, Captain," she managed, "B...but let's have some punch first." And as Mike led her away, she glanced back at Mandria three times.

"If looks could kill," Mandria uttered enjoyably.

"*Perdonomi?*" Iano said from beside her. "Did you not ask for my dance?" he teased.

"Why yes, Iano, I did! —And you must tell me, how your new home is coming along," she laughed as they stepped out on the floor...

When Mike returned Nicole to the group, she noted that Tom now danced with Lucy and Allen with Mandria; that Rizza and her father were engaged in conversation; and that Kathy was clinging to every word Mamalyn saw fit to bestow on her. ...*And why wouldn't she?* Nicole mused. *Otherwise, the bitch wouldn't be allowed in the back door. ...But why keep such notions to myself? Yes, it's time to tweak another nose—and this one will be easy prey.* "Mamalyn, why don't you dance with Mike while I finish my punch?" she began. "You'll take this impatient man off my hands for just a few minutes, won't you?"

"Well, I can try to keep up with him," Evelyn accepted his extended arm as they moved away. "But Captain, I hear you're an excellent dancer!"

Nicole then made a slow turn and honed in on Kathy. "My, your gown is lovely; —and it looks so expensive! How ever did you manage to afford it?"

"It...it was a gift," Kathy answered hesitantly.

"Oh?" she asked. "From which of your lovers; Tom, Sam or the handsome Italian?"

Kathy paled and lowered her eyes, not knowing how to deal with the girl.

"You might have asked for more jewelry, though," Nicole went on. "Something more brilliant than that quaint little locket."

"But I love the locket," Kathy raised her fingers to it. "This was his mother's."

"Such a sweet gesture. But the poor lady would never approve of *you* wearing it; —that is, after we've gone through your collection of men and discovered whose mother we are talking about."

"Miss O'Rourke...please," she uttered.

"Tell me, how did Tom persuade a man of Mr. Rizza's station to bring you here? You must know your presence is humiliating to all of us—and especially, to poor Sam."

It was difficult, but Kathy managed a reply to that one. "Then why don't you go console him? Please. Just leave me alone," she lowered her eyes again. "Oh, I wish I hadn't come. I didn't want to."

"Yes, but when Tom commands, his women obey!" Nicole laughed. "So what is he up to? —Why would he want you and Mandy here at the same time?"

"I'm sorry, Miss O'Rourke, I don't know what you're talking about!" Kathy's voice broke, as she was that close to tears.

"Stop it!" Nicole hissed, grasping her arm. "Don't you dare cause more of a scene than you already have! Just tell me what this is about and I'll gladly leave you alone!"

But her reply came from Tom and his whispered words brooked no argument. "You will let go of her! —Now!" he stepped closer. Then looking at both women he continued. "I will not ask you to apologize, Nico, because you don't deserve Kathy's forgiveness. And Kathy, there is no reason to cower before this...this person. Just remember who you are and why you are here."

"Yes, I was just asking that," Nicole said tenaciously. "Since you know her...*so-well*... perhaps you'll tell me?"

"You will learn soon enough, "Tom turned her to face the approaching Captain. But just before sending her into the Irishman's care, he could not resist a final remark in her ear. "And I hope you choke on it, you vicious little gutter snipe!"

Not a minute later, the mayor of Savannah stepped upon the orchestra riser to a fanfare of trumpets and drum rolls. "Ladies and gentlemen, its ten o'clock!" he called for attention. "Gather closely. —Up here, if you please. Now, for those of you still unfamiliar with it, let me explain our custom of Announcements. Because of the time, distance and expense involved, rarely do our friends and families from the outlying plantations or coastal islands have the chance to join together in great numbers. Happily, our annual Harvest Ball became the exception—and over the years, has come to include us city-folk too! So as we're all here for reunion and good fellowship, what better place is there for sharing and celebrating the joyous events in our lives? Therefore, I now invite all who wish to make such an announcement, to step up here and do so!"

Four young couples went forward first and while their news was told in turn, Tom kept maneuvering through the crowd until he and

539

Mandria stood beside the Rizza's at the base of the riser. From there, he looked over the room locating friend and foe. Sam had deemed it more fitting to remain apart from the crowd and Allen, as promised, was at his side. Nicole stood beside her father at center stage, of course. And though she still was in a pout over Tom's slight, she was nonetheless, staring straight at him. A little behind the O'Rourke's, Evelyn whispered quietly to Mike and Lucy as she gave each a stack of small white envelopes. Then squelching a delighted yelp from Lucy, she went to stand on the other side of Sam, clasping the most important of those envelopes in her hand. Tom smiled at his mother-in-law and her response was a nod and a naughty wink.

He looked now at Mandria, who had stooped to straighten a ridge of sea-oats along her make-believe dune. All evening, she had received compliments on her decorations and predictably, she would blush and give equal credit to Lucy and Nicole. Tom enjoyed her discomfort with compliments—mostly, he thought, because he liked seeing her blush. He smiled at that, for in a few minutes she would be in the limelight as never before—and oh, how she would blush for him then!

As Iano and Kathy stepped onto the riser, the whispers and turned heads were in evidence again, while just beyond the tittering, Sam Lucas stood immobile, trying to comprehend what was about to happen.

"*Mi amicos*," Iano began. "I am most *nervoso*…uh, nervous. *Perdonomi*! When this happens, I sometimes lapse to *Italiano* and you are kind to have…uh, patience. So, *mi permetta*, I introduce *la mia bella donna*," he laid a hand on Kathy's shoulder. "*Domenica,* we have *le nozze! —Si, nozze,* in Charleston of your Carolinas!" Silence followed, as the audience still looked at Iano in confused expectation. "Thomas!" he exclaimed. "*La prego di scusami del disturbo*—I forget! *Assistenza*…uh, please, your assistance?"

"Come love," Tom chuckled, drawing Mandria onto the riser with him—and what luck that he was able to get her there without making her aware of things to come.

So after a brief conference with Kathy and Iano, he turned to the waiting crowd. "Ladies and gentlemen, Mr. Rizza says he still relies heavily on his Italian-English dictionary and that you can not imagine his dismay, on an important night like this, to discover he had left it at home!" Tom paused, as polite laughter warmed the crowd. "For himself, Mr. Rizza asks your pardon and patience. For the lady beside him, he asks that his many good friends make her welcome, because a week ago Sunday, in Charleston, South Carolina, she became his wife: Mrs. Kathleen Morgan Rizza!" he finished, by leading a round of applause. And thankfully, a cheering response was immediate.

As the Rizza's stepped down to accept more congratulations, Tom exchanged a look with Mike and then Allen before all of them looked at Sam, watching as anger roiled through him. It was taking everything the man had to remain where he stood and not put a fist through the wall. Nicole, as Tom noted, only looked bored, refusing to grant the Rizza's even a nod when they stopped to accept Ransom's best wishes.

"Shouldn't we get down from here?" Mandria whispered. "They'll want to start dancing again soon."

"Not just yet," he patted the hand resting on his arm. For Mike and Lucy had about finished distributing those envelopes and glancing at Sam again, Tom saw Evelyn hand him the one she held. "Ladies and gentlemen; —friends!" he called for attention. "There is one last Announcement." And he saw Sam's mouth go slack. "May I present my wife, Mrs. Mandria Lyn Lucas Scott!"

"…Tom?" Mandria uttered, her grip on his sleeve tightening. As did Nicole's on her father's arm—and like Sam, she now wore an open-mouthed expression of shock.

"The keep-sake Announcement you've just received from Mandria's parents contain the details, so I won't repeat them," Tom continued, reaching into his pocket. "Instead, it would give me great pleasure to have you share a special moment with us. You see, until tonight, this beautiful lady has not worn my ring in public. …Mandria?" he turned her to face him. And lifting her left hand to his lips first, he placed the gold band on her finger while the smiling crowd looked on. Then drawing her close, admiring her most beguiling blush ever, he murmured, "I think they expect the groom to collect a kiss from his bride—and lady, I've no intention of disappointing them."

Mandria nodded, her lips forming his name, but she couldn't seem to utter a sound. And when he lowered his mouth to hers, she could barely see him for the tears of happiness clouding her vision…

On finishing his task for Evelyn, Mike had returned to Nicole's side, and while watching the touching exchange between Tom and Mandria, he felt a bit misty-eyed himself. Noting the tears spilling freely over Nicole's cheeks—assuming she felt as sentimental as he—Mike made the sad mistake of saying so, which sent her into her father's arms sobbing bitterly. All this was lost in the resounding applause and shouts of good cheer from a crowd expressing approval of the romantic gesture they'd witnessed. Lucy took part, with repeated squeals and a whole series of bouncing hops. Beside her, Allen only went through the motions, for his attention was riveted on the conversation just over his shoulder…

"God damn you to hell, Evelyn!" hissed Sam. "I will not accept this—never!"

"There is little else you can do, but make a complete ass of yourself by denying knowledge!" she hissed right back.

"No, because I *didn't* have knowledge—and you abetted this, knowing how I feel about the bastard! Well, you can bloody-well be certain I'll pay all of you back for this one!"

"But it won't be tonight, or your prestige will suffer. There are too many here with large investments in the company—and what faith would remain in your ability to manage their funds if you can not even manage your own wife and daughter? And now, dear husband, I see Mr. Brumlow and Mr. Watson coming this way. How will you greet them? As a duped fool or the proud father you *never* were?"

Sam glanced at the two men, who were very obviously seeking him out. He had been trying for weeks to get Watson's signature on a deal; and Brumlow was always good for cash and a lucrative venture. Sam could ill-afford to lose their esteem and that was a fact. Then it occurred to him, that had he allowed his angst to provoke a hasty reaction, it would have placed public sympathy squarely on the side of the enemy. He even wondered, with a fresh bloom of anger, if Tom Scott hadn't counted on that! "It doesn't end here, my dear wife," he said, straightening his coat and his posture. "All you have bought them is time—and precious damn little of it!" Then smiling broadly, Sam turned to accept those unwelcomed felicitations…

Soon, the floor was cleared and the night's honored couples led off the new dance set. Mandria's smile was radiant as Tom guided her through the sweeping steps of a waltz. "Husband, promise me something," she said.

"You little beggar!" he teased. "First, I had to promise to love, honor and obey; then never to let you fight me off—and you know how that one upset me! What could you possibly want now?"

"Well, I assume that I'm going home with you tonight—to stay, forever and ever?" she laughed.

"You damned sure are," he nodded.

"Then promise we'll spend all night and all day tomorrow in bed. We'll have our meals there and everything. We won't be at home to callers or—"

"Yes! Oh-hell-yes! Yes; yes; yes!" he expounded. "Mr. and Mrs. Scott will only be available to each other."

"Good," she nodded, "because you have a lot of explaining to do."

"Whoa now," he chuckled. "That is not what I hoped we'd be doing, pretty lady."

"Oh, we'll do that too. I'm certain you'll see to it, Tom Scott," her eyes sparkled up at him. "But even you must come up for air. Then, I want to know every detail of how this came about—and how my mother became so involved! I'm thinking now, she even tricked me into wearing these emeralds. And Father—Tom I can't believe how calmly he has behaved…"

"Hush!" Tom pecked a kiss to her beautiful mouth. "Tomorrow is soon enough for that. My love, tonight we dance and celebrate!"

And oh, how they did…

Mike spent the rest of the evening in quite a different mood and place. After Nicole's outburst, her father had hurried her from the room and tried to calm her. But Ransom returned alone to find the Captain, who was told she had one of her headaches and that he thought it best to get her home to bed. So there Mike stood, watching the happy, dancing couples, wondering what had happened. ...Why did he feel he'd missed something very important? —And maybe he was just feeling sorry for himself, but when the hell was Nicole going to answer his marriage proposal? Something else bothered him too: from one Friday to the next, he'd gone from too much sex to none. There had been time when they met earlier in the afternoon, but his kiss was rebuffed because Nicole said her hair was done for the Ball and he'd muss it. Of course, that was true, but it wasn't much helping the Captain's depressed ego at the moment.

Turning, he left the Ball and went in search of a friend he hadn't seen in several weeks: the lovely, uncomplicated, unquestioning—and uncoiffeured—Candace De Shoka...

# CHAPTER 42

Tom and Mandria were not the only ones to stay abed the next day. Mike nursed a gigantic hangover and a bad attack of conscience. After all, he did love Nicole, but he hadn't behaved like a man anxiously awaiting acceptance of a marriage proposal. He prayed, not only for forgiveness, but that she would not make one of her surprise visits, for he knew he'd have trouble looking her in the eye…

But Nicole didn't come. Her day alternated between tantrums muffled in one pillow and crying jags that soaked the case of the other—and for once, the resulting headache was of her own making…

Sam's problem was more a lack of sleep. The poison of deceit forced down his throat lay undissolved and unresolved in the churning biles of his stomach. Brooding fury aggravated his condition and he knew relief would only come with the bromides of swift retaliation. …But how? What could he do to inflict the most pain on everyone involved? The way was there and oh yes, he would find it…

By Monday, one of the ailing trio was at least ambulatory, while the other two were nearly euphoric. Feeling entirely justified by her great personal loss, Nicole accepted Mike's proposal on Sunday evening and he left for Augusta the following morning happier than he'd ever been in his life. So was Sam, for within the next forty-eight hours, his enemies would be brought to their knees—and this time, the scheme did not depend on Nicole. But her willing assistance would be given, once he told her what she most wanted to hear…

"Damn you!" Nicole slammed the suite door behind Sam. "How could you let that happen? You're Mandy's father; —you said she'd never give in! You said Tom wouldn't want her! Oh, I'll never forgive you for this! —Just never!"

"Well, no one was more surprised than I was, Nico," Sam said calmly. "But it makes no difference now. Both of those newly announced marriages are doomed."

"Talk!" she spat at him, pacing furiously. "Empty talk and empty promises—you lying bastard! I want nothing more to do with you!"

"Oh? Am I to assume you've lost interest in Tom Scott, simply because he's married?"

"You are too, Sam, so that is not at all the point!" she stopped, arms akimbo. "You saw them together! Tom is enchanted with Mandy— enchanted, I tell you!"

"You also told me you'd take him in any condition as long as he was able to make love to you. And that is being arranged as we speak."

"How?" she flailed the air with her hands. "And more importantly, when?" she demanded. "Sam, I want no more of your long range plans that never—*ever*—work!"

"Nor do I, Nico," he assured her. "It will happen day after tomorrow at the latest. Now, if you will kindly light somewhere, I'll fix us a drink and explain."

"This better be good," she plopped upon the sofa. "—Damned good, Sam Lucas!"

"It will be. For both of us," he handed her a glass of sherry—pure sherry, as he wanted her complete attention. "So, as I understand it, Evelyn, Mandy and Lucy are to meet Kathleen Morgan for lunch either tomorrow or the day after—"

"Kathleen *Rizza*," she interrupted. "I'm sure you enjoyed learning that too!"

"But not for long—if you'd keep quiet and listen, God damn it!" he bristled. There wasn't time for her antics, and his expression said so. "As I was saying, they are meeting Kathy for lunch, but she won't return to her husband. Instead, my daughter will discover her in bed with Tom. Not only will this destroy both marriages, it will completely un-do my meddling wife, who did more than her share to bring this travesty about,"

"Just where do I fit into this? You said Tom would be mine—and you said tomorrow."

"Or the day after. But you can play with him first, Nico. Kathy will only replace you before Mandy arrives. She will divorce him for what she sees—which should appeal to you, as Tom will be a free man again."

"…And engagements are easily broken," she uttered pensively. "But how on earth do you expect to do all this? Tom and Kathy may have been lovers once, but have obviously parted ways. Neither will crawl into bed and cooperate just to please you."

"Cooperation can be controlled, little Nico—with drugs," he paused for a chuckle. It was time now, to assure her willing assistance. "Yes, it's a special drug that heightens sexual desire. And we do want them caught in the act."

"Truly?" she said intently. "You can make them perform with a drug?"

"They'll have no other choice and won't remember how they got there or what went on. They will simply…*perform*, as you said."

"And I can have Tom in that very condition?" Nicole warmed to the idea.

"Non-stop, my dear—just as you like it."

"Then we must do this. We must!" she hugged Sam in her excitement. "And I want to help. What can I do to help?"

"Quite a lot, actually," he said with satisfaction. "First, you must find a red wig the color of Kathy's hair. You're to wear it—along with that veiled hat you wore here—and register as Mr. and Mrs. Tom Scott at the Lloyd Hotel, around two o'clock on the chosen day of the luncheon."

"Why not do it here? —That's a terrible place, Sam!" she began a complaint that ended in a smile. "…So notorious for illicit affairs."

"Exactly, little Nico," he returned. "Now tell the clerk your husband sent you ahead while he stayed to have drinks with friends. That way, he'll think nothing of Tom being delivered to you. He'll just assume your husband is drunk and his friends had to assist him."

"So where will Kathy be during all this?"

"Oh, yes. When you register, say you are expecting a cousin. Insist on two adjacent rooms and both keys. Kathy will be taken there—where I do intend to repay the bitch for her betrayal, while you enjoy time with your Tom. Then, we make the switch; I see you safely home; and bring Mandy back for the grand discovery."

"But they can't be left alone! —Sam, what if they escape, somehow?"

"They'll be guarded, my dear," he replied. "And with this drug, they won't be doing anything but proving themselves adulterers."

"Oh, Sam, it's going to work—this time, it's really going to work!" she rose to turn gaily before him. "But where will I find the patience to wait? I really don't think I can!"

"You do have a wig to shop for," he suggested, then added lies to keep her on target. "—And whatever else you'd care to use on Tom."

"To use on him?" she questioned with just the interest he expected.

"Yes, my dear. Didn't I tell you? Not only will he be passionate, but you can heighten his responses all the more. Massages with heavily perfumed body oils are most effective—and some men even respond to the torment of a switching. If anything, I'd say you have more than enough to do until then."

"So I must add a stop at the perfumers to my list…," she said pensively.

"And I must go and learn which day we put this into motion," he rose to leave and had reached the door before realizing she had not bothered to bid him farewell. But so what? If believing his line of garbage kept her entertained—and doing exactly as she was told, so the hell what?

But unbeknownst to Sam, as usual, Nicole would do only what pleased her most…

At around one thirty on Wednesday, Kathy was waylaid while returning from her luncheon engagement. She did not recognize the two men who roughly pulled her into a closed carriage, but in her heart she knew who sent them. And when a foul liquid was forced into her mouth, she managed to let most of it drain from the corners. It was her only hope and she clung to it as they bound and gagged her; as they shoved her to the floorboard where she had to endure not only a bumpy ride, but fondling hands which she tried desperately to avoid. Still she clung to hope, even as her struggles ceased and she drifted into deep sleep…

Upon arrival at the Lloyd Hotel, Nicole's first order was having a bath delivered to her room. Into the steaming tub, she poured a portion of the most expensive scent she had ever purchased: Mandria's honeysuckle oil, which she had to bribe from the perfumer's assistant at double the cost. After a leisurely soak, she briskly toweled her skin until it tingled with a healthy glow. Then, donning a new sapphire blue negligee, trimmed in the sheerest lace, she sat before the fire to brush-dry her hair, admiring the way it fell softly in white-blonde sheets. Next, she examined her nails and finding them in perfect repair, moved to the dressing table. Opening a cosmetic case, she dabbed more of the honeysuckle to the pulse and pressure points of her body, adding extra to her maiden-hair, the creases of her elbows and behind her knees.

For amusement, she applied overly generous amounts of rouge to lip and cheek and practiced the alluring expressions used by whores to entice their customers. She decided hers were better, but also that the rouge did her features little justice. So removing it, she sat a while longer delighting in her own unequalled perfection. But that had been hours ago and even Nicole could tire of pampering herself—especially since she'd been waiting in this room since eleven o'clock in the morning, for heaven's sake.

Making another impatient trip to the window, she rubbed away the frost of a chilly late afternoon. "Why doesn't he come?" she muttered. Kathy awaited Sam's attention in the room next door and Tom should have been delivered to her soon after school let out, but now it was nearing five. "Damn you, Sam!" she stomped a jewel blue slipper. "Where is Tom?"

In answer, there was a light rap on the door and Nicole raced to answer it. "So?" she faced Sam across the threshold. "Did you finally remember I've been waiting all day?"

Sam felt his blood stir at the sight of her slender body silhouetted against the fire. "Easy, little Nico," he allowed himself the feel of a nearly nude breast. "Jack and Harry are bringing him in by the front door now."

"But why are you so late?" she impatiently brushed his hand aside.

"Because Tom required a heavier sleeping potion than Kathy—and for a while there, I wondered if the bastard was immune to the God damned stuff!" he said, dropping his cloak over a chair.

"A sleeping potion?" she said testily. "That is not what you promised to give him!"

"Nico, I had to get him here first, didn't I?"

"Well…yes, I suppose so," she nodded. "But how did you get him to take a sleeping potion?"

"Does it matter?" he stepped aside as Tom was hauled through the door and dumped on the bed with Nicole right on Jack and Harry's heels. "All right, you two," he said to his hirelings, "check on the one next door, then wait in the hall." And they left, but not before ogling Nicole as much as they dared.

Nicole was already unbuttoning Tom's shirt when Sam went to a table that held some glasses. From a pocket flask, he poured a small amount of whiskey in one and a healthier portion in another. The larger drink was for himself and he paused to savor a taste. Into the other, he sprinkled precisely measured grains of his Zombie powder—just enough to effect will power, so that in spite of the massive sleep potion, she might be able to arouse Tom. …If she worked at it diligently enough. At one point, he really had considered giving both his captives a lethal one and a half grams—and he had it with him in case he changed his mind again. But no, this plan was infinitely better. Let them live in disgrace; let them just try to explain their adultery.

Taking another drink from his glass, he glanced toward the bed and watched as Nicole unfastened Tom's trousers, slid her hands inside and with closed eyes, uttered a satisfied sigh. Not knowing why he found that distasteful, Sam set his glass aside and took Tom's drink to her. "Do forgive me," he held it for her inspection, "but if you want more than that to play with, you'll have to pour this down while I hold him up."

"I will, Sam—oh yes, I will!" her eyes burned with unnatural light. "But help me undress him first. I'll never manage it alone."

Sam expelled a breath of acceptance, and did as she asked. Kathy awaited him—and he did owe her such special attention—yet if he didn't accommodate Nicole, she would be interrupting and complaining every few minutes.

Tom's nudity had opposite effects on the two standing over him. Flushed with her own arousal, Nicole made no secret of her pleasure as her hands roamed him eagerly. But Sam felt twin pricks of jealousy: one because of Nicole's enjoyment; the other because not in his best days had he so splendid a male body. It was hard to believe this was the same gawky boy he's once called *Miss Scott*. And as Mandria had previously, he wondered how Tom came by his muscular build? He would have been most surprised to learn he was the reason.

"All right, Sam," Nicole said huskily, all but snatching up the glass. "Let's do it. Then you can leave. I mean to bring him along from start to finish and I don't need your company."

Sam resented her tone too, but complied. "First the drink," he held Tom while she administered it. "...And now the dumb-cane leaf," he drew one from his pocket and crushed it against Tom's teeth.

"No!" she slapped at his hand. "That's what Mr. Trinkle gave his slave and the boy died—his tongue swole in his throat and he choked to death!"

"I know that, Nico," he retorted. "Trinkle just used too much on the sassy-mouthed buck. What I've given Tom will only keep him quiet for a few days. Kathy will have some as well. It's better than making love through a gag. I want to feel her mouth—as well as her sweet little red-haired cunt."

"Well, anyway, you've already done it," she said, crawling onto the bed. "So go away and leave us alone now."

Having been twice dismissed, Sam picked up his drink, stalked to the door and jerked it open. But he could hear Nicole greedily teasing at Tom's ear and unable to stop himself, he paused to look back. Now she was tracing bare, plumped nipples across his chest; eagerly tasting his lips—and all the while, massaging the stump of his sleeping desire, awaiting a spark of interest. "Damn the bastard," he gulped at his drink, for though it was Tom who was drugged and not Nicole, this time she still might reach the same heights to which he'd led her, simply because she wanted the man so badly. Going out, he closed the door on that unsettling thought…

It was then that the quiet, empty hallway drew his attention. "The God damned perverts," he nodded, suspecting Jack and Harry were molesting another slumbering body. Not that he actually cared. He was planning to let them have a turn when he was finished with Kathy. Hadn't he promised her as much during their last encounter?

But once again, Sam was denied his anticipated moment, because the room next door was empty. "Fuck!" he exploded, hurling his glass against the far wall. And from the other side of the bed, where the shards and liquid splattered to the floor, came a moan that brought Sam on the run.

"O-o-oh," Harry moaned again. "Oh, God, I'm ruint for sure."

"Talk—and talk fast, you idiot!" Sam loomed overhead. "Where is the woman?"

"O-o-oh," Harry repeated. "She kicked me—the bitch kicked me right in the nuts."

"Man, you'll think you've grown new tonsils from the foot I'll put into you! —God damn it, sit up and tell me what happened!"

"Yes, sir—o-o-oh; all right, Mr. Lucas," Harry struggled to prop, painfully against the wall; not daring to mention that he'd cut his hand on broken glass while doing so. "Me and Jack, we come in to check on her—like you ordered—and she was awake this time. Swear to God, Mr. Lucas, she spread her legs while we felt of her a little. So Jack, he loosens her gag 'cause she kept trying to talk—not yelling talk, but real hot and horny-like. Said if we'd free her hands too, she'd give us a good time—both at oncest, don't you know? Promised me a blow job and said Jack could fuck her ass, cause he likes it there, you see—"

"Harry!" Sam injected. "Where is she? —And where the hell is Jack?"

"Well, I don't rightly know. She said she'd undress for us too, if we cared to set down and watch. And true to God, she wiggled around here, showing us her tits. Then somehow, she got holt of a vase and bashed old Jack's head. —See?" Harry pointed to more broken glass. "And afore I could move, she kicked the shit out of me and run out the door! But maybe Jack went to catch her, 'cause he sure ain't here."

"He better have!" Sam began to pace. "God damn it, how could two grown men let a woman escape them?"

"'Cause she's a Jezebel!" Harry declared. "A red headed, man teasing Jezebel!"

"And she kicked you right in the brains!" Sam started for the door, where he collided with Jack.

"Mr. Lucas, she got away!" the bug-eyed man panted. "—And her husband found her too!"

"Are they coming here?" Sam seized Jack by the shirt collar.

"No, sir— No! I followed *them* back to the DeSoto Hotel!"

"All right then, you talk!" Sam shoved him away. "Start to finish, I want to know what happened and what was said."

"Start to finish? Well, me and Harry come in here to check—"

"No, Jack!" Sam again cursed the fates that forced him to deal with morons. "What happened when you went after her?"

"Oh. Well, she run out the back way into the alley and I wasn't far behind," he said while dabbing a blood soaked handkerchief to his head wound. "Anyways, she was lost, 'cause I chased her through the same alley twice. She didn't know who had her, either, 'cause me and Harry was new faces to her; and she didn't know where we was holding her, 'cause she was so lost and all. And she never seen you whilst she was awake, so you're safe too, Mr. Lucas. ...Sir."

Sam's patience was being sorely tested. "And pray tell, how did you learn all that while chasing her up and down alleyways?"

"Truth be told, I guessed the part about you, since you never come in here when she was in here, you see? But I heard her say the rest to her husband. Mr. Lucas, she run right smack into him over by Ellis Square. She was crying real bad, but I got close enough to hear. Said to him she got away from she didn't know who or where and just kept running and running and couldn't get back here did she want to—which she didn't want to—'cause she begged her I-talian to just take her on home. Then he said a bunch of foreign stuff I couldn't understand—'cept the part about looking for her all afternoon—and he acted more interested in calming her down than finding us, anyways. So I think everthing worked out just fine!"

"No, Jack, everything is not fine," Sam nodded, weighing the remnants of the situation as his mood grew more ominous. Kathy's escape meant another God damned failure. ...Or did it? Wouldn't it serve his purpose just as well if Nicole were found with Tom? All he needed was her consent to spend a little longer in bed with him—and she'd give it, or she'd be given that lethal dosage he'd been tempted to use earlier. Murder was a small price to pay—especially since Tom would be blamed for it. That would still destroy the marriage and his meddlesome wife's high hopes for it; turn Herb into Tom's enemy; and then he could cast himself into the role of consoling friend and mentor to Allen—as Tom was led to the gallows! It almost had him wishing Nicole would refuse.

"Harry; Jack," Sam reached for his wallet. "Take this money and leave Savannah tonight. I've heard the Italian is a crack shot—and he will come looking for the men who dared touch his wife. Now, go and stay gone, if you value your lives. And I do mean tonight!"

"Yes, sir!" they chimed, and as quickly as Harry was able to move with Jack's help, they were gone...

A strange sense of calm guided Sam as he began putting the room in order. He took a pillowcase from the bed before straightening the covers and into it he put Kathy's bindings and a towel he used to dab up blood and both sets of broken glass from the floor. Then, easing into the room next door, he left the pillowcase just inside.

Nicole did not even hear Sam enter and he smiled as he paused to watch. Still trying to inspire a full erection, she rode Tom from the top, urging him to cooperate with her sterling effort. "That's it. Do it, Tom. Take it from me, you beautiful bastard!" And scoring the flesh of his chest with her nails, she laughed when he flinched and rode him all the harder.

Sam saw the glazed look in Tom's eyes and knew he'd cause no problems while Nicole's fate was decided. Toward that end, he mixed his poisoned drink, left it and another dumb-cane leaf on the table before approaching the bed. "Having fun, my dear little nympho?" he whispered close to her ear.

Startled, she straightened indignantly. "What are you doing back in here? Get out, Sam! —Go!"

"I'm so sorry, but I can not do that. There has been a change in plans—a dramatic one, I'm afraid. Come now, we must talk about it," he took her arm.

"Oh, no, you don't!" she jerked away. "Tom isn't ready yet and you're not going to ruin this for me!"

"Nico, kindly uncork yourself and listen," he tried to reason with her. "Kathy has escaped and—"

"So? Go fuck some other whore," she continued her undulations. "But you will leave us alone!"

I intend to do that very thing, my dear—one way or the other." And spotting Tom's clothing beside him, he searched the pockets, removing the note he'd sent asking that Tom come by his office *for the sake of Mandy's future happiness.* "But my daughter will now have to find you in bed with her husband and I wondered how you felt about that."

"…Me?" she looked his way in confusion. "Sam, that's insane. Daddy would disown me for the scandal alone!"

"Perhaps not," he said. "You could claim Tom lured you here; that he got you drunk and took advantage."

"But Tom would know better," she reluctantly swung herself down to sit on the edge of the bed. And when Tom rolled against her hip, she drew his groping hand to her breast and held it there. "He wants me, Sam. Can't you see that? If I did what you're asking, he'd never come near me again—even if Mandy did divorce him."

"So your final answer is no?" he asked from beside the table—and her waiting glass.

"Of course, it's no, you stupid man!" she laughed. "Now, do go away," she reached to fondle Tom anew.

"Well, I'm afraid my reasons for seeing this done are more important—and at this point, I see no harm in telling you why. You see, by a bigamous marriage, Tom is my step-son. But Allen truly *is* my son—illegally—but *my* son, nonetheless. And Tom could ruin the plans I have for Allen by exposing the past."

"Why hasn't he done so already?" she rose to her feet, curious now. "—His precious Mandy?"

"No, he was only a boy when I left and has yet to recognize me," he watched her move toward him. "But I can not allow Allen's future to dangle on the edge of Tom's memory. …So like Mandy, Allen will have to turn on Tom—which means Tom must leave Savannah and in total disgrace," he added, knowing this would bring her even closer.

"Leave?" she exclaimed. "You said nothing about Tom leaving before! I want him here; and I want him free of Mandy. That was our deal, Sam, and none other!"

"Again, I am sorry, Nico," he shrugged. "But I have decided how it will be." And that brought her closer still.

"You have decided?" she challenged, hands planted firmly on her hips. "Who are you to decide anything for me—or Tom? You can't and especially, not now!"

"Can't I?" he urged her to take just one more argumentative step. "No, because I will tell your big dark secret if you make me. Now:

Tom-Scott-is-not-going-anywhere!" she jabbed him with each word. "But you may. Leave—and go lick your wounds somewhere else, Sam. I have a man to attend!"

Quick as a snake strike, Sam had Nicole by the throat, a thumb pressed into her windpipe. He released the pressure only enough for her to gasp for air and suck down the lethal mixture he poured into her mouth. Repeating the process until it was gone, he then crushed the dumb-cane against her teeth, and clamped a hand over her mouth to prevent a scream until the leaf juice could take effect. "A fitting way for a bitch to die—fucking herself to death," he fabricated the terror that would speed death through her bloodstream while dragging her back to the bed. "Look at the fine cock that awaits you, little Nico. Just a few seconds more and I'll release you to Tom. —And isn't it ironic? You were dying to know his passion and now you will die because of it. You won't escape his strong arms; and once your own dosage activates, you won't even care. Go to him, Nico," Sam forced her close to Tom's chest. "Rub your pretty tits on him now, if you dare. ...Ah, there: see his hands move; his head turn? Could he be looking for you? Go ahead, bitch—spread your legs and Tom will fuck you straight into hell!" Then, satisfied that her limpness said his stories had the desired effect, he shoved her onto the bed.

But Nicole managed two final words of defiance. "Won't die!" she rasped and ramming fingers to the back of her throat, she vomited all over herself, Tom and the bed.

"God damn you!" Sam viciously twisted her backward by the hair of the head. Never had he known such fury—how dare she try and empty her stomach! And while that was still registering, Nicole brought an elbow around, punching him in the groin. "Bitch!" he hissed, backhanding her. "Deborah's bitch!" he hit her twice again, enjoying it more each time. "But she never went against my will—never!" his blows grew heavier. "She would fuck me or any man I named—just for a dose of my power! But not you! All you wanted was Tom! Always Tom!" And the ones delivered with this tirade were frenzied, hammer-hard and unceasing...until he realized she was no longer moving or resisting them. "Stupid bitch!" he said into her bloody, battered face while gasping for breath. Then, finding no pulse in her throat, he straightened with satisfaction. "You could have died lying peacefully beside your Tom, little Nico, but for all of that, you did have to die."

As he towed Nicole back over the bed, the vomit and blood which covered her left its trail across Tom—an added touch of realism. Embellishing it further, Sam pressed Tom's hands into the gory mess before rolling his body onto hers. Going for the whiskey flask, he took a long slow swig, made a silent toast to the couple before him, and poured the rest of that over them too. Yes, the unholy sight they made, along with all the unsavory odors about them, would be enough to convince Mandria and the police that Tom had killed Nicole in a drunken rage. "…Why they might even hang him on the spot," Sam chuckled.

Then going to the bathtub, he dipped a towel in the water and wiped his face and hands as he moved on to the dressing table to check the rest of his appearance. "Shit!" he cursed his mirrored image, for his clothing was also a bloody mess. It was a tiresome inconvenience, but he'd have to go by his office for a change. …Or maybe it wasn't so inconvenient. He could burn these clothes and his pillowcase collection while there, destroying all evidence of his connection to any of this.

As Nicole's cosmetic case was sitting there, Sam took a perfume bottle from it—part of a matched set he'd given her at The Tabby House—and though he'd always hated her heavy rose essence, decided to allow himself one morbid, nostalgic and final whiff. But finding the scent of honeysuckle instead—remembering she would never change perfumes for him, but had for Tom—he was angry all over again. Turning, he flung the bottle into the fireplace where it shattered, filling the room with a puff of thick scented smoke—a burnt offering of honeysuckle and tree bark to all of Nicole's lost dreams. "But only the beginning of mine," he muttered, adding the blood-stained towel to the pillow case now. And checking the room a last time for any trace of his presence, Sam put on his cloak, tucked the pillowcase underneath and left by an alley door…

# CHAPTER 43

S am Lucas returned to the Lloyd Hotel an hour later escorting his daughter, and for the first time that day, came through the front door. At the desk, he made a to-do about seeing the register, snatching it away from the meek looking clerk.

"See here, Mandy—look at this! It's here, just as I was told: Mr. and Mrs. Thomas Scott! —Clerk?" he turned on the little man again. "I've sent for the Police already, as my daughter's husband is obviously here with another woman. She will need competent witnesses, so you'd best start remembering all that you've seen and heard about this!"

"Father, I tell you there has been some mistake!" Mandria objected, as she had during the entire ride over. "It—it's another Tom Scott. It has to be!"

"Then where is your husband, missy? You said he didn't come home as he usually does after school, so where is he?"

"I don't know," she lifted her chin. "But Tom is not here—and certainly, not with another woman!"

"There is but one way to prove that, my dear. When the Police arrive," he pretended to check the register for accuracy, "…Yes, we're going to room 107 and see for ourselves."

Mandria gave a negative nod and sat shakily on a near-by chair. …*Hold yourself together*, she thought. …*This is only a horrid mistake.* …*Tom loves me. He would not do this; —he just wouldn't!*

Then, Patrick Herb entered the lobby with three of his men close behind. "Mr. Lucas," he said stiffly, having no use for the man. "You have a complaint, sir?"

"I do. I was informed that my daughter's husband is in room 107 with a woman. And it seems a certainty, as the bastard was stupid enough to register under his own name!"

Patrick looked for himself and then nodded. "This is not a Police matter, but nonetheless…this appears ta be written by a woman. — Clerk, who signed this: man or woman?"

"Woman," he answered promptly. "Pretty one too, with red hair and all? Told me her husband was to join her—and he did. But he come drunk and had to be helped to their rooms."

"Rooms?" Patrick caught that immediately.

"Yes, sir, she rented two. One for a cousin, but that one hasn't shown up yet."

"Wh…what did the husband look like?" Mandria forced the question out.

"And who was the red haired woman?" Sam injected. "We both know, don't we, daughter? *She* is in town, after all."

Mandria gave another negative nod and looked away.

Patrick Herb wasn't ready to believe this either. He knew and respected Tom Scott. He also knew Sam Lucas… "Well, Clerk?" he said. "The lady asked for a description. Can you give one ta her?"

"He was big—and must have been heavy, because his friends had their hands full getting him in here. …Dark hair, dark suit—and yeah, I'd say he'd be what the ladies call tall, dark and handsome."

"Well?" Sam looked from his daughter to Patrick. "What more do you want? Shall we visit that room and ferret the bastard out?"

"Sorry, Mr. Lucas. As I've said already, this is not a Police matter," Patrick repeated. "We have no legal right ta enter unless foul play is suspected. And neither do you—not forcibly."

"Then arrest me!" Sam drew Mandria up and steered her toward the rear corridor. "Because one way or another, we're going in there."

"Just a minute!" Patrick called. "Mr. Lucas, you're not thinking ta take the lady in? Surely, sir, you can see how upset she is."

"Captain Herb," Sam paused to look back with a sneer, "in the past few months—at every turn and in every instance—my daughter has refused to believe what a bastard Scott is. And you have refused to be the one witness she might believe now. Man, I have no choice but taking her with me. She has to believe her own eyes, now doesn't she?" he finished, prodding Mandria forward again.

Patrick was trying very hard to keep his private and professional views separate. "Oh, hell!" he swore, hurrying after them—and his men came right along too. "Sir!" he caught up mid-way down the dimly lit hall. "I must insist you keep this legal. Me men and I will go first. We will knock and ask ta speak ta the man in 107. That much we can do for the lady."

"Then do you're your good deed," Sam pointed to a room just over the Police Captain's shoulder.

As Patrick knocked, he glanced at Mandria, who leaned against the wall beside the door looking quite pale. He felt very sorry for her—not because he thought Tom was here, but because her own father would put her through such a thing. And anticipating the satisfaction of proving Sam wrong, he knocked more boldly.

"God damn it, how much time and warning are you going to allow?" Sam stepped closer. "They could have crawled through a window by now!" And he gave the door a kick that sent it slamming into the wall.

"…Jesus!" murmured one of the young officers, staring through the doorway. "Oh, sweet Jesus!"

"Captain, that's Scott, all right, but the woman's no red-head," said another. "That's Mike's…; that's Nicole O'Rourke, sir—and Christ, but she looks dead!"

"Nicole?" Patrick uttered, stepping in beside Sam and a little behind the other three policemen. For it was then he realized this touched his life too. It had been just two nights ago—late Sunday night—when his nephew awakened him to share the joy of his engagement to this girl…

Mandria stood against the door-jam now, her face turned away. She couldn't force herself to look, but that didn't shut out the voices or the putrid, cesspool odors assailing her. Both painted vivid pictures; both were making her want to gag; —and when the youngest of the policemen did, her nausea worsened ten-fold.

"Damn, what a blood bath!" swore the third officer. "He must have beat her unmerciful! —Captain, she is dead, isn't she?"

"She appears ta be, Price," Patrick felt for a pulse and nodded sadly. "But you'd best go for the doctor. We need ta confirm cause."

Mandria heard footsteps coming and when her father's arm closed about her shoulders, she assumed she was being moved from the departing policeman's way. But that wasn't Sam's intention at all, for he didn't stop until Mandria stood at the foot of the bed. Now, she had to look and it was so much worse than what she'd imagined. Blood was everywhere; all over—so much blood! It was smeared on their bodies; spilled on the sheets; splattered on the wall; caked in the tangles of Nicole's hair; between Tom's fingers...

"No! —No!" she shuddered violently. "No, please God, no!" she agonized. And as if in response to her voice, Tom moved slowly, almost protectively—or was it...sensually—over Nicole.

"Well, Captain Herb?" Sam said indignantly—and in graphic detail. "It's enough that Scott has raped and beaten poor little Nico to death, but damn it man, you could stop him from trying to repeat the deed on her dead body—and right in front of his wife! Have you no regard for her feelings?"

"Oh!" Mandria recoiled. "I can't bear this—I just can't!" And fleeing across the room, she clung to the mantle to keep from falling.

"Captain," the rookie was gagging again, "sir, can I please open a window?"

"Go ahead, Faircloth," Patrick replied, glad the lad had spoken when he did, for himself had been on the verge of giving Sam Lucas a most unprofessional piece of his mind. First of all, Lucas was to blame for his daughter's misery. She should never have been allowed in this room. And secondly, Lucas was the one who insisted on it!

"I've seen a lot of drunks in my day," said Officer Schall, helping Patrick roll Tom away from Nicole, "but none like this one. Captain, was he really going after her again?"

"Lower your voice, for Lord's sake," Patrick advised, watching Mandria sink slowly to her knees to stare blankly into the fire. "Here: cover Tom with the sheet. I'll cover her with the spread."

"Humph!" Sam said now. "Your concern for Nicole's dignity is understandable, but I fail to see the need for extending it to Scott. — That bastard should be dragged through the streets as he is and hung in the nearest square!"

Police Captain Patrick David Herb straightened suddenly, having taken all he was going to from this man. "Mr. Lucas!" he snapped. "There will be no lynching here! Now, if you've no more ta contribute than that, I'll be thanking you for leaving so I can get on with this investigation! —And as I'm certain you're anxious ta' get your poor daughter home, you can stop by the station tomorrow and give us a statement."

"What investigation?" Sam said huffily. "This case seems cut and dried to me!"

"Maybe; maybe not," Patrick watched as Sam drew Mandria up from the floor. And because she wore such a dazed expression, he felt compelled to add a word of advice. "…Mr. Lucas, she's had a very bad shock. It might be wise ta get the poor lass some medical attention."

"The poor-lass needed a good shock," Sam retorted. "But she'll get over Scott now—and the sooner she does, the better off she'll be."

Patrick had to wonder about that when Mandria insisted on stopping beside the bed again. So, evidently, did his men, for both lowered their eyes, respecting her need for a private farewell to her husband. And what touched Patrick most, was her manner. Instead of wailing in anger—that she had every right to express—she just stood looking at him while endless, silent tears, flowed down her cheeks…

Then, as if Tom sensed her presence a second time, slowly his head turned her way and his eyes fluttered open. There was no recognition in those blue-glazed depths, and yet, he tried to speak. "Dreams! — Bad dreams!" his lips formed words no one could hear or understand. "…Mama? —No! Not, Mandria—no!" his eyes widened and his head nodded wildly. "Don't!" he began to choke. "Oh, God—don't!" he convulsed. And though all was done in silence, the strain on his

563

swollen tongue and throat sent a stream of fresh blood gushing from the corner of his mouth.

Mandria looked once at her father, took three steps toward the door and fainted…

When Sam pulled into the Lucas stable yard, Mandria was conscious and offered no resistance when he led her into the parlor. Nor had she a word to say when he repeated the tale of horror to her mother. But when Evelyn hugged her—dared to defend Tom, insisting there had to be a more plausible explanation for all that happened—Mandria went to pieces, hysterically laughing and crying at the same time. Every effort to calm her failed and finally Evelyn sent Jed for a doctor. Sam then carried Mandria to her room through a crowd of anxious servants gathered in the hall. "Damn it—get to your quarters!" he ordered. And when he returned from depositing his burden on her bed and into her mother's care, it was through an empty hallway. Going to his study, he slammed the door. He had played the concerned father quite long enough. Now it was time to celebrate his victory over every one of his enemies—and with his best cognac at that!

But before the study door had even stopped rattling, one by one, the servants reappeared and moving as a single, silent body went up the stairway to wait before Mandria's door…

It took time and effort for the attending policemen to calm Tom down too. In eerie silence, he continued to struggle against the demonic visions haunting his drug clouded brain. It was nearly choking to death that ended it. He remained on his side where they had finally been able to roll him so the blood drained from his mouth. And yielding only to life, he drifted back into a deep sleep. Patrick and Schall were left panting for breaths of their own, while young Faircloth returned to the window with another case of the heaves.

"As I said before," Schall managed between gasps for air, "Scott's not behaving like any drunk I ever saw. Most scream out in terror when they see their demons, but this one suffers in silence and bites his tongue or something! —Is he having fits, maybe?"

"This man is not a drunk, I can tell you that," Patrick wheezed back.

"But the stench of liquor is on him—along with everything else," Faircloth added, gagging again.

"What is he then: insane?" Schall asked.

"Acts more like a drug user and their demons are much worse," Patrick said. "A few years back, a local whore was fed an overdose of Spanish Fly and we found her hemorrhaging ta death in a closet—still ramming the mop handle what did it inta her own body."

"So you think Scott took something like that," Schall surmised.

"Or had it give ta him," Patrick answered.

"Either way, he must have gone crazy too. Why else would he beat a beautiful girl like that? Look at her, lying in that stinking, bloody filth."

Faircloth, who still clung to a chair by the window, suddenly leapt to his feet. "And—and look at her fingers!" he stammered. "Captain, I saw them move!"

"Oh, lad, if only you had," Patrick leaned closer. "But how could it be?"

"There—I saw it too!" Schall exclaimed. "Captain, what now?"

"Get her to the hospital! —Get her to the hospital!" Faircloth braved joining them in his excitement. "Captain, we have to take her for help!"

"No!" Patrick warded him off. "For God sake, don't touch her! Son, if her injuries were grievous enough ta slow her breathing and pulse ta nothing, moving her a half inch could be fatal. No, we'll just cover her more—keep her still and warm until Price returns with the Doctor."

"So, what about Scott?" asked Faircloth. "Want us to dress him and take him in?"

"Yes, I'm afraid so," Patrick sighed. "For his own safety, Tom had best be behind bars when this story gets out."

"Sir? …Why are you suspicious of what happened here?" Schall questioned. "I don't care for Sam Lucas any more than you, but as he said, this case seems pretty cut and dried."

"Maybe; maybe not," Patrick repeated. "But when the Doctor finishes here, I'm sending him down for a look at Tom too. What could it hurt?"

Soon after Tom had been transported to the jail, the Doctor arrived and Nicole's condition was found to be grave indeed. But she was alive and Patrick instructed Officer Price to assist in getting her quickly and safely to the hospital and then to locate her father and get him there too. Alone now, in room 107 at the Lloyd Hotel, Police Captain Herb was able to go over the place more thoroughly.

Lifting a thickly veiled hat from the corner of the dressing table, he found the red wig underneath. *Why*, he wondered, *had Nicole found both these items necessary for her disguise when one would have sufficed? Why did she register alone, take two rooms—and after searching her belongings, where was that second room key? Also, of note, from the tub of bath water, the cosmetics and remnants of the negligee she wore, she'd come for an afternoon of romance. But what woman plans for everything else and does not bring along her perfume? That her intention was plain meant she was willing, so why had Sam Lucas insisted on calling this rape? And, if Tom was willing too—and one would have to assume, as eager—why get drunk before he arrived? Then there was the strong whiskey stench near the bed, but if one or both imbibed, then where was the bottle?* Much here was not making sense…

Throughout the night, Evelyn remained at Mandria's side, trying to keep her from thrashing about so restlessly. But Doctor Kelly would only allow small doses of the laudanum that would have given her peace, because on examination, Mandria was found to be three months pregnant…

Likewise, Ransom's night was spent beside his daughter's hospital bed, where she rested, most peacefully, in a coma. And he was told Nicole's prognosis was not good; that the Doctors suspected brain damage…

No vigil was kept by Tom's narrow cell cot. No one could hear his silenced voice. None could see the terror behind his closed eyelids. And had the other prisoners been aware of any of it, none would have cared much…

Come morning, at their respective bedsides, Evelyn and Ransom read every word printed about the tragedy and both were confused by conflicting reports. The Gazette sided with the Police account, which said a thorough investigation was underway and stressed certain inconsistencies yet to be explained. The Town Crier virtually branded Tom a murderer and called for an immediate trial and swift execution. Ransom had more right than any to want justice done—and he did— but even he could not condone the title of murderer while his daughter lived and he could still pray for her recovery. The view of The Town Crier raised suspicions in Evelyn's mind, as almost word for word, it was the same story Sam had told when he brought Mandria home. But how had he been able to bribe an entire editorial staff? And why?

The morning papers were also how Allen learned what happened and he all but ran to Police Headquarters. But he wasn't allowed into the cell with Tom and couldn't rouse him through the barred door.

"Sleeping off his whiskey, the murdering bastard!" called an inmate down the way.

"Yeah, let him be, boy," called another. "He's practicing for the long sleep he'll be getting when the hangman takes him away."

Greatly disturbed that Tom had been judged guilty even by criminals, Allen went back to the front desk and asked to speak with Patrick Herb. He was told the Captain had returned to the crime scene; that he wouldn't be in until noon; and that Allen couldn't see Tom again until then anyway. So he sat down to wait, watching for Patrick each time the front door opened. —And it opened frequently. For on this particular morning, the Stationhouse was a-swarm, not only with reporters wanting the latest word, but with outraged, opinionated citizens and he did not hear one word in Tom's favor. Noon finally came, but Patrick hadn't, so Allen returned downstairs, only to find his brother's cell empty.

"Come for him near a hour ago. Likely been grilling him ever since," the informative prisoners began again.

"He's a cagey one, too—wouldn't talk. Kept holding his throat real pitiful like. Feeling the noose, I'd say!"

"And when they told him the charges, he done a right good job acting surprised. Why, I couldn't have done it better."

Allen took the stairs in twos and once more asked to see Patrick Herb, but was told the Captain was presently interrogating Tom and wouldn't be speaking to anyone for a while yet. Out of patience, Allen was still arguing the point when Sebastian Rizza appeared at his side.

"I wish to see *il Capitano* also," he told the Desk Sergeant. "I read of this unjust case against Thomas Scott *nel giorale*...uh, in the newspaper. I have knowledge of why a red wig *e necessario* to this crime. Would you say this to him, *per favore?*"

The Sergeant left and Allen gave Iano's hand a vigorous shaking. "Lord, I'm glad to see a friendly face. They won't tell me a damn thing; haven't let me speak to Tom yet; —and I don't know what to do next!"

"*Pace, piccolo fratello*...uh, have peace, little brother," Iano said. "Thomas would not do this thing. It will be proved."

"I know he didn't, and you know it, but Tom is in jail all the same. Sir, Nico has been throwing herself at him for months, but he never looked at her or touched her. If you want the truth of it, he does not even like her! He loves Mandy—and hell, at the Ball last Friday, everyone saw where his heart was. Now it's Thursday and half of those same damned people are crying for his blood!"

"There was one who wanted it then, *mi amico*: Sam Lucas—who wants it still, I think," Iano nodded.

"Mr. Rizza; Mr. Scott?" Patrick said from the doorway of his office where he'd listened with interest to their conversation. "Please come in, sirs. I'd appreciate any information you're able ta give."

So in they went, and as they talked, Patrick scribbled in a small dog-eared notebook. He had to write fast to keep up with Allen, because once started, he poured out the whole saga of Tom's troubles with Sam and Nicole—and even that they suspected the pair of conspiring.

"And when did you last see your brother on Wednesday?" Patrick asked then.

"In the morning, when we both left for work."

"Was he well? —No cold or ailment of that nature?

"No, Captain. ...Why?

"Has he ever been subject to laryngitis; —the loss of the voice?"

"No, Captain! —*Why?*" Allen repeated, becoming concerned. "Is there something wrong with Tom? One of the prisoners said he was holding his throat. Was he hurt or injured or what?"

"Easy, lad," Patrick raised a calming hand. "He is fine except for this bout of muteness. But try ta talk he certainly has, and it has caused bleeding—twice, now. So we won't be questioning him again 'til the morrow. The Doc says his symptoms are the same as those caused from eating the dumb cane leaf, but that he's never treated an adult white male for it before—only slaves or children what ate some by mistake. Anyways, he said it should heal in a day or so if no more strain is put on his vocal cords. ...But you would say he spoke normally yesterday morning?"

"Yes, sir. He taught school too, so he had to be all right then—until three o'clock, at least, when school lets out."

"I'd think so," Patrick made a note to check that out. "Do you know anything of how he usually spends his afternoons?"

"He does some tutoring, though he's usually home when I come in from work around five. But he wasn't home yesterday and before leaving again for the evening, I teased Mandy for behaving like a worried wife. When I came back about eleven, the house was quiet, so I went to bed, thinking everyone else already had. I went to work early today—and that's where I saw the story in the damn papers..."

569

A sudden thought brought Allen to his feet. "Oh, my God—Mandy! If she read it too, she must be going through hell!"

"She did, Allen," Patrick nodded. "But she didn't read it. Lucas brought her ta the Lloyd Hotel last night. First hand, she saw Tom and…well, she saw that whole awful scene."

*"Madre Di Dio,"* Rizza swore softly.

"Damn—oh, damn!" Allen rubbed a hand to his forehead. "Captain, if I can't see Tom now, may I leave? He'd want me to check on Mandy."

"Yes, lad, I think he would. …And off the record, it might help her ta know I'm doing all I can ta help, because I'm not satisfied with the way things are stacking up. This case is almost too easy and that makes me nervous."

When Allen had gone Iano said, "It is Sam Lucas behind all of this, *Capitano*. You saw what he did to my Kathy—how he beat her? He does the same to Nicole O'Rourke. Thomas Scott is much too honorable for this."

"Off the record again, Iano, I happen to agree," Patrick turned to a new page in his notebook. "So, back on the record—Mr. Rizza—let's talk about that red wig…"

# CHAPTER 44

When Allen finally tracked Mandria to her parent's home, he heard both good and bad news from Evelyn. She freely assured him of her own unshaken faith in Tom, but then told him how upset Mandria had been and that she was uncertain what her daughter's feelings were. At present, she added, Mandria was finally asleep, and under Doctor's orders, was not to have visitors yet. After Allen left, Evelyn wondered if she should have told him about the pregnancy. She hadn't told Sam. She hadn't told anyone, for in truth, she wasn't really sure how Mandria felt about that either…

Sam didn't arrive home until late that night, still not believing how stubbornly Nicole clung to life. If she came out of the coma with the brain of an animal, he was safe. But if by the slimmest chance, she recovered unencumbered, he was a doomed man. So, for most of the day, he'd searched for a confederate within the hospital walls; one desperate enough for money to feed him pertinent information on her condition; one who would also commit murder should the need arise. And of course, he found one…

Allen went again on Friday morning to see Tom and as he approached the cell, his heart ached for the dejection he saw in his brother's posture. He stood with his forehead lowered on a folded arm, while the other dangled through the bars as if he might reach out and touch the freedom he was being denied.

"Brer," he grasped that hand, trying to sound cheerful, "I told you I should have kicked your ass back to Athens."

Tom held to his touch with strength enough, but when he spoke it came as a weak, raspy whisper. "Mandria…where?"

"With Mamalyn. She'll be all right, Tom. She's confused, that's all."

"Believes it?" he struggled. "Pat said…fainted."

"I know. I heard the story," Allen fought a tear sheen right along with Tom. "But Captain Herb doesn't think you're guilty—I'm sure of it. And neither does Iano Rizza. We're going to clear you, Brer. —We are!" he hugged him as best he could through the bars. "How could this happen? —Damn it, Tom, how?"

"Note," Tom searched his pockets yet another futile time. "Sam's note; …office; all I remember. …But dreams—awful. …Oh God… awful!"

"Tom, stop—please—before you hurt your throat again? All right? Just let it heal for another day and we'll talk more."

Then, as Allen started to turn away, Tom caught his sleeve. "Mandria…talk; watch after; …for me…?"

But Mandria refused to see Allen. She would not see anyone but Evelyn, yet not even her mother could make her hear a word concerning Tom. And about her pregnancy? She wanted that mentioned even less…

That Friday found Sam feeling a bit better. About noon, Nicole had awakened from her coma with the lovely, innocent mind of a child. And the doctors felt she would never be any different…

572

Later, on the same afternoon, Tom heard a commotion down the corridor.

"I don't give a damn, Uncle Pat," Mike's voice boomed through the cell block. "I'm going to see him! —Tom Scott, where the hell are you?"

"Here! …I'm here…Mike!" he managed all the volume his throat would allow.

"Yeah, there you are," Mike approached calmly enough. But at the last second he lunged, grasping Tom's lapels and slamming him forward into the bars. "Where you belong, you God damn bastard! You Judas! You cowardly God damned son of a bitch!"

"Michael!" Patrick pried him loose. "By Jesus, you'll just be stopping that! You've heard but one side of the story—the gossip—and you're ready ta attack your friend?"

"*Friend? My* friend, Uncle Pat?" Mike raged on. "I've just come from the hospital! I've seen what *my friend* left of Nicole! She accepted my proposal—did you know that, Tom? Or that I have her engagement ring next to my heart, here? But she'll never wear it, thanks to *my friend!* No, now she just sits, hour after hour, babbling nursery rhymes and the non-sense of a five year old, God damn you! —God damn you to hell!" Mike tried to come through the bars again. "I'll kill you, Tom Scott! So help me God, I am going to see you dead!"

"Price! Schall!" Patrick bellowed for assistance. "Take Michael up ta me office and hold him there if you have ta numb his thick skull with a billy!"

Stunned, Tom watched as Mike was physically hauled away. And except for the yelling Mike did, the entire block was silent as the other prisoners watched too.

Patrick turned back to Tom, feeling sorry for the added misery in his expression. "You must realize how hurt he is, lad. I meant ta' meet his boat and tell him easy, but he come in early and heard the worst possible version. —And as you can imagine, there's some ugly ones going around; …some lynch talk, too, I'm sorry ta' tell you."

"But Nicole?" Tom questioned. "Dear God…gossip too?"

"I'm afraid not," Patrick nodded. "She is alive, but—well, it's real sad. And Mike has ta place blame somewhere."

"Mandria too?" Tom had to ask. "Hasn't come. ...Won't see Allen. —Why?"

"Tom, as far as I know, she hasn't left her father's house. I don't know what she's thinking, but you do have friends wanting ta help. Iano Rizza is one who came forward. It seems his wife was abducted that same day and—"

"Kathy? ...Missing?"

"No, she managed ta escape, but Iano feels strongly that her disappearance and your case are related—and frankly, so do I. Now, as you would expect, Kathy was deeply upset by the incident and he took her home—upriver ta her children. But they'll return within the week and I'll be looking inta her story a bit deeper. ...Meanwhile, lad, don't lose heart. After I've spoken ta me nephew—and boxed his ears—I'll send for you and go over all I've learned ta date."

So, trying to keep his thoughts hopeful, Tom sat back on the cell cot and idly toyed with a piece of string. But on seeing he'd created a noose about his finger, he quickly discarded the thing in favor of pacing...

By the following week, Evelyn would have given anything to see Mandria pacing about the floor. She had been coaxed out of bed, but had yet to leave her room. And Evelyn worried. She knew her daughter, and always before, when troubled or wrestling with a decision, Mandria had sought the outdoors. Now, she only sat gazing from her window. And Evelyn worried. Mandria was too calm; too serene; and not since the first night, had she shed a tear. Evelyn worried most about that, because she behaved as if her decisions were already made. It was to the point where Evelyn was afraid to leave her. She had wanted to visit Tom and had sent him notes through Allen— whom Mandria still refused to see, though he came daily. She would not even speak with Joleen, who came daily too. And not that Sam had made any effort to communicate, but Mandria wouldn't have welcomed it anyway. No, her daughter's distant mood kept Evelyn within earshot at all times.

Finally, in desperation, Evelyn came up with a proposal that would force a reaction from her. Mandria would either protest vehemently or passively accept, but either way, something of what she was feeling could be learned. "…Mandy, the hospital is releasing Nico day after tomorrow. But the Doctors say she still needs a lot of recovery time and preferably away from the city. So, I told Ransom—if you agreed—maybe we could take her to Marsh Haven during the week. Then, he could come out and spell us on the weekends. …Would that be all right with you?"

Mandria continued to stare at a certain bench in the square, but after a pause, she said, "You want to do this for Uncle Ran, don't you, Mama?"

"Well, he's been my friend since childhood—as our children were friends, until this happened. But you are my daughter. Your feelings matter most to me—and frankly, dear, I think you could use some time away from here too."

"So do I," Mandria made a slow turn to face her mother. "…But Marsh Haven is not far enough from Savannah for me. I am going to leave and I won't return until I've had this baby, put it up for adoption, and divorced Mr. Thomas Phillip Scott."

Evelyn was truly shocked. "…Mandy, you aren't serious—"

"Oh, yes, I am!" she said bitterly. "I'm going and I want to stay with Aunt Margery, if you think she'd have me."

"You know she would, dear—but Tom's case has not been decided—"

"Mama! I know what I saw. Thanks to my oh-so-caring-father, Tom's guilt was indelibly proven to me and I won't raise his child."

"It's your child too, Mandy," Evelyn said gently.

"Yes, but what if it looks like him? Mama, I'd just end up hating them both, so adoption is really the kindest thing. Now, I'm not going to argue the point and I am leaving here tomorrow morning."

"Please, Mandria, see Tom first," Evelyn pled. "Please. It could be for the last time ever…and good or bad, don't leave things unsaid. Believe me, you'll regret it."

"Oh, I intend to see him. Telling him what I am going to do is a pleasure I owe myself. Then I'm leaving—and Mama, you get to pick my direction. If you swear to keep my destination and my reason secret from everyone else here—even Father—then I'll go to Aunt Margery. If you can't promise me this, I'm still leaving, but you will not know where I am. So, which is it to be?"

"All right, I'll keep your secret," Evelyn reluctantly agreed. "But, maybe I should go with you?"

"No, thank you," Mandria declined. "I got myself into this, and I'll get myself out. Besides, Father would become suspicious if you did—and you've already promised to keep Nico during the week," she started for the door. "Now if you'll excuse me, I'm going to ask Jed to bring down my trunk and start packing. And isn't it convenient that I wasn't married long enough to move my damned clothes from this house?"

Evelyn nodded sadly. "My poor Mandy," she uttered. "You're hurting so badly…"

That afternoon, Mandria purchased her stage ticket, then went by the hospital to see Nicole for herself and the visit was profoundly hard on her. Nicole's beautiful pale blonde hair had been washed and brushed and hung softly about her shoulders. Her face had been sutured in several places that would scar, and was still swollen and bruised in spots, but her smile and eyes said it didn't bother her much. Nothing bothered her, in truth. She seemed content just to croon and rock the rag doll she held.

"Father, mothers, sister, brothers," she sang repeatedly. "Don't cry, wont die."

"Oh, Nico," Mandria said to her. "I should hate you, but you've suffered more for loving Tom than I have. Yes, and I'm glad I came to see you. Now I'm certain my decision is the only one I can live with. Good-bye, little Nico," she brushed a kiss to her cheek. "Be happy. Tom didn't leave you with much of a future, but at least you'll never have to think about him again. …I could almost envy you that." And she left crying for the first time since that awful night…

576

Moments later, Nicole looked at the closed door and said rapidly, "Father, mothers, sister, brothers; Father, mothers, sister, brothers! Don't cry, won't die. —Tell Tom! Won't die!" Then, lifting her doll, she smiled at it and went back to crooning again…

Very early the next morning, while most of Savannah still slept, Mandria moved quietly along the jail corridor as she'd been directed—and alone, as she had requested. But pausing before Tom's cell, she knew a moment of panic. He lay with his legs crossed at the ankles; a forearm resting across his brow; the other hand on his chest. …How many times had she seen him do that? How many times had she snuggled beneath his lifted arm and felt both of them immediately close about her? Too many times, evidently, because she could still feel desire for the man. And closing her eyes, she admitted that desire would die a long tortuous death.

"…Mandria?" his lowered voice startled her. How did he always know when she was near? And finding that unsettling too, she moved back a step when he rose and started toward her. Tom saw this, and stopped as far on his side of the bars as she was on hers.

"I thought you'd never come," he said softly, not wanting to awaken the other prisoners.

"I had to," she replied in her own hushed voice "I owe you something."

"…What?" he hesitated, confused by her staid attitude.

"Payment in full for the pain and heartache."

"You still believe…? You haven't spoken to Allen or Patrick yet? —And why haven't you?"

"Allen wasn't at the Lloyd Hotel; and Patrick Herb saw the same thing I did," she raised her eyes to his now. "Yes, I saw it all."

"Mandria?" he grasped the bars, for her calmness and coldness were having the opposite effect on him. "Lady, you saw what you were meant to see—"

"Damn you, shut up!" she hissed, stomping a foot. "I didn't come here to argue the point. I came because I'm leaving Savannah today. And when I return, if they haven't hung you already, I'll divorce you."

"No," he began to nod.

"Yes. You see, I'm pregnant, Tom. And I've decided to handle the situation just as your mother did."

"No; no," he repeated, a bit louder.

"Oh, but yes—with one small change: I don't want your child and I'm giving it away."

"No—damn you, no!" he yelled, yanking at the cell door.

"Yes—damn you, yes!" she replied with equal fervor. "You will never see this child—as you and Allen never saw your own fathers—and I won't have to be reminded every day of my life, I was ever stupid enough to have loved you!"

Now Tom was roaring his protest—attacking the door as if he'd rip it apart. And Mandria slowly backed away, certain his violent reaction only proved he was capable of the violence committed against Nicole. And while he still raged in fury, calling her name and swearing to stop her, she turned and fled up the stairway…

When Tom had begun his rampage, the rest of the prisoners awoke and gladly joined in. Soon, the entire block was rattling doors, banging anything they could lift against anything they could reach and shouting their favorite obscenities right along with him. Finally, when enough knuckles and skulls had been rapped, order was restored—in all but one cell. There, it took the jailer and four guards to gag and cuff Tom to his cot. And there, he remained, furious with the fates that would allow this to happen—and growing even more furious with his wife…

## RAPIST CAUSES JAIL RIOT

This was the banner headline carried in the Town Crier. The article to follow cited eye-witness accounts, taken from inmates, who told how Tom went berserk for no reason whatsoever; how he reached through the bars and tried to strangle a guard, injuring him grievously. Tom was described as a wild eyed maniac; a devil spewing foam from his mouth; —and one prisoner swore he bent the iron cell bars with super human strength! Naturally, the story was well-read and with prodding from Sam's minions, talk of a public lynching gained momentum.

The Gazette carried a denial of the tale, citing Police Captain Patrick Herb as their voice of authority. This report simply said no injuries were sustained and the prisoners over-reacted to a small disturbance; that it was normal for men held in detention to seize any opportunity to vent frustrations. And though this was the true version, it wasn't nearly so popular…

For Tom, time dragged by in leaded boots and to occupy his mind, he began to keep a mental list of ways to locate Mandria; —the steps he might take, checking then rechecking behind himself when a new possibility would occur. Yes, if he were free, he'd act on some of his ideas, too. But he wasn't free, the hours long and the visitors few, so he just continued to plan…

Allen's days weren't long enough between work and running errands for Tom. And he soon became baffled by Sam's attitude, disillusioned with Lucy's and disheartened that he'd been able to accomplish so little on his brother's behalf.

Sam Lucas had been nothing but sympathetic—even to suggesting attorneys capable of handling Tom's case. Allen had wanted to tell him what to do with his new found sympathy, but Tom said he shouldn't; that it might prove valuable if he stayed close to Sam and picked up what information he could.

On Tom's behest, he next went to the DeSoto Hotel to see if the Rizza's had returned, but the clerk said they hadn't and he had not received word when they might.

Then there was the day of Allen's double disappointment. A note from Evelyn told Tom she'd taken Nico to convalesce at Marsh Haven, but not one word was said about Mandria. Perplexed, he sent Allen to ask if she'd heard anything from her daughter or knew her whereabouts. On the way, Allen stopped by the Love's, thinking Lucy might also enjoy the ride, but her parents denied permission, making a polite reference to Tom's situation and their daughter's too close association. Lucy sat through this with hands folded, eyes lowered, mouth closed—and finally, Allen just got up and left. The news he brought from Marsh Haven made him feel no better. Evelyn re-pledged her love and support, but said if she revealed Mandria's destination, she might never return home again…

Patrick Herb was beset with problems as well. His investigation was no where near complete and already, rabble had formed in the squares—some even paraded in front of the jail—and all wanted a lynching. It was hardly surprising that Sam's men were reported as the main instigators. Yet he certainly was surprised to learn Mike had skipped his river run, been drinking steadily all week and was among that particularly boisterous crowd at the jail last night. Patrick just thought it ironic that two long-time enemies could now want the same thing: to see Tom hang. But neither would see it, he vowed. If it came down to a choice—even if it meant his career—Patrick Herb would not allow his nephew to take part in the death of a man his investigative soul knew to be innocent…

Things came to a head late on the following Tuesday afternoon, when an informant brought Patrick disturbing news. A lynch mob had, indeed, formed and for over two hours, Sam's hirelings had provided endless ale kegs and a lot of encouragement. Patrick hurried over for a look and returned with dread in his heart. The mob numbered close to a hundred and worse, when Sam's men faded into the background, Mike had assumed command, drunkenly swinging a noose in his hand. Yes, Patrick knew what had to be done—and done quickly—because his men could never hold off such numbers. And he wasn't unprepared. Every day for a week, he had tethered his own horse in the alley below his office window and checking to see it was still there, he had Tom brought up on the pretext of further interrogation. Dismissing the guard and locking the door while giving Tom a brief summery of his reasons, he then wished him luck and requested a final favor. But thanks to the hours Tom had spent planning for a chance such as this, he requested a favor too. Quickly scribbling a pre-dated note, which he had Patrick witness, Allen was given Power of Attorney and would now have access to funds Tom might need.

"And you'll keep working to clear me?" Tom asked as they shook hands.

"I will lad," Patrick closed his eyes. "Now, I'll thank you ta smack me a good one. It might save me job and me pension."

"Thanks, Captain Pat," Tom squared the Irishman's shoulders. "God, I hate doing this!" But he did it, catching Patrick before he hit the floor. Moments later, he emerged from the far end of the alley riding the Police Captain's horse…

Tom entered the back hall of his home, put two fingers to his mouth and gave a short, shrill whistle. There was no need to repeat it. Allen came racing down the stairway, as he'd always come when called this way by his brother.

"Brer! Oh, my God—Brer!" Allen hugged him ferociously.

"Yes, little brother, a man on the run. But alive, thanks to Patrick Herb. It seems my best friend is throwing a hanging party tonight."

"Mike? Damn it, I tried talking to him, but he stays drunk nowadays and—"

"And he, or the police, will likely come here when my escape is discovered," Tom injected. "Allen, I haven't much time, so here's what

I want you to do. Once they've searched the place and left again, pack me a saddlebag and all the money you can find. Then, without being followed, meet me on the road from Marsh Haven. I'm going there now and hopefully, I can persuade Mamalyn to tell me where Mandria is. She has to, Allen. This may be my one chance to change her mind about the baby."

"Then I'll pack two bags and go with you!" Allen declared.

"No; —No, little brother," Tom quieted an objection "I need you here. You and Patrick Herb are the only way I have of keeping tabs on my case. —And take this," he handed over a paper. "It gives you authority over my funds. I want you keep this house open, Allen. When I'm cleared, I mean to return and live right here in my own home. I'll want you to send money too, though I don't know where or when yet. But you have to stay and be my life-line," he said going out the back way again.

"…All right," Allen nodded following as far as the door. "Good luck, big brother," he uttered as Tom disappeared into shadow. And turning, he saw a sad faced Willie Luther and teary-eyed Joleen standing at the top of the kitchen stairs…

It was close to nine o'clock when Tom reached the gates of Marsh Haven. Tying his horse in the woods, he made his way down to the marsh and followed it around toward the servant's quarters. He had decided to speak with Hassie first and maybe spare Evelyn the heartache of betraying Mandria's trust. So choosing the largest of the small cabins there, he knocked softly at the door.

"…Mister Tom?" Jake stared. "They done let you go free from jail?"

"In a way," Tom replied. "May I speak with Hassie, please?"

"She still to the house. Miss Nico, she restless tonight and Hassie helping Miss Evelyn get her to bed."

"Well, so much for that idea," Tom nodded. "Then I have to speak with Mamalyn—and Jake, I'd appreciate a warning if you hear riders coming"

"This about Miss Mandy, ain't it?" Jake grinned. "You wants to find her."

"Yes," Tom answered, then thought to ask, "Do you know where she went, Jake?"

"No sir, but Ah bet Hassie do, so come on, Mister Tom," they started down a well-trodden path, "Ah take you in the back way. Hassie might be in the kitchen if you're lucky. Hope you do find that Mandy-chile'. We loves her much as you do."

Tom made no comment as Jake pointed him through an entrance. …But yes, he did still love Mandria somewhere in his heart, though of late he'd been too angry to think of anything more than wringing her neck. She had been hurt—he'd grant her that—but vowing to give away their child went beyond vengence; —and perhaps beyond forgiveness…

No one was in the kitchen, so moving up a dimly lit hall, Tom met Evelyn at the foot of the stairs and his sudden appearance startled her. "Oh!" she gasped and the cup of tea she held, smashed to the floor. "Oh, dear Lord, Tom! …But what are you doing out of jail?"

"Running from a lynch mob," he answered. "Mamalyn, give me a direction. Please?"

"They were going to hang you?" she stooped and nervously began to gather the broken china.

"Yes, ma'am," he knelt to help her. "Patrick Herb knows I'm innocent and let me escape. —But you mustn't tell that."

"Oh, I wouldn't, Tom. You know I wouldn't." Then with a lap full of broken china pieces, she raised her eyes to his. "…Tom, please don't ask me to break my promise to Mandy."

Tom gave a tired sigh and sat back on the steps. "Mamalyn, you must. Unless you tell where she is, I'll never find her. And even if I do, I don't know if I can change the way she feels about the baby. But I have to try. Don't you see that?"

"…I understand what you're saying," Evelyn rose very slowly, for as they spoke, Nicole had appeared on the darkened stairway behind Tom and was sneaking downward on bare, silent feet. "…But Mandy didn't want anyone to know her destination," she continued to watch the girl. "…Especially her father."

"Thank God for small favors," Tom commented. "At least he won't be encouraging her insanity. —Or does he even know she's pregnant?"

"No," Evelyn nodded. And now, Nicole was sitting on the step directly behind Tom. "…Mandy didn't want anyone to know about the baby either."

"Baby!" Nicole said in a little girl voice. And when Tom turned suddenly to face her, she giggled. "Baby?" she repeated, offering him her doll.

Tom looked at Evelyn, who held a hand pressed to her heart. "Take the doll, please," she murmured. "Nico hasn't allowed any of us to touch it—not even Ransom. …Oh, Tom, if you had beaten her so savagely, she'd never trust you with it. Couldn't this mean something; —something that would help you in court?"

"I don't know, Mamalyn. I just don't know what it could mean," he turned back to Nicole. "…Baby?" he said and because she still wanted him to, he took the doll.

"Father, mothers, sister, brothers," Nicole crooned, rocking back and forth. Then she looked up the darkened stairway and called, "…Mandy? —Mandy, brother's here!" which had Tom and Evelyn exchanging puzzled glances.

"Nico…baby?" Tom placed the rag doll in her care again as he rose. "Mamalyn, I can't stay much longer. That mob could be right behind me, so…please…where is my wife?"

"Two!" Nicole said abruptly. "Two wives; two brothers," she nodded. "One daddy; one sister," she smiled, as if that just explained everything. Then, rocking her doll, she returned to crooning her song over and over. "Father, mothers, sister, brothers. Don't cry, won't die. Don't cry, won't die."

"Mandy is in Aiken, Tom," Evelyn wiped at teary eyes. "She's with my sister in Aiken, South Carolina, a few miles across the river from Augusta. …But what are you planning to do?" she asked, placing the broken china on a table.

"Truthfully, I don't know yet," he answered. "I'm just going to find her—and try to talk sense into her stubborn little head!"

"She won't speak with you. If you go to the house, she won't even come down to see you. She was that adamant about the way she felt. And if she has told Trippe and Margery anything about you, it wasn't good. Tom, Trippe would set every man on the place after you if he thought you meant Mandy harm."

"Then I'll catch her away from the house," he shrugged. "May I have your sister's married name and directions to her home now?"

"Yes, but I'm trying to explain how very determined Mandy is. You may have to…to kidnap her and tie her down just to make yourself heard!"

"I know," he gave a nod of irony. "I almost had to once before. But I'll do what I must; …for the sake of the child, if nothing else."

"Your child—and my grandchild," Evelyn hugged him affectionately. "Now you stay put, Tom Scott. I've just thought of a way to give you that time with Mandy!" And she hurried toward the study.

"Good thing Miss Evelyn told you," Hassie said, as she sat beside Nicole. "Cuz' Ah would have, hadn't she. …Tell you something else—something 'tween me and you, or could still prove a danger for Joleen and Willie. But Miss Nico, she done bad things to them. She stand over them; make them do sex just so she could see. And she touch them—feel their privates, right while they doing what she say. Do things Ah never heard of too—like whipping or poking with a stick, all while they joined together. …Now, Ah feel sorry for how she end up and Ah treats her kindly, but she wasn't no good, Mr. Tom, and your trouble more than a little her doing. Might do if somebody check out a place Willie drive her to. It called The Tabby House and bad goings-on happen there right regular."

"The Tabby House," Tom nodded, trying to digest Hassie's tale. *…And Mike still believes Nicole an innocent little flirt,* he thought.

"Here we are," Evelyn returned with an envelope for Tom. "This will keep my relatives from putting anyone on your trail. It's a note from me saying Mandy was badly misled; that you are innocent of any charges she made against you; and that you've taken her—with my blessing—to straighten it out between you."

"…Mamalyn?" Tom laughed for the first time in two weeks. "Are you telling me to kidnap your daughter? —Seriously?"

"Well, if it takes that, I suppose I am!" she laughed too. "But you will keep me informed; let me know where you're going?"

"As soon as I know," he replied. "And right now, I'm not sure of a damn thing—except that I'd best be leaving here."

"But you going to bring that Mandy-chile' home, ain't you Mr. Tom?" asked Hassie.

"…She'll come home," Tom answered. "I'm sure she already misses you and her mother."

"Bad Mother!" Nicole stood suddenly, arms akimbo. "Bad, bad, bad Mother!" Then, hopping from the steps to the floor, she stood looking up at Tom, with a serious expression and said in slow staccato, "Father, mothers, sister, brothers. —Two," she pointed at him. "One, two; one two!" she twirled about, only to stop abruptly, looking confused. "…Father?" she asked him now. "Is your father here?"

"No, Nico—" he began.

"Uh-uh!" she nodded affirmatively. "Father, mothers, sister brothers! Two; —tell Tom two!"

"Come on now, Miss Nico," Hassie came to lead her up the stairway. "Time we put your baby to bed." And without looking back, Nicole obediently followed.

After a moment of thought, Tom turned to Evelyn. "Mamalyn, if she has reverted to childhood, why would she use my name? I wasn't part of her life then. It could mean she remembers more of the present than we know. Anyway, do this for me: Just write down what she says and if it begins to make any kind of sense, tell Patrick or Allen right away?"

"I will, Tom," she said as they went to the door. "But you must do me a favor in return."

"What's that?" he turned on the step to face her.

"Don't let Mandy have her way. If you have to hold her until the baby comes, do it!" she ordered. "And one more thing? Please—*please*—

send for me at the beginning of her last month. I don't care where you are, I'll come. Please, Tom, I just want to be with my daughter when she gives birth."

Seeing hope for a happy ending in Evelyn's tear-bright eyes, but holding little for one himself, Tom sighed, giving her a final hug. "All right. If I'm still free and with Mandria, I will send for you."

"Thank you—now take this," she pressed money into his hand. "No arguments. Just take it and go save my grandchild." And crying softly, she moved back and closed the door...

Tom stepped from the shadows beside the road and gave his whistle once again. Again too, Allen's response was immediate. Reining hard on the horse, he turned and came back.

"I guess you heard me and got off the damn road?" he asked, his tone sounding irate.

"Yes. It's hard to tell friend from foe these days," Tom replied.

"Tell me about it!" Allen said, dismounting. "Damn it, they came to the house—just like you said they would. First Mike with his filthy crowd—and they broke the Grandfather clock! Hell, then here came the police, who ran Mike's bunch off before searching all over again—and they scared Joleen and Willie to death barking out orders!"

"Easy, little brother," Tom soothed. "They won't be back. You aren't the one they're after."

"Well, they'd better not come! I told all of them it was my home too—and that I would protect it!"

"Good. And I hope you meant that, because if anything should happen to me—"

"No! —Don't say it, Tom. I don't even want to hear that kind of talk! ...Just—well, here. It's all the money I had with me—and Joleen and Willie put in what they had too." Then his voice broke and he turned away. "Damn, I wish it was Friday. That's payday, you know, and there could have been more."

Tom knew Allen was trying to hide tears, so he opted for a change of subject. "Is that the saddlebag you packed for me?" he asked, taking it from Allen's mount and strapping it to his. "You didn't include another surprise—like the one I found in my bags the summer I left for the railroad job? Your pet frog wasn't in too good a shape when I reached the work camp."

"No; no surprises, but here, don't forget your musket," Allen said, managing composure again. "…So did you learn where Mandy is?"

"Yes, Aiken, South Carolina," he said, climbing into the saddle. "I'll follow the river road as far as I can tonight. From there on, I'll just play it as it comes, I guess. But I will send word and an address. I have to know what's happening here."

"I'll write—I'll send every scrap of information I can," Allen extended a hand. "Brer, please be careful. That place won't be a home until you and Mandy are there again."

"Well, as I said before, I plan to live there. …And it won't be alone." Then giving Allen's shoulder a pat, he rode away.

Allen watched him out of sight before starting back to town. Having a home had always been important to his brother and Allen vowed that Tom would be proud of the job he did keeping things there up and running. He would find some way to help clear his brother too—even if it meant playing Sam Lucas like a fish because, damn it, there had to be a way of proving his innocence and bringing him home! *…I plan to live there. …And it won't be alone…* Those had been Tom's parting words, clearly stating his fondest wish. …And yet, as Allen turned them through mind he began to sense other meanings. You had to know Tom really well to catch it, because he was truly good at tucking truth into the middle of what was expected.

Then for some reason, what had happened to the Grandfather clock presented itself in analogy. There lay the tall, proud clock on the floor—and like Tom, it had taken much abuse. Next, it began to whir and gonged out the correct time—like Tom, saying all the right things whether standing upright or beaten down. Allen shuddered, for that was when the great mainspring had exploded from the heart of the clock. …Yet this too was like Tom—filled with a dark explosive anger which could very well tear out his heart. "Lord, Brer," Allen uttered in realization. He knew then, his brother's real problem had little to do with the happenings in Savannah and everything to do with the defection of a wife, equally hurt and disillusioned as he. "Oh, Lord," he groaned, not envying the sparks that would fly when those two met-up again. Yes, and settling those differences just might take a really, long, time...